I'M
DYING
LAUGHING

Other fiction by Christina Stead

The Salzburg Tales
Seven Poor Men of Sydney
The Beauties and Furies
House of All Nations
The Man Who Loved Children
For Love Alone
Letty Fox, Her Luck
A Little Tea, A Little Chat
The People With the Dogs
Cotters' England
The Puzzleheaded Girl
The Little Hotel
Miss Herbert: (The Suburban Wife)
Ocean of Story

I'M
DYING
LAUGHING

THE HUMOURIST

CHRISTINA STEAD

Edited and with a Preface by R. G. Geering

For William Blake, novelist and economist
My friend and husband, who helped me from the beginning

First published by Virago Press Limited 1986
41 William IV Street, London WC2N 4DB

Copyright © The Estate of Christina Stead 1986
Copyright © Preface R. G. Geering 1986

British Library Cataloguing in Publication Data
Stead, Christina
  I'm dying laughing.
  I. Title
  823[F]   PR9619.3.S75

  ISBN 0-86068-797-X

Typeset by Goodfellow & Egan
Printed in Finland by Werner Söderström Oy
a member of Finnprint

'The mockeries are not you. . .
The pert apparel, the deform'd attitude, drunkenness, greed,
    premature death, all these I part aside. . .

Through angers, losses, ambition, ignorance, ennui, what you
    are picks its way.'

(Walt Whitman, To You.
Birds of Passage, 1881)

PREFACE

Christina Stead paid her first visit to the US in 1935. In New York she and William Blake (who was an American citizen) were to become associated with the magazine *New Masses* and to meet writers and others of the radical Left. She and Blake were back in Europe again in the following year but returned in 1937 to the US, where they lived throughout World War II. This second stay was the period in which she wrote and published *The Man Who Loved Children* (1940), *For Love Alone* (1944) and *Letty Fox: Her Luck* (1946). *The Man Who Loved Children* and *Letty Fox* were set in the United States, as were the next two novels, which came out after her return to Europe in 1947, *A Little Tea, a Little Chat* (1948) and *The People With the Dogs* (1952). This book, *I'm Dying Laughing* published now for the first time, is the only other novel of hers which grew out of the years she spent in America.

The decades of the thirties, forties and fifties were critical times, culminating for the radical Left in the McCarthy witch hunts conducted through the House Committee on Un-American Activities, and the Trial of the Hollywood Ten in 1947–8. In a radio interview in July 1973 Stead spoke of the 'terrific convulsion in the USA' in the thirties, and then of the McCarthy period as follows:

> It was very unpleasant. So many people, good worthy people were being attacked, and it was entirely for the worst political motives, they didn't care about Reds, there weren't enough Reds. They were all making their political ways, as some have done of course. Oh, it was a terrific moment, it was worth living through, it was great.

The novelist shows out in that final sentence. From this period comes *I'm Dying Laughing*, which is based, in Stead's usual way, on the fortunes of people she knew at first-hand.

In an interview in June 1973 Stead described *I'm Dying Laughing*, which for a time she had dropped, in this way:

> It was all about the passion of – I use passion in almost the religious sense – of two people, two Americans, New Yorkers, in the thirties. They are doing well, but they suffered all the troubles of the thirties. They were politically minded. They went to Hollywood. They came to Europe to avoid the McCarthy trouble. Of course they were deeply involved. And then, they lived around Europe, oh, in a wild and exciting extravagant style. But there was nothing to support it. At the same time they wanted to

be on the side of the angels, good Communists, good people, and also to be very rich. Well, of course . . . they came to a bad end.

The earliest sketches for *I'm Dying Laughing* begin in the late 1940s. By September 1950, living in Montreux, Stead was down to serious work on the novel, then entitled *The Renegade*. 'UNO 1945' appeared in a special Christina Stead issue of *Southerly* in 1962 as 'Chapter One of an Unpublished novel; *I'm Dying Laughing*.' The writing of other books had intervened in the 1950's, *Cotters' England and Miss Herbert*, both to be published years later. By 1966 Stead had completed *I'm Dying Laughing* and sent the manuscript to the United States. Many Americans had by then discovered, with the Stanley Bursnhaw inspired reissue of *The Man Who Loved Children*, originally published in New York twenty-six years earlier, that Stead was a great writer; the time might have seemed right for another big novel. As it happened, she was urged to revise her manuscript, to make the political background of the 1940s and subsequent events clearer. This she set out to do and for the next ten years or more she worked on and off rewriting and revising. She came (rightly or wrongly) to regret this decision and to believe that she should have left the book, whatever its shortcomings, as it was. Working at it for so long she felt that she was being drawn into writing a different novel and into sacrificing some of the force of the original version.

In a letter of April 1979 to me as her future literary trustee Christina Stead wrote that I was free to publish *I'm Dying Laughing* after her death if I thought fit. She seemed to assume that the manuscript, after all those years of rewriting, was in a publishable form. What I inherited, in fact, was a huge mass of typescript ranging in finish from rough to polished and in length from page bits to different versions of whole chapters, along with piles of basic and supplementary material. The typescript for the novel presented further editorial complications. The names of characters, their relationships, their ages and (sometimes) their appearances had undergone changes over the years and the pagination was often misleading. The greatest difficulties occurred in what now stands as Part One of the novel. The opening chapter ('UNO 1945') of the 1966 version here becomes Chapter 4, since much of the re-working of the early manuscript was designed to provide in an additional three chapters more information about the earlier years of Emily and Stephen in order to account for their difficulties with the Communist Party in the US in the 1940s. In this process the present Chapters 5 to 10 underwent considerable changes.

Part Two posed fewer problems. I have incorporated wherever possible Stead's handwritten emendations and have followed the excisions she made in the original manuscript. The first draft of the novel went straight through from Chapter 12 to the end without chapter divisons. As an aid to reading and in order to bring Part Two in line structurally with Part One, I have split this large body of material into separate chapters and have provided headings for what now become Chapters 13 to 24.

I'm Dying Laughing is the most obviously political of all Christina Stead's books but it is not a political novel in the manner of Koestler's *Darkness at Noon* or Orwell's *Nineteen Eighty-Four*. Given its economic, social and political background *I'm Dying Laughing* is concerned primarily with character and morality. Stead was quite clear about this in her accounts of the writing and rewriting. Americans, she said, have short memories even for crucial events but she felt that she had neither the talent nor the desire to remind them of their political history. She once described what was originally her first chapter and its relationshp to the rest of the novel as follows:

> [It] is full of energy and [a] sort of a picture of the whole book in a way, except that I meant it to go on from fire to more fiery to fierier still; it has a very terrible dramatic end, I wanted it to be a build-up all the way through. But you can't do that putting in political explanations.

Emily and Stephen are the true centre, theirs is a story of destructive passion, misguided idealism and wasted talent; of self-indulgence, folly and betrayal. Emily now joins the gallery of Christina Stead's most memorable characters, which includes Catherine and Michael Baguenault, Aristide Raccamond, Henri Léon, Sam, Henny and Louisa Pollit, Teresa Hawkins, Jonathan Crow, Honor Lawrence and Nellie Cook.

Stead liked to think of her books as her children, to be reared and then sent out to take their chance in the world once the time came. After many years, *I'm Dying Laughing* is now ready to go. It will attract brickbats and bouquets. Predicting the responses and their justifications would be easy enough but this Preface is no place for such an exercise. This book is the last large-scale addition to the already substantial Stead oeuvre.

Some anomalies remain after all the assembling and repair work I have done. There is no satisfactory account among the manuscript papers of the Howards's move from New York to Los Angeles. Hence the gap between Chapters 3 and 4. Lennie drops out of the story when it shifts from the US to Europe, where the family is reduced to two adults and three children. I hope that no other obvious inconsistencies remain in the narrative.

As with *The Man Who Loved Children*, the title, *I'm Dying Laughing*, is ironic. Emily Howard won fame as a writer of small-town American humour. The subtitle 'The Humourist', underlines her tragic story. The dedication of the book to William Blake is reproduced from the prefatory pages in Christina Stead's manuscript papers.

R. G. Geering, Sydney, July 1986.

PART ONE

'I'm thirsty!'
(*Gargantua*, Rabelais)

1 HOW IT BEGAN. 1935

The last cable was off, the green lane between ship and dock widened. Emily kept calling and waving to the three below, Ben, a press photographer, her brother Arnold and his wife Betty. Arnold was twenty-three, two years younger than herself; Betty was twenty-four. Arnold was a dark fleshy man, sensual, self-confident, he fooled around, had never finished high school. From Seattle he came to New York after her and she had helped him out for a while. He now was working on a relief project for the WPA and earning about a hundred dollars a month. Betty was a teacher, soon to have a child. She was a big, fair girl, bolder than Arnold. She had already had a child by Arnold, when they were going together, had gone to Ireland to some relatives to have it. Arnold had never seen it, but Emily regularly gave them money for it. It was a boy four years old and named Leonard.

This couple badly wanted to go to Europe. They had argued it out with Emily in their rathole in Bleecker Street. They wanted to open an arts service somewhere around Eighth Street and Sixth Avenue. Betty's idea was to go to Vienna, Berlin, Paris, Florence and Prague to collect new notions and curios, Wiener Werkstätte, art objects, Käthe Kollwitz dolls, Raymond Duncan batiks, to sell in their store and by catalogue throughout the United States.

'In the Depression?' Emily objected.

'All the artists are working for the Government; on projects. They're spreading art through the Union. Every village has its theatre in a barn; they're getting to see there's art in Bowery bums and the old-time oil paintings in Wild West saloons. The Depression is good for art. Besides, the Depression is not so deep now.'

Their idea was that Emily was to back them and sustain them till the business made money. If they ran out of cash in Europe, Emily would send it; that is, if she stayed in New York at her job; and then there was Lennie. Betty would visit her son while abroad. He lived with Betty's old nurse outside Belfast. Emily could wait for Europe till next year; but she observed that already, in their plans, were yearly visits to Europe, to see what was new.

Emily had several times offered to bring Lennie to the States. Why couldn't she have a photograph of the bambino at least, in return for her support? But no, Betty's old nurse was a superstitious old darling. She did not believe in photographs.

'But I love Lennie,' cried Emily, 'I want to hold him in my arms. I feel as if he's partly mine.'

She could not even get his address.

'It would never do. It would so frighten Mary-Martha, the old darling. She would not understand a stranger writing.'

Emily longed for him. She even shouted at Betty.

'Are you going to plant the next one in Scotland? Maybe with Lindbergh's dear old nurse, or Lizzie Borden's dear old servant?'

This and her longing to see Europe strengthened her: she refused to buy their tickets. Next year.

'But then we'll have the child.'

She at once saw they might leave the new child with her. She rejoiced.

'If I'm lucky, kids, and sell articles on "Europe Today – Another Bonehead Abroad" to the *Toonerville Times* and the *Wabash Weekly*, I'll be able to send you and keep the kid with a nurse. But I've got to have the material first.'

'Couldn't you write it up here – read the foreign press?' said Arnold.

Emily rolled back on their divan, laughing, 'Gee whittaker, what crust! I go now, you go later.'

They gave a farewell party and were now seeing her off.

'I'm glad they haven't brought their luggage with them,' she said to her colleague, Ben Boakes, the press photographer; 'and even now, I'm not convinced. Heigh-ho, you know the famous Hollywood crack, "May you be the richest of your family! Get to Hollywood and wait for the swarm to settle on you." That's my fate. Fifty years hence, Ben, I'll be struggling for a byline, Irish Lennie will be fifty-four and spending my pittance in the dramshop and they'll be where they are today, feeding from flybitten cans in a Village one-room pleasance. Read your fate in the cloudy crystal, with Emily Wilkes.'

Now, at the rail, she grinned, pointed to the roses on her arm, shouted, nodded, wiped her eyes, with big gestures, so that they could see.

'Hooray, hooray, I made it!'

She turned to the lean, dark man standing beside her, a middle-aged man, her height, dressed as a workman. She saw his smile, and said, 'Sigh, blissful sigh! Until they unhooked that damn rope, I didn't know if they weren't going to crawl up the rope, first prize the greasy pig. Me.'

He looked quickly at her, laughed wider, and said in a low, hesitating voice, 'Who are they?'

4

New York, 'Mrs Browne, Mrs Walter Browne, the Browne spelled with an e.'

'Is this your first trip to Europe, Mrs Browne?'

The woman finished her drink and washed out the glass. No answer.

'H'm, well, excuse me. My first trip, except to Staten Island, Arbutus Beach, to study the spot marked X; and once, when I took the ferry from Seattle to Port Angeles on a stormy day of strike, my life in my hands.'

On the way up, she thought, 'Good company, I see! Talkative; verbal diarrhoea. They probably figured me out and put me in with Signora Sphinx, so I can learn to be refahned before I get to Europe.'

Warm now, though there was a fresh breeze, she walked round the deck.

Aft, lounging on a grey-painted locker, was a large man, shirt open to the waist, showing his long, sparsely hairy body. He was fair, a big face with large, open blue eyes, the eyes of a child. This big man saw her, smiled, began shaking with laughter. 'Who is that?' She knew him. She walked all round the deck and came back. He was there, but looking tired, his cheeks creased and fallen. His muscular arms burst out of the short sleeves; he had a big putty nose. 'I know him!' Five years before – a troublesome student in Seattle, shouting with students at a long table in the canteen, putting them all down, roaring with argument, sitting by himself, moody, dirty, drunk and with his books before him. As she trotted past, he looked at her purple slippers. 'He does remember! He remembers that after moving to his table, called the Circus, attracted by the circus, I started asking sappy questions. I got the attention of one Bellamy Dark, a "mediocre academic drudge" he said. Modest lad, thought I; and did not know it was an informed analysis. I went after this drudge, named Woodworm and deserted this one named Fireball. It was a chit's cowardice. I figured I couldn't rope in Fireball, I guess. Well – B. Dark is one of the reasons I'm going to Europe; to wipe out the shame. And lo, here is Fireball! Is it a reward, is it Fate? I wish I knew. Forget it girl. You're sure to lose.' She was always making mistakes – she had an impulsive nature.

'Hi! You're from Seattle,' she said.

'Yup. Just been there to see my father-in-law.'

'What's your name? I remember you. You fought fist-fights with three of the faculty; two for Sacco and Vanzetti, one for Karl Marx. Then you left.'

'I got a job as a stevedore. Then I became a sailor.'

'That was a big general fist-fight that Sacco – Vanzetti event. Even I at last knocked on doors for the shoemaker and the fishman versus the United States. Even Mussolini, to get down to the dregs, was obliged to tell Italy and the world, "I did everything humanly possible to save Sacco and Vanzetti." It was our first international trial. I mean Judge Thayer tried them, another word for the bum's rush, in this instance, and then the world tried us. The first but not the last, no doubt. Dreadful. Why was it? Why do we do it? They burned the American flag in Tokyo and Johannesburg. Thomas Mann and John Galsworthy and other worthies said, "Sacco and Vanzetti are our blood brothers." If there's one thing we know, it's how to get the banner headlines.'

'The USA was in the usual red scare; people being rounded up and deported. In the 1790s it was the French who were the dangerous reds we had to round up and expel,' said he.

'Why are we such scaredy-cats?'

'Come and have a drink,' he said, pushing himself up. She remembered more about him now. Most of the girls had avoided him, though he was a magnificent animal; because he roared, went on benders, didn't shave, didn't dance and would come towering in, full of drink, smiling strangely, separate, threatening, ready to smash-hit, or shout rough laughter, or topple. Drunk or sober, he argued and fought. He was going to London for his Ph.D.

'Why London? Plenty of Ph.Ds at home.'

'I like it where it's tougher. And I've got to talk to someone.'

'What about?'

He did not tell her then. His father-in-law was paying the minimum sum for the trip. His wife, Sue, who was at home in Seattle at present, studying for her MA, still believed he could make a good professor: but if not, they'd separate and she'd teach. When he said this, he grinned like a good-humoured lion.

She told him the home facts. Her father was a small inventor and manufacturer. He made boilers, stoves, ovens, heaters. He had invented a few things, especially noted the Wilkes Boiler. She had brought her brother Arnold from Seattle to New York, unemployed, to get a job she had found for him.

'What did he do?' She hesitated.

'He was on . . . WPA.'

'Good.'

She laughed, 'I hope it's good. He was in a small PR agency. He helped the other hucksters stuff the holes of reputations with flannel. You know, Imperial Caesar, alas, poor Yorick. Ugh, I hate and fear the name. I always felt I was poor Yorick. I am always concealing from myself that I am poor Yorick. Besides, Hamlet was poor Yorick. Clown at court; what future but a naked skull?'

He snarled, 'Who knows who's Hamlet? Hamlet's anyone. He's all

8

moods, any moods. He's a wind-and-water adolescent. It's a phase of youth I don't like. I was through it by fifteen. I was a Catholic, a choirboy. Then I changed.'

She heeded the belligerent tone and said hastily, 'My father remarried and I was mostly brought up by my granny, at least ideologically. She was a battling old lady who subscribed to the *Clarion* and heard Elizabeth Gurley Flynn when she first went out west. I got all my history of the West from her and I've always had an abject, cringing admiration for the Wobblies. They admitted life was really tough: you can't flatter it.'

'Faugh!'

'Faugh yourself. Grandma loved a Wob, that kept her straight, though I guess she was straight. I saw him at last; "my dear Tom", she called him, "my dear young man." He was a tall, straight man, seventy, no stoop, long head, bushy black hair, footballer's neck and shoulders, with big slow feet, just like Lincoln, glasses on his small blue eyes, big shapely hands, and a wonderful laugh, like all the glasses in a glass-blower's ringing downscale. He was masculine, ugly, you might say; yet I somehow thought he must look like his mother. He said he looked like his father. "I'm the only one of the boys that does," he said: "my mother had a faithful weekend visitor." That floored me for a while. Grandma loved him all her life. Ah, me. Living Man, she called him: or Deep River. I don't know why.'

'Deep River is the Ohio. It's a freedom song for the Negroes.'

Emily said, 'I bet secretly I'm looking for one like him. Girlish first impressions.'

The man looked restless, surly. She said, 'What's your name? I've forgotten.'

It was Jean-Marie McRoy, a mixture, French-Canadian, Scots, and yes, part Russian.

'You look Russian. When I saw you lolling on that box, I said to myself, "He's resting from running up the Potemkin Staircase." Or was it down?'

He liked that. He said his rich father-in-law, a lumber man, didn't think much of him.

'He says I have no imagination, no personality. That means I don't make money and don't want to. Sue thinks so too, my wife. She's stuck by me so far. She likes me, but she wants me to shine on campus, the big popular man: heads turn when I come in, sush-sush murmur, bald heads and spectacles shine with approval, they clap – the bear with the heart of a mouse. To hell with it. I tried it. I try anything. I got drunk and ducked – '

He had published an essay on population, well received except by one professor in England – the name? Growl, growl. The first thing he was

9

going to do was to go to Cambridge to seek out this professor. He had already sent him a four-page letter requesting him to issue a recantation of his review of the book, already printed in a learned journal.

'I don't know what you think? Was it the right thing to do? Or should I just take it?'

'Go and punch his nose,' she said.

'No, I'll go and show him his ignorance and question his scholarship. He's well-known as a Marxist. I'm going there first thing, won't even get a room in London first. Talk to Mann first.'

'Man?'

'Aloysius Mann!' he called out, staring at her for her ignorance. 'Population theory!'

'What are you going to do for your Ph.D?'

After a pause, he grinned,

'The two departments.'

'Eh?'

'Marxian economics. Producer goods and consumer goods.'

'Well, that's Greek to me. I've been to an American high school and college; ergo, I know nothing. My dad was a business crank; made ovens, patented the Wilkes Oven and believed in self-government in industry, that meant free enterprise by company rules; government run by business advisers; no government interference. The Utopia of businessmen – and he thought the USA could be. My uncle worked for the Eastern Railroad and Lumber Company. He was a self-respecting worker, that means no fighter; and basically he agreed with Dad. Sure, to hell with the boss; but the unions interfered with a man's freedom; so good nigger just the same. He was a veteran from 1919 and they were a bit leery of the men who came back from Europe in 1918. They thought they might have caught a light case of ideas; and ideas are anarchistic. That's why they formed the Elmers. Uncle was one. Then he got caught in the crossfire of a street-battle in Centralia, Armistice Day, 1919, marching with the veterans. My grandma always said we would pay for it – the crude inhuman brutality: sacking the IWW hall – fighting, making a victim, cutting off his genitals, hanging him – then getting in harmless women and making the jail a bawdyhouse; and then there's the romantic story of the law man who never got over it, got a neurosis. Not sturdy enough to be one of us hundred-percenters. I wrote a play about it, thought WPA might put it on. I said "inhuman". Why? It's human, it's what we do on Saturday afternoons. Didn't they hang Frank Little at Butte, Montana, in 1917, the same idea, hanged him from a railroad trestle. Merry, eh? We're a side-splitting set. It gives you confidence in sharks. Do you want to write a selling story? Man, softbodied, brave man against those devils of the

10

deep. Sharks don't march down the current, and form in vigilante groups to tear up other sharks. I hope we don't find soft, gentle jellies of our ilk anywhere else in space, progressive ones who've got a few centuries ahead of us in blood-letting and soul-freezing. Even tigers, well, don't trust my zoology, I learned it in the yellow press, tigers get on their hind legs and claw in a man-to-man duel; but we fight in a mob, get all the fun and then, "I wasn't there, Mac." I'm not saying just men; women, too, hide behind the twitched curtain, then rush out when there's a mob of fifty hellcats. That's in Zola, do you remember? Do you think we'll change some day? Will we have a Winter Palace or a Potemkin Staircase? Or blackhat, whitehat till the last President? It's fixed, I guess – leave us to heaven. There's nothing else to do.'

He was looking at her,

'What did you say your name was?.'

She told him. What was she going to do over there?

'My God! I'm going to see. I'm just one hundred and one per cent hayseed and ignoramus, the big, brainless American wonder from Hix-in-the-Stix. They've got so much culture over there they throw it away like, Uncle said, we threw away beefsteaks and turkeys in the garbage cans at Christmas around Camp Upton. I'm hoping to eat out of their garbage cans. Unless there's a sentry.'

'Eh?'

'They used to post guards around Camp Upton to see the natives didn't pillage the garbage cans.'

He laughed. 'Sure, sure.' He got two more drinks. He liked her. Later, he said he'd see her in the afternoon, if she wanted to come around. When she went down to her cabin to leave her coat for lunch, she felt elated. Her place was at a small table with three others, between two portholes. There was a honeymoon couple from Toledo, Ohio, and an eager, polite old woman from Riga, Latvia, who had been living around New York and Chicago for forty years. She was a plump, small woman, dressed in black silk sprinkled with pink roses. She was sturdy, friendly, like all Riga people. The bridegroom was a big, fair youth; the bride about seventeen, short, stout, fair and a great eater, going through all the courses at all meals, cramming the contents of her plates down her throat. Before she left the table, she swept the heap of rolls from the bread-basket into her handbag. The second day, she brought a plastic beach-bag and into this she put all the butter, bread, fruit and other things left after the meal. People looked from neighbouring tables. The bride was unconcerned, too busy, though the bridegroom flushed and spoke a word which made her laugh.

Emily said to her, 'Good for you! The fish don't need it.'

11

But the young couple did not even answer direct questions. They stared at each other, rolled their eyes, laughed. Emily introduced herself, 'I'm a journalist, write for the papers; this is my first trip to Europe; yours, too, I guess.'

The couple stared at each other, went on eating, didn't turn to her. Mrs Cullen had been in Riga in 1919, seeing her family and was there at the time of the naval battle. She had got out of the city and become a nurse for the soldiers; she had travelled through the country, gone to Georgia, gone to Petrograd, which became shortly after, Leningrad.

'What was it like?'

'The roads and villages and ruins were full of wretched wanderers, uprooted. Soldiers starved and froze. In Petrograd and Moscow you could see some night-life and middle-class people with hidden reserves, who gave parties, with the blinds drawn. The remains of a class, hoping for the best. Europe collapsed in 1919; the USA took ten years to catch up and now the USA looks a bit like Russia then – not so bad though. Roosevelt is saving them from that. He's a wonderful man – the best they have had since Abraham Lincoln.'

'But his class hate him.'

'They don't like his handouts. It costs them.'

Emily was dissatisfied. 'Golly, yes, but how did it happen? Why does it happen? The USA is a rich country; it's been plundered only by us. Nobody invades us. We're not exhausted by wars and landowners spending the bone-dust of serfs at Nice and Monte Carlo. We're worrying about farm surpluses! We're full of minerals, lumber, rivers – workers, steel mills, cattle – pigs, corn – how can it be worth nothing? How are we poor? How can we be rich, rich, rich – and then suddenly a stock market crash and overnight we're poor, poor, dying in our tracks? Then what is rich and what is poor? We made money out of the First World War: it helped us out of a depression. We're on top; and then – bang! Back into a worse depression. I feel lousy too, turning my back on all those soup kitchens and tar-paper shacks. I feel lousy leaving my brother and sister-in-law to scratch a living and me living the life of Riley. But, this is my only chance. I want to get as far as I can, see Warsaw, Leningrad, as well as Rome and Paris; I want to see Sofia and Belgrade – all, all – my favourite story used to be "The Seven League Boots". Heigh-ho! And I can't help feeling life is great and good and wonderful. I know it isn't. I'd like to be a John Reed – an Axel Oates, seeing history. I'm fed up with fires and police courts and ruin. Eastward-ho for a real life.'

'You ought to go to Russia, see the first revolution since the French!'

'And the American,' said Emily. 'But they always starved in Russia; it was an old-fashioned system: it couldn't last in the twentieth century.

Working fields by slaves and serfs is uneconomic. Well, we always had a lot of poverty and people on the roads, but not like now, better: people taking a dry crust in their teeth and a covered wagon on their backs and setting off into the mosquito-shrouded plains. Always looking beyond their noses. But now what's frightening is that the ones who sickened on the way, the failures, the shallow-lying corpses have turned into underground rot, little soaks of black misery, that have shot up into the air and are falling down all over us. We, the hope of the world – think what we look like now! Rah! Rah! Rah! Woe, Woe, Woe! Other countries have history; we have nothing but contradictions. We haven't even got a system; or if we have, no one knows what it is. American get-ahead, that's the only system we know: and now that no one's getting ahead, not even the magnates, we're like a lost dog, howling and looking for a hole. We can't remember that other people have systems; we don't know what it is. So here we are on our backs with our legs in the air waiting for someone to turn us over. And the only man who looks like doing it is Roosevelt. Is that a national philosophy? But we're full of political philosophy! We started out, like no other nation, with a philosophy, a constitution – a cartload of furniture to fix our little grey home in the west. But the landlord, know as Wolf, is knocking at the door, and even he is going to be hungry, tonight. No, I won't think about it till I get home again.'

But she was watching the long table on the other side of the dining saloon. Mrs Cullen noticed it and said eagerly, 'Let's get to know them, eh? Someone to talk to. Someone you can walk round the deck with. They're New Dealers, I know; I heard them.'

The young men at the long table were idling over their fruit and Emily saw the young man with the cloth cap she had met on deck, the cap now off; he had thick, curly hair, dark-brown with grey threads.

The bride waved a spoon at the waiter, caught his eye and held up the bread-basket. When he came, Emily put two dollars into his hand and asked him to give them their coffee at a little table on the other side. From there they were able to look at the party of men, mostly young. Facing them at one side of the table, was a tall curly-haired, graceful man, in his thirties, who was talking in a nervous, scoffing yet deprecating manner.

'The proletarian writing we're turning out is opportunist, a despairing shriek against the boot that may tread us under, just as essentially pessimist as Maxim Gorki. Our middle-class radicals are a hodge-podge, just anyone with a high school education who's been tossed out of the career machinery – and a few misfits like me, who feel guilty. There's a new society over the way – our chins are pointing eagerly; our ears hear a

13

new song – this could be a seedtime in the USA – but it's slow.'

'It's the hand-outs,' said someone: 'in old Russia they didn't have relief. Relief and pensions and WPA stand in the way of revolution.'

'Can't let them die on their broken asses,' said another.

'Hunger doesn't produce revolution,' said another, 'or the world would have been revolting since clan society broke down.'

'It produced it in Russia,' said Emily to Mrs Cullen; and she could not help calling out to the man, 'What does produce it then?' Cloth Cap turned and grinned at her.

Mrs Cullen said in an energetic whisper, impressed, 'That's Tom Barrie, the famous proletarian writer – do you know him?'

A man they called Walden, a gross fellow, middle-aged in worn, expensive college casuals, said something about the long radical tradition in American writing, 'the polemical and didactic and patriotic – like Edward Everett Hale's tear-jerking fiction *The Man Without A Country* –'

'But there's a terrible feeling around that we haven't a country, for country is family, job and dinner – and who has them?' a voice said.

The dark, graceful young man had been using a goose-quill toothpick neatly. He put it down and said,

'Hold it, Walden, that Hale story is true; it's true for me. Why must people always prove there was no King Arthur, no Robin Hood, no Paul Bunyan, no Casey Jones – for me that story is true. It haunts me. It haunts Americans. Even yesterday when I came up the gangplank, I thought, What if I never came back to my country again!'

Tom Barrie was grumbling amiably, 'I read a story about the day the sun did not rise. People cleaned their teeth, started their cars, got on the George Washington Bridge, but the sun didn't come up and they went on into the perpetual cold and dark to sell shares and insurance. Gee!' he laughed and shuddered, 'Scary!'

They began to leave their chairs and go on deck. Emily and Mrs Cullen followed them.

'I had better talk to my cabin-mate,' said Emily. 'Will you come along?'

Mrs Cullen wanted to go and get into conversation with the interesting men. 'Why don't you come too?'

Emily was bashful.

She asked Mrs Browne if she could drag her chair alongside her.

'If you like.'

'Do you want to be alone?'

'What difference does it make? Everyone is always alone.'

Emily brought up her deckchair. She said, 'We're lucky. It's a real sunny day. Grand blue sky.'

'Do you think it's grand? I should have thought a writer would find that

14

staring sea and washed-out sky very uninteresting. A painter I know claimed that there were twelve colours in the ordinary blue sky we were looking at somewhere – it was in the Bagatelle Gardens outside Paris. One colour, I told him: I told him he had to believe that there were twelve, some sort of fiction, so that he could go on painting. But I know that all art is based on a convention, a fiction between the artist and his public.'

Emily, much surprised, said, 'Well, I'm fascinated. But who started it?'

Mrs Browne looked ahead of her, over the ship's keel – they were aft and almost under the covered deck. She said, 'It may have a social use. Look at all these artists and writers employed now by the Government. Those artists are glad to have a weekly cheque and they do what they are told to do. They never wanted to starve in Greenwich Village, trying to get ideas that would sell. They're glad to get into organised society. Fantasy has no social value.'

'Well, that's terrific,' said Emily 'but just the same, society prizes its artists: it doesn't want them to go and bake bricks. There's Shostakovich for example: he's original and he's also accepted at home and abroad; and what about Paul Robeson's singing? That's not a convention. Everyone recognises he's a great.'

'Artists like that are an accident,' said Mrs Browne, 'society is organised without any relation to them: and could go on without them. They're not necessary. You can't base a theory on accidents.'

'But if they see ahead? If they belong to a convention not yet made?'

'That is impossible,' said Mrs Browne firmly, 'no one invents anything: it is there, made by the people; there is no room for individuals – an artist should interpret.'

'You're a socialist?' said Emily, quite fuddled by the woman.

Yes. Mrs Browne, born in America, was of Russian parentage and was for the Russian revolution; always had been since the great day in 1917 when the news came over and people like her parents rushed out into the streets and cried, 'Fonya Ganuf, Fonya Ganuf is done for!' Fonya Ganuf, she expained, was the word in the old country, Russia, for the detested Russian State: Fonya, a diminutive for 'Ivan', Ganuf 'the thief'. Yes, they had all been forced to be rebels, even revolutionists of a sort, their conditions in Russia were too hard.

She was going to Paris for a few days and was to wait for her husband, Walter Browne, now working in a small private bank in London. He would take a vacation and join her in Paris. Mrs Browne slowly tore off fragments of ideas, all of them segments of iron, ready for use on the barricades. Yet she seemed stodgy, conservative, prudish. Perhaps she was not; perhaps that was a Russian manner. She and her husband, she said,

15

saw through the New Deal, a palliative. Franklin Delano Roosevelt, hailed as saviour, was the friend of big business, though Wall Steet frowned on him. Wall Street could not sit at table with a friend who talked democracy and admitted that big business had mismanaged. Such talk encouraged discontent, doubt, criticism.

'So you and your husband are socialists – ?'

No, no: they were leftists – after a moment, she said, 'Communists; we're both communists.'

Emily was shaken; and looked sideways at her companion. Now the thick, pale, almond lids dropped over her dark eyes, the long lashes rested on her pale cheeks. She may have been feigning sleep to end the conversation, once she had given her downright views. Perhaps she hated to talk; but the machinery was somehow set in motion against the will? Emily turned to her book, but the wind blew, the sun shone, voices drifted about; and she was drowsy.

She went to look for the man from her home town. Jean-Marie was there. He had no deckchair and was leaning against the rail. They went to the bar. She said she felt guilty about her brother Arnold and Betty. Perhaps if it had been only her savings, they could have had the money; but she could not give them her prize-money.

'Prize what for?'

'Well, it's a wonder I got it. I write anything. I was shocked to find out how easily you can write for and against. It destroys your morals, also your ideas of truth and morality. But once I got started on this idea I had, I got quite hectic. I stayed up at night. It was an essay on Mark Twain and the American dilemma; I called it that.'

'What is the American dilemma?' he quizzed her.

'Well, as I see it, it's that you want to be free and break new ground, speak your mind, fear no man, have the neighbours acknowledge that you're a good man; and at the same time you want to be a success, make money, join the country club, get the votes and kick the other man in the teeth and off the ladder. You believe sincerely in Washington, Jefferson, Lincoln; and also know you'll get your nose bloodied if not worse, if you don't believe in Rockefeller, Mellon, General Motors and Sears Roebuck. An earthquake in your own small brain. To believe, *Send the homeless . . . I lift my lamp beside the golden door!*' and to know in your bones that the door *is* gold. We're Americans, we can't fail, some sort of covered wagon will get us through; yet we see lean and tattered misery, the banks failed, businesses taken over, dust-storms which used to be farms bowling along the roads covering the corpses of crows and men; and we despair, despair. Where to turn? For people used to turn to us. There ought to be an answer. We came over in rowboats and founded the USA, we beat the

16

old inhabitants into the dust, we won the West, and now we starve. It isn't right. Despair, despair. There's the rich man's table firmly planted with its golden legs right in our corn and oil and steel highways; and all we get are musty crumbs.

'We're worried. France was voted Most Backward Country and they had a revolution; then Russia got the leather medal, Most Backward Country, and they had a revolution. But we were always Most Forward Country and look at us. It's a hell of a dilemma. So maybe we are headed for a revolution; but who wants that? It's sickening for Americans to be living on handouts, when we're the world's richest country and believe in the survival of the fittest. None of it makes sense; and that's our dilemma. We won and we won and we've lost and there's no reason for it. The American dilemma is the essence of America.'

'Do you believe that?' he said.

'Oh, my, yes, one step inside the golden door and there's a trap door, you fall right to the bottom of Deadman's Gulch. But why? Why? We have two shovels in our hands, right for digging gold, left for digging graves. And it has always been so. We're miserable people, leanfaced, dismal Uncle Sams. Isn't our history all struggle, all terror, all bloodshed; and at the same time, all hooraying, all success? America the Golden. The dark and bloody ground, I think is our subtitle. A nation of brothers, Cain and Abel, the Fats and Thins, lined up against each other – civil war at the factory gates; and yet – we do believe in equality, fraternity. I guess we think we do. We welcomed with open hands the hungry foreigner, to join the sons of opportunity, and yet we meet the invader from the next county with guns at the county line. Move on, you Red!' Then she began to laugh, 'I've found out in my travels that when the small town bosses say, "Our workers are incited by foreigners", they mean New Yorkers. That's a united nation for you. Oh, well – fooey. Live and let live; if we only could.'

'What a pessimist,' he said laughing.

'I'm a humorist: humorists are always pessimists. They're reactionaries: because they see that every golden cloud has a black lining; so why get a stomach ulcer?'

'And that's the story of our time – you believe that?' he said more seriously.

'I believe in everything. Everything's true. I don't believe things and they turn out to be true. I believe things and it's something put out by the chain-gang press. So now I believe in everything. I know I'm the sort that always falls; but better to be a sucker than a sourpuss. But I long, oh, how I truly long, Jean-Marie, to get things into focus. I'm nearly twenty-five. I have a feeling about this year – Fate! Kismet! Nemesis! My number coming up.'

'For that have another drink!'

'Yes, let's. Oh, Jesus Q., but it's a puzzle. Yet do you know we're so communal, Americans, I sort of believe socialism must be our destiny. Do you know that Eugene V. Debs, a railroad fireman, a socialist, polled one million votes for President, in 1920 and everyone thought the robber barons were going to have to cede their fortresses. So they offered up Sacco and Vanzetti, I guess. Circuses if no bread.'

'What'll you drink? Martini? I'll buy a bottle and make my own; they don't get it dry enough.'

'I'm not much of a drinker. Anything.'

When he returned with two glasses and two bottles, she said, 'I wish you'd tell me what to read. This is my chance away from the sludge-mills to catch up a bit. I couldn't learn anything in college. I was working at night. Now I write informative articles about subjects I've never given a minute's thought to. Woe, woe! I make a living and it's not an honour-able one.'

'Make it some other way.'

'You don't think I can? I can play the piano, sing a bit, I did an act with a boy, went around. But I wanted to be a writer. Maybe I could go to Hollywood and be a gagman. What an ambition! Alas, poor Yorick. Just another skull in the charnel house, at a time when skulls come very cheap. Our life doesn't bear thinking of, does it, Jean-Marie? A flash and then join the majority.'

'Every man who says, "Why struggle? Look up there! The stars are millions of years old," turns out to be a crook; he has his eye on your pocket.'

'Ah, something starts up in my soul when I hear those sibylline words,' said Emily laughing and quaffing; 'as well as everything else, I guess I'm a crook too. Nothing inhuman is alien to me.'

The next day she wore cream slacks, a pink and white sweater striped horizontally, and her white jacket with a pink neckcloth, knotted to one side. In the outfit she looked larger, rosier, younger. Her hair she had tied on top so that the long curling strands, windblown and dust-coloured, fell over her cheeks and neck.

The deckchairs were set out, but differently. Mrs Browne was sitting in the shelter of the sports lounge and seemed not to see her. In the cabin before breakfast she had said to Emily, 'Because we're cabin-mates you don't have to keep me company. I'm a lonely person and used to it. My husband is like you, gregarious. To me such people are dependent.'

'OK,' said Emily. That's the lesson for today, she said to herself. She did not know whether Mrs Browne, who spoke only once a day, thought

18

these things out during her silent hours, or whether she had a few texts to run her life by.

Emily sat in her chair in the sun beside a man who turned out to be a Romanian and reading Henry James in Romanian.

How wonderfully exciting the world is! You just have to travel.

'I haven't even read Henry James in the original,' said Emily; and though he was polite and even gay, she felt the man lost interest in her.

The sun shone, the breeze tickled and after trying to memorize a few sentences of *The Rights of Man* by Thomas Paine, a book everyone was then reading, and her copy given her at the boat by her brother, she became restless and went to look for Jean-Marie.

'Honest contempt, bad temper, is what I want – hometalk! No melancholy damnation as with Mrs Browne, no chewed-over headlines as with Mrs Cullen.'

She found him. Presently they went to the bar lounge. The lounge, so early, with views each side of the sunny sea, full of blue-green ditches with top frostings of foam, had a fresh innocent air. The floor was clean, the chairs and tables neat. They sat on one of the long benches waiting for the bar to open.

'The sailor's snug harbour,' said she. Jean-Marie got them to turn down the loudspeaker diffusing a popular tune, which Emily began to hum.

'What was it you did? A college act?' he said.

'Better than that. I'll show you. They'll get up a concert and you'll see I'm really good.'

She had a newspaper, he had a big book in German, which he was reading, though he understood German poorly. After an hour or so, some of the Americans from the New Dealers' table came in and sat on the other side of the lounge. Jean-Marie knew the names of all of them.

'They're a delegation from the American Writers' Congress, going to the Paris Congress.'

'And who is he? The – uh – that scion with the curly blond hair, the tall one?'

'Stephen Howard. Does a column for the Washington *Liberator*, written some studies of labour problems, union leaders, use of goons and labour spies; all the details; learned it at Mummy's knee.'

'His mother's a socialist?'

Jean-Marie laughed to himself.

'I like his style,' said Emily.

'Go over and introduce yourself. You're a writer.'

She wouldn't, but became merry to attract Howard's attention. McRoy got her another drink, with a calculating look; he wanted to make her drunk, to see what she would do.

'Come on, let's have your story. More about the dilemma,' he said.
It had now become a joke with them.

'We've got so far ahead of the rest of the world that one-third of us are dropping in our tracks from hunger. Now we suddenly for the first time think about ourselves. We didn't have a system like other people, we were a covered wagon hiking towards Golconda. Now we're suddenly looking at people who have systems – the laughable British, the licentious French, the ragged Russians. What can they do for us? We wish we had a system. It's side-splitting. We're a side-splitting people.'

'No, you haven't explained about your essay on Twain.'

'Well, I started in with that sour, ferocious, bloodcurling little gem about the Boxer Rebellion, at which time we had our Bible students in China too. Some were killed. You know, *To the Person Sitting in Darkness*.'

She was talking to him, but facing the group across the lounge and talking loudly. He looked down into his drink, with a pleased expression. They were talking; she was matching them. His marvellous lively eyes, man and animal in one, were looking at her through the eyebrows, as through underbrush.

'The missionaries compelled the Chinese to pay for the murders and fined them thirteen times the amount of the indemnity; and the newspaper paragraph about it said, "This money will be used for the propagation of the gospel." It's rich. And some other missionaries – Catholics,' she said with that frontal attack instinctive with debaters, for he had been a Catholic, 'collected not only the indemnities, but a Chinese head for every American head. It sizzles. It burns holes in the paper. Well, that's the bitter truth, the savagery of life which staggers you, keeps you rooted to the spot and your outcries stop your breath; and yet it is wildly out of line with all our ideals, humanity, peace, brotherly love, do unto others, until you laugh, shout, you understand your own simplicity and wickedness and denseness and greed – that's American humour. It's better than Daumier with lumpen-proletariat gargoyles gaping. You listen to any Hollywood dialogue in a modern film and you'll hear such a mash of good sense, brashness, earthy wit, impudence – that's American wisdom, that's our humour. It's not *les bons mots* and *le raffiné*,' she said (with a strong home accent), 'it's not hissing the *double entendre* through thin lips, it's not like *Punch*, hitting with a flour-filled sock, no hit, no mark; it bites to the bone; it's not like satire which is just needling someone you're afraid to touch; American humour is another way of seeing the truth; and what a vision! It isn't giggles or smut, it isn't anecdotes about baby-sitters and chars and Uncle Brown's habits; it is homespun, godlike truth stalking in from the plains and the tall timber, coonskin and deerhide, with a gun to disturb our little home comforts.'

20

She spoke so loudly that the barman looked anxious and was hesitating at the side-door to the bar; and she had attracted the attention of the delegates across the lounge.

Jean-Marie approved her and gazed with a smile in the folds of his weather-beaten long face. He looked at the delegates and winked. She laughed at them, at him, at herself. She got up.

'Look, I'll show you. I'll do bingo-bango.'

She walked to the little piano behind the gold rail and sat on the piano-stool. But the piano was locked. She went to the bar counter and asked the barman for the key. He, small and dark, with a neat wooden face, shook his head; but she persisted, her face becoming brighter and brighter, her features pinching into a faunish mask; and a candle lighted inside the mask, as she bewitchingly, irresistibly coaxed and flattered and teased. Everyone looked. The barman looked across at McRoy, suddenly smiled, bent down and handed out the key. She went back across the little dance-floor. 'Olé,' said the man in the cap, Tom Barrie. She sat down. Her strong legs showed their muscles through the slacks, her strong arms freckled and with fair down, her strong wrists and small squarish hands looked well, coming out of her striped sweater. She opened the piano, turned towards Jean-Marie, sideways, one foot on a pedal, one foot on the floor, and genial, a little drunk, said, 'I used to barnstorm with a boy called Bim-Bam, stage name, and we brought Broadway to the hinterland, or said we did. Really we just made up our numbers out of nursery rhymes and work-songs or anything going around. This is one.'

Then beating time with one foot and using the pedal freely, she began in a forceful, calm and sophisticated style and seeming more than life-size, to give a musical comedy rendering of 'La Cucaracha', with intro-duction, aria, a comic interlude, which she said was supplied by Bim-Bam originally, though she now supplied it. 'La Cucaracha' was played every-where then. The men in the American group all sang it and when she had finished gave applause and 'olé', She bowed.

She went back to Jean-Marie, and Stephen Howard came over and asked to join them.

'I've seen you somewhere before,' he said.

'I've seen you, but where?' said she.

'Writers' Congress?'

'Naw – tavern on University Place?'

'Maybe; place with the white cat?'

'I've been there. The cat's always having kittens.'

'Yes.'

As the boat edged its way in awkwardly at Le Havre and she stood at the rail, excited by her first view of a French town, the man in the cap, Tom Barrie, came and stood beside her.

'Gee,' he said, 'I'd like to get down there and kiss the dirt on the docks. In Europe and in America too, what France means! The light of the world.' His dark face was wreathed in smiles. 'The modern world began with the French Revolution.'

'And the American,' said she.

She was to go ashore with Mrs Browne. She had not thought to get a hotel room, fancying Paris had plenty of rooms for tourists. She agreed to go to Mrs Browne's hotel in the rue St Benoît, St Germain-des-Prés, a very small place where Mrs Browne had stayed with her husband in 1926, their first year in Europe.

Mrs Browne said gloomily, 'That is, if they have a room. There are residents in all these little hotels in Paris. They live there all their lives. Paris is full of people from the country and from foreign countries who left home and now live in a hotel room. They go to the zinc for their breakfast and eat rolls and pâté for dinner and that's their life.'

'The zinc?'

'The bar counter. My husband likes that. He'd like to live like that. But I don't. I can't live in London. It's the climate and the clothes don't fit; and they always say "Are you a Canadian?" So we may as well be divorced.'

'Eh?'

'Marriage is a kind of divorce. You are just two people getting farther and farther apart. But that's true of everyone. I'm getting farther away from my mother, too.'

On the train she left Mrs Browne in the compartment. She suddenly felt a pang, realising that she had not said goodbye to Jean-Marie, who was going on to London. She stood outside in the corridor to see Normandy. A man coming along the corridor stopped beside her; it was Stephen Howard.

'I was looking for you. Come and sit with us. Come to our hotel!'

'Well, thanks, I'd like to but I promised Mrs Browne, that woman there. If I desert her, she'll say life is like that, always abandoned. She's an inspissated crêpehanger, but friendly. She thinks we're all marooned on a million desert islands and no radio, no handkerchiefs to wave. So I can't.'

He remained silent. She looked up at him. On the ship he had listened to her tirades; and when at the end she wrung her hands, crying, 'What prattle,' he said:

And gliding and springing, she went ever singing. . .
The Earth seemed to love her, and Heaven smiled above her
As she lingered towards the deep. . .'

When she blushed, he said, 'Shelley, *Arethusa arose* . . .'

He had comforted her, picked the meaning from her words, made her feel young, wise, bright.

He had fetching ways, a delicate, assumed selfishness and petulance, his life-long private joke which he shared with society, an affectation of naughtiness and self-indulgence which she, who had been brought up rough and ready, found delightful. Then, as if ashamed, he had let her know that he had been for many years an invalid.

'And when at last I walked out into the world, a living man, a free man, grown up, as good as the next man, and left behind me the doctors and nurses who had done that for me, unselfishly, because they could have been stockbrokers and typists, and I saw all the little businesses, heartache, headache, sturdy tough little lives whisking down the drain, turning into the stuff we were made from and all those good lives, gone for nothing, I had to go to work, straighten myself out, no poor little rich boy for me.'

An only son, he had already spoken of his mother, Anna, friendly.

'Anna lives in a narrow, happy world. She's not educated, though she's been to college and made I don't know how many trips to Europe. She's thoroughly Chicago and never became New York, though we live there; and I think she keeps the Chicago out of pride. She's shrewd, unaffected, rather awkward and a first-rate businessman. There's no need to make any more money, but Anna does it out of pride and honour; one has a duty towards money. For us, the dollar-fever crisis has passed. We're all gentle now, or ridiculous cranks. All but Anna and Uncle Howard Howard; someone has to mind the business.'

Stephen had been married, was a widower and had a daughter, Olivia, aged two, an heiress, in the care of his sister, Florence, so as to leave him free. He wanted a political career; thought he had it in him. He said with a satirical grimace, 'We're not ascetics, we don't mind money. My family are now lining up suitable girls for me, particularly one I was walking out with, a canned meat fortune, very suitable; and there's my cousin, Charlotte, very nice girl, went to Bryn Mawr, went to art school for four years, no talent. No money now, but in due course she will be much better off than even I will be. Mother thinks I should have just a small allowance. I'm really paying it to myself, for it comes out of the estate I'll eventually get from Mother. She's right,' he said petulantly, 'fortunes have died young in the hands of dreamy misfits who want to see socialism in their time and do not realise that there is genuine socialism here and now for the rich. My mother thinks socialism would spoil the workers. I said to her, "Look at them! They're spoiled now. No fish-knives, no boathouses on the lake with their little country cabins, no going to Groton and Princeton. How coarse and makeshift! The life of the workers' friend is not decent either. You have to see the blackfaced, baldheaded facts of half a nation on the soup-lines; you have to compromise, get insulted, fight, blackguard." No wonder Mother thinks it is no life for me. It isn't. But I couldn't live any other now. And she loves me. She puts up the money for this kind of frolic. For I'm not an elected delegate on this mission. I'm a private observer. She sees me making a mistake and she keeps me dependent to protect me. She's not buying me. Dependants never have to compromise, they can speak out. No benefactor wants to lose his toady. Mothers even less.'

'You know she is very practical. Don't think she's asleep. The Howards have seen trouble before. If by chance, the wind is the wind of change, then maybe that wind will blow a Howard into the White House even as a friend of the workers, and that can't be bad. No matter what Adams got to Washington, it was good for the Adamses.'

'But why do you talk like that?' Emily said. 'You're great and you're working for the biggest new deal of all, change the world.'

He said carelessly, 'Oh, I'm a calculator. I'd rather depend on the poor than the rich, there are more of them. I have an affection for them. They're used to bearing us on their backs, usually think nothing of it. There we go mowing them down and they shout or whisper, Hosannah! Till, of course, they get up, wipe the dust out of their eyes and have at us. A bad lot. Why can't they be like us? The rich never revolt.'

That's what he had been saying to her. She had laughed quietly that day; and that night, when she lay in her bunk, she laughed aloud and had to tell the reason why to Mrs Browne, who did not think it funny. But such cracks and blisters in the skin of the rich she had never imagined. Was he ridiculing himself or her? Was she, to him, just a yokel from Lumberville? Wasn't she worse than he pretended to be – for she hadn't given a thought to these things, in spite of Grandma and her Wobbly.

'But you sound so bitter!'

He said, 'Oh, I'm so pickled in contradictions, I'm soured. A vinegary skinflint. Can't you see me in forty years? I'm going to be a mean old recluse like Grandpa Tanner, living in one room at the Ritz, knocking on the floor with my stick because the gruel they brought me is too hot. I wanted to do the world a good turn, but it turned out of my hands. Everyone knows the workers have no gratitude. So I'll take it out on my manservant.'

24

He said this in an airy, almost girlish way.

'The air's honey,' she said to herself later, 'there's something odd about this. I'm floating.'

Now in the train, looking up at him, she said 'How tall are you? I must know.'

'Just on six feet. I look taller because I'm thin.'

Then he said, 'What are you saying, your lips are moving?'

'I was thinking about you. You do what I have never done. I've only fought for the family bread and then Emily.'

Looking out at the countryside, he talked now in quite a different way. He told her how enthusiastic he had been at college. He had got in with a group who thought they ought to use their higher education for society. He studied socialism. He engaged a tutor, a poor scholar, a Marxist, who helped him because he, Stephen, was slow and behind in studies, on account of having spent years in hospital. Stephen had thought it wrong to spend his allowance. He tried to work his way through college as his tutor did. He made himself sick again. But the determination to help the world, which filled him then with an ardour, a fever, had never left him. It burned inside him. As soon as he graduated, he went off to join a labour battle between fruit-pickers and fruit-packers; and in the battle there he met his first wife, daughter of one of the packers.

'I bounced right back into the boss class. We loved each other; but we thought a long time about it. Neither of us wanted to marry a boss.'

He was eager now to see the writers and rebels they were to meet in Paris, face to face, to shake hands with, hear from, colleagues, those who had been in battle, in jail, been wounded, founded communist groups, edited papers, written appeals, spoken to crowds; people in exile, people burning with political ambition, and courage in the present doubtful pass, tough and keen with hope for the future, fighters, new people from the new lands. Think, men who had seen socialism in action!

'What glory,' said she: 'it will be liking getting a whole sea-roller in your teeth.'

'Did you ever?'

'Yes, and swallowed to much, it ended up just a thin film on the beach.'

'Come and sit with us. You can join your dismal Browne friend later.'

She refused, 'I'm a bit scared. You're too good for me.'

'Well, I'll be looking for you at the meetings.'

'Oh, Stephen,' she said involuntarily, 'I'm not a writer, I'm only a hack, a getter-up of pars. My highest hope is a byline. I'm a westerner as hairy and horned as a bison, Emily Hayseed from Skid Row; and you are a sort of ambassador of culture.'

'I would not be there in glory without Mamma's money,' he said peevishly.

25

She turned away and began to clap her hands, 'Oh, look, France! Appleblossom time in Normandy! Oh, and I'm here. Do you care how you got there?'

There was a pause. Then he said in a low voice, carelessly, 'Why go with these schoolmasters to the council of the good? Let's get off at the next station and tramp through Normandy, catch them up in Paris in a couple of days.'

She was startled, could not speak, a little shocked too, for already she was visualising this great meeting of the new world, already reporting it. He waited, said no more and, someone coming for him from the other coach because they were in committee, he turned without a word and went off. Standing there in the corridor, a cool breeze coming through, she pictured scenes in inns, eating, walking, the night – fresh, innocent though in love, pleasant – a French inn among orchards, the broad white bed linen thrown back. Why had he said it and then gone off? A rich man's joke?

She went in and talked to Mrs Browne. There were new settlements, suburban houses, crowning and folded in hills. She was surprised, for some reason. There was in the distance a wide green field inside a square fence with trees along three sides, just inside the farm-gate an old car standing. It reminded her of lessons, 'Find the area of – '

The Atlantic was a long way behind now. At the station she saw him walking off with three other men. 'That finished me with him.'

Mrs Browne turned warmer on acquaintance. She knew the Paris Americans lived in; and offered to help. But Emily took her guidebook and Thomas Paine and set out to see the Bastille, the Place de la Concorde, Montmartre. She sat down in the Place de la Bastille in a café, surveyed the monument and read her book. Everyone was reading Tom Paine in the USA then and some of his words were as well known as the Gettysburg Address. She was surprised to see that the book was dedicated to George Washington. She began to memorize.

> The American Constitutions were to Liberty what a grammar is to language.
> Freedom has been hunted around the globe; reason was considered rebellion. But such is the irresistible nature of truth, that all it asks and all it wants is the liberty of appearing. The sun needs no inscription to distinguish him from darkness and no sooner did the American governments display themselves to the world than despotism felt a shock.

'Oh, great! I must change too. I must write that truth,' she said aloud. She was glad now that she had discovered her ignorance. She wanted to be by herself until she could learn a few of the things that were ABC to

26

the people she had just met and that were known to all artists in rebellion, all people who had been stirred up, in search of a better fate for mankind. It seemed strange to her now, looking back, that in the USA everyone was not on the march. Wasn't it obvious that the system had failed? It was; and yet what had she been doing? She had lived from minute to minute, without an idea. She would go to the meetings – one day soon. She was shy about pushing herself into what she called the *crème de la crème*, she was not fit for it. She saw now that Stephen Howard's remark about Normandy was just a joke. What was odd about it was the way it had struck to the heart.

2 LOVE STORY

Paris, June 1935

For a while Emily's home was the little hotel in the rue St Benoît and she trotted the streets around, the rue Jacob, rue de Fuerstenberg, rue de l'Abbaye, rue Bonaparte. At eight o'clock the evening they got there, after thick rain and the sun had shone, the streets, drying rapidly, were glassy. There was an old house at the end of the rue St-Benoît with four windows in the attic displaying pots of greenery, and the front of this house, anciently whitened, was patchy, part age, part wet, and next was Number 40 over which was the sign *Ébénisterie*, cabinet-work. Houses in various heights, various whites blotted out part of the washed blue sky, a *terrasse* with wooden tubs – the clouds lifting still, the air fresh, someone washing a floorcloth in the gutter, streaming with clear water released from the hydrant; and in all these old houses, people sitting in small places taking the air, but modestly, no elbowing, no outcries. Opposite the old Abbaye, before the police station, was an interior with the plaster bust of a young girl, a little Greuze, some bronzes. She was at the commissariat, frankly studying it, when a man, a painter in studio gear, stopped the three policemen going on duty, saying, 'Have you seen – ?' and later in the distance she saw the same painter in the street, anxious, nervous, shaking his hands together: and then, passing a restaurant, there he was, walking along the counter towards the table at the end where six policemen were having supper with six half-bottles of wine. The painter said to the man behind the counter, 'Can no one tell me where it is?' He said to the policemen, 'Can no one tell me where it is?' How sad.

The houses opposite the hotel were very old. There were little stores boarded up and poor laundries, restaurants dismal in the mixed tail-end of the rue de l'Université. She walked around bursting with joy. 'It is, it is, it is!' Down on the quays, where the bookcases were now shut, there was clear evening light, the smoke of the *Sansonnet* tug on the Seine, the line of trees on the Quai de Louvre. 'It is here, I am here, life, new life.' When she returned to the hotel, they said there was 'un monsieur' waiting for her. There he was looking out through the lace curtains of the dark sitting room; Howard had come for her.

'How did you know?' she asked.

'You said the rue St.-Benoît.'

He took her to dinner. They walked across the river through the courts of the Louvre to a small dark restaurant in the Palais-Royal, the famous Véfour. 'Uncle Maurice comes here.'

He had arranged for her to join the American group at the conference, as a 'private observer' like himself, so that she could go to all the sessions with them.

'But we won't go to all. You'll see Paris, too.'

She became part of the American group. When Stephen did not call for her, she went to the congress herself, sitting near the front of the auditorium. She could write it up when she got back. One afternoon, it was hot. The Russian writers, sober and straitlaced, were on all the afternoon reading their forty-page dissertations, either in Russian or in translation. She noticed the American writers gathering at the side and signalling to her. But she remained in her seat. Then she saw them laughing, and in a moment Stephen had come down the aisle and leaned over her,

'Come along, we're playing hookey.'

They had their photographs taken in an ante-room, then Walden and Barrie and Stephen and Emily marched off along the Seine. Walden and Barrie were going to the Right Bank, Emily and Stephen turned left, went up the boulevard St-Michel and sat down in a café.

'I knew your feet were tired,' said he; 'I know you by now. In a little while, when you're rested, we'll take a taxi to the Ile-de-la-Cité – it's only a couple of minutes.'

'Oh, that little island in the river that tags along after Notre-Dame?'

He said, 'I've an uncle lives there, Uncle Maurice. He's an old bachelor, an aesthete, a do-nothing and I'm like him. Or I should be if it weren't that a hellgrammite bit me once and I've been biting my luck ever since.'

'What's a hellgrammite?'

'A bug you use for fishing.'

'A hellgrammite bit you?'

'Yes, it really did. But I meant, one day I found out my family uses labour spies, goons, strike-breakers, the lurid lot. Someone told me, reproached me at Princeton. I didn't believe it. I went and found out. I wrote a book about it. I'll give it to you. A pamphlet it is – *Labor Spies*.'

'What did the Howards say to the book?'

'It was brought out by the left press and under a pseudonym – you know, Justin Clark, I told you. I knew Mother read it, for she had a quiet talk with me about all the good the Howards have done the country. She is very proud of their services to the country. Men on strike are undermining that good. She didn't put it in those words.'

'She didn't mind?'

'I'm her favourite son – the only one that is. I only mean to say, I'm really another Uncle Maurice and she is thankful I am not. He went to the Sorbonne – so did I for a year. He collects – all sorts of oddities, delicious objects that I like and admire. It took me years to understand him, for it seemed boyish to me – collecting. He goes to concerts just like me, has a faithful friend or two he loves – just a happy Howard.'

'It's such a beautiful way to live, the way you live: all with different personalities, leaving each other alone and admiring each other. A united family. I do love it. It's like a picture gallery somewhere in Italy – all the portraits, elegantly drawn by some master of the day – tray raffinay. A friendly master – a court painter – not a hater of the rich. Till now, I never knew the rich were decent.'

He laughed, 'I don't think Anna thinks so; she knows too much, but she is a good woman; she won't give her class away.'

In the taxi he said,

'I've been thinking about you, Emily, thinking a lot.'

'I'm not sure I'm glad. I don't stand thinking about.'

'I think you do. Do I stand thinking about?'

'Oh, you – you're the first honest-to-god scion I've met, on my own. My Cousin Laura met a few. You'll meet her when we get back – that is, if you don't drop me at the foot of the gangplank. But I've never called her men by their first names.'

'Are you engaged to someone back home – or, I mean, got a steady?'

'Oh, no – someone I dropped or who dropped me. Partly I came away to let some fresh air blow through me. It would have been ten dollars in my pocket if he'd never been born. Oh, I told you about him – B.D.'

'So, the post is vacant, isn't it?'

'Oh, stop kidding, Stephen: it still hurts.'

'You don't love him, do you?'

'Oh, no – you're full of love, you're sending out a beam and someone gets in the way and you think it's him; it's you lighting him up.'

'Then let the beam shine on me! Have me!'

She looked at him; she began a tremulous smile,

'I suppose this is what they do in your mauve, decayed circles. Laura would understand, I guess.'

'I don't care about Laura. I don't like her.'

'You don't know her: every man falls for her.'

'You're not like other women,' he said.

'I know better than to ask how. And what about the rich witch you're all but engaged to? And that respectable, highborn cousin with the moolah – in England?'

'I'll write to your parents if you like.'

'My mother died long ago. I had a stepmother. My father's a pillar of small town society, makes ovens. I have a brother Arnold, who is younger and married and prolific. You better write to me. If you write to them, they'll think their living's gone. Besides, what do you want to write for? To find out if I'm married? Or been in jail or am a dangerous red or have debts?'

'To tell them we're going to get married.'

'Oh, golly – my goodness. That's what happens to Laura.'

'Oh, down with Laura – whoever she is.' They got out of the taxi at the church of St-Louis-en-l'Ile and walked down the narrow high-banked street.

'Am I walking? I must be floating,' she said. 'How did we get here?'

He looked down at her, touched. She looked up, 'You look really beautiful here; it suits your El Greco face.'

'You can't tell a man he's beautiful,' he said.

'I can. The first time I looked at you, the light from the ocean was shining on your face, while you were speaking at table: and you had a toothpick in your hand. I thought, What a saintly face!'

'God forbid.'

'An El Greco saint, I saw later – those long folds and lemony look.'

He laughed, was pleased. 'There is some distant Spaniard in my family. You may see a little of him in Uncle Maurice. You'll understand him and he'll understand you. He lives in a spindling reflected light from all the windows in his museum of a home; but he understands people, he never interferes, never criticises, always knows what to do to help – if he likes you. A sort of Cousin Pons, too.' He had to explain that.

She exclaimed, 'Oh, my, oh, my, my neglected education. Oh, will I have to sit up all night on the kitchen chair, trying to catch up with you and your sister Florence and sister Brenda and Uncle Maurice?'

'Shut up,' he said in an undertone 'and here we are.'

She usually spent half a day sightseeing, half a day at the congress. She arrived at its doors each day very elated – from the faubourg St-Antoine, from the Luxembourg, from the Ste-Chapelle – what a city, what people, and here in the hall, what freedom lovers; 'the Hall of Fame on roller-skates from all points of the compass,' she said.

Programmes, meetings, subcommittees, reports, lunches, dinners given by the Americans to foreign writers, and by others to them, the great reception at the Opéra with the *Garde Républicaine* in full dress, boots,

Roman helmets, plumes, brass, straps, lining the staircase. Passing them, irregular clouds of visitors in simple clothing, street dress, the garments they wore in their rooms, at artists' parties, people whose faces shone or looked away diffidently at the shine of the brasses and arms; gauds put out by the gallant French Republic, where literature is always honoured – for the shy, awkward, touchy, nondescript but acutely observant citizens of the Republic of Letters.

Tom Barrie made a speech. The shambling, flask-faced workman appeared on the planks while the photographers crowded between legs and desks. He said, 'Our writers must learn that the working class which has created a great civilization in the Soviet Union is capable of creating a similar civilization in our own countries. The working class has heroism, intelligence, courage. We must never forget that a class which has such depths of creative power deserves only the best literature we can give.'

Louis Aragon, the French writer, said, 'I returned from the Soviet Union and I was no longer the same man. However, there remained a thousand bonds, fine as a spider's web for me to break. That I have had the strength to break them, is, I know, due to practical work, to the social work which was carried on by the proletariat of my country.'

'I am floating, Stephen, I am floating. Now I am glad I am a scribbler. There is a future. Tom Barrie is right; France sheds light on everything. We have a future.'

'Wait; plenty is to come.'

The embassies received them. In their dress of poor relations, they were announced by servants in black clothes and gloves, all the artisans of typewriter and pen, the unknown, the known, all named: 'Monsieur André Gide, Madam Anna Seghers, Monsieur Thomas Mann, Monsieur Forster, Monsieur Thomas Barrie, Monsieur Kantorowicz . . . Henri Barbusse, Romain Rolland, Martin Nexoe, Ilya Ehrenburg, Aldous Huxley, Julien Benda – Monsieur Stephen Howard, Mademoiselle Wilkes – Bonjour, Monsieur l'Ambassadeur, bonjour, Madame l'Ambassadrice.'

'Oof!'

Then sitting round the big rooms under portraits in oil, chatting with the hosts, getting to the big tables on which were the largest dishes of food they had ever seen, silver boats and coracles used no doubt by Jupiter guzzling in heaven; but at the Russian Embassy used to hold caviar.

Several times she promised to meet one or other of them, the Americans; and she did go with Tom Barrie to a room he shared with an English writer; but sat shy and uneasy in a chair while the two men flirted with an English girl and a French girl from the congress.

'I can make any man lustful just by looking in his eyes,' stated the

32

English girl, who was plain, long-nosed and big-eyed.

'Try me,' said Tom Barrie.

She sat opposite to him on the twin cot and glared.

'Pah!' he cried suddenly, jumping off the bed.

'Try me,' said Pax, the English writer.

She twisted round to face him; and after a minute, he fell back on the bed, legs and arms in the air, laughing, 'It works, yes, it works.' The French girl meanwhile was having a bath, for there was no bath in her room at her little hotel, and it appeared that she did this every day, for her toilet things were arranged in the bathroom.

'Well, comrades – ' said Emily, diffidently and with a flush, 'I think I'll get back to my hotel.' They let her go.

Others she left standing at the door of the hall. One serious journalist from Chicago made quite a face as she hurried past him, engrossed in Howard's words; his lineaments crashed together; he turned dark with disgrace.

'Now, he's going to hate me. Oh, jiminy,' she said to Stephen, 'I'm like B. D. Given a chance we'll all teasers and cheats.'

'Forget him. We're going to lunch.'

She sighed, 'If you knew the lift I get being with you. Life is a battlefield, but not a field of honour. Here at least, we are all on a field of honour.'

Stephen said, 'Every writer worth his salt begins by some notion of revolt. He wants to show people that the labels are wrong; and then there's the contagion. Writers don't write about themselves – they need others. The others – the all-important.'

'Ah!' she said. 'The baffling, puzzling, beloved others. If we could just for half an hour get inside someone else and be someone else, we'd swipe the laurels. If it didn't kill us. Maybe, it would be the fatal bolt, strike you dead.'

He said, 'Most writers, even if doing pulp and potboilers – are forced at least once or twice in their lives to say what they see before their own eyes – they wake up one morning and say, "The emperor has no clothes, and I've got to tell people that."'

'But this lot here are the best, they say nothing but the truth and they are trying to change the world. Oh, I can hardly bear it, it is so thrilling, noble, grand,' said Emily. 'What have I been doing all my life? Pulping and potboiling. Every morning I said, "The emperor has no clothes"; but I said, "But the paper runs clothing ads and they won't let me print that." How shameful! You don't know what it is, Stephen. I feel punchdrunk and ethereal too – free. I'm dizzy. I can scarcely breathe. Anything can happen now. To be with the *crème de la crème*, me, the family misfit.'

Things did get better for her, as he said. Howard took her to Langer, to restaurants in the Bois, to Véfour, to La Pérouse, to the Vert Galant, places big and small, with cooking exquisite – 'exquis' she kept saying – rare, provincial, homestyle. They ate also anywhere, in bistros and cafés, just flopping down laughing, having a drink, saying, 'We'll eat here, why not?' Talking, talking. He took her again to see his uncle, Maurice Howard.

'Oh, I love you Uncle Maurice, you are so modayray,' she said. Emily was immoderate. She found that she was a gourmet; but she was too greedy, she wanted to try everything and when she looked at a menu in a good place, not merely to know the meaning of the names but to try them all. She was so eager, delightedly gay, spontaneous, so tumultuously full of joy and folly – and with it, sharp, discerning, salty.

Stephen was satisfied. When he went back to his hotel he would laugh at her enthusiasm, smile, and tears might come to his eyes. The girls he had known knew the right things to say and eat; they enjoyed themselves, too, but they suffered from the respectability of the rich; especially if they shared his political views.

At the end of a week in which they saw each other every day and ate together at least once a day, they were thought of together; so that any group in a restaurant expecting them, left two places side by side for them. Stephen said on a Friday, when he was taking her home, 'I have sent a cable to Mother about the girl she wants me to marry.'

'Oh!'

'I said it was no use. I wrote a letter to Mother at the same time and one to the girl telling them I have made up my mind.'

'Mm.'

'If you will have me, I will have you.'

There was a pause. He continued, 'Let's go back on the same boat. We can come to Paris later, not for a honeymoon, because I have work to do as soon as I get back; but next year.'

He stopped and turned to her, his eyes full with his resolution.

She was too startled to be shaken; she thought he should have asked her before writing home. Still, there it was. He was still looking at her, waiting for something.

'All right.'

'I made up my mind a few days ago,' he said.

When did I make up my mind? she said to herself, in annoyance.

Then he said, 'I want to explain why. We are going to work together. This is a time between worlds. You could sink into pessimism if you did not have a plan. Roosevelt entered the White House with a plan, that is why he can still make out: no one else has one. Roosevelt, when he

34

entered the White House at a time when fourteen million Americans were starving, and the "tide of destitution rising" as someone said, did not promise reform, a new order, he promised revival for the business community.'

'Well,' she said, 'he promised a more abundant life, he promised the forgotten man that he would be brought to the national table – '

'Yes, Lazarus. There isn't just a forgotten man, but a forgotten nation, grudgingly kept alive. So the scene is set for total breakdown or some sort of social plan. We never had a common man's social plan before. The Constitution, though the refuge of our liberties, is secretly used in favour of the rich. Though its general rhetoric means the poor can use it too. Relief is not a social plan, it's a few sandbags against the flood. Everyone knows relief isn't the way to run a nation and make the human tree burst with flower and fruit.'

Then he said, 'That occurred to me because I worked for a while in the orchards in California as casual labour. No different from what you know or expect. And those "miserables" don't want to revolt – just one red-eyed man in a thousand – because revolt is even worse. They've had enough of fighting, black eyes, broken noses, thugs, sheriffs, and all to get rags, beans and something mud-coloured in a tin mug. The only reason they throw rocks at the overseer is to get into jail. Rather eat crow than bite the dust.

'The thing is they don't go any more for social sunrise ideas. Here we've got five or six, the League for Social Justice formed by Father Coughlin, politically dubious; the End Poverty in California clubs of Upton Sinclair, a coffee house dream; Dr Townsend's clubs for old age pensioners; there's the Share the Wealth Clubs of senator Huey Long – all vote-catchers; and two left political parties, the Farmer-Labor Party in Minnesota and the Progressives of Wisconsin. They don't fit into our political history. There's the Communist Party which has the backing of international experience, a great connection overseas and a plan – but people don't want revolution. There all you can buy is trouble, misery and daily bouts with the police, only too glad to earn their pay with steel and tear gas. "I want a job! Take this you bastard!" And he gets it in the teeth. It's a frightful cosmic joke. If you have a full belly. It's either a faceless future or some trained brute plugging you in the guts. All these people here, our colleagues, know it; but the people who get slugged don't know what it's for, can't talk, can't write.'

'They don't know? One plug on the nose and they know: it's a college education,' said she.

'But resentment isn't enough. This could have been a revolutionary situation in the USA – like Russia in 1917, but there wasn't enough preparation. In Russia the writers in the eighties expected revolution – they knew it couldn't last. Thousands went out into the country, devoted their whole lives to teaching the people, lost their lives at it. It's a terrible business to be in social reform. It gives me a pain, a real pain, in my head, in my stomach. I've got pains everywhere and I don't know if it's fear or despair or incompetence. I know I'm incompetent but I must go on.

'And there you are, Emily, full of joy and interest and love and humanity and a need to know and you are strong, can't be crushed. I know you're strong and loyal. A faithful love, a true, great woman. You have the faith I'm afraid to lack.'

'How do you know I'm faithful and strong?' she objected, feeling cornered by this belief in her, without any foundation that she could see.

He laughed.

They were crossing the Luxembourg Gardens, on their way to a students' restaurant in the place du Panthéon. First, as he knew, she would stand, read the incised letters across the pediment of the Panthéon – Aux Grands hommes, la patrie reconnaissante – to (our) great men, (their) grateful country. She would sigh with enthusiasm, say, 'Oh, grande nation, loving glory and greatness.'

He had said, 'You haven't seen Lincoln in his temple in Washington. The archaeologists to come, ten thousand years hence will find it in the rubble of time and say, "This was the American God", or they may think it is Manco Capac, First Inca – it won't make any difference, and the Gettysburg Address will be tacked on to the legend of Paul Bunyan, for things will be as mixed as Mesopotamia by then.'

'He is the American god,' she said.

'Not FDR?'

She stopped half-way across the sandy walk by the fountain and burst out, 'Stephen, I came over here to see Europe; and this is all I've seen. I don't care if it will be gopher-mounds in ten thousand years. I came to see Berlin, Warsaw, Vienna, Florence, Rome, Amsterdam, Dublin – I wanted to go back with them all in arms.'

He paused. 'Well, I could take you to Baden-Baden and Karlsruhe where my family holidayed and lived a hundred years ago; but it will be on the up-and-up, no honeymooning; the Germans know from no jokes,' (he said with an assumed German accent), 'or Salzburg perhaps. We have a few days yet before they're Nazified. But Berlin? Vienna? The pot's boiling. Last July, Nazi conspirators shot Chancellor Dollfuss in Vienna. Last month, Chancellor Hitler, now known as Der Führer, rejected the Versailles Treaty and ordered conscription in Germany. He's fired the Reichstag, blamed the communists, arrested thousands, even members of the Reichstag, who should be immune; he's assaulted the Jews and

36

promised Germany revenge. You've seen refugee writers yourself. Why go there? You don't even speak German.'

'I can say, *Ach, Himmel!* and *Gott sei Dank!* and *Sumpf* and *Pestfaul,*' she said, making explosive noises.

'Very good! That sweet song should keep you out of the hoosegow. And they'll tell you all.'

'But I do get news, Stephen. Emily the Scoop. I want to see where things are happening. Don't you? You're a political journalist: you want to meet the President, tell him forceful things. I want to see where Dollfuss was shot to death and Weimer, and where the Weimar Republic was shot to death and I'd like to see I. G. Farben and Krupp's and where the young no-good Adolf, the Spellbinder, got up the Beer Hall Putsch; yes and Bayreuth. I want to see the Reichstag that was fired by Goering, Ernst, Dimitrov, Torgler, Van der Lubbe and anyone not on your side. That's how I do business.'

'Do you think by looking at the ruins of the Reichstag, you'll know who set it on fire? I know, without spending the train-fare, by the simple deductive route of *cui bono.*'

'I know too. But I love to see the spot marked X. I used to have a friend in the firehouse at Keokuk, Iowa –'

'Were you ever in Keokuk?' he said.

She pursed her face in her delicious roguish smile. 'Maybe. He'd phone me and I'd get to the fire before they did. I even helped to save some children and furniture. Forgive the old fire-horse, Stephen. Think! You look up and those walls are soaked with incident, they drip with conspiracy, crack with fiasco and there are the blood-red bystanders, packed with queasy guilt or fear. I like to look at them and think about them. I get on with them, too: people talk their heads off to a journalist.'

'Are you going to quiz the blood-red bystanders in Berlin? Then, "farewell the tranquil mind, farewell content"! No! I don't want you to go there. I shouldn't sleep one night, worrying. All decent people with any sense are flying or packing. The Nazis are crushing opposition: the multi-millions, though humming and ha-ing are preparing to move in behind Hitler; and everyone is *gleichgeschaltet,* co-ordinated, incorporated. It's the fashion. Mussolini, Hitler, and even the USA is in the shadow of the corporate state: they're chewing their nails and thinking it over, waiting to see what happens over here, letting the Nazi terror spread its foul wing, while big business recovers. Don't you know it's like that? Do you have to go and record the dying shrieks of a republic?'

'You want to live in Washington and record things.'

He had a strange look, mournful, big-eyed, 'Doesn't it mean anything to you that we've just become engaged? Don't you want to be with me? If

I ask you not to go, won't you stay with me?'

'Engaged?' she said pondering, 'Are we engaged?'

He took her arm. 'What are you waiting for? Do you want a ring? Let's grab the first taxi and we'll go to the place Vendôme, Cartier, Van Cleef and Arpels, or place de la République, the five and ten – anywhere. I'll telegraph Anna for the money.'

'No, don't. But I must go somewhere, Stephen.'

'Go to Amsterdam, that's not far. Go to Brussels.'

'I ought to go to Belfast and see where Lennie lives. But I haven't the address. I don't suppose by asking around – '

'Well, I'm glad. I know you. You'd kidnap him. You don't want Lennie headlined in the world's press like Baby Lindbergh and Bobby Franks, do you?'

'Gee whittaker – you're the yellow journalist, not me.'

'I don't believe Lennie exists. They're milking you of his pittance.'

'It crossed my mind,' she said laughing; 'but golly, I can't say such things to them.'

'If you can get his address, I'll go to Belfast with you. There! It's a deal.'

They began laughing, he eased her on their way. They ate in the little restaurant where each student had his separate numbered napkin and they went to the Salle de la Mutualité to the congress; and in the evening they dropped in at the Opéra Comique and saw *Louise* by Gustave Charpentier, but she continued restless.

'I guess I'm not happy living the perfect romance,' she said to him; 'it's my training; it's too good; I'm an unbeliever; how can it happen to Emily the Dope?'

'But it can. You'll get used to it. You'll learn.'

He began to talk about their future – we'll do this, we'll try that, we won't have any children at first; I have a daughter and that's enough. I'll take you to the best hairdressers and *couturières*, we'll get rid of your freckles, if you like. On the way back to the hotel, he bought her a large box of chocolates.

He did everything with such gaiety, such inner and outward grace, she felt like a pleased child and yet she did not quite like it.

'It's because I'm used to the battle of life,' she said to herself. 'I'm a bugbear at the feast of life, a spotted clown, Emily Homespun, unlicked; I suppose I must learn the bong tong, the *comme il faut*. Pish! Pshaw! Can you bedizen a dancing bear? Besides, he says we'll have no children – but he hasn't said he loves me.'

He hadn't said so; and she thought to herself, astonished: 'I have agreed to marry a stranger – H'm! OK. Well, we'll see!'

But she continued thoughtful. She did not know him well enough to

38

size up the reality of this shipboard acquaintance and this sudden projected marriage.

'And your family, Stephen?'

'I was an invalid once; I'll get my way. Anna loves me.' After a moment, he added, 'And then, they're not sure!'

'Not sure of you?'

'The way my mother and uncles, the Howards that is, look at it, is, You never know. They're not taken in really by theories of sunspots and crop failures and business cycles. They know the USA started from nothing: it wasn't a business cycle, but something new. They know that after the French Revolution the rich men came back, but not the kings. If the Commune had seized the banks, what would have happened? My people and their cousins are hoping for Russia, that some day they'll have business cycles, but it looks bad at present. Europe and the USA are goggling after socialism – they've had too much of business cycles. Though, my respected family will do their best; and their best is good. But you never know. Paul Valéry wrote "The time of the world's end begins"; only a pen-pusher, true. One of our congress people said, "Some few among the greatest have already said yes to the future – but all have felt it, that a time is passing that can never come back."'

'Hitler is trying to put the clock back.'

'They'll help him, for he's our barricade against socialism; he even has to call his socialism, to fool all the people all the time.'

'People have always believed in the apocalypse,' she said slowly.

'This vision shakes us all. But we have no right to romance. Someone said those who flatter the people with false revolutionary legends are like a cartographer who would give sailors lying maps. And the apocalypse is such a lying map.'

She said, 'My God, what can we do – in the apocalypse? What an extraordinary race to belong to! Ants and bees have organised societies – so they say. It's all nicely fixed up, mother to son; they don't turn the anthill upside-down every twenty years. But we say, it's a tenet, the tree of liberty must be watered every twenty years by the blood of martyrs. Why is it? What is the answer?'

'The answer is, revolution is a necessity if we are not to be ants and bees.'

'Brr! but it's murder, it's terrible.'

About that they talked for days. In the end Emily gave up her plans and returned on the boat with Stephen. They would come back to Europe some other year.

3 MARRIAGE

At the dock they met Stephen's mother, Anna Howard, 'dear Anna' as Emily at once called her, a sallow, handsome, tall woman, with slender waist, long legs, broad shoulders. With her was a young woman, Adeline the heiress whom Stephen had thought about marrying. She was a dark, casually pretty girl, with large brown eyes and a hesitant manner, covering modest convictions. She was dressed in a dark material. Both greeted them friendly, but Mrs Howard kept Emily talking while Stephen spoke to Adeline and then Anna took Emily to her hotel, where she had a room for her, while Stephen, promising to see them later, went off in her car with Adeline to lunch.

Emily lunched with Anna Howard in a small cellar restaurant off Washington Square.

'I know you like places like this; Arthur and I come here,' said she. She did not explain that Arthur Winegarden was to be her husband: but Emily knew.

'You don't drink wine,' said Anna with a smile, after Emily, following her lead, had chosen *osso buco* with rice.

Emily had meant to order veal cutlets with truffles; but she remembered what Stephen had said about 'millionaire asceticism.' Too bad, she thought; well, I must learn – let it be marrowbone and gravy. They had cheese and coffee and then went back to the hotel. Stephen returned, went to his mother and then called on Emily, who had a room across the hall from 'dear Anna'.

'It is all settled, Mother accepts my change of plans. What can she do? So there you are, you freak – engaged to me and we'll be married right off. But do you mind going to Chicago? Anna has a summer shack the size of a department store, style cottage–baronial on the lake shore. We'll be married there and then back to NY. I want to be near the New York party. I'll work in New York. Mother wants us to live opposite her on East 75th Street; she'll buy the house and rent it to us, or any arrange-ment. I don't know how you feel about that? I'd say no.'

They went uptown to look at the four-storey building which had a gable, tiles, an attic balcony; 'a certain air of Montmartre,' said Emily.

'Yes, but good God, look at the place next door, gilded iron and heavy lace curtains, looks like a fine Paris brothel; and besides, Mother has only to look out of any front window from her house opposite to see our curtains, our car, our shared janitor and me at work in my study. One of her private ambitions is slowly to buy up four or five houses in this street and plant us all opposite, Florence, Olivia: "Howard Village".'

'No, no.'

'Yes, no-no.'

They came back, went to the bar downstairs to frame their answer to Anna's offer.

'Golly, Stephen, I can't get over the idea that because I went red, I married into the social register. I can't take it in. I know it's so, but it is just like a story by a dimwit, that any editor would reject.'

'America the Golden,' said Stephen, 'and what about me? The effete scion finally inducing some honest red blood to mingle with the watery anil in his veins?'

They were married at City Hall, with only brother Arnold and Anna to witness; and then spent a few days on the lake at Oak Park.

The Chicago country house was entered by a paved courtyard behind stronghold walls; over them, tiled roofs, below dressed stone archways. There was plenty of room inside: guestrooms, halls, flights of stairs, unexpected turns looking through long windows on to parts of the grounds and a weed-grown private pond, on which was a rowboat and in it a man hauling out weed. These glimpses were disheartening. Perhaps the landscape and thick bit of woodland could not be fitted into these long but too narrow windows – something of the air of a citadel hung about the place.

'A nice little shack situated in its thousand-acre backyard,' said Emily.

'Three hundred acres,' said Stephen, 'unless you're counting the lake, not ours yet! Actually Anna is thinking of selling off twenty acres so that neighbours, the Littles, can get to their stables from the road.'

'I'm simply not telling my folks anything about this. They wouldn't believe it. Not for Flop-eared Emily, the family white elephant. Supposing I told them that this slum was occupied by a red, someone with his name at the masthead of the leading conspiratorial weekly, an agitator mumbling slogans to truck drivers, taking down in shorthand the beefs of striking seamen about pork chops – that's what you do, isn't it? Clasping the horny hands of the sons of Casey Jones, pulling the forelock to the Central Committee – they know I'm a liar, but they'd think I was mad. For journalism is one thing, but reality – no.'

'Well, we will manage without troubling their dreams.'

'Yes – but Stephen, listen, last night I had an idea! About Lennie.'

'Who's Lennie? Oh, yes, the Irish lad, possible nephew.'

41

'Well, we'll see if he exists. We'll ask him over. They haven't room. He can stay with us. It will cost less, too. He won't take up room. He's only four.'

'H'm. Wait a bit.'

They got an apartment on Twelfth Street, three rooms in a row, bath at the side, kitchen at the back. They divided the big front room with a large steel Venetian blind; they furnished the place and bought a Chinese carpet which Emily called 'tray raffeenay,' and went to work. Emily joined the Communist Party, went to classes for new members, stifled what she called her 'ignoramus objections,' read serious books, sold newspapers, and attended meetings; a very serious learner.

Stephen even tried to restrain her. But she was in a fever. 'I must learn all, everything – for the truth will make us free.'

'We will see what the truth will do to us,' grumbled Stephen.

Stephen had first married Caroline, a young heiress. Her will left everything to her daughter, Olivia, now aged two. Part was to come to her on her sixteenth birthday, the rest at twenty-five. Meanwhile, the trustee, Anna, paid out of the estate all her expenses. Caroline, knowing her death to be near, had also asked Florence, Stephen's sister, to take care of the baby girl; for Stephen, she said, did not understand children and had an indecisive nature.

'Why did Caroline disinherit you?' asked Emily, 'disregarding the gracious words about understanding children, for the moment.'

'I had my allowance. She was afraid I would become a drone, an idler, a rich louse and she had an ambitious conscience. She wanted to do me good; she wanted me to have a clean name. Even at noonday she saw the red muckraker in the shadows. You must understand that we, the Howards, are mentioned in *The Jungle*, under another name of course; but every social-minded citizen knows. And we all know. I think she married me to keep me straight. She didn't want a servant, a class enemy in the house. She wouldn't cook or clean for me, because I didn't do the same for her. I pointed out that we would be in each other's way dusting; but she thought I was unserious. She threw herself into social work to forget the misfit at home; she got her MA, studied law, to fight class injustice. We lived in a California bohemia, marched for causes with placards, threw parties for Negroes, Mexicans and others who had no reverence for our coronets and kind hearts; they simply drank up the hooch, went away and forgot our names.'

'I can't understand,' said Emily, 'why you rich are all such do-gooders. Not one in my bailiwick. Arnold's just a Village Pink. The rest discuss the baseball scores over the dividing fence and a whisky and soda in the evening, and neck over a banana split at the drugstore, Saturday.'

42

He said, 'It's because our money isn't old enough. It hadn't been wrung from the backs of analphabetic, godfearing peasants for centuries, but from fighting bums who yelled every time we snatched a drop of sweat, the ungrateful hoods. Didn't we build up the country, as Anna says? We dream at night that they are turning round to wring it all back and build up the country on their own. Well, Caroline thought I should get a job like her, to show the world I was a man; and I guess she thought I'd get hold of another heiress anyhow, with my effete personality and my emaciated comeliness; such a change from the sportive jack-puddings of our set, who smash up their cars and forge Mother's signature and go periodically into psychiatric care or jail.'

'I wouldn't do that to my husband.' said Emily.

'But that, my dear, is how it is I am an honest man.'

'You're better than you say. She must have been bad for you. If you had her money you could go right into politics, not just hire a room and a secretary in Washington and attend press conferences at the White House. You could at least be a private secretary, an adviser. Think of all that money going to Olivia, a baby.'

'Let's be realists. There are political possibilities. The New Deal is in. I don't see us going back to rough-and-ready vandal capitalism. I'm actually indignant that my family, the Howards, the Tanners and the Drovers have organised the country so well that what we see out of the pullman window is Hoovervilles and one-third of a nation bone idle and suffering from beriberi and malnutrition. We did this, I said to Anna; are you proud of that? Anna said nothing. Anna is only a nice schoolgirl who knows nothing but triple-entry bookkeeping.'

'In a way you really are responsible – food for nightmares,' said Emily.

Emily went through her course in Marxism under Party auspices, still scrupulously studied the textbooks and held her tongue when officials came to dinner; at these times she looked younger, like a freshman. A trained journalist, she intended to write articles for the Party press. She earned a living with what she called her Toonerville tales, short amusing anecdotes, in simple language, recollections, stories about uncles, parents, cousins, grocers, mailmen, townspeople of the small towns; a doctor on the wrong side of the tracks who was always drunk but a loved, reliable bone-setter; a woman with one tooth who won the corn-on-the-cob eating contests every year, drilling her way furiously along the rows; an uncle who stewed cheese-rind with anchovies, the first eater of yogurt in Toonerville.

She sold these to big-city magazines and began work on a comedy for Broadway, called *Henry There's An Angel*. She also struggled again with her historical piece *The Bridge of Centralia*, 'Because I want to write it out of my system. That incident shows us what we can do when we're minded to. I know every detail. The worst was the dreadful shock of fear and recognition, "like us, like me". It went heart home and stayed. I know it is so. I'm afraid of America; I'm afraid of myself.'

Stephen said the title was wrong to begin with, 'They'd think of *The Bridge of San Luis Rey* and expect an appetising joggle of events of that sort, a who-knows who's-who slice of apple pie. In any case, goddamn it, why write something that will make the hackles rise? Do you want to be run out of town?'

'It's for the cause,' said Emily.

'Let me look after the cause and you do what you're good at – the uncle-grandpa comic cuts.'

'That's an insult,' said Emily and sulked. Later, she told him he was right. She was wasting her time. She had always wanted to write a great thing, truth with a bang, thrust out bricks from the wall and make a window on the world. 'I must do it sometime. I'm angry with that in me.' Then she said, 'How wonderful it is to be with you, Stephen. Right or wrong, such an idea would be quite totally impossible to me in my little Tacoma shack. They don't know what a writer is. They don't even known what a bestseller is. Think of such a sink of humbleness.'

'What about Grandma? What about this gorilla you met on the boat, McCoy?'

'Well, hooray, thanks. I'll put him in a story. McRoy.'

But her story about a tough nut in the hometown, with hard fists who fought for Sacco and Vanzetti and Karl Marx did not come off. Stephen was right: it had no takers.

She said, 'Your advice is good: you're outside it. I'm just an eager Toonerville expatriate with glory in her eyes, a high school learner.'

They spent all they had settling in and then they ran up bills. Anna Howard was generous. She gave them family silver, linen, a linen chest from the Chicago house. She made loans to her son, kept an account, reminded him of his indebtedness when he borrowed more, remarked thoughtfully to each of them occasionally on the duty of man to money, but never asked for money back. It was being charged against his estate and was his affair. She only regretted with a felt sadness, at times, that others had the money and no doubt were making it bear fruit.

'Money is not a tree,' said Emily, 'it does not bear fruit. The only way to make money is to earn it in a big way; get it out of them – I would never scrooge it.'

'Scrooge or be scrooged,' said Stephen.

Anna married Arthur Winegarden and made a settlement on him. He

44

also did not care for fruit-bearing money; though he had his own insurance business, which he ran from an office in her house on 75th Street, New York.

Her heirs were Stephen, his older sister Florence, his younger sister Brenda; and a portion each for Olivia, Stephen's daughter now aged nearly three, and Christopher Potter, Brenda's son, now five years old. Christopher's father, Jacob, a man of no estate, a soft, dark, pliable man, collected old music, composers' manuscripts, and had looked to his wife Brenda to give him money for his hobby. She gave him music for each anniversary; but the Howards, Brenda too, believed in work. She herself did social work with Anna. They made Jake Potter manager of a fashionable Howard hotel in the Adirondacks. He worked at it obligingly, unwillingly. He felt like a rich boy done out of his rights. Uncle Howard Howard owned the hotel and was a difficult character. He was persistent, rancorous, never forgave. He had once married a famous dancer and when she left him for another dancer, he persecuted the couple, trying to deprive them of work; and in the end he succeeded. So that the gentle Jake had trouble with Uncle Howard. Anna constantly praised Jake to cheer him and also because he was her son-in-law. She believed in family loyalty. She explained to Jake the duty of man to money; but anyone could see it – he worked like a fly struggling through treacle; and he had to stop for a breather, he had to sup treacle sometimes. The hotel was full of liquor; the clients were spenders. Jake began to drink and got to be a two-bottle man, a bottle of gin, a bottle of whisky daily. He would sit nodding in the lounge with the radio on and a bottle at hand, fall asleep, sometimes spend the night in the easy chair. His wife Brenda had begun to spend time away from the hotel. She visited her mother and her sister Florence in New York.

Anna had now bought two of the houses she wanted on the other side of 75th Street and Florence had rented part of one from her. The top two floors were let to strangers.

Florence was a tall, handsome, bony-faced woman built like Anna, with dark hair and grey eyes. She now had poor health and was often in bed. She lived with a lover, Paul, a sculptor, who used her as a model; an energetic man who was away half the time either at the studio he patronised on 48th Street, where he had space, advice and models, or organising exhibitions for other artists or for the Left.

Florence's apartment, reconstructed by Anna for her, consisted of a sort of studio with bedrooms on a balcony overlooking a large living-room, and under the balcony, a dining recess, the kitchen, bathroom and on the other side a sitting-room. A gilt corkscrew stairway led up from the living-room where Florence held her parties, to the balcony. Above it dangled two gilt cupids. The staircase was in a sort of open chimney, papered to resemble a green canebrake. Along the balcony ran a frail gilt railing. When Florence was out of sorts, she could survey her parties, even if she could not attend them, through her open door or from the balcony. When she was ill, Anna came over every day to look after her.

Anna and Florence had to discuss Olivia's future. Florence's apartment was too small for the child and her nanny. Since Florence had moved to this house, Olivia and her nurse had been lodged at Anna's. If Emily and Stephen could be persuaded to move to the neighbouring house in 75th Street, Anna thought Olivia could live with her father; it would be simpler. Anna herself went abroad often and she now proposed to travel with her new husband, Arthur, an amateur archaeologist, who, every year or so, went on digs. Besides, though she did not complain, the nanny did not belong to her staff; she felt her to be a supernumerary, too much in presence: and the staff disliked her.

'Even if you had room,' said Anna to Florence, "there are all these parties. I thought when you moved up here you might do less. I was thinking of your health.'

'They are my life, it's my contribution,' said Florence. 'It's what I do for the Party and it keeps me in touch. I quite see that Olivia can't stay permanently with you. Then if she lived next door, I could see her every day. There really is not room for her here, with Paul here.'

'That's what I thought,' murmured Anna. She had arranged the move, in fact, so that Olivia would not live in an irregular household. Uncle Howard Howard was discontented and he did not like Florence's political views, but Anna said nothing of this.

Anna went down the narrow staircase to get some light lunch for Florence in the kitchen, a mere closet that had no daylight. When she returned, climbing the stairs with difficulty, with the tray, she meditated, 'Emily loves her home; she is a homemaker. Caroline didn't care for housekeeping at all; they ate out.'

'Hamburgers in diners,' said Florence, 'no wonder Stephen has stomach trouble.'

'He was a sick baby,' said his mother; 'and he starved himself in college to keep within his allowance. He has will-power. I did not realise – the consequences. The only thing is, I wish they would have a plainer diet. If Olivia went to stay with them, of course, she would have her own planned meals.'

But when Florence found out, as she did through Brenda, that Uncle Howard was behind Anna's manoeuvre and that the idea was to protect Olivia from crackbrain ideas, she became indignant and hard to persuade. Caroline had given Olivia into her care. She needed Olivia to love and guide; and her hope was to bring Olivia up as a communist, so that their part of the Howard fortune, all of which she considered blood-money, would be used for the workers' cause. Anna did not discourage her: she did not believe that the national hardship would continue: the economy had improved considerably. When the time came Olivia would do as all girls of her class did. Olivia was a dainty child, with platinum blonde hair, a fair, thin skin, rosy cheeks, a straight neatness and beautiful eyes, with a ring of dark blue outside the iris of china blue; and her manner was charming. Anna looked forward to her adolescence.

Florence spent her money on her parties for the cause, on cheques for charity dinners and in other reputable ways; but occasionally she would go out with Anna on a little shopping spree. Then Anna would buy a handbag, a small jewel, some gloves, persuade Florence that she needed perfume; and they would lunch modestly in some little place Anna and Arthur liked, never in a showy place. On one of these trips, Florence displayed energy. She took her mother in a taxi to a building overlooking the East River and showed her a large ground floor apartment for which she had the keys. Paul could have his studio there: and there was room for Olivia and a nursemaid.

'I need a child,' said Florence: 'it will keep me straight. Paul cannot have children.'

Though Anna listened gracefully, she was discouraging and she went home, herself very discouraged. What of her dream of looking out of the window of her house and seeing her dear family opposite? What about the irritable Howard? She said no more and hoped Paul would object. Olivia was now five: it was 1938.

4   UNO 1945

Emily and Stephen had been free-lancing in Hollywood four months when they sold their second script. The morning they heard, on the telephone, from their agent Charlie Goldhammer, that it was sold, they telephoned a house agent to find them a house in a better district of Hollywood. They were then living in a rented house on Rexford Drive, a fairly good address in its upper section, which was about a thousand yards long, but in its lower section an address for newcomers.

The Howards' rented house was in the lower section. Only a hundred yards from that house the good addresses began. There were the houses of two long-established movie stars, and two other houses rented out by Mollie Pearcorn, private secretary to Ind Pellikan, the ranking director on the MGM lot. His top rating meant that he was the director who then had the conduct of the largest section of allotted expenses, who turned in the largest profit to the company and who knew prudently and as a man of the world how to make suitable losses.

It happened that Ind Pellikan was the director to whom Charlie Goldhammer had sold Emily's story *Sally In our Alley*, for which she also wrote the script, her first sale when she reached Hollywood. The news that Emily had now sold a second script, *Oh, Sally!* to Ind Pellikan and for $35,000 plus $1,000 weekly for three months was known that same morning throughout Hollywood; that is in well-paid writers' circles.

When the Howards, after house-hunting, reached home, they fell into raptures. There was a list of telephone calls and invitations from some of the best names of their sort in Hollywood. Emily may have laughed a little, with scorn and contempt, at their sudden rise in the world, 'accepted at last by the forty-niners', but she was, with Stephen, touched: for this same society, some of the best names, and people who got the highest prices for their scripts, the most screen credits, had something a little more honourable to recommend it. It was fashionable leftist society, people who without giving up their beliefs had made good in a highly competitive and sometimes hidden game. There were messages too, from the famous Jim Holinshed, elegant radical who had written a novel about the sufferings of some young Nazi soldiers, in a lost company in a citadel which was to fall; and from Godfrey Bowles, a celebrated radical who had written several novels translated east and west. Jim Holinshed for several years had worked with and shared an office and stenographers with Godfrey Bowles. They often wrote scripts together and the names Bowles and Holinshed were treated with respect in the studios; they were considered men of talent, who knew the business.

The Howards spent the next day looking at suitable houses in good districts and arranged to buy a house in Pomegranate Glen. Ranging from the flat seacoast of Santa Monica are a number of sandhills, covered with sparse scrub and the almost pure sand held together otherwise with logs, ivy, desert flora and a few trees. The hollows between the hills are called glens, narrow shallow gullies which decline rapidly towards the place called Beverly Hills.

There were bungalows of all kinds and little houses in all these glens. But the glens varied in social meaning and architecture. Guava Glen was a poor man's glen, with bungalows and huts built of clapboard and fibrous plaster and other poor materials, and they were sold or let to those who had just arrived in Hollywood and as yet had sold nothing to the studios and had no job. The very next glen, Kumquat Glen, was a little more esteemed and had solider bungalows, newly painted white or yellow and ranged close together on the valuable hillside. Here lived people with regular jobs in Hollywood or Westwood, or writers in the brackets, with long contracts who had jobs, year in, year out. Persimmon Glen, next, was for fastidious writers who had a position in Hollywood society; and here were found also a few agents and architects. Pomegranate Glen was next to it and here were people who were graduating from excitable and unsure radical groups to long-breathed Hollywood society of the stabler sort, people who had had jobs in the studios for many years. Some actors were here, even one director; and here Moffat Byrd, the five-thousand-dollar-a-week man, leader by common consent of Hollywood progressive society, had one of his houses. He was not a foolish spendthrift, no gambler; he invested his money in real estate. He had other houses out in the valley and in Rexford Drive.

The house the Howards saw, in the afternoon, in Pomegranate Glen was exactly what Stephen wanted. He had made up his mind to plunge now, select a house that would suit them, no matter what successes they had.

The Howards gave a house-warming party for the new house, inviting friends in the social stratum they had moved to; they entertained at the new house several times in the week.

The Howards attended the 1945 UNO conference but left before it ended and set out to drive back to Beverly Hills. They had spent all this time and money on the conference to write reports for the New York *Labor*

Daily and the Washington *Liberator*, at a time when Emily's Hollywood agents were waiting for two scripts; and her New York agents for the manuscript of a new book in her moneymaking series, *Mr and Mrs Fairway*, humorous books of family life. The couple quarrelled before starting, about the opinions in Emily's article for the *Labor Daily*; but she posted it unchanged. As soon as the car started, the tiff began again.

'This is not for money, Stephen, and I'll say what I like; it's the truth.'

'Oh, damn the truth and damn not for money. You'll offend the left and you've wasted a week rewriting your article when your agents are screaming. But it's OK, your soul is white and the children won't eat next week.'

'Your goddamn article was a palimpsest by the time you'd finished achieving a wise, dry, prescient tone. You had to telephone it to Washington,' said Emily, but she began to laugh. 'In Europe contributors to radical sheets go without soles to their shoes and gnaw a dry crust in freezing attic rooms; and we live on the plunder of the land, best hotels, three-room suite, long-distance calls, swell car to run us home to our latest residence; that's American radicalism I suppose. They can't pay us so we pay them.'

'Well, it's worth it to see my name flown at the masthead,' said Stephen nastily.

'That's a petty, selfish view. If we waste all this money, it's what we owe the country for our unnatural luck.'

They quarrelled again and the last part of the journey was passed in silence. When they got home, Emily went round the house fast, talking in a lively way with the servants, the children, neighbours' children who were in. She looked through the children's clothing and the laundry, checked the contents of pantry, icebox, deep-freeze and bar, ordered dinner and took her large bundle of letters up to her room, a little room at the stairhead, and overlooking the side and back gardens. Manoel, the manservant, brought up a pot of black coffee; and she locked the door behind him. Her room was furnished mainly with steel files containing copies of her voluminous writings of all sorts, her diary, her correspondence, the material for many novels and stories, copies of all her lectures and articles, bundles of clippings, household bills and the children's school reports; as well as the exercise books in which she carefully went over their lessons with them. Besides this, there were wire baskets, a few reference books, a chair and an excellent typewriter. She drank the coffee, took a pill from a little drawer in the table and began to read her letters, with shouts and great guffaws and sighs. She began typing replies at once.

Downstairs, in a large front room well furnished as study and library, his own workroom, Stephen sat discontentedly going through the notes his research worker had sent him. He had a partner's desk, a pale blue-grey carpet. The panelled sliding door communicated with a charming living-room decorated with chintzes, French paintings and flowers arranged in Japanese style by Stephen. Stephen found it hard to settle down to work, for Emily's agents, the studios and her publishers kept telephoning her; and every conversation in which, in her jolly, loving, languishing manner, full of good sense, outrageous hope and *bonhomie*, she promised and put off, threw him into a frenzy. Last year, she had, without effort, made $80,000 in Hollywood. Yet she consumed hours, weeks in all, writing to friends and otherwise wasting time. A river of money was flowing through the telephone: she had only to direct it into their pockets. The thought poisoned him and stung him. Their expenses were large. The Portuguese couple who managed for them cost considerably over $400 a month; his own research worker had cost more than $5,000 in the course of five years.

Yet upstairs Emily flirted with the idea of writing a great novel. She sketched out one idea after another, and in each of them she wanted to tell some truth that would offend some section of the community. Some of the truths would offend everyone and get them on the black list. Also, she prepared lectures and courses for workers' and students' education. She wrote impassioned letters about her troubles to her friends, gave advice to young writers, worked harder on articles for 'those snoots' on the *Labor Daily* than on a script for Twentieth-Century Fox.

Emily came downstairs, very cheery, bustling the children to wash their hands, fix their neckties, come in to dinner.

'What have you been doing?' he said sourly.

'Writing a letter to Ruth Oates.'

'The house is full of unpaid bills, and Hollywood and Bookman Bros. are telephoning and telegraphing every hour. You've got a market shrieking for your work. Why don't you do it?'

He said this before the children and Manoel the butler, who was serving. They always talked with the greatest freedom before intimates.

'My writing's crap,' she shouted, 'I don't want to do it. I'm not proud they pay me gold for crap. That *Mr and Mrs* stuff is just custard pie I throw in the face of the mamma public, stupid, cruel and food crazy. I find myself putting in recipes – ugh! – because I know they guzzle it. They prefer a deepfreeze to a human being; it's cold, tailored and shiny. I don't believe in a word I write. Do you know what that means, Stephen? It's a terrible thing to say. You believe in what you write! Why should I work my fingers stiff to pay off the mortgage on this goddamn shanty with electric lights on the stair treads so that the guests don't roll down when

51

they're full – let 'em roll – and with dried sweetpea on the airspray in the linen closet – '

'That dried sweetpea makes me gag,' he sang out irately. 'All right! Let's get out of the crappy place, though we've only just got in, and find something cheap and nasty with no towel rails. Let's go to one of my family's modest little tax-saving apartments or a cabin in Arkansas. Let my family see I'm a failure. Let's get rid of Manoel, who's my only friend, and get a char smelling of boiled rag and with hair in her nose. I'll do the buttling. Why not get a job as a butler? I'd make a good sleek sneak sipping the South African sherry in the outhouse. Let's wear our shirts for a week and save on the laundry.'

'You're eating my heart out with your aristocratic tastes,' she roared, beginning to cry too. 'Moth and rust are nothing to what a refahned young genteel gentleman from Princeton can do to an Arkansas peasant girl, when a spot on the carpet to him is like pickles to a stomach-ulcer. Oh, Jee-hosaphat, what was the matter with me, marrying a scion? You've ruined my life, darn it. I want to be a writer. I don't want to write cornmeal mush for full-bellied Bible belters. Did I leave my little Arkansas share-cropper's shanty for that? I was going to be a great writer, Miss America, the prairie flower. Now I'm writing Hh-umour and Pp-athos for the commuters and hayseeds.'

She helped the children with their homework. Both parents went up to sing to Giles in his cot, a song invented by Stephen.

Oh G, oh I, oh L, oh E, oh S!
Sle-ep, sle-ep, sle-ep, sle-ep!
Oh, Gilesy, Gilesy, Gilesy, sleep!

Stephen ran a bath, while Emily went downstairs; and after writing out the menu for the next day and saying, 'I will make the crêpes suzette,' she went to the butler's pantry where she mixed herself a strong highball. Just as she was carrying it into the living-room, Stephen came down in fresh clothes. He scolded her for taking a drink and for the expense of some new handmade shirts which had just come in for the three boys; Lennie, aged fourteen, Christopher, twelve, and Giles, four. Emily defended herself; what was he just saying about a char with hair on her eyeballs? She was in a good humour. 'I've got an idea that will work for my script; it's so cheap I blushed for shame.'

Stephen picked up the evening paper and glanced over the headlines. They began once more to tear at the great wound which had opened in their love, mutual admiration and understanding, and great need for each other. This was an equally fundamental thing, a disagreement about American exceptionalism; the belief widely held in the USA that what

52

happened in Europe and the rest of the world belonged to other streams of history, never influencing that Mississippi which bears the USA. The flood of American energy could and perhaps would swallow those others: the watershed of European destiny was far back in time and drying up. To this belief, Stephen liked to adhere. Emily accused him of servility to a system which had made his grandparents and parents millionaires; and Stephen would not have been so tenacious, if the Government, and all the political parties right across to the extreme left, had not agreed that America's reason for invading Europe, joining the conflict in 1939, was to spread America's healthy and benevolent business democracy everywhere: the western answer to communism. Stephen had everyone at his back, but a few.

'We'll help them make the big leap: they won't have to go through the secular agonies,' screeched Stephen.

'Daddy!' called Giles from the stairs: 'Dadd-ee!'

Emily found this 'a pill too big for a horse to swallow' to quote Michael Gold; and she declared that the local doctrine held even by the communists, was wrong.

'The Oil' (Earl Browder) 'has adjusted Marxism to US Government Policy.'

'Dadd-ee! Mumm-ee!'

Both went up to Giles, put him in his cot and sang the song again, upon request, several times. Emily kissed the boy and went downstairs to get herself another highball. Stephen came down and reproached her. She said 'Let me live!'

They went on about the mistakes of policy.

'The quiet man from Kansas' (Earl Browder) 'is quiet because he needs his tongue for asslicking; and the Seventy Sages are waiting in a queue behind him.'

'They know their theory better than you and me,' said Stephen querulously; 'at any rate better than me; and I don't know what to answer them. I can only follow blindly; but I intend to follow. I went into Marxism for personal salvation. I know, a despicable reason; but I have to stick to it, or where am I? Just a failure; not even a playboy.'

'I'm not going to follow anyone into a quagmire; and I don't want to be saved.'

'You're an individualist; individualists become renegades.'

She sprang up from her chair. 'Don't you dare call me a renegade! I'll scratch your nose. I won't stand that.'

They quarrelled so bitterly, and such unforgivable things were said that she got a seat on a plane going east the next morning and telephoned the studio that she'd post the scripts from New York. 'And I'll be able to work there,' she shouted to him, 'not worried to death by a limpet throttling me. Maybe I'll give up the whole crazy game, and get myself a hall-bedroom and really write.'

She went upstairs to pack; and on the way went into the nursery and looked at the family portrait photographs of all the children; and of them all, including Anna, 'Dear Anna', Stephen's mother, who had had it all done by a fashionable New York photographer. Dear Anna wore a modest afternoon dress in silk from Bergdorf's, the boys had tailor-made suits and Olivia, their half grown girl, an imported silk dress. Emily herself wore a simple dark suit imported from France and chosen by Anna. On the wall opposite were two photos of her cousin, Laura, both enlarged from snaps. Laura did not appear good-looking in these pictures; she looked downcast and thin; but she was debonair, cool at heart, had the cupid's bow mouth which implies sex and intrigue, and 'the smile of smiles' when she cared to smile; she was loved but did not love; she spent all her time thinking of how she would appear to men, had many personal recipes, rituals, taboos; in company she was nonchalant, offhand, she was always moving out of sight and earshot with some man; and she would never be found surrounded by women; and women bored her so that she would never go out with them or go to their parties. 'I want the musk of male,' she said, 'it's what I live for.' Behind her, in her many snaps, were always things fine to see, a long new car, pedigree dogs, a handsome man, a cherry tree in flower, the terrace of a private house, the Sound with a sail; or even an old jalopy with Laura, her hand to her mouth, laughing like a child at a man lying at her feet.

Laura had lived with Emily for years and Emily knew her recipes, her secrets; she wholeheartedly believed in her ways, and she loved men, too; but she could not apply Laura's ways. It was by some inner power, she thought, that Laura was always successful with men, while she, Emily, was always a failure. 'And I hate the waiting game!'

But Stephen said Laura was not attractive at all; 'our friends, Axel and Jimmy and Mike don't like her.' This hurt Emily. 'She's like a best of breed and I'm like a big unclipped sheepdog.'

In the beginning of their marriage Emily feared Laura. The trio went to shows and concerts until Laura said, 'I refuse to go with you and Stephen again. I don't play walk ons.'

'But he likes you!.'

'But he married you!'

Stephen disliked all these photographs of Laura and when Emily raved, he said, 'What was your cousin but a third-rate whore?'

At such remarks, Emily would for a moment become silent and then sadly, 'Ouch! Oof! You know, you never appreciated her.'

54

'You don't know that she told other people she would gather me in. That finished her with me. She said I was worth a one-night stand, a scion stuffed with straw.' Then Emily would smile, throw her arms around her darling Stephen, whom she had gathered in for more than one night and laugh, laugh with freshness, candour, charm and what health!

'Oh, Stephen, I am not nearly as good as she was. You never knew her. I knew her. There never was anyone like her.'

Emily now looked across the room at Laura's cheesecake photographs (as he said) and her eyes sparkled. Laura, with all her conquests, had in fact, been sure she would tip up Stephen, play with him and throw him away. 'Stephen the Scion,' she called him.

'Laura never had a chance,' said Stephen.

Emily now walked lightly up and down the room in which her own little son, Giles, her only child, slept pleasantly. He was a square-faced, rosy, dark-haired lad, with large dark-seeming eyes, really light hazel, which opened wide between long dark lashes. He had a well-shaped mouth which opened to smile and say wise things. He was like Laura in some ways. Emily sighed gustily and stood at the foot of her son's bed.

'Ah, dear Giles, what will you be? Mystery of personality! Are personalities developed so young? They are though. Each pregnancy I had was different, a different soul was there. Is it possible you see something different from us all and not even a shred of what Laura saw, or me? And nothing of Stephen? It's possible. Can you go your own way so young? Yes. And you're a mystery, a deep mystery. Why be parents at all? And I was always afraid I would never get a chance to be a parent! And I'm the writer, supposed to understand people and fix up their destinies. Ah me, I don't even know the next critic who's going to shy coconuts at me. Someone smiles, I think he's warm and good. Then the smiler attacks, he's indecent, inhuman, he contradicts all decorum, kills all hope in life. But destiny itself is a smiler with a knife. I haven't any animal instincts, ah me, and yet I'm all animal.' She sighed naturally and went on, in her soft, husky, resonant undertone, looking at the sleeping child, 'I know you inside out! How can that be if you are so different from us? I won't like you if you are! You have no right to be!' Although she respected sleep, she was so excited that she went to Giles and kissed him, threw her arms round his head and when he woke, in his usual good temper, she said, 'Giles darling, Giles, my own sweetheart, what would you do if Mother went away from your for ever. Went a long way away?'

'Do you mean died?'

'No, no, good heavens. I mean went away to New York and stayed there.'

Giles smiled, 'I'd go and live with Grandma, and Grandma would take

Olivia back and Uncle Maurice likes me too: he has money and he has no children. He could pay for my education and put me into business.'

Emily was shocked, surprised, and hid a laugh, 'Jee-hosaphat, wouldn't you cry for Mother?'

'Oh, yes, I'd cry; but what good would it do? Where would you be? I could telephone you. I could take the plane and come on my birthday.'

Emily smiled, 'H'm, very true, my child, but you oughtn't to say those things to parents.'

'I thought about it when you were sick.'

Emily laughed, 'Go to sleep, Giles. I oughtn't to have waked you up. What were you dreaming about?'

'I dreamed a black lamb came and lay down beside me in bed. It seemed so real,' and his eyes filled with tears.

Emily's eyes filled with tears. 'Go to sleep, my darling, and then the black lamb will come back.'

'Oh, no, it will be something else; it's always something else.'

'Then a white peacock,' she said impatiently, covering him up and rising from the side of the bed. She rarely dreamed. She felt uneasy when she did, as if the dream were a portent, even a threat.

She stood in one part of the room biting her lip. Supposing she did get a place for herself in the east and write? She would have to provide for them. All Stephen had was his quarterly allowance from Dear Anna and they thought of it as a windfall; they always went and spent it at once. Stephen did not know how to save, would never consider it. Dear Anna might help him, but then Anna would insist on taking two of the children, Olivia and Christy. Emily was not going to let Anna have the children, and nor Stephen either.

There tumbled into her mind details from several best-selling books of the humorous housewifely kind and the family kind which accidentally, she held, had been successes. She knew that they appealed to the 'mamma public'. She must do something along those lines. She saw the books as poorly written, vain, cosy, dull, ignorant and pitiably lacking in self-criticism, as were their readers. They did not know the elements of writing. 'Neither do I; I'm qualified!' Those writers do not repeat themselves; she could. Almost all, it seemed to her, since the success of her book *Uncle Henry*, had stolen little things from her, a detail here and there only – they were vetted only for flagrant plagiary. She murmured, 'Oh, there ought to be a way of proving the colour of plagiary. Then I could collect from them, thus making – ' she smiled with joyous venom – 'thus making yet more from poor overworked Uncle Henry. Why not? They're by-products.'

Uncle Henry was hers. She had invented him. At least, he had been

56

her Uncle Henry – her mother's. He was a new feature in American humour. Perhaps after a lifetime of bashing it out on the typewriter, she would be remembered for Uncle Henry, as the author of *Pinocchio* – what was his name? – Collodí – Pinocchio had been given a statue; and Tyl Eulenspiegel – didn't the author get the idea from an old book he picked up on the bookstalls? There was a statue to Tyl. Too bad then if all that was left of me was a statue of Uncle Henry. Such is life. If the Uncle Henry vein went on yielding, she would one day get enough, she would triumph solemnly, sullenly with a loud roar of victory, with golden divine contempt for –

'Emily!'

'I'm packing!'

In James Thurber – in – this and that – she saw faint shades of herself. American humour based on the American dilemma, based on, what you want most, you'll never have, but the plastic makeshift – ha-ha-ha! She laughed, biting her lip and allowing a dimple to appear on each side of her mouth. Her mouth twitched, her eyelids fluttered. How really successful and triumphant she was! Small-town girl – she had left her impression on the language, on the nation, on the USA, a great nation of humorists. Emily Wilkes Howard, Emily Wilkes, as herself, the Humorist – 'Or – let's see – ' She began to ruminate.

'Emily, come down.'

'I'll be right down.'

'Are you taking those damn pills?'

'No. Leave me be, goddamn it.'

Meanwhile, she said to herself, I need success for another reason. I really can't give Stephen and the family an ultimatum until I've cash in hand. *I don't need you, you need me.* The fact, the heavy-loaded truth is, that with each book, I've unconsciously prayed for a success, not for crass commercial reasons. I can always eat. But to get rid of Stephen. Let him go back to Mamma or find another woman to support him.

At this she frowned and kicked the dressing-table, looked at her son and frowned. 'They say there's no good prison and no bad love. This is a prison and he loves me; figure it out. What a dilemma!'

'Emily! Emily!'

A proud smile arched Emily's lips and eyebrows. She did not answer. Stephen came running upstairs, panted at the top and stood there a moment, catching his breath. Then he said nastily, 'How many of those damn pills have you taken? You're a drug addict. For pete's sake come downstairs. The coffee's there and Axel Oates has arrived.'

She pouted, smiling, 'I had a good idea for a story, that's all.'

'Come on down and stop crapping around.'

She said, 'The fact is, I was thinking of your quarterly cheque. Every time it comes, though it's only $3,000, we start living inside the rainbow. What creatures born for joy! And when it's gone, we're back in the subcellar with the toads – faugh – living for money! But money is joy!' He had started to go down but now came back to the head of the stairs, clasped his hands and looked pathetically at her. She laughed quietly and said to him, using a phrase from his German governess, 'I'll put in an appearance.'

Emily pranced into the living-room, all coloured solid flesh, like a circus horse and, on top, her fair hair full of man-made curls, with pink ribbons in them, like a ballerina on a circus horse. Said she, running to Axel Oates, 'Darling, thank God. Oh, why didn't you come to dinner on Sunday? I should have telephoned you. This week was wasted. I feel so lousy and low; I have so little time and that wasted, when it's you, Axel, I should be listening to. Jesus Q. I've been in a low state and Stephen says it's because I'm dieting too much. But I haven't his elegant storklike physique. I eat like a cormorant, an elephant, a pelican, otherwise I can't think, I'm famished and he has the divine figure of – a – '

'You said it, stork,' said Stephen.

'Are you dieting again?' said Axel, who had to diet too. He was a middle-sized, thickset, fair man, with long limbs. He was a rebel journalist, who had been through wars in Europe. He ran a little weekly of his own, bought by journalists and intellectuals and financed by himself. He had published a few books and had come to Hollywood to make money to run his weekly, *Evidence*.

Said Stephen, 'Dieting! At the end of a splurge, as now, she lives on black coffee and benzedrine, if that's all it is. Then she groans all night because she's starving and gets up and roams the kitchen. Has breakdowns and hysterics and says she's going to leave me and curses out the Party; says we're creatures of straw used to light the forest fires, she's a denizen not of the new world but the world of bourgeois corruption; she's hopelessly frustrated. And I have to live through it all.'

Emily exclaimed, 'Oy-oy, what am I to do, Axel? I've the figure and avoirdupois of the Child of Moby Dick. I am down with sinus. Damn my short, stuffy nose. I had that operation five weeks ago – five minutes it would last, said the Doc. He cut a nerve leading to my eye or ear or brains and all I've got is fire up there. I feel as if a sledge-hammer is whacking away all day and night on all these bits of anatomy – and I look so rosy or peony, not to say like a sugar pig. And then, oh, jiminy, I started eating too much the week before, on the theory that I work better. Your theory, Stephen, don't deny it – stand up like a man. So I ate butter, sweet corn, potatoes, mashed with cream-butter-onions, cheese, baked like a cake,

58

delicious, yum-yum, brie creamed with butter and spread on porterhouse. I read about it and that's what started me off, then, a glad, glorious, grand week with whipped cream on strawberry shortcake, cheese with pie and cream; Viennese coffee, flaky pastry made by me with a secret wrinkle of my own, not to mention the banana split when passing, but not by, the drugstore downdown, nutbread, sherry flip – I thought, all right, this is my week. Oh, what the heck, why can't those who like to eat eat and those who like Stephen are astringent – '

'Ascetic,' called out Stephen.

'I like astringent better, it sounds stringier. What a world! And on top of everything, this Olivia plot.'

Axel sympathetic, began to smile, 'How goes the plot?'

'It thickens,' said Emily, 'like night in the rooky wood. Now Christy's grandparents are trying to prise him off us. Inspired by press revelations about Olivia, Mamma and us I suppose they thought there was a good chance of Christy marrying the Howard safe deposit vault – '

Stephen checked them by saying, 'You know we were given Christopher by his father Jake – Jake Potter, after my sister Brenda died. Jake had a breakdown, was in hospital for weeks, came out, a nervous wreck, was downing two quarts of whisky and gin a day – said so; and agreed with us that he wasn't a fit guardian for his boy; so he signed him away into our care. So Christy is with us. He's a problem; a moody sort of boy, like his parents.'

'Oh, he's sensitive and ruminates about all this, that's all. He's growing up,' said Emily, 'and this world is hard to understand.'

'So now you have four children, that's a big burden,' said Axel.

'Oh, what joy, what blessedness!' sang out Emily. 'Even though we must keep our noses to the grindstone.'

She stopped prancing, poured herself a drink and said, 'But Axel, what is your news? What about the big party? Fancy you a star of Big-time Society in the Seven Suburbs! Oh, what an event! Groucho never gave us so much as a nod; and we're much better – h'm, well, evidently, we're not. Tell us Axel!'

Axel told what happened.

Mervyn Spice, a Hollywood agent and talent scout who was a political radical and knew of Axel's reputation on the East Coast and in Europe, had paid Axel's fare to Hollywood, as a speculation, believing that he could place him and that he would make big money; even though Hollywood in 1944–5 was far from as radical as it had been, because of the fear of investigation running through the studios.

But the agent was disappointed. 'Everyone tells me that guy is a genius, but I don't see nothin'; I never heered him say anything I like,' so the agent said; and it was quoted about, laughed at, and Emily laughed in glee, though she did think Axel was a genius.

'Come on, Axel, tell us, tell us –' she now said, with a brilliant, sarcastic, joyful expression. 'And how is the script coming along?'

'Well,' said Axel, 'the *magnum dopus* is now being revised and I am grooming myself for another week of decision, which I am sure will be two weeks. I thought the story was a mere movie stunt, but a glorious swindler is a great subject; and McTeague made, according to unanimous opinion here, the one great picture turned out of Hollywood in the silent days. It was the favourite of Erich von Stroheim, who directed it under the name of 'Greed'. But for George Graham Rice, I must write in the apparatus of the woman versus rival feature.'

Emily listened, her eyes sparkling. 'But the Party.'

'Yes, Groucho called up; I couldn't believe it.'

'Why not?' said Emily.

'You don't know,' said Stephen: 'very peculiar rumours preceded you out here. For instance that the Party had made the move, and that you were sent to set us right out here.'

'What bullshit,' said Axel, but he was pleased: 'to the Party I'm a maverick, a copperhead.'

'This is the land of Cockaigne, remember,' said Stephen, 'but even I believed it. I thought they had taken thought. Everyone was waiting for you to speak.'

Axel smiled, then said, 'If they thought what I said last night was a message from the Party – they didn't! Last night at Groucho's I had a discussion with the most touted and best-paid writer in Hollywood, none other than super-odious Lucius Lewin. That man has a stench as deep as a sewer trench. He declared that all writers were better off as writers and did better than others after they had gone through the great experience of Hollywood. The old Paris street girl's reply on a café terrasse, "Oui, quand on fait l'amour pour de l'argent, même, mais l'on y donne tout de même toute son ardeur, on apprend mieux son métier. On se respecte parceque l'on assure le bonheur d'une famille inconnue." "If you are enthusiastic about the stories you have to write here," said the great Lucius, "then you know how to shape anything else better." I said, "Bogus stories, fallible psychology, the inevitable twist – it's good for everyone? The introspective, the painters of man and nature, rare understandings between man and man, or historical analysts?"

'Then Lucius said, "The individual writer is leaving the scene: or he must adapt. If Shakespeare were alive today, he'd be in Hollywood. Hollywood isn't the cause of writers' failures. Look at Sherwood Anderson; he disdained movies and he poohed out about forty-six. Men have their

60

menopause, we spend all our emotional capital when we are young; all we have left now at our age, are the dregs of emotion, but through experience we can turn it into what's acceptable – raw emotion and raw writers are not suitable for public entertainment. So, make a good thing of it by selling out for $250,000 a year!"'

'But Lucius isn't a sell-out,' said Stephen: 'he's a business. That's all he can do; make *schmattes* and sell them, in Huckster Alley.'

'Lucius was the hope of Broadway when young,' said Axel. 'Then Lucius said, "What's the use anyway? The age of literature is over. As the sciences grow and our perceptions become more exact, our type of writing will become extinct – the vague, poetic, symbolic will die; it is amateur, ignorant." "No," said I, "the rise of science, by releasing a million unknown facets will increase the range of literature beyond the present, our tools will be so many more. All the numbskulls shouted that photography would antiquate painting; and look now!" This was met by silence from the Bone-tired Champion, King of Hollywood, in his rusty side-slipping crown. Then, next cliché. He said, "What's the use anyway? We live in an age of danger. Those ages have never produced great literature."'

'Oh, what a dying dog,' said Emily. 'But he can still tear out the seat of your pants.'

'"Like," I said,' continued Axel, '"the England of Elizabeth, always on the cliff-edge, about to slip into the sea; the Athens of Pericles. Think of the tremendous writings that emerged in the age of reason following upon Newton, Descartes, Bacon, Locke: think of Diderot, Voltaire, the *Encyclopaedia*; and how all literature was influenced by the scientists and the French revolution. What are you saying, man?" "Well," says Lewin, "it must soak in. The political obsession of our age means there will be no literature for a century." Everything showed his dread of age and decline: that he knows he has spent his small mental capital and has nothing to show for it.'

'Such men are time-servers,' said Stephen. 'He has never helped a fellow-writer. That is why he says there are no writers.'

'To him Groucho said, "Meatballs",' said Axel. 'And I asked Lucius whether he understood that politics is a specific form of strain between men in which both sides play for the realization of vital impulses; and that these passions, these conflicts are the essence of drama, the stuff of new literature. Shelley thought so, too. "Shelley was a horse's ass, he believed in mankind, the shit," were the memorable words of the defunct genius of the American stage. After which I annihilated the decaying pontiff of the studios, showed up his rottenness and contradictions pitilessly, showed that everything he said confuted previous statements whose implications he had never begun to understand. I built up a case for literature and said he was defending his own pitiable defeat.'

'He countered very feebly. "Well, my medium, the theatre, is dead. The Stage Hands' Union did it." "No," said I, "the tsarist silence in the studios has done it. You can say nothing tragic or humane; you're King of Hollywood because you're selling moth-eaten old clothes and that's all they can take at present." "Oh, hell," said he, "a good drunk is better than all this crap." The conversation smashed him. Groucho told me this morning that this guy has walked all round Hollywood owning that he was smashed, and he is out. As everyone detests him from bosses to errand boys, I did no harm.'

'He will smash you,' said Emily.

'For all that, he is the god of clever, decent men here, like Nunnally Johnson and Gene Fowler, his former associates,' said Stephen.

'But only journalistic types,' said Emily.

'We're all journalists, every man jack,' said Axel laughing. This was true, so they all laughed.

'The party was strange at Groucho's,' said Axel, laughing as he improvised. 'It shows that the commies are a chosen people. It was full of typical apolitical Hollywood celebros and the Beany-Simon test would show their mental age as pre-embryonic. They gather round the piano and sing ditties for which the police raided the feeble-minded home in the days of William McKinley. So, from now on, I stick to folks like you and others at whose homes I meet people at once charming, friendly, humane and reasonably wide awake. Groucho said in parting from me after dinner, "Goodbye, Mr Oates, you cost me a pretty penny tonight".'

'With love and kisses from the Anti-Lucius League,' said Stephen.

'I bet he meant it,' said Emily: 'Lucius will think Groucho got him into a trap to show him up.'

'He wouldn't: I wouldn't,' said Axel: 'and who can hurt Groucho? He has us all in the hollow of his hand.'

'H'm. Stephen, pour us some drinks.'

'Axel doesn't drink.'

'But I do – if I can't eat.'

Stephen said, 'Yes, Emily wants to leave me and Earl Browder together. It's the dieting. If I say, "It's a bread and butter life," she gets up and walks to the icebox. If I say, "The union have no ideals, they just fight for pork chops," she starts to drool.'

Now she said, 'The bread and better life. I'm going to New York tomorrow.'

'To see your publishers?'

'To get out of this smoky and flamy abyss. That's why I eat so much.'

Stephen ran Axel to his little downtown hotel in the car; and Emily, taking a drink with her, went upstairs to pack. When he returned Emily said, 'That settles it. When did Lucius Lewin attend a party we went to? We're second-class citizens here. And Lewin's star is setting: he actually said Axel beat him. He must be on the slide; after playing so close and neat. Pooah! I am not going to stay in this pitiful suburb of six-car clapboard palaces and browbeaten male Scheherazades, suffering insult, injury, envy, backslaps and horselaughs.'

'I cancelled your reservation,' said Stephen.

'Then I'm getting another one,' and she telephoned the air company at once.

When Stephen came up to bed, she told him she had her reservation for the next day. Then she said, with a queer gay grimace, 'Axel is finished: he won't get any work here. You must say, "It's the art of the masses"; or else, "I'm a punk, and my god I wish I were honest"; but you can't show them why they're cheap and nasty.'

Stephen said, 'Axel has to speak his mind. That's his life.'

'He can't do it here. He'd better go back to New York.'

'The town here is full of his admirers,' objected Stephen.

'But if it's MGM or Axel, it will be MGM. He won't get work here. I know them. Why is he here? Because he wants to be a punk too.'

'He wants to get money to support his magazine.'

'I'm a whore because I want to keep my dear old mother. Fooey.'

Before it was time to leave for the airport next day, Stephen took the car out. Emily telephoned for a taxi. But Stephen returned with a jewelcase, in the velvet lining of which lay a deep amethyst necklace from Russia. Emily loved stones in yellow, green and purple.

She was dressing and sat before her looking-glass in a linen slip with a square-cut neck embroidered in small scallops; and a bronze silk dressing-gown, fallen round her hips; her hair was disordered, pushed back in spikes. Arranged on her rosy, solid bosom, set in the low bodice of white embroidery, the gems looked superb. Seeing her comical, robust fairness in the glass and Stephen beside her in pale blue, pliant, placating, absorbed, she began to laugh with tears in her eyes.

'Oh, Stephen, it's so beautiful and it's such a filthy insult, to think you can buy a writer's soul with money.'

Stephen said, 'Don't let Browder and such bagatelles separate us, Emily. What can I do without you? I know you can live without me.'

She sat thrown back in the dressing-chair, looking at the necklace and her grotesque fair face. 'By golly, I look like a Polish peasant dressing as a countess,' she said laughing, her blue eyes bright and flushed, lucent, wet.

'I look like any kind of peasant, I'm so goddamn earthy, no wonder I fell for a silk-stocking. I like to hear you talking to waiters in icy tones, "This Graves is not cool enough, wait-ah!"'

'I do not say "waitah".'

'The prince and the pauper.' She began to take off the necklace, tugging impatiently at the catch. 'Help me with it, Stephen,' she continued in a hearty, husky tone, 'it's lovely, I love it, but get thee behind me, Satan. I guess you don't know me after all. Hasn't any woman ever told you it's a damned insult to try to buy a woman's affections with Russian crown jewels and a fur coat? Is – our – whole – future,' she continued, breaking into sobs, 'to – be – built – on my selling out my belief in the future of the world for some gewgaws of Tsarist Russia? It's a symbol, all right. I guess that's the kind of women you've known though.'

'Oh, Lord!'

'Of course, your mother and your sister are like that; they believe in Cincinnatus labouring the earth with a golden plough share. And what is the harvest? The corn is gold. The country's rich and right. Why Dear Anna, your mother, would think it the hoith of foine morals intoirely to give up dirty radicalism and wear a clean fortune round your neck. I don't say sister Florence. Florence is not all lucre. She'd pawn it at once for a hundred cases of Bourbon – '

'I got this from Florence. I've got to pay her for it, somehow.'

'Take it back. It's for her sort,' said Emily decisively pushing it along the table. 'I like it; but after you saying you'd divorce me if I didn't believe in the American way of life – '

'I did not!' he shouted.

'American exceptionalism! What else is it? And you'd leave me for not believing in Hollywood, the art of the masses; do you think you can buy me back with a stick of candy? I don't think you could have done that to me, even as a child. The only thing you could buy me with then was affection. I loved people. They didn't love back.'

'I didn't mean to hurt your feelings; I don't seem to do anything right. So I've lost you!'

'Will you give up your belief that revolutionary Marxism is right; and consent to be led by the nose by the quiet men from nowhere (Earl Browder) all for an amethyst necklace?' said Emily loudly and scornfully; and throwing the box with the thing in it on to the carpet, where she kicked it away. 'Pooah! What triviality! Is that what you think of me, Emily Wilkes? You can buy me with a string of beads? When I whore, I'll whore for plenty, for the whole works. They'll have to come to me with the whole world wrapped up in their arms! And with the Bible too and the whole of revolutionary history, man's struggle too, and say: "Debs says

64

you can, and you can prove it by the Haymarket Martyrs, the crimes of Cripple Creek; lynched labour organisers led to it and Sacco and Vanzetti died for it." Manoel! Is the car ready? Put my bags into it. Drive me to the airport. Stephen, I've left everything arranged; the children's diets, their dentists' appointments, when to change their clothes; everything; I've paid all the bills, I was up all night. Now, this is final. You can divorce me if you like.'

'Forgive me, Emily,' said Stephen.

'I don't forgive you. I'm goddamn mad and I'm going to stay mad.'

But Stephen ordered Manoel out of the car, got in himself; and while he was driving Emily to the airport, he talked her round. In tears, quite overwhelmed with shame, Emily was brought back to the house. They spent the day together talking over many things quietly and sincerely; kisses and endearments were exchanged in the vegetable garden, down by the shore, behind the trees that screened the barbecue, by the children's swing, in the dark of the garage and while they were spraying the vines with DDT against the Japanese beetle.

Not far off, Manoel and Maria, in their rest house, could be heard talking and laughing; once they screeched with laughter. Two or three times Emily ran to the children, who were being kept together by the English governess named Thistledown. Emily hugged them all, kissed the eldest, their adopted child Leonard, in the dark curls that fell over his pale narrow forehead. 'Oh, my darling,' she said to them once, 'if you only knew what a mother you have! You'd do better with a snake, a Gila monster, than an earthworm like me. Oh, Miss Thistledown, I'm a poor weak woman without character.' She hugged the governess. 'Let me kiss you,' she said, pressing her wet round cheeks, rough and warm as fruit, to the middle-aged woman's thin face. 'You English are all so strong, you're just and strong. My God,' she said, turning away, and aloud, 'if my fighting forefathers heard that blather! I'm fat with the buttering and the licking afterwards.'

At dinner, Emily made the crêpes suzette as planned. She was wearing rings, a hair-jewel and bracelets. She was flushed and her tongue wagged frenziedly. 'Oh, if only we were Jewish,' she cried; 'we'd stick together. What a beautiful family life the Jews have, so close-woven; and they make more of blood than we do. It's beautiful, that tree of life with all its branches, under the mantle of all its leaves. Oh, how lucky you are, Lennie, to have had a Jewish father. If only I had Jewish blood I'd make you happy. I'd have the art of keeping the fire in the hearth forever. I used to go down to the Jewish quarter as a child and just stare in, glare in hungrily through their windows on Friday nights, when they had their candles in the windows! Oh, how tender it was, how touching and true!

The family is the heart of man; how can you tear it open?'

Stephen listened, smiling, grinning: 'Christopher's father, my brother-in-law, Jake Potter, was a nasty little man! Family life is poison. I'm sure Miss Thistledown and Manoel think they're having a season in hell. Read what Plato said about the family!'

'Plato was a homosexual!' declared Emily. 'Stephen, listen to what I say! Family love is the only true selfless love; it's natural communism. That is the origin of our feeling for communism: to each according to his needs, from each according to his capacity; and everything is arranged naturally, without codes and without policing. Manoel, why don't you bring in the coffee? This coffee is not like we get at your sister Florence's. But of course, there's only one liquid that means anything to her – '

'Stop it!'

But she did not stop and held them at table while she discussed Stephen's family and their money habits, for a long time. Christopher's grand-uncle had dieted himself to death, being a miser; having apportioned his estate among his children to escape death duties and family hatred, he found them all sitting like buzzards around his semi-starved person to tear the pemmican from his bones. Stephen's mother, Stephen's sisters, the rich girl the family wanted Stephen to marry –

Miss Thistledown, embarrassed, half rose from her chair. 'Stay where you are!' roared Emily, 'I haven't finished speaking. You're the children's guardian. If I leave, you'll be their mother! You may as well know what's in them!' At last, with an imperial gesture, she dismissed them, the children to their homework or beds; and when they had sung the Giles song, she said to Stephen, 'Let's go to the movies; I have a need to sit in the dark with you.'

They went downtown. At night, they went to bed but did not sleep. In the film, the word 'fascist' was used and Stephen exulted, 'There you are! Hollywood is not all poison. Reaction is on the way out, when the radical writers in the studios can put over their ideas like that.'

'Oh, poohpooh,' said Emily: 'people don't even know what it means. It went by in a second! Who heard it but politicomaniacs like us?'

And with this one word, the bitter wound opened again.

'I shall be ill if you don't let me sleep,' said Stephen. 'Last night too – '

'Sleep! When our futures and our souls, I mean that word, it's all we have that's worth fighting for – we've got to think this thing through. We can't sleep anyway.'

'I could if you'd let me. I've got you; my children are with me; I have no other wants. I don't want to have ideas. Ideas are civil war. Let us drown our ideas, Emmie. Let's live in a friendly fug. I'm sick of it.'

'In the first place, what are we fighting about, Stephen? Let's get that clear. We're mixed up. We like New York, but you want us to stay here and make a fortune in the movies, so that Dear Anna and Florence the Fuzzy and your English Uncle Shongo – '

'I have no Uncle Shongo!' he squealed.

'Your English Uncle Mungo and Uncle Cha will see you are not a failure; you, too, can make money. I don't mind being a failure because my people remain in the mud of time; but you do. I'm from *hoi polloi* and you're from hoity-toity – '

'Stop it! Was there ever such a fool! I married a clown!'

'Anyway, for some reason, we've got to believe in MGM and the mistakes of the left.'

'Goddamn it, they are not mistakes. Who are you and I – '

'For myself, the writers like what I write when I like what I write; but the agents don't and you don't and even – but leave certain names out of this shameful story. If I write the way I like, it'll be poverty for us; not this monogrammed sheet, but mended shoes and tattered pants and not enough vitamins; and that's not fair to the kids.'

'We're not philanthropists. It's theory and practice for everyone in the world, except the unquestioning and thankless rich – lucky dogs! You don't want our kids to grow up like Clem Blake's, eating out of cans with many a fly twixt the can and the lip.'

'Golly!' she laughed: 'I guess they'll grow up, too.'

'If they don't die of botulism.'

'I thought that was from botflies.'

'What are botflies?'

'It shows I'm a farmer's daughter. Well, they'll grow up, too.' She sighed. 'Oh, well, what the hell! Maybe the oral hygiene and the hand-made shirts are just hanky-panky. Maybe that's no way to raise heroes of labour.'

'I don't want to live with heroes of labour,' he said pettishly. 'I've seen lots of them. Starvation and struggle are no good for the soul; nor the stomach. What are we fighting for? Not to make people like the workers are now. Good grief! I had a "love the worker" phase; but I wasn't sincere. I walked along working-class streets and saw their stores and their baby-carriages and hated 'em. I wouldn't raise anyone to be like them. Why are the French so revolutionary? Because of their good cooking and good arts of life. And what the devil – you can make money, so make it! If we starved, it would be a whim, the whim of the rich. Why should we starve? You've only got to do two days' work and we'll be in for $30,000. It's a whim and a selfish one to throw that kind of money back in the studio's face and talk about art and poverty and your soul. And if you're a red, you ought to show you're one just *because* you can come out on top; so they can't say it's grousing. You ought to be a shining – red – light. The rest is just moral filth, mental laziness and infantile behaviour. You want to be back in Tacoma, the schoolgirl who read through Shakespeare once every year, and dreamed about making a noise as a great writer. Fooey! You know I hated Princeton. Well, one of the reasons was, I spent my time trying to live up to the noble secular trees and noble secular presidents. I starved myself trying to live on what I thought a poor scholar would live on; and fancied my parents admired me for spending so little. Rich imbeciles like me think there's something mystic, some intellectual clarity and purification of the soul in sobriety, austerity and poverty. I got over that. Now anyone can keep me, my family, you – ' he said bitterly, 'or Christopher or my son.'

'Christopher is your son,' she said.

'My lazy vampirism feeds on my nearest and dearest: I gnaw their white breasts.'

'Oh, Stephen,' she wailed, 'oh, don't say that. I love you. Don't say those things. If I have a vulgar streak which enables me to make more money than you, aren't I, in those moments, like your moneymaking grandfathers that you despise? And I feel I'm tanned like a tanned rhino hide: I'm secretly afraid you'll leave me and get some decent woman who never sold out. Despise me; but don't despise yourself, Stephen. What else am I working and selling out for? You're my whole life, my *rayzon d'ayter*. If we haven't got each other, we've got nothing. Our life is so hideous. With each other, we can work it out, we can hope. Otherwise, what has it all been for? You gave up millions, I gave up my hopes, dreams and ideals; and our hearts are being squeezed dry.'

'You've made me better than I was,' said Stephen. 'First out of Princeton, I used to hang around with those wistful, carping critics of the critics' group. I was young and stupid and I think I still am. I hated those arty people, Emily – all – with the bitterest hate of envy; and then I took up Marxism because I thought it gave me a key they didn't have; it raised me above them. I got out of the grovelling mass in the valley and felt the fresh air blowing on me; but it was all selfish – '

'It was NOT,' roared Emily, 'don't be crazy!'

'Yes, it was. They seemed to get women without even trying.'

'Jee-hosaphat! Did you want to get women?' She began to laugh, rolling about on the bed and looking at him with her red and yellow face, surrounded by loose fair hair. Her face was made for laughter – a pudgy comic face with deep lines only when she laughed, the deep lines of the comic mask. 'Oh, Stephen! And you so beautiful! Why on earth you picked a puttynose, a pieface like me – '

'A what?'

68

'I look as if some slapstick artist just threw a custard-pie in my puss – '

'Don't insult the woman I love!'

'And those freckles remind me of the oatmeal in a haggis – '

'You're the most beautiful woman I ever had in my life, that's all. It's the beauty of the mind – '

'Oh, if we could wear the mind inside out! I don't get it. You're fascinating, Stephen.'

'Well, the only women who go for me are those who wriggle down to the platform after meetings and ask me to explain. You know what that fellow in the bistro in Paris said to his son that day? "Don't fret son, study cats. The females always go for the ragged, bleary-eyed, whiskery, dirty old tom with cobwebs on his eyebrows."'

'But is it true?'

'I envied them all,' said Stephen sourly, 'and you provide the final revenge against them. You're so wonderfully, truly, profoundly potent and you're nothing like them. They were so genteel; they wouldn't be caught in an enthusiasm: the sad little band of *nil admirari*. I had my intellectual revenge when I studied a few scraps of Marxism too. I learned they stood for nothing. They, if they learned a bit, they dropped out halfway. They married a bit of money, a schoolteacher with cheques appeal, took a house in a restricted suburb; no Jews, Irish or Italians, they're all too enthusiastic. They begin to owe money and have plenty of nothing; they get sleek and terribly bright and wise – and so terribly empty. There's nothing to prevent them jumping off Brooklyn Bridge right now. Because only an idea and a belief can prevent you doing that.'

'Oh, well, who the hell cares for them? You got out.'

'Yes, but they've no doubts. I employed a poor scholar, a tailor's son, to teach me Marxism: the old noble getting out an insurance policy against the revolution! You're real. I knew right off you were a genuine person, a wise and rich woman, strong and meaningful.'

'How did you know that?'

'That awful dress you wore!'

'Stephen!' she cried, blushing; 'and you always said you loved it.'

'So I did and I do. I made you keep it forever. I love it. The vines and the grapes and the flowers – '

'Stephen! I did think it was lovely and warm,' she added thoughtfully. 'I loved it too. I still don't think it's awful. Of course, dear Florence wouldn't have – '

'Don't spoil it. And the story you told me of your growing up and the things that happened to you! The man in the house that fell down when you were in it: Jimmy – the man who rented out condemned buildings and introduced you to Donne – well, I never met such people. And then the rotten men – whom I understood, with all my failure, better than you. It all showed me the depth of life and love and passion and ability that could be. And lacking just one thing, the ability to be warped.'

Emily said nothing.

'I felt so cut off from the rest of mankind and you bridged that for me. I felt I was still up in that hospital in the snow slopes and pines, where I was cut off for three years. But I know I'm down on earth again when I'm with you. And I live for you,' he said obstinately, 'and only for you. Would I live for myself? You don't like me to say that; but I must. I want to call it out, to shout it out. I thirst for what you give me. My life drives me into sterility; I can't give and nothing bears for me. But you did.'

Emily turned about restlessly. 'You musn't say that. I told you not to. It makes me feel ill. Suppose I died? Anyone can die.'

'Don't say that, please.'

'All right. But you mustn't found your life on one person. It's dreadful. You throw yourself on another person's back and bear them down. They bow right down to earth with weeping and sobbing for you and them. You kill them. The feeling's unspeakable. I'll die.'

Stephen laughed. 'Well, that's me though. Too bad. You must live for something. I think I'm lucky. A lot of those men I knew had nothing to live for and now they're slipping along a moral skid row. They're looking sideways furtively at the milestones. I guess the only thing that stops them putting their heads in the gas oven is that all they've got is an infra-red grill. I know what I'm living for: for you. For anything you live for. I don't care what it is.'

'That's fabulous. I won't have it,' said Emily angrily.

'Perhaps I could be different in another society. I wonder. But I think a bad man, a real bastard but a strong villain, would be better for you than me. At least, he wouldn't pretend to be an intellectual or a moral hero and take up your time and waste your affections.'

'Oh, I don't know what to do,' said Emily frantically. 'I'll give you a beating. It's more than I can stand. I'm going mad. You're killing me.' She threw herself from side to side as if avoiding bees. 'I'm burning. Don't, don't, don't!' She threw herself at him. 'Stop it, do you hear me! It makes me feel desperate. I'll burst.'

She jumped out of bed, opened a small drawer in the dressing-table, and he at once snapped, 'What are you doing? Taking some of those damn pills?'

'I've got to calm down. How can I work tomorrow? And I've got a lecture in the evening.'

'What lecture?'

'Adult education.'

'That's it, that's it! Your whole life is filled with giving, doing, I'm nothing but a barnacle on the wheel of progress.'

She jumped back into bed and kissed him furiously, all over face, neck, hair, chest, arms. Then, she lay back and began to reason. 'This life doesn't suit you, Stevie. It's a gambling, race-course crazy life for touts and bums, not for you. You're a scholar and should live in peace. This double or nothing, boom or bust scares you and nauseates you. Your attitude towards money, so different from mine, is disturbed in this mad Hollywood carnival. You respect money. You shouldn't. Fancy respecting the filthy reeking stuff. I don't respect it. To me it's not part of a highly organized respectable society, the just reward of pioneering valour; nor a medal pinned on the virtuous starched bosom. To me there's just as much virtue in skid row, or as little. Moneymaking is gangdom, grab or someone else will. Of course, you're right too. It's the high established church of our great land. Lincoln said, "As a nation of freemen we must live through all time, or die by suicide." Suicide! Oh, God! A great nation cutting its throat! Could it really happen? As long as the razor is of gold and the noose of amethyst – '

'A country can't die,' said Stephen indignantly. 'We can, the poor lice on its hide, but thank God the country can't die. If I thought it could, I'd die of empty horror. Do you know the story that has haunted me since I was a boy? *The Man Without a Country*.'

'But that's bamboozle.'

'I think I can even understand the cranks and crooks who are put out of Russia and write lies for bread. They want to be noticed; they're Russians too. It's the infant screaming for its mother.'

'Don't waste your sympathy,' she said drily.

'I suppose it's envy too,' he conceded. 'They're best sellers; though it's a nasty, mean way to make a fortune, running down your country. I know you don't believe I am as good as that. I couldn't write a book that would sell, in any terms. So I ought to be out earning a living and giving you the chance you want.'

'I wish I could,' said Emily, thoughtfully and gently. Then she began to fire up, 'I'd like to write a book about the revolutionary movement, the way I see it and what's wrong with it. Here we have the greatest organization for socialism in the western world. Look at the size of the labour union movement! A state within the state. When it says, "Go", we go; when it says, "Stop", we stop. Organized millions of conscious workers: what would the early socialists have said to that? The millennium! Though, it's not. But isn't it a great big poster saying, "It can be done!" Or is it already too late? Are there too many labour opportunists, too many finks and goons? I'd like to write this book. I'm dumb enough to think it would be good. But who would print it? We would all of us end up in the railroad wreck and not a single finger lifted to take the engine off our neck.'

'You could do it,' said Stephen without force; 'but you'd get nowhere. I ought to build fires under your ambition. It only shows the kind of punk I am. But I'm representative. You could have me for one of the characters; a clay figure covered with the fine patina of soft living, a radical, arguing man, busy with top secrets and who's who in Washington, soft-shoeing in the antechambers of the lobbies of Congress, a radical dandy, dispensing the amenities of another caste, paying his way into the labour movement, following a boyish dream; take the underdog along with you to the White House; heel, sir, heel: misinterpreting everything to suit the silk-lined dream and with laughable ineffectiveness exhorting a stone-deaf working class out of the blind alley of pork-chop opportunism to lead them down the blind alley of rigid righteousness. For what have we to offer them? Something we don't believe in ourselves; socialist austerity and puritanism for the better building of steel mills.'

'I wouldn't see it that way,' said Emily slowly. 'This would be a cruel book. I wouldn't spend much time on theoretical errors or an analysis of our peculiar applications of theory; but I'd try to put a finger on essential human weaknesses; the ignorance and self-indulgence that has led us into Bohemia. On that score, there's plenty to say. Ought we all to live well, have our children in private schools, training them for the *gude braid claith*? I ought to say how everything becomes its opposite not only outside the besieged fortress but in: how we misinterpret the mission of America, the position in the unions, ourselves; and what our lives are, that are going so far astray. We sneer at Utopian communities; but we are trying to live in Utopia.'

'It might be an epitaph of American socialism: I'd like to see it,' sang out Stephen.

'No, no! It would be for the real rebels, the real labour movement, against all vampires who take all that's best in the world, even the name of the most sacred causes and use them for promotion; shepherds killing and eating the lambs. That's it. Socialism can't die! Don't we believe that? But it can die – suffocated, here! By us! That's horrible.'

'It's horrible; especially when we're in it up to our necks,' said Stephen restlessly: 'if I had to be born in these days, why not a Russian, where it's all settled?'

'Why not a Yugoslav, a Frenchman, anyone but us? Yes. The world's going to be implacable towards us, Stephen. Let's face it. There's going to be a lot of stuff in between; but that time, the day before yesterday, was IT, *die Ende, Schluss, Fini*. I keep seeing the weirdest thing dancing before

72

my eyes – like a dagger, like a cup of poison: choose fair maid, but both are death; ha-ha! Gromyko round the big table, eyes straight ahead, shoulders back, jaws grim, pad-pad, round and round, silent, but brain radiating what we all felt only too damn well: "If there's a war you can't win!" Oh, God! And we have to be on the *wrong* side in the bad time coming! To be in America, to like America, to want to be an American and to be wrong, to be martyred by Americans – because by golly, how the Americans love to make martyrs! They make them wholesale, they never notice. Every few years some innocents have to be offered up on our altar, the giant footstool before the infinite altar of the brass-faced philistine god. I know my people; I'm from deep America. What did Lincoln say in that address before the young men's Lyceum in Springfield, 1838: "till dead men were seen literally dangling from the boughs of trees upon every roadside and in numbers almost sufficient to rival the native Spanish moss of the country as a drapery of the forest." I read that often as a child and I trembled. Later I thought, things have improved since then. But I now know they haven't. Can you see us as martyrs, Stephen? I'm not made for that. I don't believe in it.'

'Neither do I,' said Stephen, 'but it happens. Every day someone's name is called and he is conscripted into the army of blood.'

'I don't like to be a martyr, I won't be a martyr. I don't want to be on the wrong side. I wasn't born for that. How short life is! And what about the children? Oh, my, my! For them, one can't be on the wrong side: and yet we have to choose. What's the right side? I mean morally, and in terms of our natural lives? Oh, Lord! We can be torn to pieces. I won't give up the kids; and your mother and Florence will drag Olivia and Christy from us like lightning; and Giles and Lennie will be homeless. They'd have every right to grab them if we became outcasts, outlaws with the community riding us on a rail and throwing stones through our windows. They're taking the children from guilty communist parents, "communist" meaning guilty. The court would be enquiring into our bank accounts and laundry baskets; and Grandma and Florence would be seen white as snow, for guzzling is not considered wrong in this country – '

'Oh, for Pete's sake!'

'All right, Stephen,' she said, furious; 'you know you want to keep the children!'

'Yes, I didn't want them, but now I do. I love them and I need Olivia's money.'

'You can't touch it: her mother left it in trust,' she said.

'I can charge her for keep and education and foreign travel: you always do it with rich children; and we can travel maybe. I can influence her, I hope. Imagine, two tots in my household will be millionaires; and I'm a poor man. Life hoaxed me.'

'If they were settled, our hands would be free,' said Emily without joy. She sighed, 'It's the damnedest thing! But I won't let them go. And besides, with us they'll escape the tumbrils!'

'What tumbrils?' he said testily.

She sighed, 'Oh, well, if we weren't socialists, I suppose *agenbite of inwit* would make heroes of us anyway. We'd have to start out and join Daniel's glorious little band marching to extinction. Ugh! But that would finish us with your family. Now, we can contend with Dear Anna and all our dear lucre-men, that communism was a youthful jag, "our Spanish civil war phase", as the renegade hath it; and they can see it as an enthusiasm we're too decent to abandon. But, start in now and it would be crystal clear that we're middle-aged delinquents, not mad but bad. Yet we can't abandon and join those other bastards whose names are writ in shapes of crap.'

Stephen lay rigid and was silent. She became silent too. They went to sleep.

Emily rose early, ordered the food for the day, and, taking a tray of black coffee up to her little room, she began on one of her scripts, a story with humour and pathos about a freckleface in the big city. She worked hard through the day, drove down to the village to buy some bottled French sauces and herbs from a specialist, visited a workman's coffee-stall, the owner of which was a political friend, and hurried back to make over her UNO article into lecture notes for the evening.

In the evening she drove to downtown Los Angeles and in a small hall addressed forty to fifty people, among them Mexicans and Negroes, giving her impressions of the San Francisco Conference. Emily spoke in public as she spoke in private. On the platform, she was earnest and incisive and also rollicking and fatly funny. At the end she said, 'A man I know in the Middle West had someone in City Hall tip him off about condemned houses; he rented them out privately as flophouses for whores and bums. He showed me a few and he used to recite John Donne to me – "But since that I, must dye at last, 'tis best, to use myself in jest".' An ambulance-chaser I knew in my newspaper days used to sit outside the emergency waiting-room and read me William Blake. The first I ever heard of either poet! The way I collected my education, my high school having no use for same! Ha-ha! Very funny! I'm dying laughing. Imagine I have to go to work now, parsing and pluperfects, in my old age! Well, to the point, friends! I see you there and I am here and I see something ahead. The choice will come, the choice has come. Perhaps you don't see it clearly yet; but one day it will be as obvious as the cop's club and you will weep by tear gas, because it is then too late to choose. Some of you will be in jail, some will be silent with the silence that grows over a man like fungus; and some will be successes and able to appear anywhere in broad daylight. The choice is already taken out of our hands. Well, anyhow, this is the way William Blake puts it in one of his cloudy epics and I'm damned if I can remember anything else but this; and I'm damned remembering this, anyway, maybe. It goes:

> But Palambron called down a Great Solemn Assembly . . .
> That he who will not defend Truth, may be compelled to
> Defend a Lie, that he may be snared and caught and taken.'

After a pause, there was acclamation. She was forty minutes getting away from the meeting afterwards, for she talked with anyone who wanted to talk with her. Stephen was waiting for her in the car. She got in and they drove uptown. She remained silent.

'Did you wow them?' he asked.

'Were you in the hall?'

'No, I was sitting in the car.'

She grumbled, 'I recited to them a quote from William Blake.' She repeated it. 'They probably thought Palambron was an Indian chief,' she said, laughing. The laughing turned into uncontrollable sobbing.

5 THE HOLINSHED PARTY

Soon after the Howards gave their house-warming party they received an invitation in return from James Holinshed to dine at his house in the next gully, Persimmon Glen. Holinshed, like Stephen, was said to have money from his family. It was to be a small dinner party, just for them, the Bowleses, and the Moffat Byrds. Others would drop in later. This was very gratifying.

On a Saturday, about five in the afternoon, the Howards, in their new dark-blue car, climbed Persimmon Glen and found the Holinshed house where it was perched on a table cliff, with very little ground, neatly arranged by Japanese gardeners. There were observation windows, a sun porch, rockeries, a steep flagged path, terraces, and a pretty drying yard up in the air above the roofs, on another table cliff. The Howards were in their best mood, Emily bubbling gaiety, Stephen with his smooth, slightly invalid walk and unexpressed smile, giving his wife a feeling of discreet alertness, satisfied satire. Though a delicately pale man, he glowed in repose, with ease and achievement.

The large living-room was attractively disordered, with chairs, divans, cushions and children's toys spread about. Paintings hung on the walls. They found Godfrey and Millian Bowles and the Holinsheds talking.

'What will you have to drink?' said Holinshed.

Godfrey Bowles said, 'Let's have some fun, let's drink. You must drink, Millian,' he continued to his wife and, in succeeding chatter, it turned out that Millian drank only milk and orange juice on account of the children, but that this once she would have a martini cocktail.

Said Emily, 'Why on account of the children? They're not here.' Millian smiled to Godfrey; and answered, 'We don't want our children to feel we have a life they can't participate in. It's enough of a trauma that we must explain to them later that they're adopted. We don't want them to begin feeling insecure now.'

'Just the same there are lots of things they can't participate in – yet,' said Stephen.

Emily said in an undertone, though with a smile, 'I believe in toughening the children. Only I don't do it. Why should the children be

76

taught they're the same as we are? They'll soon find out it's a lie. Wait till they meet the world.'

'We're hoping it won't be the same world.' said Godfrey.

'What – in fifteen years or so?' asked Stephen.

'I don't know that you see things as we do,' said Godfrey smiling.

Emily exclaimed, 'Look here, Godfrey, I have at present four children. I guess I see the problem as well as you do. I have to take their temperatures and get their breakfasts and get them to school.'

Godfrey and Millian became serious.

The Japanese manservant Katsuri came in with the drinks. Millian took the cocktail, the others took scotch and soda. James Holinshed held his drink up to the light; Vera, his wife, looked down at hers sadly.

Godfrey said, 'Well, that's the heart of the question, Emily, these children and the trauma of change and insecurity in their present background. Yours have come from more to less security, especially your house-guests Olivia and Christopher. Ours – are being given the only opportunity that could ever come their way. Their parents were poor.'

'Come on, what's your argument?' said Emily, waving her glass.

'Godfrey – later, not now,' said Millian.

Stephen took off his jacket and hung it on the back of his chair. He said, 'Millian – what is this "later, not now"? I did not come here to discuss children. I came here for a rest from children. But just to get this straight, let me say that my house-guest, as you put it, is my own daughter Olivia, whom I am planning to take back from my sister, and we got Christopher from my crazy brother-in-law Jacob Potter who is a drunk, a night-owl, a wastrel, who loses his driver's licence and doesn't know his name; and even before he mashed my sister in the wastelands one moony eve, their marriage was on the rocks. And on the rocks is the subtitle too, of the life of Florence, my other dear sister, who is childless and claims I should give her my only daughter, because Bertram Baldwin is looking for himself elsewhere.'

'Your brother-in-law Baldwin was struggling towards integration,' said Godfrey.

'My brother-in-law Baldwin by a freak will was worth five million dollars. And he couldn't be integrated with that. I could. And before the court I objected to my sister bringing up my daughter Olivia, who is now twelve, hence or not hence, as you will, on the verge of pubescence, in a night-court atmosphere.'

Emily burst out laughing. The others looked grave and prudish.

Godfrey said, 'Let's discuss this later; let's have some fun now.'

Stephen said, 'I don't want to discuss it. Leave my family out of it.'

Emily laughed; the Holinsheds laughed too. They also had adopted children.

Godfrey laughed formally and sipped his drink. Millian had established herself in an armchair, where she sat relaxed and with a quiet smile. Godfrey moved his chair closer to hers and patted her arm: she responded with a warm smile. She was a rather plain, soft woman in a black dress, about fifteen years older than her husband. Godfrey was strongly built, sombrely dark, pleasing and with a curious manner of looking not at the people present, but offstage, just as if he were on a stage playing a part.

Millian said comfortably, 'Godfrey's contention was, to the psychoanalyst, that he never was frustrated; he liked being the way he was when he was a child and whatever he wanted to do, he did; without ever infringing the nursery laws. You see, we thought it better to know where we stood before we adopted the children. The psychoanalyst simply laughed at Godfrey, and said he showed a double frustration; there was not even a normal reaction and Godfrey was too anxious to prove he was normal. That is not at all normal. Godfrey told Dr Stumpf that he'd always been loved at home; he'd had everything he ever wrote printed in private editions and his parents circulated them to all their friends. You see, his father being a writer, they did not want Godfrey to feel underprivileged and inferior about his own writing. Godfrey played with boys and girls alike; he'd never had any infantile curiosity or doubts or fears about sex. Dr Stumpf asked him why, in that case, he had married a woman twelve years older than himself. I'm fifteen years older than Godfrey; but out of gallantry, which you might call a repression or inhibition, I suppose, he told Dr Stumpf twelve. Godfrey has an obvious Oedipus complex, I suppose; but so far we have not found out why.'

Emily said, 'I don't get it, Godfrey. Are you unhappy or unrepressed or something? Why are you going to this Dr Glumpf-glumpf? I think it's unhealthy.'

'Godfrey adopted the two children so that he wouldn't be able to leave me and he still wanted to leave me afterwards; so he went again to the psychoanalyst; for he says I represent his ideal,' said Millian looking at them and patting Godfrey on the arm. Godfrey put down his drink, which he had only sipped, came behind her chair and kissed her several times in the hair.

Emily shrugged her shoulders. 'Say, listen, folks! I'm damned if I'm going to a psychoanalyst if I split first; if I'm not smart enough to figure what's wrong with me, I'd better die. I know a psycho in New York, he's a friend of Stephen's. He says he never psychs artists or writers: they get it out of their system the simple way. I'm with him. What's all this worrying about your psyches? I don't think it's Marxian. I don't. I don't see how it helps the working class. I bet working mothers don't run to a fakir every time their three-year-old gets a cold. No such fun. They give an aspirin and if little Annie dies, they are prostrate and next year they have another. It's boogoy – it's anti-Marxian.'

'I think so too,' said Stephen.

Godfrey called out, 'Emily! Stephen! How can you say psychoanalysis is anti-Marxian?' James Holinshed became serious for a moment, 'Why, Godfrey's cure is the most celebrated cure on the West Coast. Dr Stumpf made his fame out here with Godfrey's cure. The stars and the directors go to him now.'

Emily began to laugh good-naturedly, 'Well, as long as I know Godfrey's cured. But what did he have wrong? He seems the same to me. Maybe I'm short-sighted or something.'

'I'm afraid human nature is a little different from the superficial grimaces of a cardboard comedy,' said Millian.

'Ouch, what a push in the puss, Millian!' said Stephen.

Emily flushed, 'You mean I write for the *Post*, well, what's wrong with that? What does the Party say? My book *Johnny Appleseed* offended *les belles dames sans merci*, the uppercrust, the good ladies and gentlemen on the central committee, because no good man ever looked twice at an extramarital woman if he was married already, if he belonged to the socialist movement. His mind is set on higher things. And do I even say this blasphemy? I imply it. And by jiminy if I'd made you the hero, Godfrey, I wouldn't even have implied. And it's you who have to go to Dr Glumpf-glumpf to get exorcised! Oh, ho, ho! Oh, ho, ho! But I'm in good standing. I'm a good Party member because I'm a funny writer, writing funny family stuff for the *Post* or the *Kallikak News* because that way I make good money and help the workers' cause. But the Party and you, too, Godfrey, and all the rest of you here, you don't like my serious writing which is about and for the working class, because each worker and each Party member shall be the husband of one wife. Thus saith Holy Writ.'

'And please leave my wife out of this,' said Stephen scowling. He unbuttoned his suspenders and hung them carefully under his coat on the chair. He then sat cross-legged in his chair, ran his hand through his hair and smiled gaily.

Godfrey said in a cautious low tone, 'We were all very disappointed in you out here; but then later we understood. We had all seen great changes in you.'

'Stephen, I'd like you to look at a manuscript I have,' said James Holinshed in a diplomatic aside which changed the conversation.

Bowles came in, serious now, 'Yes, we'd like your opinion, Stephen. I think James has done a very fine piece of work, it's about the social status of the progressive intellectuals just preceding and after Pearl Harbor. Pearl Harbor was, of course, a qualitative change. Jim shows the radical movement fought the reactionary tendencies in America, the various streams of thought, the idiosyncrasies – that's his poetic approach – I make no comment; and how they all united for the war effort, for the one front against fascism. He begins with his idealistic and even petty-bourgeois postured youth in eastern towns – he even had a project, resurrecting the memories of the dead towns along the fall line – nothing could be more reactionary and socially useless – how he met socialist and communist groups in New York, how he chose between them, by the force of ideologies and circumstances; and how after fighting in what might have seemed a bywater he found that this bywater joined the general stream of mankind, flowing towards progress on the day of Pearl Harbor. The general background is Persimmon Glen. He does the rest by flashbacks. The last scene is Persimmon Glen, formerly lighted by the headlights of cars and the floodlights from private houses; now lighted only by his torch as he goes up it in his blacked-out car, in uniform, a man working for his country, which is united with Russia and all progressive countries in the fight for democracy. I'd like your opinion of it. Moffat Byrd thinks it's the best progressive novel we've turned out here. We were under pressure here. We face the Pacific. It might have been us. We haven't had a really outstanding left writer. I think Holinshed fills the gap.'

Said Emily, 'Well, by golly, Godfrey, you yourself are supposed to be a leading left writer, leaving out others present. What do you mean? No left writers? That's an insult to the whole outfit here.'

Godfrey flushed slightly, 'I say so and I think so. I think Jim is beginning to fill the gap.'

'The thought does you honour, God,' said Stephen.

Holinshed pursued, 'But I want your honest opinion, leaving all this preamble aside. Moffat Byrd and others have seen it and think it has the right line but I want real outside opinions. I consider a work of art is social, it should be submitted to the people.'

'The people thank you,' said Stephen.

'Stephen,' said Emily flushing, making a grimace and draining her glass.

Vera Holinshed said, 'Let me freshen your drinks.'

'That's Vera's painting up there over the chimney,' said Godfrey.

'Is it really? Why, it's wonderful. What is it? Where did you find those huts?' cried Emily.

'In North Africa,' said Vera, in an undertone, glancing at the picture and away.

80

'When were you in North Africa?'

'Oh, you know Vera was married before to Bathurst Pemm,' said Jim.

'What?' Emily checked herself and looked at the picture. 'You were both painters – ' She glanced at Stephen and continued, 'It's wonderful, Vera.'

Stephen said in an amusing manner, 'I knew Bathurst years ago, when I was hanging out with the Trotskyists and he was a rough-and-ready artist from the streets and had just chucked his job in lithography for people's art. I didn't know you then, Vera.'

Vera said, 'I was there though. I was doing a social welfare job and painting weekends.'

Jim said, 'Bathurst and Vera grew up together, same street on the East Side. It was one of those things. But Bath wasn't her first love. It wasn't as unconscious as that. She really picked Bath out of the bunch as a comer; and she kept him for a couple, for five years and she paid for the trip to North Africa – didn't you, Vee? I forget the whole route – Spain. Looked wonderful in his one-man show. Vera made Bathurst; so of course he left her.'

'But that's really fine art,' said Emily, choking over her drink and waving at the mantelpiece.

Jim replied, 'Oh, Vee's an artist, but it's the way with women – kids, progressive schools to be paid for, orange juice, all-night baby-sitting – I don't know what it's all for, but it's necessary for women; otherwise they have repressions. If women don't have children, their art's cramped and if they do, they don't have art. So men have the art. Fair enough.'

Emily looked at him angrily, 'I take that amiss, Jim. Damn it, that's an outright stuffed shirt viewpoint; so you get it straight all the time, eh? I can beat any man alive, I bet, in my writing, and children and house and all. I think it makes a woman an artist, it doesn't hinder her. If she's hindered it's her own fault; she or her husband doesn't want her to win. Stephen has always helped me and it's because of him I can have a full life and I believe in marriage and children for women and art, too. I think it's possible for a woman to be a wife and mother and woman and artist and success and social worker and anything else you please in 1945.'

Emily sighed, 'I don't say it isn't the goddamnedest problem, but it's no more a problem than being a wage-earner in a factory with kids at home, or a working mother or an unmarried mother, or a deserted mother, or the winner of a beauty contest in Dayton, Ohio, who comes out to Hollywood to conquer the box office and spends the rest of her life hash-chucking in a hash-house for other failures. I grant it's terrible to be a success in literature and the movie trade along with being a wife and mother, but it's not so terrible I can't stand it.'

81

'Very prettily said; the voice of Pomegranate Glen,' said Stephen. There was a silence. Everyone was thinking that Pomegranate Glen was in better style than Persimmon Glen, they wondered if Stephen intended a crack.

Emily was flushed. She simpered at Stephen, 'All right. I'm right. Millian and Vera and I ought to know.'

At this moment the Japanese manservant announced dinner.

'Thank you, Katsuri,' said Vera.

They went to the table. The dining-room opened out of the living-room and was a long, wide room lined with glass shelves and glass cupboards let into the wall and filled with ornaments. Some were toys made by the children, in wax, straw and wood. There were parts of an old French dinner service, some Bohemian glass. The polished refectory table was decorated with lace mats, with monogrammed china, plain and cut glass and four hand-painted candlesticks. They had a light dinner, grapefruit in ice, chicken with potato croquettes, peas, salad and ice-cream, hot freshmade southern popovers, served in a linen serviette.

'I love these,' said Emily, taking three at once and looking hungrily at the wartime butter ration, which she did not touch. They drank some white California wine. Emily remarked, 'Um, um, this is a nice dinner, Vera, wonderful chicken, yum-yum. Is Katsuri your cook? Stephen's dream is to have a Japanese butler and maid. So far what we have is two Portuguese. They seem to use up a lot of laundry. We pay $400 a month for the pair, plus laundry, bed and board; it seems a lot but I suppose it's worth it.'

Stephen frowned, 'When I was a youth and getting psychological mumps, my best friend was our Japanese butler Nakai and I know from experience a butler can be a friend. I'll get one yet. If they think he's a spy they can come and investigate me. Nakai taught me to make flower arrangements. I know that's degenerate. My sister Florence despised me; "Just like Stephen," she said, "he would!" They expected from me the effete, wasteful, useless, pretty touch.'

Stephen smiled to himself and twined his legs round the legs of the chair. He speared a piece of chicken and swallowed it invisibly.

Vera said, 'Heavens, well you've got to pay high out here and in wartime.'

Stephen said, looking round, 'Worth it, worth it. It makes me happy and when I'm happy I'm paternal. I don't nag at my wife and children. If the poor only knew about Japanese butlers there'd be no divorce in working-class families.'

Vera, who was sitting at one end of the table, looked at Stephen in surprise and after a moment smiled. He smiled at her and biting into a piece of roll, showed his even white teeth; his curly fair hair shone its gilt threads in the candle-light. James Holinshed sat at the other end of the refectory table. He laughed, softly.

'There are other cures – for not nagging at the wife.'

'Marry a dumb husband,' said Stephen.

Emily laughed, 'My mother before she died, told me to marry a Jew! She said Jews make the best husbands. I don't know what it meant in her life, of course; probably – some – '

'Probably some Jew,' said Stephen.

Emily laughed, 'She was right, though, Stephen. When I was reporting for the *Kallikak News* there was a sort of Jewish quarter in Kallikak, not a ghetto exactly, but where the Jews lived. I used to look in there on Friday nights. You could tell because they had a seven-branched candlestick either on the windowsill or on the table or sideboard and the most surprising houses had that candlestick.'

'Judas Maccabaeus and his six sons, it's the Manorah, that's the meaning of it,' said Godfrey.

Emily broke in, her eyes glowing, 'I always looked in.'

She leaned back in her chair, to free her body from the table and free her arms. She began to declaim, 'There's no people on earth so lovely in their family life, the children love their parents and honour them, there's none of our American goddamn it, get off the earth, old has-beens, attitude; and the parents love the children and spend their lives on them; and for the mother, the father is not only the father of her children – '

' – and the uncle of her nephews – ' murmured Stephen.

Angrily she cried, 'Stephen! But the crown and glory of the house. And he's not just a breadwinner, bringing home the bacon – '

Godfrey sat up, made a gesture, but said nothing.

' – but he's an honour to her and, if he goes, the whole house falls down, she breaks her heart and the children cry round her knees.'

'A man I went to college with now has a job; he's stationed at the Canadian Pacific Terminal in Montreal picking up the fleeing Jewish fathers from the States. He's in league with a waiter in the first kosher restaurant around the corner.' said Stephen.

Vera laughed and eyed him gaily. Jim smiled, and Godfrey said gloomily, 'Stephen, I don't think that could be proved and should it be said? I think that in a time like this, of united national effort against fascism – '

Emily did not tolerate this, but continued briskly, 'It's a sin to forget the death anniversary of the father or mother. There's a firm of merchants of woollens in New York City, Fourth Avenue, that have a light on before their father's picture, day and night, the whole year round. You can go along any time of night, any holiday and see it. That's a parent cult that is very touching. It's preserved them in poverty, it's tied them to each other, the parents had something to work for, not just a kick in the pants. There's no family as united as a Jewish family. You ought to see them at Rosh Hashonah and Yom Kippur – '

Stephen laughed. Godfrey looked gloomier still.

'You should see the joy on their faces, their faces shining as they all sit round the table and laugh. The father wears a black cap, the mother wears a white cap and a collar and calls her husband "Jacob my crown, Jacob my little bird" – Stephen, my crown, my king – ' she said turning to him, with tears in her eyes, very flushed and smiling – 'doesn't it sound wonderful? And so surely the growing up of those children is the father's and mother's reward?'

Now Emily's eyes were sparkling and her lips twitching with suppressed merriment, 'Try to find me a picture like that in an Irish family or an American family, where everyone's trying to squeeze the last nickel out of the old man because he's an old-timer anyway and if he had any heart, he'd die and let them have the insurance to get through college; and where Ma's weeping her eyes out at Clark Gable and thinking how Tommy Firefly III nearly proposed to her at Junior Prom in the Year 1899 and how – '

'Emily!' said Stephen loudly.

'You shut up a minute, Stephen,' said Emily gathering speed; but after a few moments, Stephen broke in again.

'As long as Emily hasn't seen it, she can describe it in detail. What Emily saw, she experienced through the window of a bungalow while she was racing past in a racing two-seater to get a fire-story from a pal she had on the payroll at the Kallikak firehouse.'

Emily said angrily, 'You are a liar, Stephen: I did see those things.'

'Sure you saw them.'

Stephen grinned at Millian who was sitting beside him, 'Emily had to work so hard and so long for the *Kallikak News* rag and the *Halifax Weekly* and the *New York Evening Crimes* that she got into the way of seeing things. She had to see things or she didn't hold her job, and believe me Emily is the best seer the other side of the Rockies.'

'That's true,' said Emily.

'I know it's true.' said Stephen.

Jim Holinshed, who with various grimaces had been toying with his ice-cream spoon, was making signs to the servant to fill the glasses, bring coffee; and now continued in a gentle voice a conversation he had begun before.

'Vera has her memories and I tell her nightcap tales of the days of yore.'

84

He smiled at his wife with lowered eyelids, his face forward and his pretty hand poised over the lace mat. He murmured clearly, 'I believe I have a son in Denmark, so I have been told, and I went to see him some years ago. Heidi's married and the boy doesn't look like me, though his name is James, quite an elegant name in Denmark. That was when I went to Paris, just before the war; Vera and I were married, but Vera let me go. A girl-friend of mine from other days was crossing on the same boat and Vera and I thought it would be a good thing if I were to test our marriage; for I'd always felt – had a yen, you might say, unlovely expression – been attracted by this girl physically. I didn't tell Vee about the girl at the time, well, not this particular girl, unnecessary to cause useless mental stress and insecurity without good reason. If we clicked, I thought I could tell Vera later, after we'd tested it. Well, I was justified. We didn't click. She was quite a bitch. I found out – where babies come from – of course – and thought I was caught; but she turned out to be a four-alarm bitch. She landed in Paris with some professor she'd picked up on the boat. She was a – very pretty girl and had real physical charms – for others as well as for me; and she was no virgin, even before I met her.' He paused and smiled round the table with an air of boyish grace and saluted his wife delicately, with his lifted glass. He laughed, 'Vera won, didn't you Vera? This – dame – ' (every time he used a vulgar expression, he did it with a refined, amused air as if conceding himself courteously to popular taste) 'this sweet little rounded blonde tigress – got typhoid. The professor quit and she had me tied so that I ran round Paris looking after her, might have caught it myself – didn't think of Vera and the children, or if I did, I thought Vee'd had a man before and she'll get one again, if she's good enough. And I knew I had enough life insurance for the kid – my kid if the pregnancy comes through; and there are the war bonds – plenty of them. So I thought, if she recovers, I leave the goddamn – bitch. And if she dies, I'll die too, of love. Just to show it can happen here. She got better. I followed her to Berlin where she had a man to look up – and there she turned out to be – more of a bitch than before. In the meantime, I wasn't frustrated, by any means – but even I finally told her I was going to check out and I did, in good order. I took the first train that came along – to Hamburg and there took a boat to Denmark to see if it was true about my boy James. Heidi was a nice girl too. I left her in the lurch; but you know what women are, they're tenacious. Coming along the quay I found a girl and I was so fed up, I asked her to come along. I took her along. I asked her her name, "Regina," she said; the queen. So I took the little queen along. I forgot the Berlin nuisance right away and when I got into Copenhagen I was quite embarrassed, for I didn't want to go and see Heidi and her child any more. But I took the little queen along and I told Heidi, "This is my wife". Heidi put us up too; for a couple of weeks. It was really amusing, the girls playing against each other and neither knowing everything. In the meantime, I was writing to Vee, telling her everything. That's what's good about us, I tell Vee everything. You see marriage – after a few years – had begun to drag me down. Vee had been married before and she was quite motherly about it. You understood, didn't you, Vee?'

'Yes,' said Vera, looking at him directly and then quietly at the others.

'And that – with one thing and another – some episodes I've left out, not really printable – must be censored except for Vee's ears – was how I came back home just before the war broke out.'

'Yes, yes, really, fancy that,' Emily had been saying, fidgeting in her chair and drawing on the plate with a bit of bread. Stephen had been listening quietly, smiling occasionally. To Godfrey and Millian the story evidently was not new.

Holinshed laughed tranquilly, 'There was a girl in New York who seemed to know a lot but I would have missed the plane. I was coming back to Vee – and I refused. To refuse experience is wrong.'

Emily, all of a sudden, said loudly, 'I don't think experience is something outside you you have to seek. I think experience is inside you.' She opened her mouth, shut it, then said, 'Well, anyhow, I don't see how married people can betray each other: to me, it's betrayal. I don't call it old-fashioned. I don't see how a woman can look at her husband, if she's even thinking about another man. How can she look him in the eye, how can she speak to him in an honest tone, discuss the weekly bills with him? It's dishonest. I think it's the same with men. After all, being loyal is an experience, too.'

Millian looked across at her with a faint superior smile; and Vera said, 'Let's go into the other room, shall we? The Byrds will be along soon; and a doctor and his wife, they're progressives, and a man called Evans and some others.'

The two friends Bowles and Holinshed began consulting in low tones by the piano and Stephen was talking to Millian. Katsuri had arranged bottles and glasses for the evening's entertainment. Emily and Vera went in to look at the two young children, who were sleeping. The two women did not come back for some time. They looked at the house, the kitchen, the linen closets, the larder, the small backyard built of stones; at Vera's pictures, the library where Jim worked when at home. There was a private class in socially significant writing organized by Holinshed and Bowles. These classes and intimate political meetings were held in the bigger rooms. Vera worked on two women's committees, and twice a week worked on a voluntary committee which collected clothes for the British.

Emily exclaimed, 'Why the British? I wouldn't give them our torn underwear. Well, we haven't any. They're our enemies; there isn't one of them that doesn't think we're ignorant savages, a dollar in one hand, a stick of chewing gum in the other and a bottle of Coca-Cola clenched in the teeth; and in our pants pocket a writ of dispossess, pay up or be damned!'

She burst out laughing, 'Well, they're right! That's what we do. Goddamnit! Why do we go out of our way to prove we're just like foreigners think we are. Well, OK, I'll give you some clothing for the British, not torn either. It does me good to think of them going about in what Giles and Lennie wouldn't wear.'

Vera laughed but said sturdily, 'They're our allies. We all believe in the united front.'

'For my money, the united front, the way it's being worked, is a pentagon front, facing five ways, but all against Russia. Look at all the intellectuals who felt they were out on a limb, who got into $600 hand-made uniforms and sat in Hollywood-land doing important secret work in firms for which they were paid not only by the studio but also by the Government. It was an unmixed blessing for the brainy reds who were tired of being called un-American Kremlinites, fifth columnists, fellow travellers and Russian agents. I don't blame them. Who wants to be called a traitor to his country? Though it's only the communists them-selves who are true to their country, real patriots who see the future of their country – '

She stopped a moment, burst out, 'It's in this country that the word traitor means most of all. A traitor in England is just one of a long line of shabby individuals who had no guts; but in this country, it's the blackest and lowest.'

'Don't you think that when we're working for the war effort and buying bonds we believe in the united front?'

'I think they were sick of being out on a limb and they fell on spy-watching and social services and desk-militarism with a glad cry.'

'Well, I disagree with you there. Jim's new book is to show how ten years of work in the people's movement brings a man logically on the day of Pearl Harbor to American loyalism.'

'What does he do then?'

'He joins the fire patrol.'

Emily yelped with laughter and 'Oh, ho, ho,' said she, 'excuse me, Vera.'

Vera reddened.

'It's as plain to me as the war memorial in Kallikak. It's philosophic decadence; and the unions' no-strike pledge was betrayal. We're all just glad to belong.'

87

Vera said coldly, 'You'll see it won't turn out that way. Why should there be war between the worlds? Unity and eventual peace is the best pledge either of our worlds has. It's the best refuge for American progressive democracy and Russian recovery.'

Emily burst out with, 'Not one of you can see a stone's throw around the corner! Haven't the words meant anything to us? Surely the Russian system is the bitter enemy of everything our system stands for! And surely it's us or them! You mean it isn't as bad as typhoid to every congressman and his flock that we're the allies of Russia?'

'So you really have been against the united front and the second front and a peaceful solution?' said Vera, in a very hostile manner and going towards the door.

Emily chuckled sadly and said, 'Oh, I guess it's maybe the sere, the yellow in me. I feel like a poor old cracked and tarnished buggy in my Grandpa's shed. I don't seem to understand politics, though I always thought I did. I'm some kind of dope. Still, is there anyone you know who can explain to me, not yell at me, why in the USA alone of all the world, a Marxist-Leninist-Stalinist Party of the working class is considered unnecessary and even harmful? Why are we friends with every political crook because of the lesser-evil policy? Why do we hush-hush on the good old class struggle? You mean all that's abolished for the USA? I thought Lovestone got thrown out for being an American exceptionalist? Are we just going to sit down to a love-feast? No advantage taken, no profit, no imperialist urges? Are the contradictions of capitalism all solved now and leading Marxists are going to get a chance at the presidency? But isn't the fight won in a way? Isn't this the hour of triumph of the Soviet Union? And shouldn't we say it? That we've got what we fought for? And why is it wrong, if we believe it, to say "Up the Labour Republic"? I suppose I'm just an Old Bolshevik and ought to be retired.'

Vera had become stern, cold, very pale. But she said, 'Moffat Byrd's going to be here this evening and he'll explain to you how we feel. But you ought to be careful what you say. I'm saying this as a friend. As a matter of fact, Emily, I'm against this evening's meeting. They're coming here tonight for a specific purpose, to straighten you out, both of you, I mean. I think it's wrong. I think you should have been told.'

'What is it? They're going to give us a working over? Why? I'm just as much a Trotskyist as the green man in Mars. Stephen agrees with you absolutely. Hence I'm driven to mumbling to myself in my workroom, and I make seditious speeches at the anniversary meeting of the Soviet Union. Do you know what I said?'

'Yes,' said Vera looking at her fixedly.

Emily laughed, 'Yes, I guess you do. Everyone else too. I guess I've

88

made trouble in this duck-pond. But no one has yet given me a good answer. The Soviet Union is winning and we're to say that Lenin said Rockefeller is progressive.'

'He did say that.'

'Well, then our martyrs were all wrong. They should just have laid down and let the American progressive steamroller squash them flat. Let us all be slaves here, wear gags and we'll be honourably serving American progressive capitalism.'

Vera said, 'You're very much in error. Let's go and join the others. I think this discussion should be general and I think Moffat Byrd can show you just where you're wrong. But you ought to get closer to the people, hear how they think and you ought to read the *Labor Daily* regularly.'

'That's the last straw. I write for the damn rag. I'm an editor.'

'I know you are; and when you first came out, you and Stephen, we thought for one thing you'd been sent – ' She bit her lip and hastily continued, 'There was some confusion, we thought your opinions were official. But Moffat Byrd soon realized they were not.'

She had paused inside the door and looked at Emily a little more friendly. She said quickly, in a lower tone, 'Don't you think you ought to accept more discipline? Do you think your own individual opinion is so important? I don't believe you're just a Bohemian; and for that matter, we've all talked it over and put it down to your coming from New York. Everyone here knows that New Yorkers are more Bohemian, more individualist than we are; especially writers. There you've got the nine-teenth-century view of writers. Here, we've got a mass of working writers who are unionised, work for big bosses, just like factory workers. The writer working in a cellar on his own ideas, is almost unknown: it belongs to the handloom epoch. This gives us a different and more modern viewpoint. We understand that New York writers, when they first come here, bring along a heap of out-of-date fetishisms and individualist attitudes. We've put it down to that; and we're conscious of your importance as a humorist and family writer. It's very important that you shouldn't go wrong. Your family books appeal to the people. You're important.'

Emily turned red and began to shout. 'What about my political books? What about *The Wilkes-Barre Chronicle*? What about *Johnny Appleseed*? Why are my serious books not mentioned?'

Vera said painfully, lowering her eyes and raising them appealingly, 'They didn't sell. They didn't communicate.'

Emily was shouting, 'Three times a week, I get letters from miners and seamen and such non-executives of the Party saying that my books, my serious books, put fresh heart into them; and before they felt the struggle

89

was too hard but now I've given them fresh hope and a fresh wind has blown through their lives. I can show you these unsolicited testimonials to the value of my books and my communication. Why, I had letters this week from a group in Wilkes-Barre saying that everyone there was arguing about Johnny Appleseed. They said he wasn't a symbol but a real worker; a miner said he was a miner and an ironworker said he was an ironworker he knew. What about that? Aren't you just a bunch of intellectuals yourselves?'

At this moment, James Holinshed with a smile around the eyes in his pale smooth face, stood in the doorway. Emily saw him but went on to say, 'Who cares about the purity of a bookworm in a heap of gold? I think that's wasting time and the time of local X of the Printers' Union. What's the apotheosis of this bookworm? It takes all Pearl Harbor to make him the fireman he meant to be as a boy. Well, so did the grocer's lad, didn't he? Or, to put it in the terms of your industrial, not handmade epoch, the cashier at the superstores? Or didn't he? Do the intellectuals in Hollywood join a separate branch? The writers' branch of fighting progressives in Hollywood is by long miles separate, isn't it, from the vulgar Mexican worker downtown?'

'Labour unionism is based on the division of labour,' said Vera.

James Holinshed came smoothly into the room, 'Oh, we're segregated. Let's all get together. The Moffat Byrds are here. Katsuri's handing out drinks. Clare Byrd has reeled on to her favourite sofa: she's got a yellow dinner dress on and she's just spilled her drink down the front and she's hiccuping from pure embarrassment. Byrd's waiting for you, Emily. We consider you are two of the leading intellectuals here and you've kept us up at night; you're a maverick; or else it's your simple innocence from Wilkes-Barre, Penn? Was that my book you were castigating? We're intellectuals and they don't want us to corrupt the honest Mexican worker of Los Angeles. First with our money; then with our ideas.'

Emily said, 'That's wrong. We might teach them something; or they might teach us something.' Holinshed said, 'I know, that's often discussed; but we see no way out. Our subscriptions are so much larger, to all causes; we have cars; we do so much more, we have more time, more influence. We have connections all over the country. We'd overwhelm, discourage and then drive out the ordinary worker.'

'In flat words, we're rich and he's poor. What good can come of it? Pooah!' said Emily. She flounced out, nearly fell down the three steps leading to the dropped living-room, where the guests were. Standing on the bottom step a moment to wrench at her shoe, she heard the two behind her whispering.

'What about the letter? When is Godfrey reading that?'

90

Holinshed said, 'That's later. Byrd is very anxious to speak. She's making deviationist speeches every time she opens her mouth. It's a very serious thing.'

Emily sailed down into the room and looked gaily and impertinently at Jay Moffat Byrd, the political leader of the rich progressive writers of the studios. The screen writers were organised into a professional guild apart from the guilds of the pulp-writers, photographers, actors and stagehands and others. This gave them a corporate interest and a curious, conscious self-interest which she had never met before.

She changed her mind about him when she looked into the large, dark, fleshy face of Jay Moffat Byrd. She was afraid of him, not because of his strict ideas, nor his political and studio position, but because she was in the presence of a quality she did not understand and shrank from. He was in the highest moneymaking market of any writer in Hollywood; he was a 'faithful Party Communist' as they said. His explanations, however unexpected, of political happenings and the changes of political line, and however difficult to follow and explain, were accepted; and his political incubations, his views of the other world, the non-Hollywood world, were at least always seriously discussed; though by no means slavishly followed. There were a few, though, well-paid writers, like Godfrey Bowles (called by the Howards in private 'God' or 'Godfrey the Good'), who abdicated and asked Byrd for guidance. These were few, but strong. At the same time, there were barely any who went so far as Emily in thinking that serious mistakes of policy had been made by the American progressives, out of thoughtless patriotism perhaps and by the American Labour Movement, during this wartime crisis of opinion: few who thought so; fewer who said so.

6   THE STRAIGHTENING OUT

The women sat about among the men, saying very little, huddling in groups and talking quietly about their children, well-dressed, modern, polite and most somewhat drunk; and the men, also drunk, took many postures, horsing on the backs and arms of chairs, striding up and down, leaning on the windowsills, on the high mantel of the bogus fireplace. As they passed, the women drew in their feet; except for Clara Byrd, lounging now on a large brocade sofa, dressed, since she had spoiled her dress, in a borrowed white and red wrapper and red mules, her strong arms bare, her hair loosed on each side and her bright blue eyes starting from her head. Clara Byrd and Emily were boldly drunk.

Every time Emily took a drink, Stephen, who was sipping brandy, gave her an angry glance and said, 'Emily, quit drinking,' or 'You've had enough.'

Mrs Byrd was left alone and the mood of the party was dull, but restless.

Stephen had taken a dislike to a newcomer, Everett Maine, the son of millionaires who owned property near Central Park in New York. He had joined the Party and been disinherited. He was working, rolling barrels in a brewery. He had been expected to dinner but was late because a jalopy which he had bought for twenty dollars had broken down at a street turning. He would have to get up early to walk to work the next day. He was a fair, tall, good-looking man, and appealingly, with something of Stephen's own manner, described his parents' ways. In the private suite at the top of the apartment house they owned, were hints and glints of gold; a gold-plated toilet seat, *goldwasser* in the bar, a banknote in *trompe-l'œil* in the lounge, 'maybe so that some guest will break her fingernails trying to pick it off the wall.' They insisted on his coming for Sunday dinner and Christmas.

'If I did that I could even join the Party.' But he had refused.

Stephen didn't respect pettish ways with parents.

'What are we fighting for if not good housing, central heating, free entertainment, peace, prosperity, the cocooning of all from the cradle to the grave? I never met a communist yet who wasn't fighting for a bourgeois way of life for himself, his family and the rest of mankind. He just varies the full-belly Utopia to suit his tastes.'

He was acid. He could not endure another like himself; he hated himself; and he was trying to provoke Everett.

Everett said, 'You can't buy the revolution. It's just bourgeois American to think you can buy everything. You can't buy people: not all the people, all the time.'

'You can try,' said Stephen laughing.

'Yes, how about giving it a try, buying the revolution? Enlist some tender-eyed Midas,' said Jack Smole, a writer.

'I consider you've let the revolution down and ought to be censured for giving up your family money; you could have given it to the Party,' said Jay Moffat Byrd.

'So you too think you can buy it,' said Everett disdainfully. 'Is that Marxist or just MGM? A plot for Robert Taylor?'

Fair, small-faced, forty-year-old playwright, doing well as a screen-writer, Jack Smole continued, 'Everything can be bought and why not? As soon as you know there is value you put a price on it. The thing is to recognise all values. Money's only a means of exchange; what you get for it is your business. Here we've reduced all values to one. That's going to simplify things for us later on. You can take out the money and substitute the value ticket. The revolution's made; and no one hurt.'

'Supposing there were someone, a nation, rich enough to buy out Hollywood and the monopolists of America and he were a communist, wouldn't he be right to buy them out, tell them to go play hoops and hand it over to the workers – or the Russians?' said another writer, Bob Beauclerk.

Byrd, a heavy dark man in dark clothes, rose and moved his armchair, towards the centre of the room. A silence of consent followed.

He said, 'Stephen, would you move over next to Emily? We want to talk to you.'

'What is this?' said Stephen. He moved beside Emily. Emily was bubbling over with mirth, talking furiously, and had not noticed Byrd's portentous move.

Stephen said, 'Put down your glass, Emily. You're higher than a kite.'

She put down her glass, her face swam at them. Jack Smole crossed over, put his face close to hers and said, 'We've all discussed your book *Johnny Appleseed* as a screen possibility and we feel we can't do anything with it out here. We've changed our minds. We feel you made a mistake writing it.'

This was said in a considerate but determined tone. Emily stopped laughing and stared.

Byrd cleared his throat, moved his chair a little to face them directly and said, 'This has all been discussed and we want you to know how we feel. Our feeling is unanimous. It is with some regret that we have decided to speak to you. But for some time, since 1942 in fact, when Stephen was roving reporter to the *Western Weekly*, he was observed by some to oppose the policy of national unity pursued by socialists throughout the world, a unity embracing all, including capitalist elements who sought victory over the Axis. In a series of articles he wrote, which the editors of the *Western Weekly* rejected in their original form – we have taken the trouble to have this confirmed – Stephen attempted to narrow this policy and to develop an approach which would have divided the anti-Axis forces and disrupted the war effort. The Howards, both, in divers articles have described as reformist what we term progressive, and call all reference to pro-Roosevelt forces "reformist illusions". They have demanded the casting away of the present political structure of the Party and the formation of a class-conscious Labour Party. Now is not the time for any such trial and error tactics.'

This was delivered in a final solemn tone. The guests, except Stephen and Emily, sat in a tense quiet, their eyes fixed on the rug, or on the pair they had already judged. Only Mrs Byrd, sprawled on the brocade sofa, a magnificent body, a gay, inflamed face, paid no attention. She got up now and went to the drinks-table to fill her glass. The convention among them was to take no notice of Mrs Byrd's behaviour.

She returned, joy in her face, tipsily treading, and sat down without spilling a drop.

'This is a straightening-out, I take it, and you are the treble-dated crow to sing the requiem over two dead souls,' said Emily.

'Emily,' said Stephen.

Byrd emphatically continued, 'All of us, reading your articles and hearing Emily's lectures, have reached the conclusion that you have a consistent plan; that you are attacking the basic lines that we defend, slandering the leadership, taking up the position of petty-bourgeois pseudo-radicalism and maintaining sympathetic contacts with anti-socialist forces outside our ranks. There has been a consistent campaign of destructive, factional attacks.'

He paused and everyone sat in silence. Stephen looked at Emily. Byrd said, 'We have refrained until now from making public our views, in the hope that the passing of time and the grave national and international problems confronting the American people and its socialist patriots would cause Stephen and Emily to abandon their puerile leftism and place the fight for peace, democracy and socialism above personal pique and petty individualism. Instead, they have developed their ultra-left posturing into an approach to domestic and foreign affairs which is in conflict with that of socialists fighting for peace and unity in this and other countries. No,

94

Emily and Stephen, we know your value; and your loss would be a great loss to the movement and to us all; for you are fellow-workers, good fighters and valued acquaintances, where you are not friends. We want you, therefore, to consider that this is not a warning or an admonition, not a preaching, but an exhortation, a friendly gesture, to make you reconsider all that you have written and said in a, perhaps, intemperate, ill-considered personal way; and asking you to reconsider and to make amends. It would be thought a good thing if this were in the form of a signed document which could be circulated. All this has caused us much heart-burning, much regret, and it would make us all feel better. It is the time now. You have enough influence to influence others. It would be a pity for us to lose that influence. Outside our movement, what influence can you have? I ask you very seriously to consider your position and this most grave conjecture, which is perhaps the most serious in your lives.'

He finished and the silent audience, like only half-living things, retired into themselves with quiet and greedy satisfaction, was yet appalled at what was going on, at the awfulness of it, at the fates of two people they could see, being suspended like that, by a hair, at two people hanging in the air by a thread. They relaxed slightly.

'May I leave my seat, please?' said Emily, getting up and going to the drinks table. 'Katsuri, I need a good one, a stinger.'

'That was the wrong thing to do,' said Stephen, 'to get us here on a pretext and then turn it into a trial with the judgment and sentence all arranged. That was a lousy thing to do. Lead us on and put us on the mat.'

'We want you to know we are all your friends; and if you are with us, you would not want us to hide things of this nature from you. Of course, you are on our side, or we would not trouble to give you this chance. You see we think we know what has changed you. We understand why you have taken this diversionist road.'

'If you know it, tell me the secret,' Stephen shouted.

At this Godfrey got up and sat on the settee beside Millian, his wife. He had in his hand three or four sheets of paper, covered with single-spaced typing. He said mildly in his fine round voice, 'Sit down Emily, this concerns you both.'

'Holy mackerel, not another parson at the graveside,' said Emily.

He said gently, 'Sit down, Emily. It concerns Olivia, the rape of Olivia.'

'The – WHAT – of Olivia? Oh Jehosaphat – '

Stephen hushed her. 'Let's hear this indictment to the end. For I assume it is another indictment.'

Godfrey put his hand on Millian's arm as he began to read, 'This has not been written without long and careful thought, painful thought, and has been discussed with others.'

He looked up and then at his wife, 'Millian and I have been over every idea expressed here, every word, you may say.'

He went on to read, 'I have the permission of those others to read this; and it incorporates their view of a situation which may seem private, but which, on account of elements in it which have social implications, affects us all. This concerns the little twelve-year-old girl Olivia Howard, who now resides with Emily and Stephen Howard and is introduced as their daughter and is Stephen's daughter. A court case is pending in which Florence Howard Baldwin and Mrs Anna Howard, the grand-mother, are also asking for joint guardianship. We have been asked our opinion and this is the testimony which Millian and I have agreed to give, as neutral observers. I must add that we are friends of all parties, friends too of Isaiah Higham, a close friend of Bertram and Florence Baldwin; Higham agrees with us.'

He put the papers on his knee and looked thoughtfully at Stephen and Emily; then said gently, 'I ought to prelude by saying that it is known that Stephen and Emily, for personal and to pinpoint it, mercenary reasons, fraudulently obtained possession of Christopher Potter two years ago, when Jacob Potter, the true father and a widower, was under the influence of alcohol. There can be no doubt of this. Stephen and Emily have several times related the circumstances in public. We admit here that Jacob Potter who is now in the hands of a psychoanalyst, is a compulsive drinker, subject to fits of deep melancholy and is even morose at times; and that Stephen and Emily may have had also an admirable or at least fully excusable motive for taking the child from him. When he was incapable of clear thought, however, an agreement was presented to him by them and signed by him and when the grandmother made claim they showed this agreement, and testimony as to Jacob Potter's unfitness, which appears unassailable.'

'Well, by golly, this is the limit,' said Emily.

Godfrey put up his well-shaped hand. 'Listen, Emily, I have thought of you, had your interests at heart, too; and Millian too, when thinking this through.' He continued, 'Four years ago, Emily and Stephen had a son of their own, Giles. They had already adopted Lennie. Two years ago, they adopted in the manner I have shown, Christopher. Now, they wish to take back Olivia, who had already been handed over to Florence Howard Baldwin and Mrs Anna Howard, the grandmother. What is the reason underlying this avidity for adoption, this child-catching? It must surely be part of that aberration which makes young women steal children from their baby-carriages, from their beds.'

'It's horrible, it's horrible,' said Emily.

He continued, 'We all know since Emily Howard is of a free and frank

96

nature, that Emily has always longed for a daughter; nothing more natural. In a way, her motherhood spent on boys only had been suppressed. Suppressed motherhood in itself constitutes a claim. But I am not a formalist. Social formulas and prejudices are embalming of what was once useful to society.'

'If I had any gold ink I'd take it down in shorthand,' Stephen sang out.

'What I have written to the referee is as follows:

'"Mr Referee: it is our opinion (that is, Millian's and mine) that Stephen and Emily Howard are unsuitable guardians for Olivia Howard, the daughter of Stephen Howard and his deceased wife Caroline. We do this without the diffidence that might be thought prudent, because of our concern for the child and for the psychological comfort and affective needs of her aunt, Florence Howard Baldwin, who is very well known to us. We cannot judge accurately of a domestic interior. Marriages contain infinitely varied relationships and no one can pass judgment upon the satisfactions which may or may not be received in a relationship so intimate and indeed secret. But this thought is only for the man and the woman, the adults. The child caught between the two, undergoes not only the strain of his or her own adjustment to the world, which varies with every day and every year; but also the tensions of parental conflict in a context he cannot yet understand; not to mention strong intimations that filter through every conversation of an upset world."'

'Heard and approved, God,' said Stephen; 'go to the head of the class.'

Probably Godfrey did not hear him.

'Too many facts of an interior and exterior world for which he has no slide-rule are shuttled before him. And we are speaking of a little, sheltered girl. Conflict and economic and psychological tensions, and even suppressed conflict will produce mentally or even physically battered resentful and rebellious children, who will not adjust to any norm. Yet what is more normal than the family relationship? And where it concerns children of a sweeter more pliable nature, as for example Olivia Howard, whom we all have seen, it may produce either victims, masochists, or natures which become double-dealing, secretive, unstable, furtive; or insinuating and deducing natures; children who are not frank and self-reliant, or too much so who sit in judgment – '

'What a cast of characters!' said Stephen.

'Won't sell,' said Emily, 'too morbid, not for the suburban mamma.'

' – in silent judgment; in fact, strangers in the house and in the world, sneaks, cowards, those who triumph in malice and suspicion, the voyeurs of others' troubles. Is this the best way to bring up a child? Perhaps Olivia is Stephen's daughter – '

'Perhaps! Cicero, you will be sued for that – ' said Stephen.

'That was rhetorical, I withdraw it. We know Olivia is Stephen's daughter – '

'How do you know?'

'But if other claims on him are greater, if the family background fails her in her deepest needs, would she not be happier in her grandmother's or her aunt's peaceful and well-ordered, if more conventional households?'

'That is the question!' said Stephen. 'Say an aunt who comes home drunk every night in a taxi? Is that good for the young psyche, a goodnight kiss of that flavour?'

'Stephen,' said Godfrey, 'since what is at issue here is the care and future of a girl, a beautiful, enchanting little girl, who is by reason of her background and her own personal fortune and her large expectations, entitled to expect the very best this country can provide for her – '

'You mean a further million and a half in government bonds at the age of sixteen? I believe you! What more could her country do for her? Two million? That will come. She attracts money. My daughter Olivia will be of intense interest to all; but I come first.'

Godfrey said, 'Yes, the money is a factor. But it is real; we must deal in realities: it is part of the child and her future; and it makes her more interesting to you admittedly.'

'Godfrey,' said Emily, 'get it over with. Chop off our heads. Where are the tumbrils? Let's get out of here, Stephen. This is simply the Paul Pry Committee in executive session. Come on, Stephen.'

'I am sorry, Stephen,' said Godfrey, 'to make direct references to Emily; and her possible motives as well.'

'You mean because Emily's father was originally an automobile worker and what money she has and what money is in our bank account, she has made? We grant it all. Good for her! Bad for me!'

The other guests were fascinated by this trial without jury, entirely in the spirit of mid-century and of their society; but they were helping themselves to drinks, also. Emily, in spite of Stephen's cranky whispers, made trips to the table too.

'Why can't we go? The play must go on, eh? If I stay I **get** something out of it.'

Godfrey was speaking again, 'Emily, like myself, is a member of the lower middle class and what money she has made is a credit to her. But where is that money? It is spent in a reckless manner, in accord with general incoherencies of speech and behaviour, and inconsistencies of opinion. We can only regard her behaviour-history of the last few years as a kind of rake's progress – '

'A rake? What rake?' said Emily recrossing to her chair.

' – intellectually, morally and politically; financially as well perhaps. Is

98

not the present and expected fortune of the child regarded by Emily as the finger in the dyke? Can we not say that?'

Stephen said, 'Say that too: say anything. I've often wished I could sit in one of those high booths in a Chinese chow-mein palace where the lights are low, and listen to all my friends in the next booth talking about me. So you get your wishes. It's as good as the little play in *Hamlet*. The king sees his crime done in public.'

Godfrey said, 'Let me get to the end, Stephen; I didn't come to wound you or to get into a battle. It was thought necessary by us all to get you here and be frank and clear; not to work against you behind your back.'

'The evil that men do lives after them; the good is oft interred with their bones,' said Emily, draining her glass and laughing. 'Godfrey, I know how you feel, everyone talks about Godfrey the honest man, we call you Godfrey the Good.'

Godfrey flushed, 'I'm glad of that!'

Stephen took off a shoe and exercised his toes; 'Yes, I was thinking it would make an epitaph.'

Godfrey scarcely heard this. He continued, 'Emily refers to herself always as Olivia's mother. Is she equipped for the task? Compared with a real parent and putting aside for the moment the notion of biological motherhood – what is her equipment in this field? She is a woman, she is the guardian of two boys and mother of a third, she is an American and she can by her earnings provide a background of reasonable comfort and security. But Olivia's social obligations will be large in a few years. We have here not merely a little girl, but a girl who in her adult years will have the control of an estate, perhaps two estates; and so we hear, will come into a large inheritance later on. We are not living in the ideal commonwealth, though we are living in one in which adjusted people can be happy. Is Emily by nature and training, by the way she makes her living and by emotional maturity, by present psychical state, a fit tutor, guardian, custodian, mentor, a fit all, for a mother is all, for this girl of great estate? That is to say, we know that on her twelfth birthday Olivia will have an accrued monthly income from government bonds of four hundred dollars. Now, with Millian and friends, on the information we have had from Olivia's aunt and grandmother, we have carefully considered this situation, discussed it in all its intentions, over many nights and days, ever since we received the request.'

'What request?' said Vera.

Godfrey explained patiently, 'Isaiah Higham wrote to me and I saw Florence Baldwin a number of times. Mrs Howard Senior and Florence Baldwin want custody of Olivia. Stephen some years ago made them her guardians; then two years ago he took her back. Not only this but we have studied everything and reached a conclusion and we stand by our judgment that Emily Wilkes Howard shows an advanced and progressive case of mental confusion, a disordered psychism, though whether this is accidental or constitutional psychopathy, we cannot say.'

Stephen, putting on his shoes, said, 'Say those words again! Do you mean to say you put your name and Millian's to this goddamn trash and sent it to the court? Who are you? Freud? Jones? How would you like to go where the good niggers go?'

Godfrey drew back, appalled, 'What did you say? What word did you use?'

'Skip it. Forget it. Is there much more to your indictment?'

'It is not an indictment. It is a conclusion, a series of observations.'

He read from his papers, 'A natural classification of universal application is really impossible at this moment. The unreasonable self-indulgence, the exploitation of her own personality for which Emily Howard is known, disturbs the nervous system, if it is not a result of a disturbed nervous system. We do not believe that such a person with no self-control and no self-criticism, a pronounced cult of her own individuality and of all or any circumstance connected with her life, acquaintances, name, pursuits, amounting almost to a delirium of self, can be a good guardian for any child, let alone such a child. In any case, the almost kidnapping that took place two years ago seems to show that Emily and Stephen themselves were aware of their real impropriety.'

Emily put down her glass, got her strong bulging form off the sofa and said, 'I've been thinking, Godfrey, what is behind all this. I like to let things sink in and then I see the basic reason. What I see is that you are an ally of the big money, the real big money, I mean the Howards' and the Tanners' money. They have got at you through your virtue. Money can always get at anybody through some damn thing. You adopted children; but you adopted poor children. We adopted rich ones. You're probably jealous. I'm making more than ever you made and I've just come out here. But you have sense enough to prefer established money. Good man. What an instinct! You goddamn hypocrite you – what's the name of that man, Stephen? – who crawled into a family and – '

'Tartuffe,' said Stephen.

'Tartuffe,' said Emily sinking back again. She was wearing a long silk dress of yellow with slanting stripes of purple and silver. She rolled over towards her neighbour, the man called Beauclerk, put her head on his shoulder and began to cry.

Stephen said, 'The man says. But I will get others to say different. Look at my wife sobbing her heart out. What would you think if I came to your house for dinner and started attacking your wife?'

100

Godfrey said, 'This is an interesting reaction. I am not attacking your wife.'

Stephen said in a mean voice, 'OK, it's just a suppressed wish to attack my wife; on top, philanthropy.'

Godfrey remarked, 'It may be. But to the proof, this is a paper I prepared for the court. I thought it better to prepare you.' He took another paper out of his pocket and read, 'We knew the Howards well in New York. We did not see them for some time, since we had gone to Los Angeles to make a living; and during this time we ourselves had taken on the duties of parents and had adapted ourselves to the new social and family setting. Here, in California we met members of the Howard and Tanner families, who have their businesses and have made their fortunes in this state. (Excepting for recent acquisitions and accretions in Texas and Illinois to the large family estate.) In fact, we became friendly, even intimate with Florence Baldwin, Stephen's sister, with others. Later, the Howards followed us to California.'

'Followed you is not strictly true, merely coincidental,' said Stephen.

'We did not see them during this time of absence. When we met them again, after they had shown their customary instability by taking first one, then a second, then a third house in Los Angeles, we observed the signs in Emily Howard of a degenerating psychism, of intellectual lesions perhaps, perhaps even physical, though we are not competent to say. There were verbal incontinence, detailed recitals of insignificant events, a general excitement, incoherencies of speech, unsuitable confidences in public – '

'By golly, what do you call this?' interjected Emily.

' – a wish to dominate the scene, a refusal to let anyone intervene, an irresistible urge to talk, shouting and ill-temper, public quarrelling with Stephen, an inability to report faithfully events she witnessed, false and ridiculous ideas. Examples: Emily calls all birds, even swans, "snakes" because she thinks they have descended from snakes; she says that men descended from monkeys because monkeys had to climb out of trees to retrieve the coconuts they threw at snakes and tigers.'

Stephen said, 'That idea was in the *New York Times* and how do you know it's not true?'

Godfrey went on reading. 'The temperament was the same, though exaggerated, the grasp of reality feebler; though no doubt all this is a monstrous growth of inborn characteristics.'

Stephen thoughtfully took off his shoes. Godfrey remarked, 'I see you recognize this?'

Stephen said, 'When a first-rate psychologist hands down an opinion, one listens respectfully.'

Godfrey read on with more calm: 'During this time of absence,

America had entered a fatal struggle against fascism, and our own lives had been knit with that of the nation. During that time Emily Howard had made much money and become known throughout the progressive world; one might say, a satisfying, contenting, a healthy factor. During that time Emily Howard had had the joy of motherhood, given birth to a boy and had the other joy of giving a home to a lonely child, her adopted son Lennie. To become a mother, surely for a woman is the solution of many conflicts. But it had not sufficed. Her conflicts were deeper still; the subconscious itself seemed to us to be rising to the surface through a profound cleavage.'

'Well, what do you know about that? I'm amazed,' said Stephen.

'Surely worldly success and the satisfaction of a woman's deepest instincts should give equilibrium; it has cured many a woman.'

Stephen, listening, dropped his head, became reflective, then said, 'I want a copy of this.'

Godfrey replied, 'I have one for you.'

'We're not going to trial without a knowledge of the indictment, at any rate.'

Godfrey continued, 'Yet where were the signs of this happiness, this security, this health? Instead we saw signs of a marked insecurity, one might say, hints of an internal terror. Where was this adjustment and clearer perception of the real world? We failed to see it. We were shocked and upset. Here was a person whom one might call a success in the best sense of the word. But we saw unhappiness, distress, insecurity and at moments, something approaching the psychopathic, horror in every trait, in every inflection. This is not going too far. Surely before, she had had a lively good humour, a natural comic spirit, a broad general wit, an almost gargantuan perception, an unrepressed genial flow of animal spirits distilled upwards into true wit – '

'Golly, thank you, Godfrey,' said Emily, her fat, mottled red face laughing, though it was set in seriousness.

' – observation, reflection, something unique, the word is not too much. And what is there now? She stammered, stuttered, emitted long parade speeches turned on instantly as if prepared long before; and yet, how could they have been, unless prepared in the unconscious, and rising to the surface, the necessary and healthy inhibitions having melted in the fire and disappeared, as is seen only in the unstable.'

Emily seemed torn between anger and hilarity.

Stephen said, 'I'll say one thing for you, God: you'll never be unstable.'

Godfrey said he hoped not; and continued, 'There were coarse, hasty blandishments, and arguments whose strong, greedy intention immediately crudely appeared: a verbosity approaching surely morbid conditions,

102

a repetition, excitements false and real, frenzy, and almost delirious monologues as if the words came out without any censorship.'

'It's like Shakespeare,' said Emily.

'In the meantime, two of the children under her care have developed marked speech defects, lowness of response and bashfulness and this no doubt is due to the neighbourhood of this chronic verbal excitement which arises apropos almost of the feeblest immediate cause.'

Stephen rose and walked about in his socks.

'Godfrey, Godfrey, don't. Don't say you wrote this dreadful and partly true story to the lawyers! Is this your idea of truth and the role the friend and the writer plays in human life? You're asked for an opinion and you get up like Life the Prosecutor itself, like a prosecutor in a reign of terror, like – oh, hell. Is that your role? Your duty? What sort of heart have you? Stone, engraved stone and on it engraved: To the glory of Godfrey.'

Godfrey was hurt: 'I am thinking of the child, the little girl.'

'The little golden girl.'

Stephen came to a chair, turned it to face Godfrey and sat down, 'Don't you feel how horrible all this is, Godfrey?'

'Of course I feel it: I wrote it. Why did I write it? Because I deeply felt it.'

'Yes, a true writer.'

Godfrey continued reading, 'But now though her ideas are still often sequent, they are no longer fertile; they are second-hand. She may not recognise their source.'

Stephen said loudly, 'I won't allow it. I won't allow Emily to have these things said about her, and particularly in court where her enemies are and particularly in the presence of my family. My sister Florence comes home or sits at home every night drunk. I suppose she has sequent and precise ideas?'

Godfrey said, 'Poor woman, drunkenness, as we all know nowadays, is a substitution for and indicative of other lacks, such as sexual satisfaction.'

'Oh, I see, poor Florence. But not poor Emily.'

'My letter deals with that immediately. We remarked that Emily Howard was repeatedly ill, given to hysterical fits of weeping, bitter moments when she condemns her husband, whom she considers parasitic –'

The husband said, 'Oh, heavens, yes, she does; and so I am. And that's not a poor Emily to you?'

'Only her high intelligence and strong will managed to conceal thinly these fits of despair and fear and misery.'

Stephen said, 'You saw all this and you have no pity? Because, it's true, of course. And that I suppose will appear in your next report to the court, that I said so.'

Godfrey said, 'Please, Stephen. In one or two years, she has had repeated colds, rheumatic conditions, aches and pains, to us psychogenic, stomach upsets, sore feet, swollen legs, headaches, eye operations, a motor accident, abdominal surgery, all, for us, resulting from abnormal psychic conditions and possibly with no physical cause.'

'And not resulting from the goddamn high-minded, supercilious, dollar-crazy doctors? Any Hollywood person is just a dollar-bearing animal to the average specialist.'

Godfrey said, 'Let's not indict American medicine, admittedly in advance of the world. Let's grant that others, especially the Soviet Union, what you will, are good, but Americans are surely world leaders in certain things and medicine is one. If some things are discovered abroad, it is only like the principle of the pump being accidentally stumbled upon by an ingenious farmer's boy – '

'Like Leonardo da Vinci,' said Emily.

Godfrey held up his hand ' – the applications, the deductions from this lucky guess are made by organized American science.'

'Like the atom bomb, America's gift to the world,' said Emily.

Godfrey became solemn, 'The atom bomb may prove to be America's greatest gift to peace.'

Someone, who? Beauclerk? said, 'Are the dead at peace I wonder?'

Godfrey's eyes were on the paper, 'Let us go on. Let us comment for control, upon Florence Howard Baldwin's psychic and mental growth in the last few years; this is something we have been privileged to watch and understand, with wonder, with delight. She was timid, broken by an unhappy marriage, by the complete failure of her first husband in his duties as a husband, and she had been several times under treatment for nervous diseases, a result of her long tribulations and unhappy youth. She is a very attractive woman; beautiful, but she was an unwanted and neglected child, though living in luxury, ridiculed by her mother, given into the care of nurses and maids, and a child who, in spite of the great fortune she expected, had been told she was too unattractive to marry.

'Probably because of this fear, she made one disastrous marriage after another; and from them, one child, only one, a girl, Augusta, who by the court's action was taken from her, because of her alleged behaviour at the time. She was even characterized in public before the world, since a multimillionaire is a public character and allowed no privacy – as libidinous, dissolute and a disgrace to her family. This young woman, Florence Howard, has striven for and succeeded in achieving maturity. We have known much of her struggle and triumph; we have been the privileged confidantes of this growing psyche and mind. She has always had a simple, almost childlike health and clarity in dealing with her own

104

and family problems, even in her understanding of Stephen's and Emily's viewpoints, which we found simply delightful. Her life is calm, pleasant and, if marked still by some deviations, it shows a growth, a progression which is utterly lacking in the other household. She has voluntarily returned Olivia to her brother Stephen, an act of conscience; though she longed to take Olivia, to replace her own child. Some wild parties were given by Florence, an accepted thing in her set and there was some outside attachment, a natural thing upon which a scandalous construction was put. This has all changed. Florence has developed new qualities. Her life is orderly. She is a normal, sensitive, intelligent woman, if more delightful, more humble than most.'

Emily said, 'Well, we say that a woman who was living openly with a Mexican political leader has no business adopting an innocent little golden girl, as you put it. We said that to the court.'

'It is just four years since she was in a – a rest house,' said Stephen.

'I don't think we need take notice of these damaging and unnecessarily spiteful comments.' said Godfrey.

'All right, all right, I'm not to tell you, oh, fair and impartial judge, what I think about this,' said Stephen chewing his lip. He got up and went to the drinks table. He looked through the bottles, and around.

'Goddamn it, Katsuri, don't stand in the shadows listening like Mephisto. Where is the whisky? Bring me a drink, please. I don't care what happens to me. I want to have a highball and exhibit a degenerating psychism. But when it comes to court, I'll say God made me do it.'

When the butler came back with a new bottle of whisky, Godfrey said, 'I'll have some now, Katsuri, if you don't mind. I don't mind having whisky at this time of night, just once.'

He continued to read. Stephen turned round in amazement.

'This young woman, Florence Howard, has developed into a mature, thoughtful, studious and, we should like to say, good woman. We have seen her with Olivia, when she was allowed to see her – it was a happy moment, a happy weekend, for it was a weekend; and we were there to see it. This was our own witnessing. It is true that we have never spent a weekend with Olivia and her father Stephen and Emily. We cannot comment upon their actual relations. We all know well what the companionship of other children can mean to a child. Nevertheless we feel that though Florence Howard is still in the process of formation as a character, she can provide a simple, tender, human, unaffected and normal home for the girl Olivia, her niece; whereas those in whose charge she is at present, exhausted and distracted by financial and personal troubles, cannot possibly avoid affecting, even wounding permanently the psyches of the children, we mean their own child too. Though

105

Stephen may preserve a certain emotional measure, is in some sort, a man of the world, Emily, in her intolerant, wild, irresistible self-obsession, in her near-manic states of excitement and depression – we do not attempt a psychological or medical analysis – in her struggle and in her cries of dismay or shrieks of pleasure in the various currents which at one time and another bear her off in all directions without compass and without destination – cannot possibly guide the destinies of children, more particularly one which has just emerged from the larval state of helpless childhood and is about to cope with the outside world; whatever may be, in parenthesis, her earnest desire to do all she can and her natural female love of children.

'To conclude, Mr Referee, this was written at your request and instigation and has caused us much heart-burning, much sincere pain; for though written without partiality and putting first the good of all concerned, it does incline to one litigant more than the other; and to found our reasons well, we have had to invade private lives, which are not fit for discussion, except in private circles. What profit do we get from it all, will undoubtedly be asked. None at all. This letter will poison our relationships with some people, alienate some we are fond of and even will perhaps be misunderstood by Emily and Stephen Howard. About Florence, we have no doubt, because of her humane sophistication and the kindly philosophy with which she regards all dilemmas, all problems. But this is a situation where one must take a stand; and personal considerations are nonsuited. The future of a girl, an important girl, a girl who will take her place in society, is concerned, and so we have put aside our personal feelings. We have tried to abstract from all this personal matter the essence of the situation. Yours sincerely, Millian Bowles, Godfrey Bowles, Los Angeles, 1945.'

Godfrey took the yellow second sheets and handed them to Stephen. 'That is the copy for your files.'

'You're very kind.'

'We decided that the higher ethics was that you should not be taken unawares in court.'

'Thanks for that. Tell me why you had to read it and in this company?'

'I thought it would cause less pain if I gave it to you myself, read it, so that you could attack me if you wanted to. It seemed cowardly to put it in the mail, almost an anonymous letter: and in this company you will understand that it is disinterested. We do not want a prominent member of the Party to go into a disgraceful court fight for a monied child. Florence and Mrs Howard Senior cannot be accused of money interest.'

'I see, rob the poor because they show a need for money. Rob a man of his child. How do you know I haven't a tender affection for the brat?'

Godfrey seemed surprised and hesitant, 'Well, you understand my motives.'

Stephen said, 'I don't know if I understand anyone's motives. I get balled up any time I try to understand people's motives. Maybe that's why I'm such a bad writer. As you kindly said earlier this afternoon, there are no great writers on the people's side and I'm one of them.'

Godfrey was silent, his head hanging slightly; he looked at the carpet. Then he roused himself to say, 'I thought I'd set it out very well. Perhaps it's discursive? Florence liked it as it is. They liked it here.'

He looked round at the guests. Beauclerk said, 'I don't know if I like it. It's too personal. Let's keep our noses clean. What's it to us?'

'Florence is a Party member; Olivia will be trained as a humanist.'

'We're Party members. Not humanists. Godfrey, you ought to have seen us first. You saw Florence.'

Godfrey said to the Howards, 'I could come over on Friday. Perhaps there are other issues to discuss; I want to be fair. I want the whole picture.'

'I'll let you know,' said Stephen.

The oak door and the swing doors presently closed on Godfrey and Millian, who had to go home, because they had a baby-sitter waiting for them. They went down the steep path to Godfrey's little car, Godfrey with his arm under Millian's.

Stephen said to his hosts, 'Well, thanks for the evening. I'd like to reciprocate some time.'

'I'm putting the last words to the manuscript of my new book. I'll send it to you. You'll read my manuscript and let me know what you think, in perfect frankness,' said Jay Moffat Byrd.

'Oh, frankness is what I like myself. I'll do that,' said Stephen.

He shook Emily, who for some time had been sleeping on the shoulder of Bobby Beauclerk, her neighbour on the sofa. Flushed and fat, her hair in hanks about her, she woke up, 'Is Godfrey still here?'

'No; the stone guest has gone.'

'Isn't there a drink on the house, after that?' asked Emily of Jim.

'Come on, Emily, you've had enough. We'll get a drink at home.'

'I'm going to kiss you, Bob Beauclerk, you spoke up,' she said and kissed him. She turned to them, 'Well, goodbye friends, if that's the word. Come down and see us sometime. Come over and have dinner next week, a dinner for the little Olivia. Alice, Jay! Jim and Vera! Maybe we'll ask Millian and God. We'll celebrate! Caviar fray – consommay – patty with troofs, lobster with thermidor – the works; champagne! Hooraw, hooraw, hooraw! What a world!'

'He can crack the unconscious but not a smile,' said Emily.

Stephen helped her down the path.

7 AFTER THE PARTY

In the car, Stephen said, 'I'm going to read it all over and then go over and give him a punch in his righteous puss. Or, better, I'll seduce Millian, for it would make Godfrey's private life more absorbing still. Look at him seduced by Florence's millionaire charms, so mature, so sophisticated. But I don't intend to make Godfrey's life as interesting for him as he makes my life interesting for me. I haven't the talent.'

There was a silence, when Stephen said, 'He's a good boy; he means all for the best. I bet he'd take it in good part if I did analyse his motives.'

'Simple; he's just voting for the family money. He'd like to lick every cent of it.'

'He's honest.'

Emily said, 'Everyone's honest; but about what?'

They reached home. When Emily poured herself the promised drink, Stephen said angrily, 'Don't drink so much!' She held the glass in her lap and her eyes moistened. She looked with pathetic indignation at him.

'Now, don't you start on me, too. I carried it off well. I pretended to be asleep. But I heard it. He can't laugh. That's a bad trait. I'd laugh even if I were dying. What a joke! E. Wilkes bit the dust. I'm laughing at this evening.'

She began to drink and laugh.

'Bottom the Weaver or Malvolio the serious man, take your pick. These are my great C's, U's, leave out one, and T's. At the last writers' meeting Godfrey said everyone must streamline his writing in the studios, accept directives from national leaders and the Party, and the same in private life, to further the war effort. Then James Games got up and said, if Mr Bowles would instruct him, he'd be glad. "My whole life I've written Westerns for the struggling studios and I don't know how to adapt white hat and black hat to the war effort." And Godfrey answered him in simple faith. He said the boys overseas would recognise themselves as white hat and the Nazis as black hat.'

Stephen said, 'If American boys in soldier-suits are going to keep going over there to further social unity and prevent nationalist deviation (read economic imperialism) to oppose the Soviet sphere of influence, if they are going to die abroad so we can get fat at home, I don't see why we shouldn't send them millions of feet of horse-opera and situation comedy so they can die happy on some French Boot Hill with a letter in their

108

pockets to Mamma; and if there are some nuts of homely truth stuck in this cake, good.'

Emily poured herself another drink, 'Godfrey doesn't reason at all, though he's sententious: he just has a heart. He's probably good all through. He's one of those people who oughtn't to reason, who are fatally attracted by reason. But what reason? There are all kinds. I don't believe in reason. It can lead you anywhere. The same man can argue on both sides convincingly: each side has its reasons. Listen to them and you're the ass with no hay. Only madness can get you out of some situations someone said.'

'Let me brood unreasonably. I'm thinking if there is anything I can do to Godfrey the Good, now that he has got all my family on his side.'

'We won't give Olivia back to Florence and Grandma no matter what; his literary effort is wasted, so is his asslicking. I know your family. They don't really care for any scribbler who has to make his living in the studios. They don't like workers. Good sense.'

'I'm going to get witnesses too. If Florence has her good boys I'll have mine. I'm not going to be the only one in the family without a cent. I'm not letting a millionaire kid get out of my clutches. I married a poor woman, I'm not a gold-digger, and I'm not going to be a hanger-on of my own wife the rest of my life. If I bring up Olivia, maybe one day Olivia will do the handsome and remember her poor old Dad. Goddamnit, Emily, how many bottles a week do you get through? Call me venal, I am.'

Emily put down her glass and lit a cigarette from the butt of the first. She said timidly, 'I'm not venal. I don't think so. But I'm haunted. It's the way Lennie listens at doors and on the house-phone and sometimes when I think he's off with the baker's boy, he's really hanging around the porch wondering what we're saying about him; trying to get the hang of things. Who is he? I feel conscience-stricken. I often wonder how the children feel. I don't dream much. If I do dream it's about the children or my illnesses or my "Cousin Laura". You know I was brought up with her. Her mother Loretta was a widow and a kind of servant in the house. I feel terribly guilty about that. Loretta could have been an actress. She would stop in the middle of cooking the dinner and recite:

> O, Romeo, Romeo! Wherefore art thou Romeo?
> Deny thy father and refuse thy name.

and she would also recite:

> Of all the girls that are so smart,
> There's none like pretty Sally:
> She is the darling of my heart
> And she lives in our alley.

109

'She laughed and sang; and would cry if anyone said they were waiting for dinner. She never meant to give us burnt dinners. Several times lately I've dreamed that my Cousin Laura came in through those folding doors. Doors are frightening. People knock: who is there? The knocking on the door! It's your heart knocking. You open up and a stranger comes in, a killer, Death or a ghost, or someone you've forgotten or done wrong to. I dream I'm sitting here and Laura looks at me with her big oval eyes. She's just as she used to be when she was fifteen, and lovely, a bit fat but shy and sweet. She asks me, "Where is my child? You can't keep my child." I ask her, "What child?" She says, faltering and timid just as she used to, when I shouted at her, "You know I mean Giles, I've come for him." She says terrible things to me just like I imagine Florence saying about Olivia. I can't stand it. I never say things to people like they say to me. Like Godfrey. People don't tell them the harm they are doing and so they go on, haughty and hard, wounding and lashing. I worry about it. Am I a child-stealer? I took Lennie from his father. I know my brother Arnold didn't want him; but I took him. And I am taking Olivia from Florence. Maybe Godfrey is right and Florence does need her.

'The other night Laura came and said to me, "I've come for my son"; and she meant Giles. I said, "But Laura you know Giles is my real son." But she just moved towards the door and said over her shoulder, "I'm going to get Giles." Oh, my God! I threw myself at her feet, I screamed and sobbed. I hung on to her knees. "Laura, Laura! He's my own son, my child." I was helpless. Laura always gave up things for me, anything I'd ask her; I made her play second fiddle till she became a sex-success. It's there in my mind, that I shouted at her and she opened her eyes and took a step backward and she was frightened. I was playing some game; she said, "You've cheated!" Laughing. I shouted, "Do you know you can get killed for saying that? People kill for that." She didn't understand. After that, I never could understand her: maybe, she went underground. Now, this time, in my dream, she left me there on the floor and went upstairs. I got up and ran to the foot of the stairs, calling, "Laura, Laura, Laura!"'

'Is that what you were saying? You were screaming,' said Stephen.

'Yes, I am sorry you woke me up. It means that Laura is still going upstairs to get Giles. What frightened me was that she was a soft-hearted girl and never stood up for herself: she'd cry. I stole the show. I feel guilty now.'

'I knew your Cousin Laura very well. Dear Aunt Loretta tried to net me for her when you and I got engaged and I sized her up the minute I met her. She's dull and she spreads boredom around her fifteen inches thick and anything the man says is right. But because you always underrated your sex appeal, Auntie thought if you could get a man, Laura could get him faster.'

110

'You were prejudiced against Laura from the start,' said Emily.

'I couldn't stand the name Laura; and her mother trying to hook me when it was you I was after. She told me what a good cook she was: Laura would have no need to spoil those lovely hands: in other words, marry Loretta and daughter.'

'She had lovely hands and a soft, hesitating, throaty voice and – '

'When all I wanted was you. You had just scored a bull's eye in the entertainment field and I figured I could live off you for the rest of my days.'

Emily laughed heartily, 'Oh, Stephen, let's get malicious: I need to laugh. I've been so dismal. Laura haunting me, my brother Arnold wanting money again and I can't refuse because of Lennie, Godfrey denouncing me, Lennie eavesdropping, owing the butcher, the governess quitting to get married, so that I'm sure Florence will have the court dropping in when there's no one to iron Olivia's dresses, so I have to iron them. But I've got her. I do adore her. It's your daughter; it's you.'

'Godfrey made you feel dismal. He made me feel like a louse too.'

'Not me. I hear he thinks I'm boring. I said to myself tonight, surely that is Godfrey boring me and not me boring Godfrey!' said Emily.

'Everyone bores Godfrey, because they can't keep on these high heights; they keep falling off. Godfrey deprecates those falls. He wants man to rise on his former self to higher things: like sister Florence's bank account. Just supposing Godfrey had sister Florence's living-room to perorate in. That is why he has had to revisit the psychoanalyst to make good his union with Millian. All the rhapsodies! My Florence, her ducats, her ducats, my Florence!'

Emily said thoughtfully, 'No, Godfrey's really disinterested. He spreads that kindly universal shadeless light all over, till your soul is dead.'

'If you will consent to my going over and knocking Godfrey to the ground several times, it will be very good for his all-seeing, all-knowing psyche. We all forgive him. The one time he doesn't get forgiven will be an eye-opener for him.'

She laughed, 'Oh, forget it. He'll probably kiss you on the other fist. Can you risk being kissed by his good lips? Manoel!'

The man came in.

'Manoel, we'll go and have a picnic early tomorrow. Get a picnic lunch packed, roast chicken, salad, white wine – ' she grinned towards Stephen, 'cheese and fruit. The youngsters want to swim. Then we'll come home, put on the record-player and play poker. I'll be out in a jiffy, Manoel, and see what else.'

Suddenly she became wild with excitement and pleasure. She jumped up, 'Begone dull care! I'm going to paper this whole house before

Christmas. I'm not going to let myself be pulled down by Moffat Byrd, Holinshed, Bowles and cohorts. We'll make a lovely Christmas for Giles, Lennie, Christopher and Olivia; perhaps it will be the last Christmas Olivia will be with us.'

'I'll see it isn't; I'll write a report too,' said Stephen.

Emily said, 'About her drinking. About her husbands, lawful and unlawful, about her being a communist. A communist nowadays isn't allowed to bring up children.'

'Let's keep the Party out of it.'

'We'll say she goes down south to incite the coloured people. She does,' said Emily.

'She's just a progressive like us; won't they point that out?' said Stephen.

'A progressive! Everything a progressive does is treason to the republic in which we live. We can get her on a hundred counts. What if we too are guilty? We can point that her shining witness too is a communist; his statements aren't worth the paper they're typed on. We can do anything. And we must, for we must keep Olivia; I need that child as I never needed anything.'

'Not even me?'

'Oh, oh, I need everything so badly so much, Stephen. I can't do without anything. I need you all. Stephen, let's get a new wallpaper, a good one, and French curtains.'

'When we're so broke, that's the last thing we need. We have to pay for the lawyers, too.'

Her eyes sparkling, her face lively, enchanting, begging and teasing, she said, 'Come, we must have a home suitable for Olivia, the others don't matter to the court. And oh, think, darling, Olivia's birthday party is coming; we're having twenty little boys and girls; and oh, let's make the place bright. I'm going to ring the man in the morning. These drapes don't go with our pictures; we'll have to get another rug, this is shoe-worn.'

Emily went to the kitchen to give advice to Manoel and Eva, then went to the telephone and told several people about Godfrey's noble action in jackalling for Florence Howard and she invited them all to come to dinner on Friday when Godfrey and Millian and the rest were coming.

Stephen growled, 'I can't stand that woman, Millian. I don't want any of 'em.'

Emily began fluttering and teetering towards the door, 'Oh, yes? I have invited everyone who was there this evening except one or two.'

'It's late. Come on.'

He went upstairs. She ran into the kitchen through two heavy swing-doors and found on the red-tiled floor, a stray cat. The kitchen was in

112

order and faultlessly clean; but an unwashed baking dish had been put on the floor for the cat to lick at. Emily shouted, with an ugly expression, 'Who did that?'

She took the cat by the scruff of the neck and hauled it to the door. It was a bluish, shorthaired animal with a white hourglass on the belly. It had just had kittens. It was almost starved to death. She threw it out on the hillside which rose behind the house. There were always stray dogs and cats in the hills. People, when they were leaving, took their pets there, hurled them from the cars, and raced back down the glen. At nights, cats howled in the glens and sniffed round the doors. The cat threw itself against the bolted door. Emily put on an apron and scrubbed the floor all over again, saying, 'Ugh, fooey!' and scrubbed the baking dish inside and out. She dried it, scrubbed the draining board and sink. Stephen came through the door with a scowl and asked her what she was doing: the servants were paid to do that.

'You took a drink while I was having my bath, I suppose.'

Emily said, 'Manoel, your best friend, let in a stray cat that dirtied up the floor and it licked germs all over the baking dish. I pay four hundred dollars a month to your friend and your friend's wife, and have to do all the housework twice a week, while they go to town to bank their savings, but at night the kitchen's like a pigsty.'

'Don't talk to me about money,' screamed Stephen.

'Why not? Don't we live for it? Isn't it our be-all and end-all? Money! I hate the word! The damn people in New York look at me with a sort of crappy patronizing regard, because I write for money; at the same time, they don't give a damn for my two serious books. I'm Emily Wilkes the famous writer, because I had a box-office success on Broadway and they tell me, leave that serious stuff alone, it's out of date, muckrakers are dead, leave the labour problems to the deep thinkers, you go ahead and write comedy so we can panhandle more dough for our causes. Everyone to his trade: yours is to make money. And you, Stephen, instead of standing by me, you only want me to write for money, more and more money, too.'

Said Stephen, 'How do you live without money? Do you expect to live off my family?'

Emily howled, 'Oh, that is the absolutely final last limit of horror: that makes the evening totally complete. Oh, how can you speak like that to me of all people! What has your rich family done for us? And doesn't it despise me, because I work? I'm classed with the ditch-diggers; and I don't mind. And at the same time that I am keeping this whole goddamn circus going, you speak – ' She began to pant and wring her hands, 'you speak of money to me, you make me live for it, when I hate it, I swear to you,

113

Stephen, I hate it. I'm known as a money writer, but there's nothing I hate and despise, and know – '

There was a deeper tone and with a faint ironic smile looking him in the face, she said after a slight pause, 'There's nothing I know more than money. I've never given a damn for money. I can make money. I'll borrow it or steal it if I want to. No one has a conscience about it – '

She burst out laughing in an agonized way, and leaned on the table, '– but I don't do it. I work like a lowdown Chinese coolie, much much harder than your friend Manoel and Holinshed's friend Katsuri and I'm writing this grade B and not even good grade B, cheesy, smalltown stuff – for you, for us, for Manoel and Eva and our millionaire kids. God! I'm certainly a success. Wilkes-Barre girl makes bad. That's what I've come to. I wish we were back in New York or Chicago. Chicago is gentler than this dump.'

She turned to him with a noble resentment and vision, 'Stephen, you'll never starve! We've done these stories, some of them have sold and I have got a great reputation for selling. But you know – and in fact all Hollywood knows – otherwise, they wouldn't have dared attack me tonight, you know, they wouldn't, you know these bastards – that I've got two stories circulating and at present neither has sold and it frightens me to death. When they started in on us, I knew they knew we hadn't sold. You say about money. But I'm frightened to death, blasted, done for, withered up. Oh, I know I sound baffled and upset. I am dreadfully miserable, Stephen. You are my best friend; isn't a husband a best and only friend? But how dreadfully the son of a rich family you are! You don't even understand my misery, my agony, my hysteria. I know it's hysteria, but it's me; it's the only way I can live – the Wilkes way of life and death.

'Look, Stephen, I know your work requires a decent standard of life and we can't keep the kids without a show of money. How right you are really! I am just all money. But think of my wasted weeks and I'm really raring to go. I want to work on a decent piece of work even if the back-room boys laugh at the poor humorist trying to go highbrow. I know damn well, Stephen, they take you for a real highbrow and good reason to; but why, for this reason, are we obliged to live beyond our means in a hellhole where everyone is tearing his neighbour's skin off his back as he hauls him down to hell with him?'

She stopped and came up close to her husband and said in a tense voice, lifting her fists, her blue eyes shining with passion, 'I am not as bad as they make me out to be, I mean, my work makes me out to be. This story I'm doing, Stephen, on which I have got a retainer and I have to do, is the most degrading thing I've ever done; including all the years I worked on scandal stories and gossip columns and night-court reports for

114

the small-town newspapers – it's so cheap! Jesus! I gag. I wake up at night in a sweat and think, "Is this me?" And I want to give up everything to write good literature for the working class. They need it and I can do it and I'm going to. What is the good of being a rebel at heart? And you think, they think that I'm like them, I care for money! This dreck! No wonder they pay you so much money. They ought to. For spewing filth in public they ought to pay you money. And we ourselves don't say, "Throw it in the ashcan", we say, "It's the new art." And we know. And what now? I write it. And this other thing hasn't sold and I wake up in a sweat at night because the trash hasn't sold. Stephen, think of my wasted life!'

There was silence for a while. Stephen looked sick. His eyes were shut. He at last exclaimed painfully, 'If I'm ever allowed to say anything! How do I like the insult that I throw in my own face, that I'm living on you as a parasite? Aren't I allowed to defend myself or is it only you? I'm trying to do a good job for the working-class movement for us both. Where would I be without this work?'

Emily shrugged her shoulders and hissed, 'Phtish!'

'Don't hiss like a snake at me. If you're paying your doit to capitalism, surely I have a right to try to earn it back, the shame, I mean, by doing good work. And I can't do good work away from people. People have a message for me. I can't think away from people. Maybe, that means I can't think. Maybe, it means I'm just hanging around stealing and composing their ideas into a crazy quilt that's only acceptable because it's current scraps. Well, I can't help it: That's me, as you say.'

Emily made another odd sound.

He continued, 'Don't hiss at me. I know what you think of me; and goddamn it I'm going on just the same, drearily without meaning, but I'm going to do something on theoretical lines because if I didn't I'd die. You've got some bee in your bonnet, you've got to do serious work, too. When it's quite clear to everyone but yourself that you're a humorist and just that.'

'That's what it seems to you,' Emily groaned.

'This idea of writing serious work, it isn't you. You got it in school and thus far I agree with our friend, the New Yorkers, Easterners are Bohemians, they're playing around; they all want to write their novel or their play. Here at least you're in the centre of mass writing. You're in a different business. Forget about the great American novel. Why should you write it more than another? Forget it, I tell you. You can make money. So make money. When we make enough money, we'll go away, OK, goddamnit, we'll go away and rot in some one-pump town, and you'll write your great novel. But why you with your smart horse-sense should do it, beats me. Still, all I ask is that you make money first and let's

115

have some security and peace; and then we'll see about the novel. The idea's not you and not yours though. You're not a social satirist, or a big time rain-in-the-face. You see things otherwise. You say your say in your own humane way and luckily for us it's a selling way and we don't have to starve in a shanty, while you're revolving the novel of the century.'

Emily sat down at the table and looked across at Stephen, who was sitting in a large armchair. He had thrown his shoes and then his socks across the room.

She said, 'You simply don't see how cheap is this life we're living.'

'All right, I apologize, I have the cheapness of my forefathers, without their ability to turn it into business success.'

'Oh, shut up. Don't I love you and understand you? I wake up at night and think and think. I don't get enough sleep.'

'You'd get more sleep if you didn't take those pills.'

She began to laugh, 'What a stupidity is a woman's life, those true women and mothers Godfrey was mewing about. Didn't you gag yourself at his bold words? I know you do. You screech at me but then you go and hide your head in the library out of shame for us both.'

But Stephen began shrieking at her, 'You make me mad: shut up! Do you think I'm so thick-skinned? And what are we to do? The Party is out to get me, God knows why; and here you go around making things more difficult for me. That attack was on me, not on you: Godfrey doesn't know it. They think you're a side-show already and instead of hanging your head and listening to the great man, the great stone faces of the Party, you argue back. I blushed for you tonight. Why can't you let Moffat Byrd act the little tin Jesus and have his say. Suppose it is the line that Lenin said Rockefeller was progressive! Suppose he did say it? Suppose for once you're wrong, the wisdom of the lumberjacks is cock-eyed and American cannibalism–capitalism is progressive. Suppose the Russian system is a leap and we're going round the easy way! Here I've come out, upped stakes in the east, come out here in a keenly competitive market where everyone's watching every move and we've committed the unpardonable sin of really making big money as free lances, which no one said anyone could; but the goddamn Howards did it and that's why they've got it in for us – and so they're trying to get us out on Party lines – '

'Stephen! Stephen!' shrieked Emily.

'OK. Sacrilege! But you know it and I know it. So instead of bowing the head and keeping in with the boys, you're sassing them all the evening and asking them about primitive socialism. Primitive socialism is just about as useful as primitive methodism in the war of the worlds. That's all over. OK. I'm not going to give up the Party or the boys'

116

favour, because if I didn't have that, I'd have nothing. I must have their esteem. I gave up my family, its money and its esteem. I must have something.'

Emily said, 'Then it's like religion or a desperate love affair, akin to waving the stars and stripes at the end of a Broadway flop, it's a neck-saving, soul-saving device. I'm not looking to anyone to save me. Why? Because I've got my two fists, just like any Irish worker or bohunk back in the rolling mills. I'm sorry you were converted to socialism. Now you feel that there's no ground under your feet. And so, though you hate and despise Browderism and you were always against it in the east, now you're as mild as a ewe-lamb. It's the Party boys or me.'

'You've put it in a nutshell: the boys or you. I'm not going to fight with the boys. I didn't go through all that just to be hoofed out on my ear by a lousy lot of opportunists that I know the inner smell of. I'm going to stick around till they acknowledge either I'm right or I'm so sticky with piety and holiness that they'll have to keep me on even if it turns their stomachs.'

Emily's broad chest was heaving and her cheeks were red. Her eyes sparkled and a tic continually lifted her mouth as if she were smiling ironically. Her tears dried up. She thoughtlessly began to make some coffee and laid out cups and plates, on a clean cloth. While the coffee was heating, she turned to her husband with a smile, 'I'm prepared to fight Hollywood: why not you?'

'I don't give a goddamn for Hollywood. It's my family. I've a kid worth ten million dollars; I'm not going to lose her or let Florence laugh at me.'

Emily quietened down and poured out the coffee.

'I want to do work I believe in, honest work,' she said sitting down.

'Florence is chortling because they say you're on the road to Trotskyism and your honest book is frowned upon. It doesn't even sell to reds and who else would look at it?'

Emily said, with that strange merry twitching of the mouth, 'But the letters I get from workers. Isn't that what we're for? I mean Stalin says "The writer has a function: he's an architect of souls."'

'Pah! Not in the USA. The best he can do in the USA is to make money and communicate in some smaller or more picayune way. We're Americans. We must try and make do with that. My family and kids are millionaires and that's the highest ideal this country has: so let's stick to what we have and breathe life into that mud: Man.'

'That's a good expression,' said Emily smiling at him. She drank her coffee at a gulp and poured out more.

'You won't sleep,' said Stephen angrily.

'I'm going mad with headache and 'flu and I don't know, maybe even

117

rickets, with working and never getting out for a break except in a night-club with our agent, Charlie Goldhammer, or a mantrap called a dinner invitation in these parts,' said Emily laughing. 'So if I have a few cups of coffee and can think and think, I'm better for a moment. Let me be.'

Stephen said, 'I'm getting an ulcer and I'm going to be sick for a week after this. The misery I went through tonight with all those jackals howling. I'm not taking their side. Let you put enough money aside and I say you take a year of freedom and write any funereal working-class crap you like.'

'Jesus, Stephen, I don't think it's crap. I sweat when I read those letters from workers who read my book. You know what it costs; $3.50. They either got their club to put it up or they got someone to buy it; and they worry about it: they send me advice. It's the happiest and best moment of my life, except when I had the baby.'

She began to sob loudly.

'Oh, shit,' said Stephen between his teeth.

She shouted, 'All right, all right, you write for the middle class, you've never had one letter from a worker. Because what you're writing, whether you know it or not, is university tracts. It's good. I know it's better than mine, anyway as a contribution to knowledge; and you're a library scholar. But it isn't enough. We ought to give people something to live for. I had that remark from a whole group of workers in Wilkes-Barre, Pennsylvania.'

'A whole group of shits in the land of Cockaigne. Maybe they're kidding you. It wouldn't surprise me, after the Party attack. A come-on to get you to write off one of your well-known effusions, in which you will really put your foot in it and they can show us the door.'

She said suddenly laughing, 'Look, this evening's attack. In the first place, it wasn't. I don't believe they're going to really attack one of their prize moneymakers, a Broadway success. They just want me, like you, to keep on writing belly-laughs and so make them money. I understand it, OK. And then their fright and scorn of my serious writing – it has a sort of basis. It's a hangover from Wobbly days, when culture was spit on as bourgeois. I knew that and that's why I first wrote the labour book, *The Wilkes-Barre Chronicle*. I made it as reportage with statistics and police incidents to appeal to the Wobbly in them. And then there's something else that frightens them. You've got more of it, Stephen, because of your background and having spent a year at the Sorbonne and because you're not a deep-dyed tarpits New Yorker and that is, gosh, that's why I'm so attracted to you, Stephen; that is, I think communists should be renaissance men and women, not just fanatics or dreary committee-people or rabbinical post-graduates. To make a new world, requires men and

118

women – of catholic interests – of a rich – and deep – knowledge of all sorts of things.'

'That lets us out,' said Stephen.

She paused but went on with greater vigour, 'You think there are historical jobs and then there are easy quick sideshows to get in the luridly, pruriently curious and the applause and guffaws and in any case the dimes: and that is what I can do. That's not an insult. You don't know the business. It's shit but not quick. It's taking as much of my lifetime to write cheap, easy shit as to write a good book.'

Stephen said, 'Well, I'm not allowed to say anything. I just have to keep quiet here. I have opinions too, but I can't open my mouth. I'm jumped on and it looks as though I'm a louse. I'm employing my wife to write shit so that I can read in libraries. I have nothing to say. I'm not allowed to open my mouth.'

Emily put her head on her hands and immediately looked up, 'Oh, heavens, who can fight with you? It's the electric chair. Little Ikey makes chalk-marks on the sidewalk; in two days he's a gangster; he ends up in the electric chair. Oh!' She writhed between laughter and helpless hysteria. 'Oh, you won't listen to what I mean. There's no getting round you. Oh, you drive me crazy.'

'I don't notice it. I don't see you crying,' said Stephen.

Emily sighed noisily, 'I'm dying laughing. That means something to me, not just a joke, Stephen. You don't know what I mean.'

'Well, what do you mean?'

'I lay awake enough nights to know what I mean. I lie awake and try to find out what I'm going crazy for: what the struggle is for.'

'Well, what is it for?' asked Stephen.

She sighed, her pink face turned towards him. Her hair had come down on one side, out of the ribbon: the other side was bunched up in spikes and curls. She looked like a Holbein woman. Stephen looked. His face changed. He laughed.

'What's the use? You're laughing at me,' she said.

'I'm not.'

'Yes, you are.'

'I'm laughing at you because I love you. There's no one just like you. I'm laughing with joy because I was so clever, out of all my family of high-minded or dead-headed shnooks, to pick a woman original and with genius and who would not listen to my sour-pickle line of talk and believe it.'

She smiled, 'We love each other, that's true. Look, this Hollywood game is not good for marriage. We're always shrieking at each other and when not battling about effective clinches in the script, by golly, we're making unrecorded scenes offstage. A dead loss. Let's quit the gamble of salaried literature. It's the same as shooting craps for a living.'

119

'That's life. I don't want a sheltered existence. I want to destroy my enemies in the family and outside with the terrible acid of success and melt them to bone-dust and with your help I can do it.'

'If we don't tell the truth, what's our function? We're just fancy icing on the oatcake.'

'Oh, shit!' said Stephen.

'I'm not laughing. I know it's like shouting, "What is Truth?" in the middle of a cocktail party; that is to say a business meeting of two-thousand-dollar-a-week men, or political mahogany-heads who think a writer is there to write slogans. We get into money habits and we forget the tremendous responsibility a writer has to tell the truth – '

'I don't know what you're getting at, and I've a headache,' said Stephen getting up and putting the coffee-grounds into newspaper and then into the garbage-can.

'Stephen, what are you doing? You know in Los Angeles you can't put coffee-grounds into the garbage: they won't collect it.'

Stephen reached into the can and brought back the packet, 'Hell, and there's still that wartime ordinance against incinerators that might make smoke signals. Are we crazy? Well, I guess.'

Emily went on in a low tone, 'I know that you don't think so much of my talent and I know – ' (her voice became firm) ' – I know that your esteemed confrères on the Washington *Liberator* don't think my views matter a cent because first I'm a woman and they're ex-Cedar boobs; and next I'm just a comic writer, let me stick to my last joke; but I've been through the mill – oy! what an expression – but I mean, I do know the writing trade. I think a writer *has* a tremendous responsibility to tell the truth and tell it with all the skill and ability and experience – he has – to rise above himself – not like I'm doing, Stephen, going down to the sod-digging level of my grandfather. To be better than he was for the sake of others. That's a funny thing, but every night I wake up and I think, I want to be better than I am by nature. To be a writer in an age when the truth will set us free – means to be a writer of the truth; or to be an utter, utter, decadent damned soul.' She put her head on her arms on the table and cried.

At this Stephen turned round and shouted uneasily, 'For God's sake, that's enough drama. You don't have to act out your soul-dramas in the kitchen do you? You've probably woken up all the children and Olivia is going to write a letter home to Grandma tomorrow about how we fight and Florence will put that in her report to the court. Jesus, the scenes you make! Anyone would think you thought human beings were good, kind, decent, generous and the friend of someone.'

'I do think so – I really think so,' sobbed Emily.

120

'Well, that's fine. Write that for the weeklies and we'll really make a living. I'm going to bed, Emily. I've got a stomach attack and I've got to rest.' He pushed the swing door.

'Take your medicine and I'll be in in a minute,' said Emily, partly raising her head from her arms and looking after the door still swinging. She slouched there a moment and then raised her head. Stephen had left some coffee-grounds on the tiled floor. Emily got a pail and washed the floor there, washed out the pail and stood it to dry. Then she washed the drying rack again, smelled the dishrag, soaked it in vinegar and boiled it and hung it to dry. She sniffed. The kitchen smelled of various cleaning agents. She looked happy. She lit a cigarette and sat down at the table with an ashtray and a long drink. The cat hurled itself against the kitchen door. The locked door rattled. The cat rushed through the grass and with a bound landed on the kitchen windowsill. She saw its phosphorescent wild eyes through the glass. She heard Manoel and Eva moving in the room overhead.

Stephen shouted, 'Come to bed!'

The cat crouched on the windowsill staring in. She turned off the light and, after tidying the rooms, went up to the bedroom. Stephen was already in bed, groaning faintly. She looked at him.

'Goddamnit, don't hover,' he cried.

She tapped a new cigarette on the table.

'Don't do that,' groaned the sufferer.

She grimaced to herself in the mirror. She put a swansdown jacket over her nightdress and opened a book. 'Don't wear that tickling thing!'

She put on another bedjacket and got into bed with a glass of water and her reading lamp, two tubes of different pills, a pen, a notebook and a box of face-tissues. This room had windows on two sides, one set facing the hill rising in the back. The cat threw itself against these windows and, after several leaps, managed to settle on the windowsill. It stared in. Emily drew the curtains.

'Open the curtains. You know I can't sleep unless I can see the sky.' She opened the curtains, took her pills and put out the light. The long night of pain and restlessness began. It seemed to her the cat was part of it. She got up and banged the window till the cat went away. 'What are you doing?'

'I hate cats. I'd have them all killed,' said Emily.

'I thought you liked them because they killed birds.'

'We could kill all the birds ourselves. Send out a plane to spray the woods with DDT. What use are they?'

'They kill the insects.'

'You wouldn't have insects with DDT.'

'Leave them all alone.'

'What use is all this trash in the modern world? Let's get rid of them and organize the world. They don't belong to anyone, they don't like anyone – they're marauders. They eat our food. City people are sentimental. They think milk grows in containers. Farmers don't like birds. They eat the food they grow.'

'Go to sleep.'

'The world belongs to man or to animals, doesn't it? It's them or us. Look at the roaches, thousands or millions of years old. We're inefficient. We're letting them and all the other pests and the snakes and the flying snakes – '

'What flying snakes?'

'Birds are flying snakes. It shows it in the Natural History Museum. Get rid of them and you can do fertilization with a spray. Spray from a plane. Let's get rid of the old-fashioned world. We want the world for ourselves. We're growing at such a rate there won't be enough for us if we let them maraud and rob and steal. I'm a farmer's daughter – '

'Go to sleep.'

'I can't bear to think of our garden and our place on the river at home and our wood-lot full of these creeping things that we could destroy. What's the matter with us? Why don't we – '

'Go to sleep.'

But Emily went on fretting for a while about the laws and measures against the free-living part of the world, those who spoke with other tongues than ours, who hissed, chirped, rattled, scuttled, flew, slid.

8 BACK EAST

The next morning a parcel containing a bound typescript was delivered at their house before breakfast. It was for Stephen. He opened it at breakfast and found it was Byrd's 'homework, a necessary job to get things straight', the essay on America's new task in Europe, that he had promised to Stephen the night before.

With it was a pleasant, cajoling, almost humble letter from Moffat Byrd, ten or twelve hand-written lines asking Stephen's opinion 'on this rough draft'. He said, 'The discussion yesterday evening did me good; I made some alterations before I went to bed and strengthened the tone of the argument. I know your plain dealing and will value any comment at all you have to make. We all believe in autocriticism, we all make mistakes. You are among friends and I, like all the others, value your opinion, coming as it does from a comrade devoted to Party and country.'

Stephen was deeply pleased. To conceal his pride and pleasure, he fluttered the pages, smacking his lips with contempt, but with a glowing face, said a few words and then, packing the typescript neatly by him, he confessed that he was glad.

'Perhaps after all, Byrd was ashamed of the comedy of last night. I will take him at his word. I will read it thoroughly and make a sincere criticism. Up to now these deep thinkers have not seen fit to consult me. But they know who I am. You caught that, about how they thought of us, when we came out first; that they thought the Party had sent us as censors, scrutineers, to straighten them up. Byrd will get a scrupulous –' he began to smile; 'Byrd will get a petty, titivating, meticulous, nit-picking, fine-comb report.'

He looked merry and stretched in his chair.

Emily was at the other end of the rectangular breakfast table, which was set by some windows; in front of her were a number of letters, mostly answers from her correspondents.

'If you do anything but flatter the brute, you're sunk. Elementary my dear Watson. It's the oldest rule in the book.'

Stephen spoke petulantly, 'Say what you will, Byrd is a man of real quality. He's Party leader in the studios, he's highest paid scriptwriter and he's no yesman. I see what it is – he's trying to prove that it is economically necessary for us and for the Europeans to accept American industrial organisation, until Europe rises from the ruins and is ready for its own pattern. To undertake a revolution now on the Russian pattern, after such a disaster, would be a disaster to the revolution itself. Take France – there is nothing to seize. Revolution must seize a going concern or seize a state in the making, not a heap of ruins.'

'In Russia, they did.'

'Let's not be primitive socialists. It is no longer 1917. It is a good idea for America to protect and nurture the diseased, famished nations till they can look after themselves and find their own way out.'

'Uh-huh,' said Emily, reading.

'Well, it gives me a real chance to defend my views and show them where they are mistaken. They are asking me for an opinion. And you can just see it, Emily – if my views are accepted or even partly compatible, if he invites me over for a talk and I can put it over, the other Party boys will follow tamely enough, you know that. It is my big chance to be acknowledged, to get in with the top boys; and once I'm accepted here, I'll have the prestige of being a leader here, when we go back to New York.'

'Hollywood prestige! Alackaday! They think the Hollywood boys are a lot of merry andrews, jack-o'-lanterns, harlequins; plain nuts. Besides, it's a trap. You don't see it and he doesn't mean it – maybe. And maybe he does. If he squashes you, no more chance of getting on the central committee.'

But Stephen took no notice. He set to work and in three days he had prepared a long commentary and criticism of Byrd's paper. He read it to Emily, who agreed with the ideas, but said it had no chance.

'This paper of his is going to be published over his name. The local Party's thirsting for it so they can drink another full cup of obedience. He's advertised it in all our set. The studio faithful are waiting for it; and he's going to print your ideas? What he wants is to get you on paper. He'll show it around and say at last he has proof, a statement under your own signature, that's you're a traitor to the Party and to America, first to him.'

Stephen said, 'You don't know how men think. There's another sort of fellowship. Men really want to have a sympathetic, intelligent consultation when they're framing a new policy statement. It's necessary. All prime ministers, all presidents, all heads of corporations do it. It's also good Party doctrine, criticism by colleagues and equals. It shows, Emmie, it pays to stick it out. In the end you get your chance. Appearances sometimes to the contrary, the Party is a democratic institution and Jay is not our enemy; he's our colleague and he's a loyal Party man.'

He was jubilant at the work done. It was a bright morning. The breakfast-room overlooked a short paved terrace, a grass slope, running down to other slopes and then to the canyon. Emily was good-tempered, too. She had received two fan-letters, one from a woman in Seattle and one from an American roadworker who went to the evening class she taught, in downtown Los Angeles.

She laughed and conceded, 'Perhaps you're right. This fighting for a living is bad.'

She began to laugh, 'See what I've got for my next lecture downtown:

> "They have created a social life based upon pitiless rivalry of interests, which instead of excluding, actually completes itself, when these same interests require it, by a ferocious group solidarity . . . on fête days, they exercise themselves in trials of strength; pride, emulation, interest and boasting are mingled and confounded, the rivalry is more bitter in proportion as the rivals are better known to each other: conflicts multiply, lawsuits succeed one another."

'That's from *La Terre du Voleur* by a certain M. Tammsaare, about some miserable backward community. It's us. I cut it out of a book about denunciation and denouncers: awful subject, but very domestic under Hitler and under us.'

'Where are the lawsuits?' he asked contemptuously.

'Aren't you afraid of people writing in to the Party about your being a traitor to them; and to the FBI about your being a traitor to the country?' She shrieked with laughter: 'This way the iron maiden, that way the guillotine.'

He got up to pack up the typescript and commentary, saying negligently, 'I suppose there's some reason why a humorist has to see life as Grand Guignol.'

'Yes, it's the struggle. But struggle is life, as someone said. However I know I'm wrong to get suspicious and sardonic. There's more good in the world than we think.'

'This will be a turning-point, I feel it,' said Stephen comforting her. 'To think of our holding our heads up again and having, as well as good faith, which is a ticket to the gallows, good odour.'

He took his car out and delivered the package to Moffat Byrd's house. Byrd, a punctual hard-working man, was at the studios.

But it was only, it seemed, a leader's conciliatory gesture. Byrd wrote back that night saying that he had allowed Stephen to read this as yet private paper, to get his reactions, for he, Byrd, had not been able to accept the idea that Stephen 'and his spouse' were in such complete disagreement with the Party. The Party said that American aid was necessary for broken Europe, the Party's chief said that cartels were not an evil of capitalism, but at the moment actually necessary for the health of society, that cartels were a form of socialism, a new form and that would

125

pass into another socialism. How could Emily and Stephen quarrel with the Party on all its fundamental views, formed not idly, but in the crucible of war, in the fight against fascism (Stephen having written that cartels, American industrial capitalism, the control of one country by another, were a form of colonialism and opposed to all Marxian doctrine)? How could the Howards form a fragmentation of two, and still claim the respect, loyalty and comradeship of the Party members? Byrd's views were the accepted views and he had been so shocked by the 'wavering, crumbling Howard viewpoint', another form of Trotskyism, puerile incendiarism and little better than provocation, that he was going to take counsel about them. The country, the Party in the lead, and along with it, its elected leaders, was going ahead to set up a new regime in Europe, where all the past had gone down the drain, America, the best organized society in the world, was gallantly and generously about to rebuild her allies – and the Howards, playing at revolution, sticking to a few texts out of context, like Biblical students with 'God is Love' on their walls, refusing to look at the world about them, wanted the Party to follow them. They were right, millions of other Americans were wrong, the Party was wrong. What could happen to them? They could only become outcasts with no function, unless they saw the abyss opening before them.

'My God, I thought the function of the Party was revolution,' said Stephen; 'I have been wrong. Goddamn the comfortable temporizers. I'll stick to it, if it kills me.'

But he did not sleep at night and he suffered more and more from his indigestion and his teeth.

Emily still had two scripts going round; and now Stephen wanted her to get into the studios as a regular writer with a good weekly wage, such as Godfrey Bowles or Moffat Byrd had.

She ridiculed it. 'If I'm one of a regular team with one of those offices like a bee in a cell, I'll have to give them my work for say $2,000 a week – I won't get $5,000 to begin with; and so for $104,000 a year I'll give away work that's worth $160,000 even in a bad year. You're not allowed to free-lance.'

'But we'll have a regular income. I wouldn't cry at getting $104,000 a year.'

'You're giving up a goldmine for a pension.'

But they were hard-up and presently Olivia's custody case was coming up; they would have to show their earnings. With regret, shame, but hiding her feelings, Emily went to see an agent who had already been interested in her, Walter Simpson; she had also been approached by Bergman, an agent with a good string of writers in the studios, all of them

126

leftists as was Bergman; but she avoided him.

'I want a good job,' she said; 'I don't want to wear the CP brand; I want a job on merits; you get more.'

Walter Simpson, a handsome, stalwart Englishman who had once been in the paper business, took her round to studio after studio. Cocktail parties were given for her; they all watched her; all thought she would be a success. Some of 'the greats' came up to her lunch-table in the canteen, talked and smiled: they were seen with her, for them an act of charity and promise. For some reason she was not accepted. The dinner invitations fell off, stopped. It was explained in this way: she talked too much, she was too bright. She would go in to a producer or director, interest him, charm him until a contract seemed certain; and then the sale (of her person and talent) did not take place. She was sorry and glad. She did not want to work in the studios. All her money was made on plays, books and independent scripts, all free-lancing. With any luck, and putting in the hard work she always did, she could hope to make very large sums outside the studios; whilst inside, her income would be limited. The contract offered by the studios was, in reality, a peonage contract, and therefore illegal, though no one challenged it. The contract Stephen had hoped for was a seven-year contract, under which every moment of her life belonged to the studios. They would pay for all her time, twenty-four hours a day and 365 days a year; so that, in theory at least, if she did any independent writing while there, it was theirs.

One day Emily was called to the studio to see the secretary, a strange, long-headed man who looked as if his head had been cast in two pieces, in two metals, silver and bronze and the pieces carefully but not reassuringly put together. He was a hated and ridiculed man; ridiculed out of hate and fear – he had great power, throughout the studio; he was the hatchet man. He had an odd manner, mild, courteous, strained, not at all brutal and nasty as she had heard. He asked her about her projects, her books; then said quietly that writers of her sort should go to New York and write their successful plays and books and come out with them on quite a different sort of contract, to see them through the studios, when they were bought.

Emily did not argue: she heard her sentence and though this was exactly what she thought herself, she was dashed. She had lost the job; she never wanted the job; she had never wanted to be a studio hack, sitting in conferences, haggling over every word. This was what she did with Stephen, but for more money. She trotted through the large reception hall, down to her office, telephoned Stephen, left a message for him. Then she went back to the town centre by bus, looking indifferently at the wretched landscape and with the feelings of a man who must go home to wife and children and tell them he cannot pay for their bread at the end of the week.

127

They were out of money, they had spent Stephen's allowance, the lawyers looking after Olivia's case had sent in a bill, doctors and dentists were unpaid. In her trouble she began to imagine conspiracies – already, she thought, Jay Moffat Byrd had given the word in the studios; it was through him that her last two scripts had been rejected.

She telephoned Stephen from the bus terminal; the maid said he had already left to meet her. She stood there waiting for him, her heart dry and painful, tossing projects and arguments about in her fancy.

When Stephen drew up in their second car, a little cream one, and opened the door for her to get in, she saw that he was perplexed, moody. She did not want to break the bad news till she got back home and had a drink; she could not bear his reproaches.

'I called from the studio, but you were out.'

He did not answer.

'Anything wrong, Stephen? Olivia lost? Lennie sulky? What's wrong?'

'Byrd telephoned me to go over; he said it was critical, emergent.'

'What is?'

'Discussions are going on. Down with the Howards. If we don't conform, they'll oust us.'

'We'll fight them.'

'I won't. You can't fight the ultimate, the final justice,' said Stephen. 'I'm going to put my pride in my pocket. If I lost the Party I'd have nothing. I wouldn't know where to go, where to look. I can't live without the Party. I've built my life, my philosophy, my affections, too, on it.'

'We'll fight them. They have no right to do this to an honest man like you. I'll fight them. We'll write them a manifesto, if we have to sit up all night. We'll show them they're wrong. Maybe it'll take a week, or more, but they won't go through with this. This is Hollywood. Not New York. We'll write to New York. This is the land of Cockaigne, the cave of Adullam. Here they don't cut ice with the NY central committee. Who are they? Illusions, daymares, oases – '

'Oh-oh,' he sighed, not listening to her.

'Not oases, that flapdoodle in the desert – and it comes from that white headachy plain – mirage, mirages,' she shouted.

'I've given my word to Jay to write him a letter retracting all my errors.'

'You won't.'

'Yes, I will. I couldn't bear to be put out of the Party. It's my whole life. If that happened what has my life been for? I couldn't have spent all these years for nothing.'

'What about me? The children? What about your work – you've got your name on books.'

'You know damn well,' he said between his teeth, 'that tomorrow

128

morning, if I don't do full penance, those books won't be fit to line the garbage cans. No one will read them. No one in the Party and no one outside the Party will care about them. No one will stand by us. You and I will be alone, ridiculous naked people, one fat, one thin, under a thundercloud. You know what Thurber said about the man who left town under a cloud. That'll be us tomorrow. Well, it won't be. I've given in. I have got to be taken back into favour, I won't let my work be destroyed. I'm not going to let them destroy me. We'll stay here, be accepted, you'll get a regular salary, no more of this huckstering; Byrd will help us, he said he would, if we listen to reason. It's all settled.'

'It's not. I'm not wanted in the studio; I'm out. No job.'

His hands trembled on the wheel and he began talking in a high-pitched voice. How were they to face up to everything? They were ruined, no ground under their feet.

It was a miserable evening, one of their worst; and yet with all this, they had to think about their appearance in court, the following week. They both had to fly east, with Olivia, to explain their way of living and their plans.

In turmoil, Emily quickly made up her mind what to do. Their chances with Olivia were very good. Florence was in a nursing home; Anna was out in the Sinai Desert with Arthur. Either the case had come on before they expected it, or they had decided between themselves not to fight. This was likely, for they had strongly disapproved a headlined custody case.

Emily let Stephen take Olivia to the zoo, though they both disliked animals, to the movies, to the museum; she herself was very busy; and when the day came for them to appear in court, she informed Stephen that she was going to say that they had decided Hollywood was a poor setting for the little girl and that they were moving east for her sake, bringing with them all their establishment, Lennie, Giles, of course, Christopher, the servants, the cars –

'With my face, I can't tell such lies,' said Stephen.

'Ah, but it's not a lie: the house is bought, or spoken for. It's a lovely old house in White Oak Shade Road, in New Canaan; it's on a millstream, a house built round three sides of a square, with an orchard, a vegetable garden, a field; and I have bought a nanny goat for the children. We can give them goat's milk. It's healthy.'

'Who's going to milk the goat? How did you pay for the millstream? I don't want to live in New Canaan.'

'I sold the house in Beverly Hills.'

'Sold it? What about my signature?'

'I said it was forthcoming – you'll airmail it.'

Then she began to explain all her idea to him. In this way, they slipped out of the noose (as she said) prepared by Byrd, they got back to the old company who knew them. The West Coast had gone mad since Pearl Harbor, with 'it might have been us'. What happened in New York the day of Pearl Harbor? People were upset. In Los Angeles the railroad terminal was crowded with people, 'including some of our well-known friends' with just paper parcels under their arms, anything to get out and go east. 'That's their state of mind, mass hysteria delivered with the milk and necessary for them to be able to write their absurd patriotic scripts. Easterners are saner. You won't feel ill, your life wasted, your aims wobbling over here. Connecticut is calming; it's also fashionable enough. And you'll love it, Stephen; it's a lovely old house, with bits built on, galleries, a balcony, a separate stone staircase going up to a wing with airy rooms – it's genteel, *tray raffeenay*, a gentleman's place – and all around are people you can talk to, there's a couple of writers who've had a radio serial running for five years, right next door; and all about, New York radicals, that is to say, sensible, honed-down, adjusted radicals, not people out of *The Cabinet of Dr Caligari*.'

He was attracted, though he refused to be consoled till he had been in to see some Party colleagues to whom he told his troubles on the Coast. In a mild, blurred indifference, they made him feel at home; and though he felt sure that an unfriendly description of him had reached them, by their noncommittal words, he also felt soothed by the feeling that though sincere they might be, those theatrical mavericks were scrutinized without love by the cold, clearcut, cut-and-dried 'boys' on the central committee.

'There's always been a suggestion that the central committee should be moved out to Chicago or Pittsburgh, away from the soft cosmopolitanism of New York. How glad I am it hasn't happened. Here they soothe me because I'm just a poor, rough, Chicago type; Chicago they'd cut me down with a blunt axe.'

They moved into the new house in New Canaan and, blithely and with the usual invigorating arguments, went about furnishing it to their taste, leaving it pleasantly airy, with plenty of room to move; and at once, to show Stephen that he was still *persona grata* with the Party, they set about entertaining the radical set. They were pleased to find that their absence in Hollywood and the exaggerated stories of their moneymaking there gave them a warmer welcome here; it had also helped them that Olivia had been given to them by the court and that the sweetly obeisant little Christy was living with them too.

'Are you happy, Stephen?' said his energetic wife, the first morning at breakfast, as he sat with his paper, letters, cornflakes, toast and egg in the temporary breakfast-room. They had yet to sort out the rooms.

130

'I could be,' he said, 'but all this commotion and the worry about whether Jim Burgess really meant it when he said I was with them just as I had always been – you know how he sits there, talking, not looking at you, chucking lumps of sugar into the sugar-bowl and then digging them out again and chucking them in again, so that it looks as if he doesn't mean what he says – '

'What a worrier. What will be, will be!'

'I've always been afraid of that.'

'Tut-tut. Listen, sweetheart, last night I was reading *The Blithedale Romance* – '

'You had the light on all night.'

'I didn't. I have to catch up. I'm a leftist, and I don't know anything. I have no backlog. I started to laugh – '

'The bed was shaking; I thought you were crying.'

'Listen. This is you, oh-ha-ha, don't be mad at me, it's so like. Listen:

> "In this predicament I seriously wished – selfish as it may appear – that the reformation of society had been postponed about half a century, or at all events, to such a date as should have put my intermeddling with it entirely out of the question . . . What in the name of common sense, had I to do with any better society than that I had always lived in . . . My dinner at the Albion where I had a hundred dishes at command . . . Was it better to hoe, to mow, to toil and moil amidst the accumulations of a barnyard; to be the chambermaid of two yoke of oxen and a dozen cows . . . "'

'That's me? It isn't me at all. I don't want a hundred dishes. I don't want to milk the goat, that's another matter. Did you ever milk a goat? You've got to throw her down and tie her legs! A bestial, repulsive slavery of a goat.' After this outburst of amusing peevishness, he said thoughtfully, 'It would have made no difference to me what time or place, I would always have been what I am. I know I am a gnat, a mayfly, I know I haven't the stamina or coarseness of men who succeed, but I must be a revolutionary, not just a rebel; for me, it's a kind of love, a better kind. I love you and the children, when the house is quiet and they've had their food, I love you most, but there is more; and it isn't love of mankind, it is just love, but this Party and this movement is the body of that love for me. Not better – it's not better to love the Party than you – you are two, strongly loved.'

Emily looked at him markedly. 'Stephen, Stephen! I don't deserve you. But who really deserves their friend? I adore you. And, do you know, it's not the first time, you are a saintly character, too.'

'Oh, not that milky-watery picture.'

'Oh, you are very different from me. King Cophetua and the beggar maid.'

9 THE MAGIC REFUGEE

The determination and violence of her nature called on Emily's physical reserves; more than that, because she tended to obesity, she had to diet, though working hard. During the day she lived on black coffee, barbiturates and, in the evening, a good meal and wine, whisky and soda and liqueurs. She soon heard of a refugee doctor in Park Avenue, who had taken the name Doctor Park and who gave injections of the Bogomoletz serum, a Russian product which was said to prolong life, particularly if taken before the age of thirty-five, and Emily was just thirty-five; she had no time to lose.

She persuaded a neighbour and friend of theirs, Ruth Oates, to go with her twice a week to get treatment from Dr Park. Axel Oates ran his own mimeographed weekly, called *Evidence*, full of rumours, tips and the secret news, which was bought by every bright journalist at home and abroad and by a good many left-leaning economists and others. His news was good and he said the things they wanted to say but could not; in other words, he had achieved the aim of many a gagged journalist. He had a small office in Eighteenth Street, in a loft: Ruth came in from New Canaan four days a week to do the considerable office-work. She was a husky, good-looking woman, thirty-five or so, who worked hard in their house and garden and at the day's end liked to drink. Axel was a teetotaller. Ruth and Emily became very friendly. Ruth did not drink at all on her days in town. Emily now drank a good deal of whisky: she found she was able to – and, in fact, her manner when drunk differed little from her manner when sober. Stephen, with his delicate stomach, drank very little though he had a favourite cocktail which he served at the parties, which he called the Howard Bomb, a disagreeable, harsh, throat-twisting concoction which he had made up one night by pouring the ends of several bottles into the cocktail shaker. People would take it because it was like an explosion: then they went back to their usual tipple. Apart from this joke of his, Stephen frowned on drink in the daytime. Emily liked to drink now and took advantage of being alone in town to amuse herself in any way. Stephen refused to take the Bogomoletz treatment; 'I'm too old,' said he: 'besides, who knows? Bogomoletz died at 57.' He was very busy in the city, working with and for the Party; he never met Emily when she

132

went into town twice a week for her guzzle at the fountain of youth, the Bogomoletz injections. Dr Park's waiting-room was full. There were also people who wanted the treatment for their animals; but the supply of serum was limited. Emily talked with everyone in the waiting-room and came home full of the grotesque vanity of these peculiar people who wanted to live for ever, 'not to mention their hound-dogs.'

She and Stephen were soon invited to one of Dr Park's 'salons' as he called them, there to meet some famous New York progressives, Jan Jones, who defended clients in labour victimisation, NAACP and civil liberties cases, lawyers for International Labor Defence and a popular radical psychoanalyst and his wife, a producer, speakers for the exiled Spanish Republicans and one or two, but very few, literary people.

Every time they went home from one of these evenings, they laughed, jeered, compared views and were consoled; 'How different from that intellectual coal bin Hollywood, everyone black, dreary and the same.'

Before this Emily had never known doctors: she came from a family that avoided doctors because of the expense. Before her confinement she had not known the exotic, strange, magic world of medicine: she had not known the back-kitchen and disease-infatuated world of women who regard their own bodies uneasily and are district nurses for the family. She had heard in hospital, for the first time, woman-talk, dirty talk, superstitions like witchcraft, but perhaps, who knew, partly true. She had her baby Giles and with her usual enthusiasm, though her modesty was offended, she accepted it all with laughter, humour, malice, ridicule but without hatred – material, after all, for her future stories. It was not venal. She liked people. She swallowed down all the new woman's world of aching, haunting fantasy and concern with the loins, the bowels, the digestion. She saw, for the first time, the brain as a wet, slippery, red palpitating animal inside her 'thick peasant-shaped skull' and she had suddenly appreciated the difficulty of living, breathing, surviving, the infinite possibilities of death.

'It's a wonder I'm alive,' she breathed one day, thinking of all the accidents to children, their infant hazards, what she herself had narrowly escaped. She said to Stephen when he came to see her, 'Here's a ward full of women who have just side-stepped the potholes; and they have no foresight; they're going to blunder along. Upstairs is a ward full of what they call "the screamers", dying of incurable diseases, hideous, dirty – the nurses neglect them for good reason. I have no sympathy for them, Stephen. We must live: our children must live. I won't die. As soon as I get out of here I'm going to make money in fistfuls so that I'll have all the attention I need, all of us: so we'll never end up in a public ward, not die among the screamers up there. They disgust me. I have no sympathy with suffering and death. If we weren't cruel, Stephen, we'd die.'

'I elbowed diphtheria and suspected plague when I was a journalist. I was always in too much of a hurry and tripped and fell on my nose countless times. I turned a corner in a car dizzily on the ice and knocked down an old man hobbling along on a cane. The cane slipped – he slipped. Oh, it was funny. But I hated him lying there, looking like a bag of old trash. "Why not run him down," I thought. Stephen, I never want to be old, withered, hideous. There is no dignity of old age or disease. I hate the stench of death, I hate death. There must come a time when we conquer death. What's the point of tinkering with salves and bandages? Just to help us to be a cadaver in a mortuary. Life is such a wonder! How did it come about? I'm breathless thinking about it.'

'When you're through with this we'll get you to a doctor to see why you're breathless.'

That is how she became interested in the doctor who offered her long life and good health. Her appointments interested her. Laughing and joking in her usual commotion, she told him her old ideas, extemporized others. The doctor sat quite still with his large dark eyes fixed on her. He had a young rosy face, though he was forty; he had thick chestnut hair. She saw his notes once when he was called away. It said, 'Excitement, hysteria'. He had a pedantic, alien manner. He was 'European'. She thought of his soft, rosy, round face; his type was new to her. She thought of his small mouth, his stubby, rather hairy hands with clean nails. He twiddled his thumbs and one thumbnail was bitten.

'He's the giver of life, he's the giver,' she said to herself. But she felt colder towards him after she read that he thought her a hysteric. 'Those European doctors,' she said to herself, 'with all those neurotic middle-class women. I'm a worker, not like them.' She despised him a little.

Although she told Dr Park she was taking no other injections nor medicines, she was still taking her pills, the synthetic drugs she had first got in Hollywood and which called up the energy she needed to lead her arduous, passionate life. When she came home to New Canaan from the doctor, she talked for hours to Stephen, relating everything to him, what people she had met, what they had said, all with vocal effects, smirking fun, ridicule, exhortations as if to them, analysis, all that had happened to her during the day, what she had read, felt and what strange incidents occurred, the streaming, storming thousands of New York streaming towards the black hole of their destiny and fabricating inadvertently the history of the day. She was a wayward casual scandalmonger, or as she said 'sca-mongerr' and would relate with amused contempt and curiosity too, some family break-up.

One day she said eagerly, 'Oh, how can a woman betray her husband,

134

how can she break up her family? Surely if she does that she has no sense of honour, nothing woman left! I don't see how she can look at people: and think of looking across the room at your husband – or, golly, looking at a man sitting on the other side of your own hearthrug and thinking you had – you'd blush so – there's no word for it. And how could he look at you? The shame, his and yours, thinking what you had done, betrayed everything, your whole world. I can't understand it. Surely everyone would know by your face; and how could you meet his eyes? I don't really dare to think about it, it's so unnatural. How can she ever get back to home life again? Perhaps as a result of much, much suffering – but you could never get back to that beautiful country where you were so happy. But what indignity! How could that ennoble? And then forever to have a nasty secret. Surely, somehow, the children would feel a change? Oh, I think about it and can't understand it. Sometimes at night, those times when you wake up and worry – I shudder, I'm quite frightened and I blush. I just think of meeting those eyes – and I know it would be impossible.'

He stood looking at her, considering. Here she laughed, shaking herself all over like a young tree, 'But the other day I met Hortense at Longchamps and I said, "What happened to you, Hortense? You're absolutely shining, like smoke and fire, you're radiant, you're ringing like a Chinese porcelain bell." And she told me she had a lover. I said to her, "Does he know?" I meant Carlo, her husband.

'"Husbands know most things, but I don't know about this; I don't care," she said. Think of Hortense so devoted to Carlo! We know she's devoted. I only know for me it would be impossible, unthinkable. My honour, all my happiness would be lost, that feeling I have – I think – of being good bread with a golden crust – it would be burnt in the oven to ashes.'

She stretched out her arms, her legs, embracing as much of what she saw, as she could in that instant. 'Here I know I can be happy.'

There were others there, friends from the district, she had met at the Parents' and Teachers' meetings, who listened without rapture; and indeed with slight grimaces of disdain, boredom, disbelief and surprise.

Emily broke out again, that she loved those people with perfect home lives; the Jews where the mother was a queen, the father a king; the Irish, happy, wasteful, hard-working, joyous, knowing how to sing and act; the Germans, such devoted family people with pious fathers, simple-hearted mothers, close to their own blood, jolly healthy children singing folk-songs and going on nature tours; the French, who under the Code Napoléon, made the family a revered, honoured thing, a thing that stretched from end to end of life, like an unbroken chain; the Italians, who died on the battlefield with the words 'Mamma mia' on their lips and

135

who had really invented the devout family idea, mother, father and child.

'And what about us, the Americans?' said Mrs Wetherall, mother of two little boys who lived across the road and who were Giles's playmates.

Emily laughed and said lustily, 'Oh, my mamma public! That good old respectable pie-eating Middle-Western family with papa and mamma, taking colonic irrigations and the children twice as big as anything in Europe – but the Russians maybe – the dreary, thick-skulled, fat-backed, smug, pig-eyed hog-calling Middle West. I guess I like it too, when I'm not with my family. Oh, to hell with aesthetics. I guess we're all right, too, with our orange juice and schools and bathrooms and pie contests and baseball, as good as the rest, if not better. Yes, because civilization is built on the family. That's how it began.'

She told them about her new book, making them laugh with the episodes she was putting in it. It was called *The Life of Murphy*, a family story. They had high hopes for it, thought it would sell to the movies, Broadway, serialize. It ought to pyramid, found the family fortunes, pay for a trip to Europe and for buying a better house here.

She had finished four chapters and sent them to her agent. They had been turned down, surprisingly, by two magazines which had been her surefire markets. American small-town family life, simply, touchingly, gaily treated. What could be wrong? She asked their guests and after the guests had gone – they went early in this middle-class village – she and Stephen sat discussing it. She had had a long talk with her agent, this very day, on her trip to town.

They wrung their brains and later, turned in their bed. Her humour and simple humanity, her formula, pathos, good sense and the drop of honey, were all in it. Lincoln said that the bitterest truths could be made palatable with a drop of honey. She and Stephen saw to it that there was a pot of honey in each book. Sometimes, the drop of honey was a good Catholic neighbour, a journalist of the knight-errant sort, drunk but loyal, an uncle who was the *Deus ex machina*; and the characters never deviated from good American family morals, nor from loyalty to the country and flag. The certainty of the cut-and-come-again sales arose in their observance of these rules.

Was it turned down because one of the characters was a freethinker and a trade-union fighter? Yes, but he was an old man, a bachelor, eccentric; surely, the town atheist was always allowed. Was it because they had made the jokes about the small-town neighbours a bit acid, a little near the bone? Because in one aside there had been a complimentary reference to a Russian scientist? Next morning at breakfast they fine-tooth-combed every line, every paragraph of the four chapters in their carbon copies, and this heart-rending, exhausting anxiety went on each day of that week, when no news came from the agent and each evening when Emily had finished her work, each night in bed.

'My God, what will become of us if you've worked out your vein, if they're tired of it, if you've lost the touch?' said Stephen in an agonized voice, at the end.

Emily said harshly, 'It isn't that. Sales aren't automatic. But they are stealing my market, they're copying from me and there isn't room for all. You know that the last two best sellers are straight steals from me. Oh, what suffering! What a struggle! Stephen, I love you and I often say to myself that I ought to kneel to you for your goodness, understanding and patience, you're a true helpmeet, a real husband – how did I get a man like you? – and yet, Stephen, perhaps we'd be happier if you were a simple salesman, or would go and work for your family at an ordinary desk-job.'

'I can't do it. I've always worked for myself.'

'But Stephen, I don't write what I like! I write for the crappy, shameful money-magazines and I write an LCD type of thing. I'm not writing for myself, but for them – for you and the children.'

'I can't, I won't – get another man! Throw me out, I'm not worthy of you, get another man,' Stephen cried.

What was to be done? Only work, work, work, closing her eyes to the drudgery and calling upon her enormous strength and contempt for disaster.

When she had finished the fifth chapter and with tears, insults, shouts and, near to blows, they had both revised it, to see that all the ingredients were there and nothing to harm, nothing about atheists, Russian science, or anything 'but family hokum, a belly-laugh or two and a shovelful of sentiment', they sent it to the agent. At the same moment one of the first four sketches sold.

At once their sorrows disappeared. They began to laugh. They went to New York for an expensive lunch. In the restaurant they saw Somerset Maugham, two or three editors, a publisher. They had to sit at a table for six and with them were two young men known to Stephen; one of them, an editor who lived in New York, was named Davy and was very attractive to Emily. Stephen took Emily to buy a bracelet and they were very gay on the way home.

Emily asked, 'What did Davy mean? He said, "There's Bennie Tuck-away with three vgb's." Then the Trotskyist husband, your old friend, said "One vgb, one fgb and one ngb." I've been trying to figure it out. I know it isn't blonde.'

Stephen blushed, 'Never mind; and the Trotskyist husband isn't my old friend. Everyone who's disagreeable I notice is my old friend.'

'I saw another man there I recognized, a friend of Dr Park. His name's

Alfred Coriolis, he's a refugee, a laboratory worker and he's been here since the fall of Paris.'

She grinned.

Stephen said, 'Ugh! Refugees now in my happy home. Don't look so coy!'

She continued with excitement, 'Stephen for shame! I meet him every Thursday in the afternoons at Dr Park's.'

'A rendezvous every Thursday!'

'He's a patient; he's always there waiting when I am.'

'So now he naturally comes to lunch with you and your editors.'

'He's a European with taste and refinement. He's had the most amazing adventures with women,' she said, laughing.

'What gall!' said Stephen.

'He's had these adventures because he's innocent, he's naive about women. He can't go far with them because of a heart condition, at least I think that's what he meant. He lived with, that is alongside, a rich woman for six weeks. She regarded him as a mascot. She lived in a villa at Menton and took him to the Casino at Monte Carlo every day to bring her luck. She bet a certain amount, a limited amount, and always won, every day. On the last day she played for him, she won a hundred thousand francs and she gave him ten thousand. That was a bit mean, wasn't it?'

'Give me the address of this bastard and his telephone number. I'll kill him. What was he doing in the Ritz? Did he have a woman to pay?'

'He was with a woman but he paid,' said Emily.

'I don't want any mascots with heart trouble hanging around my wife.'

It passed off in fun and the Thursday patient did not occupy Stephen; but Emily's face was bright next Thursday morning. When she returned, Stephen asked about the Mascot and was told new adventures. She spoke excitedly, brimming over, keeping nothing back. He had been a well-known scientist and society man in Germany, had foreseen the rise of Hitler and had guessed what would happen when Hitler's party began to decline at the polls.

The Mascot said to Emily, 'I knew the international financiers would put him in by force and, after trying unsuccessfully to persuade my colleagues to leave, I myself left and went to Paris.'

At some time before this, he had known a wealthy woman who wore emeralds, always emeralds. He met her through the laboratory, where one of the technicians had done a TB test for her. The society woman asked him to go to Switzerland with her as her personal physician – he was a qualified doctor. He had done so.

Emily said triumphantly, 'But as a physician, that was all.'

138

The woman paid all expenses and his salary. It only occurred to him afterwards, when she sent him home after five months, that she had been disappointed.

'I'd be disappointed too, paying a gigolo for five months,' said Stephen.

Emily exclaimed hotly, 'He's naive, innocent. It never occurred to him that women would pay for – h'm – love, as it were – '

Stephen said irritably, 'And he tells you all this about his innocence. You're a foolish little girl, he found a nice American little girl. Don't let me see you taking him off to the White Mountains to cure your bursitis.'

Emily expostulated, 'But he is innocent. What reason could he have to deceive me?'

> 'Ma mither does constantly deeve me
> And bid me beware of young men;
> They flatter she says to deceive me;
> But wha can think sae of Tam Glenn?'

said and sang Stephen.

'But he knows I'm married with four children and a public character and a believing communist. I couldn't do anything – out of the way, dishonest, could I?'

Stephen got up and kissed her, 'At least you're a very sweet, young, innocent fool, my own idiot wife. To hell with the Mascot. He'll never get you. Tell him that next time you see him.'

The adventures of Dr Coriolis were unfolded week by week. Stephen became sulky and bit his finger when they were told, but nothing stopped Emily's babbling. Breathlessly she related every detail.

'Oh, Stephen, isn't it fascinating? Life is different, it's much gayer, tougher, stranger, more complex in Europe. Here it's just dull corruption, drink, drink, fornicate, fornicate, no love, no romance, no adventures, no mascots. Once when Alfred was in jail – '

'Oh, he was in jail, too?'

'Yes, why not?'

'I can't think why not. How did he get out?'

She laughed, 'A woman came to see him – '

'Of course. He was guileless and couldn't remember who it was.'

Emily laughed with delight.

'That's funny. Yes, he didn't remember her name and she said, "Don't you remember me, councillor?" He had been a town councillor, a liberal, and wanted a rent restriction on slums, or slum-clearance, I forget which – his own family owned slum properties – and he went about making speeches and the other landlords framed him. The woman said, "I'm Countess Werreli" or some such moniker. He said, "I'm sorry, but I don't think I remember you." She said, "Don't you remember the woman in black who stood up in the gallery and threw you a bouquet of red roses when you made your last speech, when the police came in?"'

Stephen said nothing but stared at Emily. Emily continued, 'This countess went to another man who had loved her as a girl and said, "Don't you remember me?" He said, "Yes."'

'A better memory than Alfred I see.'

'And though it was years since they had been in love, he got Alfred out of prison for her. Alfred called upon her at one of her at-homes, took tea, thanked her for the roses and the other service, bowed and never saw her again.'

'Let that be a lesson to you,' said Stephen.

Emily went on chattering. Stephen took to walking up and down the room. Finally, he said, 'Emily, I'm trying to think of my Roosevelt book. I've done ten pages today but there are two or three I ought to revise.'

'Oh, very well, I'm sorry,' cried she and left the room in a huff.

After this she said no more about Coriolis. If Stephen said, 'Did you see Coriolis?' she would answer impertinently, 'Yes, I did.'

Stephen was ashamed and encouraged her to talk about him. He said, 'I do understand, Emily. You ought to have got this out of your system when you were fifteen. But you were working too hard.'

Another week he said, 'Is Coriolis a friend of Dr Park?'

He was an old friend, from Europe.

'Why don't you invite Coriolis and Park down to our next barbecue? Maybe the mosquitoes will eat them both.'

Emily hemmed and hawed, brightened and said she would ask them. They accepted the invitation. Emily began running about the house like a luminous beetle, shining, flashing back light, busier than ever before. Whom would they ask? Who ought to meet these brilliant Europeans? Axel and Ruth Oates, Max Wilvermine, Edward Nonesuch the chess champion (Coriolis played chess), dear Anna, Maurice – all their best, hand-picked guests, with one or two other friends who had lived in Europe and would make Park and Coriolis feel at home. Stephen helped with the preparations, allowed the extra expense without grumbling.

'How good you are, Stephen, to me!'

'I'm not really good at all. I'm a bastard.'

'But you're so good to me, I know you don't really like these two.'

'I don't know them.'

'I'm a dope, I suppose,' sighed Emily.

'You work hard and I'd be a criminal to say no to you. And then I've been a husband much longer than you've been a wife. I ought to try to make you happy.'

140

Emily sat down and looked at Stephen. Stephen looked at Emily. A serious silence fell. After a moment, Emily, with a sober expression, got up and went into the kitchen. He soon heard her bustling, commanding, laughing; and the servants' laughter and loud chatter. He sat still for a moment, thinking. Presently he got up and, going into his study, started looking gravely at the last pages of his manuscript.

The party was a success. It was a warm Saturday, slightly cloudy and damp; this the only hitch, for the damp brought out the insects. While Stephen prepared the barbecue, Emily went to the station twice, once for the foreign doctors, and Hortense and Carlo, once for Anna and Maurice.

On the way up the station ramp to the car, Emily took Hortense's arm and said, 'I'm so glad you came. I want to see you. I want to tell you something.'

Ahead of them were the two dark, middle-aged men. Emily's eyes moistly lighted, ran to them and back. Hortense, a fair pensive woman, with a brusque manner, said, 'You told Coriolis you loved him.'

'Yes. How did you know? I wrote to him this week.'

'I knew it.'

'How did you know?'

'It's obvious.'

'It's obvious?' Emily chortled.

She was very excited all through the day.

Carlo was one of Stephen's oldest friends, a short, plump New Yorker with round head and face, who loved Europe and would have been living there then, but for the war. Emily walked the two doctors round the field, then went off with her arm through that of Coriolis.

Stephen stood by Carlo and said, 'A man like that will get nowhere with Emily. She's sturdy; this is just childishness, a sort of dare; a prank she's playing on me. At most it's a passing fancy. I'd like to spank her, but that wouldn't help. I have to laugh at her instead.'

'Emily's serious and completely loyal,' said Carlo.

'I know she is.'

Meanwhile, Emily was walking around the grounds with Dr Coriolis, showing him the hen-yard, the orchard, the vines swarming with Japanese beetles. Then she took him through the wild patch down to the stream and beyond, to the old mill; and all the time she was waiting for Coriolis to say something about her letter to him; pleased with herself, glad of what she had done. She did not believe for a moment that he would reject her. He said nothing. She chattered.

Coming back they looked at the cultivated patches. On one grew sweet corn, rows of vegetables. The fence was draped with grapevines ruined and burned by the DDT spray. Between the green cornstalks, six to eight feet high, Emily and Dr Coriolis walked, picking cobs to be cooked right away for lunch.

She said, 'And for supper, lobsters fresh too – just caught. That is the only way to eat them. And I am making cardinal sauce. Do you know it? It's exquisite. *Exquis.* One pint béchamel, half pint fish *fumet*, truffle essence, finish with a lot of cream and some lobster butter. Wait till you taste it, Alfred! It's my *shay doover.* I'm a very good cook, Alfred. I even put it in my mamma books, though I blush at that. Alfred, watch it. Beetles have got into the cobs, the tassels and leaves. Alfred, didn't you get my letter?'

'Yes.'

'Yes; is that all?'

Leaning from one row through to the other, she thrust her rosy face into Alfred's, and kissed him twice above the moustache and to the side where there was a descending ridge of soft flesh.

'Alfred, I've had an obsession about that, just kissing you there.'

She laughed, blushed, turned her back and went along the row. She looked through the corn at Alfred, who caught up with her. He said thoughtfully, 'You know I was afraid of you till just now.'

Emily laughed and walked on. 'Oh, I was afraid of that. You see I am so nervous I broke this cob in two.'

'Are you really nervous?' he said wonderingly, looking her over.

'Oh, yes, terribly.'

They came out of their rows at the other end. Here the fence divided Emily's house from the neighbour's. The fence was overgrown with heavy grapevine, quite sterile, swarming with beetles.

'The neighbour is responsible; they do nothing about pests,' said Emily.

Old trees grew along the fence and the vine had reached up to them. At one end was the rest of the vegetable garden with tomato plants protected on one side by plastic sheets; then there was a light fence with shrubs and trees, beyond which could be faintly seen the children's lawn. Here Miss Groyne, the new governess, was playing with Olivia and Giles.

Emily stood looking, then said, 'Put down your basket.' She put her own down.

'Don't you want to kiss me?'

He was hesitant but put his arms around her and kissed her, a cold, loose kiss.

She put her arms round him and hugged him, stood back, said breathlessly, 'Alfred, we are all going into town to an opening next week. Dear Anna has a box and you must come too.'

'Dear Anna is your mother-in-law?'

'Yes. She's full of money. They all are, all but us, we're the underprivileged Howards.'

'Is your father-in-law here?'

'The real one's dead. Twenty years ago. But there's a new one. Anna lives for the family. When there's no war, she goes over to Paris and London every year to visit far-flung branches of the family tree. Ah, Alfred – '

He put his arms round her and she flung herself on his chest, kissing him on the jawbone and neck without thought of self, quite wild with affection. Then she withdrew and said, 'Let's go back to the others. I need three more cobs. Let's get them.'

At the end, she had a few cobs over, but they piled them all into the one big palmleaf basket, which was lined and overflowing with cornleaves. She said, standing back, 'Oh, that looks grand. Everything must please me today.'

She put the baskets on the ground and led him towards the fence near the hen-yard. The hens heard her and became excited. She pulled Coriolis by the hand, as he stood in the furrow of warm earth, with his back against the thick rusted vine and began to kiss him all around the mouth.

He closed his eyes. Emily laughed and rubbed the lipstick off his mouth. Coriolis frowned, and looked sharply at her. Emily ran, picked up the baskets and hurried before him through the opening into the big lawn which stretched from there towards the barbecue. People had strayed among the flowerbeds, and into the goat-field in which the weeds had grown high.

She yelled, 'Look out, poison ivy. Stephen, did you tell them poison ivy?'

She said to the doctor, 'Join them!' and ran towards the kitchen with a triumphant smirk. She said to herself, laughing, 'I cornered him, I made him pay up. Well, a good job done. I'm damned if I'm going to lie awake for Coriolis.'

She had muttered one thing to him while they were kissing under the ruined vines,

'I began to stay awake because of your long lashes – they sweep your cheek.'

'Yes – ' he said.

'Yes – ' she repeated giggling; 'So that's what the other women said? Do you know they say arched eyebrows are a sign of deceit?'

'No,' he said crossly.

'And eyebrows that meet are and narrow eyes are and feminine buttocks in a man are and you have them all.' She shrieked with laughter.

She smiled to herself as she delivered the corn to Paolo, the new butler, gave orders about the steaks, the hot dishes. The tables were already put outside, and the baskets of linen and silver and the trays taken out.

She kept away from Coriolis the rest of the day; but noticed him having long serious talks with Anna and Maurice. She could not help thinking him funny from a distance, a middle-aged, middle-sized podgy man, dark and eager, yet passive, like an invalid in a wheelchair. She detailed his defects to herself with malice.

This Coriolis affair went on till the Labor Day weekend, when the Howards always gave a big party.

Their Labor Day lunch was one of their most festive and, for the Howards, for long memorable. Anna had no car, as she always lived in a hotel when in New York and took taxis. She drove out for the Sunday and Monday with Dr Park. Dr Coriolis arrived by train on Monday morning; Paolo went to the station for him. Emily had been gardening, fixing the barbecue, and still wore washed-out denims with a tublike white middy jacket, white socks and brown saddle-shoes. Her sleeves were rolled up above the elbow showing her strong, fat arms. Her face was a freckled rose and her fair hair hung untidily but comically round her face. She was smiling, laughing all the time. At the corners of her wide-open blue eyes were two small wrinkles. Her hair, the colour of yellow loam, fell over half her summer-baked broad forehead. She was on an eating spree. Her face had become queerly caked with flesh, thickened, yellow and red. The middy jacket emphasised her portly figure, but suited her. Emily had not seen Dr Coriolis for some time. She knew he had had a heart attack; but she had not telephoned. She rolled forward to meet Alfred Coriolis and Ruth Oates, who had come up from the New York office on the same train. She kissed Ruth, Alfred was next; she kissed him on the cheek twice and rolled back on her heels making a sound of jovial relief. As they entered, guests with Anna came out into the hall.

'Haven't you something to wear, Emily?' said Anna, in her usual cool, brief style.

'Oh, this is just a picnic, but if you like Anna – '

When she got upstairs, she quickly put on the new dress she meant to wear, all black with a draped skirt to conceal her prepotent belly, a black, fringed bolero to conceal her bosom. It was well made, it improved her looks. It had a low square neck and short sleeves. She put on a necklace of small rubies with a ruby sunburst given to her recently by Stephen, to match Anna's. She combed her hair back and up; it fell loosely down the back and curled slightly – nothing could be done about it. She fixed in half a dozen small combs carelessly, made herself up lightly, and stepped

144

into her small black slippers. She looked much the same; but now she had a coquettish, cunning smile and her eyes shone piquantly. She put on some gold bracelets, some drops of fine perfume, took a new lace handkerchief from its envelope. She did not even now seem like a woman, but like a thick, loamy sprite, taking advantage of feminine forms and tricks. When she entered the newly-papered living-room with modern paintings in it, she smiled and waved her plump hands, she swooped across the room, behaved as she had often seen her cousin Laura behave. But her cousin was an ordinary siren with nothing original, and this same air and behaviour in Emily was quaint, even breathtaking. Everyone looked at her and laughed in sympathy. She began to chatter, to talk without stopping. Dr Coriolis had been talking intimately with Cousin Charlotte, one of Stephen's cousins, a woman poor and a rebel from her family just as Stephen was a rebel, then an amateur playwright and actress, who was at present dressed in a splendid blue and black, corded silk suit, a French hat and shoes, the gift of her Aunt Anna; she looked liked the heiress she would in the end be.

'But I am poor, really poor,' Cousin Charlotte was saying to Coriolis, with a delightful artificial laugh, a stage laugh, with a roguish roll of her large, tired eyes. She was about forty,. She was made up as ladies are made up, not actresses, she spoke with a drawing-room tinkle or drawl: she behaved modestly as if Anna were her protectress. She drew out a monogrammed black and gold vanity case with a cigarette compartment and offered a cigarette to Coriolis. Emily, seeing this, bounded over to the couple and began talking fast. She saw the eyes of Dr Coriolis fix themselves on her own ruby necklace and star brooch, her bracelets and rings. She was gleeful. She hurried Paolo to bring the drinks, to get Olivia and Lennie to present the hors d'oeuvre, she offered Alfred a cigarette, from a handsome wood box presented by Anna.

She said possessively, 'Did you know we are going to Europe to live as soon as we can get a boat, Alfred?'

Cousin Charlotte said, 'Are you really? Oh, how wonderful, oh, how good for all of you! Oh, I shall come and visit you. The five years of war have been nothing but a waiting period. We have all missed Paris so much. And there is London. Dear battered London. And even Brussels. Do you know I once played in Brussels, Emily? Oh, shall we all meet there next spring?'

The talk continued. Charlotte wailed fashionably, 'Yes, but what am I to do? I'm so poor. I won't ask Mother to keep me. I must get a job. I really must, Dr Coriolis. But it must be something in the theatre. That was my job with the troupe. I organized theatre.'

A discussion started, some saying, How could anyone go back to

Europe with the danger, uncertainty and shortages and revolution around the corner? Dr Coriolis said that there were dilemmas. For instance, though he himself had had to run away, if he went back, he would find enemies who would blame him; and then the gulf of experiences and years between him and those who had stayed would be too great. Some friends had been Nazis, come collaborators, some in the Resistance, some passive and glad to survive 'like the Abbe Sieyès'; and some, like the English, out of it, except for the bombings, the mute dread and death.

But Stephen said Silvermine, their Washington friend, had proved that fewer had died in England from bombings than from motor accidents on the bad English roads with the feebly powered English cars, 'they boil over on a 1 in 8 gradient.'

Emily laughed and said enthusiastically, 'And think of the young people who died in the army and the bombings, who will never die in childbirth, from bad English medicine, from lack of sulphur drugs, from corrr'nry thrombosis, canc'rrr, advanced arrthritis and the diseases of old age. Dr Park was telling me about old age. It's the worst disease of all, so think of the statistics saved on that alone. After all they had to die sometime, it just bunched the statistics.'

Dr Coriolis laughed, while cousin Charlotte looked frightened.

Emily cried, 'Heirs and murderers waiting for fortunes would agree with me – and why, it reduces the murder rate. Think of the murderers who died and of their victims who won't be murdered.'

'Because they were,' said Stephen.

'But think of the injury to health and the genocide,' said Dr Park, feeling ashamed because he had laughed, too.

'What's that – genocide?' said Emily.

'Killing off a race, as the Nazis did: and preventing people from having children. And other things – American soldiers in hospital suffering from social diseases either ruin the maternal chances of clean women, or themselves may never become fathers. Syphilis and other diseases, like tuberculosis were almost ceasing to be plagues; now they are raging. All this has genocidal tendencies. The USA won't feel it, we have suffered so little.'

Emily said roughly, 'So what do we care? We will survive and work out our destiny. We don't want Europe on our backs. Let them die and genocide. Russia can take care of herself. It won't make any difference to Asia. And the American soldiers who were infected, let them stay over there and infect foreign women. We don't want them either. What do these plagues and epidemics and the wars mean? It's nature protecting us. It's the balance of nature. We breed too fast anyway. There isn't enough to eat in the world anyway. If anyone gets a disease or a woman can't have

146

children, it's because they're unfit anyway. Let them all stay over there till no one is alive but the fit and clean. Look at the Black Death! A lot died, but a lot survived. The ones who survived were our ancestors. The others were born to die; they were weaklings. Of course, I realize,' Emily hesitated, 'h'm, well I know that under socialist methods of production we'd have more to eat and not have to throw coffee into the Gulf of Mexico and burn up elevators full of grain as we had to do until we had war to pay for everything. But supposing under socialism every woman could have as many children as she wanted and they were taken care of, no infant deaths and all healthy, no childhood deaths and growing up – there's going to be a terrible problem. We won't get enough to eat. I don't see that it's such a bad lookout for us that Europe has been decimated, as you say, Doctor. There were too many people, hungry, dirty, weak, ignorant, anyway. And they'll spring up again. That's one of the awful powers of the human race, that they're like birds, or roaches or weeds. Gee – it's a terrible problem. It frightens you for us. There are too many of us. I don't see why they don't permit abortion. Any foetus that aborts is abnormal, weak or something anyway.'

'But this is not scientific fact,' said Alfred, laughing somewhat.

Emily said jovially, 'I don't care about scientific fact, I care about survival. I can't weep for victims or abortions; it's bad for me. It's not my nature. It weakens me. I don't like misfits and sick people.'

Coriolis said seriously, 'This is a different matter. This, I understand.'

Emily took him by the arm, saying, 'Phew, phew, the heat. Come and walk around the garden, Doc. There is still some of Stephen's garden left.'

Coriolis hesitated, glancing at Cousin Charlotte's fine silk revers and the lace frill of her blouse, at the earrings she was wearing.

'Come on, Doc, I want to talk to you!' Emily marched him out of sight into the small orchard.

Anna was talking with Axel and Ruth Oates about ragweed, sheep, rose-pollen, blankets, cats. They all had allergies and did not like to go into the garden, even in September. Paolo could bring their food inside to them, from the barbecue. Anna and Cousin Charlotte thought they would try the garden. They both had allergies, and went out discussing the merits of sea-trips and mountain resorts.

'You're going to stay in the States?' said Emily to Dr Coriolis.

'Yes. I like it here. If I go back I shall be a has-been. I am bringing over my daughter too. She is now in Holland. She was married to a Jew; he escaped and they let her alone. Now we will be reunited.'

'Three cheers, put out the flags,' said Emily drily.

They could see the barbecue party. The evening was cooling. The sun sank below the treetops, the mosquitoes were thick, everyone was jigging and slapping to get rid of them.

'Well, then we won't see you any more, Doc,' said Emily calmly.

'I am sorry. You are a thrilling woman,' said Alfred.

'Ah, you can't warm me up again. You let me get cold,' said Emily.

'I was sick, Emily. I was in the valley of the shadow.'

She said, 'Yes, Anna told me the old ticker was on the bum, Doc. Too bad.'

'I think I will go inside now and lie down if you permit.'

'Sure. Go right ahead. Call the ambulance. Call the district hospital. I'll tell Paolo to go and look after you.'

'You are angry with me.'

'I don't give a damn for the whole thing, Doc. Include me out.'

Alfred Coriolis, deeply offended, left her and went into the house. Emily watched him go in; and then herself went upstairs to get one of her pills. She came down in a reckless mood; but she did not feel angry, defeated or sad. She felt that this affair, which had at first seemed to her real love, was just a springboard: she knew more about life now. She was full of an unknown, a fresh energy; and was able to look abroad for some new affair.

'But it has taught me one thing. I am not going to be the little girl I was before. Through Coriolis I grew up.'

She went over to the people near the barbecue. It was getting cool and darker. She took a drink from Paolo and said to him, 'There's a man inside lying down. Don't bother about him. Let him rest.'

She went up to Maurice, hooked her arm through his arm, and walked about feverishly.

'I've got an idea. I'm going to write a horror book, about that most-dreaded figure in American society, a failure. There she is, my Aunt Rose, with quietude, lassitude, hopelessness, accepting her fate – she is despised by the family. And then there'll be a girl who makes the world her oyster like my Cousin Laura and my Grandmother Jane Morgan; and the different ways they do it. And there are those who are cunning in a way and sneak up on American life, like my sister Beth, who's always looking round corners, for a man; and one who accepts the world and lives for it like my Cousin Fivie, an ideal wife and mother, and the brown working-mouse like me – yes, I am that, Maurice, though the others are rolled up in me, and God I envy them and try to imitate them.

'Sisters? Eh? And the terrible aching poignancy of knowing, in a way, for they know, it's all a mistake, and these hectic, drab lives are living for nothing because the country's mindless, and life here is without a system; and it could be better. What waste! Oh, what a splendid book though.

148

Eh-hay, maybe, I'd hit the publisher's jackpot – maybe not, too bitter, too true, eh? We're all so pressed down on every side, like a fish at the bottom of the ocean, as Mike Gold says, with dollars, dollars – I guess a flounder doesn't know why he is flat and has two eyes on one side. He thinks that's fishrightness. Of course, life is not a dream, it's a nightmare.'

Maurice asked her about it and said he liked the sound of it. She knew he admired her and she fired up, especially as she saw in the distance Cousin Charlotte being genteel with Stephen. She said, 'It is pathetic, touching, eh, the way they have been hawking Cousin Charlotte for twenty years. Why don't they get her married?'

'The young men used to wait for her father to die, to get more money. He's always been ill; but he's still running the business.'

'What business is it exactly?'

'Nitrates.'

'Millions?'

'A few.'

She said, 'Oh, Maurice, life, life! What it is. I have a lovely husband, children, home and good servants. I'm a good cook, I'm a success. I've just come through a wild, impossible love-affair – oh, Stephen's not blind, though he didn't know what I felt – who would? Anyone to look at me – ' She changed this unprofitable line of talk. 'Yes, every one of my clan is fascinating and gives me the horrors, fills me with love and pathos. And a great curiosity. The dilemma is great, Maurice. If you stick to the rules, a woman, I mean, you know nothing and you're in actual danger of being a bore, a moral tyrant. And if you don't stick to the rules, you learn something, but you're in danger of sinking very low and having nothing to judge by, no standards. Oh, my family are all magnificent. They have standards and they escape by being mad. Every one of them is mad, even if it is a madness of sameness. They are not, thank God, though, of basic floury goodness with tasteless insides, like commercial pies. They are humans and strange. Oh, I hate the ads, Maurice, showing the lady wondering whether her wash is telltale grey, or her toilet paper crude, the man going home to mother because wifey let the sink get stopped up and the young couple who drift apart because he had dandruff or she – excuse me! And then the mother who reunites them by mentioning trade-names and baking an old-fashioned, fluffy, dee-licious bunch of goo with banana whip and ice-cool guzzle. That's the only life my family *admits*. But they have another. And why not? Can't Americans, too, have passion in middle age and die for love at seventy? Oh, Maurice, Maurice – the lovelessness of our lives.'

She said this earnestly, gave one sob, said, 'Never mind! Tell Paolo to bring me a drink, darling. Pretend it's for you, or Stephen will yell.'

149

She walked about feverishly while waiting for Maurice. When he returned she said, 'For example, Grandma's sly boasting, her slanders, lies, the dramas she concocted quite without foresight, so that she got into messes, the way she kept her friends apart, so that there was no comparing of notes: the manoeuvres, the chances she took. It was magnificent. She was trying to live. In my "Mama" I have to make them so mediocre to make them credible to my public. Americans are not mediocre but they love the ordinary. It's socially safe. Do you want to know a good formula? An ordinary girl meets a man, maybe unusual, but he's a failure, he tells her so. She's an ordinary, pretty girl, that goes without saying, she likes ordinary things, soda-shops, dates, little jackets, a little hat and high heels, and she's got a little nose, not much of a hair-do, some – there's a fascinating story opening; every editor and movie director would fall for it. Let's see? H'm-h'm! She goes for an ordinary job on an ordinary bus and there she meets an ordinary jerk, in fact a regular fella this time. He sells iceboxes, not too successful, of course. She gets into ordinary unemployment and has a damn ordinary time . . . Isn't that melancholy, Maurice? Take another start. A damn bright precocious girl, graduates high school three years ahead of the others and is as well valedictorian. She's not erudite, never read Ben Jonson and Shakespeare, I mean she doesn't wear horn-rim glasses. She gets a magazine scholarship, goes to town, gets the year's prize for journalism, goes to New York, wows them, goes to Hollywood, licks the cream off it, marries the handsomest man she ever saw, and they inherit more or less ten million dollars! That's a true story but it don't suit. It won't wow them. It's not ordinary. Even though the town itself is full of small-town successes, with swimming pools, Japanese servants and governesses. But I've got to write about ordinary punks. Pah! What a dull life! Maurice, I long for another life. Will someone explain why our country, which is crazy for success, is also crazy about the ordinary punk and failure? Why is it? Oh, Maurice, I'm so unhappy, so miserable. I said I had a wild love-affair. It isn't true. It was just a flirtation, nothing but a tease. I couldn't credit it. A European, a man of experience, a courteous, refined, cultured man, with sweet manners, behaving like a high-school tease. Maurice, why, why am I so dumb? The freckled valedictorian always hungry, for some reason, met her fate, and had the wildest good luck and can't be satisfied; but now must dream of exotic and mysterious romance, of someone who lives in your heart.'

She turned to Maurice, put her head on his chest and sobbed. He looked down at her for a long moment and then put his arms round her, 'Don't cry, dear.'

She lifted her red face streaked by wet hair, 'Maurice, I've a hunch. At the end of my road, there's a smash-up! I'll run into a rock and never know what hit me.'

He soothed and consoled her.

'Oh Maurice, I know that you are always there. The thought of you consoles me. I know you are my friend. I don't see you often; but you stand there, in my heart, good and kind. If you knew my gratitude to you. You help me to live. My life is such a struggle. Thank you, dear Maurice, for being my friend.'

Maurice stood back, eyeing her quietly, but with shining eyes and a faint smile. They stood looking at each for a few moments; then both turned and went towards the guests.

When they had all gone, Emily, who was very tired, could not sleep. Her ideas, both for a new book, for a chapter of her present book and for a movie, restlessly moved about in her skull. She had to go upstairs and work on the typewriter. It calmed her and made her feel worthwhile and fit. She wrote a letter to one of her friends who had been at the party. This finished, she sat thinking of Maurice, how kind he was, how he helped her to live. She intended to play him, keep him always by her side. She needed someone and someone in the family was better still.

Stephen, in his flannel dressing-gown, opened the door and stood there. He said weakly, 'Come to bed. You're doing nothing. Are you going to stay up all night thinking of your romance with that fellow?'

She broke into a smile. 'Oh, he's out. He's a nasty little man. I've got to have some time to myself, after the people have raged and gone. I've got such a good idea for a book.'

'You can think of it just as well in bed. I must sleep and I can't sleep when I think you're here with puerile, giddy, spoony nonsense between your ears.'

She burst out laughing, and said meekly, 'Oh, all right. Not a minute to myself.'

In the bedroom, she undressed fast, then sat in her dressing-gown before the mirror looking into her own face, though not at herself. After a while, she said in her warm crusty tones, 'I've got the characters mixed, I must untangle them. With three girls you have to do a superb story-telling feat, so it's not We Three, or Girls Together. One is led into a first sordid adventure, more from exasperation than curiosity even, just so as not to be cheated; and one believes all the rules, no necking on the side; she holds out till the fellow marries her, she has children, she follows all the rules and then smash-up, something goes wrong and she never knows what hit her. She read the ads, she washed her kids' clothes with No-work, she didn't have telltale grey. And now? It's too bitter, eh? Or so

151

real they'll lap it up? No. No.'

She cried, crushing out her cigarette. 'No, it's cheap and wrong. I want a human book people will read. Would she be exhausted in the end – the vital one? Or would she just subside into a normal life, take it all for granted? It's a grand ironical end in a way. But my public's used to the consolation end.'

Stephen screamed, 'I'm ill, I'm ill, my ulcer's playing up. For God's sake, come to bed!'

'The other. Would she relapse into some kind of sex racketeering or social success? Or whine, be embittered or sick or suffer a fatal boredom? Would she too lapse into the wife and mother game? Then suppose she could. Think of the meaning of it! That all she went through, her sorrows and struggle meant nothing. We put up the youth, energy, hope and agony but society gives us nothing in return, only the age-old treadmill? One becomes a prematurely aged cynical sex-racketeer, though of course she's married. One tries everything and is a success and then, just when life opens out – well maybe it does. Let's have a picture of all the hopes offered to any young one who wants to take them, the wave of the future, Poh-poh! Pshaw! As they used to say and with truth. Take the living pants off all these chattering pompous sinister dopes, these semi-skilled radicals. A capsule analysis. . . and oh, the freckled one, the valedictorian, her deleerious sweeping through those easy long ago days of youth, the élan, the bravado and the packaged millennium for tomorrow, the enthusiasm, the easy success of belonging and belonging to heaven and the angels. Oh, my God!'

She burst out crying.

'What's the matter, you goddamn nuisance, stop shouting and come to bed! I'm so sick, I'm ill,' said Stephen.

After waiting for some time, Stephen said drily, 'It's nearly three in the morning. Don't you think it's time you got some sleep?'

Feeling callous towards her husband and with some contempt for him, Emily got into bed and, thinking of the incident with Uncle Maurice, she slid into a blessed sleep, full of light and harmony and without sound. She woke an hour later, in the middle of a dreamed conservation about a classic figure of a young girl in America, a sort of figurehead for our ship, for all her tragedies are explicit in the dying corrupt civilization of our times. 'She is a victim, I am a victim but I have grown up –'

No, no: she must sleep. She thought again about Maurice, whom she now suddenly called 'saviour' and again suddenly fell into the same magnolia-white sleep. She woke an hour later, with early dawn, and her brain went to work at once, for work was calling; but fatigued with the dreary soulless writing she had to do, she began to think once more impatiently of her new ideas.

'She is a victim, an American woman, exactly as an exploited steel-worker is a victim of the American modern imperialism he cheers for. He cheers for it because it feeds him. Her husband sees she's exploited, but he thinks she gets away with it. And who is there to sympathize? Greed is the recognized value; greed is personality, quantity is success, possession is what prevails. Any hopes she had as a child are crushed, foolish as kites which only fly when there's a breeze. She's Mrs Blueberry-Pie now, prematurely white-haired with a big white apron over her big white stomach. . . Freckles is her daughter – she tries to escape and evade. Must this struggle forever end in nothing? Their sufferings are real but are laughed to smoke and powder. Who says any one of us is cheaper than the others? We spring from the same fresh dark water of tragedy. Well, some of us are cheaper: those who know, like me. Alas! Oh, hell, I've got to get up in the morning – oh, hell, I must sleep. Oh, hell, hell. And I'm a success! What would you call a failure?'

Supposing she had married Maurice and not Stephen? She thought of Maurice, the kisses, the kindness, and was asleep again before she knew it. Coriolis had asked her to telephone him. She did not know what to make of it. She was tired of his teasing. She had to compose menus for that week, get up the laundry list, check Olivia's clothes because she was growing out of them, call up Bonwit's about some new clothes for Olivia, telephone Giles's teacher at the break to see if he was getting on all right at school, telephone dear Anna out of courtesy. She should, she knew, have been telephoning people about their manifesto, as they called it, finding out their 'reactions'. Now that it had gone out, she could think of a dozen things wrong with it, or that would sound a false note with others. She could recite many of the passages by heart. She would think of them for a moment:

> William Z. Foster states in his report to the national committee that the most important of all questions is the fight to maintain world peace. There is no world peace. There is already in the east a focus of world war being fanned into fire by the United States. The civil war in China is already an international war – the diplomatic or so-called Cold War being waged by the US against the Soviet Union and all workers' governments, consisting in some part of the occupation of territory which is now or would at once turn democratic if not socialist, without American military occupation and intervention and is tantamount to shooting hot war – what is the use of speaking of preserving peace? Let us fight for peace but not pretend that peace exists. . . The fact is that the flabby, vague and perhaps disingenuous announcements of the committee conceal only very slightly an intention to do nothing at all,

153

to bide their time, to pursue the old line of 'notorious reformism', to quote. Browder has gone, Browderism remains. Indeed Browder himself is only the casualty of the Duclos letter. . . We must mobilise labour's allies in other sections of the population. What sections? And what elements in the labour movement itself? They are all porkchop chauvinist when not self-satisfied, scared for their deep-freezes.

She remembered it hopelessly. All was lost. This manifesto of theirs would get nowhere. 'Forget it. I've got Olivia's party and Anna coming and the whole house to turn upside down. I'm crazy, I guess, I guess.'

That day she did not work on the typewriter at all. But all day she had ideas. Supposing, she thought, while ironing a Swiss muslin for Olivia, I wrote about a woman's life in 1946? At last she hastily put aside something she was doing and ran upstairs to her workroom. She wrote two-thirds of a page of a letter to Maurice, inspired, joyful words; and then downstairs, full of gratitude to Maurice; and she thought, 'What is wrong with our current morality? It deplumes all joy. Look how I can work! Why, with my energy – I could turn out ten times the work if I were happy and in love. What is wrong with passion for others? Our lives are dull and Stephen and I even fight, because our lives are drained of all true joy, the kind you are allowed to have in adolescence before you're tethered to one adult. Then everyone smiles, beams with fellow-feeling. And now it's wrong. We grow up longing for men, we slowly and with what miseries get to know them; and then just when we know them, we must never know them again. Men and women meet each other all day. They talk and laugh and kiss. But how can they know each other except by sex or divination, and I'm no mind-reader. Sex is easier and surer. Oh, how stupid now my wails and gnashings of teeth and what I said about married women who fell in love. Maurice, oh, my darling, you've cheered me up tremendously. I've written a beautiful page which you won't see, but I'm full of ideas, I'm rich, I can work, I'm a full nature, a joyous woman, a full-grown fruiting tree, fruits and flowers and leaves. I've found out a secret and if ever I lead a dull monogamous bachelor life again I'm crazy. No more guilty feelings for straying from the pen. Oh, a crown of roses for you Maurice and even for poor Coriolis, dead stinking roses, and of laurel for me and even for Stephen – poor Stephen, who's so glad when I feel strong, but I don't give a damn for him! He's my jailer. He caught me and he's going to keep me. As a dog-owner can't bear to observe that his dog likes anyone who hands him a bone. A good old nag between the shafts, the blinkered ox treadeth out the grain. Love story. Boy meets girl, but girl mustn't nip a mean husk. Oh, poor Stephen, there he lies asleep at last, poor angel, with his nerves, his flu, his rheumatics, his clinging love, such a darling – 101.2° fever, I ought to worry; but oh, well, he'll get better. In the meantime, I must love and work hard; there's only one way. It's economic. Only, Jehoshaphat, how I've ridden women who've gone astray.'

Stephen got out of bed. He came down to lunch because he had to go to the dentist's. A tooth had begun to gnaw in the night. He was for the moment feeling better. They laughed at lunch and wondered if they might not carry the decision in the Branch.

Stephen said, 'You look well, you look simply sparkling this morning. I guess I'm wrong about you. I ought to let you go your own way. But I'm afraid you'll break down one of these days. Of course the secret, you poor old horse, is that yesterday you had a good day's feed and hunger's always the explanation of your deep psychological revolts, your mental abysses.'

Emily said, 'Ha-ha. I don't mind work, one can say. I worked like a demon yesterday and all morning. I'm glad you're going to the dentist. I can clean out the bedroom. Paolo and Maria-Gloria are off today. I don't know what we pay them for. Maria-Gloria simply scamped the bedroom last time. I wish we could pay on result, but that's unproletarian. I should have the stern nature of my stepmother. Why don't I pay myself at $350 monthly as I pay them? On myself I don't spend half that much each month, not a quarter. Listen, Stephen, stop toying with that milk and go to the dentist. Clear off. I'm busy.'

'Oh, I hate to go to that sadist and you're a sadist to send me. I see a regular gleam of pleasure every time I enter his office. He knows I'm a milksop when it comes to teeth. I'm going to find a tender-hearted dentist who has a nervous breakdown every summer from seeing his patients suffer. Last time I told him, "Ben, I know you're a sadist. Don't save on drugs with me; I'll pay you extra. Why should I suffer? If I were a pretty girl you wouldn't make me suffer. If you hurt me, I'm going to squeal, the first prick and you'll get a thin and pathetic squeal, and if you really hurt, I'll roar. It may please you but it'll drive away your clients." It's so funny, but there are no masochists among dental patients. He promised he'd never hurt me again. I said, "No, and you're not going to hurt my children either." Now he's probably going to give me a damn good jab. I can see his milk-fed, white jowls faintly smiling. He'll keep me waiting while he strokes his hair back and smiles at himself in the surgery.'

Stephen was lounging in his chair with a self-satisfied pretty languor. Full of coaxing petulance and gentle graces, he lounged about the house for a while and then went off to the dentist's. He said, 'Ring me up in about three-quarters of an hour. Find out how I am. If he fills me full of dope, perhaps I'll want you to drive me back.'

Off he went, strolling down the path along the street, in the sunshine, with a small snap-brimmed hat, the picture of the elegant young college man, a very youthful forty. Emily, running upstairs to look at the bedroom, watched him from the small-paned window through the curtain frills. She saw his curly blond head, shining like a dog's coat, gliding along the fence in the side-street. When he turned the corner she went and telephoned Uncle Maurice. After waiting, she got him.

'Oh, Maurice, I want to thank you for coming yesterday and the wonderful time we all had, oh, how lovely. You were lovely, Maurice darling! Oh, how happy you made me with your trust. Listen, darling, will you try to come up for the next weekend? You know the political crisis I told you about? You know nothing about that, but I'm going to need a friend. We're not having a big party; this is select, practically only you, darling, and Anna of course, and the Oateses, they know Europe. It will be the last time we cook outside, this year and maybe forever. We bought citronella and will spray the whole place with DDT in the morning and midday and it is definitely not one of these big routs we seem to have been perpetually getting up this year, with all kinds of people undesirable to each other and sometimes even to us.'

But she telephoned Dr Coriolis and spoke to him in almost the same words. The doctor murmured, 'Oh, next weekend? But you know I must go to Pittsburgh to meet an ancient colleague from Frankfurt, and his lady too. I must tell you that I very fond of his lady once, but of course nothing happened because he was behind her and now it has all passed away. But I have a certain natural wish to see how she looks now. I am sure she looks much older! That will be disappointing to me. Women disappoint when they get older. Except you, Emily. You are such a bewildering, fascinating woman and then – an American and forever young. And then you have such strength, so much of the frontier still in you.'

Emily said, 'Say, Doc, things that might have been said otherwise.'

'Please?' said the doctor.

'Skip it! Well, too bad. Are you sure you couldn't go to Pittsburgh on Monday? You could fly, couldn't you? Listen, Alfred, this former Frank-furter and his lovely pain-in-the-neck – '

'Please?'

'Listen, Doc, I don't like 'em, see? I don't like this Frankfurt and his wandering cutie, for she must be if she was flirting with you. Give me their address and I'll send them a box of exploding soap powder. Why can't you go Monday?'

The doctor laughed, 'You are so original, it really is the frontier; Oklahoma Purchase, no Louisiana Purchase, and Oakley Annie. I have been reading about it, you see.'

'Listen, Doc, don't read so much. We'll have the party inside if you like.'

'I should like this better. They are many mosquitoes now. Ha-ha.'

'OK. It's a deal. Inside; and listen, we'll just sit around and talk to each other, no walking round the corn-rows. Oh, joy, joy, I'll make it a real event, only for ourselves. I'm not even inviting your colleague, as you call him. I am sensitive, Doc, about my parties, since you frankly told me I was greedy for self-expression and that it could degenerate, and that company was bad for me and produced a pathological excitement in me. But still – people do have parties, it's quite an American weakness, it isn't really pathological.'

The doctor still demurred. She exclaimed, 'Oh, please, please, please Alfred! Don't spoil it for me. I work so hard and if you're not here, there'll be no joy for me. That's a truth I only found out yesterday.'

She laughed hysterically, 'Imagine me, I've always had hundreds of friends and belonged to things and worked for things and if you're not there, the whole world is black and I'm cynical – the day's so bleak – oh, Doc, Doc, what have I come to?'

She was between laughing and crying.

He said reluctantly, 'Well, but I have a guest. I was just trying to make up my mind to put off my Pittsburgh trip. Could I bring my guest?'

'Oh, Doc, oh, how delightful! Will I write an invitation for your guest?'

'No, this is kind. I'll send you a telegram if I can't come.'

'Oh, yes, but do come. Oh we both hope so, Doc, so loudly and passionately and truly. Oh, I'll compose the most urgent, endearing, insistent invitation for your guest so that you both can come.'

'Perhaps I must go to Pittsburgh.'

'Oh, Doc, oh dear, oh dear! Oh well – frustration again! Very well. Well, don't forget to telephone me. Doc, you must come. I'll send you a telegram every day till then.'

He laughed, then, 'Don't do that. I'll come all right. I'll persuade my guest.'

She said laughing, 'Oh, Doc, darling, how grateful, passionately grateful I am. I have something to live for. *Salud, Salud!* Goodbye, my darling.'

She turned away from the telephone crossly, 'These Europeans all play hard to get. You have to lick their boots before they'll stir. I can't bear him and I beg and pray him to come. Oh, well – Maurice will see I have a beau.'

The rest of the week she was feverishly gay. Stephen said, biting his lip but hiding his smile, 'What is it now? Are you going to get married? Leave me and get married?'

Later he said, 'It's this damn footling idiot, this magic refugee, isn't it? What has he got that I haven't got? Anna's money? Just like me. He's

157

apparently trying to get Anna to put up money for some laboratory or some such thing. I don't mean he's a gigolo.'

'Stephen, I don't give a damn for him.'

'What can he offer you?'

Emily looked at him in contemptuous astonishment. 'Offer me? That's a real American question; or maybe that's how men see it. You don't suppose he offered me anything?'

'No?'

Emily stood looking at him, torn between anger and amusement.

Stephen said, 'Well, I don't offer you much; why shouldn't you look for a man who'd do more for you? There's nothing strange in that. Only I don't think Coriolis will. If there was a better man about, I'd understand it only too well. There are – only Coriolis isn't one of them.'

Emily said, 'What am I? To be bought with offers? Well, that's silly, I guess. Still, I'd like you both to go somewhere and out-offer each other; it's a man's idea of love. Go on, go and out-barter each other and I'll get two other guys. Men are supposed to be the passionate sex. I'd like the idea of you two shut in a little room outbidding each other. Tell me, if the other man did outbid you, would you yield gracefully?'

Stephen said nothing.

'Oh, pfooey,' said Emily.

'Well, is Coriolis coming to the party?'

She bragged, 'Yes, I telegraphed him and telephoned him every day and I left a note at his house when I was in. The bastard wasn't in although we had an appointment. Maybe he'd gone to Pittsburgh to see this jane of his. The maid seemed mum. I wonder if she is one of his seducees.'

'You haven't much confidence in him.'

'Golly, you don't think I'm serious.'

'I don't know; and I don't think you know.'

'If I were serious I'd pick on Uncle Maurice, not this flirtatious trimmer.'

He looked at her in surmise. She said saucily, 'Uncle Maurice could be a great help perhaps.'

But they changed the nature of the party before it came about. Fourteen members of the branch were invited and Emily, wanting their favour, had made a great effort for the cocktail party and subsequent supper. It was Olivia's eleventh birthday: they were nearly all parents: they must be touched by the child and the loving efforts of Stephen and herself. There she was, as she really was, a family woman. The children were drilled for their parts; and Christy had invited his closest friends. The house was in beautiful order, with not only Paolo and Maria-Gloria, but a butler for the occasion. The house, always fresh and beautiful, was at its best, the windows shining, the flowers arranged by Stephen and Olivia, a striking modern picture. The members of the branch were of all sorts. There were impudent people, devoted followers with no minds of their own, a noisy but ever loyal Connecticut editor, who was rude to all intellectuals and particularly rude to communist intellectuals, because he was one himself; and people from New York, Emily's own editor, a man in tweeds with a pipe, a large British type, Holcombe Oldtown, with a big nose, a mole and swollen lips, a young medico from Bellevue Hospital, the district organizer, a man suspected by everyone of being the police spy in the branch, a self-described 'real worker', who had been expelled from a labour union, the garage owner, the Negro gardener lately joined, some factory workers from newly established light industries, a woman house-cleaner. Some, including the garage owner and the gardener, were shy. There were more than thirty guests half-drunk and shouting when Dr Coriolis arrived. It was about five-thirty.

'Oh, at last,' cried Emily, who had been on the alert.

Coriolis was unlike himself, fresh, slightly excited, bashful. He pulled from behind him a fleshy young woman with fair hair to her shoulders, a long, peachy, oval face, large blue eyes, a round chin; a very sensual girl. She wore a silk dress, a three-quarter coat in blue, and in her hair a wreath of small blue velvet and ribbon flowers.

Dr Coriolis said breathlessly, 'This is my friend, Dr Camilla Bruce. Camilla did not want to come but I told her, at my friend Emily's place she would get the most wonderful things to eat. There is no place in New York, I told her, where you can get for no matter what money the delicious food my friend Emily always has.'

Emily said drily, 'You're welcome' and left the maid to take their coats. Drily she said, 'Come and get your drinks. You've a lot to catch up.'

She became adult suddenly. A good-natured, ironic smile played in and out. She brought them the drinks, sent them the canapés, sent Stephen to them. When she came round with Lennie to give them a second drink, she served the doctor and, seeing the girl in the middle of the floor with a good many people around her, she said to her, 'You must meet people!' She turned, 'Ruth Oates, this is – what did you say your friend's name is, Alfred?' He frowned and told her. 'Ruth this is Dr Camel; Mrs Thornton, this is Dr Camel; Alec Brown, Dr Roberts, Holcombe Oldtown, you must meet Miss Camel, she's a doctor of some sort –'

Alfred's young friend shook hands with everyone, correcting her name, emptied her second drink and herself went to get a third.

159

Dr Coriolis was angry. He kept away from Emily and her guests, talked most of the afternoon to Dr Bruce, and some of the women. Emily was on her high horse, sparkling, dimpling, and embracing her more intimate friends, jolly with the children. She swept by Dr Bruce without seeing her. Stephen was very happy: he smiled like a bridegroom. Every time Emily saw this, she bit her lip. Presently she went upstairs (when Stephen had gone into the garden with Axel Oates) and came down in a much changed mood, challenging, laughing, imperious. She neglected Dr Coriolis and his guest, grew into one of her wildest moods and began to circulate furiously among the branch members, exhorting them, saying the strangest things about the Party, the central committee, characterizing them as men who lived off rich women, all cripples, or with heart disease, saying she had last seen the chief crossing University Place, peagreen, a new-drowned man, spineless with fear, supported on each side by a gorilla, with the fear of the devil in him; and describing his family life; his wife, a foreigner who declaimed socialism while terrorizing and tyrannizing over the servants; one of the servants, a faithful follower who had worshipped the leader for years, and worked free for them, now afraid to go even to the post office. She was not allowed to post a letter for fear she would ask for help, tell someone how she was tortured and sneered at. She was sneered at for her peasant ignorance, her worship of the leader. And the new leader? An immense ball of dough, with an unknown past. And the sacred and famous Albert Coster, one of the Inner Heaven of Sick Men who had not shaken hands with a worker for fifteen years, and their newly furnished office in brocade, plush and thick carpets; their parties, the sacred seventy who were invited to everything; all the scandal and gossip about the Party brass for ten years, during the time she and Stephen had been in the seventy, as well as things found in the mud stirred up by the Browder crash, divisions, quarrels, private matters. Then on to the policy of the Soviet Union.

Almost everyone was drunk and the usual brutal personal attacks, parlour analyses were going on, along with all brands of economic and political discussion.

It was quite impossible for a foreigner like Dr Coriolis to tell friend from foe, the loyal from the renegade. He gave it up and took Dr Bruce into the garden, showing her the place as if he were the proprietor. In fact, he believed himself passionately loved by Emily. He knew she had bought the house and kept it running and thought he could be master of it and her if he liked. He hinted this to Dr Bruce.

Meanwhile, there was scandal at the cocktail party. The words, 'wreckers, saboteurs, Trotskyists, bastards, petty bourgeois poseurs, rich crackpots', had already been shouted at Emily and Stephen by certain

160

partisans led by the suspect district organizer; and this man, suspected of being a spy, coming into the middle of the floor, with a drink in his hand and a cigarette in his mouth and facing Emily, who was drunk and calling to Stephen, spoke as follows, 'I've something to say to you, Howard.'

'Uh-huh, all right, I want to hear it,' said Stephen, who, on account of his ulcers, could not drink and was sober and sour.

This man they called Bake. 'We know all about you,' said Bake, smiling broadly.

'Everyone knows all about us,' said Stephen.

'Yes, I bet they do, you lousy traitor.'

'Do you call this a discussion? Do you want to discuss my ideas?'

'Oh, well, no. I've read all of your stuff. I wasted three lousy hours on it and I think it's terrible; you're a splitter, a damn dissident and I know why.'

'Why then?' said Stephen coldly.

'Come on, make good,' said Emily.

Bake laughed up and down the scale theatrically, 'Oh, yes, you theorists! Don't you know it isn't theory and brain-beating, but action that counts?'

Stephen said, 'We can discuss this some other time. After dinner, if you want to stay with the rest of the branch. As well now as any time.'

He looked round at the members of the branch, some their friends and some friendly acquaintances who had gathered about them, with anxious expressions.

Bake roared with laughter. 'Oh, no, we don't. I read the paper all the time, the daily; it's all you need to read. Why don't you leftist theorists shut up for a while, come off your pinnacle of purity and do a little work for the movement, eh?'

'Well – ' said Stephen

Emily said, 'That's colossal brass. Why don't you? What do you do? Didn't you get thrown out of two or three unions for the sad wreckage that occurred in your coincidental presence? Is that action?'

Stephen hissed, 'Shut up! Let him get it off his chest. It amuses him. Let's see what's in the bastard. Did you ever read my stuff in the *Weekly?*'

Fright and doubt, anxiety and pleasure were now written on the faces around them. The guests had divided. Some had moved away, some outside, others gathered quietly and silently around the arena.

Bake declared, 'Yes, I know they've had their fingers crossed for you since 1945 if not earlier.'

He began shouting with laughter, 'But I didn't waste much time on your stuff. I don't go for the heavy stuff. I hope *not*. And I don't stick my neck out. I should hope *not*. I don't read, I don't think. I work for the Party.'

161

'What do you do?' asked Emily.

'I leave it to you theorists and fancy guys to stick your necks out and get it where the chicken gets it – me, I stay in the Party. Ha-ha. In the Party, not out. Ha-ha. In like me, not out like you. Ha-ha.'

'Good God,' said Emily.

'Listen, we'll have an impromptu discussion after,' said one of the members.

'Not with me, you don't, no unofficial lobbying for me. *Bonsoir!* Goodbye,' said this extraordinary character; and he took himself off, laughing wildly.

'Drunk as a peacock,' said Stephen, turning on his heel and looking at the others with a slight smile. 'If any of you want to discuss this report now, let's go into my study and go over any points you want to raise. I would welcome discussion or even a good beating. If you can show me I'm wrong, I'd like that too. It might get me out of a lot of trouble I'm not looking for,' he ended with his usual self-confessing petulant grace.

In confusion, some of the branch members went hesitatingly towards the double doors standing open; and others walked there resolutely. The district organizer followed them with a sarcastic expression. When they were all seated, Stephen, as if elected chairman, went behind his desk and sat there with a pencil in his hand. He said this was not a meeting but a group of friends, whose advice he was seeking. He asked any one of them to speak up. No voice was raised. Stephen asked them one by one, if they had read his report and what they thought of it, what suggestions? Then each one said either that he had not had time to read it, or was only a quarter through, or could not understand it, or was not theorist enough to judge, or could not make up his mind, or was shocked or puzzled, or would read it before the day set for the next meeting, or thought it better not to take a stand on so extraordinary a document, or thought such things dangerous and whatever the good intention, showed a desire to split and divide, 'the road to hell is paved with good intentions'; and the district organizer himself when all had spoken, said he had read it, and not only would he reserve his opinion and criticism for the proper time and place, but that he intended to do what he could beforehand to show the other members the tendency, that 'of a confused, vicious, mistaken and dissident document'. At this most of the other members looked relieved, although the garage worker and the factory worker said each that he thought he had better read the document carefully to make up his own mind.

One said, 'We must not take the opinion of the organizer or of the Howards, or of anyone. If we have not enough theory, we must use this as an opportunity of sharpening our minds.'

162

A third branch member, a woman who worked in a bookshop, said they must remember that they themselves at a meeting some weeks before had asked the Howards to make a report in writing, explaining their criticism of the committee's report. Said she, 'Since this report is made at our request, we ought to consider it seriously; and each member take the responsibility of his own criticism and his own views.'

Stephen said he would read the report at the next meeting. At this they all rose with relief and almost all left.

But the Howards still had with them Axel and Ruth Oates, an Argentine engineer, Porrez, friend of Axel's, staying overnight; Silvermine, out of a job and about to go into hiding. They were all passionately interested in the Howard document and in the Howards' situation. They were all Party members but believed that the reformism then current, had vitiated the leadership and press of the Party; they thought a housecleaning was needed and might come at this moment of hesitation.

The Howards thought that it was wrong to choose between the old reactionary parties, Republican and Democratic, the same party under two names; they should attempt to found a third party representing labour; that it was wrong to support the quixotic erratic millionaire Henry Wallace, who would change his mind when he pleased, like other rich romantics; that Rooseveltism had not been the hope of American labour, but a romantic form of capitalist consolidation, that Roosevelt had saved American capitalism from its sharpest threat and had only been opposed by the Republicans and Wall Street, opposed merely on gang principles by what they called the Black Hand or true fascist tendencies brought up by war and oppression.

'The next few years will probably prove us right,' said Emily.

Said the Argentine Porrez, revolutionary from childhood, 'Your friends will go to gaol being wrong and be martyrs. It has often been seen; and they will lead the whole army of children and rats into the fastness with their piping.'

The notion that the police had infiltrated the branches, that there was a spy in every branch, was discussed. 'In our branch there is a man who will never be photographed. . . I am sure one-third of the top are police spies, but what does it matter? Why, in any case, do the rank and file stand for their policies? It is the duty of the rank and file to rebel . . . Yes, but no true communist wants to rebel and risk being expelled, it's his life. They know it, these bastards, the supine and the crooked and the blind and the office-holders, and they hold on stubbornly and always will to that sacred invulnerable name. It's theirs. And you can't set up another one. They've got the sacred name. In gaol, out of gaol, wrong or right, they are what they are and you can't take it from them. That is their strength.'

163

Some said 'spy fever'. But Emily said, 'No, we'll end with every citizen on file, like Tsarist Russia or the Nazis.'

'No such files ever stopped revolutions,' said Porrez.

'What no one foresaw,' said Axel Oates, 'was this immense white-collar class, which has to be supported somehow and jobs made for it, as service agents, ad-men, and secret service spies.'

They began to laugh, and told amusing stories.

The Argentine, who lived in a suburb among green hills, red barns, dust roads and pied herds, said his neighbours, his employees and his friends had been called upon by plain-clothes men for information about his habits and his political views.

Emily said in rather a melancholy and sullen way, 'They have no need to question us; our views are only too well-known and they'll be even better known before the month is out. I know we're going to be blackballed. I know we've got our feet on a road from which there is no turning back. I don't know where this road is going,' she said sadly, 'but I know in the night, one night, we passed a signpost, I dreamed about it and when I woke up I shuddered. I shivered all day long, for we had passed the sign in the night, in our sleep and there was no going back.'

'What is this road?' said Silvermine, looking at them intently.

Stephen said, 'Emily is afraid. She thinks she knows we are going to get no quarter. At least we're giving none. She thinks we're going to be expelled. What did that crazy nut yell just now? "In like me, not out like you." I think she is right. But what is to be, will be. The only road I won't take is to be an enemy of the Soviet Union and an enemy of the Party. My belief in them is my life. And if I didn't believe in that, what would I believe in? It would be as if I suddenly did not believe in the ideas of Galileo; or after being an atheist all my life, woke up one morning believing there was an old bearded tribal God. I should become a stupid, doddering old man, I should sit on a bench outside the village store and talk about my rheumatism. Perhaps that will be my end anyway. I won't be a stalwart old man, I'm sure.'

Silvermine said quietly, 'Well, that will probably be my end. You know I've been before the McCarthy committee three times, now; and they have got me out. My answers were good, my work is good. I have never betrayed the USA and never could. I would not spy for my own country, let alone anyone else's. However, you will see. Every single one of my friends has been approached, you, too, no doubt – and most of my friends are afraid for themselves.'

Emily said discontently, 'I don't know. I believe this fight with the Party will bring us only ruin. What use is ruin? Communists should not be ruined: they should stay on top. I have a sense of tragedy for us and you,

164

Silvermine, for us all. I feel ashamed before real revolutionists like some of you, who would live on grass rather than give up; but I wish quite a lot that Stephen and I had just been yea-sayers. We could have sat this one out. Those about to die salute you. I never cared for that. To die for one's country is so fine a fate, that everyone would wish for it, but to die knowingly, meaningfully. H'm, and yet I don't care for that either. I don't want to die or go down battling bravely, while the ward heelers win. Ho-hum, there's bright old Wilkes, who knew all the answers and she's dying for the most up-to-date lost cause.'

To the surprise of everyone, Silvermine, one of their heroes, said, 'Yes, it's hard. No one accepts that willingly. We should win, not lose. We should fight to win. It's stupid to fight to lose. But we have not fought very much yet in the United States.'

'We will fight and we will lose,' said Stephen.

Emily said cheerfully, 'Oh, who would believe, who reads about the USA and the gilded lives of writers and the middle-class, that it is so intricate and full of fantastic difficulties? It's unbelievable. And we're men of goodwill and try to understand the world we live in. It's confusing I guess. Don't notice me. I'm gay. We didn't sleep last night till four in the morning but it suits me. I've been dieting for weeks, so I went off and now for two days I've been eating melted butter, sweet corn, mashed potatoes, mushroom cream sauce, hot popovers, chocolate sundaes, glazed orange slices and chicken supreme. So I can't be as blue as I should be. Stephen, we're making our guests blue.'

She turned to Porrez and said with a laugh, 'But the situation is really getting desperate, isn't it, Porrez?'

When the 'customers' as they called them, had all gone, the Oateses home, Porrez to bed, Stephen begged her to come to bed, not to clean up as usual. The servants were all asleep. She refused.

'I can't get breakfast tomorrow morning in the muddle; and I still have the puritan conscience of my old stepmother.'

When she had finished she went into their bedroom and found Stephen awake. He said, 'Oh, I'm relatively calm and happy. We've passed the first milestone on the way out. It's a rough road and we're going to be sore and angry. That was a nice girl Coriolis brought with him. Is he going to marry her?'

'The Doc never marries. I was furious with him for springing that girl on me. That was why he was so coy. He behaved badly and he knew it. How ridiculous she looked with that intellectual, sad face and those harems in her hair.'

'Those what?'

'Harems. (Hair-ribbons.)'

165

Stephen laughed a long silvery laugh, 'I thought she looked a nice, lovely woman, very pretty, very sexy.'

'You're hideous,' said Emily.

Stephen laughed.

Emily turned her face away.

'Don't be angry with me when you're angry with him,' Stephen giggled.

'Oh, you're a sickening bird-brain; I'll explode,' cried Emily and began quietly to weep. Stephen said no more but soon was sound asleep.

Emily was in revolt and thought of Coriolis only with cold revulsion.

'I have his measure, I understand him now. What a life! How sinister! I've made a fool of myself and I'm a bad mother, bad wife, bad writer. I'm every day more corrupt, we're every day older, the children we're fighting for are every day growing away from us and there we will be, the typical failed American middle-class couple.'

She tossed and groaned. Stephen woke and complained. She said, 'What are we to do? Stephen, help me.'

'We'll talk it over in the morning. Let me sleep.'

She sighed, put on the bedside lamp and took some aspirin. After a few days' respite, her sinusitis had come back.

'Why do I enjoy squandering money when I know the misery of getting it and in such quantities? A worker on weekly wages worries too, but not like we do. With us quantity changes to quality of agony. There he sleeps and breathes at my shoulder, a man who is incapable of helping me, who is only a burden. And Coriolis is lost. I must have someone, even a dream, to help me. And I am thrown back on this breathing, armless log, my fate. Oh, my, supposing I picked the wrong man; and that there is somewhere the right man for me? And yet we're as happy and as well off as anyone in this howling American swamp. Are people really happier in Europe where they don't call names? Or are they suppressed? More suppressed, I guess.'

Her thoughts faded in and out of the sinus pain. She believed her last operation had made her disease worse. New Canaan was a low place with much water about and they all smoked and drank too much, but Stephen. Sinus trouble was the white plague of New York. Everyone had it.

'I can't nurse this damn thing, I must work.'

When it was like this, with dope and pain, she knew that the next day she would be nauseated and groggy, but work she must.

'What I want to know is, is this going on for years; for the rest of my life? I'm wasting time on such thoughts. I've no time to be ill and self-sorry.'

At five-thirty, she looked at the time, took more pills and, thinking through a web of pain, she sank into unconsciousness, a sick groaning

166

sleep. At six-thirty the alarm rang and she got up. Paolo and Maria-Gloria, having worked yesterday, had today off. She had to get the breakfasts, see the children to school. She could scarcely see, black waves of nausea rose over her; but she had driven a car from the age of twelve and had a strong physique, a solid back. She picked up a neighbour's child. When she got home Stephen was up and pottering cheerfully round the kitchen.

'I started some coffee, Em. How do you feel?'

'I feel as if a sledge-hammer has been operating all over my head and neck. I've got to have another operation. And I've got to reduce. I put on five pounds yesterday I know.'

'Oh, that's nonsense. Have some coffee. You're always impossible as a wife when you're reducing. I'm happy. Don't depress me. The waiting is over. The wheels are beginning to turn.'

'I wish to God I could live like other people, like the Oateses or Silvermine. Why all this agony? I shall never understand. If only I could understand. I'd feel better, I think. And this operation, I wish it were over. I must have it. Dr Tripod said it would take three days to heal the septum and it still hurts. The last time it was such damn agony, I'd rather have another baby.'

'Don't say that, for God's sake. That would put the cap on. There's the toast burning.'

He had the mail open, including Emily's letters, and he handed her her letters, commenting variously upon them. One of her stories had been rejected by a high-paying magazine, not funny enough. Another was a letter from Gordon Pymble saying that he was not accepted for a Wall Street press job which Maurice had suggested for him; but that he thought he could offer it to Stephen. Stephen's experience was good, his reputation high, even thought his books were progressive, his family background so good that 'even during the present witch-hunt' they would like to have him. It was a mere suggestion; but he had happened, as a friend, to hear them complaining that now Stephen had no occupation and was troubled by it. Stephen just glanced at the letter and threw it aside.

'Listen, darling, you might like this; just listen, darling, it'd be wonderful if you could work in Wall Street.'

'Why? They wouldn't take a man with my record.'

She cried, 'Oh, damn and blast it, you can listen.' Then she softened, 'Poor old Gordon: it is decent of him. It's 4.30 p.m. to 11. Bad hours of course, but still – you could drive home or get a room in a hotel. It's a high-sounding title, Foreign Financial Editor. Not bad eh? You'd be the New York man. There are foreign financial correspondents in Paris, London, Tokyo – ah'hm, maybe elsewhere. And the idea is that the man in New York would co-ordinate the despatches, edit the currency quotes, translate them into dollars, write a daily leader to go on the financial pages for financial events abroad; and of course, you'd be syndicated. Wow! A coast-to-coast name in Wall Street, that's damn good. Your family would respect that.'

'Thanks! You think that shnook Gordon Pymble knows what it's all about? All he knows is that he didn't get it.'

She stuck out a rebellious underlip. 'Why, I think it's decent of him. He's trying to pay us back for helping him with the house and the money loan and Uncle Maurice.'

'What a crawling bastard, trying to shove me into a desk job and thinking it's wonderful. Well, I guess I deserve it. Who am I to criticize? Probably they all, including this masterpiece of slime, go about thinking I'm a snake, toad, living on my wife. Why not?'

She said gently, 'Listen, Stephen, I know it sounds dull. I've done newspaper work and plenty. I've worked hard for a lot less than this and it's the same pay as you got on the workers' paper. It's $90 weekly, chicken feed right now in NY financial papers, and damn cheap and low; and he says he knows it is a lousy outfit to work for, poor pay, rotten hours, no security, no gratitude, bosses hate you and treat you as Senegalese hirelings and – still Stephen, you wouldn't be planning a career with them; it's a dead alley, everyone knows it. I mean I know, darling, you know about eleven million times as much about foreign finance and finance in general and about general conditions than they'll ever print; and you've got even a sort of knowledge of rewriting cables, making the deadlines, what? They couldn't hope to get another man like you.'

'Don't flatter yourself. There are a hundred men in Wall Street who know more than me; who've spent their days there since they started at fourteen carrying packages, and know the Big Board standing on their head and can do arbitrage asleep, things I just know the names of. I don't even know about stocks, and bonds. Even as a rich man's son, I'm a failure.'

'Oh, Stephen! I wonder if life is worth living. Our life, especially. You don't have to stay there. Tell them you're wildly interested and stay as long as you like.'

Stephen was absorbed in a letter; and merely threw Emily a postcard. She whooped with joy.

'Oh, goody. And he's a gourmet. Of course, we'll go.'

It was an invitation from Uncle Maurice to a restaurant in town to celebrate the birthday of dear Anna, his sister, Stephen's mother; and it was for the following evening. They expected a very lively cousin of Stephen's, Lilias, and with her a famous English journalist; Maurice's friend William; some other members of the Howard-Tanner family.

168

10 ANNA'S BIRTHDAY

It was a restaurant for the rich, built in a horseshoe, with room for the floor-show. Everyone was there but Lilias and her escort.

'She's late as usual,' said Stephen, 'just to show she had a good many other appointments.'

'I don't think that's very funny,' said Anna.

'No, I don't either,' said Stephen.

The others were drinking their cocktails. Uncle Maurice had been directing two waiters and looking at the wines and, after pinning a flower to Anna's dress, he looked brightly around.

'Well, we won't wait for Lilias and Des. They're at a reception at the Russian Embassy. It may be any time.'

'The Russian Embassy? Lilias at the Russian Embassy?' said Stephen.

'Well, I know those, the mink coats torn in the rush for the caviar. And the caviar! Pyramids of the real McCoy piled in cutglass dishes the size of washbowls. They won't leave till dawn. Ah, me. Gone are the days,' said Emily.

'Des? Is it Des Canby?' said Stephen.

'Yes.'

'Des! Oh, marvellous,' cried Emily, clapping her hands. 'We haven't seen Des Canby since the UNO meeting in 1945. Is he here? Why didn't he call on us? Oh, he must come home and stay with us. He'll tell us whether you can go to Europe and when.'

'Lilias wants to meet you. She read *Uncle Henry*,' said Maurice, politely, to Emily.

'It gets me down the people who want to meet me because I'm selling stories by the piece or pound, like sausages. I'm always embarrassed with such people. I'm gladsome, I grin and all the time I'm thinking, I'd gladly choke you.'

'Why should you feel that? Surely you like admiration,' said Charlotte, the English cousin.

'Now you help out in hospitals, voluntary work; why do you do that? Is it for admiration?' said Emily.

Charlotte indifferently was eating hors-d'oeuvre. She took a little white wine. A thin string of diamonds which she wore only in the family ran softly round her faded olive neck. Emily's eyes gleamed. She began to laugh, slewing her eyes at Maurice, who was dressed, slim and neat, by a French tailor. She said, 'Then Lilias does not care for you at all, Maurice? You haven't had a single best seller. Only an honourable mention in scholarly papers. And footnotes in the standard works.'

Maurice smiled and said in his discreet, chattering style, 'Lilias asked me why I wasted my time on that old stuff. If I must write, why write about archaeology? Why not something modern? Something people are interested in, that would sell better. "Why don't you write in the magazines, so that I can show my friends?" she said.'

Dr Edward Tanner, a cousin, said, 'Well, you know, there might be something for you to do Maurice, about our most recent ruins. All Europe's a ruin now. And plenty buried, bones and jewels. They're all antiques now.'

Maurice did not like Edward Tanner. He said softly, 'But surely, Tanner, Europe's out of date, horse-and-buggy. You wouldn't read about it.'

Edward drank his second glass of white wine, 'Oh, surely, that's wrong. I go to Europe every year when there's peace, we visit the medical congresses and the British Association. Surely you can't claim they're wholly behind the times. I would lay it down as a general rule that Europeans invent but we manufacture, use, develop and apply. Take penicillin and radar and DDT.'

Emily objected, 'Surely you can't mean those has-beens invented penicillin and radar and DDT. Those are pure American inventions.'

Edward laughed and said otherwise.

Stephen said, 'You read a Russian encyclopaedia and you'd find they invented them, no doubt.'

Emily said, 'I can't believe it. They maybe got some little angle. But Ed, the diagram of a steam-engine isn't a steam-engine and the fantasy of Odysseus flying through the air, I mean Briareus – '

'Icarus,' said Stephen.

'Isn't aviation.'

But now Lilias and Desmond Canby appeared, and all began to rejoice.

'Let's have lobster mousse and more wine,' said Maurice.

'Oh, we have enough,' objected Anna.

'No, let's have more.'

Emily laughed, 'Quite right, what's the purpose in moderation? What shall it profit a man if he eat a sour crust and gain a long snout? Oh, I should love to be joyous. Bless you, Maurice. It's so miserable to calculate, cut corners, suppress, deny and yawn. It fills me with fury. What I have to take in humility, I give out in pure fury, pure rabid hate.

170

Let's have everything in quantity. Maurice, you know communists believe in that. They think the world's a granary and why shouldn't we all eat?'

Lilias, a big young woman dressed in white lace, said, 'Like rats. They want to eat what doesn't belong to them and what they didn't grow.'

Emily burst out laughing, 'Well, doesn't the world belong to the rats?'

'Rats are rats,' said Lilias.

Emily said seriously, 'Roaches are older than rats. I read somewhere that they are the oldest living things, ginkgo trees, too.'

'Ugh', said Anna.

They were serving out the lobster mousse. Maurice said, 'Let's see how you like this, Emily. I thought of you! Stephen, I never count on. He always has something wrong with him, but you're the dream of a man who wants to give a banquet. Lobster mousse; later you'll have chicken. I know you'll stay the courses.'

'And there's the champagne,' said Lilias.

Emily kept giving out creamy laughs, 'Oh, I know I shall go out looping the loop. But I shall do justice to your splendid, poetic, wonderful banquet, Maurice. I love you, Maurice: you're appreciated in this quarter. Oh, dear, if I am a sort of candidate for the tumbrils in the end, still it is worth it. I can see why they did it.'

'Why are you a candidate for the tumbrils?' enquired Charlotte.

'Oh, dear, the company I keep. You dear people, in fact; and the things I eat. The workers will get me yet.'

'You are a donkey, Emily,' said Stephen, beginning to laugh.

'Why, what are you laughing at?'

'At the way you see an ordinary birthday party.'

'Lobster and champagne. There was a time when I had them every night; but that was when I was working the fashionable restaurants. I see behind the scenes. Why shouldn't I see both sides? Tumbrils coming and going.'

Emily began to laugh heartily, the three other women seemed less amused, and Lilias said angrily, 'The workers in America are really just capable of anything, of any crime, to be greedy and lazy and I don't believe you know what you're talking about. I do. They're vicious and dangerous and I think you're crazy to go to these meetings and even go anywhere near them. I told Des so. You're just children playing with fire.'

Edward Tanner said, 'No, writers see, but they can't do anything about it; so they fret about it more. We're professionals, or people running businesses; we govern workers and it's a practical problem every day.'

Emily said with admiration, 'How ingenious! There's a lot in that.'

Lilias said, 'Well, take my opinion. I've met official Reds and people who know them. I know the embassy crowd in Paris and what they tell me would make your eyebrows turn purple. And Americans are bad enough but when it comes to Europe, especially the French, what they need is discipline, hard treatment. As soon as the Germans quit, the French start rioting again. They're monsters and you've no idea of what goes on over there, in Belgium and France.'

'She hears the tumbrils, too,' said Emily grinning.

Charlotte said, 'I don't believe in tumbrils. The French had them but no one else will. I really see the people, more than you do, Lilias. I went all round England in wartime and for the most part, they're quiet, too quiet and easy to deal with. Well, I mean the English people. I think it's a question of dealing with them. They do anything we tell them to, in the main.'

Edward said, 'The trouble is there are too many of them. It would not be a bad idea to spread a few biological diseases that would gradually weed out the weak ones. We need strong workers. Take places like South America, Puerto Rico. Get rid of them and start again. They are such poor stock, if all the money in the USA were turned to treating them, you'd get nowhere. With the US counselling and aiding, we should start again there. We could even send our own Negroes who have been reared here in the United States' conditions and plant them there. We'd get rid of our problems and make South America healthier and easier to deal with. They'd understand us. Instead of sending all the State Department health visitors, the journalists and professors. They just get infected with the moral diseases down there. I've been down there with a medical party and I assure you there's nothing to be done except to treat them as a museum of pathology. Apart from their clinical value for us, they have no reason for living. It's not worth all the time it takes to go through medical school and all these years of experience to make a slight improvement in a case of yaws. It's a waste of medicine and men. Let's bomb them out with some germ easy to die with and restock the place. We can do it.'

'By golly, Ed, I call you a regular Nazi,' said Emily.

Charlotte wagged her head and fixed Edward with her deep, tired eyes. 'I grant this biological warfare has its uses. Why not wipe out all the germs that are no good, that our children can catch, infantile paralysis and diphtheria and whooping cough, lice and roaches. Why I think it's degrading for us to let them live. You could wipe out the ants and bugs, but other people, Edward, I wouldn't subscribe to that. Even the Nazis didn't do that; well, not entirely.'

'If you wipe out people where do you stop?' enquired Emily loudly.

'What I like about you communists is you're such romantics, it's the human race first last and always, even criminals and diseased natives,' said Lilias furiously. 'And then you parlour reds, like Des and you and

172

Stephen, you make things worse by letting them think they have friends among decent people; that gives them encouragement. I don't know what the FBI is doing. I don't sleep at night. I wake up, get into a sweat and walk up and down. I wonder what the hell it's all about. I wonder if I'm crazy or you are. Look, you kids don't know, that's all, what the workers are like. They like the way they live. You give them more money, they spend it on drink and joy-rides. They don't want to live decently like us; it would kill them.'

Stephen said, 'Me, too. It kills me. It's all wrong.'

Lilias looked at her cousin and said, 'Frankly, Stephen, you make me sick. One whiff of those gentry and you'd fall right over backwards. Why don't you pick out a nice cellar in Chinatown and go and make love to gun-molls with lice in their hair? I know a man from Poland whose brother was carried off in the middle of the night and no one has heard of him since. This man from Warsaw introduced me to a lot of people who were over there and know. This Mr – I can't pronounce his name – said he saw the reds put out a man's eyes and left him to stagger through the street with bleeding eyes. No one would feed him, because they were afraid. At last someone in the middle of the night led him across the frontier and now he weaves baskets as a blind weaver in Vienna. One of his friends was kept in jail for five months and questioned every day. They patiently tortured him trying to get him to confess that he'd sabotaged by working for the Germans as a spy.'

'Well, did he?'

'Don't be silly, Stephen. How do I know? And I wouldn't blame him. I would do anything myself to get them.'

'So you mean he was a spy?' said Stephen.

'I mean you don't know what they're capable of. You never listen to my stories, for instance. I was told at the Ruritanian Embassy the other night – you don't know what crimes the French underground are committing. The Germans are justified in what they're doing. A man absolutely above suspicion, was taking a night walk and a German sentry was found in the Seine. The Resistance was guilty but that man and fifty others, innocent, good citizens were taken. The Resistance were simply provocateurs. I call that mass murder. And then three ladies, I actually heard of, were taken in a car across the Finland border and were stripped and murdered in cold blood, for no other reason but that they lived in a private house and had two servants. That's a crime according to your famous reds.'

Stephen laughed wildly, 'Oh, really, Lilias, you don't sincerely believe that these ladies were dragged about naked and then shot.'

'I know for certain they were dragged screaming from their houses and their servants shot as collaborators because they were working for the rich; they were all taken, servants and ladies and stripped for jewels and shot.'

Stephen laughed.

'Do you really think it's funny?'

'Look at my fangs dripping with ladies' blood,' said Stephen.

Lilias said, 'You're kidding? Well, don't kid so fast. I'll live to hear you goddamning the day you ever knew one of them.'

'Listen, Lilias, a little reason. Here we all live, automobiles and fur coats and orange-juicers and servants and the workers don't have that. Maybe they want paediatricians for their children; they don't want to drink blood.'

Lilias said, 'All that is no excuse for killing people in cold blood. There are a lot of things I want but I don't hold up people in the street. I'm astonished at you, Stephen, defending muggers and knifers.'

Stephen said angrily, 'If you need a job at any time, Lilias, you can probably get one as a reporter in the yellow press; only I warn you there's a lot of competition in your line of political romance.'

'Stephen,' said Emily.

'It's my own lousy family, I don't have to take it,' said Stephen.

Charlotte was not talking. She was bent over her plate of roast chicken, which she was deftly and rapidly consuming. She finished it long before the others and sat there self-contained as always with her brilliant, still, nervous look. Adeline was fond of Stephen and there had been talk of a marriage. She smiled at him; Lilias was truculent.

'If it were not for your labour unions, Steve, we would not have to have spies and security police and goons and strike-breakers. Look at the extra expense for industry! In the USA people are happy unless someone makes trouble. There's enough for anyone if we have industrial peace. I know the men in our own business. We have to have company police and they have to be armed; it's a kind of private army, and there's an arsenal, guns, gas. That's all your fault, Stephen. People are working and you make them greedy. You can make anyone want what isn't theirs with your kind of hot air.'

Charlotte said, 'Well, I don't see it that way. They have rights, the workers, I mean. I'm really on their side. I'm really with Stephen.'

Lilias said, 'Then you're a pair of nitwits or hypocrites or traitors, or all that.'

Stephen turned pale. Emily began to laugh and glitter, in a hurry. 'I was with the police once! Yes. I was out with the state police on a story in the San Bernardino. They let me ride in their car. I was alone, I had to get the story. There was a packers' strike, oakies were in it and oakies were news as well; goons were roaming round the orchards and the packing

174

plants, getting in the way of strike-breakers and strike-breakers getting in the way of the cops. No one knew who anyone was. I shrank literally from going on the story; but I had to get inside and find out what was going on; so I went with the cops.'

'But your sympathies were with the strikers,' said Charlotte simply.

Emily laughed with unsteady heartiness, 'Oh, I don't know what I was then. I was just a working stiff, a crazy, knight-errant reporter, seeing life in the raw, scraping the seamy side, getting material for the Great American Novel. I had to do something like that. I was working my way through college.'

'I didn't know you did that. Edward did that,' said Lilias.

Emily continued with frenzied jollity, 'Yes, yes, yes! Naturally a journalist's sympathies are with the victims, not the oppressors, more with the corpse than the murderer, the sidewalk Venus than the man who picks her up. He's got a safe job, she hasn't. It's a romantic viewpoint, the mysteries of the underworld, sorrows of the underdog.'

Anna said, 'Yes, I can understand that – in young people.'

Stephen looked down at his plate. Emily said hurriedly, 'Well I was looking down one of the apple-chutes and I slipped and rolled all the way down the chute with the apples! The cops had a gala day. Something funny happened! Put out the flags! I was their favourite girlfriend. Ha-ha-ha.'

They laughed at this, except Anna who said, 'There might have been a pulper or a parer at the bottom.'

Emily laughed heartily, 'Yes, there might have been: that's the joke. There was some kind of chute leading somewhere, but I was too fat to go through.'

Stephen laughed. He laughed and laughed.

'You are laughing at me, Stephen!'

'Because I love you.'

He got up and went round the table to kiss the hair that curled round her ear. He said, 'She's such a fool, that's why I love her. I'm behaving like a schoolboy, Mother, but that makes me well. Makes me laugh.'

'You laugh?' said his mother, not understanding.

Edward said, 'We need the cops, I don't care how many J. Edgar Hoovers there are in the world. We need protection. We're producing enormously and the world needs production. Look at Europe now. They need everything we can give them. All strikes should be stopped. We're just encouraging greedy, inefficient people to think they can benefit themselves by halting production.'

'I'll say for you, Edward, you never stop, you're never diverted,' said Stephen. Lilias was well ahead of the others in her drinks, flushed and confident.

'I can *pay* for what I want, for everything I want. So I've got no questions to answer to anyone. I didn't steal it. I'm not in debt. I've never been in debt. If I didn't work, my grandfather and my father and my brothers and my husband worked and they made enough to keep me. Out of their honest labour, I'm honest. I don't fall for that honest sweat line. The reds don't want anyone to benefit from work; and that's the story streamlined without a lot of talk. I get by. I've always done every damn thing I wanted; but I never ran into the law. If you do that, it's because you want to.'

Anna said to Stephen, 'But Lilias is right. You must have aspiration.'

Lilias said indistinctly, 'These damn unionists with their reds come along and want to take my father's and my grandfather's and my husband's hard-earned cash. I stand by them even if my husband left me, the *schwanz*.'

'*Wanze* is the word you want,' said Stephen.

Lilias giggled, 'OK, I got the wrong number. Castration was a slip of the tongue, doctor.'

Anna blushed. Charlotte looked with an enquiring smile, 'Is that a joke I don't know?'

Edward laughed. Maurice said, 'This is a very boisterous party, isn't it? I never thought with Anna here we'd become so suggestive.'

'We're not suggestive, hardly the word, we're frank,' said Emily.

Lilias said, 'I'm not going to be side-tracked. The workers here are vicious, really vicious. I know from a man I know that Edgar Hoover's got everything organized to take over, and I hope he wins. He's all we've got. Hats off. I'm drinking to the best man. To J. Edgar Hoover. Now come on, you parlour pinks over there, and you, Des, I don't think it's fair to eat with us and drink with us and all the time conspire behind our backs; so drink – '

'You're right,' said Stephen, very pale now and rising from his seat.

'Sit down, Stephen,' said Emily.

Anna looked at them both with hollow eyes.

Maurice said, 'Lilias, you oughtn't to make trouble. We all believe in freedom of opinion. You know this is Anna's birthday party.'

Anna said, 'Poor Lilias is sad now. She's just lost her husband and she's drinking too much. We mustn't upset her. Let her feel she's got friends.'

Lilias said, 'You don't *know*. I heard them once in Paris in 1936. I was at school there then. Singing the "Marseillaise". You know I understand French. It says, "Drag them away from their homes, drag them in gutters of blood and hang them to the lampposts." Now by them they mean us. Drown in blood the enemies of the people and the damn aristocrats and the people with money; that's us.'

176

'A spirited bit of verse, if that's what it says,' said Emily.

Stephen said, 'Now listen, Lilias, you're drunk but not stupid. Supposing you had to live on $200 a month – '

Lilias broke in firmly, 'I'd hate us. And I'd try to take it away from us. But I wouldn't join any union. I'd be either a movie star or a best seller or an oil millionaire like I am now, or I'd marry a million. If you think I don't understand the proletariat, I do. I came from there. I know the road. So does Emily. But she got herself all balled-up in some screwy ideas. The workers are gorillas.'

Everyone laughed and the discussion broke up. Anna was taking Lilias home; and the Howards asked Des Canby to come home and stay with them. Their old friends Axel and Ruth Oates, also old friends of Des, were visiting them over the weekend and this was a great chance to 'talk over everything from every point of view'.

Stephen said, 'God, what an ugly life! I'm sick of it. We want to start again somewhere else. But can we?'

Emily said, 'I always had a theory that people get what they want; and here we are – what about that? That's what worries me. That we'll always get what we want.'

When they were getting ready for bed, Emily said, 'Stephen, I was really celebrating for myself, for ourselves tonight. Didn't you notice?'

'I noticed something. I thought you were sky-high.'

'Oh, it didn't matter. I know nothing will dislodge this one. I feel so safe, so sure. This will be a girl and my own darling daughter, just as I want.'

'What?'

'Yes, I'm pregnant. Oh, it's so fine. It's what I want. I always know because of this splendid rich full feeling, this wholesome creating feeling. Stephen, perhaps we will be happy with this one. Do you know a woman feels different each time she's pregnant? I suppose that is the basis of personality; or it's connected – well, this time, I feel as if I'm swimming in a bed of lilies, like those floating islands in Mexico.'

'Oh, this is terrible,' said Stephen.

'Wonderful! Be happy with me.'

In the morning, Des Canby, the Oateses, Porrez, Paolo and Maria-Gloria, the butcher, the greengrocer and the policeman on point duty congratulated Stephen. Emily, passing in her car on her way to school with the children, had told them all.

PART TWO

'Renounce, renounce, on every side, I hear'
(*Faust*, Goethe)

11 TWO LISTS

Des Canby was a British reporter, who attended wars, revolutions and congresses and was famous in many countries for his reports and scoops. His grandfather was Lord Cockaigne, a Victorian Queen's Counsel, his father was once a Tory cabinet minister and Des had been educated at Oxford. He knew everyone at home and abroad. He had met the Howards at the UNO conference in San Francisco in 1945 and was now highly pleased to meet them again in such good society.

'Of course, I remembered you from San Francisco, Emily. Brockhurst and I were sitting at a table and you were crossing the courtyard below, laughing, with a round face and round straw hat with poppies on it, your head nodding and the poppies nodding, and you nodding on your high heels.'

They asked him where he was staying and he said, in a dull, dear, dubious, mid town hotel. His paper didn't give him expenses; he was freelancing.

'The reason I know everyone, my dears, is that I can get into embassy parties on both sides and have a free meal.'

They begged him to come and stay with them. They wanted to discuss so many things; they were at a moment of great decision. They needed his advice.

Said Stephen, 'We're standing now where you stood a few months ago.'

'Where?'

'When you left the Party but left the door ajar to get back if need be. How neatly you did it.'

Emily said, 'You know how to survive. The British do, we don't – an American failing.'

Des said, in the delightful, asinine, British manner he thought would most captivate Americans, 'Oh, I was hoping to sponge on you, stay with you for a night or two. I was fascinated when I found out Lilias was your relation, and it was sweet of her to bring me to your party. I must tell you about my new wife, not the one you met in San Francisco. You know I've had three; not my fault. Number One wrote fantasy stories and so we parted amiably. Then I met a girl on a plane; trouble was, I had only a Mexican divorce, it didn't work. We married but how could I get

181

divorced? I don't think we've divorced legally yet. I do wish you could meet Manthea though. She's a darling. An Honourable, she's a blue-blood, darling girl, beautiful long hair, very impractical, our house is a pigsty. But she's perfectly right always. How can she run a house in London? And we can't get a maid. They're all undernourished, or see ghosts – yes, I assure you, there is a ghost in our house, well, it's a mansion flat – or they get pregnant. Manthea is wonderfully good at managing maids: but she cannot stand second sight or pregnancy or malnutrition.'

'Where is she?' enquired Emily.

'Oh, she's staying with her relatives, squires who ride to hounds, and all that, in a very unfashionable part, I assure you; oh, but Manthea doesn't care, she likes dogs and horses in any part, and she was brought up that way. There's an old castle somewhere, all falling down; old retainers falling to pieces, rattling their gold teeth, starving to death; ghosts rattling their false teeth, but where the ghosts hung out, it's fallen down; nowhere to haunt, poor devils. They have rooms to live in and they don't bother to repair anything. And it's not good enough to become a national monument. Wonderful girl, Manthea. You must meet her.'

The Howards picked up his bags from the midtown hotel and took him home with them, rejoicing.

'We're grateful to you, Des. I thought the aftertaste of that banquet with the harpies' shit all over it would stay with me for a full week,' said Stephen.

Desmond laughed, 'Think nothing of it. That's just social talk. They're simpler over here, that's all. It's *la bouchotte*.'

'What's *la bouchotte*?'

'An American noticed a French friend taking a little spray of hair out of his pocket and smelling it. "What's that?" "Zat eez ze pubic air from mes amies. Eet smell so sweet and eet ees so fine. Eet remind me of many lovely zings." The American is very much impressed. Next time he meets his French friend he hauls out of his pocket a bouquet tied with rope and the size of a bunch of leeks. "You see! I did like you." "What ees zees *bouchotte*?" "Well, friend, I did like you. But yours was too small. I like something I can appreciate."

Des had many stories, but he did not tell them in a string. He placed them. And the Howards began to call things American *la bouchotte*.

They told him their friends Axel and Ruth would be over.

'We're glad of it. We've so many things to decide. And the Oateses, like you, are outside, but inside, inside-outside, and that's the only way you can help us.'

The next morning they told him all their troubles.

He murmured, 'I know, I've heard.'

'Where did you hear?'

'In London somewhere.'

'Oh, of course, we're already internationally infamous,' cried Emily. 'In that case we can go right ahead. So what do we do? The Oateses want us to go to Europe as soon as we reasonably can, remembering we have a family of very refained children to bring with us,' said Emily.

The Oateses had come over. It was a hot, sunny day. They sat inside in the large airy living-room, decorated with broad flowered cretonne, light curtains and Cézannes, had long drinks in front of them, and Stephen displayed again his fears; that he would not be happy in a foreign country, that he might feel like a traitor, that it was not right to desert the country, the cause, the friends he had, in trouble.

Emily pooh-poohed all this, 'We're not traitors and we can have friends everywhere. Communists have friends everywhere.'

But Stephen did not want to fight, to join anything. He wanted to rest: to be a communicant, but to rest. But he wanted it to be known to everyone that he was not quitting.

'I don't want to be thought of as a traitor. Do you know that when I was a boy I wanted to be President of the United States? I thought it was the noblest thing any man could be. To be thought of as a quitter, as leaving the United States – and the cause, too – that would be the end. Nothing – my wife and children, success, family, money – nothing of that would mean anything to me. That's my honour. That's my soul. It is. There would be no future. It would be the black day: *dies irae*.'

'Why worry about it? We're not going to be traitors,' said Emily.

Des Canby, who seemed embarrassed, though perhaps, Emily thought, by their candour and simplicity, cleared his throat and said gaily, 'Well, you've had so many chances to step out and you didn't, why think about it now? You just want to step out for a while. Good idea. Have a holiday.'

Emily said, 'Oh, yes, indeed. We're still on that all-stations train. That omnibus. How many stops has that train got, that started at the Finland station in March 1917? At every whistle-stop people got off. Not us.'

Stephen said, 'Romantics and mystics and people like ourselves looking for new energy, a new aim from the revolution. All there with a personal aim. Well, we're still on the train that started from the Finland station.'

Des seemed bored. He emptied his glass and looked at the drinks table. Emily got him another drink. He drank it thirstily and turned to them,

'Ah, the omnibus! The crimes of the Soviet Union! I know the full calendar. The ones that dropped off at each station as you put it, throng like all the dead of the world. I think about the dead. The dust we walk on and breathe must be the dust of dead men since the beginning of the world, mustn't it? Well, that's how it is with the tribes of the awakened. Those who woke up one day and found the Soviet Union had betrayed them. Do you know how often the Soviet Union has betrayed?'

The Howards were embarrassed now; but the Oateses began to laugh. Axel said, 'Well, I know. March 1917, Lenin went through Germany in a sealed car; hence he betrayed the Allies and democracy.'

Des said, 'Right! And February, 1918, the Treaty of Brest Litovsk, Russia abandoned her allies and became the servant of kaiserist imperialism!'

Oates laughed; he said, 'And March 1918, Lenin dissolved the Constituent Assembly and in mock democratic elections was revealed as the new dictator. May 1918, Lenin in public said he regretted the assassination of the German Ambassador von Mirback, which proved Russia was lickspittling kaiserist imperialism.'

They all began to shout and crow and to throw dates and events at each other.

Said Stephen, 'And 1918 *passim*. For example, Lenin's book, *State and Revolution* demanded the dictatorship of the proletariat, dictatorship, you see, not liberty – '

'I waited months to get that book: it was the title,' said Emily.

Said Stephen, 'The betrayal of everything sacred in socialist democracy. Kautsky cried for war. And what happened in 1919? Russia failed to invade Germany, a clear case. She abandoned the world proletariat. 1924, Lenin is murdered, Stalin takes over the party machine, the State does not fall to pieces as all are hoping; and we have a great weeping and wailing for the betrayal of the greatest revolutionist, Trotsky. All the capitalist states weeping because the only true revolutionist does not get into power. A fine scene.'

Des said, '1923, the party purge – '

Oates said, 'And 1926 the Soviet constitution, a fresh betrayal, for it gave more votes to the industrial workers in the cities than to peasants; this betrayal of democracy was too much for the liberals.'

Emily said, 'And 1927, Trotskyists expelled from the Central Committee; crucifixion of the old Bolsheviks, they cried. The revolution was betrayed definitely this time. 1928, Trotsky was expelled from Russia, Stalin became a grisly murderer, though no one was shot. And then, and then – in the USA and elsewhere began the legend, the real legend. Emma Goldman, old trouper, leading anarchist, could not bear the Russian tyranny and started violent propaganda against Russia and she suddenly was adored by the middle classes; and after living miserably and precariously as an outlaw, she sold her books. And Spiridovna and Matushka, the mother of revolution, a social revolutionist belonging to

184

the *narodniki*, all the old fighters, the romantic revolutionists who had shed so much of their own blood, didn't recognize the revolution once it was organized as a state. Yes, they got off the train in shoals at every station, giving the ticket-collector their paid-up tickets to the real revolution; and settled down – bought little houses in the suburbs, on the way. At each whistle-stop they found the social truth.'

'I shall go on with that train to the end, the bitter end,' said Stephen.

'Where will the end be?' asked Emily.

Ruth Oates was drinking her drinks, laughing often, but saying no word. Emily said in an aside to her, 'I didn't think of giving up my ticket, but it was a shock to me when the Soviets stopped legal abortion. The mother, not the State, should be the one to decide that.'

'Oh, I agree with that,' said Ruth Oates.

The three men were still laughing heartily, throwing dates and historic events, long famous, to each other. Emily listened to them a moment; said, 'And 1934, I remember that. It worried me at first. It was the era of the artists-in-uniform cry – people crying their eyes out over artists! – as if anyone ever cared for artists in or out of uniform! But the crocodile tears!'

'And in 1936, in 1937 – *mille e tre, mille e tre*,' sang Des Canby.

The men went on talking, Ruth listening; but Emily had sunk into reflection.

Towards the end she listened to them again.

'In the Pacific war, she failed to declare war on Japan, leaving us to bear the brunt of the war. She won the war, she could not have done so, but for large American lendlease aid and she is showing total ingratitude to the only country who saved her from extinction, the USA.'

Axel said, 'And what about the twenty-five million to forty million slave labourers – figures varied with passions – exterminated or worked to death in prison camps, the biggest slave system known in human history, not excluding the Romans and the Nazis?'

Emily said slowly, 'Well, honestly there have been moments when my heart failed. By golly, what a canticle you have made! We talk about the crimes of the USA, but, well, with that list, put that way, we've got a shining morning face compared with them – at least you can't blame readers of the morning papers for thinking so. And to think we're losing our shirts and our face, standing up for such a nation, such betrayers of all that's dear to the romantic hearts of the parlour pinks. It's quite a record, isn't it? It wouldn't look good set down in black and white and pasted on the walls of the town. But we all have a terrible record, looked at that way. Think of the British. Well – heigh-ho! History doesn't bear scrutiny!'

They sat a long time over lunch, discussing the family problems of Emily and Stephen; and in the afternoon, while Emily was working, and Stephen out with the children in the car, the Oateses had a talk with Des Canby out in the garden, as they walked up and down from the riverbank to the orchard, or sat in the garden seats. The weeds were high and ripe, the autumn leaves falling. They were old friends, they talked about a lot of things. The Oateses were going to Antwerp as soon as they could get passage on cargo boats. There were few people going to Europe at that time. Desmond Canby was returning to England the following week, for the marriage of 'an old girlfriend'.

'If I'm not there, I'm not sure they'll marry. I have to go. I'm best man.'

The Oateses expected to sail about the end of the year. They begged Des to talk to the Howards and make Europe attractive to them, press them to go soon. Desmond asked why. Axel and Ruth were both quite frank.

'The last few months their names keep coming up. They're going to be called before the Investigating Committee very soon. We know this. They can't stand up to it. You see the way they live? The American dilemma is tearing them apart and will tear each one to pieces, if they stay here. Something very bad will happen. How do you think they will stand up to days of hostile pestering? One of them will break, if not both. It would not only ruin them with their friends but smash them. For what? Let them go. Insist on their going, Des. You can do it. Say you'll look out for them. We will, but then we're poor and without name or fame. You'll have more influence, son of lords and ministers!'

The keen, dark, jaded face of Des Canby smiled. He chattered in his most Oxford manner; but he promised, 'I agree, I agree. I see your point. I'll talk to them.'

The Howards listened to them all; were tempted and then enthralled. It was what they had had in mind and it was such an easy way out.

'People in Europe have seen so much history, no nation has ever been always in the saddle, they understand failure and terror, they aren't like the Americans, who can only win and, if they don't, wring their hands in bleak despair. You'll be all right there. No one will question you or your motives. You can live out your lives happily and return home when the trouble is past.'

This was the theme of their conversations for the next week and when Des left for England, they went to the boat to see him off. They gave him a bottle of brandy, some other presents, were giddy and gay and called out, 'See you soon.'

They meant it.

They discussed Emily's pregnancy too. Stephen said, 'If we are going to

186

Europe soon we simply can't have the baby.'

There were long discussions. Emily cried. But after Des Danby left for England, she had an abortion and she convinced herself that it was right, for she had read a book or spoken to someone who said, 'All foetuses that come to nothing, the abortions, are defectives. They would not abort otherwise. It proves that there is a defect.'

And when this operation was over, she and Stephen had a discussion about the inconveniences and embarrassment of her being a woman. She refused to have a hysterectomy, quite a fashionable operation then. She said, 'Without my sex and womb, I'm not a woman, my character would change, I'd be nothing and I wouldn't want to live. I'm a woman all ways. I like it; and I won't have that.'

Stephen found her a surgeon who ridiculed her ideas, 'That's super-stition, that's an old wives' tale, that your character changes.'

She felt she knew better. 'I know where my feelings spring from, not only the brain, but from everywhere, I am myself everywhere.'

But they found another way, another operation in which the fallopian tubes were twisted so that no more ova would pass into the womb and she would no more become a mother. This she endured. Because of this perhaps, after this, she suffered many pains; another operation. She said, 'The doctors have got their hands on me: I'll never be free of them. Doctors have never been a good thing for me.'

She was still in bed from an operation, this time an appendectomy, when the Oateses sailed for Europe, travelling on a cargo boat, a rocking toy of shallow draught, built hastily for war purposes only and soon to be laid up forever in some weedy harbour. The tall bare masts rocked against the dim stars over a stormy Atlantic and the master was without storm warnings, weather services having ceased during the war and not yet been restored. But the Oateses, Axel a reporter, for his own business, Ruth for him, and a few Europeans, long stranded in the USA, were pleased to return to the bleak, hungry countries, where coal was scarce, milk blue, baths rusty and houses cold; and where some of the quays, docks, streets, city squares, looked still as they had the day the Nazis left them. The Oateses took with them a few valises and a trunk; and in Ruth's purse was a memorandum from the Howards.

'Darling Ruth and Axel: these questions will probably seem silly, but they are the sort of little things that bother Stephen and me and we would appreciate a hint on them; as we are now, thanks to you dear ones, going to move to Europe with our family. I shall keep a carbon copy, dear ones, and if you answer just by number, indicating only yes or no, plus or minus, that would be of inestimable help to me in packing. The difficult ones first.

187

1. Stephen had pneumonia several times, last year twice, and we thought it very serious, because you know the illness he had when a student. He was helped by penicillin and this seems essential. Is it possible to get penicillin in France or anywhere in Europe? Should we have it sent regularly?

2. I have had throat, head and ear infections, helped by sulphur. I need it. Should I bring a supply with me or have it sent regularly?

3. Our children are and we all are, except for the above, big husky people; but we are used to American food and we are afraid that too abrupt a change to European standards may harm us, the children particularly, who are not yet formed. We have heard that Europeans are living on soya bean extracts cooked with vegetables and such things, that potatoes are scarce, while bread is black and indigestible and causes bowel upsets; and milk is lacking. Do such real shortages exist? Is there any way of getting round them, such as black market ways? We're ashamed to put this down, but our children are not used to hardships. Should we bring, or have sent regularly, such items as the following: canned milk; canned orange juice; canned fats; sugar; chocolate; powdered eggs; cocoa; jam; canned meats, as ham, hamburgers; ice-cream; frankfurters? Any suggestions? Are all necessary? Is it true that Americans have special privileges and can import freely without duty, either through their consulates, embassies, or the American army canteens, or otherwise?

4. Should we bring in quantity or have shipped regularly: toothpaste; toothbrushes; aspirin; toilet-paper; simple household drugs, such as bicarbonate, boracic, adhesive tape, vitamin pills for the children, usual household medical supplies? The adults in our household take several drugs regularly by prescription. Should we bring or have these sent – benzedrine, thyroid extract, belladonna. Are such things obtainable in Europe?

5. Household furnishings. We would bring a few books and personal things. But will you please say whether any of the following, or all, are obtainable or at such expense that we would do better to ship them from here: electric refrigerator and deep freeze; electric stove (we don't like ours but still); mattresses, bed springs; chairs, dining-room table; small rugs; simple glass curtains and drapes; lamps, standing and table; vacuum cleaner (Hoover or not); electric bulbs for lamps; electric transformers; sheets; blankets; pillows for beds; sofa pillows; big furniture; chests of drawers; hand- and bath-towels; general household linen; kitchen linen.

6. Kitchen equipment: pots and pans; kitchen knives; services; knives, forks and spoons; plates; cups and saucers; platters; general kitchen equipment, such as mashers, graters, slicers, mixmasters, can opener, mops, brushes, pails etc.

7. Clothes. We would stock the kids and ourselves up with necessary underwear, sweaters and complete outfits and would expect to get changes from the USA as they outgrow; but we are not sure of the timing and want to know if we could buy washing materials and other materials such as cotton, rayon, silks, wools, stuff for play-clothes and dresses, aprons and so on. Should we bring a reasonable supply of such materials to last for a year or two?'

With this was a letter from Stephen, saying, 'The Pilgrim Fathers once again! Here is a letter from the Reverend John Jones to Chief Squahunk: "Greetings! Before we decide to come over on the *Mayflower*, please let us know whether we should bring with us, the following: buskins; camlets, hollands, cambrics; spinning wheels; looms; ewers and brocs; black physic – whether you have or can have obtained by runners or otherwise, the following: mulled wine; mead; cyders – we understand you live on roots and leaves and fire made by rubbing damp sticks together; need we bring flint; tinder; also sheep; fowl?"

'Or my great-grandfather coming from Central Europe to the goldrush: "Dear Smith, Engineer of Mines, I intend coming to your goldrush and at present I have only a small tin box; kindly tell me if I should pack in it, the following comforts to which, although by no means green and tender, I am accustomed, for I am afraid my health may suffer in California: *videlicet*, one large German central stove, tiled and decorated, one suite each Biedermeyer, dining-room and bedroom furniture; warming pans; slippers, one grand piano; sets of meerschaum pipes and so forth?"'

12 LANDING PARTY

The Howards, naturally, travelled first class. They gave a big landing party the evening before the ship docked at Le Havre. When this was over, they received several invitations to dinner in Paris, Brussels and elsewhere in Europe; Johnny Ledane, a banking friend, wanted to see them the next day to help them to get settled; British Mr Scope conferred a favour upon them by asking them to meet him for drinks at the Scribe next week; the Valais family asked them to dinner in Passy, the following week; and Mr Mernie Wauters, a Brussels businessman, said they must really see each other, they must really be friends. Brussels and Paris were as close as suburbs.

After the party Emily went down to finish their packing.

Instead, she sat down to her portable typewriter, wrote some reflections on their last day at sea, a comic description of the party, some political views, with unflattering sketches of the guests. 'Cake-eaters Worrying,' she wrote. 'They feared they were going down and down, but they were going up and up. Faugh is the word and phew! (Or Scope! and Blough!) Caviar contributed by the management, while in the cabin, Madame is typing away on a commissioned article. *What to do when your young man leaves you.* ('Shoot him,' said Stephen. 'Then you get in the newspapers, the vaudeville stage, the movies, and marry a regular guy.')

She wrote to Ruth Oates, now in London, 'Stephen was not very Homeric at the landing party. I would scorn to proselytize such *canaille*, the mean of *passé* European culture. (Also he could not. He had to be *le sophistiqué*.) Johnny Ledane, the banking character, thinks of me as a writer, extremely famous and rich, *cela va sans dire*. I too am getting European culture, you see. He pictured me as a redheaded glamour girl, he said, fresh from the carboniferous jungle (Wilkes-Barre, Pa.) But now he's seen my clownish features (he didn't say that), he thinks, he says, I look more like Simone Simon. I do *not*. Ah, *l'infatuation, l'amour*! He's in love with the daughter of the Prefect of the Seine, if I got it right, maybe not. Perhaps it's the daughter of General Pétain – too old, probably. Anyhow, she's wowed him. It's forever. He wants me to meet her. I said, "They'll be astonished by the American way of making love, no dowry! I think they're dancing hornpipes every night as the boatloads of green

190

American greenhorns draw nearer. What did she do in the Great Muffle?"
I asked nervously. I am afraid she must have been a collabo. Maybe she
sang in a night club for German officers. There's something he won't
mention: so beautiful, but fishy! Well, I have an idea for a new book on
Myself, good, fat, funny, sincere, dramatic, tragic, also a picture of the
USA as seen transparently through me – how is that possible? I'm fatter
than Hamlet. I *never* believed he was fat. Emily Wilkes, in *Double or
Nothing*; by Emily Wilkes. Well, this is the result of fame, however
decayed, shot through and mistaken. I started to tell a certain passenger,
Warner Warner, about myself and he's wild about it and me. He's going
to comb Paris for suitable *appartements* (as they call them), or *petits hôtels*,
that's just a sort of brownstone affair, I gather, and he's going to put us on
to the right agents. Seems Passy is a good place. The catch is the *reprise*,
means hold-up sum for handing over. Oh, well, we'll have to break into
our nest egg with a sledge-hammer and buy a *reprise*. (A *reprise* is also a
mend in your stocking.) I am not going to start on Europe from an attic in
Bohemia. Of course, Stephen did his part, the easy manner, the Princeton
silkiness, the general manner of *le bourgeois gentilhomme*, which quite
carried the yapping stiffs and M. Ulysse Savary away. We invited Savary
to dinner too. Crazy, I think it, as we are going to throw him our
exchange business; but we must take off with some friends and then weed
out. Alas – there is no doubt that Savary was a collabo and he seems
proud of it. Mr Warner knows a wonderful house with four bathrooms, if
it isn't taken, eleven rooms, sixty thousand francs monthly, cheap,
prewar, but of course, a million francs in *reprise*. We'll see.'

She finished this letter and got up to comb her hair just as Stephen
came in.

'Did I interrupt your work?'

'No, some junk.'

'You've made an impression on this bank guy. He's being staggeringly
helpful. He believes in us. I felt my eyes getting rounder and rounder. But
doesn't he see, I thought, that I'm in opposition?'

'Ha-ha. Effect *totale* of the *grande dame*, only show given by me this
afternoon, my best birthday necklace, my fifty-dollar hat, oy-oy, bought
with Anna and I had to pay for it myself; a case of mistaken identity, who
pays the bills? Skip that. My one and only Hattie Carnegie suit, a few
jingle-jangles of the better kind on the freckled and muscular wrist. Well,
I guess I put it over. I could feel it. I ain't handsome but I charm –
sometimes.'

Stephen said, 'You're original, you have style and stop insulting the
woman I love. Ledane's fascinated. Thank God he's engaged to the
daughter of the Prefect of somewhere.'

191

Emily sighed, 'Another American sucker conquering Europe, while he is conquered. Oh, well, I heard you doing pretty well, sneering gently, an easy man-to-man chuckle over the vulgar tourists, in town to see the French starve, and then go to nibble a snack at the Tourte d'Argent.'

Stephen said irritably, '*Tour.* It's *Tour.* We went there on our honeymoon.'

'Well, *tourte* is something – it's a tart, at any rate.'

They wrangled over this for a few minutes.

'Let's call it Touriste d'Argent,' said Stephen in the end.

Disappointed about some rooms they had engaged, they put up at the Hôtel Continentale at first. Emily had to go to work at once on her writing. Stephen went out home-hunting. Most of the hotels had been used during the occupation and few had been cleaned up or renovated: the plumbing had gone wrong, the baths were old and dirty. Stephen saw a few with the requisite number of rooms for his family; but in one, the flush toilets worked slowly, or had to be filled with pails of water; in another the bathroom and toilet were across the hall, accessible to any guest; in another the separate bath with excellent arrangements had not been cleaned since its occupation by the Germans and later by the American troops. Then the curtains, carpets, bed-furniture, dusty and spotted, were unsuitable.

'The children will go mad if I give them their first view of their new life this way,' said Stephen desperately over the phone to Emily.

'Oh, what shall we do? I've spent the whole day on the phone with agents, who not only don't understand my French but speak the strangest dialect, which they insist is English.'

After this, came for them a procession of despair and uproars they had never seen before. Hitherto, though they had often searched for houses, they had done so in their own language, in a country they knew, where they had respect and a bank account that could be checked. Agents who understood that they wished to view and not to rent or buy at once, would drive them for miles in any direction; but here the agent tried to sell them the first house they saw. They kept getting houses that never became theirs. Not only the half-cynical agents but the Howards' friends from the boat kept bringing them to houses. Sometimes they did not find the house. At other times it was so unlike any they had lived in or even seen, that, stupefied, they would agree to take it only to get away from the agent; and then they would run to the hotel and groan themselves into a frenzy. Stephen already regretted their moving. His mother had been for it. Indeed, without her help they would never have got away, with their two hostages, Christy and Olivia. She said that in Europe, away from dangerous associates, they would settle down, forget their bohemianism.

192

Stephen groaned; 'My God, you're not Marie-Antoinette and I'm not the Comte d'Orsay and our kids are not even too bright. They've had, what's worse, the supreme disadvantage of an American education. It's enough to be an American, the future belongs to us; so what the hell does it matter what those frogs over in European swamps know? It's all long hair, anyway. But the fact remains that here our kids are terribly handicapped, they've got to start life over again as ignoramuses from the frontier and I can't ask them to face up to bad food, stomach-aches, bad plumbing, typhoid, too.'

Emily groaned, 'And Anna would simply take Olivia and Christy right back to America. She'd be right. Those two aren't like Giles and me. I guess we can't get stomach-ache. Once he ate two marbles and a shoe-button and absolutely nothing happened. He looked even better the next day. I could ask Giles to live on black bread and he'd probably arise and shine; but the other two are too old. They're used to two quarts of milk a day and meat twice a day. Maybe we made a mistake. Maybe that's why Yanks crack up. Woe is me. But I'm an American and so are they. You have to have generations of dirt and hunger, to survive here: they're like the roaches and the rats. And we're nature's newcomers, for better or for worse. We've got to live near supplies and the American canteens and good restaurants and no matter what, even if the sound of the tumbrils rings through the cobbled streets, oftener than the garbage collectors.'

'What tumbrils?'

'The tumbrils. Sure, oh boy, I guess we're doing our best to qualify for them. Jehesus-Jehosaphat! I'm always doing the opposite of what I want. It's dialectical, I guess. The latest word for selling-out. Ha-ha-ha. Do you know what struck me as so awful, on the boat, Stephen? Those guys didn't even know we were any different from them. Don't you think if we were different, it would show?'

'Oh, bunk. Stop worrying. They go by the clothes and the caviar. They forget when the Soviets win we'll all have caviar. Except for the general.'

Emily said mournfully, 'Ha-ha! I don't know. Don't you think we too have a lot of that *Übermensch* psychology, we're just Nazis with Roosevelt music? All those guys on the boat loved us because they thought we were coming over as natural spies and snoops and overlords and American agents, practically. Those Valais people boasting they were no longer French but Americans and flattering us about the superiority of our culture and our cooking (think!) and our movies, our heritage, our everything – supposing they knew what we think? But Stephen, if we were straight, they ought to have been able to see what we think.'

Stephen said crossly, 'How? That mob never sees the revolution till it's walking up the front stairs. Why blame us?'

193

Emily said dismally, 'I feel guilty. They seem to think we were over for an anti-red drive, or part of the crusade at any rate. I lost a lot of sleep this trip over that.'

Stephen was suddenly depressed. 'God knows! Maybe our trip is a mixture of bragging cowardice and inept retreat. Maybe I'm doing just what Anna bids me. What would we do at home, Emily? The reactionaries are really in the ascendant, they're in, strong, confident and smelling blood. It feels like Munich.'

Said Emily, 'But Munich with the atomic bomb. Ay-ay. Our name is mud, but no one, except in New York City, in the entire surrounding world knows it. Even those crawlers on the boat eating our canapés are not going to spring to attention for us. They'll take our caviar and leave us in the soup when the time comes to play their own game.'

'Let them play their own game and push us out and we're saved. To think the world is not run by Joliot-Curie and Einstein but by small-town, pettifogging birdbrains who think Europe ought to be like Kallikak, Ohio.'

'Maybe we exaggerate,' said Emily hopefully.

'Yeh? What was Hiroshima for? Naughty boy stuff? To show the Russians what we could do if we got real mad. I'll bring along my big brudder the atom bomb.'

'Well, everyone at the cocktail party, except Mernie Wauters and that weight-lifting girl, agreed as to that. Why not bring over the atomic bomb and wipe out the Russians, wipe out Europe's troubles in one big stinking blast! Gee, we've got to get out of this crowd, Stephen. Did we cross the water to get in with the enemies of mankind? Oh, let's quit wailing and get settled in and we'll make the right friends. In fact, we'd better, or it will be tumbrils for two.'

'Oh, shut up, do,' said Stephen.

'Well, I've got to do the laundry list. Bring the dictionary, Stephen. I suppose this time next year, I'll just rip it off on the typewriter in perfect French with subjunctives. What's the word for underpants?'

'We didn't learn that kind of French in Princeton,' said Stephen.

The telephone rang. Someone had found an apartment of five rooms. This was the eighth of that sort.

'Oh, let's take it,' said Emily.

'How can we fit into five rooms?'

'The battle of life continues, then,' she said, working at the dictionary.

At first, the children settled into Paris faster than the adults. Olivia started to collect photographs of French movie actors, Christy bought a beret and Giles began to hate the Catholics, according to the philosophy of the grocer's boy, who managed to make himself understood to Giles on

194

this new and strange subject. The parents found a respectable English woman who stayed with the children in the evenings, when they had dinner-dates.

Their first dinner-date was with a shipboard acquaintance, Madame Valais. She told them, 'It will be potluck. But you Americans will understand that there are shortages and forgive.' She also proposed that they should mull over together the problems of schools and tutors. She had three children of upper elementary and high-school age. Three boys. 'Alas! We are training them for the professions, law, medicine and the professorate; but really in an age like ours, we should make them steam-fitters. First, there will be another war; they will some or all be taken. If they are taken by the Russians they will be sent to the saltmines. It would be better if they learned mining, I suppose; how to blow up bridges. But we do our best, we follow the old tradition. We live according to history – let them have ten years of western civilization and then let the deluge roar!'

Emily sighed, on the way there in a taxi, 'Poor thing! After all, she is a mother. What can we do with ours? Make them steam-fitters? No, Christy must study something. Law or Sanskrit or anything. How lucky the English are. Any boy like Christy just goes naturally into the Foreign Office. Maybe I'll make Giles a steamfitter but Anna would never speak to him. Oh, faugh, Giles has to be at least an architect. Oh, dear, dear, why weren't we born fifty years back or fifty years forward. The Chinese are right. It's unlucky to be born in an exciting age.'

The house was in a small street off the boulevard St.-Germain. Madame Valais had built up a story about how Bohemian they, the Valais family, were, not fashionable at all, living on the Left Bank and among the Americans, who had already started to come over in thousands and occupied the quarters that their generations had occupied for a hundred years. It was an old narrow street with high stone walls on each side.

'Why, it's a sumptuous manse,' cried Emily. There was a tall iron railing mounted on a low stone wall and you could see the flagged courtyard built in carriage days, and unsheltered steps where the porch had been. The front was now smooth, a pleasing, rather low, three-storied façade with classic plain windows and a low, pitched roof. The concierge lived in a lodge at the gate. The Howards admired it. The Valais family did not occupy the whole building. The ground floor was occupied by an antiquary and through his old carved doors, beams, stones, his wooden saints dislodged from churches, his vases and odd pieces, a stone stair led up to the stone landing of the next storey, where the Valais lived. On this landing there were three oaken doors, low and broad, an old carved-oak wardrobe and a large carved chest with wrought iron metal fittings. A rubber plant stood in one corner. A small window looked out through the thick stone wall, to the courtyard. They rang. Emily shifted her feet,

'I'm nervous. What do you suppose a dump like this costs?'

Stephen said, 'I'm freezing. Ye old yule logs, I suppose; or just shortages.'

They were greeted by a maid, with Madame Valais and her daughter crowding hospitably behind, and amid gracious and complex greetings and compliments, they went through a hall in which Persian carpets covered stone flags, into the reception rooms. The hall was very cold. Emily put her wraps in one of the bedrooms, a spacious dark place, also cold; and returned shivering to the warm sitting-room. This room was kept warm all the time, they said, because of the fine pieces of furniture in it. Emily and Stephen sank into deep, somewhat worn easy-chairs and were complimented on the amount of French they had picked up. This encouraged Emily to go into furious French in her Western accent; while Stephen became more and more discouraged and in the end appeared to know no French at all.

Fortunately Madame Valais knew English well. Mademoiselle had spent three years in New York City studying art; and perhaps looking for a husband. Monsieur Valais had learned English at school and had frequently visited the United States. Beside, they said, in the friendly company after dinner, everyone would speak English. There were a few from the boat, a few Parisians Madame Valais thought the Howards should know; among them Madame Leclerc, of an old French family, who ran a small school for the children of foreigners, diplomats, businessmen and rich exiles. She had most modern ideas of education, 'a little leftist perhaps, extremist even perhaps, but a really nice woman and I am sure most dependable'; and Mademoiselle Valais, whose name was Irene, had a friend, named Suzanne Gagneux, a widow, who was a good tutor. The elders had lived in the house in Paris during the German occupation. Madame Valais had gone away with the family for the first eighteen days; but hearing that if they stayed away, their house might be taken over by the Germans, they sent Irene to the United States and returned; and having nothing on the slate against them, they lived quite peaceably under German rule.

'Indeed, it was not too bad; bad, of course! Ah, you Americans can have no idea how bad! And as for the English, they talk of their part in the war, but what did they suffer? I assure you, Madame Howard, there were genuine privations and irritations; and yet we lived as quietly as possible and did not make ourselves objectionable. *A la guerre comme à la guerre*. Things would have been much easier in Paris, for the Germans

196

respected Paris and were quite happy here, had it not been for the hotheads, ill-advised, so-called patriots, thoughtless, selfish people, with improper, disgusting revenge tactics, for which we all suffered. Because of some thoughtless, conscienceless act against a German soldier doing his duty, we had to go in fear of the firing squad. And there you were, sitting at home, quite innocent, while some streets away some unhinged mind might be perpetrating an act for which they would take you hostage. I assure you! These people did not think of their fellow-citizens! When we saw the German police in the streets, every one of us trembled. We were innocent, absolutely innocent, no sabotage, no blood on our hands, yet we might be shot before morning. Yes, it did you no good to have a house, a business, a military career as my husband had. If a German was shot in the next street, they opened a dossier on you, too. Yes, you learn home truths in times of terror.'

Emily, feeling embarrassed, answered Madame Valais, 'Yes, yes, well, well, very true. Well, I guess it's different under an occupation. Yes, indeed.'

Madame Valais said, 'You are such a free independent people, full of initiative and such good organizers! If you ever have troubles over there you will organize yourselves, your communists will be shot at once, your foreigners put into concentration camps and your state will be free to act. You think straight. We, alas, are degenerate. We no longer have any enterprise. What we need is organization, order, as the Germans well saw, although of course, I certainly did not wish to go so far as to become a German state, as some did. They felt that would be a purification. The republic had gone rotten. Only the worst elements came to the top. We all felt it. If it could have come from within of course – alas, the times we live in! And then the Germans did not have a free hand, a fair chance. With the Russians hammering at the gates, how could they organize? And now we must look to the Americans to give us new ideas, new blood, new direction.'

Emily cleared her throat, 'Yes, that's very flattering. I'm glad you think so well of us. Of course, we think we could be improved a lot. Well, well – '

Stephen began with an air that Emily particularly detested, the smooth outdrawing air of a society special agent, 'And so, you remained in Paris during the occupation?'

Madame Valais said, 'Yes, with Madeleine my sister,' and she nodded to the younger woman sitting, without conversation, beside her. This woman now spoke up, in a voice like that of Madame Valais, but a softer, more hesitant voice. 'We had our house here you see. I can't live away from Paris. I can't breathe away from the Paris sidewalk. That is what my

197

brother-in-law always says. And we all agree.'

At a slight, almost unnoticeable movement between the women, Emily was struck by a strange thought. Why was it that the two sisters behaved like twins? Jealous twins? Madame Valais was about sixty, but in appearance much older, excessively wrinkled perhaps by war privations, and with a starved and vulture look, which had nothing to do with her character. She had high cheekbones and high nose, and a little bun of hair on her head. Rags of skin hung round her slender, firm jaw. Her sister Mademoiselle Madeleine de la Roche was younger and was evidently critical of Madame Valais, looking at her sideways when she spoke, evidently thinking her words and ideas misplaced.

Mademoiselle de la Roche said, 'Of course my sister went out little and saw little. We lived walled-in, you might say. My brother-in-law took care of everything for us. He was afraid for us. We knew very little of what went on. We breathed, we lived, that was all. But we were in Paris, we lived on the sidewalks of Paris.'

They began with asparagus soup, made with fresh, out-of-season asparagus, and with cream which could only be got on the black market. This was accompanied by a rather ordinary red wine for which the host apologized.

'One just can't get the right sort of thing these days! Don't you find it a little green, a little rough, Monsieur Howard?'

Stephen said he did, but it was pleasant to find a passable wine at all these days. Then they had poached salmon with mussels sauce, little new potatoes, English style with parsley, and with this a little white wine, white rolls and butter; all black-market of course, as they explained, for at that time nothing but the coarsest yellow or black bread was to be had. Most people were eating it and some feeling ill from it. Everyone but Stephen ate two helpings of everything. The thought of the difficulties made them hungrier.

'Good this, it's swell,' said Emily. Emily's face shone. She said, 'It's poetic! And to think that I thought I was going to reduce in Europe. I bought two satin girdles two sizes too small, thinking I wouldn't get those things here and that as I'd be shrivelling – '

'Uh-huh,' said Stephen.

They were then offered their choice of waters, sparkling and still, and the Americans all took a deep glassful, Emily's still, and Stephen's sparkling, which began to make him ill at ease at once.

They next had cold jellied chicken encased in pâté de foie gras and truffles. The guests who had felt well-fed before, now became hungry again.

Emily said to Monsieur Valais, 'I think that I must soon start to reduce.

198

What a surprise! Me! Who came to Europe to reduce and live high-mindedly.'

'*Tiens*, did you mean to do that?' he said.

'I am delighted. This dish is our personal family house speciality,' said Madame Valais.

Emily said, 'Mighty, mighty good. I'll try to imitate it, the first chance I get.'

Monsieur Valais said, 'This wine now is a nice if not a great wine.'

'It's Lucullan,' said Emily with great pride.

Stephen said, 'I have a little, not much education. I'm not much of an eater, but when I read some of Horace's Lucullan banquets, I myself feel tempted to try. In my opinion, both Horace and Cicero were dyspeptics. Excuse me! Not the word to use here. Now Horace mentions'; and here he gave one of Horace's dinners.

'I thought they ate lampreys and slaves,' said Emily.

Monsieur Valais said, 'You're making us all hungry.'

Stephen said, 'I once cured Emily when she thought she was dying. I read her the specialities of Tours and Blois. She regained her appetite and became well within two hours. She determined she must live to eat those dishes.'

'Really? That's superb!' said Monsieur Valais.

They had then a few slices each of roast fillet of beef with a heavier red wine, and with green beans, and after this a salad of lettuce, eggs, tomatoes and shrimps, of which Stephen wrongly took some. Then came a platter of cheeses, unobtainable of course, except by such people as had friends in the black market, and a wine with that; and then a zabaglione with Marsala wine, and with this the champagne was brought in. Stephen was feeling worse and worse, with a paler and bluer face. He sipped more sparkling water, which hurt him more. Emily took her third glass of dry champagne, Mademoiselle de la Roche took her third glass of sweet. Cake was brought; and then the guests were taken to the salon where they had small cakes, coffee and cognac or liqueurs. Emily got into an excited friendship with a Belgian girl she had met on the boat, and offered to give her introductions for her next visit to the States. She said,

'We know everyone. Stephen is a *fils à papa*.'

People stared, and Stephen, feeling ill, laughed feebly, 'My wife doesn't know how she is painting me.'

Emily cried, 'He is the son of millionaires and not ten-cent millionaires.'

'Real millionaires with a hundred thousand dollars,' said Stephen.

Emily, drunk and resplendent cried, 'Who live under the big top. There's a kind of Howard-Tanner network, coast-to-coast link up. Stephen's family have got their fingers into every pie, they're always married to someone and there are even celebrated Gold Coast reds in his family.'

Stephen was trying to forget his stomach-pain. He said to himself, 'It's no good. And that's how the water comes down at Lodore.'

Emily took three or four of everything, coffees, cigarettes, cakes, glasses of cognac.

Emily was telling endless tales. She said she had bought her typewriter from a fine, honest young salesman who had begun his career in Nevada by squiring women divorcing in Reno. He had had several offers of marriage but wanted to make his own way. 'Original, eh?' said Emily. They laughed.

A young American salesman said that something funny had happened to him in Chicago on his last trip east. He'd had to sleep in the foyer of a big hotel because there was a firemen's convention. A fire had broken out but everyone was so drunk that it caught the whole east wing and several firemen were burned to death.

'That's excruciatingly funny,' said Stephen gloomily.

'Well, I know a thing as funny as that,' said Emily. 'A whole plane-load of pilgrims were going to Rome and they flew into the side of Mont Blanc, and bones and charred flesh and holy images were strewn for miles. There were three Muhammedans there too.'

This funny story cast a gloom. Presently people began to leave. Emily said, 'But I don't want to go home.'

Everyone laughed.

Emily said, 'But I don't want to go home. Don't be so rude, Stephen. I could stay up all night. What are you doing, Stephen? Another half hour and then I'll go.' This remark was received curiously. Emily could not make out people's expressions. She said, 'Oh, all right; I don't know. Perhaps you keep shorter hours in Europe. Well, OK, I'll go home, but I'll come another time. And you must come and dine with us as soon as we have our house.'

Handshaking, goodwishing now began, wishes for success, health, a fine house, good servants and teachers, and all kinds of counter-invitations were given, more courteous than pressing, for 'in these days of shortages, we all know the difficulties'.

The Howards took the Belgian girl in their taxi. She said she thought she would like to practise law in the USA, where democracy affected the laws. Emily said she knew a Supreme Court judge. Stephen said he personally knew quite a few people who had been to jail or who were going, if that would help. One was his Uncle Benjamin, who had been in Teapot Dome and another was his cousin, Felicia, who refused to pay a fine for speeding, without even a licence. Another was a Hollywood friend of his who refused to pay alimony and then there was his sister,

Florence, who had gone to jail during a strike for picketing.

Emily was beginning to laugh, 'To think that we imported a water filter from the USA in case we wouldn't even get good water, here! Haw-haw! The master race. We've got food packets coming from three points in the States by every boat. And we thought we'd have to fill in between the cans with boiled grass and soyabean powder, and perhaps surreptitiously catch pigeons on the public squares.'

Someone belched, but who? She hiccuped. Stephen gasped.

'Most of them do live on that sort of trash,' said the Belgian girl.

Stephen said, 'I know another funny story. I knew a man knew a man who used to go to the Café Royal. Here he met a man named James P. Hudwant or something, originally a Viennese, who wrote operettas and had an immense fortune in Europe, where his music was a hit. When he came to the USA to make his fifth fortune on Broadway, no one knew him or wanted to know him. I used to lend him a dollar or two. He had a story. He had an inheritance in Vienna and it was coming through any time now and then he'd pay back and eat in good restaurants. He had lawyers' papers, letters which he showed. I didn't bother to read them, didn't believe him. He got into the papers because he died of food poisoning. He'd been getting a living picking food out of garbage cans. Three days later the inheritance came through. Three hundred thousand dollars or so. We all used to laugh like hell at him behind his back. America, land of opportunity. Funny, isn't it?'

Said Emily, hiccuping, 'It is funny. You'd die laughing at the poor shnook. Why didn't he either go back or get heard on Broadway?'

'God, answer that one,' said Stephen.

When they dropped the girl at the hotel where her parents were staying, Emily exclaimed, 'Oh, Jee-hosaphat! What a wonderful evening! We're going to love Europe, Stephen.'

When they got in, the lights were on and Mrs Fortescue, the baby-sitter, waiting for them. Giles was pretending that people couldn't hear him and he wasn't going to speak any more. He hid under the bed and said he was going to stay there. Olivia and Christy had fought over a cushion! Giles was in bed now but Mrs Fortescue had had to spank him to get him there. 'Spank him!' Silent with anger, but anxious, they tiptoed in and saw Giles's flushed face in sleep. They paid Mrs Fortescue and sent her away.

13 SETTLING IN

Next day they felt ill. Stephen had sinus and rheumatism, and Emily had sinus, rheumatism and headache; but they spent the day trailing Giles round town looking for agents and answering advertisements.

On the second day they left Giles at home with Olivia (Christy was out on his own looking at Paris) with lunch ordered for the two children, to be served in their rooms; while they went to have lunch with a fellow American, named Harrap, in some way connected with the Embassy. He took them to a restaurant near the Embassy for lunch, where Stephen, who was feeling better, ordered an omelette and cherry tart. Emily and Harrap had little river-trout, taken from the tank and plunged alive into boiling water, head joined to tail, poached and served with butter sauce, then roast pigeons and peas. Mr Harrap then had French salad, but Emily, whose appetite had been wide awake ever since the French dinner party, ate also veal and ham pie, a salad, strawberries and Chantilly cream. They gave up their bread tickets and received in exchange, not the ordinary black or yellow bread (the famous *friandise*) but small white rolls. These, the butter for sauce, their fresh table butter, the cream and a good many other things were of course black-market items; but compensated for by extra charges, which they gladly paid.

Emily, after eating, said, 'I feel rather low at eating so much and in the black market, when in fact people outside are starving partly or totally.'

Harrap said, 'I wouldn't worry about that. They'd still have the Boche if not for us.'

Stephen said, 'One of these days we three will get shot along with the other aristocrats and you'll give up worrying.'

Stephen did not feel well and was sad, downhearted, despairing.

Harrap said, 'That's old stuff. The Germans beat it out of them. They'll never have the guts for that again.'

'I guess you're right and after I've eaten all that, it's too late to worry: they've probably got photographs of me stuffing, taken through the swing-door,' said Emily. She cheerfully filled her glass with wine again.

'I know a good steak place, I heard of it from some Belgians,' said Mr Harrap.

'Yes, me too. It seems Belgians dote on steak. Isn't that staggering,' said Emily. She took down the name of the steak place; and that evening after passing another depressing afternoon looking at addresses which either they had mistaken or were non-existent, or at places which would not suit them (seven rooms, walk-up, bad-smelling, furnished, as Emily said, like the waiting-room of a pre-Pasteur doctor, or four rooms with bath) Stephen said he was going home to drink some milk and go to bed.

Emily said that in spite of their sorrows which were heavy and manifold, she had to eat. She took Christy along to the steak place. She said, 'Thank goodness he is too young yet, or looks too young, for them to think I'm the queen who loved the page; and then, I'm getting so old and fat and ugly, they'll probably think I'm the Ugly Duchess with a secretary, or else I'm his great-aunt.'

They took a taxi for which Christy gallantly paid. Christy recited Shakespeare in the taxi, to Emily's delight, and behaved like a pretty boy of wealth and elegance.

'Mademoiselle Valais on the boat told me that mussels are the speciality of Brussels and we must go there just to taste them – 107 ways of making them! Let's take the train, muscle in on Brussels,' said he.

'Oh, how clever of you, darling!' exclaimed Emily, genuinely surprised.

The restaurant was a small room with shaded lights and delicate flowers, where almost everyone sat on the plush benches. Emily and her son were not noticed till Emily began to call out in her unabashed sonorous French, aided by Christy, who had more accent but less confidence. Nevertheless, a well-dressed captain, a wine waiter and a sourlooking but correct waiter, all spoke to them in sufficient Anglo-French for them to order sole with white wine, rare steak with sweet butter melting on it to compose the sauce which tasted of chives, cauliflower, sauce Mornay, french salad and then profiteroles with which Emily once more had *crème* Chantilly.

Said Emily to Christy, who was paying, 'Oh, my goodness Christy, and what is the price of this after all, in dollars? To think of the time we ate with Anna at The Bell-Glass, just before we left, ten dollars a crack, and nothing to eat, just a whisper born on the air, a hint of what was going on in the kitchen; how to serve a thousand New Yorkers on two loaves and five fishes; and The Racecourse, a beggarly midtown coffee-pot for office-lunchers where you can't get out under four-fifty a head, with cocktails, wine, champagne, coffee, bread, butter, cream all extra. I'm going to live in Europe forever! Garr-song! *Savez-vous* that it's not dear here at all. *Amérique* is much dearer. You couldn't get a jambong sandwich in New York for the price of this superb feast! Banquet superb!'

After, she wanted to take Christy to a café but the cafés closed early in those days of shortages, took in their chairs and tables, closed their shutters. So they took a taxi and went back to the hotel. Stephen was wretched and disagreeable. Giles had been unhappy. 'He's turning into a neurotic! He thinks we'll have no roof over our heads and I won't get a job and we'll have no money. That's the upshot of all this.' He seized Emily's large handbag, which as usual was open with its contents showing, handkerchiefs, letters, wads of bills, rings, in the pink satin pouches.

'How much did you spend this evening?' She told him. He was angry.

'I can't help it. The more trouble I have, the more I eat. I'll take off ten kilos as soon as we get a home. My eating keeps the family together; it keeps me cheerful.'

The following day they started out again. Said Stephen, 'Everything's hideous beyond belief. I wish we'd never started out on this wild-goose chase! Where is it getting us? Do you know how much we've spent the last week? Entertaining, being entertained, running about celebrating to get relief from our miseries. And not counting the hotel, we've already run through as much as would last a month at home. We came here to save money.'

'We will; and besides we've got to find a place soon, for I've got to settle down and make money. We've simply got to get this place on the avenue Président-Wilson. I'll pay more than he's asking just to get a home. If only we didn't have this hideous business of our three wretched, sad darlings. Hotel life is not for babies. And Jeehosaphat, I feel so fat and ugly and Giles thinks people can't hear him; and Olivia is getting neurotic because she doesn't know if they're complimenting her in this foreign lingo. I don't want her to turn into a sour, suspicious coquette and a bitter flirt. Oh, lor, children! I'm morose as well as you, Stephen. Of course, it's a healthy, enjoyable, wonderful neurosis, the one I have; it's not like taking to drink or drugs, which get you hangovers and bad moods and suicidal impulses and make you betray your best friends and fawn on the police, so that you become a social problem. But, oh my, though it's enjoyable, I daren't run for the bus because people laugh and God knows the others, the hungry ones, probably want to stick a knife into my ribs to see whether truffles, sausages and pâté de foie gras will run out; as surely they will. The food's superb – the situation's terrible – and look at me!'

In the evening they heard from their two agents that apartments they had hoped for were out of reach. This created domestic disorder, real trouble in the Howard family. Giles wept, under the impression that they would never get a home and be too poor to pay the rent in the hotel. While Emily and Stephen took it in turns to calm him, Olivia and Christy began to quarrel again, with shrieks, scuffling and hard words. 'Is this our serene, sweet little princess?' said Emily, sadly, to Stephen; 'and

204

look at Christy drooling insults! In the taxi the other day he was a genuine scion. I was so proud of him. Stephen, the family's breaking under the strain.'

Stephen separated the two, found them at it again in a moment, sat down dismally, ran his fingers through his hair and, dragging off his tie and shoes, threw them into corners of the room. He whined, 'And if that house, that little den, had come through – what about the ton or so of cargo that's coming by the next boat? Eh? Store them with the concierge? The water-filter, the record-player, the records, Christy's piano? We're crazy. If I could, I'd go back to the USA tonight. All right, let the bogyman get me.'

Immediately after this, Mr Harrap, who thought of the Howards as very rich and distinguished persons, rang from downstairs, waiting to take Stephen to see a small house to let. Stephen beat his hands on the table.

'I won't, I won't go about the world taking houses.'

'What about the children? What about the furniture? What about me getting to work? Let's take anything, provided there's a flush toilet and a kitchen. By gosh, I'll buy a rubber bath, I'll install plumbing, if there's a toilet or two, for the first couple of nights.'

Giles stopped wailing and asked if they had a house. Olivia came in looking wicked, but she said gently, 'A house! Oh, let's take a house!' Christy came in and looked with melancholy sweetness at them.

'I'll go, all right, all right, don't scream at me,' said Stephen.

Emily asked, 'Because how are we going to fit in everything without a house? Maybe we could go to the Côte d'Azure. We'd have a garden too; and I could be quiet.'

Stephen flew into a rage, 'And what would I do in a garden? You want to keep me for a pet? Of all the damnfool adventures I let myself be persuaded into – OK, OK, I know we're political refugees; but maybe we could simply have bought our way out of it with less money than this. Just bowed out and said nothing.'

'And Florence? What would she think – ?'

Stephen seized his hat and made for the door,

'Don't say another word or I'll fly back to the USA tomorrow. Oh, God, if only I could. I can't see the kids suffering in grandeur at these towering prices. You don't count; I have to. We'll soon be kaput at this rate. Pieces of eight wouldn't keep us alive with this band of kids, a week. There's my nephew, a relative of the Federal Reserve Bank in my sight, and I have to buy cellar to attic to keep up with him, and my daughter, a dainty midget, relative of the Rothschilds and Rockefellers, you might say, and I must get a sixteenth-century china-closet to put the Meissen beauty in. Shut up, Olivia. Papa's mad. You moneybag kids ought to be ashamed of yourselves seeing Papa suffer.'

He began to laugh. Emily dimpled. 'Oh, Stephen, you should be ashamed.'

He was presently back, telephoning from below saying he had a car. Their friend had a little house in Auteuil, which seemed just right for them. Off they went, after cautioning the children, and found a house with three floors and basement, completely furnished with Persian carpets, silk damask and lace curtains, Louis-Quinze and Empire furniture, engravings, candelabras with crystals, linen, silver, central heating and even a stock of coals and wood. The price was very high, but it was to let for a year and possibly renewable. At first they were rejoiced. A rather large guarantee had been asked by the owner, a Spanish nobleman for the moment in the Argentine; and they had to sign an extensive inventory and pay for wear and tear. The owner had been anxious when he heard Americans might tenant it. 'They throw wild parties.'

'And where is the room for our own furniture and goods?' asked Emily sadly.

'But look at the coal! It needs a strong man as well as a butler,' said Stephen.

Emily said wearily, 'Oh, what stupid harassments! No, we can't take it.'

On the way home, Emily declared she could not go home to the battling and disappointed children. They could telephone Christy and tell him to look after his brother and sister. The hotel would send up food and drink if they wanted it. Stephen said, 'I'm in despair. Why the devil couldn't we have got something before we came? What was Uncle Maurice doing to let us come here like this with all these children? Damn his eyes.'

He raged, beat his knees, loosened his tie. 'I'm ill, I'm really ill, Emily. I'm not joking. I can't stand any more of this. It will kill me. I've suffered too much for the only decent thing I ever did, giving up my country for my family. Why didn't I remain at home, a quiet little louse, like the rest of my family, except Florence; but she has moneybags and the demon rum to console her.'

'This is an occasion to celebrate, how we turned down our last palace and I'm too nervous to go home,' said Emily. She opened the taxi window and told the driver to drive to the Ritz.

Stephen said, 'I won't. It's vulgar and we haven't the money. Ask him where's a decent, modest, quiet place.'

'Take us anywhere that's decent, modest and quiet and don't spare the expense,' said Emily, to the driver, a gaunt, ragged man with dry hair and a harsh foreign accent.

206

He took them to an American night-club, where Stephen sat nursing his stomach and looking miserable and Emily got very drunk and jolly and made a few friends.

The next morning early they went shopping to get some extra clothes for the children, berets for the boys, ribbons for Olivia. The Printemps, the Galeries Lafayette, the Trois Quartiers and other shops up and down the Madeleine and Opéra quarter were even at this moment well-filled with household and luxury goods.

Emily, and Stephen too, kept saying, 'Oh, for a colour photograph to send to the old folks at home!'

For many days they lived this life. They were robustly, angrily but gloriously employed in inspecting empty houses, even small palaces, attending auctions and visiting shops for antiques. They bought books on fine furniture, pictures and old silver, they ate here and there, drank apéritifs, wine and brandy; and all the time hurried, argued, spent, but with the serious feeling that what they were looking for was a place for a quiet, well-organized life, tranquil rooms for themselves and the children tucked away with tutors and schools, so that Stephen and Emily could attend to their real business in life, writing. At last, said Emily, in so inspiring a city, where artists and writers were respected, not for the money they made but in proportion to their achievement, at last they would settle down and, after tossing off a few things to make their bread and pay their rent, she would turn to her serious aim, write good books, make an honest fame, become a master of her craft. At last. And Stephen too. Now he would have the leisure and atmosphere to indulge his learned bent; and he too might try his hand at something lighter. He was very amusing when he wanted to be, a real sour wit, but laced and decorated with fruits and cherubs like the old ceilings they saw; the mark of what she called 'his scionage'.

Emily said to him enthusiastically at a breakfast, 'This is not wander-lusting. It's our future life, our work. We're preparing for it as you prepare for a family; the work's in the making!'

The children however, were getting spoiled. They had only to ring a bell to get any kind of service; their parents kept buying them novelties to pass the time; they went out a good deal; they looked after themselves. They developed perhaps, but they needed a home and a more modest life. Christy worried about the amount of money they spent. They found a long record of accounts in the back of his diary. Olivia, reticent and clever, passed primly before the expensive novelties she coveted, as a desirous woman passes before Molyneux, Worth, Cartier, not revealing her great needs and her small purse. But she became more irritable because they did not spend enough. Stephen kept them occupied for a few days by telling Christy he must make his sister understand how the rich kept accounts and watched their money, compared prices and avoided waste. The rich 'brother and sister' travelled round Paris for a few days, looked in shops, visited other rich children in the afternoons and Olivia had a chance to see how girls her age behaved and dressed. She at once behaved like them and wished to dress like them, in the simple and expensive clothes they wore.

The Howards, meanwhile, took Giles with them to view small houses at Fontainebleau; Fontenay-aux-Roses, a suburb; a villa at St-Germain-en-Laye. They considered villas on the Côte d'Azure, near Menton and Cap d'Antibes, Juan-les-Pins ('we would save the expense of holidays'), they thought of buying a house near Montparnasse: and near the War Ministry and elsewhere. At Fontainebleau was a complete house for a million francs, suitable, but cold, dark, furnished in a style fifty years old, and with a bleak garden back and front, not yet awake to spring, perhaps never awakening to spring. Yet it was near the magnificent forest and the frozen ponds, trees blue and grey and green rising slowly in the distance. Near the Arc de Triomphe they found a large six-room apartment kept by the concierge for an American tenant who had not come back; and in Neuilly, a little house in a garden belonging to a woman who had got it from a lover and who had gone to live in the south forever, disgusted, frightened; a woman who had been a Pétainiste and collaborator and now feared the people of Paris.

Emily said, 'Again the tumbrils. She's afraid!'

They began French lessons and yet could not make out the headlines, and the headlines were on the wrong pages. They disliked the make-up, found the information obscure, the presentation grandfatherly, the local passions absurd. They tried to participate, but they remained, they were as yet, tourists. In the end they took all the newspapers written in English and began to spend more peaceful mornings as they scanned them.

They severely criticized the French. But Stephen said, 'This remains capitalism. It is in its way as good a capitalism as ours, perhaps better. I don't know what would survive in Oshkosh and Painted Post after an invasion, after we were stripped of everything. Here at least there have survived the thick walls of villas, the polished floors and the engravings of Louis XVIII. After all, all the world is capitalism but one experiment in the East – '

Emily exclaimed, 'Experiment! If all the world was in its dotage and there was one young person alive, we would say, an experiment in living. And after all, too, the USA is for Europeans still an experiment. Especially for the sour old English. It's a point of view, it's arguable, too. And let's not backbite the boys who stayed at home. Someone has to stay at home. A country is made up of people who stay at home. We can't all run before the storm. One ought to like one's country, even with its faults. I feel quite guilty. What the hell! Who kept France alive? Not those who ran but those who stayed, collabos and Pétainistes and all, they stayed. They stayed through the long night; and the refugees were out wandering in another night.'

Stephen sighed, 'I wonder what we are doing really wandering round the dead suburbs of a devastated foreign city whose wars we didn't fight, sorrows we didn't suffer, whose cemeteries we aren't going to fill? I'm here to eat their groceries, I'm not here, for one thing, to eat off their sorrows, or hurrah for the revolutions they make in blood and despair. We're bastards. We're lowdown bastards. I feel like a louse.'

They were at this moment crossing the Seine. It was night and the Seine, from recent rains, was a plump broad satin flood with long trails of red and white coming down to them from the Pont-Neuf. It was cold. There were miserable people about. The taxi-driver, who had cursed them in bad Russian French, the thin ragged porters at the station, the people hanging around outside the station to pick up fifty devalued francs for finding them a taxi, the scarecrows with nowhere to sleep, depressed them.

Stephen went on, 'Are we any better than the Germans, coming here like a master-race, full of money, eating like swine, with schemes for their improvement which happen to suit ourselves?'

Said Emily, 'We make our money somewhere else and spend it here. The fifty francs we gave that man was to the good.'

Stephen wrung his hands and shrieked, 'But I don't want to see it. I'm a coward as well as a parasite. At home, I don't see the poor. I'm used to my country. It's perfect. I don't see what's wrong. I live there in a blue daze.'

Emily asked harshly, 'What are you going back to? To prison, contempt and sneers – because you couldn't make a go of it abroad either? Every one of our old friends is an enemy now. We're just as lonely there as we are here; only that here it is they who said the American Party was wrong; people have opinions like us here. Listen, Stephen, you'll learn French and get in with the heads of the Party here; and if not here, we'll go somewhere where you can get in with them, to England or somewhere, we'll go to the east if you like, anywhere, so that you can feel yourself fulfilled. You've got to, Stephen. Otherwise, I'd feel guilty at having dragged you abroad.'

Stephen replied, 'Oh, you didn't drag me. If I'd had any serious objection I wouldn't have gone. But where are we going? What's our aim? You're full and I'm empty. Wherever you go, you've got a full cargo; but even at home and rusting in the old harbour I'm empty. But you expect to find empty hulls in an old weedy harbour. There are plenty rusting away there and no one knows whether they didn't in the time of their youth bring in full freights and get a great name for heroically battling the storms. If we had only thought of that – a greening, rusting old harbour and waiting for our old age, till no one knew our names any more.'

Emily said after a time, 'Gosh, I'll never be able to forgive myself if I've brought you abroad and you don't find yourself here. But let's find a home and we'll settle in, you'll work and I'll work and you'll have responsibilities, a future, you'll find the Party again. You're tired. You're not used to being without a home. I am. I wouldn't give a damn if I had no home. But you would and so would the children.'

Stephen said, gently, 'I'm grousing again. I'm not fair. If only we could get a house! I feel like cutting my throat when each evening brings the hotel bed and the children backfiring next door.'

Emily burst out laughing. Later, when they were sitting on a café terrace, she sighed, 'These unwanted houses make me feel all the terror and the horror of the years. I begin really to hate the Germans and I'm afraid of them, too. All those outhouses and fences and all these attics have seen such fear, hideous terror of death, hunger; the dusty boards of a stage of such misery! I've never felt such terror. Europe is all fear. We have a budding terror, we have a youthful inquisition, we have the lynch spirit, hale and healthy, and we've had to run, but we haven't got this feeling of the blood running cold in old, vacant rooms, these haunted holes in history, through each of which a man or woman fell, shot, starved, self-murdered in despair. And each man is history, you can't talk about history; we are history, each thudding heart. Oh, my! Oh, I can hardly stand it! What they have been through! And they're so quiet – the very way they stand in queues for their food breaks my heart. I used to get furious with the old-time French who quarrelled about everything; but now, this sweet people, who are fair about seats in trains and buses, move their luggage on the rack, move over for you, never quarrel with the post-office clerks, it's dreadful. Because they know they aren't any more *La Grande Nation*; and the English, too, know they're finished. Their histories are written down to the last word. Oh, God, oh, God, I suffer so terribly. The Americans had trouble, but they aren't blasted. I hope we never are. I hope I never see America like this. Oh, God, I hope it lasts fifty or seventy years, more, capitalism, I mean, even if it is brutal and fascist, not to see such blasted souls, the sweetness of defeat!'

'I think we ought to see the destruction of Europe. After all we came here to learn something, too. No good shutting your eyes and praying like a maiden aunt.'

They found a telephone message at their hotel from one of their house

210

agents. The proprietor, who had been in America, had returned and was willing, he thought, to rent them a large apartment in his private mansion in the rue de Varenne. The premium and the rent were high; but the agent thought they were sure to get it; their references in America were excellent.

'My references in America would push me out the window if they knew we were spending so much money,' said Stephen gloomily.

Emily jubilated, 'Thank heaven for the break. I have to celebrate. Let's drop the kids and eat something splendid.'

They took a taxi accordingly to the Touriste d'Argent. Said Emily cheerfully to the head waiter who came up to speak in good English and assist them, 'My husband, mong marry, is in a sick despair, Monsieur, because we cannot find a house to live in, our children are getting paler every day from hotel air and I'm very hungry. What can we eat?'

In the end, Stephen played with shrimp rissoles and salad, while Emily, exhausted but happy, as she said, ate cress soup, Armorican lobster, roast duck, asparagus sauce mousseline, and ice-cream.

She sighed as she supped the ice-cream, 'What I'm costing you! But this is divine, worth ruin.'

'I'm glad one of us can eat,' said Stephen.

When the head waiter came up to ask them if all was well, she said to him, 'Yes, colossal, poétique, Monsieur. We ought to come here every day. Only I hope we won't be so miserable every day. Imagine three miserable babes and the intense hell of – '

'H'm, h'm,' said Stephen.

' – the intense and utter horror of hotel life. Are you a father, oong pear? You'll understand what it's like. It's the revolting business, Monsieur, of watching them suffer and my husband suffering too. Their sense of security is – shot – to pieces. It isn't the same for me. Oh, your grand, colossal, poetic food. Oh, dear' (she turned to Stephen) 'I guess we're suffering in grandeur all right, like the old Romans when they feared a slave revolt.'

'Stop talking,' said Stephen, between his teeth.

Emily laughed outright. People were listening, taking notice and smiling. Emily, rosy, very fat and sitting bolt upright, began laughing and said she couldn't face the cruel world unless she had coffee, brandy and cigarettes. The waiter went for these.

Said Stephen, despondently, 'Oh, well, what does it matter if we go broke now or in a week from now? You and I will go hand in hand begging through the American colony.'

Emily was laughing on and on, 'Oh, I feel guilty. But what the heck! Eat, drink and be merry for tomorrow we live on bread and water. True, eh? Howard menu: financial soup, poor fish, plenty of beef, hot corn, candy on the pill, drink of Lethe and start over.'

'A New England boiled dinner,' said Stephen.

Emily said irritably, 'As long as I can keep on turning out hot corn in Europe.'

'Don't call it corn. It's your way of seeing things. Some comedians spend their lives yearning to play Hamlet. They'd make him funny too. They couldn't help it. You're a funny Hamlet. Be satisfied. It's you.'

Emily was insulted. 'Then why is so much I think of hangman humour? Why do I hate to write it?'

'You don't. You have to be solemn in order to laugh at them after. All humorists are gloomy, cruel bastards. But at least they're not dull. They have both worlds. They see the sinister truth and they can laugh.'

Emily said, 'H'm. Laugh, clown, laugh. How is it that the masterpieces of the world are all gloomy – tragedies, no less?'

Stephen was irritated, 'Because they all belong to the bad old world, which was black. You're a real American, the new world. For Christ's sake, if I thought you were going to turn arty in Europe, I'd go back on the next boat.'

'What about Melville and Hawthorne and Poe, eh?' said Emily sadly, looking down at her small muscular hands.

'Oh, don't keep dragging up those boneyard types. That was another age.'

Emily said, 'And besides the wench is dead. I don't want to live this way in the bright lights, going to the gilded palaces, unable to tolerate a waiter who's been eating sour cabbage, or a waitress who hasn't washed, unable to bear a hotel if the manager doesn't scrape to me, suffering if my girl doesn't change her dress twice a day. I don't want to be like that. I am like that. Why? Because I see the funny side, I'm a wise guy. I've got the angles. I know the score. How despicable! Money's filthy. It is filthy, Stephen. Don't look down your nose. And when you think that my humour, which is me, I admit, is really the way I see things, laugh at everyone, sneer at everyone's troubles – I really am cruel. I often wake up in the night, Stephen, to think out what I am. I'm like a doll with two faces glued together. They used to have those. I disliked them. One back, one front. Mark Twain wrote some terribly unfeeling, heartless pieces. After all, to write *The Man Who Corrupted Hadleyburg*, you have to have a really hard heart, you have to be a cynic. Whereas a natural tragic dramatist is always weeping for humanity. And here I am, supposed to write for the proletariat, or at least be a friend of the people, and I can't live except this way, moneybags or what's just as good, enormous debts. I'll give you two quotes that hang heavy on my heart. Someone was

212

making up an anthology and wrote to Jack London to ask him for something, anything lying around, some little piece. He wrote back and said he hadn't written an honest word in twenty years. Damon Runyon –'

'Who's he, after all?' said Stephen irritably. He was very tired and he felt himself attacked obscurely.

'That's it, isn't it? Who's he? He wrote a review of his own works. I copied it from *Time*, August 1, 1949. "By saying something with a half-boob air. . .he gets ideas out of his system on the wrongs of this world which indicate that he must have been a great rebel at heart, but lacking moral courage. He was a hired Hessian of the typewriter. . .I tell you, Runyon had subtlety but it is the considered opinion of this reviewer that it is a great pity the guy did not remain a rebel out and out, even at the cost of a good position at the feed trough." Runyon on Runyon. The Hired Rebel. My life too, eh? Pretty.'

Emily began to bawl, cough, hiccup, sob. After a while she calmed down and said, 'Yet to be in Paris is a sort of achievement. I guess I could be happy just to live here.'

Stephen said, quietly, 'I feel like a heel.'

'Oh, it's this total hell of hotel life. I feel so despairing at times. We're not used to feeling like homeless dogs. I'm glad we quit America, if there's a way out, just the same. There always is a way out.' She said, with a shudder, signalling the waiter, 'If we'd stayed here, all the frightfulness, the calvary, that would have been ahead! I should never have done any more work in my life and I should have joined, we should have joined that long list of martyrs, so many names on the list you can't remember them, just a hunger for anonymity and death. If you want it and are ready for it. But it's failure. The object of life is to live, to survive. After all, those here are the resisters, the martyrs, the victims aren't here any more! The next generation comes from those who survive! I can't go out like a light. I like the life of the mind; but life is real, actual, factual, tangible, life is children and making a go of it. It isn't being crucified. Of all the crucified ones in this world, millions and millions, I shudder to think of it, only one got any following, the others have no names. I can't love the humble and desperate. I can live though, my own way, anywhere I guess. Oh, how selfish! I should be thinking about you; I have no psyche, no nerves compared with you. Your sufferings are as real as their bombings and their barbed wire.'

'Oh, bunk! Let's take a walk.' But he had cheered up; and they went walking and talking happily, tired, but unaware of the miles in the fine evening, calm blue light and quiet streets.

Stephen named the streets they passed in the darkness. They discussed strange lights they had seen, here on a river at sunset, elsewhere with the trees and clouds blowing, a silver pass of wind in gardens, roughened waves, the reflection of sunrise on children's faces. And somehow it came up again, the life of art and the monied life; the old debate and as always, no resolution.

But by three the next afternoon, they had rented the part-furnished house in the rue de Varenne. They instructed the moving and storage company, rang agencies for servants, ordered two taxis for the next day, found black market coal, got in cleaners and went to buy enough linen for the first week. When the costs mounted and Stephen had an acute attack of mental and physical pain at the big sums to pay out, Emily said, 'What does it matter? This linen is real linen, not deodorized pre-shrunk, previtalized, superduperquality, all-American easy-sleeping cotton, guards your loveliness the night through; it's just plain linen that will last a lifetime.

They took a taxi to the hotel with a load consisting of four double sheets of the largest dimensions, one dozen single sheets, two dozen square linen pillow-slips, all solidly hemstitched, one dozen bath towels and a few other things. The children stared. Emily said, 'When you get married, Olivia, I'm going to see you have old-fashioned fixings, we're going to right away start a hope-chest filled with things like this.'

'It's stiff,' said Christy, thoughtfully examining the goods.

'It's like iron, it will last twenty years,' cried Emily.

'Well, I guess Europe has some things left,' said Giles.

'Ah, my loves, your troubles are over; ours are just beginning. This has made a whale of a hole in the cash-in-hand and Mamong has to write three books, one cheap-as-dirt to sell, one humorous for the record and one good, for honour's sake; and maybe two boy-meets-girl scripts before the others.'

'Maybe nothing but boy-meets-girl with all this junk,' said Stephen.

Emily went on heartily, 'French for us all, tutors and schools for Christy and Olivia and a sort of miscegenation school for Giles.'

'A what?' said Stephen.

'Miscegenation, school that takes all nationalities.'

Stephen lifted his eyebrows and shrugged, 'As long as you keep these epithets within the walls of this room. It means mixed-race, like the bi-coloured python rocksnake, or a striped child, half chocolate, half cream.'

They had a fierce argument on this and Christy produced his ever-present dictionary. Emily would not yield.

'I don't care. In a humorous or allusive way I'm right. And never mind, we're going to learn real French. Giles is probably the only one who will pick up ler Frongsay and Mama and Papa will be known as the

214

Silent Sioux! Hooray. Put out the flags. Run up the skull-and-crossbones. We're on the high seas at last and fortune is but a stone's throw around the corner.'

Next day, about ten, they piled their baggage, three children, three typewriters, new linen, into three loaded taxis, and made off for the rue de Varenne, faubourg St-Germain ('you must speak of le faubourg only,' said Stephen) where they had found their little house. They rang at the gate, were admitted by the porter, crossed a small, semicircular paved courtyard and found the doors open, the agent waiting for them.

There was a small, slow, creaky elevator, (at any one time, two adults or three children) serving the three floors. On the ground floor were one large room, two small rooms, closets, and a long, cold corridor lighted by numerous windows; the same on the next two floors with small unheated rooms in the attic for servants, a cellar dug in the backyard for wine and coals. The division of the house was difficult but they arranged it in this way: no dumb-waiter, so the dining-room next to the kitchen and pantry, ground floor. First floor, Stephen's library and study, the largest room; a sitting-room and bedroom for Christy. In Christy's sitting-room was a bath, covered to look like a trunk. On the second floor would be Emily's small study, Olivia's large bedroom and a bathroom. They just fitted in. They had to have two servants, a housemaid and a cook. They had scarcely got their baggage in downstairs when the porter introduced a plump, middle-aged woman with grey hair, a cook, named Fernande Morand. They engaged her for next day: she was to live with them. She investigated the kitchen, the backyard, the attic and, with good-natured phrases which they found elegant, she went. They turned down several more cooks that day. They also engaged a housemaid, not the first, but one of the first, for the next day.

Meanwhile, Emily was hurrying round, jovial, harassed, exclaiming over the stupidity of her life, the gaiety, the happiness, the anything you like. The sun was shining and Stephen was happy rearranging the furniture and making a list of all the extras they needed: so many new bulbs, where to put the iceboxes, running out to telephone about the telephone and taking Christy with him (Christy's French was esteemed the best), buying salt, pepper, herbs, flour, oil, butter, paint, nails, hooks, a hammer, a chisel, shelf-paper, towel-rails. Giles and Christy came back loaded several times and darted out again for forgotten items. Olivia was supposed to unpack. She unpacked her dolls and her own clothes and refused to do more, arguing that at least several cases were now out of the way.

Stephen said, 'Ah, you're adorable, my pet, a real woman. Grrr! What are we to do, Emily, with this revolting success in life, the perfect woman?'

215

While Stephen tried to find out what was in the packing-cases (lamps, skillets and casseroles?) the success in life was reading with negligent grace, an article in a movie magazine about the sex-life of one of her Hollywood favourites. One of her favourite dolls (she was too clever to have only one favourite) was held in the crook of her arm.

Stephen sighed, 'What a repugnant sight, to see one's favourite daughter so perfect!'

Olivia smiled faintly as if at what she was reading.

'Come and help, Olivia!'

Olivia looked up, made a charming grimace, put down her doll and magazine, and came over. She helped them for thirty full minutes, in a very practical way. She knew where things should go, she was orderly, sensible, had a natural sense of housewifery and a very good conceit of herself. Often they were surprised into taking her advice, only to change everything a few hours later.

Their household goods not having been unpacked, Emily sent Stephen to buy a frying-pan and some fat and meat. The butcher asked, 'Why do you want to chop the steak? It's good steak and you spoil it hashing it.'

'I like it hashed,' said Stephen with dyspeptic asperity.

He bought some wine for Emily, some spa water for himself and orangeade for the children. He bought bread, coffee, a coffee mill, a pepper mill. There was no milk to be had. He got some American canned juices and powdered milk. They managed by taking a taxi round Paris, to get some white bread too, some real butter, and salad. Their first meal, on wrapping paper but with orange juice, hamburgers and fried potatoes, coffee and cakes seemed to them home. They had got the heating going. The porter had been wonderfully helpful.

Emily said blissfully, emptying the bottle of twelve degree 'van ordinary' (so she called it), 'Home at last. Is it possible? After being beggars and tramps, pleading and weeping, humiliated and disgraced, sneered at and flouted, deceived and disappointed, the humble, the desperate, the "noo churchon see voo play", the esperanters, the exhausted, insulted and injured, is it possible that we are fervently feasting in our own home? Oh, I'm glad my supposed pre-war famousness made Mr Johnny Ledane's trusting nature expand at the American Trust Company. I'm glad we missed all the other houses because still, oh boy, it's something to have a porter and two maids of our own and a house in Paris and I guess we're giddy with success; I am. To us! To us and to Mummy who's going to work like hell to make money fast so that we'll all be happy and to Daddy who's going to work and make public and financial and political glory! And to our darling Christy who's going to work and be a great Latinist, able to repeat all Cicero backwards and go to the Sorbonne; and to sweet,

216

lovely Olivia, our darling, our own little beauty, who's going to be a genuine Parisienne and speak French like angels (if they speak French of course) and to my little Giles and Daddy's little Giles, who is our heart's darling!'

'But what am I going to do?' enquired Giles, who had followed all this attentively.

'You are going to be a doctor or a lawyer or even an engineer perhaps,' said Emily.

'Why not a writer, an artist, a scholar?' said Stephen laughing.

'Oh, God, never. It's too much agony. It's unsafe, a gamble. Then to be, at one and the same time, gimlet-eyed and rapturous, profound and sophisticated, sentimental and wordly-wise, a success and not afraid of living in a dirty backstreet on crusts, it's a tightrope trick you have to be born for. Most writers are shnooks, stinkers, bores, fatuous, eloquent on a single subject, me; or stuttering only with their ultimate unique profoundness. Ugh! Double ugh! No, no, no; not for Joe.'

They all at once began to sing this, one of the Family Songs, taken from an old blood-and-thunder recently revived in the Village, so they said:

> 'No, no, no: not for Joe, Not for Joseph, if he knows it;
> No, no, no: not for Joe. Not for Joseph, not for Joe.'

This ditty had been arranged for them by Stephen at the time of the SHAPE (Supreme Headquarters Allied Powers Europe) Pact. The children took it up now, led by Papa and with Mamong chorusing away, out of tune. There was beating of spoons, kicking of chair legs, with Giles doing a double-header beside his chair.

Emily said, 'A good thing we didn't take any of those satin and brocade mausoleums with the family heirlooms all ticketed. Not for our brood.'

Papa now obliged with a little song he had known as a child, taught by his French governess.

> 'Ah, little Bi-bi-bi-neah,
> He sucked his mandoline-eah!
> And played his tangerine-eah!'

This they all sang, too; and :

> 'I am a little Italiano!
> I do-do-do on my piano!'

Emily exclaimed, 'Oh, how glorious, restful, to be at home at last!'

They cleared up, made the beds, gave the children lukewarm baths, sent them to bed.

217

Stephen sang evening songs to Olivia and Giles, both of his own composition:

'Oh-livia, livia, livia, livia-livia, light!
Methinks she makes the candles to burn bright!'

Giles shouted, 'Me, me, me, me, Papa!'

When Stephen went in, Giles asked if this was now really their home. Really, for good. 'Yes,' said Stephen.

'I'm glad of that. But anywhere's home when we're all together isn't it?' Giles was studying the painted ceiling, encrusted also with ornamental plasterwork.

'A truer word was never said or sung,' said Stephen and went on to Giles's bedtime song.

Christy was downstairs studying French, a dogged, gentle, ambitious lad.

'Go to bed by ten, Christy.'

'Oui, Maman!'

Emily beamed, 'Oh, he is going to be so French.'

Stephen said, 'God knows what we're doing. When they go back to the States, they'll all be out of step, they'll offend, they'll grizzle and growl and make nuisances of themselves.'

Emily said, 'But they'll get jobs in Washington, they'll be attachés or diplomats. Olivia will marry some rich man and shine in society. Anyway Christy's a gentleman, he can live abroad forever if he likes. Like Uncle Maurice.'

They soon went to bed and slept tranquilly.

The next week was taken up with servant worries. Servants came and went, or did not come. Emily, the ambitious, enquired about courses at the Cordon-Bleu cooking school; they found schools and tutors. One tutor declared Christy was dull-witted, another said he could never make up for lost time; his answers were either ludicrous or heart-breaking. Stephen began to explain the case beforehand: 'An American boy without any advantages: he's been brought up in America.'

They engaged a French tutor for themselves, a dark, thickset, middle-aged woman, unmarried, who called herself Madame Gagneux. She came to them nervously and dubiously; but she was a woman of experience and seemed to understand them at once.

'I was afraid to come to teach Americans, but I see that from you I will learn as much as I can teach.'

They were pleased. She soon began to manage the children's schooling calendar and their outings; and now, though Stephen was unwilling, Emily had time to think about their first dinner party. They invited the

218

Wauters, who had not yet gone to Brussels, Madame Valais, Mademoiselle de la Roche and others to whom they owed a dinner. They were nervous, as they had never yet seriously tested their cook, Fernande; but they obeyed her when it came to their dinner menu.

> With cocktails, sherry, port wine, hors-d'oeuvre of 20 sorts.
> For dinner:
> potage queue de boeuf (oxtail soup),
> turbot hollandaise sauce,
> tournedos chasseur,
> poulet rôti,
> salad,
> new peas, French-style,
> orange soufflé
> With this: wines, champagne, still and sparkling water, white bread, butter, coffee, liqueurs, petits fours, chocolates etc fine champagne.

When Stephen complained of the expense, most of the above not only being dear but black-market, poor Emily, who wished to show she was not an American barbarian, as she was not in fact, but a gourmet with a fine palate, hurried out by herself in the car, in the intervals of resuming her book, and so built up the food she felt was necessary. When Stephen made a fuss, she explained, 'Yes, but this is just practice for Uncle Maurice, who will be here next week and for dear Anna when she comes in the summer. Once they see us, à la frongsay, they will be convinced we've reformed and have quit the fifth column for ever and are members of the Howard nobility; they will even give people our address.'

'Leave my family out of this,' said Stephen.

'Can we?'

'God forbid! We've got to pay these bills some time.'

'Oh, in Europe they let you run on three months or six months. We'll give them our references. The whole aristocracy of every country has always lived on debts. What are banks for? Not for savings deposits. Forget it. Quit worrying, Stephen. We're going to live high, wide and handsome and to hell with the consequences. When the revolution comes we'll have helped to hurry it on.'

'We oughtn't to talk like that,' said Stephen thoughtfully.

'Oh, I'm going to say what I like. I won't be hemmed in for any conventions. Let's live first, think afterwards.'

They had been tormented from the first by a mysterious quarrel that had broken out between the indoor servants, the porter and the daily cleaner. These four seemed to know all about it – angry, sneering, witty, and low, biting voices floated round them: they could not make out what was wrong.

The housemaid, Marie-Jo, was thoughtful in their company: she served poorly and was edgy, worse, hysterical in the company of Fernande, the cook. The porter took her side, the cleaner seemed to be mediator.

Giles reasoned about his new, strange surroundings. People did not understand him; he drew deductions. Olivia wept because she was not appreciated. She did not like the French and did not try to learn the language. But for the hour before the dinner party when she was to see the company, Stephen bought her, somewhere in the rue St-Honore, a delicious, ruffled muslin, with new socks and shoes, so that Olivia, who knew all about these things, at five o'clock was ready to appear as the modern French girl-child, her curtsies and her small-society French ready. 'Bonjour, Madame, bonjour Monsieur,' she said, curtsying to the pier glass; and the boys were ready, Giles in a new French costume and Christy in a tailor-made from Uncle Maurice's New York tailor, to whom he had written his new measurements. They and a temporary governess were running about the courtyard while Emily finished dressing. She wore a silk muslin in pinstripes of pink, silver and white, gay and oddly like herself. This was Stephen's present to her for 'our home in Paris'. Stephen had just received his quarterly allowance of $3,000.

The party and the evening were a great success. Fernande was so good a cook, and Marie-Jo, for the occasion, so good a waitress, that the ladies, after dinner, settled down to a plain-faced discussion of what she cost and where she must have cooked during the occupation. They then went on to the prices in the black market and the simple fact that it was their duty to keep up their strength to resist the threat of revolution, while the Americans were perfecting their plans for saving Europe.

Mademoiselle de la Roche said, 'It was the fifth column which lost us France. But it is too much to expect the Americans to do everything for us. It is true, with the atom bomb the problem is different now; and one wonders why – tell me why, your President doesn't use the bomb now, before it is too late, before things can leak out and be copied by the other side?'

Monsieur Valais was an elegant, long, amused and vain man who, it seemed to the Howards, was laughing at them and their undercover tactics. He said, 'Yes, unfortunately there is no way of keeping science secret. The Russians will either catch up with you or invent something else. I am certain they are experimenting in two other ways – with radioactive rays, that is, death-rays; and that their atomic research is directed towards industry. In a few years, if they don't have the atom bomb, they'll have an industrial efficiency in perfection and output to overtop the USA. In ten years say.'

He laughed at the long faces of his hearers. 'I am sixty-eight. It's indifferent to me, you understand. But it is to your interests to stop it

220

now. I don't think you can stop Russian progress with biological warfare. The Germans tried genocide: it seemed so good; and now the French birthrate is going up.'

Johnny Ledane, from the bank, said, 'The fifth column is the X-factor. Things are blowing up now, every few months, an armaments factory, a war-experiment-plant, in Japan, in Spain, in England, in Germany – I attribute it myself to fifth columns, an anarchistic band determined to leave Europe defenceless against the Russians. You Europeans have got to get on your toes and root them out. It isn't the collaborators who are the danger; they were realists. It was the damn Resistance; they're all reds. Everyone's trying to say he was in the Resistance now. I'm damned if I know why. Why not say they were all reds and try them for treason.'

Madame Valais agreed, suddenly, briefly, 'They were not fighting for us, but for the Russians. They expected to stir the country up to revolution. They expect it now. France would never have been invaded if the reds had not so divided the workers that they didn't want to work. They thought only of Utopianism, no work and all pay.'

Ledane said, 'What's needed is a house-cleaning and America has the right to demand that of every nation it helps get on its feet.'

There was agreement on this.

'Jealousy made the French revolution!'

'My grandfather built up a business with his own hands and anyone could do the same but they prefer to take. The Russians hold out the hope to them that when they come here they'll hand it over free. They've got a big surprise coming to them.'

'They won't come here. The Americans will see to that.'

Emily turned to the immense double-cabinet radio-phonograph with automatic changer, which had been Stephen's present to her with his previous cheque; and brought out some of the private Beethoven recordings, which had been her present to Stephen after that. These she put on full-blast, using the amplifier. The audience had stone-struck expressions, like people about to fall through a crack in the earth.

'Oh, heaven, not so loud,' cried Mademoiselle de la Roche.

Emily sparkled and impudently grinned. 'But this is the latest American machine. You hear the same volume as in a concert hall.'

'But we're not in a concert hall,' said Monsieur Valais, looking uneasy but firm.

Emily cried, 'But you must imagine you are in a concert hall. In this way you have the full beauty of the music.'

She was shouting, for the music was very loud.

One lady got up with an aching expression, 'As for me, I can't bear anything so loud.'

221

Emily shouted, 'Sit down, come back. You'll lose the beauty of it all in there. Here you get the full sonority. Just imagine you're at a symphony concert.'

The lady said, hesitating, 'I have very small ears, I can't bear noise.'

Emily roared, 'Sit down. Don't go away.'

Stephen turned the amplifier down. Emily shouted, 'Stephen, let them hear the values! There isn't a better machine!'

She turned it up, Stephen turned it down, she turned it up. The astonished and troubled guests sat fixed on their chairs; one woman had put her fingers to the side of her face. Stephen disconnected the amplifier.

Emily put it back again, 'Stephen! You're ruining the music!'

Monsieur Valais said, 'But it isn't music! It's roaring like Niagara.'

Emily smiled at this praise, 'Well, now you can see what we can do for volume.'

They had to sit through till the end of the record. Common protest stopped Emily from playing another Beethoven. One woman said, 'Oh, I feel as if I'd been under a railway bridge.'

Ledane spoke with slow patronage, 'Naturally, here in the war, you had to tone your radios down so low that you're not adapted to modern systems any more. It must take a long time to get over that kind of inhibition. It's fear of the Germans.'

Emily said roguishly, 'Well, we have some Macky (Maquis) songs too. Do you want to hear them?'

They hesitated. She put on 'Le Chant des Partisans', the principal song which even they knew; and this too she played as loudly as she could.

Madame Valais said, 'It's a good thing you have no neighbours.' She smiled bravely however; and when the record was taken off, she said it was well done, 'Really, one can't help feeling something.'

When they had gone, about ten, and the place was cleared up, Emily said, 'Faugh! What sleepy-heads! Still, I think it was a splendid success. One of the two or three best dinners I ever ate in my life. I wish I had a recording, a dictaphone of all that was said tonight. We could send it to dear Anna to prove that we've bitten off a large hunk of the upper crust. Say, how did we break into Cold War Society?'

Stephen was sitting down, worn out. 'What stinkers! In a half-starved city we spend what we haven't earned and we rifle the black market, too, to feed a pack of wolves, bastards, dogs, villains – phew! Why can't we invite some honest guys? I loathe entertaining people I despise. I grudge every bite. Smile, smirk: "you don't say so". Draw them out viciously and dishonestly like a spy because you can't write the evening off, after spending so much money – "I'm finding out how the other half lives," you think. You don't fool them. They eat and wait. One mis-step and they'll have us dissected. Old Valais has an inkling now. We look like fools and we're living like rakes. We passed the offices of *L'Humanité* on the way down from the station the other day. Why didn't we, if we had to give a dinner party, drop in and ask twenty of the fellows there in for a feed? What we stuffed down these collabo gullets would have fed twenty honest, starved men.'

Emily pouted. 'Oh, I hate the way you denigrate and belittle. We can't live in a charmed circle, swopping slogans in a tower of glass, through which we see the rest of humanity making strange gestures we don't understand. They are just living; but we don't know the signs. Oh, don't grouse. It was wonderful. Poetic. I'm able to live up to your family now. I know it. The Howards in Paris, famous for their French cooking. Yippee! We'll hang out the flags and have one last grand gala for Uncle Maurice when he comes, and then to work. Am I happy, Stephen! In Paris, all we want, our heart's desire; and we'll ask the twenty starving from *L'Humanité* if it will soothe you; all this and communism too.'

She paused. The night was quiet. An old cart was going past, cloppity-clop, rattle and squeal, drawn by an old horse. She shivered.

'How sinister! Isn't it still here!'

'This quarter is famous for its silence, the Grenelle quarter – '

She said, 'H'm, now it's going back again. Is it parading in front of our house?'

It stopped and then went on. She said in a low voice, 'Jesus! Tumbrils! Maybe the Resistance watches those people we had here tonight?'

Stephen said, 'You're superstitious and over-tired. Get to bed. You read too much Dickens as a child.'

Emily said, 'Yeah – but the French revolution really took place. I guess I understand why some Americans are camping on the Lake of Geneva, Swiss side; no tumbrils. It's an awful thought that we are here like mayflies on a volcano.'

'Go to bed.'

Emily slept soon, but started from her bed in a fright. What horror had she dreamed, something drawing around the corner, something leggy and material? 'Stephen! Stephen!' He comforted her and in the morning she could only remember that something horrible had happened.

She said, telling Stephen about her dreams, 'And yet I feel calmer. I've slipped out of something. Now there's nothing but work ahead. We've taken on the responsibility of three miserable babies. Work is called for. Productive years and maybe forgetfulness. Heigh-ho!'

Stephen looked gloomily into his cup of coffee, said nothing.

'Is anything wrong, darling?'

He shook his head and grunted. She continued impetuously, 'Ah,

223

America was like being in a hospital with an operation hanging over you. Everything with sense, reason, is subordinated to physical fear and agony. Or it's blotted out, you're down to the animal level and you think with desperation of either the next meal, or next injection or next nurse, or next hour, or even next survival. Here, life goes on. It's amazing when you think what they've been through. Shows man can survive. It heartens me. It seems to say, "You can survive". In USA those last few months everything has been down to LCD, will we survive, will we go to jail, can we ever escape the Terror in time?'

'Ah, the hell with it,' cried Stephen.

'What's the matter? I knew something was wrong.'

'Listen to the servants quarrelling! America had at least one thing, it had Paolo and Maria-Gloria. My real friends. Here I have no friend, they don't understand me. They gloat over me behind my back and they probably hate us because we're rich Americans, trying to steal their country from under their feet for some miserable handout and Shylocking them all over the place. I hate it here. I hate being hated.'

'They're fawning on us.'

'I'm not Louis XVI. I haven't a deer-park. I don't want fawns.'

'Is it headache?'

'No, pocket-ache. Our finances are kaput. We've almost emptied out our bank account. Our son and daughter are sitting there – they'll never starve and yet we're keeping them while their percentages and their premiums and the value of their stocks go up. And what little we have, we waste feeding those who don't need it.'

Emily said, 'I know. I was thinking of you, Stephen. We have to see that you have an honourable and satisfying career over here.'

'With my French? If I didn't learn with a governess and at Princeton, will I learn it from Madame Suzanne Gagneux? And Madame Suzanne, we already learn, was in the Resistance, another Resistance type like Wauters. What are we doing living in the peace and plenty they won? I hate it. And Europe is just a war-waste anyhow. The next party you give to these goddamn lice I'm going to speak my mind.'

'Look, I heard you and that bank official, Johnny Ledane, gently sneering at vulgar Americans who come to Europe for business. We didn't. I laughed to myself for I thought, that isn't us. I'm starting right off with my *Journal of Europe 1948* and I'm going to make every patch of waste evening fertile, so it doesn't bother me. Yesterday evening will pay a profit yet.'

'$700 expenses for $500 return – our usual economy.'

'Oh, let me work without gibing. The bailiff's voice hearkens.'

'You mean calls. It's all very well for you. The Case of the Racing

224

Typewriter. My work's long and slow and then I'm only regurgitating pre-digested stuff. I put it in acceptable prose and I hope people will call it my point of view. Pouah! Why am I here? Running away like a cur!'

'What does it benefit the human race if you sit in jail?'

'Am I here for the human race? I'd like to believe it.'

'Well, Stephen, I must go. I've all the meals to order for the week. That's the way they do things here. Fernande told me. Then I must start work at 10 o'clock sharp. Today!'

Stephen stood up, 'Yes, what an egotist you are! Think of me! Think of something for me to write! Start me off. That's all I ask. I'm despicable but I want to work too.'

Emily came up to him and said gently, 'Oh, dear. I wish I were a good wife to you. I wish I weren't getting so hearty and fat. But I'm so afraid of Fernande, the porter and Marie-Jo, that they'll leave us together or singly, and we'll have to go back to canned hamburgers, pork and beans, that I daren't give up eating. I must diet, Stephen and then I'll be more human, I'll suffer agonies, just like other people. Why don't you keep a Journal?'

'I'm damned if I'll write down all the small beer of my life. I go along with you every day and you see everything as large as life and twice as natural. You see what I don't see; things that never were on land or sea and you make it real. I'm stunned, abashed, melancholy, every evening to see what you've been seeing all day and I've been there and haven't seen one-hundredth; I haven't seen it at all.'

Emily burst out laughing, 'Oh, that comes from being a journalist. I had to see things or I didn't eat.'

'It comes from genius and I'm not one,' said Stephen, in a low tone.

'Oh, hash me hash! What bunk!'

'Would you say I was a genius?' asked Stephen, in a low tone, looking at her sarcastically and in the eye.

'Of course you are. You're the only real talent in the family. I'm nothing but a shameful scribbler for the mamma magazines. I'm ashamed when I think of you my darling, the only real writer. I don't care what I write either, as long as you have time to think things through and get things down on paper. It's only the question of finance. Oh, things are so complicated. Here you are, one of the best men alive, an angel, no one knows it as I do, and you've got to be tortured this way about earning a mean living, while thousands and millions of people are on government payrolls. I wish you were, just to ease your mind. What about the UNO?'

'I won't do that; that's flat.'

'Well, go to the Sorbonne.'

'You can see me tottering along waving my hickory stick, old grandpappy in the students' demonstrations! Ep-ep-ep! Our comrade St-st-stalin!'

Emily burst out laughing: 'Well, I wouldn't give a damn. I'd start in at forty or fifty if I wanted to; I always wanted to study medicine. Why in the Soviet Union granddams and grandpappies are starting to learn to read at seventy.'

'This isn't the Soviet Union. This is highly sophisticated Paree.'

Emily was tracing invisible designs on the tablecloth, 'Well, look, think it over. Take a nice walk to the Invalides or the Seine. I've got to get my work started. It's like dry rot if you put it off from day to day. You think, do I know how to write at all?'

'All right! Send me out to play. Don't think about me!'

'Don't be a donkey, dear. Write a book! Like me!' She laughed.

'OK. Let me rot! What book? I'm sick of my dull books that bore everyone and that everyone sells as soon as he's read it. I see them at the second-hand dealers.'

'Oh, go and Micawber for the morning, Stephen. Do help me out.'

He shouted disconsolately, 'I am Micawbering. I'm here in Paris on a Micawber errand. Maybe I'll write fiction and end up by shooting myself.'

Emily was going downstairs. He leaned over the stairs and shouted, 'Don't buy anything. Let's live on the leftovers.'

226

14 COMRADE VITTORIO

Emily tried to fit in American habits with French family eating. Fernande said that for economy, and with the queueing, it was better to arrange things a week ahead and *grands dîners* had no part in this schedule. Christy and his tutor had a tray lunch, so did Stephen. Emily did not eat when working, taking only black coffee until cocktail-time or even dinner.

She told Fernande, 'It makes me feel a beast, *une bête*, not to cook for my dear ones myself. *May say impossible.*'

At first she accepted Fernande's suggestions. Enough bones to make stock for several soups for the week, bean, peasant, village, housewife, vermicelli, tomato, onion. She drew up a large menu for each day of the week. Fernande said it was a fine menu for a high-class boarding house. Emily cut it down. Fernande approved: 'It is a good, modest menu for a family.' Emily took it to Stephen, who said it was a fine menu for a large hotel but not for them. Stephen was still aggrieved over the small attention paid to his destiny and the large interest taken in Fernande, her opinions and her kitchen.

'Get things to stretch the food,' he shouted. He told how he and his brother and sister had been brought up. 'We're living like the American army, with garbage cans overflowing with roast turkey, steaks and pork-chops.' At his home Father asked each one, starting with Mother, 'Will you have fish soup or cabbage soup? Then, 'Will you have a slice of roast beef or shoulder of mutton or stuffed veal?' as the case was. 'Mother asked, "Will you have creamed turnips, boiled potatoes, sauce?" as the case was. Anyone who hesitated even a moment, lost his rights. If we hesitated we had no appetite.'

'That's why you're dyspeptic now.'

'In England in the old public schools they let the brats eat out of a trencher in which they have sardines, stew, bread and blancmange.'

'That accounts for the graveyard look of Englishmen.'

'Our kids have to have discipline and some austerity. I want them to be like youngsters from a rich family, not kids who wolf every mouthful because they think it may be their last.'

Emily said, 'I despise the way your family eats. Leaving half a plate, not touching the lobster mousse because they just haven't the appetite, finding a plate of soup is enough tonight and taking a thin slice of mutton and nibbling the dessert, and just half a glass of the best Pommard.'

'You're simply greedy.'

'So was Rabelais.'

'I'll bet. Shakespeare was dyspeptic.'

'OK, Shakespeare.' She burst out laughing.

'Now don't run off. Stay here and worry with me. It fills up an empty life for me. Besides, we've got money. We're living off our nest egg. I've got to get down on my rheumaticky knees and crawl to Anna. That will be my manly part in our economy.'

'Well, do it, Stephen. They've got it. Why not?'

She went upstairs, and they still shouted exchanges with each other till she shut the door. Then she took several pages of a long letter from her bottom drawer and put it in the typewriter. It was to 'Dear Anna' and began, 'My darlings, it is now four days after the famous dinner party and I am a criminal writing to you but I must keep you up-to-date. After this, Wilkes melancholy, which is what I call my working-mood. We entertained at that dinner brilliant Cold War Society. With my French teacher, who was in the Resistance, I am studying André Malraux and de Gaulle. Just fancy, they are no longer kosher. Stephen is miserable with dismal wails about the budget and indeed it took us more than we thought to settle down. But I think he will be all right with a little intellectual and political *vie sociale*. He must find the right friends; then he will cheer up. He is miserably unhappy, a martyr because we are feeding social-democrats and ex- and not so ex-collabos. Why do we meet them, when we come abroad, dear Anna, as you know, to preserve our revolutionary honour? Well, that is life, as Stephen says. And then no doubt if there had been no social-democracy, no doubt the communists would have invented it. Joke, eh. . .?'

She kept writing just as she thought and as she and Stephen talked to each other. Then she put away her unfinished letter and went on with her work.

Meanwhile, Stephen had told Fernande not to send lunch in: he would be out for lunch.

He studied the city map, packed a satchel with some of his writings and evidences of former standing and good faith and walked from the rue de Bellechasse all the distance to the room of the Central Committee of the French Communist Party in the rue Lafayette. There he asked to be received by some member of the committee. His card, with a carefully written inscription in French, was taken in; and then he was invited to see a man who, though friendly, was watchful. Stephen's French failed him but he tried to say that he had come to France with his family and wished to work for the Party in any capacity, to work as a volunteer in any way, as an outside contributor till they got to know him. He had the good fortune to be in the office when there came in a celebrated Italian communist, who spoke five or six languages well, among them English. Stephen caught the name as 'Vittorio, our well-known comrade Vittorio.' He was unknown to Stephen.

Vittorio was a middle-sized man, soft-bodied, with thinning, sandy hair, surprisingly ugly, ugly as a seamed, sunburned claypatch, and that was his colouring. He had been gashed twice over the side of the face, past the ear to the jaw and from the brow to the jaw on the same side, cutting the eye which was now a blind blue and turned upwards. When he opened his thick, light-red lips, he showed a magnificent set of large creamy teeth. It almost seemed that there were too many of them; in some parts of the jaw they were set double; but they appeared in a beaming, affectionate, charming smile. Vittorio's fleshy face lighted up with an expression of love and he came forward and held out to Stephen a large hand. He limped slightly, one shoulder had been injured and he was partly deaf; he shouted.

'How ugly,' thought Stephen. But Vittorio seemed unconscious of his appearance. He came to Stephen with eager friendship, generous confidence. He told Stephen again who he was; he was cultural director in one of the largest Italian cities. The Party there was now housed in a magnificent old palace, three sides of a courtyard, and the workers and Party workers climbed the carved stairs where formerly gloomy, sour and wicked landowners had climbed. He said enthusiastically, 'You must come and see it. It'll cheer your heart up. You must come and see me.'

He knew all about the Howards, mentioned the names of their books; and when Stephen said deprecatingly that he feared they were in bad odour now with the American comrades, Vittorio only laughed enthusiastically, waved his hand and shouted, 'That's of no importance. You came to us. Talk to me about America.'

He bent his head forward as Stephen spoke and listened attentively. Stephen became more and more explicit. The other man in the room, young, strong, dark, with an ironic smile, also listened and took notes. When Stephen stopped, the other man said, 'I'm making a speech tomorrow evening and I will use some of these details.'

Stephen was astonished, flattered at being believed; he felt like a messenger from a far land. He said, 'I'll write some articles for you if you like. I have someone who would translate them.' He meant Madame Suzanne.

'This will come later, we will see,' said Vittoria, cheerily.

229

Then he said they must meet again, they must fix it now; and thus it happened that Stephen himself fixed the date for the next dinner party.

Vittorio said he was sorry that leading members of the committee were not there then, but Stephen would meet them soon.

Stephen walked home swinging his satchel, stopped to gaze lengthily at the beauty of the Champs-Elysées, the Tuileries, the Louvre, the Seine. He was speaking to Emily in his mind, 'And you were the one who was beating the breast the other night, because you had brought me abroad. I am being fulfilled, I'm going to be justified. If this is the way we're received, then they're getting ready to sink the American Party.'

He drank in the mild, cool spring air, was grateful, felt younger and more mature.

'A man is less apprehensive than a woman, who sees corpses hanging from every bough. You take a decisive step and all the phantoms fade. Emily will be happy for me.'

He ate his lunch in a small restaurant at the corner of the rue du Bac and on the quay, was surprised at the prices but found the cooking very good. He walked back to the house in happy mood. Emily was to be seen next to the window upstairs. She peered at him with his satchel, waved, and went back to her machine.

She was not writing a chapter of her book at this moment, nor even a 'pork-chops' boy-meets-girl story. She was writing a sketch, something amusing that had happened to her, the history of a really fat person who, though alway dieting, keeps getting fatter; one who, alas and of course, loves to eat. She had run away from home, left school at fourteen, got a job and attended night-school. At the same time she wanted to take up dancing to meet boys. She had been valedictorian, voted the one most likely to succeed. A snap in the school paper showed her with her mouth open, a bright, malicious wrinkle to her mouth, her eyes sparkling, a lock of hair streaming down one cheek, folds of adolescent fat around her short solid neck and chin. Making her speech, prepared beforehand, she had not stuck to the text but had gone on, laughing, joking, carrying the school with her for nearly an hour, and with everyone then getting more restive she became imperious. At last someone spoke. She turned and shouted, 'I am Sir Oracle and when I speak, let no dog bark!' It had no success: no one knew it. Fired by this, she had prolonged her speech. In the end, she caught the eye of a boy she admired, saw his sneer, blushed and stopped. Like many another ambitious, gifted and healthy girl, her first love was a mean second-rater, a crawling careerist who kept referring to his unworthiness, only to get help and climb another half-inch higher. She only knew this later.

'And all because she was fat,' she now wrote, telling this story.

230

While writing this she had had another idea and made a few notes on it before she gave up for the day. She also meant to work at least one hour on her next funny chapter. She knew she was wasting time, financially speaking, and yet she took such full joy in trying one thing and another. 'I like a full quiver.'

But this afternoon, Stephen kept shouting, 'You've done enough, come down, come down, you don't know when to stop.'

At last she came down, protesting. Stephen told her all that had happened. They were excited, charmed by Vittorio's friendly advances. What did it mean? That they had friends in the USA who had written? That Vittorio had written to the American Party and found out their situation and now from his European viewpoint, sympathized with them? For if it meant that they were forgiven, no, that their cause was taken up by the Italian and French Parties, that these repudiated the position of the American Party and were anxious for ammunition to pounce on and set right the political and theoretical errors not to say crimes of the American Party, and were ready to pursue farther the path opened up by Jacques Duclos, then it might mean that the Howards were in a way supported even by the Kremlin and that in the end the thunders of the Kremlin would be directed against, would even demolish those in University Place who had led them to shame, disgrace. Stephen was so joyful and Emily so proud of him, Emily so triumphant and Stephen in such a gay teasing mood that they decided to leave the children, the work and even Suzanne's lessons and go out for dinner to a very dear, very 'rayshershay' place they knew, Véfour. Madame Suzanne had been in the house since ten o'clock. They went to explain to her that they would take the afternoon off.

But Madame Suzanne knew Vittorio very well, by name, reputation and by sight. And what wonders she told them of him! In the first place, before the troubles in Europe, he had been a society lawyer, sought after by all the society men and women for their difficulties. He had charmed endless women. 'Charmed! Charmed women!' Stephen almost shouted.

Madame Suzanne nodded her head. 'Oh, yes, I assure you. He was very seductive. I don't mean he created scandals. Women fell in love with him. He had an enormous practice out of it. And he himself is an odd type. He used to fall violently in love and go through agonies for the beautiful women he met. To love and be loved by Vittorio was an adventure every society woman wanted. Or most wanted.'

'Women loved him?' said Stephen, still astonished.

'Of course, he has changed, he is dreadfully disfigured. But women still love him. He can still charm and win them. He had been married four times.'

'I don't understand it. But then I never did know what women wanted,' said Stephen.

And she told them much more about him. How brave he was, how, once convinced, he had dropped his fashionable practice, joined the Party and done their legal work, organized their cultural work, how good his memory was, infallible, freakish, how he sacrificed himself, how he was sought after by the police, what he had done in the Resistance, how he had been caught and put into a camp, where he was ill-treated. Much more. The Howards were entranced by their capture, their new friend. They must have him at the house as soon as possible, and they began to discuss with Madame Suzanne or as she now already was, Suzanne, what sort of people they could invite who would not hurt the feelings of this hero. She said she knew many such people; she could easily fix up a congruous party for them. They went out for their walk enraptured. They sat on a café terrace later, took a taxi to Véfour in the Palais-Royal and liked it so much that from then on they called it their Véfour, 'our dear Véfour'.

Emily was delighted with the character of their new friend. It was pleasant to know that such a hero, a man so highly regarded all over Europe, had once been a man of Stephen's own background. Emily said, 'At last you are vindicated! Now you realise that what you did had meaning and worth. You really fought for freedom and theoretical purity. I always believed in you, Stephen. I let you down at times and wished you had not touched the theoretical questions, but now I see you were right, we have not only got out of the whole mess, but with clean hands. Oh, I am so happy and proud! Oh, my dear, dear husband! You are really wonderful. I'm deleerious, this is the new life. God bless Vittorio and Jacques Duclos and all the people here. I am so enchanted and excited. It proves this wasn't just an escape. It always hurt me bitterly that they called us escapists and Bohemian adventurers. I was discouraged and now I'm in a dream-world of glorious joy. Oh, what a gamble! It seemed like a gamble, worse, a delusion; but even for us it's worked out perfectly. Oh, what a cave of Adullam we escaped from. And to come straight into the arms of the Party here – in Paris, the loveliest city in the world; and I have everything straight at last, and am happy.'

Stephen said with a proud, repressed smile, 'I wouldn't be so enthusiastic about it until we can check up. A few facts won't hurt us. But you, Emily, don't need facts to work on, only enthusiasm. However, I feel a lot better. He's in such a high position in the Party that he couldn't, wouldn't visit us unless he thought we were clean. He couldn't do it for his own reputation! No need for us to be hangdog any more, though.

What a smack in the nose for the old die-hards of University Place.'

He became silent. His wife said hastily, 'We're celebrating, darling. Don't start to fret.'

But his face had clouded over. He said, 'They were my friends. I know them. They're really all right. I hate them to call me what they do call me, a goddamn bastard, an apostate, a Benedict Arnold – I left my country and my Party. They are right.'

'Oh, don't groan like a Jew in the subway.'

This was a family joke with them. Stephen said, 'And yet he had a right to groan. It's the ones who don't groan who are wrong. Six millions, many more, put to fire and sword and bullet and torn by dogs and buried alive – he is right to groan and so are we.'

The next day they ate out as well. They went to the Museum of Modern Art, one of the finest buildings of modern times, in pure, perpendicular marble, unspotted and airy, an angelic gate where they saw old paintings, new copper, ceramics, a 1910 revival and the strangely beautiful tapestries of Lurçat, living as blood in a sunlit flask, with the thought of a tree, glowing in its pattern of life into the austere and innocent web. There was a lot of walking to do, and many steps and few exhibits. France of the artists was just lifting its splendid head from the Nazi night. On this day, the sun shone, the Seine flowed as brightly as any young river, the sky was blue and the trees along the rue de New-York were in small leaf. Emily skipped along with the daintiness of the fat, on her small high-heels.

'We have spring in New York but it isn't like this, wine and food and spirit. There they suddenly push down a funnel over the city and that's it, spring, wilting and burning.'

Stephen was opposed to the list of guests she and Suzanne had drawn up for Vittorio.

'I don't feel at home with social workers, French teachers, sombre or slap-happy Resistance types and all that crew. Can't we have a little fun? He's a very entertaining man. He's polished, thank God.'

'But they would have something to talk about!'

'Bunkum,' said Stephen.

But in the end he had to yield. He himself wanted to have some good Party talk with Party leaders and now he was to have his own servant, a dull but good woman, a pedestrian heroine, Suzanne, at his side.

'But you like Mernie Wauters!'

Stephen cheered up. Emily explained, 'We'll have to have a right circle and a left circle. We need both.'

'Yes, I need people. I don't believe the brain flourishes in isolation. I'm no hermit nor masturbating thinker. Thinking is social.'

'What about Darwin?'

'Oh, he's English. They are never the same. And that's horse-and-buggy. The Soviet thinkers and scientists are proud and glad to think socially in a laboratory and for the State. These old countries need socialism to wipe off all that smear of solitary thinking, which is just the ornament of a class state. But in the USA, as in Russia, we think socially. We have a lot in common.'

Emily said, 'That's very true. I wish we could work in Russia or Yugo or somewhere over the border. It's hard to keep on fighting for what you know are the merest ABCs. I do hate to yes-ma'am a lot of snobberines here. Why don't we come out with it? They do. I guess we're in a mixed world. That's why we must have a right circle and a left circle. I don't want to cut myself off any more as we did in the USA. I want to live in the whole world.'

The people they invited were delighted to come, 'to spend an evening with Vittorio, with Vittorio more than with us, nobodies, American theoretical ignoramuses.'

'What do we care? We've got hold of a real person,' said Emily.

'But it's our soup they're eating.'

'Those are the risks of entertaining,' said Emily.

'When in Rome burn the candle at both ends,' said Stephen.

The preparations took up a lot of time: the expense would be no less than for previous parties. Stephen groaned, 'Who got me into this? How do you know he doesn't like a cup of coffee? If he's a real communist who spent years in the Resistance and in concentration camps, he'll be glad of a baked bean or a lamb chop grilled over a campfire.'

'Stephen, don't be so miserly.'

'Well, we represent the American relief for wilting Europe.'

Emily said, 'Besides, I know from Suzanne that Vittorio is a very good cook; and even when he is living in one room with kitchenette in a closet, he gets up elaborate dishes and invites gourmet company.'

'Well, your admirer will get enough to eat here, with that menu.'

'My admirer? He's never heard of me.'

'Yes, he has. He's heard of you. He's a one-man encyclopaedia. He'll probably come here armed with more facts about you and your books than I ever knew. He told me he particularly admired *The Wilkes-Barre Chronicle*, he's convinced you'll be a great serious writer and he thinks you're a great humorist too.'

Emily had a sunny smile, 'Did he? Oh, I wish I'd done that hunger-march better! It should have been better. It's just cheap journalism.'

234

'You did it nine times before it went to the printer. You're a great writer.'

'No, I'm not. Not in the hunger-march. And here's a man who knows much more than hunger-marches. Well, well. Stephen, I sent off three chapters of my funny books this afternoon and I ought to get five hundred dollars apiece; and maybe a movie bite. I think they're medium-funny.'

'They're uproarious. You ought to hold out for a better price. Listen, why don't you write travel articles, show all the society we meet, make it funny as we see it next day at breakfast. We could travel more, see more, it would keep paying for itself. We'll make a go of it. I don't really worry about you. I scold and worry and beat the breast and insult you – it's only superstition! I don't think it's right to tempt fate.'

'Why can't we live like dear Maurice? When I think of the lovely dreamy mornings we spent last week with him here, just talking at the breakfast table, blissful – '

'None of us working,' put in Stephen.

'Ah, my dearest, to think that compared with the meanest continental or English schoolboy, I'm an old woman of the wilds, a hairy ape, an ignorant buzzard who can scarcely write her own name. Oh, I must study to keep up even with my own right-wing guests whom I so deeply despise. America, my own: what have you done to me?'

She went on merrily, unable to stop, cheered beyond limit by the news that her books were admired by Vittorio, once the darling of the best-cushioned, best-dowried, best-titled, Catholic society, a man of dangerous charm, guile and success in any world he chose. She ended sighing, 'Ah, my dearest, these weeks are the nicest things that have happened to us in years and years. Goddamn it, in Europe communists and relatives don't have to be all tattletale grey, spots of gloom, festering mildew and unbarbered sextons intoning anathema and looking out for the bottle of scotch. Europe and I agree about everything. Here they calmly survey their own downgoing, the advent of the Red Terror with reasonable fortitude, resignation or reasonable fight. Whereas God knows we come from a country of writhing, groaning, torment. Reeling and writhing, what the tortoise taught us.'

The next day they took their usual three-hour French lesson after lunch with Suzanne. She lunched with them and during lunch they spoke English; but after that they worked very hard, like college students.

Suzanne had been teaching them for some weeks and after being surprised by their whirling life, their expenses and their domestic brawling, she had come to understand them. She said to them now, in French, 'You know when Mademoiselle de la Roche asked me to give you lessons, I hesitated. You seemed so strange to me and I could not make out whether you were real radicals or the shallowest of parlour pinks. But now

I understand better; and if I have taught you, you have taught me.'

She laughed harshly and went on, 'We are so many. You can imagine, I got to know a good many people during the occupation. I had many surprises. The people who betrayed were not the ones you would have guessed; the people who took in Jewish babies and Jewish refugees, political refugees, who ran the real risks, were not the ones you would have predicted. Your own reactions were not what you would have thought. And there were so many factors of nationality, training, personality, family situation, love and fright that you can hardly trust yourself, let alone anyone else. And you must take chances with strangers. But you come through and others come though. I do not know if the same people would come through again; or if I would come through again. And so I have no prejudices, or very few. I'm very anxious only to know more people. I could never have guessed at the existence of people like you.'

Emily who had worked hard at her tenses, understood and was very pleased with this speech,

'What do you think of us now, dear Suzanne?'

Madame Gagneux laughed, 'You know, I am not really French. I am Belgian. We're a mixed and weighty people. Weighty in bad and good senses. You've heard from me of *l'esprit Belge*, the Belgian approach, that means heavy, taking things wrongly, misunderstanding French, it means a crass approach. I can't help being Belgian; I don't mind it. I think we're different, we're more medieval, we're lustier, we joke more in a genial, kermesse way, the primitive market-day peasant and farmer way, we see things as ludicrous and coarse rather than otherwise. And we're not good psychologists for nowadays, so I leave that aside. You are very Belgian, Madame Howard; and your husband, Mr Howard, does not like me much I know.'

She said this without flattery and without resentment.

Emily fluttered, 'I think the only reason for that is that you're our teacher and so his role with you is a humble one, that of learner, of a tot. Oh, we're not linguists. I work, I'm full of French, I have my lesson, I do my writing and by six in the evening I can't think of the French for tomato juice. Alas! You may be Belgian but you're a linguist.'

Madame after a moment said gently, 'Well, now, reciprocate. Tell me what you think of me, and why you ask me questions about myself.'

Emily struggled, '*Eh, bien* Madame Suzanne, vooz ate not amie, you have become our friend and because I heard some hints – what's that, good God in French? – I felt all the time this great vacuum, not knowing exactly what nameless and terrible things, *shows terrible*, had passed in your life – well, I can't say it in French – what painful and awful times your life has encompassed; yet, because I know you and you are part of us,

236

we have dinner with you, you know our children, you are ours as contrasted with the *purple anonyme general*, the anonymous vague general people; and in spite of the pain of remembering, in spite of the *honter freeson*, I mean the shameful shuddering away from (God knows what I'm saying Madame Suzanne, *vous comprenez?*) the sufferings and heroism of those people I don't know are less pressing – you might say honestly I don't care any more for the sufferings of people one never saw or cared for, they're not real sufferings, they are *fetts diverses*, but because of knowing you, and knowing you have been through all that, I feel – somehow strange, terrible, very ill, even guilty. *Vous me comprenez, n'est-ce pas?*'

'*Je vous comprends parfaitement,*' said Suzanne.

Emily paused and said, 'I shrink, Suzanne, terribly from this knowledge. I don't know what will be the consequences of knowing.'

'I must say, if your French is very inadequate, I understand your feelings,' said Suzanne.

'I feel a positive horror, a fear to know these things and to know that these things happened to someone I see with my own eyes and my own children see with their eyes; and my husband sees with his eyes. It happened to someone whose voice I know, whose eyes are watching me. My God! My God!'

Madame Suzanne said, looking at her with wide-open eyes, 'It's bizarre. You, too, give me a sense of horror and yet I felt none then, except at any given moment. Is it because you are a writer?'

Emily continued, 'This afternoon, just before I am to meet Vittorio, this famous man and hero – '

She paused a moment, looking questioningly at Suzanne, who was non-committal. Emily continued, 'I feel this reluctance, this shuddering and, at the same time, a sense of duty, is it? Of being forced? So I must know, it seems to me, what you suffered. Will you tell me please? Tell me in French, as part of the lesson.'

'Well, I know you have heard many accounts. You were a journalist, you went and interviewed widows of miners and of men dead in accidents, orphans, all kinds of people, so I am not going to tell you sad stories. Besides, it's not my way and it's not of importance. These are realities. No need for window-dressing.'

Stephen was called away at this moment for a telephone conversation and he did not return. His French was better than Emily's but he would not study and he resented Madame Gagneux.

Emily said, 'Yes, Suzanne, I understand. Oh, go on, hurry, I can't wait to know. Tell me before Stephen returns. Do you see, tonight I am going to meet people who know about you; or if not you, the life you led and I am outside. *Je suis dehors.*'

Emily looked at Suzanne, thinking about her. She wished that Stephen would return. Madame Suzanne was perhaps ten years older than Emily, poorly dressed, as always, (and perhaps for that he doesn't like her, thought Emily), an intellectual, surely, with fine half-grey hair in waves, her face solid, dark-eyed, if not handsome. They were what Stephen called scornfully, 'no-doubt-soulful-eyes.' They were large, dark eyes quite startling in what Stephen called her 'pasty, meaty face'.

Emily declared she was beautiful: Stephen found something detestable in her. Suzanne was saying, 'And tomorrow, the day after tomorrow, you must prepare a speech for me, all about your life in Hollywood. Have you your notebook, Madame Howard?'

Emily said, 'I feel ashamed to write notes about the words in a story of this sort.'

Suzanne smiled, 'Oh, this is quite unimportant. As I no doubt mentioned, I was a member of two underground groups, one for the hiding of Jewish children from the Nazis, the other the demolition squad for the *actifs*, Resistants on active service. Good.'

'Ah? Good,' said Emily.

'I had a war name: we all did. Mine was Mademoiselle Marie-Charlotte Broun. Of course, I had false papers and a baptism certificate. I am atheist from childhood. From 1940 to 1944 I hid 2,134 Jewish children and I lost fourteen of these children.'

'What do you mean by lost?'

'By lost I mean, fourteen of these hidden with families were discovered by the Nazis and transported to a crematorium where they were changed into burned bones and ashes. Of these, nine were under ten years old. The other five were between ten and twelve. After the war was over, I helped in the work of returning the children to their parents, if there were parents. You see this was very hard; just as hard as before; and then I had to tell them, myself, some of them, about the lost ones. It was my duty; I could not blame others. Returning the children was not easy. Many years had passed; some could not remember their parents, they loved their foster-parents. They had to pass as non-Jews of course and did not know they were Jews. One, for example, had to be sent to a distant uncle in the Argentine. I criticize no one. For the Jews, nearly extirpated as a race, these lost treasures, a grandson, a nephew, these were treasures, you see. I understand. But it was very hard, for those who had put their own lives in danger and fed and loved the little ones during those years. You are crying. I do not cry. There were so many hard things. It is no use. It is all very hard.'

Emily looked at the woman before her. 'It is simply strange and

238

wonderful. How could you have had the courage to do it?'

'Oh, in the first place, I look like so many other people. And then we found we could all do it. There were times – I'll go into that later. I was plastered all over the walls as Mademoiselle Marie-Charlotte Broun you know. The Germans knew my pseudonym, my work with Jewish children and the demolition squads. But I take a very bad photograph. I look like others.'

'What did you do on the demolition squad?' said Emily looking timidly at the dumpy grey-haired woman, whose voice was tired now.

'Oh, I organized, helped get explosives. I was in a sector where, frankly, there was not much of that. The population was not very enthusiastic. There were such sections, especially near German head-quarters, and apart from general and special regulations such as special curfews, the Germans were not too bad to the population. It is a pity to say it, but mere truth, that some people got used to living with them, living as a sort of serf or client. I was in a not very heroic section, like that. At the end, just before the end, our chief was sent to Buchenwald and died there, a professor of mathematics at a college. I must tell you it was not only us, though. There were complete strangers who helped in an emergency. Once I had a list of eleven Jewish children in my handbag. The Gestapo came and started a search of the café where I was sitting, waiting for someone. They searched the woman next to me, found nothing. She was completely unknown to me. I got up to go, leaving my handbag on the seat next to her. They stopped me and searched me and she had taken and hidden my handbag; and when they went she gave it back.'

Emily, after a silence, said, 'My heavens, this is a wonderful, terrible story. Yet the way you say it, it is not exactly spectacular; they would not put it in the movies. So this is Europe 1948. Most people have lived through something like it. So this is Europe 1948.'

'No doubt of that,' said Suzanne.

'How strange it all seems. I look around and think, the Germans have been here, climbed this staircase, bought at this shop, this wheelbarrow has been used to transport their goods. This man in denims has worked for them; these streets were their streets. I think this and hate them. How I hate them! I hate them that they were here in Paris with German lettering on the Opéra. How did it happen? It's so hard to understand.'

After a few more minutes of conversation, Emily said, 'I don't know if my French is improving, Suzanne, but I understand so much better.'

'It's because you want to understand and you want to say something. Strength of expression gives grammar. You will learn French. I do not think Mr Howard will learn it so easily. I read your fine book, Madame

239

Howard, and I think this was a fine, forceful work. Vittorio lent it to me.'

Emily jumped up from her end of the table and came to throw her arms round Suzanne's shoulders, 'Oh, Suzanne, you encourage me. I need it. I have so much writing-for-money to do. But hope is in Europe, where values are different, where heroism is part of the human heart. I really hope to write the good books I have in my heart. A writer is his work, isn't he?'

Madame Suzanne began collecting her papers and books, 'No, a writer is his relation to society. You know that someone wrote contemptuously about Gustave Flaubert or the Goncourts, I forget which, 'Si le bouquin marche, tout marche.' They didn't care; they wrote. This at a moment when men, literary men, jewellers, bakers and shoe-makers were dying for the Commune.'

Emily said, 'You depress me: this is depressing.'

Suzanne smiled, 'Alas, most of the writers I admired before the war, proved to be poor creatures during the occupation and some of the actors too. Cheer up! What has that to do with you? You cannot answer for me or them; I cannot answer for you. All is to be tried out again, every time again. There is no fatality, nothing sure; you will be all right. I leave it to you.'

Emily got up from the table, 'If only we could be sure of ourselves. How difficult it is! How can we be sure? I don't know how I'd behave.'

Suzanne said, 'Everyone asks himself that question; and no one knows.'

Emily had some things to do herself. she had no time to change, and for dinner and most of the evening she wore her afternoon costume, a pair of short blue linen trousers, tight and somewhat faded, over this a blue butcher's smock over a turtle neck sweater over a white silk blouse; and a blue ribbon off a chocolate box tying her hair into a top-knot. From time to time she adjusted in her water-fall of hair, little combs which did not hold it. There was her very red and yellow face smiling, her naturally light-red lips, her bright blue eyes, rounded and wide open. Stephen looking at her, smiled, as others did; her costume was comic, original and becoming. The blouse, intended for a short, solid, rotund butcher, covered her large bosom and thick waist. She had put on a lot of weight.

When Vittorio was announced she felt a qualm. She ought to have put on a dress. The Europeans like women feminine. Stephen's argument against Madame Suzanne was that she wasn't feminine; she didn't try to appeal to the male. There in fact was Suzanne in a black dress, unfeminine, looking stolid, not the romantic heroine; and there was she, a butcher-boy. The door opened and Vittorio walked in, with a red-and-white smile. Speaking in a bubbling, happy voice he came towards her,

240

holding out a large bunch of pink roses in white paper, his glasses sticking out of his breast pocket. He kissed her plump, dimpled hand.

'I have just come from a meeting, dear Madame. These are for you. You see how I have come.'

He had not shaved, his small, sparse, reddish whiskers could be seen. He was uncommonly ugly, half-blind, half-deaf. His voice, when not shouting, was a chirping, reassuring, cooing, cozening, honeyed song, warm and hurrying; and when he wanted to explain something, he shouted. He was as confident as a much-loved child, went quickly to and fro in the room and, if he did not know what to do, he at once asked, in an agreeable, friendly, but self-reliant way; there was a very faint hint that if he was at a loss, his host was at fault. He greeted Suzanne with real enthusiasm. He was early. Emily wished she had asked more people. The room seemed hollow. The echoing green, she said to herself; and no more to be seen on the echoing green.

'The echoing green,' she said to Stephen, laughing as she turned to the drinks tray and began to fill the cocktail shaker with cracked ice, gin and vermouth. 'It just came into my head. I used to stay awake at night when I needed sleep,' (she continued to her guests) 'reciting the poems I knew. In one afternoon I learned 110 poems straight out of the anthology we had to study. I bet I was the only one went to the examination room with those 110 poems by heart.'

Vittorio said, laughing:

> 'Such such were the joys,
> When we all, girls and boys
> In our youth time were seen,
> On the Echoing Green.'

'Oh, Vittorio, what is that?' said Emily in surprise, turning to him and coming over with the cocktail shaker in her hand. She poured his drink first.

'Why you know, of course, it is William Blake. I was at a cultural conference only a few months ago in which he was attacked by an English writer; and I got up and said he knew nothing at all about Blake. And so did others, I assure you. He is considered a very great poet on the continent. All the *Songs of Innocence* are so simply purely music.'

He held up his glass and drank with his scarred but smiling eyes to Emily. 'But I am so tired, I am wandering,' he said.

'Imagine you knowing it so well. You put us to shame,' said Emily.

He smiled, 'But you must know *The Gadfly* by Voynich. A woman, you know, is the author. The man is disfigured and the man and woman only recognize each other, though they never are sure, after many years, by

241

means of some stanzas of Blake's.' The stanzas go:

"Am I not a fly like thee?
Or art thou not a man like me?
For I dance and drink and sing,
Till some blind hand shall brush my wing.
If thought is life and strength and breath
And the want of thought is death;
Then am I a happy fly
If I live or if I die."

Emily said, with eyes sparkling with tears, 'I feel so ashamed; you know it a hundred times better than I do.'

Vittorio said, 'But you create it. I am only a consumer – though I have written some plays and one philosophical story'; and he went on to tell the story, which Emily described as purely dialectical but diabolically amusing. It was a true story of a society without lawyers, which had trial by ordeal. The ordeal was to exhaust your opponent by extemporizing verses in a public assembly. Vittorio said:

'But Palambron called down a Great Solemn Assembly,
That he who will not defend Truth, may be compelled to
Defend a Lie, that he may be snared and caught and taken'

and he laughed.

Emily, flabbergasted, said nothing. He went on talking. He advised Emily to read Diderot's *The Blind Girl*, to go back to Voltaire, to read the memoirs of Mademoiselle de l'Espinasse. He told her Marx was full of ideas and explanations of things for literary people: that St Just was an expert in political psychology. Socialist literature was full of the most exquisite masterpieces, sealed in silence, rarely translated. He mentioned the novel about Auguste Blanqui, *L'Enfermé*, the man perpetually in prison; others. Emily, listening passionately, with eager, inflamed face, her hair blowing in the invisible air currents of the room, and the breezes of her own ardent life, declared she was going to read every one of them, a new life had come to her; 'I have been looking for a new road and this is it. How you help me!' Stephen listened too; but as if it were a play and with a satiric expression. Vittorio seemed unconscious of his drawbacks. Stephen smiled a little sourly. He was relieved when Mernie Wauters was announced. Wauters was a dark man in his mid-thirties, slender, stooping, a little above middle height, sallow, with liquid brown eyes under well-curved eyebrows, and a poignant, expressionless, sick face, which some woman had called soulful. Wauters was a successful businessman. He and Madame Suzanne knew each other well.

242

'He was my associate in the Resistance,' said Suzanne.

'Old warriors reunited,' said Stephen ironically.

Stephen felt restless. Suzanne was shabby, Vittorio shabby and un-shaved and Wauters looked like a foreigner, a Jew, a Pole. Emily was finding a rich flavour in this assortment; her love of adventure, her natural courage, her old training made this assembly appeal to her. But this flotsam and jetsam of war, occupation and near-revolution made Stephen feel untidy. He had come to Europe for peace and quiet, peaceful vindication. He had always detested Bohemia. However, he showed nothing of this. He had a natural pleasantness of manner which deceived even other charmers, he was the perfect master of the house.

Emily, though knowing his feelings, suppressed her animal spirits, her ready affections and tempers, when she could, and made the soft lights and music play around him. It was his house, she loved him, he was her child and her husband, a man who had been sick and given up a fortune for the revolution; who had placed himself on a level where he might meet a woman like her, had rejoiced in her, been her great stroke of luck. She never forgot this.

Now observing his mood, she said to herself, I must not spend the whole evening admiring Vittorio. She swung away from Vittorio to Wauters, who was talking to Madame Suzanne, with her life-knowing, plain air. Emily thought to herself, I'll get her some kind of a dress, and Stephen will like her better. And it's that wiry hair looks like a touch of the tar-brush, Negro or Algerian or something. Could I do something about her hair? And if Stephen likes her better, he will learn French easier and we can have the kind of company in this house in which he is really happy.

She thought this with a wise smile playing round her mobile and rather thin lips, and meantime listened to what was being said. Suzanne and Monsieur Wauters were, to Stephen's discontent, exchanging reminiscences about the Resistance. She thought, 'This is dull. It can't go on all the evening. Perhaps Vittorio is my best bet after all.'

She said to Mernie Wauters, 'But tell us one of your stories. I know you tell wonderful stories.'

She handed round some more cocktails though they were getting watery; and went back to the table to fill the cocktail shaker. This time to liven the party she put in so much gin, so little Vermouth, that Stephen called warningly, Emily! Emily! With a pretty grimace, she took no notice and went around filling glasses.

Vittorio, roseate now and not hearing what she said to him, turned to her energetically and smiling, 'You are magnificent, you have a mag-nificent chance. Very few are the humorists today. It is not a humorous age, though if incongruity is the soul of humour, there should be millions. But we live in an age of fear and fear is not funny. You laugh. In a time like this, you know how to laugh. How admirable! What a gift for humanity! But you must apply it to the day and for the workers. The world is full of incongruities, things difficult to explain. The humorist can explain them; he can cheer people up, they no longer feel contempt for humanity, for the world and for life; such things as lead to moral despair, moral and biological suicide. The ranks of our enemies are being filled every day by those leaving us, who can no longer cope with the terrors of the world; so they throw themselves into the arms of their enemies! Jail me, gag me, blind me, make me deaf! They will be decapitated physically as they already are in spirit and mind. What misery! But you laugh. Laugh my dear, charming child. Show people things are living, pulsating with life; and they won't so easily join the others out of despair and fear. Think what there is in the new democracies; something we don't know yet, joy and belief, a positive move forward. You can't restrain them in their youthful eagerness, they bound with joy like puppies, they want to love and be severe and reform in love and severity. Perhaps they don't show enough joy and life for us to see, but they are young. There are solemn children too, children who have destiny in them. We need people like you, Emily, among us. I see your humour is really you. There's no boundary to your spirit and you can express this. America is a land of humorists with stout, rich, philosophical humour: you belong to a great race. How I admire this talent!'

Emily was excited. She said,

'Oh, those who go over to the enemy, it's like climbing up the gallows-tree to get away from a bear, it's like pulling the gravestone over your head for shelter from the gritty wind, it's like escaping from a fire by jumping off the nineteenth storey and finding there's no safety net – ha-ha-ha –'

She was roaring with laughter, rosy pink, 'Ho-ho-ho, I said that once, I threw a scare into them. I felt them shudder and roll towards me; I said, You will eat the spittle of a class that knows no pity and it will poison you.' As Emily spoke habitually very loud, Vittorio was able to hear all she said; and at this he applauded, crying 'That was magnificent. I wish I had heard your speech.'

Emily now had to go to the kitchen and when she returned a dismal conversation had begun about American politics. She began to laugh,

'Oh, the greenhorns! I only just found out what a capon is. Fernande was giving me her recipe for fat chicken or capon and I said, "Why that's the same!" "Oh, no, Madame." Poor Fernande! I wish you had seen her expression just now. She thought Madame had changed into *le tailleur* or le trailing-chiffon by this. *Eh, bien, alors, tant pis, des Américains, quoi!* She's wonderful, Monsieur Vittorio. Even when we run out of everything, and we do owing to the disinterested attitude of Madame who is fabricating les bestsellers at fifty dollars *la page* and Monsieur, who is out trying to see what he can do for the working-class – '

'Emily, you fool!' said Stephen pleasantly from his throne. He always made himself a cradle or throne in his little armchair, by drawing up both legs, crossing them over the arms and displaying his handknitted wool socks. He had as usual cast away one shoe here, one there; from his pose he smiled at them all.

Emily smiled roguishly and went on, 'Even then our Fernande can run up a dinner of *potage*, veal with mushrooms, potatoes with chives, cauliflower with cheese sauce, the little cakes, the coffee, yum-yum. Is it possible, is it *vraiment possible* that Madame Howard will be able from now on to attend to *la littérature?*'

'Probably because you allow her the bottom of the basket,' said Suzanne.

'Well, it seems Fernande has the most unusual number of relatives I ever heard of and all in the provision trades or the house-manicuring trades or windows mending or – well the lower branches those are, I guess.'

Emily laughed, 'Oh, well if we set our relatives to work the way the French do. Instead of getting hired help we'll get Uncle Klotz to paint the house and Uncle Potz to build the shed and Aunt to scrub the floor – the rich like Stephen always do it.'

Stephen said, 'Well, naturally! Otherwise, what's the point of going through the hell of being a rich son-of-a-bitch if you don't put the halter on them and crack the whip! Sons-of-bitches, cousins, uncles, work for me!'

Stephen was in an excellent temper now; and the evening went on and on about American ways and French ways. They had a good dinner, julienne soup, sole cooked with a sauce of mussels, oysters, mushrooms, large shrimps, little fried gudgeons and white wine, veal birds, vichy carrots, milk-fed lamb and French beans, and the usual desserts.

During dinner Emily eagerly explained to Mernie Wauters and to Vittorio how they felt about their political ties at home.

Stephen ate a little, murmured politely and looked occasionally out of the window. It was true that he and Emily had eagerly discussed what could be done with Vittorio. They considered he had already fore-shadowed the promise of a vindication by the French, an association with the French Party, which would make their enemies in America bow their heads in shame and defeat; but that this would be a new beginning for

245

Stephen too. He could perhaps become a consultant on American affairs for the French Party, become a well-known foreign journalist, totally re-established, write for the American syndicated press. Perhaps Emily was right in talking about it right away. She was bold, ready and ripe; she would have made a first-class businessman. Born in Stephen's setting she would not, like him, have gone in for any second-rate intellectual life, she would have gone out and made another million dollars for herself.

Emily was now arguing with them about their cultural press. They wanted her to read *Les Lettres Françaises*, *L'Humanité*.

Her face had clouded, 'There's no real news in foreign newspapers. Stephen and I for our daily fodder, our morning fisticuffs, must have the home papers. We get the *New York Times* by plane and the *New York Herald Tribune* Paris edition. Why don't you read them? They're more informative and much better planned than the foreign press. It's so old-fashioned. They fill the front pages with queer things here, studies of plants, or literature or Roman culture. Fooey! I want the news.'

'She's an old newshound; she hates culture,' said Stephen.

Emily said testily, 'But I look for culture elsewhere, not in the daily newspaper and certainly not on the front page. A newspaper is for news. It was because I understood that, that I was a great success as a journalist. A newspaper is not culture or humanism or philosophy; it's the news angled to strike your eye and amuse you, if possible. I hate all this wandering palaver; I can't get anything out of it.'

'Just a savage, excuse her,' said Stephen, smiling.

She looked black. She shouted, 'Stephen! Go to hell! You couldn't write an acceptable news-story to save your life. All you write are long, watered-down, philosophical and economic canting scriptures that don't even express your own opinion. Fooey! I'd like myself to show the editors of *L'Humanité* how to edit a paper in the modern American style. It would make them more readable, get up the circulation.'

They then had an argument about the circulation of various workers' papers. It turned out that European papers did astonishingly better than the American and British. Emily was beaten.

'Oh, well, all right, all right. I suppose it's suitable for a lot of old style horse-and-buggy era workers with out-of-date factory systems; but it doesn't do them any good.'

She began to shout, 'They oughtn't to be left there back in the past, with all this dead stuff. Workers read the newspapers wrapped round their lunch in between shifts and they're too dog-tired to worry about philosophy whether pink, red or black. Think of the lives they lead. No fun. Not enough to eat. Can't pay for the wife's confinement and the boy's school books. A lot of academic intellectuals are trying to get off on

246

them the old stuff they learned in college, so it won't be wasted, so it will pay a dividend. Pages and pages of learned junk no one can follow. Give them pictures, snappy captions, title the paragraphs, lots of *fetts diverses* and people won't think communists are a lot of dead monkeys. I mean extremists, conspirators full of academic bull. I mean like this Blanqui, Vittorio. Where did he get? Or people drinking blood, or sectarians or crazy fanatics or rabble-rousers or careerists trying to get ministerial jobs through the blood and broken bones of poor men, or even cheesy Utopians and a horde of ivory towers, long hairs and squares with a sort of religion, slinging slogans like old Russia at Eastertime.'

This denunication made the guests, though not Stephen, who was embarrassed, laugh uproariously. Madame Suzanne said,

'Why don't you write it? You would make a wonderful speaker.'

Vittorio declared, 'But she does write like that, only you have not seen these wonderful books. These are the books I wish you to read. I must translate them for others, too. I have little time but I will devote myself to this, for we in Europe must know that there are other writers besides Hemingway, a silly writer about blood and battle, promoted by a snob sect, and Steinbeck, who is a poor writer and an ignorant man. Madame Emily has written a wonderful book called *The Wilkes-Barre Chronicle*, the story of a strike; and another very fine book called *Johnny Appleseed*. As well as this, she is a remarkable natural humorist. Humour cannot be manufactured. It comes from the marrow. She has also written a very funny book called *Uncle Henry* which was a great success on Broadway called *Henry, There's An Angel*. It is very, very funny. I beg you to let me translate *The Wilkes-Barre Chronicle*, I will show it to you. You will see if it is in good enough French. You will see that I appreciate your genius, too, I hope.' He bowed slightly.

Emily was in a great state, blushing and exclaiming, 'Oh, Vittorio, oh, of course, oh, Vittorio, what an honour!'

Emily burst into tears, got up and went round to embrace Vittorio, kissing him on the cheeks, 'Oh, Vittorio, how good you are. How beautiful and good! What a great heart! Oh, to say these things to me! Do you know the American Party despises *The Wilkes-Barre Chronicle*, I must hush-hush about it. They only want me – oh, never mind, never mind. They have a deep grudge against me because of *Johnny Appleseed*. I wrote about them and it sold only 5,000 and so I wasted the time I could have spent writing a best seller from which I could have given a cut to the Party. Yes, that is the truth,' she said to Wauters.

Wauters said, 'Yes, I am sure it is. They are businessmen. Businessmen think that a bourgeois can only give money. But this is not true of people of genius. I am only a businessman; but our Party did not look upon me only in that light. I was to them an all-round man.'

And he told them some of his experiences. Wauters' wife had been in Dachau, himself in Sachsenhausen but only at the end. 'I knew I was being followed. This was the experience of everyone. As for joining the Resistance, one is terrified at first, suspects everyone, every passenger in the train, but eventually you get used to it and smart at knowing who is who. And then, at the end when you are being shadowed, again you suspect everyone, every car, every truck, every person outside the house – you understand, you're like the paranoiacs. It can't be helped. It's a sort of relief in the end when they knock on your door.'

He laughed, 'I went into the local concentration camp and then to the south of France and in this camp I found a lot of gypsies who had been arrested, I can't imagine why, except they arrested everyone who had any personal ideas or way of life. The gypsies had the worst conditions and also were terribly suspicious of camp conditions. They would not drink the camp water, would not eat the camp food. I spoke to them, I became their spokesman, as I speak both French and Romany – '

'What?' said Emily.

'Yes, he speaks a good many languages, it's a foible,' said Madame Suzanne.

'I induced them to use the camp faucets and beds, to make some demands as a group. They did not know a Nazi from a Resistant; they were suspicious of everyone.'

Emily said, 'And you all knew this dreadful form of living, camps, exile, terror? I talk of terror in the USA but so far all we've done is to finger-print a few aliens, move a few Japs and Germans.'

Vittorio smiled, 'As they say in the Bible, "As ye do it to the meanest of them, ye do it unto me." When you fingerprint aliens, shut them in camps, you fingerprint yourself.'

Emily said restlessly, 'Yes, I know it's so. We are guilty, Stephen, we're guilty and we're in terrible danger.' She looked around at them, invited them to go into the next room and have coffee. She said discontentedly, 'And you, too, Vittorio; you were in concentration camp. They caught up with almost everyone, didn't they?'

Vittorio took his coffee, leaned back, stirring it. He said, genially, 'Do you really want to know what it was, the concentration camp?'

When the two Americans assented, he said, in a crisp, telling voice, 'The Germans, you know, became a nation of thieves, highwaymen. They stole flocks and herds, the contents of granaries, barns, warehouses, shops and mansions, wool, wheat, sheets, furs, pictures, china from the Sèvres factory at St-Cloud; and art and learning; though they pretended to despise it. They also stole human labour. This is the explanation of

248

many absurd arrests. I know. I was an educated man and spoke German as well, and they put me on the books. You know how they are finding out the final disposal, the eventual address of thousands of children and other waifs and strays of this last disaster? Through the account-books – I'm not joking. It was a question of calories, kilograms and grams of human resistance, the kind of flesh and fat. The nutrition problem they calculated was how long a man of a certain type and weight, fat, bone-structure, would keep working on a diminished provision of calories and vitamins. I saw the books of accounts. I am serious. A working-man, road-builder, factory worker, automobile engineer, weighing such and such, receiving 1800 calories a day would last so many months, when he would be good for nothing and sent to the gas chambers. A new type of efficiency. How long would they receive a profit in energy-units? Use up the surplus accumulated during a part-lifetime? Their food was always insufficient. When the detainees and deportees came into camp, they would treat them in an ordinary, official style. Who is sick? Who is well? It was pathetic to see old people hold up their hands tremblingly, in a weak voice say, "I am sick." "What is wrong?" "I have such-and-such." These people would immediately be sent to the gas chambers. Then the well ones would be examined. Any really well would be asked, "What work do you do?" Any specialists were given that work. A man like myself, an intellectual (I was a lawyer, I did nothing useful, so they sent me to the factory to work on the line), an intellectual who knew no profitable work, nothing that could produce a genuine profit for their system, was set to work if he could do it; and if he was inefficient, his diet was gradually reduced until he had given out all his surplus and then he was packed off to die. Fortunately I had not only strength but a certain physique which resists. I eventually became a straw-boss and got a little more food; and then, because I knew five languages and accountancy, I was put in the office. That was not common. That was how I saw the accounting system. I worked on it. Each man and woman was calculated as an animal or even as a production unit, utilizing his spare fat and energy. That gone, that stolen, he was killed. You understand? Of course there was more accountancy to it than that. A certain amount would be allotted to each camp manager. Naturally there was a lot of graft. In the first place, the commandant or manager cultivated the fields round the camp, as well as he could, to feed the camp, to reduce his costs and to sell outside to the town or village for a profit. He naturally starved the camp to sell outside. These fields were arranged around the camp almost like the fields of share-croppers and serfs around the ancient manor. The unpaid workers, the concentration-camp people, worked these fields as long as they could. There were always new workers arrested to take their

249

place when they failed. Indeed it was like the chain-gang system in the southern USA, where negroes are arrested to fill new contracts for labour.'

He said all this cheerfully, speaking of things known, to people who knew them. 'You must always keep in mind, not the horrors, the barbarities, the inexpressible savagery, and not the sadism and madness, but the meaning of this system – unmitigated stupid barbarous plunder. To plunder the earth and mankind while giving no return. A system without a future but bad and bitter for the enslaved, the overrun.

'Perhaps my knowledge of languages, perhaps, of course, my society connections – I managed to survive long enough, two or three years, that is, to graduate as an examiner in the machine-shop, for which I got a few more calories daily, though not sufficient. Then I was sent to the office; I got a little more. There were some from my class, who had eaten as well as I, who, because of their physical constitutions, faded away like wax in the fire before this conscientious malnutrition. It was luck. I was not then a member of the Party. The notion that I was of no use to anyone and that my profession was really superfluous came home to me.'

He laughed equably. 'My father wanted me to be a lawyer: I became one. I'd wanted to be something else, but I did not want to upset my father. And because I hated criminal law, I stuck to society cases, harmless enough I thought. But of no value to society, harmless – ' he laughed gloriously; 'now you see I have reformed. The intellectual always feels semi-skilled, as Madame Howard says. And people think that of him too. Unless he is active in society too. And so we have the Renaissance man.'

Stephen had listened to this with discontent and gloom, though he nodded his head.

'You've had doomsday. We haven't had ours. Have we got to go through that too? Is it necessary? Capitalism they say is revolutionary.'

Emily said enthusiastically, 'Yes, in America during the Browder backward step, this was said; but they did not say that capitalism had been revolutionary and now is not. On the contrary. It is in the sense that it is rushing headlong to a world-wide catastrophe, it is still revolutionary in the most fantastic anarchist or nihilist sense. I understand that. Not to know the USA is not to know the most extraordinary problem that capitalism has ever presented to the world and its worst obstacle to progress.'

Stephen waved his hand, Emily rolled her eyes roguishly. Madame Wauters cried out, Mernie changed his seat at once but carried on, 'The economies in Poland, Czechoslovakia and Yugoslavia are of three distinct kinds with three distinct approaches to the socialist future. I foresee a development of the Yugoslav State directly into socialism. No wonder Mademoiselle de la Roche hates Marshal Tito and Yugoslavia. Yugoslav capitalism was always of a semi-colonial nature. The fight against the Germans was a fight against the only capitalist class that then existed in Yugoslavia.'

He went on for a long time. He had travelled a good deal since the end of the occupation for his business in leather, met all kinds of people; especially businessmen who had no opinions or opposed opinions but all of whom wanted to do business.

'The businessman is the first healer after war,' said he.

'You should have worn your sweater, I saw you shiver,' said Madame Wauters drily. Emily rushed to get a cardigan, which Mernie tranquilly arranged over his shoulders, looking at his wife enquiringly.

'That is not the same,' said she displeased.

Mernie continued, 'Oh, Tito is a magnificent intellectual, a great, true genius of Marxist development, one of those accidents of history. How is it that epochs produce the men they require, we say? Not always, but now this is so. There is genius everywhere in the new democracies. History produces when it must.'

Vittorio said stoutly, 'Well, that sounds like superstition. What the people needed has been produced over and over again, because the genius was there all along. The legend of the mute, inglorious Miltons and the Einsteins lost in the cow-pastures is true. The new socialist countries are like young men and women who feel this unexpended genius being put to use. What is sadder for a writer, say, than to find his genius being distorted, enslaved, for him to have to write for criminals, warmongers, cynics and real murderers, or for the most venal, ignorant and corrupt of men, men who run or permit the running of houses of ill fame, who build atom bombs and such things. He knows all the time what he is doing and that it is a double suicide of himself and his talent, his joy and his future all in one – he weeps all the time in his heart, dust falls in his brain and he is dead long before they bury him, because his cynical masters know his price – a low one! A low one for human genius! Whereas the socialist writers are known everywhere, published everywhere, honoured everywhere, they write even better and they are recognized as good men, working for the common good, fertilizing the earth and risking not one bit of their talent or genius or poetry. This is happiness, this is heaven. And where the people themselves are educated and have a future to themselves, horizon-wide, not secreted with a narrow few, there comes a harvest of genius. Now why that is, is clear. They believe and know that though they must struggle, they will conquer nature, themselves and their individual weakness; this is man understanding the universe; this is the new world, the seed time of genius, not only what we need, but what they need for themselves, for one, for all.'

251

And they went on and on, men who have lived through history and understood what they were living through. Emily thought it was a wonderful evening. Stephen was very tired; and suddenly Mernie Wauters sneezed.

'Aren't you warm enough, Mernie?' said his wife and sprang up to examine the windows, stood about the room and said, 'Decidedly, there is a draught here.'

Emily hurried out to get a warm drink for Monsieur Wauters; and in the meantime told Fernande and the butler to bring in glasses for whisky and port, which she had been told to offer after dinner, with herb teas of various kinds. Madame Wauters specified linden tea: Emily had none.

'People always have linden tea,' remarked Madame Wauters.

Mernie, in good form, was raving about Czechoslovakia, something wholly new in Marxist history. His dark, long eyes were the colour of chestnut buds; they shone.

'A Czech businessman I know, faced with the horrid but practical fact that he has no future in the so-called west, is willing to ally himself with the inevitable power. The Czech capitalists are in no sense romantics as the Poles are; and our French friends of the other night, so foolishly royalist, are dreaming; and even the Americans about China, the British in Greece – the British are old-fashioned romantics in this, wishing to re-establish monarchy for the sake of the thing; and yet realist enough to hold on to Franco and other dictators, where the planting of a royal sprout would bring about social upheaval.'

Stephen said, 'This is fascinating. It's a new world to study and digest.'

'Oh, Stephen we must do a book together about it: *Inside the New Democracies*, all the stages on the road to socialism, all the turnoffs, all the milestones, until you get to the one that says, *No Turning Back*. Oh, what a shudder! I'd like to stand on that road and look up at that signpost. *From here no way back*. What would be my real feelings? I mean, without romance, without hazy illusions, without the idea that one day if it didn't suit I could go back to the USA? It's a fearful idea. For us all, socialism, even Russian Marxist socialism is a somewhat Utopian dream; but there – at the dread signpost – '

She laughed.

'Dread!' Vittorio said, laughing.

'No turning back is always dread. Oh, many hearts must hesitate. And think of the terrors you must pass through – the misery, starvation, torture, the countless awful deaths, perhaps our whole generation will have passed before we even catch sight of the new world! We will die on the road! And our children – they'll be lost in the Dismal Swamp! Oh, what dread to turn from a world we know well to one we don't know.'

252

'I don't feel this,' said Madame Wauters, looking at the door to see if the hot drink was coming for Mernie.

'Oh, but I understand,' said Mernie.

Emily said, 'Oh, I understand, too. It is like the first time I was pregnant and meant to have the baby – which was lost on the way. Oh, Lord, the sweat and terror! I saw myself right at the bottom of a mine and away up a little daylight, the size of a nickel and I had to climb up that weak ladder, up slowly and painfully and as I got to the top the walls pinched me and I felt I would die of the labour and lack of breath, suffocated. Oh, dear! Because, to think – you must lose all you have – your children too – all they're used to, bit by bit, strip-jack-naked, throw away all you own and the things you love, even the books you've written which aren't worthy – all in the writhing coffee-and-blood-coloured rivers that snake through the Dismal Swamp, and at last arrive naked as newborns in – another man's world. For they will have built it and we will be Rip Van Winkles, old-timers, horse-and-buggy cracker-barrel socialists. Do you know, just before we left, we were coming out of a big meeting of the party, with a dance to it. Some youngsters were taking the air on the sidewalk, they said our names and looked behind for their friends. "All the squares are coming out," they said.'

Stephen said, 'You never told me; the bastards! I'd have gone and knocked their heads together.'

Vittorio laughed, 'My daughter is a very pretty girl and she is twenty-four. She is very annoyed now, for she finds that there are beautiful girls of sixteen and seventeen everywhere.'

Emily said, 'Well, it would be like going through the ruins of the world. And what is strange is they all behave so differently and have different arguments. You say, it's very curious, the Yugoslavs have simply expropriated all foreign and domestic capital on the bland pretext that it was German – I understand it. But my God, think of the night simply coming down on an entire class like that. It's volcanic, it's an eruption that cuts off everything, vineyards, backgardens, fishing-nets and towers. And two thousand years after, they discover us, mummies crouching in the cellars – chained, yes, chained to our long-gone ideas.'

Stephen handed Vittorio a drink and said with grace, but earnestly, 'The reason I'm an amateur, although I hope I make sense politically, is that I wasn't ever trained to do anything and I don't know anything. I guess that even to know all about machine-tools, or how the cells divide in plants and animals makes you suddenly much more of a Marxist and a better thinker. I'm an old Party journalist, I've met everyone, I was worthy until – ' he stopped and went on 'but I have the feeling I'm faking. How well I understand your giving up your profession! And yet you had one! It was a hard and noble one and you were a great success in it and yet you felt yourself worse off than a mechanic. It's too late for me to learn anything. I thought of going to night-school during the war with all the other has-beens, but I felt it was useless.'

Vittorio said, 'Why not teach? Give courses on the American economy, which you say, and I believe, is so hard for outsiders to understand.'

Emily was enthusiastic. They argued about this for some time; but in the end, with Stephen looking more cheerful, the Wauters and Madame Suzanne thought they might organize a group of sympathetic middle-class people, students and perhaps writers, for Stephen.

Before the guests left they gave two invitations. The Howards were to go to the Wauters' home for dinner in a week or ten days; and they were to go to Vittorio's room for dinner the following Saturday. He had only one gas burner he said, but he was experienced with it and would stew them a chicken. He thought he could get one from a friend in the country.

Stephen said, 'We feel very low and blue about using the black market so much. But the youngsters would feel the change too much and we too have to work. We can't waste time adapting ourselves.'

Suzanne said, 'Where is the sense in starving for principle if you can eat?'

Stephen for the first time was delighted with her. He shook her hand. She apologized for not having them. She lived alone in a very small room and was not a good cook. She meantime promised to find an artist to give Christy lessons in water-colour painting.

'You see I am like Fernande: I always know someone.'

The whole company was taken to see Christy's water-colours, sailing-boats on a windy afternoon on a blue sea, a little cabin in a springtime wood, a corner of a wood with fields and distant mountains; poor but sensitive work. Christy seemed ashamed, but Emily raved about it and the guests were more than polite.

When they had gone, Christy said to Emily,

'Mother, you should not have shown my sketches, really. I know how bad I am.'

Emily exclaimed, hugging him, 'Oh, what junk! You've got real genius; a perfect eye. How many colours are there is an ordinary blue sky, remember, Christy, I told you the other day?'

He hesitated, looking at her bashfully, 'You said, eleven, fifteen perhaps. But I don't see that many.'

'Eleven! Isn't that wonderful! That's absolutely right. Oh, Christy doesn't that prove it to you? Only an artist can see such things, a whole palette in a plain blue sky, which is only washing blue to the ordinary jerk.'

254

She lectured him for ten minutes on his own aesthetic sense, what his teachers had said about him, what his future might be. He could go to the Beaux-Arts, to Rome, he might be the *Prix de Rome*, who knew? With the chances he had and his wonderful, delicate, original talent and the perfect eye for colour! When the child had gone to bed, the couple sat up a little later discussing the evening happily. They interpreted the meaning of phrases, topics, attitudes, the co-operative friendliness of the guests. They believed that it meant that not only these but the whole central committee of the French Party was friendly disposed to them, that Vittorio had just been sent to test them and that seeing their decency, their loyalty to the Soviet Union and to Marxism, they would be invited to work and speak for the Party, secret emissaries but approaching the plenipotentiary. They embraced and looked youthfully into each other's face.

Stephen said, 'I'm glad we came! Oh, to be human beings again; and not enemies of the people!'

They went on to discuss Christy and his education. As a gentleman's son and rich man himself he did not have to work, but they wanted him to know how to do something. Stephen's family contained one or two aesthetes and scholars; Uncle Maurice being one, and an old lady who went out to dig in Mesopotamia in her eighties was another. Christy was the one person who had a chance to have a happy life. He was not fit for professional life, not very clever, but very kind. Now there was his adolescence. Emily and Stephen were unwilling to part with him, but they found him maddening. He had his solemn thoughts, which he produced in company, his rude manners with the servants, his new found young-mastership, his oddly placed, awkward learning. He needed the company of the right kind of girls. Never would they permit Christy to go to prostitutes or loose girls with vulgar ideas. True, in New York a poor boy, an ordinary boy, had to content himself with the coarse, flippant, cynical sex-life of the city; but here they were freed from that. He could make the grand tour, have innocent love affairs, study and dream.

Stephen said, 'I want him to be like the English *grands seigneurs*, the juveniles of Voltaire's and Charles James Fox's time, when an Englishman was respected, though we needn't have the expenditure and the follies. I'd like him to be a mild but not vapid milord. Americans have always had their gentlemen abroad and our son Christy shall be one.'

Emily laughed and clapped her hands,

'Oh, how life has changed for us! We should never have been able to think of such things in New York or Hollywood or Connecticut.'

They hated to part with the boy so soon; and they couldn't consent to his renting a small room by himself, a *pied-à-terre* off somewhere in a

255

respectable but consenting quarter, where young men meet women. Stephen said,

'He can go so far astray. I feel such a fool. The boy knows all he should know, but I can read a book about the atom bomb and not know the first thing about it: and such is sex. I suppose the best thing would be to introduce him to some nice, friendly, pretty, clever, married woman, fifteen years older than himself. That's what they do here.'

Emily cried, 'Oh, I'd rather see him drop dead!'

'Well, all women start with men older than themselves!'

'Oh, how revolting, putrid and corrupt, I'll never let my boy so much as take a bunch of violets to an older woman; if I see him picking up her handkerchief, I'll box his ears.'

Stephen laughed and looked at her appreciatively.

'We'll ask Madame Suzanne. I wish I'd had a little apartment with a side-entrance. I should have started off as a regular beast but a healthy one and been a sordid old man now making money in the nitrates business.'

'Oh, Stephen, and not met me?'

'H'm, well – there's a drawback to everything; and as you know, not to have met you would have ruined my life entirely.'

This was one of their happiest nights for many years.

Next week in the mail was a letter from Stephen's mother, Anna Howard, saying that she was coming over earlier this year; she would put up at the Ritz for a few days; and she wanted to talk to them about their plans. Her letters were never more than a few lines: this one almost filled a page.

Stephen read the letter several times. Emily said, 'Oh, we must really welcome her. Give Anna and Maurice a party and show them our friends. I wrote to dear Anna all about our new friends, our new hopes and how you are going to give courses in American economic history and Christy is going to the Beaux-Arts.'

Stephen confessed though, that he had written several times to his mother about money. She had advanced his next quarter's allowance; besides he had asked for a loan of $5,000. He grumbled, 'I can't think why not. They can take it out of my share of the estate. When Mother dies. I don't mean I want her to die. Anyway she looks good for twenty years, to me. So it's only reasonable. I'm not asking for it twice over. Also, I told her I thought Christy and Olivia should pay all their own expenses, housekeeping, servants, teachers, clothes. Why should we? We're good guardians, we're devoted parents. But our high style of living is because of them. I'm not going to be talked out of it by Mother. I'm poor, she's rich, they're rich, they're all rich but me. Why should all the burden fall on the poorest member of the family? And just because we're poor, we have to put on a bigger show than anyone else would, to show we're not starving the kids.'

Emily did not worry about it. She felt they would make a good impression; and that Anna would be very glad to have them in Europe.

Madame Suzanne came as usual at ten o'clock for her lessons with the children. After one hour of French, she gave private tuition to Christy in Latin and other subjects; she lunched with the family and after lunch she taught French to the Howards for one to three hours depending on their free time. Stephen was anxious to have impressive arrangements made for Christy before his grandmother arrived, so that she would not be tempted to take him back to America. The adults were to use as a book for study *L'Enfermé* (*The Prisoner*) by Gustave Geoffroy, well-known socialist, the story of Auguste Blanqui who spent most of his life in lock-ups, gaols and fortress prisons, the world's greatest agitator, one of the world's greatest revolutionaries. The picture of him drawn by Madame Suzanne already had kept Emily awake tossing – the frail, small man with wretched health, living on vegetables, bread and water who accustomed himself to cold, want, misery from childhood and who, when deprived of all books, all manuscripts, all learning, was able to invent systems of thought, new worlds of imagination; the cruelly treated prisoner of Mont St-Michel and other prisons, whose struggles, work and classic failure led Lenin to formulate, with the lessons of the Commune of Paris, his own successful theories of revolution.

Emily made up her mind to study the French Revolution and the Commune too. Now that she had shaken off the curse of the narrow, prejudiced, and corrupt American radical ideas and the hate of former friends, she would start all over again. 'I am like a pioneer and I've come to the young countries. The USA is getting old.'

She fell asleep in a gentle daze of white, soft light, slept with the angels all night, told Stephen on waking that for once she had had sweet dreams but could remember nothing.

'I was happy, all day, all night, all the week, think of that! There are people in our lives who have strange meaning for us – Mernie Wauters and Suzanne and Vittorio do that for me. And perhaps for you too?'

Stephen said drily, 'I am not so romantic. I haven't a rich nature like yours, full of hope and finding themes everywhere. Only for God's sake, remember we have to eat while you're wandering in the Paradise Gardens of socialist beauties. We have to eat and there isn't one word in all those books Vittorio and Suzanne gave you, which will be of any use in a book intended to sell in America. Wait till your book's finished. For I know you, it will creep in, they'll smell the fish and it won't even sell to your favourite publisher, let alone the magazines. They can smell socialists, enemies of their dear police state miles off. Read your socialist romances later.'

But that day Suzanne brought a copy of *L'Enfermé* and they began to read it paragraph by paragraph. Stephen had written several biographies and was at first interested, though it irritated him to read a book so slowly. In a few days it was impossible to conceal from him that Emily spent almost all her time on the book. She was many pages ahead of Stephen and had already formed a plan for dramatizing the book.

She declared, 'I'll do a libretto for grand opera. I'm surprised it hasn't been done.' Hastily, she told them, in her stumbling, strange French, her plans of scenes. The boy's naked bedroom in winter, the open window with snow drifting through, to begin with: the marriage, romantic and unhappy; the plodding son of the great revolutionist; Blanqui, little figure, standing unmoved in the fiercest battle scenes; the lonely man, denied everything, pacing the platform under the stars at Mont St-Michel and inventing for want of better things, a new theory of the universe –

In those stars must be loves like ours and their life flows along by ours, like a sister sun.

Blanqui had only a manual of algebra and from this he built up a new solar system. Dragged step by step down the stone stairs, his head bumping on the flags, tortured and tied in a low, filthy hole with rats about, in one position for days on end and coming back to life, a man so frail and living so long – for what? To go from one prison to another.

'Look at the splendour of the prison scenes; his lifelong love for his unworthy wife, a mere bourgeoise!'

Stephen after an hour of this, unable to take part, left the room and from then on took part only erratically. He was furiously angry now. He saw that Emily had done no work for over a week. Her latest 'obsessions, her socialist jag' had drunk up all her energy. He went up to her room and found some books, recommended by Vittorio. He came down and heard her shouting joyfully, inexhaustibly, and declaring in English, her French having vanished, that their next book would be that wonderful, superb, gorgeous book; and she called out to Stephen to come in, while breathlessly she described a book Suzanne had brought her. It was the autobiography of Jules Vallès, small but famous three-volume story: *The Schoolboy, The Graduate. The Communard.*

Bubbling over with laughter, she held Stephen by the sleeve, 'Only listen to this! You'll die laughing.'

'Jules Vallès had shut the mayor in the closet and even the guard pleaded for him, saying there would be a lot of trouble in the closet if he was not allowed to go to the – shh! – so Jules Vallès let him out and told him, run along.'

258

Emily shouted, 'A big mistake! A big mistake. And typical of the gentle revolutionaries they were. They didn't take over the Banque de France, a primordial error. They wanted to prove revolutionists didn't grab. Prove to whom, pray? And no one ever thanked them for it. And it ended up at the Mur des Fédérés. Oh, what a story! Stephen I am going for once in my life to become a specialist on something – on the Commune! Lenin learned about revolution from it.'

She waved her arms, got up, walked about the room, excitably called for coffee, glasses of water, and for over an hour she described her future studies.

'I am going to study all the children study and more. More, because I should know more. They'll absorb it naturally, just by living here. Am I going to sit round with my mouth open, yessing and noing? Dumb Madame Howard, a typical American; knows nothing! Eh? No!'

She hit the table. 'Stephen, it's all very well for you. You're learned. You went to Princeton. But I came from Arkansas. They don't ever teach anything in America, Madame Suzanne. They're afraid you might question the eternal values, like ice-cream soda. They're tripping over themselves racing farther and farther backwards into the Ostrogoth age, determined that whatever happens to the world, the Chinese people, the Kashmiri, the Kirghiz shall all know more than the average American.'

She raved on like this for some time to Stephen's annoyance. He was proud of his country, regarded himself as a representative American, a sample American abroad: he would analyse the country but never deride and belittle.

After chocolate and bread with the children, Madame Suzanne went on to Christy's Latin lesson. Emily sat in on this. She had worked over the lessons in order to keep up with Christy. Stephen had forgotten his Latin. He growled, 'Go ahead. I'll be the dumb American cluck reading the comic strips while you three talk monkey-Latin to each other.'

'You don't study and you're not learning French, Stephen. Madame Suzanne says I am improving. *Allez-vous coucher, Monsieur. Je vous parle comme à un chien*, because, that is *parce que*, you are a *chien*. That is, *vous êtes un chien*.'

'Nice,' said Stephen.

'That's what I heard in the street today. And listen, that old iron man says *O! Du lapin-mo-ort; du lapin – qu'il est mort!*'

Mad with hilarity, she took Olivia in her arms, kissed her soft, warm hair and sang:

> 'Fais dodo, ma poulette, dors ma mignonette!
> Quand tu auras vingt ans passés, tu vas te marier,
> Avec un homme sage, qui fera ton ménage,
> Avec un homme de Paris, qui fera ton petit lit.'

'That's frank isn't it? Marie-Jo sings that and with such hysterical fury. It's dreadful to have people in the house who aren't married, who haven't children, who can't share our joys and have to take out their miseries in stealing sugar and having murderous friends around and talking about whether God thinks they're dutiful if they wash the stone floor of the basement on Sundays. Ai-ai-ai. Why must our happiness, joy, wonderful fulfilment be built on the sorrows of others? What are we to do? Oh, life is cruel, cruel.'

In the evening Madame Suzanne was still with them. After a few such evenings, and with 'Madame Suzanne always underfoot and exercise books even in the toilet' Stephen declared he was fed up. He was going to invite some lousy reactionaries to get a breath of stale air. He couldn't stand the new hope and light blazing all round the joint. 'It's too sweet and good here, pure thought and love of humanity. I'll scream if I hear one more story of the Resistance and if Christy begins one more time on the tragedy of man under capitalism. Let man die under capitalism or any other way. I want to meet some funny people, some witty, lousy people who backbite and whom I can sneer at and hate.'

Emily called out, 'Oh, good, a real party. The Wauters couple are depressing, I agree. Who'll we ask? Not that boat crowd! Let's ask Suzanne.'

Stephen said, 'Oh, God, never!' but in the end they did and Madame Suzanne coolly agreed to introduce them to other friends; 'neither teachers, benefactors, child-study psychologists, nor librarians' Stephen specified, smiling engagingly to Suzanne.

Emily enquired, 'Well heavens, we have enough introductions around the American and British Embassies, not to say half literary Paris, and even people at the Louvre – won't they do?'

The three of them sat down to work out a list of interesting people who would not talk about the food situation, nor had suffered in the Resistance. They were all laughing, Stephen insisted gaily, 'And not a single poor person, not a single honest person, no one who is suffering because he is honest or dumb. When I'm with the lousy corrupt subsidized rich and other such depraved humans, I feel safer, they're not criticizing me and I can think, I'm better than you, or at least, not worse.'

'Stephen, Stephen! You're loyal and pure. You know that.'

'Oh, to hell with that. You and Suzanne work out a list of lively, likely, lousy coots in your French lesson and I'll go and do some work. And remember that Uncle Maurice and Mamma will probably be in on this party. So do some modest high-stepping, too.'

In his room, Stephen began the calculations, which he did daily, weekly, monthly, yearly: what Emily had earned, his allowances and advance, and all the rest. He also consulted his expectations: tickets in the French lottery, the French sweepstake, a ticket in the Belgian lottery got for him regularly by Monsieur Wauters, and the Swiss lottery, a full ticket of five Swiss francs got from Monsieur Savany. He bought a full ticket in each lottery and when there were special lotteries as at Easter, in France, he bought the expensive or double ticket. His own money was in family property, respectable industrials and a few warbonds. He also ran the accounts and investments for the two rich children living with him.

He was appalled at the amounts they had already spent, were now spending.

15   ANNA'S VISIT

Preparing for his mother's arrival, Stephen spent the whole afternoon and evening casting up their accounts, and several times was on the point of calling off their 'Evening in Cold War Society' which he himself had proposed. Yet he thought that his mother would like this company, that he had better get a job in Europe, say correspondent; and for this he had better move in the best circles. When he came down after the children were in bed and Christy was upstairs studying his Latin and ancient history, Suzanne was just leaving and Emily was full of beans.

The list for the reception now lay on the table. She had something to tell him about Christy. She was bubbling for a reason he did not yet know. She had asked Suzanne many questions about Vittorio. They had both agreed that it would be safe to ask such a polished, keen man to meet Anna Howard. Needless to say, by now, Suzanne knew all their affairs.

Emily said, 'At least you can write to dear Anna about this lot. These are the *crème de la crème* of cold war society and she will see you are living like the very parfitt *bourgeois gentilhomme?*'

'Don't you know he was absurd, the *bourgeois gentilhomme?*'

'Oh, what does it matter? We're absurd.'

Stephen saw Suzanne across the courtyard and came back to have coffee with Emily. He was sulky because of the accounts, because of the *bourgeois gentilhomme*, and he pushed the list of guests aside crossly.

'What I want to know is not their names, but what is the cost; and what profit any damn one of them is going to give us. What do we expect to get out of it?'

However, in the inevitable way of their parties, the lists were checked and rechecked, invitations were telephoned and written. As well as Wauters and Vittorio, they had asked the Communist Party chiefs, whom they did not know but for whom they had been angling. Emily had not spoken to Vittorio about it, but expected them. Stephen counted upon the 'Resistance types' as refusers.

Stephen said irritably to Suzanne the next day, 'But how can Wauters himself meet the "Enemies of the People Union?"'

Suzanne smiled, 'Well, aren't you meeting them? You will be surprised at the number of "Resistance types" you will meet at parties. You didn't have to wear a torn shirt to be in the Resistance.'

'Of course,' thought Stephen, looking at Emily hastily. Of course, Emily had already told everything to Suzanne; for instance that he called them 'Resistance types'. He groaned.

'You will be surprised,' said Suzanne sardonically.

She had gradually, and now suddenly, acquired power over them. For instance, Emily had in principle agreed, yesterday, to the following: Madame Suzanne was to move from her mean room and take an apartment, in which apartment she would accommodate Christy, who was to have study, bedroom, bath of his own. Suzanne was to have her own living-room, bedroom and bath as well as kitchen; and if he could not have separate bath, Christy would use the one bathroom. Suzanne would supervise him, feed him, teach him, see that he led the life of a French youth of his age, not too free, not too circumscribed. Christy himself, now that he was reaching eighteen, would pay for all this. It was a fine arrangement for Suzanne. She promised that she would find the necessary accommodation within a week. It could be unfurnished; Christy would buy his own furniture, the Howards would advance her the money for hers. Stephen, anxious to have Christy settled when his mother arrived, accepted this entire arrangement with little cavilling. It suited Christy very well too. Stephen had a talk with his foster-son about his responsibilities now that he was about to come into his first inheritance. Christy, never exorbitant, was rejoiced to hear that as a rich youth he had duties to society and to his family and his own fortune and at once said that he would keep accounts and save money. In fact, he showed a small savings account which he had started as soon as he came to France. His question was only, whether it was better to walk and save bus-fares; or ride and save shoe-leather. Stephen said privately to Emily, 'My God, Emily: he's the dead spit and image of his grandfather John Tanner. The same ways. He'll starve to death at eighty-five.'

'Goody, dear Anna will like that. Let's get him settled in with Suzanne as soon as ever we can,' said Emily.

Stephen said, 'You're looking very well!'

'Oh, the weather's wonderful and I feel I can work. The work's going well.'

'Have you done any work for a week? Haven't you been spending your time on the books Vittorio told you to read and working up that damned *L'Enfermé*? There's not a cent in it.'

'Oh, Stephen! It makes me so happy. I feel simply rosy.'

'We have children. We can't afford to be rosy. Do you know how much we have made since we got here? The money for your last book was spent coming over here; and we didn't pay over two thousand dollars in outstanding debts over there, on the grounds, our credit is good. Since we came here, another two-thousand dollars, say, in unpaid debts, our credit still being good; thank God for the Howards' reputation; and your book has run into another edition but we won't collect for six months – well maybe we can, but spent is spent and when it's spent, we're bone dry, unless they take it for Broadway. Of course, we've got old Doc Hack working on it. Besides this, there's the promise of five hundred dollars for one story for *The Gothamite*, but you're obliged to take out anything about your uncle Henry since he was a Henry George addict and who knows what that is? And just leave in the hens and the neighbours' cats; and maybe a thousand dollars for two articles on Paris 1948 for *American Summer*; no promises and they've taken just one so far.'

Emily said huskily, turning a cheerful, red face, 'It's very promising. When you think we're exiles and our name stinks, it's wonderful. That's a wonderful in, the *American Summer* series about Europe. We'll make them an offer. We'll travel around, do Europe, go to Belgium, I'm longing to go to Belgium to taste those 107 ways of doing mussels and everything Mernie Wauters tells me is good to eat. Ledane and everyone says the food is superb. And who knows? It's a revelation. Little Belgium. Fancy! Then there's Switzerland, they've never even seen the war, the food must be good and there are the mountains and the ski-slopes. Then Italy – they're claiming they want Americans; and I'm sure they do – h'm. Well, anyhow five or six countries, taking in England. It won't pay for the hotels and car-fare and minding the children but it's a beginning. Why not *The Howards Abroad* and turn out a sort of Baedeker for Americans, all they want to know, not the old three-star stuff. Call us the Wilkeses. H'm, not good enough. Anyway, I feel it in my bones. I'm on the right track. And you will either get a good job in the Louvre or with the Party or write that wonderful novel about your early struggles or about our family – it's so charming and wonderful when you tell it and who ever did? A scion in the USA. In Europe they still think we're cowpunchers: they'll be fascinated; or you'll become a famous European correspondent, or someone will take you as private secretary, a diplomat or deputy – '

Stephen declared, 'Never! I've had a secretary myself and nothing doing.'

Bubbling still, Emily went up to her room. Stephen called after her, 'Work, goddamn it, work! Don't write letters, your journal, ideas for new books or thumbnail sketches. Write what your agent's waiting for.'

'OK! OK!' she laughed.

Emily went into her room and sat down in a pleasant day-dream. She had fallen in love with Vittorio, who thought her magnificent and who was the toast of society women. While Stephen was upstairs with the

264

accounts, she had nagged, amiably pestered, buffeted Suzanne about the ears with questions about Vittorio. Suzanne had only consented to answer if the conversation was held in French. Thus Emily had heard, but as through a swarm of bluebottles, stories of Vittorio's love affairs, all with unexplained, unexpected women, not at all as you might think with 'haughty, gorgeous, society belles' as Emily said. No. Since early days he had had an affair with the beautiful daughter of a Brussels financier. She had had many lovers since, married twice, it was not only men she loved – 'Then who? Then who?' said Emily puzzled – but she often went to see Vittorio even now, though he was so changed and so poor. 'Women can't forget him,' said Suzanne, in a fault-finding tone. Now Vittorio was in love with a girl twenty years younger than himself, 'Not at all suitable,' said Suzanne. 'Did he say anything about us here?' 'Ah, he admired you as we all do; and then he said, about the child, "Oh, what a delicious little woman."'

There was more of this; but Emily had not understood that Vittorio had said about Olivia, 'what a delicious little woman': she thought that Vittorio had said it about herself; and her strong inclination turned to passion. She was glad. She sat, looked out at the old gardens behind stone walls across the street and felt at peace.

She thought, 'At last I know what love is; I'm a woman now. I'm not foolish any more. I know he's been in love, I know men must love; and I feel such a deep, new, creative viewpoint. I understand. If I had stayed in America I should never have understood Vittorio. What shall I do? I don't want to do anything. Only to love him. Of course, I can see he loves me; he's fallen for me; it's my energy and strangeness. I bring him something; and the money, the luxury doesn't hurt. Men are weak. They like success. But oh, what am I saying? What a beautiful nature he has, what a deep soul always in motion, full of pity, humane understanding. And think what is required of him! Oh, Stephen is good to me but I have always felt deprived; some kind of block – and I always knew that love ought to be the crown of life. Now I have the crown, flowers, leaves, laurels, golden apples – I am covered with garlands – beloved, Vittorio, beautiful, rich, loving Vittorio!'

She lay down on her couch, put her arms over her face and fell into a waking dream, ecstatic and tender. Perhaps Vittorio too had waited for a woman like her, for her, to deliver him from the far past, the recent past, his nervous affairs with unsuitable women. She was sure he loved her. Stephen, unfortunately, seemed ordinary and bloodless compared with Vittorio. She said to herself, 'Just like me. Emily Wilkes, in *Double or Nothing.*'

Emily had an open secret, her journal, *Journal of Days under the Sun* she

265

called it. It went everywhere with her. It had now reached its twelfth volume. She had the irresistible duty imposed by her nature, her verbal excess and her genius, to record all her life in her great diary. In this she first wrote all that had happened to her; she recorded not only the flattering letters she had written to the rich, to kind and complimentary reviewers, the loving and generous letters to friends, sarcastic revelatory letters, tender and tough letters to editors and agents; she not only wrote all this in her journal but at times she made extracts from it and sent them to persons appropriate or not with a good deal of recklessness, devil-may-care or innocent freedom; her views of this and that; and the outcries of her passion, disappointments, their anticipations, follies and venalities.

Stephen feared this journal as nothing else. He was not allowed into her study when she was working, so he could not control her. He never knew whether his golden goose was laying golden eggs or merely reading to catch up with the children or to please Vittorio, sporting with her journal, writing letters to a hundred different people, old and new, or reading novels voraciously.

The morning mail the next day was unusually rich. All the letters produced some disturbance. Maurice wrote to say that Anna had something very special to say to them; he wanted to warn them. Another letter said that Billy and Grace Haydon, radical friends, whose paper had been closed down, were coming over at the same time as Anna and hoped to stay with them. They were two of their closest friends. They could not turn them down. Hollywood had refused one of Emily's stories. She had been a radical and it was time she made a plain statement about her change of heart; she ought to say, to reassure editors and public, that she was finished with the reds and was ready to laugh at them, that is, in her popular writings. Another popular magazine which had paid her a lot of money at various times, refused a 'surefire' story. It had dug up from its files a nasty, heady letter Emily had once written to them; and regurgitated it for her to read. Letters from friends in Washington assured them that their names were on the black list with the leftists because they had deserted the Party. They would end up as 'the fools of time'.

They had just time before Anna's arrival to start off on the first of their European expeditions. They went to Brussels, leaving the children in charge of Suzanne and the servants.

They were always happy when travelling, spending money freely, living in the best hotels, eating in the best restaurants, eased of the many cares of established living. Not only were the Wauters couple in Brussels at that moment to guide them about, but Stephen had observed Emily's excited interest in Vittorio: he thought she had been too confined. And yes, yes, it was true, she said: she too, just like any other woman was housebound. In Brussels the Wauters took them to a small, good place that few knew, they said, near the Grand Place where there was a special dish of mussels.

It was a small white-walled restaurant with marble tabletops and the menu written on a slate over the counter. A man dressed like a waggoner took the orders, and his wife, striped apron, straggling hair, brought the food, which was good enough. During the meal, Mernie carelessly brushing his sleeve across the dish, while spilling wine on the table, dropped mussels on his lap. Madame Wauters cried out distressfully that Mernie would catch cold; and Mernie was greatly embarrassed at the state of his clothing. They decided to take a taxi home at once. The Howards stayed after them, paid the bill and, half sick from the cheap meal, the disorder, took a taxi to an expensive brasserie near the station where they spent some time eating, drinking and sneering at their friends the Wauters.

'Oh, well-named the Low Countries,' cried Emily: 'and we have got into low company. First mussels in his pants and water in his sleeve and then skipping not to pay the bill: or do you think that scene was prearranged by Madame? They have rich relatives here and business acquaintances; and who ever heard of asking people out, without taking them to a café first and the theatre afterwards? Oh, *l'esprit Belge*, I guess. Let it be a lesson to us.'

They ate with the Wauters family the next day, and again in a small restaurant which Mernie said had excellent cooking, 'You must be careful in Brussels,' he told them. And again there was trouble; and the bill was low. Mernie paid this time, but the price was too low and the Howards felt cheated. The third time, they themselves invited Fleur and Mernie, and to show them real entertainment, they took them to the Place Louise where was one of the most expensive restaurants in the town; and only then were they satisfied. Emily wore a new, expensive dress in water-blue, Stephen had a silk shirt and a flamboyant tie, they were in the highest spirits and were delighted to see how depressed Fleur and Mernie were. Emily had insisted upon sitting next to Mernie and at the first opportunity upset a whole glass of wine over him; when she began exclaiming in distress, oh-ing and ah-ing, and saying, 'Oh, poor Mernie will catch cold', calling the waiters and the *maître d'hôtel*, sending him to the washroom and sending Stephen after him, bringing him back, arranging a napkin on his lap and calling attention to his misery as uproariously as it came to her. When they thought they had better go, she commanded them to remain seated, ordered fresh dishes for them, more wine, coffee and brandy and kept looking down into Mernie's lap and asking how he was, if he was still wet there. Fleur and Mernie were exhausted by this scene, allowed Emily to call a taxi for them (though they never took taxis, but buses) and went off in silence, with stricken faces. Emily and Stephen stood waving till they were out of sight, when Emily turned suddenly to Stephen and exclaimed, 'Pshaw and faugh! What wretched little fleabites of people, what sweepings, what muck' and she kicked them away and turned up the street with disgust; crying, 'Brussels, with these worm-eaten second fiddles. We made a mistake. Stephen, from now on, we'll accept no invitations till we find out how people spend. Oh, how vile, shabby, scrubby! I wish it had been Vittorio!'

'Vittorio?'

'He comes to Brussels! He's never squalid. He's precious, *crème de la crème*, rare, rare.'

'I don't want to go to his place and eat off thick, white, fish-restaurant plates either.'

She sobered, 'No, we won't do that either. Oh, how overweening we are, Stephen, unblushing, towards Vittorio, a man like that. We should be glad to wash his thick, white, fish-restaurant plates for him.'

'Hang it,' said Stephen.

She was tapping along on her high-heels. They took a taxi to their hotel. In the taxi, she exclaimed, 'Stephen, couldn't we give him a decent service, for a present. We know him well enough. A fairly cheap but good dinner-service. So that you could be happy too. I'm happy just looking at Vittorio.'

'Let's ask Anna,' said Stephen.

This week, when they returned, they posted off the first finished draft of Emily's book, for which the publishers and agent were asking. To celebrate this and Christy's birthday and to greet just once their poor friends, the Haydons, Billy and Grace, journalists who had lost their little weekly paper in New York, and Axel Oates, then in Paris, and to suit dear Anna, tired from her trip, they changed their evening party to an afternoon reception for Stephen's mother. To this, Emily, with extensive telephoning to Brussels, invited Mernie and Fleur Wauters. Mernie was an old friend of Anna, good company, a sensible man. Mernie was fond of them, and not reluctant to combine a business trip to Paris with a visit to them; but Fleur, who was often ill, said she was not well enough to go along. Emily was elated; she had captured Mernie, eliminated Fleur, found a companion for Anna. They also invited Suzanne without whom they could now do nothing, and Christy's new Latin tutor, Monsieur Jean-Claude, who had become very friendly and wanted to arrange a Swiss tour for them. Monsieur Jean-Claude had been told, with great vivacity, by Emily, about Uncle Maurice and his friend William, who had edited a book on Cicero; and he now understood that Christy was obliged

268

to become a Latin scholar, especially in connection with Cicero; and that one of these days, Christy had to dazzle Uncle Maurice. Therefore, Christy (and Emily too) had now begun on selected works of Marcus Tullius. Emily often sat in on the lessons; and Monsieur Jean-Claude had been so far amused and then stupefied by Emily's interest in and insistence upon the strength of character and uprightness of the great orator. 'He was high-minded, resisting tyranny' – and such things she would declaim; 'He hated totalitarian rule, his heart was free, he loved freedom,' she said. Monsieur Jean-Claude, whatever his private opinions, was employed by this wealthy woman and he was obliged to accommodate his views to hers. So the house rang now with her appraisal of Cicero; and the tragic end of a brave and brilliant man's life.

To the party were invited a few other English-speaking people, including the Trefougars, British Embassy people they had met at a reception, with Anna, at the Crillon. The Howards had been fascinated by the easy manners of the Trefougars, had since visited one of their parties and had them over one evening. They always behaved delightfully and with diplomatic discretion, even though Trefougar was occasionally a heavy drinker, said Stephen. Vittorio was in Paris after an absence, but too busy that afternoon to come, although Emily bombarded him with letters, telephone calls. She even sent him long telegrams to Party headquarters, saying he must come, oh, he must come, why they would either make it an evening party to suit him – or, no, they would give another party especially for him to meet dear Anna Howard, Stephen's mother, and they invited him to an intimate family lunch, to be given by them to Anna, Uncle Maurice and William, and a few others at the Pré Catalan in the Bois-de-Boulogne, in a short time.

Stephen was annoyed at this eagerness; but Emily said Mamma could not fail to recognize his charm and breeding.

Stephen hesitated and said that Vittorio did not hesitate to laugh about western society to society dames. But that was his charm in part, said Emily; he could do anything he liked, say anything he liked, he always won their hearts. Stephen said, 'Well, I don't want to see Anna carried off by love or hate either for Vittorio.'

Emily was struck, 'Love for? That would be a dénouement! In a way I'd have to cheer. You mean Vittorio could charm dear Anna into giving money to the poor? Yes, he could.'

'I am very much afraid of Vittorio,' said Stephen smiling.

Stephen and Emily, with Christy, met Anna Howard at the airport, brought her to the Ritz, told her to rest; and that Stephen and Christy would call for her in time for the afternoon party. Anna, when she came, seemed pleased by the house, the servants, the quarter, the party and the

269

guests. She was a tall, slight, gracefully formed woman with French-dressed grey hair, large, dark eyes and a diamond brooch on a neat grey dress. All paid court to her. She had been brought up in Paris and spoke good French. She was sixty-six and showed no intention of retiring from active life. She had now financed an archaeological expedition to North Africa for one of her cousins. The family thought her eccentric, Stephen called her crazy. He needed money so badly and she threw a 'young fortune' into cracks in the earth in Africa.

'Neither the Pharaohs nor God will thank her, but the income tax will be less.'

To his mother he said, 'Mother, you live better than I do, Christy and Olivia live better; even Giles in a sense does, because he lives on my back. And you see I've done what you wanted, I've got out of that New York-Connecticut radical set. Here I am, Anna, a dutiful son, ensconced in Paris like Maurice, like all the finest of the Howards and Tanners, except dear sister, that recognised red, who sells atom bomb secrets to the Russians and whom you like so much.'

His mother said, 'You're very smart, no doubt and Florence is very misguided, but remember that that money she gives to causes yearly, comes off her income tax: it's allowed as charity.'

'I wish I was in line for that charity, Mother. As it is I just received $1250 unexpected taxes for New York State; and they can whistle for it till I return, and am in the money. Unless you want to consider it a charity.'

His mother listened without interest.

Stephen continued cantankerously, 'I'm as good as Florence, you should take an interest in me too. I made the headlines, when I lost that despatch case in the New York subway, containing a cheque from the League Against Racial Discrimination, the said cheque addressed to the Collector of Internal Revenue and in the sum of $8,540. That really frightened the complacent, to think the reds, for of course anyone who even thinks there is racial discrimination is not only a red but is a sour, blue cheapskate and a foreign agent, to think that people who protect Negroes, Mexes, Japs and – hush, Jews – and even possibly at some later date, Irish, English and Rhinelanders when they get lined up for finger-prints – could have $8,540 to hand out in income tax. My God! Preserve us from the rich red within our gates, the plump Russian rouble. Because it's self-evident, no real American would protect Negroes, Mexicans, Swedes and Irish: it must be a foreigner. This is the country which is now trying to charge us some $5,000 each, without counting Christy, Olivia and so on. Even abroad we are working for the dear old USA, and its way of life. Just like Florence.'

270

Mrs Howard looked angrily at her son,

'I don't admire either Florence or you. I don't know what's the matter with either of you. I can't understand why you have not my ideas nor your aunt's ideas, not your grandfather's ideas, but your father's idea, about equality. In our family there is equality between us. If you shared it out with others there would be none at all, there wouldn't be a cent apiece.'

Stephen said, 'In a better world I might have been born a good son to you. But it's a worse world.'

'I want to talk to you seriously later on, Stephen. Tomorrow morning. Come to the hotel about ten,' said his mother, turning from him impatiently.

She was soon talking agreeably to Uncle Maurice, who was getting on well with Fleur (who had come after all) and Mernie Wauters and the Trefougars couple.

The party had a good tone, Anna seemed happy. It was a success. Mrs Trefougar came up and asked a question about Mernie Wauters; Anna Howard was taken with him, 'an interesting man' she said.

Emily said to Suzanne, 'Suzanne, isn't Mernie Wauters a kind of quick worker with the women? I don't know if he means it.'

'I am sure he means it. I've known him for years. He knows it.'

'I must be a real farwest hayseed,' said Emily.

'You surprise me. It's so obvious.'

Emily stuttered, 'But – but – Oh, well, he's not an American type. Yeah, well, those great big eyes. Of course, I like him, but not that. But look at Mrs Trefougar! She's crazy about her husband, she told me; and look now. She'd be afraid to dance with him! She'd probably swoon.'

Suzanne said drily, 'Oh, they swoon and they recover. I think one of the reasons Fleur doesn't come out very often is not only that she's in ill-health, but she's tired of seeing the old comedy being played out. For it all comes to nothing.'

'Nothing at all!'

'No. It's to make Fleur take an interest in him. She's the one who is really of interest. He's jealous of her.'

Emily was staggered, 'Oh, poor Mrs Trefougar. I'm shocked at a woman who deceives her husband – but still – to be betrayed into a passion – a cheated love – I don't know. Tell me about him.'

'He fascinated women during the Resistance and it was both useful and dangerous. Now the accounts are cast up, I can't say he did any harm. I know most there is to know about Mernie. And about his wife.'

'Do you like him or don't you?' Emily enquired, astonished, looking at the cool and wise woman.

'Naturally, I admire and respect him more than almost anyone except the Party chiefs.'

271

Emily longed to ask her if she loved Mernie herself, but she did not dare. She said, 'I suppose it is not really wrong to get women to admire and love you. But I feel it's wrong. I see nothing and know nothing. The most obvious things go on under my nose. But if a woman is in love with her husband – and happy – how can it be? – oh, I'm talking in circles. It's a mystery. Let's leave it at that.'

Suzanne laughed. Emily touched her arm and took her over to get her a drink.

'Suzanne, how good you and Mernie are to us. We're very lonely and as you know my dear Stephen likes good society. But with you we have the feeling that living is easy, we feel one with you. It isn't true. We know nothing of your lives, but it seems so. I wish I could do something that would bring me nearer to you and Mernie. You tell me about your life. How can I shape mine? It's difficult for a writer. I'm active all the time, but all the time I'm sitting between glass walls. Life is outside those glass walls. Strange fish poke their mouths at me, I see seaweeds floating without wind or current. I see it, but it's a mystery. I must do something!'

Madame Suzanne answered at once in her rather harsh voice.

'Yes, Mernie and I have been talking about it.'

'You've been talking about it?' Emily exclaimed.

'Yes. We thought you might begin by writing an account of how intellectuals resisted and suffered and died and survived during the occupation; and it might lead up to a study of the concentration camps going on now – '

'Now!'

'Yes, and perhaps Stephen – I heard him explaining American affairs to your boy Giles the other night – might give a course for us, as we said before, on the American viewpoint and a general description of what is behind this, to us, very strange viewpoint. Lecture, questions, discussion.'

'Oh, Stephen will be delighted! As soon as dear Anna has gone we'll start in; but now she is here we owe some of our time to the family. After all, Suzanne, they do tolerate us!'

'Yes, of course; you must.'

The party went on a long time and right at the end Vittorio came in. Emily beamed. She ran across the room and kissed him and then led him with great pride to Anna. It seemed that Anna liked him. The afternoon was a great success.

The next morning at ten Stephen called at the Ritz to see his mother. He telephoned home that he was lunching with his mother; and he returned about three, his long legs measuring the courtyard, his eyes on the ground, his hat slightly to one side, his satchel swinging. In the satchel were his accounts to date, and all he had done in trusteeship for Christy and Olivia. Emily saw him from her window and came running down. He threw his things on the table,

'Oh, we had the usual row. Anna always hated her only son; and I – I don't hate her; but what have I to say to her? Of course, she brought it all up again – I hate the family, want to ruin them, throw mud at them. Florence is mistaken, but she's a rich woman, can do what she likes; though she was always obstinate and lacked culture. That means you and I lack culture but we're not rich enough to excuse it. Oh, skip that. That's the overture. Well, two things. First, that little chit Fairfield, Christy's second cousin, Fairfield Tanner. She's Mamma's ideal. I told Ma she was a beastly ignorant smug little chit who isn't worth a damn to man or beast. She wants us to put Fairfield up so that she and Christy can get acquainted, with honourable intentions. She's glad we're going to park Christy with Suzanne. She approves of Suzanne, the perfect governess; she can honourably shadow Fairfield and Christy while they're courting.'

'Courting! Christy's only a child.'

'Fairfield's even more of a child. But those are the grandmotherly plans.'

Emily declared violently, 'She just wants money to marry money and keep it in the family. How revolting! How medieval! I'll never permit it, after all our trouble, all our agony with this stupid lad, to make him into a gentleman and a scholar, to make him into a painter, to teach him languages and give him a bit of culture. Never, never will I allow it, for him to be married to that simpering AAA rich little bitch.'

Stephen said, 'Still, it's the usual thing for money to marry money. Christy will never marry a poor girl, though he walks in May Day processions now. And maybe it's better for Anna to get her way and marry them and let them divorce in their springtimes and then get a regular mate. If Christy gets in the State Department – who knows? There are worse dubs than him in it – well, Fairfield would be a great help. And frankly, why trouble? Who is Christy? A nitwit we happen to know and whose millions we are cudgelling our brains to nick a bit off? Just as everyone else always will. Look at Suzanne edging in on them now! Why be fooled by our own schemes? I see no shame at all in trying to chisel and bamboozle my own son, or nephew, whatever he is now, when he's so rich and we're so poor. The more he thinks about the poor and needy, the softer his heart will be and the more likely to help his poor old parents one day.'

Emily said, 'I brood about it. I don't know. The rich don't seem to hand out. After all, for a kid of seventeen to walk in May Day processions is a cheap entertainment – it's just the shoe-leather. But to keep Mummy and Daddy who have such expensive tastes is another kettle of fish.'

Stephen said, 'Let's have a drink. Worse is to follow. We have to sign an agreement.'

'What agreement?'

'About the company we keep. We can shed them politely, the reds I mean, but immediately. When Anna comes back here on her return from Egypt, no reds of any kind. Only your sweet little friends the Trefougars, and for the enchanting Wauters and Vittorio, a *laissez-passer*, as far as Mamma is concerned. She says Mernie isn't a red at all, that we're so blinded we fancy everyone's a red. We'll have to lead a double life, as far as Anna is concerned. She was told we were coming to Europe to cover our past; and that was why she was agreeable to it and helped us out. That was why she let us bring Christy; to get his dossier disentangled from his mother's madcap dossier. Well, she threatens that if we go on being reds and seeing all kinds of riff-raff like Jacques Duclos – she thinks we're bosom friends, that's your goddamn gabbling – ' he said genially, 'all those indiscreet letters you pour out – she wouldn't believe we don't know the guys, that they're not touching us – well, if we don't sign the agreement, she'll take Christy under her own wing and throw him straight, of course, at Fairfield.'

Emily thought it over, sighing, 'Yes, of course, it's dreadful. We'll have to sign. We must keep Christy for his own good and because we love him too.'

'Anna is getting us invitations for the American Embassy's next big do and we have to go, she says.'

Emily tossed her head, 'Oh, well, what the heck, why not? We're Americans and they give a good show. We can't live cooped up with French servants and *ad hoc* cronies we don't understand. I'd be glad to speak even to a bunch of bad Americans, like even the bank-clerk, than never be able to crack a joke that's understood, never get my sentiments off my chest. We don't have to toady to them.'

'Well, if I can tell Anna that, it'll cool her down a lot; and if when she comes back, I can tell her we've been to the Embassy and are accepted, she'll be placated. I'm glad you agree. It's only until Anna sails. She might even remember the expense we've been to for her. She's agreed to pay Fairfield's expenses. She's making us a loan and, in general, she's being pretty open-handed, for her. I do think we owe her something.'

Anna had prepared, from Emily's letters, a list of their friends, which she had given to Stephen. He had it with him; and they now pored over it. Anna had scratched out the names of all their radical friends but two – Axel and Ruth Oates, because Axel at one time, when in Wall Street, had done business with grandfather Tanner; and Desmond Canby, the

English journalist, because he was related to Lord Cockaigne. She left in the names of Fleur and Mernie Wauters and of Vittorio – 'not radical', she had written: and next to the names of Suzanne Gagneux, and Jean-Claude, she had written 'governess', 'tutor.'

Anna was with them on May the first, and there was no question of their watching the Paris procession; though Christy, saying he was going to the American Library, slipped off to see it and cheer some of his new friends, marching in the ranks. It turned out later, Emily and Stephen were chilled to hear, that he had joined and marched a long way with them. Emily and Stephen talked it over that night.

Stephen said sorrowfully, 'As for me, Emily, I'm really glad. We are dead politically. It's awful to feel yourself dead. I blush privately and I'm sick at heart to think what I have become, not a renegade of course – but no one. I feel like cutting my throat. I've often asked myself how I would commit suicide. I don't think I'd cut my throat. Think of the mess. Now I ask myself what good I am, every time we get those left publications from the USA. What's more, we have to stop those; Anna insists. We can get the Left Press here, but it doesn't seem the same here. After all, we're just onlookers. We can't ride to victory on the backs of the long-suffering ranks of the French working class.'

'To victory? If only I believed that,' said Emily.

'We can only congratulate ourselves that the world seems gradually to be learning what US imperialism means. When I think about it too long, I am terrified of the future – of the inevitable and unimaginable human suffering that is planned, so detailed, and yet so lavish, wild, hasty, and that is sure to be so effective, that must come. In our country, all has failed. Who will resist? And who am I to say this? What am I? Hiding my head in a foreign country where I have just agreed to mix with villains only. And I know I'm going to keep doing it. She says so. What is the use of a man like me? But perhaps you can escape. No matter what you do, people will say, she has genius, she's mad or bad or dangerous or wrong, she's – ' he hesitated.

Emily, with eyes sparkling, face intense, grinned, 'Well, go on, she's – '

'No,' said Stephen; for he had been going to say, she's a renegade, she's deserted all she truly believed in; but he could not say it. He felt his gorge rise. He foresaw their slow separation from the Party, the beliefs of the Roosevelt era. He had a suspicion that Emily, who had jibbed at all marking time or trimming, would throw herself bodily over the Rubicon, would jump, laughing and hurrahing, the narrow deep river while he might forever hesitate on the banks. He thought to himself, Emily's bad, she doesn't hesitate; and I would be a villain to say the words, to encourage her to make that jump.

275

'Why are you looking at me like that?' enquired Emily sharply.

'I didn't know I was looking at you,' he said, realizing that he had been finding in her features the face of her powerful, practical, small-profiting business father.

He got up and walked to the window, thinking, where will we be in ten years? I wish it were all over and done with, the decisions taken, the steps made and the howling over. For there will be dreadful, painful howling. And I will betray myself. And we may all end up in jail or the madhouse or the hospital or the poorhouse.

Emily filled up her drink again and said ferociously, 'We're confronted with a simple decision – Christy or a bunch that has rejected us and keeps sending around emissaries, political teasers, leaning on us but not taking us in, letting their henchmen eat and drink with us but not asking us even to a single *vin d'honneur* such as they have in any mean *arrondissement* for any bunch of ragged workers. Who are we to Hecuba, what's Hecuba to us? Whereas Anna and Christy and Maurice and even Fairfield and all the Tanners want us; they're saying, "Join us." They've forgiven us. They want us. I hate being mealy-mouthed. It gets us nowhere. When Anna comes back, we must make the decision, Christy or outer darkness. For no one wants us but the rich and the conformists. If I don't state my change of heart in so many words, *The Gothamite* won't take me. If we don't give up a bunch of *noli me tangere* foreign reds poisoned by Florence, we'll lose our own dear Christy. Christy isn't only the money, he's our life, he's what we've poured into him with such belief, such love, such enthusiasm, such hope, all that you give to a child. He's one of our young things, the only contact with the future we now have. I don't believe Marxism is our contact with the future. We have only Christy. The decision is plain. And what's more, I believe if I said, "Don't take Christy, let him go" – then I think you'd go with Christy.'

Stephen was bewildered, 'I? And all the time – ' He collapsed, 'God knows you're right. Christy's my son. If I hadn't been around, Christy wouldn't have had a cent. I saw to that. I looked after him. I petitioned the courts. I actually saved Christy's life one night, when my sisters were out on one of their lousy escapades. The nurse had gone out. It would have been five million dollars in someone's pockets if I hadn't been there that night. I wasn't married then and I was sorry for the kid. That's true, I never told you that. Never mind the sob-sister story; though I can see you're all agog. To hell with that. It's because of me though that Christy's alive to be a millionaire kid. I'm not ashamed to be Christy's gigolo. Surely he can help his poor old dad, now incapable and mindless.'

They both laughed. Stephen continued, 'I'm really not ashamed. I'll petition the courts. They'll be getting used to me anyway. The legal lot

276

like recidivists. They understand them. Here I am, I'll say, my wife used to keep me and now she can't, and there's my son rolling in gold and saving money hand over fist. I'll incorporate myself for instance; Christy's Dad Inc. and show Christy how not to pay income taxes by keeping me.'

'That's a good idea,' said Emily.

'Sure it is a good idea. But Christy's slow to catch on. He's not even as bright as I am, because I'm poorer.'

Emily laughed; then said seriously, 'Well, we're cutting close to the bone, Stephen. They ought to pay us something for these signatures. Anna's visit has nearly ruined us in cash – in credit! I'm not sentimental. Don't the Howards ever pay a profit?'

'That's a goddamn sneaky remark.'

'It's an outright remark. We're selling our souls; let's make a profit in cash.'

Stephen said, 'Kings never contribute, their subjects contribute; capitalists, too. Or are you a Marxist for nothing?'

'Oh, well, I'm damned if I'm going to see Christy slip through our fingers after giving him the best years of our lives,' said Emily.

'Me, too.'

Emily sighed, 'Gee, you wouldn't believe it. Such a lovely, quiet boy, almost too quiet, such a sweet lad. If they'd only leave him alone, he'd be ours for life. He wants to be a communist and help people. Gee, I wish God would throw a thunderbolt on all the goddamn rich. It's too much. What does your mother want money for?'

Stephen said mechanically looking out the window, 'Money is a sacred trust. If it isn't, we give the envious ragged a reason for pinching it. You'll hear Christy use that bright phrase one day. Watch and pray. Here I am, here we are, a couple of big-con men, trying to rob a rich boy by blood-ties and by the whore method or any method; we love you and we are your best friends. Don't trust people who only want your money. Ha-ha. I call myself an economist. I can only bloodsuck. I can't sell a pair of socks.'

'You could sell socks or diamonds at Tiffany's if you wanted to,' said Emily.

'I'm sick of being told I'm worthless and a parasite,' shouted Stephen.

'I'm sick of handing out a thousand dollars to entertain your family, just to be told how vulgar and coarse I am because I work for a living,' shouted Emily.

'A thousand? It'll be two thousand by the time she goes back. She told us to cut down expenses, too.'

Stephen, going out, paused at the door, 'But then – she does go to Egypt and boasts to Aunt Phillida about the receptions she's had. For it always irked Ma that Phillida married ten times the money Mother had. I don't know. Perhaps you're right and it pays. Be – well, what's the use. Go to hell. Go to work, goddamn you! Who makes the money round here? You or me? Go to work!'

'Well, I'll be floated on a sea of mud,' said Emily, looking after him with her mouth open. Neither saw Christy, who had heard all of this on an upper stair. Stephen banged the door. She sat down and began to pencil their next guest-list. And the next thing she did was to write to her mother-in-law, Dear Anna, a tongue-in-cheek letter of grovelling flattery, which could hardly please Anna. Yet she did not mean it that way. Her outrageous humour, bad or good, knew no limits. She had little under-standing of others, unless the electric discharges, negative and positive, were of a kind. Where her general and unspecific sympathy and affection did not guide her, she had no guide.

She wrote to the woman who regretted her being, 'Ah, darling Anna, our little resources can't nearly make up to you for the company you're used to, but (woe's me!) you enchanted us, you were so magnificently, superbly good to us, not showing your ennui, that I sigh with joy, with success. Woe's me, so superficial the success; for you could not have been really thrilled, happy with our trivia of entertainment. But you said so! And we were touched. I almost wept with joy. Ah, Anna, veritably and really, I wish we were closer together; but when this necessary time of separation is over, we and our dear ones and your dear ones will no longer have to endure this bleeding agony of separation, this waste of time and space. Me, ah me! So many good days – lost, all lost! And I'm so backward, dear Anna, that though you are so dear to me and I feel all the agonies and miseries of my beloveds I can't put a finger on it like you can. What do I need more than your advice and your caution and your experience? I sigh, I long. If only I were brighter! Still, dear Anna, when the long, weary, woeful time of our quarantine is over, we will move, we will be near you or you us, and we and our beloveds, and I mean you, too, our angels so bitterly separated will celebrate in a glorious, gorgeous, creamy, dreamy way the beginning of a new, totally, absolutely united life and we'll be no more the disinherited Howards. Divine prospect! Endless, enchanting, blessed prospect! And to think I dream of it every time we have the happiness to have you with us, dear Anna! And it must take some time to come. With this awful, yet necessary, quarantine. When we are out of that and no longer lepers to our friends and foes, we'll become private people and live the ordinary good life of the ordinary good American family. Oh, let it come soon. Oh, exquisite, magnificent hope of endless, daily, loving and tender relations between us all. I'm pro-foundly moved by your visit and your words to us, so wise, so impressive, to which dear Anna, we give fullest value. I'm depressed, passionately

278

sorry that we can't follow them now. But you can be sure that as soon as it's possible we'll be at your side and leave our shivering shocks and forget this grim reality which is no reality and live like ordinary, sober, sophisticated and loving people. Oh, dear Anna (long long sigh!) what pleasure you gave us – and what pain! My simple, sincere wish is to be at your knee like a child forever and to give you pleasure in everything. No matter what other success I have, what other successes I may have, that will be my superlative success. Alas! To have been born in a small town in a low rice-swamp in Arkansas and to be so low. But you, dear Anna, never sneered at me and my squalid origin; you were always so good, so loving. And it's only through my own stupidity that I haven't so far, with all my trying, been entirely successful in pleasing you. But I will. The thought torments me day and night. Your traditions, your intelligent, sensitive decisions, are what guide me. Believe me, Anna, the few weeks you spent near us in our new home were the most touching, the finest, the very ultimate pleasure in my life. Whoops! Joy! Ah, wonderful, you're coming back to us. I have as a friend, an elegant, fine, tasteful and tender-hearted woman.

> With love, love, love, my dear good adored Anna,
> Your woeful (because I didn't entirely please you),
>
> EMILY'

Emily was very pleased with this but hastened to the post with it before Stephen could see it. And now that that had gone and her mother-in-law perhaps struck by it (for she believed firmly that you can never flatter enough) she turned to work. She had two days' work on an article for *American Summer*.

16 SUBJECTS FOR EMILY

Anna, 'that incubus' was to leave the next day. As soon as they were free they had decided to have another private party to take the taste out of their mouths, and to look for new subjects for Emily to write about.

The Trefougars came to their house that week for cocktails with Mernie Wauters (Fleur was ill again), Suzanne and, in spite of Stephen's objections, some more Resistants who had been in concentration camp. Emily, stimulated by Suzanne, had it now in mind to write for Americans a terrifying book of the concentration camps, the occupation and, in simple terms, to describe the tendencies that led to and away from the capitulation to fascism, and that might lead in those directions again in other countries.

She said at night, drumming her fork on the table, with Christy there, Suzanne gone now, indignantly, 'How can I serve America better? If my countrymen don't realize it or even seem to hanker after the Germans as the papers say, it's because of the way the things are written up, either as horrrr (horror) stories, gruesome incidents which beat the cheap shock thrillers, blood-thirsty descriptions which arouse a thirst for them – we all have evil passions. Or it is so weightily and accusingly written as to make people resent your righteousness. But it ought to be put humanly and with a certain amount of humour. So that people don't feel the writer is getting at you, that he wants you to suffer and drop maudlin tears. That's all wrong.'

Suzanne therefore had introduced some 'Resistance types'. Violet Trefougar, consulted, said she'd love to meet them. She was lonely, bored; a friend in Paris was like a loaf of bread on a desert island and she didn't care what Johnny (Mr Trefougar) thought. It was good for Johnny, he moved in a rotten, gilded set, all Jew-hating, pro-Nazi, pansy-cultivating, 'a marijuana set of rotten, twopenny hotspurs.' Emily was electrified to hear this. 'How little I know, I thought them devoted,' she cried to Stephen.

Stephen said, 'Oh, they're devoted, but she's bored. Well, bring them along. A gilded, rotten, pansy-loving hotspur will be a relief from your historic heroes. Next year you'll have the salon full of cripples and lepers. It reminds me of Hollywood when it was full of exiles from Nazism.

280

Punks. So kind and so helpless, mental basket-cases, morally in oilbaths. Well, wheel them in.'

'Stephen, you're really mean.'

'You know the chronic sick are not sorry for the others. But what do I care? Why grouse? I'm merely the accountant and see we're headed for bankruptcy courts. As long as you can canoodle with every police spy in Paris.'

'Police spy! Oh, Jeehosaphat! I don't know one.'

'We will, Oscar, we will.'

They had the party as soon as Anna had landed in Egypt. Mrs Trefougar had a smooth, French dress. She was a handsome, blonde woman, with large lean bones; hollow-eyed, young and nervous. She was nervous, thinner than ever, drinking and smoking excitedly. She followed Mernie Wauters into a corner and listened to him hungrily. Vittorio was invited, but put them off at the last moment. Axel Oates had been visiting Marshal Tito and was there, full of enthusiasm for the socialist possibilities in Yugoslavia. The two Resistants were friends of Wauters, a Jewish merchant from Brussels, who had just returned from a visit to the United States – and a young, strikingly attractive man called Clapas, dark, small-headed, with nervous tics, his hands and head moving, who had spent several months in Dachau, escaped, been a commando, been sent to Buchenwald for resistance work.

'And you lived through that and came back,' said Emily, avid for news.

'To get the better of them. They were my enemies. I'd do the same for any enemy.'

'Over the Nazis, you mean?'

'Over men.'

'I thought you were a communist,' said Emily.

'Certainly. I loathe and despise – capitalists. The rich. The poor things they have made out of the others. The men they made and the woman they made. The officials I have to talk to, the society women – all I've come back to as well as all I've left.'

'You're a cynic and nihilist then?'

'In the civilization that produced and tolerated, and is trying to put cosmetics on and forget, the concentration camps, and meanwhile is preparing more – let me destroy it with my own hands, as they tried to tear me apart with their teeth, their nails – their hands! They were men. . . And women.' He laughed.

Emily backed away, 'No, no. Not men, not women. Fascists, brutes, unhuman. In socialism such people, if they exist, will be put away. Be injected with something to make them better. With a brotherhood serum, eh?'

281

He laughed insultingly, 'I don't care whether you or I or the rest here or the rest of the world lives or dies. What does it matter: tell me? Let your freedom-loving nation atom bomb. We all thought such things hadn't occurred since the ages of the pig, the Inquisition; since the medieval burning of Jews and Protestants and Negroes – and the jails in India and the jails in South Africa – and the chain-gangs and the Chinese tortures –' he laughed excitedly, 'and now – I didn't know, I never saw it, say the good Germans – too goddamn good for them, say the Americans – and they're taking hints. And what is modern war? War dogs tearing men to pieces? Flame-throwers burning men to cinders or burning them so deep that if they live it's in agony, threats of dysgenic warfare, killing, maiming, starving and scorching, stamping out ordinary men and even burning the tender, rich, maternal breasts of the earth, scorching, burning, plunging in deeper to make sure it can't produce any more plants or children – bah! It was because I despise all men– that I agreed to exterminate one small part – the Nazis. And when they caught me, because I despised them, I told nothing; but I laughed along their lines and jeered along their lines. They weren't sure. And you see here what we are. Your Madame Suzanne! What an idiot! Do you know what she is! And Monsieur Wauters! A weak, sliding fool! Monsieur Jeepers, a businessman only caught because he was a Jew, not because he had done anything good. Such are Resistants. And now everyone is struggling to get into their ranks. Yes, those who would have given them up without a flutter. The excuse – you mustn't make the innocent suffer! Such people! And now we are all Resistants! So don't make me a Resistant. . . But you know! Everyone like you knows about the United States, their gaols and chain-gangs. Do you care? You live well. You live on that, don't you? On that. So did we, only more so, because there was more of it and time was shorter and it was more concentrated. Listen, see! Why are we alive?'

'Luck,' said Emily.

'No luck. Arrangement. Madame Suzanne had done good service and her life was bought by heavy bribes. She told you they were lined up each day and the heads counted and the names called and she never was called. It's true. She was bought. She knows it. Bribes, money taken by the Resistance from the poor and hunted, taken from communists and Jews and given to corrupt Nazis. They were bribed, the payments came in each week – for some, only for some; and in the end the Americans came in time. Meantime, hundreds, thousands of women and children from that camp went to the gas chambers because no one bought them; and all the money taken from their friends, relatives, sympathizers, was given to save Madame Suzanne. See, there's a pillar of blood-money. See there! She let burn hundreds of babies, hundreds of women were mangled and

282

tortured and buried alive and – for her one life. All blood, all blood, she's only a human blood bank!'

Emily stared fearfully at him. 'Don't! How can you say such things!'

'I am the same. I was chosen to survive because of my services! Darwinism! The fittest! Not most horrible, cruel, beastly. Here I stand a pillar of blood and there she moves and talks, a fountain of blood, without thinking of all who died in her place, every day.'

'But if she'd died too? It would only have been one more. And through her hundreds of children were saved, the lives of over a thousand children,' said Emily emotionally.

'What sickening claptrap such talk is!' said Clapas.

'You don't care if the children were saved?' cried Emily.

'I care. But only because I'm sentimental; there's a trace of it left in me. Yes, I am glad they were saved. Perhaps they'll be better than we are. But look at them. They're already half grown up. And their world is worse than ours. They will perhaps be worse and create more camps. Perhaps everyone here will become an informer, a torturer, a guard in a concentration camp later on.'

'Oh, this is too dreadful to think or say,' said Emily, staring at the man.

He laughed scornfully. 'But not too dreadful to be true. You who did not see it are living in a dream-world. And some of those who were in the thick of it continue to live in dream. Like your Madame Suzanne. She saved lives of the innocents. She loved it. She walked in blood and a fiery storm and an iron hail and she loved it. She was calm, collected, true, loyal! How beautiful! How stupid! One can save but not with emotion. One can save and resist only with cynicism. Mankind believes in the good and glorious and see!'

He bellowed a laugh and turned his back, rolled theatrically away. Emily looked after him, not believing him. But now he was on his way back with a tall, good-looking, fair youth whom he introduced as 'Stanislaus Breslow, only son and heir of Professor Breslow, the leading expert on international law, one of those consulted by the Avenging Angels in the Nuremberg Trials. Stanislaus, as the son of a Jew – ' he said, looking at the boy and smiling sharply, 'was thrown into a temporary camp and landed at Maideneck where he lived quite comfortably for some years. He will tell you all about his experiences. He has views of mankind like mine, but acted differently. Madame Howard is an American journalist. She'd love to hear about it, Stan. Mr Breslow wants to go to the States where he feels sure he'll make his way because he understands their psychology. The sap, the essence of American psychology is, What's in It for Me; and that's his too. And I'm told that's the title of a British communist pamphlet, so we all think the same. Very nice. Your communists must have some very modern realists among them.'

Emily, left alone with this youth, felt tongue-tied. Breslow had a drink in his hand, was very affable. Emily said, 'Where is Clapas from? Is he really cynical or is that his company manner?'

'He's from the south, Montpellier, and he's really like that. We get on famously.'

'The youth sneered. 'He met me in Maideneck. You know we were on opposite sides, but we merely laughed at it all when we met again on the outside. Both survived by a fluke.'

'And what was your fluke? Were you a communist, selected to survive?'

'No. I was a student, a brilliant student of course, being the son of a Jew. My father was a brilliant professor. He was an atheist and I had not been circumcised. When the Nazis came I immediately denied that I was a Jew. I had from the first given another name. I denied, denied, denied. I don't look like my father. I'm not officially a Jew. He didn't want that; he wanted me to be a modern man, no out-of-date superstitions. They tried to make me confess. Nothing doing. Couldn't get me. I was brilliant, remember. They were not. They took me over for medical examination. The doctor decided I was not a Jew – fell in love with me, perhaps. I don't know. Someone fell in love with me. I was preserved. But someone came to the camp who, hard luck, knew me, started to speak to me and that person was a Jew. I had to denounce him. That's a Jew, I said to them. I told them I was head of a secret anti-Semitic society at the university and that we had them all numbered and described. I'd pick out every secret Jew in camp for them.'

'And of course you really saved your Jewish friend,' said Emily.

'Oh, what romance! Naturally, I denounced them all. I would pick out any Jew, even yellow-haired Nordic ones like myself. I became a thorough expert. I was their secret Jew-expert. I became very friendly with the guards and officers. I got on splendidly. They were fascinated by my imaginary anti-Semitic society. They gave me very light jobs and they put me in charge of a museum of horrors they had, samples of what people looked like who had been gassed to death, women's hair, teeth, crystals which form. It was behind panes of glass for they were still very dangerous and could have poisoned us. I used to look and gloat and think, I got away with it. They never had the slightest doubt – or if they had they liked me too well to show it.'

'And your father?'

'Oh, I'm in touch with my father. He's very busy, his name's in the papers. He showed that it was not international or war law for soldiers, even private soldiers, to obey their officers, if bestial or brutal orders were given. So the soldiers too were guilty. When my father heard how I was

284

saved, he became very sick, poor man, he got jaundice. I believe he will never recover from the shock one way or another. Jaundiced, yellow as the Jew he is.'

Emily looked round for Stephen to signal to him, 'And you? What will you do now?'

'I'll go to America, I understand the country perfectly. It's like Germany under the Nazis, but more force, more power. They're a great wonderful people and I'll get on there. I'll find a rich girl, marry her and sit on top of the world.'

'Supposing she won't marry you?'

'Oh, I'll get round that; I'll find out something, get something on her, get hold of her some way or another.'

'You don't know American girls,' said Emily.

'It won't take me long to find out.'

'Look, here's Stephen. He'll get you a drink; I've got to get to the kitchen, excuse me.'

On the way to the door, she ran into Clapas who teased her, 'A perfume, a flower. Isn't he? Now you see what I mean? A Resistant! And is there anyone alive today who's been through that who isn't distorted in some hellish way? Even the kids in your country are going to the devil; they don't care who lives or dies; they only want to burn up the world in liquid fire. They're all like he is. And you want them to be happy; you and Madame Suzanne.'

Emily said, 'I don't care. Let us die then. Who cares about us? We've had our time. All right, I don't care about the adults who died; it's too late. Even about those you call blood banks. But the children must survive and be given ideals. If our generation can do that to children, the whole generation should be wiped off the face of the earth. Let us die. What do we have to live for? Oh, hideous, horrible world!' She burst into tears.

Clapas laughed, 'Just so! To remedy it, you weep and Madame Suzanne loves. She loves!'

Emily dried her eyes, blew her nose, said indignantly, 'She did more. She walked the streets when the lion was in the streets and the skies thundered, she's as brave as a Roman virgin – '

He said contemptuously, 'Bad poetry, that is. For a writer everything is fixed once he's fixed a little phrase. Phrasemongers! You're responsible too. You'll never tell what you know. You'll fix it up. You corrupt language. It will take generations to purify the language you have soiled. To make it saleable – what do I care besides? For this is hell and we're all damned souls. How do you know this isn't hell, just a cosier suburb of it? Answer!'

285

Emily said, 'I know it isn't. Because – perhaps I ought to be apologetic about it but I live and hope to live in a better world somewhere. I don't know where. I hope and I pray that my children will never see those things. There is a chance of it, and so it isn't hell. I love my children, my husband, we're happy: there'll be some other happy people left I hope. And some brave.'

'Just some more blood banks, then,' said Clapas.

Emily went to Suzanne, 'My God, Suzanne, why ever did you bring these terrible men, these furies, here? They're demons.'

Suzanne said sensibly, 'They're tortured souls. They'll never recover. It's a malignant disease of the heart.'

'I don't believe it. I believe they were initially bad.'

'And yet Clapas was one of the finest men in the Resistance.'

'I don't think I'll ever understand human beings; I don't want to,' said Emily turning way, irritated.

'The hero is a very dangerous animal,' said Suzanne smiling.

'And you were one,' said Emily turning back and cocking her eye sharply at her.

Suzanne said in that dull way which irritated Stephen, 'I feel as if I've nothing more to learn, just like Clapas and Breslow. I told you how parents denounced children who irritated and disobeyed them, or who they thought were thieves or murderers or Resistants. They denounced their own children to a certain death. Little children, sweet little girls, with long hair and blue eyes and angel faces, but sharp little hearts and hungry bellies and vanity, denounced their parents, because the underground of children had told them that they'd get chocolate, money or other food or a pretty dress for denunciations. Wives denounced their husbands to get extra food or the property – it came to them direct, no questions asked. Husbands denounced wives to get property or another wife. It was so simple, so sure, so sudden. Some concierges denounced just to get the bonus; and others held on to protect their tenants banned and fled. Many dainty, respectable, fat little pouter-pigeon bourgeois wives "yes-m'-dear" and "no-m'-dear" denounced their servants if their servants were rude, or their neighbours if the neighbours had a better carpet, or they denounced the butcher who didn't give them enough respect or the landlord they owed money to. You can imagine,' said Suzanne cheerily, 'it was so very, very simple. Others denounced simply to get sugar or butter or tobacco or absinthe or drugs; especially drugs.

'And you could never, never tell. And one thing we learned, the informer was never the one you suspected, always someone else. People denounced because they owned someone else too much gratitude. A tubercular employee was taken in and petted and supported by his

286

employer; and he kept a diary from the day he entered the house, for five years, of the daily doings of his employer, and wrote a statement so twisting all the facts that the Gestapo took the whole family. A pathetic young woman abandoned and betrayed, kept as a servant with her child many years by a decent, conservative family, denounced the daughter of the house of whom she was jealous. Denunciations poured in – they were infinite. One of our chief services was in the post office, opening letters and sending them on again and getting messages in time. We destroyed some, you couldn't destroy all. They'd come in again; poison-pen manias developed. And you couldn't help everyone. Some had to perish. Again what Clapas so bitterly and brutally called the blood bank.'

Emily exclaimed, 'What a brute he is! I hate him. You've seen as much and you aren't like that!'

Suzanne said simply, 'I don't know what I'm like. I should like to be in another world where I would not have to ask myself, where society was interested in the future and not this post-mortem and this preparation.'

Emily took her hands, 'And I couldn't live through it. We must escape. Excuse me, I'm not as brave as you. I couldn't stand this test. I should give in.'

'No one knew until they had to; and then most were able to meet this test.'

'I could not! Perhaps – but no – oh – what a dreadful dilemma! What a cruel party!'

The Trefougars waited longer than the rest, the man because he had taken a great fancy to Stephen and the woman to see Emily, for she had come to her when it got late and begged her to let her stay, 'I am so miserable and afraid. Let me stay with you and confide in you. This place is a desert of friendship and Johnny just laughs at me.'

Emily was annoyed and flattered; she invited them to stay to dinner. She had been anxious to see Stephen alone for a few minutes to rehash the conversations they had separately had, to tell in her breathless, detailed way all the Resistants had said to her, to get comfort from his manly views. At the same time she was puzzled by the Trefougars. Violet she thought happy and devoted to Trefougar and yet Violet was dazzled by 'Mernie's bedroom-eyes' as Stephen called them, his drooping, delicate, insinuating manner. The Trefougars complained bitterly about their expensive way of living and small pay; and yet that afternoon Johnny Trefougar had described a magnificent Italian car he had just got through diplomatic priority and paid just on three thousand pounds for. The car would be delivered shortly; and then the Trefougars intended to take a trip to the south of France where the food was better and there to buy a villa. You could get villas now if you had connections. Violet was expensively dressed; yet they said they had hardly enough to eat.

For dinner they had two bottles of wine and Violet drank rather a lot considering the whiskies that had gone before. After dinner, when Christy had gone upstairs to study with Madame Suzanne, who had dined with them, Johnny went off with Stephen to his study to drink more whisky while the wife went upstairs to Emily's workroom on the top floor. There they had a drink and Violet, after twisting her handkerchief and behaving very nervously, burst into a flood of miserable confidences. Johnny was now drunk and would get drunker; it was the beginning of a four-day binge. He left her for three and four days at a time and was often brought back by the police. The car made it even worse. Now he could get away from her to Rouen or Dieppe or Marseilles, Toulon, all the low and dreadful murder hotels, old-fashioned but dangerous dens of vice, and if he had little time, there were some just outside Paris, where thieves, prostitutes, drunks and drug-fiends gathered.

'Oh, you can't be right; he doesn't look like that,' exclaimed Emily.

She stared at the poor, thin, elegant woman in front of her. Violet was now weeping: she trembled from head to foot. Emily listened on with widening eyes as the misery was related.

'Last time he went away he had over three hundred pounds in his pocket and came back penniless. The police brought him back. He was beaten from head to foot, his clothes torn; he said he had been robbed. Yet he only enjoys himself away from me in the thieves' dens where I couldn't go and in the company of young, strong sailors, or drug-sellers or low blackskins and such horrible people, always caricatures, never real people. And every time he is robbed. He was robbed when we were in North Africa, robbed in Honolulu, robbed in Singapore of all we had. That's one of the reasons we're so dreadfully poor.'

'But the car?'

'Oh, a friend got it, it's almost a present. But there's the upkeep. And I can't think what it will be like after he's used it for a few of his dreadful absences. And I never know if he will come back alive. And when he comes back, he weeps, he cries for the people he's left, for those animals. He blames me for tying him down. He says he hates me; he'll kill me; he'll do anything to get back to them.'

'But how does he hold his job?'

'Oh, they're very good to him. In London they warned him. Of course, he's charming, you can see. He's fascinating, especially to men. Some of his family are very high-placed. You know they put up with almost anything if a man keeps up appearances. And he can. You'd never guess, would you? You see he never gets drunk in good society. That's why he goes off to those hellish dens. "I want the stink of crime and filth in my

288

nostrils," he says. And then he gets so drunk, for he can't drink, that the first prostitute, or criminal or thug who comes along robs him and there he lies for days together, in some bunk crawling with lice, starving, until someone finds him. Oh, he comes back in such a state. And now this afternoon, this evening, when I saw him drinking, I am terrified, I hardly dare go home. He'll be raving mad by the time he gets home. You've no idea how he's able to hide it. And then as soon as he's in the house he locks the door and begins to scream and curse. We can't keep any servants of course.'

Emily wiped away the tears of the unfortunate woman and took her trembling hands on her breast. She begged her to stay there that night, not to go back;

'We'll keep him somehow. We'll see that he doesn't get into the hands of such desperadoes.'

She wailed, clinging to Emily, 'Oh no, no, no, then he'd kill me. He'd know I've been telling you; and his pride is so ferocious, so Spanish, so violent, he'd kill me at the mere thought that anyone knew.'

Emily argued that a lot of people must know, since there had been scandals in so many places. His family knew.

'But he always prides himself on being able to carry it off and impress people, especially new people, with his cool head and his manners – '

Emily murmured, 'So he does. I'm astonished, stunned. But you know he doesn't show the slightest sign of drunkenness now. Well, perhaps he's a little excited, but considering – well, that's far from drunk. He's not more excited than I am in hearing this story. I'm thunderstruck. I don't know what to do.'

Emily was full of dread for the poor woman. 'You're in danger, don't go home. We'll say you're sick, had to go to bed.'

Violet broke away from Emily, 'No, no. He needs me. Perhaps if I'm there he won't go. If I'm not, he'll go certainly. He'll stop at some place on the way home and that will be the end of him for days. He's been warned several times by his chief. No, no.'

She seemed scared beyond reason, 'Oh, he loves me, he loves no one but me, in his own way. It's just his temperament, his savage moods. Don't give me away. He'd kill me.'

Emily promised she would not and again begged the woman to stay with them. Violet sat down, taking Emily's hands in hers – Emily shrank back, not being of the clutching kind of woman, but she kept her hands there to help. Violet said, 'Oh, I'm naughty; I'm hysterical, forgive me. I said too much. I betrayed him. Don't betray me. It comes on me, almost like a longing, as the longing for horrors comes on him. It's being so long alone and tight-lipped and having to save our faces before everyone and yet knowing that everyone knows – or will soon know something worse. I run ahead of trouble sometimes. I want you to like us not to hate us, if there's a scandal. Don't shut me out. You're sympathetic, you're a writer. If the worst comes, at least I can come to you.'

Emily's great heart swelled. She thought, Oh, heavens and I was on the point of sending this poor sufferer home, of saying we had guests to dinner. This is a lesson, never to refuse an appeal for help. We don't know.

She felt 'ashamed, bitterly ashamed' as she said to herself, already composing what she was to write later in her *Journal of Days under the Sun*. To think she had never guessed what this smooth, nervous, elegant woman had been living with; daily horror. She thought to herself, and wrote it later, 'I'm so smug, so satisfied, so happy with my darlings, such a real success as a woman, that the human race is just a passing show to me. Clapas is right. All writers care about is their work. But we ask more of a mechanic. We expect him to save the human race via socialism. Oh, my God, save me from being a philistine in my old age.'

While she had been thinking and composing these reflections, Violet had dried her eyes and now said in a strange voice, more distant, almost hateful, 'Why do I say he loves me? He hasn't been near me three times in seven years! Where are my children? I had one baby which died because he stifled it with a pillow; he was jealous. I must be the only love in his life, he loved me so passionately. He is beautiful but a monster. I am afraid of him. I sat at home frozen with terror like an ice-maiden, in an icefield in a glacier. Frozen to death, freezing – and it will always be so' (her voice rose higher) 'always be so – sitting cold as ice till they bring him home to me dead from some den of vice. If you knew the dreadful cold – '

Emily exclaimed, 'Oh, this is dreadful, appalling. I can't stand it. We must do something for you. What? Say something. You must have thought out a hundred things.'

'I cannot escape. I'm ruined. He ruined me. I don't even dare touch another man or woman. Think of what kind of people are in those places? And the poisoned liquor they give him will turn his brain; it's turned already.'

Emily went out on to the landing to make sure that Christy was not there, that no child was there to hear this sufferer. When she returned, Violet had recovered somewhat. She turned to Emily with a faint smile, 'And you see I must go out every day or have people at home and pretend that we are a loving young married couple. When he dies or when he kills me – ' her voice wavered again, then she became morbid and in the end began to weep quietly, 'our friends and our chief will hush it up, the

290

scandal will never reach the papers; and they will say, Who would have thought it, such a happy couple? No, no one but you will ever know the truth. I will have to keep up the comedy for ever. I want you to know the truth. Oh, it is terrible to think of dying there alone, him killing me and no one knowing what I have suffered, he's too charming to get the death penalty in any circumstances. It will turn out I am to blame. Five years later some other woman will begin to live in this hell.'

Emily heard the men moving downstairs. She was frightened and had not made up her mind what to do. Had she better consult Stephen now? For it was this night that Violet was afraid of, 'Most of all this night, it's a premonition, it's precognition, as if I had lived through it all before and knew exactly what is going to happen.'

'Oh, don't go – or go anywhere but home.'

Violet said stormily, 'No. If he wants to kill me, what is there to hope for anyway? I loved him. He was the love of my life. Let him kill me. There couldn't be another one. I'll just look into his eyes tonight and if I see it coming, and I think I've seen it coming, if I see that look in his eyes, I'll lie quietly, sit quietly, I'll say to myself, I always knew it, I've always heard in my brain since I was a little girl, that awful strangled yell – '

Emily got up and took her by the arms, 'It's madness. You're going to your death.'

'Yes, I am. He needs me. Leave me alone.'

They went downstairs, Violet tranquilly, Emily stony with her unaccustomed feelings. Violet was charming to her husband and Johnny was sweet, almost tender to her. Violet smiled kindly to them and when she held out her hand to say goodbye, she murmured, 'Oh, thank you so much, we have enjoyed it so much,' in quite the ordinary way, nor did she give Emily any but a casual glance.

Emily seized Stephen's arm, led him into the sitting-room and threw herself suddenly into his arms, 'Stephen, oh, Stephen, I have heard such a story! Listen, quickly. Perhaps we will have to save a life tonight. Can you get the car out? Listen!' She told the tale. Stephen was puzzled. 'I spent the whole evening with him and he seemed neither drunk nor crazy; very sensible. Is she crazy?'

Emily said of course, Violet was tormented; but anyone would be.

They discussed it. 'It's a dreadful mystery,' said Emily.

They sat there for a long time going into details, worrying; and at last they took the car and rode out to Auteuil where the Trefougars at that moment lived and, having found the house, they rode round it for a while. There were lights in the house, windows were open, but no sounds were to be heard. Should they knock at the door? Perhaps she was already dead? Or were they drinking, thinking or – a word that rhymed, said Stephen.

'Can you believe her?' said Stephen.

'Could she invent a story like that, even half of it?'

After some time they passed the same two bicycle police they had passed before. The police looked back at them. They decided to drive home and telephone. When they got home they had not the courage to telephone. Supposing a murder had taken place? They had been seen near the house and they were the first to telephone – and at that hour? Emily said they would telephone first thing in the morning.

She slept badly and when she thought Stephen was awake, she said, 'We didn't do our duty.'

They had got out in one of the streets, to come nearer to the house on foot. Coming down one of the streets, Emily heard a man shout from the third storey of an apartment house, in English.

'He-elp, He-elp! Murr-der! Murr-der!'

Three doors away a policeman was standing at an immense carved door leading into a courtyard. He was talking amiably to the woman concierge.

'Shouldn't we tell him?' said Emily.

'He can hear it as well as you. I didn't hear it.'

They rode home. On the way home Emily began to laugh and said, 'That makes two murders tonight on our heads. Or do you suppose the streets ring with murder now, just the memory of the stones, the walls and doors? And supposing it's some hashish dream?' She began to laugh helplessly. 'Oh, what a world. It's funny and terrible.'

In the night, she said to Stephen whenever she thought he was awake, 'No, it wasn't fancy. It was real. Someone was killed in that house tonight, that other house. We didn't do our duty. That's why these things occur. It's collusion. We're all collusionists. That's why they can take place. That man who chopped up little boys in Hanover, everyone in the house knew. Even that was collusion. And all those cops about. But they collude too. And Violet – oh, we should have gone in. Because what she said about precognition, a feeling of having lived through it before, which is a warning, she explained to me, one part of the brain is functioning faster than the other – that was terrifying. I hear her voice now. It's running through my head.'

'Take an aspirin and go to sleep. We can't help it. Their friends are guilty, not us. Their friends, the officials know.'

'Supposing we're the last people to see them alive.'

'What about the maid?'

'Violet said Johnny had told the maid to take the evening off.'

'Oh, Lord. Just like the stories.'

292

In the end, Emily took several tablets and slept heavily till past eight o'clock. Stephen had got up, got the boys off, and started the house going. Emily put on her dressing-gown before she remembered. She seized the telephone and called the Trefougars. The maid said that Mr Trefougar had already gone out and Madame was still in bed. She was not well. Emily asked if the maid had seen Madame. Yes, the maid took her tea.

'How is she?'

'She'll be getting up soon.'

The maid was calm and correct. Emily said to Stephen, 'I'm baffled. Unless that maid plays along with the husband.'

Stephen shouted, 'Quit building up your usual devil stories and get to work. And don't first of all write a brief history of all the criminals in your life or your journal, or study Latin and French and algebra to keep up with the kiddies; or socialism or write squelchy letters to my mother – work, damnit. We spent enough time with lunatics and other sandwich-snatchers.'

'What are you doing?'

'I'm writing an article for Vittorio, all right it isn't economic, but I've got to have some reason for living.'

She said heartily, 'Listen, Stephen, I think yesterday was a lesson, a sampling of what we oughtn't to know. Let's go back to being interested in the labour movement. I'll go out of my head if I have to spend any more time and money on Sir Clapas, Sir Trefougar and their merry men. Even your mother – '

'Leave my mother out of this: what next?'

'Stephen, do we understand Europeans at all? Aren't we like invertebrates crawling out on the primeval mudbank and looking up at primitive man and not knowing what he's all about?'

'Go and work.'

'I had an idea in the night, Stephen. Why shouldn't I write *The Personal History of Bill Blank*, one of the most original, fascinating, startling, gifted and delightful communists in America, so that people over here will know everyone over there hasn't their finger in their eye and in the pie.'

'It will find hundreds of publishers to turn it down. Go ahead! Christy can always go back to Grandma and Giles can sell newspapers!'

She said, beginning to cry, 'Oh, all right. I'm tired of being the workhorse, always patiently jogging along in the shafts. One day I'll break the traces and the cart can jolt downhill by itself into the ditch.'

He got up smiling and put his arms around her, 'There, there, silly girl. Who loves you? But you aren't practical. You're lovely. I adore you. You're a funnyface, and you're a genius; but not practical. Now we have

293

to eat first. I mean unless you want us to find some sort of a two-room hovel with wooden floor with a hole in it and chicken-shit on the boards, and newspapers on the walls down in the sunny south, a nice old crumbling stone hovel. . .you can wash the dishes, the floor, the clothes, the children's behinds in the running brook, or tug water from the village pump, which is sure to be at the other end of the next hamlet; and we can grow our own food, with the aid of one pear tree gone wild, one crab apple tree, some turnips and three rows of straggling grapevines. Giles's hair will stick up in dusty sticks, Christy will have to go out and steal hens at night. Olivia will get freckled and stupid, flies will blow in her nose, Giles will get sandy blight and when Christy goes down with his next attack of pneumonia or snakebite or appendicitis, there won't be any penicillin for a hundred miles and we'll bury them all by the henhouse.'

Emily laughed. 'Oh, stop, stop! From drawing chalkmarks on the sidewalks, comes marijuana and then the electric chair, I know. I know, OK you're worth it, darling: you're all worth it.'

'Oh, don't pull that. I'm willing to sleep on sacks if you are.'

'Oh, you brute. You know damn well I'm not.'

They went to their workrooms. Emily spent the whole day describing her adventures in her journal and fixing up her card file on her friends. In her journal she mentioned today as every day recently, her feelings for Vittorio. She thought about herself. She'd worked for her mother, then for a sick sweetheart, then for Stephen and the children. The life she was leading was not the life she wanted to lead. This journal and the letters she wrote to her friends were her real companions, she thought. She was glad she did not dream; she was afraid of dreams. One of the men she had known and been fond of, had said to her surprisingly enough, 'Why don't you break off from your job, go out and do something?' She was very surprised; and mentioned it to a woman friend. 'Oh, when a man says that – ' said the woman and stopped. What did she mean? It had taken her breath away. She'd been a firehorse all her life; but to him, this man, she'd done nothing; she was in leading-strings, like a toddler. 'I guess I develop slowly; and here I am downhill to the forties, something missing I guess.' She thought of her long years of 'fire-eating, snorting, sweating, slogging.' Now she was a lady, Madame. Still the same though. A great triumph, of course, considering her mother had been nothing but a floor-washer with pretensions and she'd worked her own way up with a pickaxe, no tears for bloodied heads. And Stephen – she smiled sweetly – a love, a darling, a great catch – her relatives were still thunder-struck in Arkansas, at Plain Jane, the Worry of the Wilkeses marrying into the 85% bracket. What a girl! When she did a job, she did it. She'd never fallen down on an assignment, failed to meet a deadline, turned in a bad job. Only – she died laughing thinking of her ways and means. What the hell! Die and let die is the good old American motto – what the hell, we're *banditti* – people admire Corsicans for it.

She laughed to herself thinking over her exploits. 'Yeah, very fine. But now I'm grown up. I'm supposed to be a writer. I've got somehow to get out of this fur-lined foxhole I'm in, playing hanky-panky with dear Anna and letting Stephen have an aim in life. Oh, golly. Supposing I'd met Vittorio in time and he'd fallen for me, then. He has a purpose. And he's not worried about what Anna thinks or anyone else. I'd never have left the left with him. Oh, dear; heigh-ho. A woman's life.'

She got up and stretched, looked out the window. A narrow asphalted Paris street with high walls each side. 'In socialism they'd throw the damn things down: or, I don't know, maybe if those walls herded social-minded characters and the town was ours, they could stay up, have some peace and quiet.'

She pondered. She didn't mind now, whether gates opened before her – and a good many opened. They were doing the European Phase in the grand way. It had not been difficult for them to move from New York society to Paris cosmopolitan society – if Anna would stay out of it. After all – Vittorio – 'Vittorio! That's the word,' she said to herself, sitting down in front of her typewriter; after thinking for a few minutes, with her hands poised, she wrote:

'Dear Vittorio: we hung out the flags (*pavilloné*, eh? How's my French?) the other day when your card arrived from Florence and your card from Bologna. How nice of Vittorio, so busy and so famous! One of the superb events of my life, Vittorio. I'll treasure both, I'll frame them. And after the revolution, I'll show them round, the Commissar for Literature and Fine arts was my friend in the bad old days. Ah, Vittorio, Italy sounds splendid, even the cooking! And we're going there. We'd gallop there now but for Mamma who has left for Egypt but will soon be back. And then – long sigh of relief – ah, then the Howards are going on a short consolation trip and when your letter came, we said, It must be Italy! But Italy in June-July? And then you won't be there, but back here. So we'll wait for you. Only, alas – a book in being and a serial to finish – the working life. Stephen is doing some articles for you, I think, and very important indeed for him and, I hope, even good for the paper they're destined for. And so we must snatch a brief repose, while we can, though so deeply longing to see you again. You don't know how we miss you. We've been partying with people Mamma would like, but who baffle us. We do live in the twilight of the gods, don't we? I wish we didn't. I wish the agony was over and dawn was breaking. But there's the long long night. Ah me. Woe, woe! Vittorio, I wish you were here. You give me

295

courage. I'm not built to be a cynic or satirist. I despise them, heart and soul. But having to keep a family going and with expenses the devil's long pocket could not meet, I'm doomed, I fear, to assassinating myself, to never doing what I want to do or to putting it off till doomsday. And sometimes I'm very much afraid I'll become despairing and then get cynical and wiseguy and empty. Well, Vittorio, come soon; I want to talk to you. You know everything these well-nourished types don't know and more. You survived the sea of blood and the shores of bestiality and cannibalism and here you are as lively as a cricket. You give me courage even when I think about Europe. It was worth coming to Europe for. Trouble is, in the USA we have no ideals worth a cent. Yes, see how it all comes out in money. "Worth a million, looks a million, feels like a million, not worth a cent." That expresses it. Well, I think of my youth. Was it I, that girl with flaring hair and freckles battling in the streets for Sacco and Vanzetti, addressing meetings and roaming the country, shouting, "Up the Revolution!" Was it I? Golly, the years get us. Here I am, a bourgeoise. Is it old age, the fat forties? Do I love money? Well, I guess I don't despise it. But I don't live for it and I could live without it. When I was a girl I was just bursting to say something, my heart was simply bursting with joy – no, with love. I was always in love, but I had no one. When I got moody I used to try girdles and ropes, nails and hooks, Will I use this one, Will that hold me? A man has just been here telling me the whole human race (except perhaps you) ought to die. He wouldn't care. A war-ruin, not a fascist. He nearly convinced me. It's only instinct, because I want my children to grow up and be sane, that makes me revolt. But such a thought has never entered your head, Vittorio. That's noble of you. Poetic, lovely thought – '

She stopped and thought, What am I writing? My diary? It's a love letter. Stephen would hit the ceiling if he saw this. I must be crazy. she suddenly became angry; the worst thing about a husband and even kids is they cut you off from humanity. You're a nun, you're gagged, your mouth's full of soap. I don't want that. She felt shame; she squirmed and thought, Oh well, what the heck, I've got to learn, you learn so slowly when you're married.

The letter wouldn't do. She put it in her journal. She had only just put a paper in her machine to begin the day's work when the clock struck six. Time to go down and see the children and Stephen.

She had a drink with Stephen, explained all she had been doing including the letter to Vittorio she was not sending. 'I want to see him all right but clean hands, clean heart – I don't see why we can't ask him again to meet dear Anna when next she comes. He was in Roman society. He's very polished and refined, a lot more than her New York friends and her Chicago family – '

Stephen said, 'Don't talk about my mother's polish. You know Vittorio would come out with anything he pleased. He relies on that diabolic charm of his, split eyeball, scars, bald head, bad skin and all, he's a deuce of a charmer. Mother would fall and you can't stop Vittorio talking about the great adventure of his life, how he gave up all for the communists. By dinner-time Anna would know it all. I don't know what she'd think. She'd love him and afterwards make me guilty. On the other hand, she'd hope he was after you – perhaps he is – then she'd hope I'd lose you and she'd have me back in the old walled orchard. Do you realize I gave up millions for you, Emily?' he said comically.

She said, 'Listen, I could have been the leading socialist writer of the USA – I gave up millions for you. Fifty-fifty. I'm not sure about it, though; maybe one rabbit, one horse.'

They burst out laughing. At this moment the maid brought them the evening mail, which changed everything.

There was a short, stiff note from Anna Howard saying she was going to England to see her cousins there and coming straightaway after that to Paris. She enclosed a note from Christy saying that she felt Stephen and Emily did not understand the boy and did not care about his feelings. Christy's note explained to his grandmother that his studies were so far behind the French boys of his age that he would either have to spend several years slaving day and night at them to catch up and then enter the Sorbonne behind the others, or else give up all hope of the Sorbonne. He reported simply, 'My tutor says that he has never met a boy so far behind. I'm afraid to tell Father and Mother' (he meant Stephen and Emily) 'and so I'm writing to you to ask what I should do, do you think?'

Anna said she thought the shift to Europe and without adequate interest and affection from people engrossed in their own affairs, had been too much for the boy. He was too old to start acquiring a foreign tongue and they had better send him right back to his native country. She didn't want the boy to feel inferior.

Stephen's face darkened as he read the boy's note and handed it to Emily.

'The damn little hound, sneaking behind our backs. Don't tell me he's naïve. I know what tricks I was up to at that age; I knew the use of naïvety too. I was no record-breaker in class, but I knew my ways and means. I'll thrash the boy. Christ, listening at doors and trying to sink us; selfish little brute. We're killing ourselves for him. What a thief! I understand this gentleness. I'll break the guy's neck. Christy! Of course he hears me, Emily. He's listening on the stairs for repercussions. Little savage! He's like a half-trained dog. Isn't he too sweet! And then he bites the hand that honeys him. Christy!'

Emily anxiously ran after him to the door. 'Shh! Don't say anything. Supposing it is a little plot of the boy's? Let him be. So it won't work. Too bad. Look, he's only a child. Like a young dog, he enjoys blow-ups. You know what he said to me when he came back from the walk in the Louvre the other day. I saw all the Rubens, oh, boy (he said) and a fat priest examining the worst and an old American lady copying one of them. Oh, boy! Shall I tell Daddy or will he kill me? It's days since I saw a real show at home. You're losing your grip.'

'Impudent young bastard,' said Stephen.

'Oh, gee, I thought it was a hell of a laugh. He's on to us. It's killing! I told him, "Your father loves fat ladies, look at me. That wouldn't bother Stephen. He'd think you were just following the family line." That finished that, you see. Don't let the kids see they've got you. They're all great kidders.'

She laughed. 'Let's just watch the boy simmer waiting for us to break out. But frankly it is bad that he's so far behind. I know it. I've sweated over his algebra and his Latin and I know I could have covered twice the ground myself starting from nothing. He just doesn't get it. Maybe disturbed by spring, sex, you know.' She laughed.

Meanwhile Stephen was opening other letters and was in a worse temper.

'They didn't take the serial! They want revisions, it's got to be cut and they don't like the character called Handout Mike, because he talks like an agitator, so they say. I told you, Emily, it wouldn't go. You can't run with the hares and hunt with the hounds. I told you that damn Vittorio stuff would get into it!'

Emily snatched the letter and read it, muttering, 'What bastards! But they ordered the serial!'

Stephen muttered, 'Go fight City Hall. That's the straight tip. Obey or you don't eat. A message from Legree to Uncle Tom.'

A letter from *The Gothamite* said that in the two sketches submitted, which satirized Greenwich Village intellectuals who called themselves leftists, the author had not made her own political position clear and that her attitude towards her characters was merely unfriendly or slightly critical. Her criticism of them must be sharpened, she must make clear her dislike and contempt or derision for such people and such a movement. This was the implication, almost the terms of the letter.

Stephen said haughtily, throwing the letter to her, 'They're putting on the screws.'

'What do you want me to do? You yourself want me to sit on the fence. If we go too far right, you know Florence will cut you out of her will. Besides, darn it, I don't want to let the Oateses and a few others think I'm a louse. I ought to can it and write innocuous stuff. . .I've done all right so far. Oh, this problem of selling out. A lot of those who talk about it can't sell out. They're too far in. There's nothing more I despise than the writer or artist who tells you what he could have made if he had not been a communist. Either he couldn't have, or he's just about to turn the corner and sell out and work his way into a million. But think of them sitting there, the spiders, in a closet, in a broom closet and adding on their fingers with greed on their faces, "I could have bought me a house in Larchwood, I could have had three cars, I could have sent my kids to Harvard, I could have had fur coats in the family, and sent them and the blankets to storage in summer, I could have had two servants each costing me $220 monthly, plus two dailies costing me $90 monthly, plus washing $120 monthly, plus two iceboxes, plus caviar and champagne, I could have made $120,000 yearly, with my talent," and the saliva dribbling down his chest – faugh! and I did all that, Stephen, I did that without selling out. And you yourself appearing at press conferences as representative of the Party press, you met the President of the United States, you were in all the sancta sanctorum and you weren't a wolf in sheep's clothing – '

'I was a sheep in sheep's clothing, the way I'm acting now.'

'Well anyhow it can be done; I've done it so far. Their story is a lie. I wrote my way into Hollywood. I can beat all those best-sellers, Edna Ferber and Upton Sinclair. Did they make a pact with the devil? That's a proof. If you hear a writer say he's a failure because he's despised because he's on the left, you can take it it's proof that he's a failure anyhow; or right next week or the week after, he knows they're going to make him an offer; or he's crying his eyes out they haven't made him an offer yet and they have made Joe Blobb, his neighbour and competitor, an offer.'

Stephen said irritably, 'All right. But we've got to make a decision today. There's Mamma. And there's the publisher and there's *The Gothamite*. Don't make noble speeches. Act. Start from now. The past is dead. Our Ten Years in A Vacuum. So snap into it, Howards! The whistle blows! Forward to the literary assembly-line. Subsection, *Gothamite*.'

Emily said, 'Well, I suppose they're scared shitless. They at one time or another published all the one-time and the still-unregenerate leftists in the literary life of New York. Because who but the leftists had the bright ideas and were so up and coming?'

'Yes, no wonder, they're after us to get into line. They published an article about my second cousin, Dr Marie Tanner, leading red medico, who likes social medicine and says they have life-giving drugs in the Soviet Union and can put a dog together after they've taken him apart

299

and can make a chicken liver live and live and live by itself – think of the destruction of the chicken-liver trade in New York alone! And my sister, Florence Howard! And they wrote an article mentioning my humble name, Stephen Howard, who lost red thousands in the subway and plenty by you Miss Emily Wilkes author of *The Wilkes-Barre Chronicle*. Goddamn, Emily, why did you have to offer up your two cents? Why couldn't you have stayed an honest-to-goodness lowdown, night-court, Hearst reporter? You've ruined my life. Here, I gave up millions for you.'

Emily did not laugh. She said coldly, 'There is a problem. Your sister Florence wouldn't know you if you ratted on the movement, and goodbye Christy. We've trained him to be a sincere, soulful red too; and Christy's a sticker. He has a sort of damp, honest character like mould and mildew. When things are bad and old and damp he sticks and grows to it. So for him too, we can't turn.'

She sat down and read, weighing every word of the letters before her. She said, 'There's no doubt, it's conform or go hungry. The usual freedom of the individual: free to think and starve.'

Stephen cried out in a high, imperious voice, 'This upsets my calculations. I'd already counted in the money for those three pieces and, as for the serial, we've already spent that money; and in my accounts I made it appear to Anna that we'd had it.'

'I guess we had a right to count in the serial,' said Emily almost to herself. She was biting her lip, in her mind revising the serial.

She did not listen to Stephen, who went on raving, 'And that goddamn skunk, our agent, what is he doing? We write, cable; nothing happens. Out of sight, out of mind. The New York manner; if you can't telephone and bawl hell out of him, he doesn't give a damn. He's still raking in percentages of *Henry*, *There's An Angel* and *Mr and Mrs Middletown* so why should he get into a mess with our goddamn red writings? Don't we know any better, he thinks?'

Emily said thoughtfully, 'Well, there's nothing for it. I must rewrite it.'

'Bring down the copy. We'll go over it tonight and see when we can send it off.'

For taxation purposes, Stephen appeared as joint author with Emily of her money-making writings; and he worked hard with her on revisions.

Emily suddenly laughed, 'There's no doubt it's the depths of crime to spend your days writing a thing which doesn't sell anyway, commercial filth, which isn't even bad enough or good enough. Oh-ho-ho. What a fool I am! The fool of time, who died of hunger though she lived for crime. I guess the lives of all crooks, except when they climb into government, are short, nasty, brutish, eh?'

Stephen snarled, 'I'm not feeling funny. All my calculations are out. I

300

cut a fair figure with Anna because of this serial. We'll have to mail off your new set of stories this week.'

Emily protested that she could not. She had been working on a new idea that she felt was not only very good but would sell; it was in her best style. Stephen raved and then asked, what was the new idea? She eagerly told him, 'The Sorrows of a Really Fat Person like Me, only fatter if possible. And who can't really weep about it, who has to laugh; and then sometimes wants to crawl in somewhere and hide herself. She's afraid she'll never get married. She always misses the bus going to work, because she can't run, but she provides entertainment for the bus passengers. At work, it occurs to no one that she might be sensitive; fat people are so jolly. Then I'd bring in my mother who was so tiny and was deeply shocked and offended at my appearance; and the dieting, pills, forced athletics, how I love to eat; picture of me sneaking away to eat. Temptations to be a fat woman in a circus and really eat all I want. Morbid thoughts; over-eating is a substitute for sex, or something else. Counter thoughts; but I feel fine when I eat and I don't mind sex, I like it. How I was always attracted to living skeletons, like you, Stephen, so refined it seemed to me to be only a question of days perhaps, so thin, so ethereal. Oh, that this too too solid flesh would melt. Only not a chance. H'm! Eh? It doesn't sound good put that way. But I've got a couple of really funny sketches. Do you think it would go? USA is crazy about diets. I could put in some diets. USA is crazy about recipes, hints. Put in some of them. eh? I've got one episode, it's a pippin, I think. Of course, it's back home in Arkansas. You might call me a regional writer, ho-ho! There are three enormously fat people there who live over the hill. I'm morbidly attracted and often go and gaze through the fence to see them. They've got high hedges, never saw that before in Arkansas. No one sees them. Once a month they go shopping, but in general the food's delivered in a truck; and they grow stuff too. I thought a lot about those people. They consoled me and frightened me. And I thought, But they don't earn. I suppose you have to be fatter still to earn a living in a circus. I used to go to see the fat ladies in circuses and they made me sick. They had a special truck for one on the railroad. They just hooked her on and she sprawled all over a car as big as a coaltruck, without the sides. Then, me showing my infant pictures. Me at twelve, in a silk frock, about ten yards of material in it and three double chins, and an immense horse-tail of fair hair reaching below my large buttocks. H'm. And then my joy! Wha-at! I got a boy to look at me. I became his slave out of sheer gratitude. When I caught a husband I thought the whole of the Wilkes family must be staggered at the news. My revenge for all my humiliations. And then the misconceptions of a fat girl. I thought all women were pretty fat, until I found out they were pregnant. You can put that it. And then of course I was pushed aside; Flossie's child. Send Flossie's child outside. I had a fear of hurting myself, having to have an operation. The surgeon would never be able to find the place; they used to kid me that way. When I used to be at my aunt's place, they'd send me outside when the others were eating. Gee, how hungry I was. "You look as if you're always stuffing." I couldn't say I ate the same amounts; I really ate much more. I stole of course – '

She sighed. 'How else could I get enought to eat? We never had enough at home. Mother had a birdlike appetite and she didn't feed me enough on account of my figure. She was deeply ashamed of me. When people shouted, "What legs!" some mothers would have been proud, a prize pig, but mother was so refined Heigh-ho! Well, there's plenty and it's damn funny too. And now it's the same. Special clothes. I have to have a dressmaker come in. Skirts that can be run along a patent band, taxi-skirts with several whistle stops, double-breasted blouses. Well, I prefer to live in a dressing-gown or a butcher's smock.'

She laughed, 'Oh, my, sometimes I have fun. These glorious splurges, this mad eating, those glorious feats that I say are for Anna, for Vittorio – and the week later, when I find I've put on twenty pounds at least. Oh, my! And the reduction wrinkles, getting old, no more satiny skin, ugly one way or another, oh, my, oh, life, life! What are you! A Gargantua that was allowed to eat and spend his life groaning, his belly ached only from emptiness and wind. Rabelais was the only man who understood me. He's dull and reported to be vulgar; but you can't high-hat the classics, you can just say they're dull. But they're real! Well, the episode – And then my dream to have a lovely little girl, a perfect doll. I hope I haven't deformed Olivia. Oh, well – '

She laughed, blinked her fair lashed eyes, 'Some gruesome, funny details. All sorts of superstitions. That fat is associated with madness. I was proud and afraid. Well, they were thinking of diabetes. Diabetes was a word I heard from my cradle. Then they could strip blubber off me like a whale, Moby Dick had a horrid fascination, I hated the book. A man died in the town horribly by burning himself to death with an alcohol stove. They said, I'd have made a lot of good fat if that had happened to me. My God, the brutality, the bestiality of people, of your own folks, the savagery – family humour is bestial and savage and that's the real humour, too, the kind the people like and I wouldn't dare write.

'Then, that I'd never marry, of course, that was an axiom. How could I get a job, mother used to wail. They showed me pictures of those captive balloons they used in *Mardi Gras* – me again! Ha-ha-ha. I got one for a birthday card. Ha-ha-ha! Though it is funny. People's humour really is funny. One of my uncles was very much insulted by my looks. One of my aunts said that fat women could never have babies like other women. And me eating – oh, my, the legend of the family! Flossie's child; the whale. I learned dancing, I made up my mind not to be left on the shelf. Mother began to pity me and got a local dressmaker to run me up a creation of my own; I bought the materials. It was pretty. I still think so – but not for me. Something suitable for an elfin child, powder-blue chiffon over powder-blue silk, with black chenille rings and sprays. I made the design up myself. It was really lovely of mother. And I sat the whole evening through in the dancing-class social and at last the dancing teacher, a woman, danced with me. And my Cousin Laura of course, who had some little brandy-brown outfit, ugly, had plenty of boys. Then, of course, I proposed to a boy: that was four years later. I was still running around in things that appealed to my rich taste – little bits of cotton goods, that appealed, designed like French wallpaper, Chinese roses mixed with birds and lattices. I had one yellow one I loved, yellow-ochre-and-claret-coloured linen. It was handsome but I never had the patience to finish it and I wore it till it dropped to pieces, with the tacking threads around part of it. After that, I lost patience, with *le classique* and went back to large roses on white georgette. H'm. A galleon in full sail, some boy called me. Kaleidoscope Annie. *Look At All Those Roses!* The time I got into my aunt's cement fountain to drown myself and the water overflowed and the fishes came out on the grass. There they lay gasping and heaving. A lot of them died and some frogs hopped about. Another crime. Ha-ha-ha! The fishes and I were gasping and heaving our last. I was about to go to heaven with a lot of small fish. I stuck my head into a fishbowl once before that to suck the water. Couldn't get my head out. I had crazy tastes. I liked the soft, brackish, weedy taste. That's why fish like it! The fish pools of Heshbon, I guess, were like that. I couldn't get my head out. I nearly passed out for good that time. They could hardly crack the fishbowl over my face. They pulled all my hair out first and me after it. I was terrified taking bus-rides! Supposing there was an accident and the doors would not open? The others could get out through the windows, not me. And then the shame – practically always taking the seats of two people. I used to pay double-fare very often, not to have the shame. Heigh-ho. Some troubles, eh? And billed as lazy and greedy when I didn't have the dough most times to eat a full lunch; and I worked my head off, ten times as much as the thin rails I admired and who sneered at me and went off hoofing and spooning. *Hard hard the cat world.* Well, and I've got a gorgeous episode, it's the central episode, I think. So far at any rate. I climb into an apple tree, romantically, to look at the next door boy; down it comes, the whole tree, with a crash! I liked to be a hoyden, too. I had fears of suffocating, getting into some little hole in a cellar or dirt-trench, or under some planks and dying there. I used to read those accidents that were always happening to boys, with absolute terror. I thought of practising yoga so that I could hold my breath like fakirs do, for a week. I was terrified of being locked in a room. How soon would I die of the H_2O?'

'What H_2O?'

'The bad air.'

'CO_2, you mean, you die of.'

'That's it. Mother used to say, "Stop it! Go put your head in a bag!" It haunted me. It stifled me. Well, the gorgeous, funny episode I think will put the book across, is this. There was a girl called Ida Nass – '

She began to giggle, 'W-w-would you b-believe th-that? A g-girl c-c-c - oh, he-he-he, c-ca-he-he-he, c-ca – ho-ho-ho. Ida I-oph-oh-oh, I ha-ca-caN'

'You're just a schoolgirl,' said Stephen smiling.

She said emphatically, 'Ida Nass and another girl called – oh-he-he-he, C-c-Car-Carlotta Katz, o-ho-ho, he-he-he, Ida-na-na-nass and Car-l-l-lot – oh-ho-hohunh-hunh-it's funny. Ida Nass and Carlotta Katz. Ha-ha-ha!'

She threw herself on the sofa and laughed helplessly.

'For God's sake, stop giggling,' shouted Stephen, laughing.

'There was one called Hed-oh-oh-oh, oh dear, oh, dear, I'm dying. Help me, Ste-ph-phen. I can't he-help it. Oh, dear, I'm dying. I'll die; oh-oh-oh! There was one called -ha-ha-ha-ha, Hedda, Hedda! There! Hedda-Hedda-Meyer! Oh-ho-ho!' She rolled on her belly. 'Oh-ho-ho, I'll die, I'll die.'

The boys and Suzanne Gagneux came in, hearing this uproar, looked at Emily, looked at Stephen and started to laugh. She saw them, waved her hand, cried, 'I was telling P--pa-pa-pa – oh – about a girl I knew called, Oh, called – Hedda Meyer – oh, dear, dear! – Christy,' she said in a feeble voice, 'Help me up, darling!'

The children were laughing but Christy sympathetically helped her to sit up. 'Oh, Lord, Lord,' she kept saying, taking breaths, 'Oh, Lord, I nearly died laughing.'

The boys were very interested, 'What's the joke? Tell us! What's going on?'

'Oh, nothing, only about a girl I knew called – ho!'

'Emily!' said Stephen.

Suzanne looked at Emily.

'Suzanne!' cried Emily opening her arms. 'Come here. Oh, I have such a pain with laughing.'

304

'What is it?'

'I don't know,' said the boys.

'A girl at school called Ida Nass,' she said suddenly.

The boys giggled.

'Ida Nass!' said Suzanne.

'And Carlotta Katz.'

The boys shrieked with laughter. The teacher seemed surprised. Emily cooled off and said, 'I was telling Stephen about a side-splitting episode in my new book I've conceived and which is going to be terrific, my darlings. Oh, this will be the one. I never felt better. I believe I can get $8,000 out of them for it just on outline.'

She had recovered and seemed very much in form.

'What's the episode?' enquired Christy, fascinated by so much money for an outline.

Stephen said, 'That's enough. I don't know what it is. Go and wash your hands for lunch.'

Emily pressed her breast, 'Oh, what a pang! I suppose you really could die laughing, Suzanne? It's an awful rolling spasm, you're out of control, but madly happy, inhumanly happy, you feel as if you'll go over the edge of the precipice in another minute, and at the same time, delicious, strange, only you. You feel as if now you've escaped, it's you and you're dying because it's you. I suppose you could go into convulsions? Oh, I think it was because I was just talking about my physical sufferings as a fat girl and I was given over entirely to remembering my sufferings physical, so very physical. And the body gets up like an immense giant and grabs me and balances me over the cliff, threatening to toss me over. Oh, heigh-ho, nothing in my life compares with my physical feelings. How often are we physical in life, Suzanne? A hot bath? Pouah! A childbirth, well, yes, it is. Sex? I mean compared with what I felt just then? I wanted to love, Suzanne, I madly wanted to love but I wanted it to be like that. But it can't be. And that's an intellectual for you. I guess I know how coal-heavers feel on Saturday night.'

They were very merry at lunch. Christy declared he had a friend in the States called Nass T. Fall; and so forth. They exhausted themselves with laughter and after lunch Stephen turned gloomy, felt ill and retired to his study. He asked Christy to come to his study with him and, before this, said dismally to Emily, 'I'm afraid I'll have to revise my calculations.'

To Christy he said, when the door was closed, 'What's the idea of writing tales about us to your grandmother?'

17 TRIPS

After two hours' work, Emily felt the humour dying out of her. She turned and looked out the window. A fine Paris evening hung over the roofs. The streets were dark except for the lights at their corner. People went home early in those days. Emily thought about the households all over Paris beginning to pull themselves together from war privations; people were still coming back from the concentration camps, from abroad. The first foreigners like themselves were settling in. Real money was beginning to flow more freely, the cabaret and restaurant life was as high as ever and even more shameless. But you still saw queues, and every restaurant, classified by category, was obliged to put up and serve a minimum menu for the poorest clients. You could get cakes at most shops on certain days only. People would still say, 'Do you know there are spiced cakes at the little shop on the way to St-Lazarre?' And yet the terror, the frenzy, the heartache, misery and nervous tension, the dread of the future which they had felt at home in America was gone. They had come to a starved and beaten continent, bravely expecting the worst. They were living, except for the shortages of milk and coal, better than they had at home.

At that time they expected revolution in Paris. The spirit of the resistance was still strong, so, of course, was the spirit of collaboration, active or passive. It was still uncertain which would win. Vittorio, full of hope, had felt strongly, until April 18, that the people would win in his country. The Belgians were as ever, torn by their national conflicts, but England where the class feeling had taken a big blow, they said, from the years of suffering in common, might be headed for a new life; and France – she was almost certainly ready for the final struggle. In America they had simply given up the struggle. Emily muttered to herself, 'Not-in-our-time revolutionists, like us.'

She looked down at what she had been writing, took it out of the typewriter.

'Worthless.' Like the people she was writing about, 'Not-in-our-time revolutionists, on-and-off revolutionists, keep the deep-freeze safe revolutionists.'

'But we're still marred by the Civil War. We can't go through that

306

again. We must escape! We've had more than a colour photograph, a demonstration by others of what it's like.'

If only it were all done, gone by. But the Europeans who had been through it all were much more cheerful and hopeful. They were making plans again.

She muttered, 'Because it's over I suppose. Maybe we're like women before they have the baby. Perhaps in two or three years here, we too will achieve the calm, the long view, the tranquillity, even the culture. What's wrong with the American mind is a raging barbarous fear behind the super-finish. Here the middle class is ruined forever – and it's a question of let's face it.'

At these words, she felt very tired, afraid and helpless. But where else was there to go? Italy? Where the sanguinary class-battle, Vittorio thought, might come up again, even after the setback of April 18, bought, they said, by American money. But why go where Americans were hated? Switzerland? A sanitarium no living and healthy soul could endure. England – starving to death and no prospect of betterment; England going down, never again to appear as a great nation. Belgium? Belgium was a consideration. Everyone said the food there was much better and the black market was better than France. But who went to Belgium? Spain? No, no. They could have gone to the Côte d'Azure, some pleasant, wealthy or not so wealthy resort village on the sea; but Stephen, like all big-city men, was terrified that he'd lose his mental activity there, he'd be out of the mainstream. The mainstream carried him along like a chip of wood, but he loved the movement.

If it had been Vittorio? Why do I let myself be dominated by this clinging man? Fate of the big, tough woman? I'm just bashful. I'm still a little girl. I still think no other man would look at me. She sighed.

Downstairs, Stephen was fuming, fidgeting, waiting for her with his accounts and his plans for Anna's return. She got up and took one of her benzedrine pills. She took more and more of them; not to faint, weep, collapse from overwork and excitement. They did her no harm. She was strong enough to take anything. She went to the window, hearing footsteps and there she saw Madame Suzanne crossing the courtyard. She hailed her, 'I'll join you. Hang on!'

Putting on a thin jacket, she ran downstairs, all merriment, smiles. She sailed past Stephen, rushed out into the courtyard and took Suzanne's arm.

'I'm walking home with you. Let's go to a café for half an hour.'

'Emily!' Stephen called.

She said laughing, 'I'm taking a walk'; and to Suzanne, 'Like a rat in a trap, I am.'

307

'Emily!'

'He's scared! He thinks I got away from him. I never take a walk. I explain my every move. I'm a prisoner of sentiment.'

Suzanne took her arm, 'Come, walk a bit of the way. But you'll be tired.'

She laughed, 'I'll find a taxi somewhere. I don't care when I get home. Isn't there somewhere we can go?'

Suzanne had to visit her invalid sister, then get home to the apartment she was getting ready for Christy. Emily was irritated. Here was a woman she paid a big sum to monthly. Christy was going to pay her full board, lodging and part of her furniture. Christy alone was paying Suzanne more than the average worker's salary, in American money. She laughed lightly however, saying, 'There he sits, a man with light employment as a husband. Oh, well, I guess it's not so light being my husband. Like a querulous wife with his hand-out, and a poisonous tongue accusing me of waste, when who makes the money?'

'Let's talk of something else. Here you are taking a walk,' said Suzanne.

'Thank God. That stone pile weighs me down. How is it, every time I move I drag mountains with me to suffocate me? Stones, debts. Why can't we live simply? Oh, well – once a sucker always a sucker. I'll never get what I wanted. Do you know what I thought as a girl when I wanted to be a great writer? I thought, then, at long last, all the men would run after me, as a bonus you understand, crowd round my door, stand in the courtyard, all the morning with bouquets and in tophats. Of course, Stephen did. Poor lamb.'

'Let's talk of something else.'

'Yes, yes. Let's talk of Vittorio. I wrote him a letter. I don't know his address. I don't know his private life. I haven't heard from him. Where is he?'

'I think he's in Rome. I saw it in the paper.'

'He's in Rome. And I want him here!'

'Why?' asked Suzanne drily, looking at the bounding, rosy woman.

'Why did you bring such strange people round me? Aren't there others?'

'Why are they strange?'

'They never have time to see you. They're such bores. Philistines in a way. No one must laugh because they were in the Resistance. Too damn serious. Heroes. Faugh! But Vittorio's magnificent. He knows the world has two sides. Oh, I understand him and he understands me.'

'He's going to Switzerland. He'll be there for a week about the end of June. There's a cultural congress on. Only I don't know if he'll be allowed to stay the week. Petty little police everywhere. He gets in and out invisibly.'

'Oh, if I could go to Switzerland. But we have to wait on Anna.' After a moment she said, 'Is he married?'

'He was married; but his wife died in concentration camp. Just a bore.'

'Oh, lord, I'm sorry,' said Emily with tears in her eyes. Then she said, 'He showed me her photograph the first day he came but I didn't know enough French then. Poor Vittorio. So he's a widower.'

Suzanne did not answer at once. Then she began to talk about Vittorio's loyalty to his wife, his long passion for another woman, a lifelong connection with an infamous Roman society woman. And now a young girl –

Emily said nervously, 'Oh, heck? I suppose so. But he's so ugly.'

Suzanne laughed at this, 'I know a beautiful society woman who wanted to marry him ever since the liberation; and he wanted to marry her, but he gave her up.'

'Why?' asked Emily sullenly.

'She belongs to the most corrupt society of Rome and Paris. How could she reform? He had to give her up. He sacrificed his passion to his work.'

'But he's so gay, so exuberant!'

'Well, everyone weeps in private. Like you. And works hard to forget it. Like you.'

'Yes, like me. Oh, I'm glad to be here. To understand myself,' Emily thoughtfully said.

'They scratched and blew up and smashed his face. The charm they could not take away.'

'Oh, this is frightful,' said Emily.

Suzanne laughed, 'You know you wouldn't marry Vittorio. Leave your country, and Stephen, your husband's family, the children! Would you?' she enquired lightly.

'Suzanne, you despise me. You're right. I'm not good enough for Vittorio. But then he loved that degenerate woman. She was good-looking, I suppose?'

'Extraordinarily beautiful. She's a friend of mine. The strangest thing of all is, she's been married in the meantime; and she still wants to marry Vittorio as he is.'

Emily began to sob, 'Here I am out in the cold. No one loves me. Suppose I lose my grip, my market? Did this Devil Dame, who was so cold and bestial, have any money?'

'Her family was ruined. She lived off men.'

'Good God. How could he? He so pure!'

'Vittorio must have seen something else in her.'

'This love of Vittorio for this cold devil is terrible. It kills me.'

Suzanne sighed. Emily besieged her with a hundred more questions.

She wanted to walk and walk, to frighten Stephen. But when she left Suzanne, though she hesitated in her thoughts, her steps hastened homewards. She was soon as the gate. He was pale and serious.

'Did you have something to say to Suzanne?'

'I need more exercise! Look at my figure. I'm like a pig.'

'You ought to take up gymnastics.'

She burst out laughing, 'Think of me in a tunic! Tomorrow I start serious dieting. Dear Anna will be back in a few days and that means more stuffing. I shall be like a pig when we get to Switzerland and won't be able to puff up the mountainsides. A typical American Middle-Western Mamma, with a beer-barrel waist, overstuffed dewlaps, panting about looking for an ice-cream soda. I'm going to become sylphlike. Sylphlike and vicious, then men will run after me.'

'What have I been doing the last ten years?' enquired Stephen plaintively.

'Let's eat! This is my last meal before martyrdom.'

Stephen said he wouldn't bother her with the accounts. She had to get to bed. They had to get to work early tomorrow. They had to get the serial in, revised. Anna was coming within a few days, another set of ten lost days.' Not to mention the days you always waste beforehand getting ready; all quite unnecessary and lost on her. She doesn't know a house is even in disorder; so she doesn't know what it takes to get it ready.'

'Oh, well, everyone likes attention.'

'Mamma would like a bank balance better. She's a typical small-minded rich woman.'

'Well, let her help us out.'

'Why should she?'

They quarrelled bitterly. She asked why should she entertain a millionairess. She'd borrow or steal and go off to Italy or Switzerland by herself. 'Or if you want me, borrow from Anna. Don't sing me your sad, sweet song about pride. Tell her I'll pay her back. I'll give her an IOU and I'll honour it. When I can. Why not? When Anna or some Tanner or Fairfield or any other Jiminy Crickets come here I have to entertain them like princes. We have to go out with them to restaurants where you can't eat under four thousand francs a head, to put it at a small figure. Four or five of us, as much as a worker gets in a month.'

'What have workers to do with it? Anna is not trying to live like workers, neither are we. All right, hate Anna and hate me, but don't give me that about workers' salaries. Because we don't give a damn about them or we wouldn't be living like this.'

'No. I know. We're rotten to the core. We're not fit to mix with people like Suzanne and Vittorio.'

310

'Oh, my stars! Again!'

They had a cruel quarrel. While Stephen sat in an armchair draping his legs and arms in various ways, like a human spider, Emily walked about, went in and out, put a big platter of food in front of Stephen. He ignored it and she cleaned up the platter herself. After that, she drank several glasses of beer, ate half a box of the best French chocolates. She told him she was sick of him, his mother, his phony sister.

Emily said, 'She'd go to jail, face sentence of death just to get in the news as the red queen of the revolution. Don't I know? People risk death, climb to the top of the Empire State, just to annoy or get in the news. Well, I'll have a fine funeral, they say.'

Emily walking about, eating and drinking, laughed. Stephen said he wished he had the guts to do it. She said, 'Well, that's not such a bad idea. If you're such a pill. Well, OK, go ahead, take poison or the big jump, what do I care? I used to make my living out of types like that. There are all kinds of ways of committing suicide, did you know? I used to know them all, some are quite ingenious. I believe some of them think up ingenious ways, so they'll be sure to get in the papers. You can take it that all suiciders are neurotics with a publicity hunger. I know a man went to Spain to fight in the civil war and it was suicide.'

'Fred,' muttered Stephen. 'He ran right into the shooting.'

She burst out crying. 'I'm sorry,' said Stephen.

She wiped her tears aside with both hands, 'Oh, boloney. I'm a bunk artist. Putting on a scene. When they come back they're misfits; so it's suicide either way. Not for all. Look at Vittorio! He has everything against him but he's all over the lot fighting. He's lecturing in Rome, lecturing in Switzerland – '

Stephen said, 'Ah, that's why we're going to Switzerland.'

She turned on him a vapid smile which grew; she flushed and burst out laughing, 'After all, Stephen, if we were there, we could hear him, see what he's got. So far all we've seen is a salon monkey.'

'The simple fact is he's a man of tremendous ability and he fascinates women with his male energy and I have none of that. No woman ever went to Switzerland or anywhere else to hear me speak.'

She sat down complacently, 'Oh, I went to Philadelphia to hear you speak. And that girl who used to follow you around pawing you.'

He shrieked with a nervous shudder, 'No girl ever pawed me!'

'She did so! I used to wait and then sail down the aisle, or roll down the aisle, and she fell back palpitating. Obviously I could have laid her out with one blow of my ham fist!'

Stephen's mouth twitched.

'I used to sit in the back – I have long-sight anyway – and I could hear

311

you all right and I used to watch their backs, I'd look along the rows and see their open mouths drinking you in; and I'd wait for the ohs and ahs, swimming around the Party silk-stocking, oh-ah! And then Red Mike would appear. They couldn't get over it, such a nice man and Emmie with the fat red face. I heard it said that you had an Electra complex, not electric, Electra, not electoral.'

They both laughed. Stephen got up and kissed her, 'You're a wonderful girl, I'll kill any gut that takes you away from me. If the Germans didn't get Vittorio, I will.'

'You're crazy. I don't like Vittorio. He's plain, he's repulsive.'

'Yeah! I noticed.'

Five minutes later she was eagerly telling him about the corrupt society woman and Stephen deduced that this was the reason she wanted to slim 'to cut out that Roman candle'. He urged, 'Stay as you are. I like you that way; and if Vittorio doesn't, he's not your man. You couldn't marry Vittorio under false pretences; you know yourself that three weeks later you'd blow up into a captive balloon.'

But domestic winds blew harsh and cold during the next few days while Emily was dieting. The children, the servants, Suzanne and her friends reproached her with such excess. Stephen raved. She kept it up. She caught a cold, became very ill, with aches, swellings in her head, heart palpitations and she moaned, 'I can't go on like this. This life will finish me. I can't keep the whole world on my shoulders. My book may sell but it's you who'll enjoy the profits. I won't be here.'

They tore the serial to pieces paragraph by paragraph, word by word. She reproached him, cursed her choice of him, her own weak will. She wasn't making money and she was going down-hill.

'Talent is a thing that doesn't stand still. You've only just got it by the tail if you've got it. If you let go the slightest, it's away from you and off to the woods. You'll never catch it again. How many in Hollywood found that out? I've let go, Stephen. It's got away from me. It's off in the glens ferreting around having a wild time and I'm here without it, lost. It's your fault. And it's my fault.'

Anna's visit approached and Emily began to recover and made her usual preparation. The month of June passed by in this trouble. Paris was lovely. Emily dictated her revisions from her bed. A chapter sent off by airmail at the beginning of Emily's illness had been accepted by one of her magazines and though it was only for $500, the Howards cheered up. They needed $30,000, but it was a promise.

While getting ready for Anna they had a note from a friend, Henri Villeneuve, a French writer who had gone to Hollywood during the occupation and done well there. He had been laughed at a little, for

312

saving his money; but now, as soon as it was possible, he had returned to Paris and bought there a small apartment in the rue Bonaparte. Henri was about Stephen's age, forty. Immediately upon returning to France, Henri joined the Party. He lived with his new wife and their small child in these small quarters, wrote all day and night for the Party press and endeavoured also to write novels as well as making translations. Hong-ree, the Howards called him. Hongree had done very well in Hollywood, quickly adapting himself; and now, because he had gone back to his former life, he did very badly, in money. They asked him to the party for Anna. But first he insisted they must visit him at his apartment. They were to call before lunch. He was unable to invite them, as yet, to eat there, because of the shortage of goods; but they had with him, they told Suzanne, 'a sweet children's drink, a mixer they call San Rafael.' They then had him to dinner. They had known him in Hollywood, a well-paid successful writer. Hongree was to come to dinner with his pretty little dark-haired Viennese wife, who was twenty years younger than he. Though he was still a radical and working in the Party, they thought he had enough *savoir-faire*, knew enough about American ways, not to irritate Anna; and they invited him for the big afternoon party. Vittorio was invited to all their dinners, all their cocktail parties, all their evenings and to private dinners, too. But it happened that Vittorio had to turn down their afternoon party. He had to leave for Italy. Hongree had invited them to dinner by this; and to get ahead of him, they decided to fill in his vacant evening with the Villeneuves.

Stephen said, 'At least Hongree has a daily woman and a European wife and he's French, so he'll probably have something to eat. It's too much for me to face indigestion for the sake of comrades.'

They were disappointed however, and laughed lugubriously on the way home. Hongree had not had cocktails but had served two sweet drinks, the ladies' sweet drink called *porto* and a sweet mixer, Italian vermouth. They had to take their choice of these. Naturally he was saving money: but after all, for a company dinner!

Emily said to Stephen, 'And probably up since the crack of dawn with the entire family, the cleaning-woman and the concierge to make these titbits.'

They had vegetable soup, called saint-Vincent, lamb's brain fritters, roast pork, tomato salad and a home-made rice and cream cake covered with chocolate and whipped cream, but the whipped cream was confectioners' cream. They were offered, but did not take, the national bread, yellow; and the national coffee, bean. With this they were offered two bottles of poor, sour red wine. Emily was very angry. 'But if that's all they had, why did they ask us? If they want to even accounts with us, they

313

can't do it with vinegar.'

Emily found it hard to understand how a man who had succeeded in Hollywood and was a leading man in the Party in France, could behave in such an awkward uncivilized manner. 'He was in Hollywood for years – didn't he learn anything? But of course he always was niggardly: they never gave parties in Hollywood, they had a bad reputation for that; they were mean.'

However, when they got home and had something to eat and drink, Emily's natural good humour rose and she saw it was funny enough as a episode. Hongree returning from 'Hollywood luxe' to wear a frayed clerk's suit in Paris 'of all places'. His wife, apparently dressed in the remnants of an old rose brocade curtain, was sitting on a seat which was really a travelling trunk covered with a hand-made, stuffed cover and on this was the same brocade or something very alike. Perhaps both dress and cover had once been a bed cover? The kind of thing they had in old-time Vienna? And what was in the trunk? For they showed them: old family heirlooms in the shape of pounds and pounds of heavy curtain lace, miles of hand-worked embroidery, several pairs of hand-embroidered curtains and everything old, rich and out-of-date. 'Her hope-chest, you could see,' said Emily screaming with laughter: 'musty old Vienna saved from the barbarians.' Madame in rose brocade sewn together with trembling hands for the rich Howards, tossing together lamb's-brain fritters, things they could scarcely touch ('I'm glad Christy was not there, with his sensitive taste,' said Emily shuddering), and roasting pork. 'It was just like a fine old Harlem get-together, black and white unite and bite.' And then the hit of the evening, the rice-cake affair with melted chocolate on it, mushy and gluey. 'And we're in Paris and they're in Paris!' They compared it with the real French desserts they had had in Véfour and the Tour d'Argent; and even, after all, compared with the desserts Fernande made for them; even the ones Emily made.

Emily sighed, 'Heigh-ho. I suppose it is because she is Viennese, Germanic tastes after all. And always boasting they are small-town – well, they are!'

Stephen said his stomach was bad but serve him right for eating with the poor. The poor didn't know how to eat and hadn't the materials and if they did where would be revolution? Why improve them? If every ragged Frenchman knew how to cook like Véfour, why not leave them alone? Why a revolution? The French revolution produced good French cooking because the cooks of the nobility lost their jobs and had to go and cook in cheap wine-cellars. 'Come the revolution Fernande will have to cook not for us but for Hongree; then you'll see.'

Emily was still repelled and fractious. 'How can a man who has had

314

money, really been in the money, had a decent house and eaten properly, had a servant, how can he serve a dinner like that? Or how can she? After all, she ate darn well in America. After all, we were often at their house. They had servants, she did nothing but hand out the drinks; the drinks were all right, the hors-d'oeuvre were passable. We really enjoyed ourselves talking politics, revolution, Marxism, talking Europe, the Europe we were going to see after the war. And now – Hongree has forgotten all that. He's gone back to grubbing in a cold-water apartment eating food for the concierge's dog and letting his wife dress in old curtain lengths. He knows how to make money.'

Emily fretted. They talked in their immense kitchen downstairs. She was eating, he was drinking coffee and a little cognac which always made him feel easier. Emily ate and heaved sighs of relief.

'It's bad for their digestion. And if that's their company food think what they eat when alone! I don't wonder she's sad, looking at him. It's not only the food but the feeling of oppression, the feeling you get they've been up since dawn rubbing cabbage into bits and hunting round for the peas for the soup, running down the street for a bone to improve the stone-broth, tasting and smelling and calculating. will it be enough? And of course the whole musty, dirty old place, though it's cold as paupers, full of the smell of centuries of such cooking. Oh, my God, I see why you have to go to a decent restaurant to eat. No old boards with mice, lice and leaking toilets in the offing. And then the guests have to worry, but this is a feast for them, otherwise they wouldn't have invited us; and they'll probably have to live off the leavings for a week. Well, let me tell you, I didn't. I ate all I could, even if I didn't want it. And when I went into her room, I took half her bottle of perfume. I think it's so paltry, scrappy to make guests feel humble and try to choke them off. And then the wine – ugh! – why have wine? I'd have swopped the party drinks and the wine for a single spot of whisky. God, they could have asked us for it. "We're too poor to buy drinks, won't you send us some?" I'd have preferred that. I didn't feel myself till the thin brandy came and it was mixing brandy. My goodness, why make your guests miserable for the sake of a social ritual? It's vanity. I must repay. And I repaid with a full course meal and drinks. Good heavens, never again! And you were right about Vittorio. Imagine eating stewed fowl off a one-lung burner. How can they? I don't get it. I didn't enjoy it when I was a cub reporter and lived on franks and orangeade.'

She walked up and down worrying about Vittorio and Hongree. 'But I don't get it, Stephen, I don't get it. And they're men I like. If I didn't, I wouldn't waste my spit on them. But these ought to know better.'

Then she began to laugh, a full-throated laugh of enjoyment.

'What are you laughing at?' he said suspiciously.

'At the side-shows! It's like going to the local fair in some one-pig town. You think about it for weeks, you get dressed up, you fight with your parents: "I've got to go!" You're hot, sweaty, everyone runs, shouts himself hoarse, little sister's lost her ribbon off her pigtail before she's off the streetcar, the car wouldn't start that morning; but you've got to get to the fair. When you get past the wooden gates, you pay your money, you're in an enclosure where you're going to see the side-shows – hot-dogs, dry rolls, dirty lemonade with flies in it, steaming coffee with maybe coffee in it, at the beginning, and such sad eastern harem girls, with steamy bits of veiling on their fat, dirty haunches, looking hungry, as if they don't believe in it; hideous, revolting monsters which you can see are put together with cardboard and glue; but at the end of the day you've had a hell of a good time, you had fun. We ought to take Hongree and Vittorio in that spirit.'

Stephen growled, 'I never went to fairs. I hate them. I never ate hot-dogs even in Hollywood parties or Connecticut barbecues. What's funny? My belly aches.'

'You'll have to see the doctor.'

'I know. I'm putting off, hoping it will go away, but it won't. I know.'

Anna came with the news that Fairfield was very anxious to come and that, if they could make room for her, Fairfield could come over at once and stay with them till Christmas. Anna, it was clear, was anxious for the marriage between Christy and Fairfield to take place when they were both very young to avoid other attachments. They were to receive Fairfield in September. Anna also suggested that if Christy could not make his way at the Sorbonne he might go to his English relatives, the English Tanners, stay with them, or under their tutelage and make his way at Cambridge or Oxford. If he could not make the grade, she hinted, there were ways of getting him in; tutors, friends of the Tanners. Emily was very indignant.

Emily was sick and worked, and Stephen was sick and worked, but when Anna had gone at the end of July, Emily found she had sold her book for a good price and that they could have a holiday in August before Fairfield's arrival. The Trefougars had visited them several times during Anna's stay and neither had given any hint about their sad domestic secrets. In fact, Anna thought them very fine people; and she softened towards Emily and Stephen.

Before they decided where to go for their holiday, the Trefougars invited them to go along with them to Belgium for a short trip. Later they were going to Switzerland, then Italy. Perhaps they could travel together, expenses shared; Stephen by this had become friendly with Johnny

Trefougar and the Trefougars, like all their friends, knew all their troubles, political, domestic, literary and financial. Trefougar had introduced Stephen to an excellent broker and had first-rate financial connections in all the capital cities. He was a great speculator, said Johnny: he had tips and helped his friends too with currency troubles and restrictions. Stephen and Trefougar came from the same setting; Trefougar was a little poorer but with more manner. Trefougar's sister had gone to school in England, married a viscount before the family lost its money in the '29 stock-market crash.

Trefougar said, mincing, 'Since then I've been a worker.'

Stephen said quaintly, 'Since then I've been a red. Lord, it didn't look as if the States were coming back ever; it looked as if the reds were the straight ticket. It wasn't till 1940 that we raised our head again. With Roosevelt began and died the forgotten man.'

Stephen had not had a crony, even a friend, since college days. He drove out with Trefougar in his magnificent new car, they took tea at the Ritz, at the Scribe, met people. Trefougar found someone who introduced Stephen to a 'funny little man' who was something particular at the Louvre, another 'funny little man' who was something in economics at the Sorbonne, a 'funny little man' who was editor-in-chief of a serious literary paper, another 'funny little man', rather a big man physically, who had just been elected to one of the literary academies and was chief literary man in a famous publishing house in Paris. Stephen was joyful. At the same time, daily, hourly, he ran in and out of the house making contacts with people introduced by letter or telephone by Vittorio. He felt his life was full.

He looked forward to this drive with the Trefougars and to meeting more funny little men who would serve his purpose in one way or another in Belgium, Basle, Florence and Rome. Emily grubbed away at her typewriter until he said, 'I want a wife, not a typewriter'; she made the money but Stephen was weaving a necessary pattern in a new society. Their whole lives would be woven into that pattern. His long, thirsty dignity, his famished ambition, misunderstood by the backwater of New York radicals, was being satisfied in Europe. He liked Europe; and they understood him. Suppose Trefougar were strange, his wife enigmatic, their politics anti-Soviet, suppose it was strange indeed that an attaché should have that expensive car and live so well – his connections explained it. Did he do little commissions for friends? Who would not? Everyone in this world, left or right, made use of diplomatic protection if they could get it. Even the Resistants.

Emily thought otherwise. She was pleased about the funny little men. Stephen might get a job. Stephen was angered by this.

317

'Do you expect me to walk in, hat in hand and beg for a job from people in that position? These are contacts. What can they offer me? Clerical jobs? One of Vittorio's friends,' he continued, looking at her with spite, 'offered me a rewrite job in a telegraph agency. Where did I hear that before? Why should I do better than a bright lycée boy of sixteen? Look at my training, my education, my experience. I must get a job in which I wouldn't look ridiculous. People won't employ a man like me in subordinate positions. They feel uncomfortable. I feel uncomfortable. The other employees feel uncomfortable.'

Emily said, after a moment, 'Well, who's going to drive? Maybe they're both crazy. I'd feel funny getting into a car with those two and leaving the children behind. I'd think, Oh, hell, I'm crazier than they are. Supposing we get smashed up on the way?'

Stephen thought Emily simply wanted to stay in Paris to see Vittorio. He said, 'Do you want the children to get smashed up too? Well, we can go by train and meet the Trefougars in Brussels.'

No, the Trefougars were passionately interested in taking them along. Stephen thought they were afraid to be alone with each other. Emily said, 'I don't want to be a buffer state. I don't want to leave my children here and go motoring with two maniacs.'

Stephen was angry. If there was a maniac it was that idiot Violet and not his friend Johnny. Stephen said, 'You only want to stay behind to canoodle with Vittorio; you'll have him here every night for dinner.'

Emily brightened. She laughed, 'I never thought of it. Besides, he's fey. He's probably in Rome again. And what about Christy's Latin?'

In the end they agreed to go with the Trefougars and take Christy with them.

'Send Christy to Uncle Maurice; he knows Latin. If you don't want to leave him with Suzanne.'

Emily frowned. 'I don't want Maurice to regard Christy as his own. I'm bringing up Christy to be my boy. Giles and Olivia can stay here with the servants. Suzanne can come every day.'

'No, no, Christy must be along.'

When the big Alfa Romeo car started from the house, Emily sighed and said, 'Oh, I feel liberated, though. Leaving all that behind. It isn't my life really. I know something will happen, too; but I won't be there to see it.'

They thought Violet had a hangover. She was at first irritable, then rude; later she screamed. She shouted at her husband, at other drivers at every crossing: she wanted to take all kinds of short cuts. She wanted Johnny to pass every car. She took no notice of speed-limits.

'We're different. You damn well know it. You're only going slowly to irritate me. You know I'm not feeling well.'

318

The Howards, who often behaved quite like this themselves, sitting in the back seat with Christy between them, were ill at ease, frightened too. They had not been going long before, in trying to double round a big car, they almost ran into oncoming traffic; brakes shrieked, there were recriminations. They were not yet out of the Paris area. 'Damn French. Don't know how to drive,' said Violet.

Emily leaned across and breathed to Stephen.

'Let's change our minds. I'd rather lose them for life; and take a taxi back.'

Trefougar with his eyes on the road, began speaking to Stephen, 'I'd like to know what you think of Daniel Hoogstraet, you'll meet him. He's supposed to be the smartest change man in Brussels. He'll do anything for you if he likes you. I never heard a complaint. He's absolutely reliable, no signatures, no witnesses, but absolute reliability and anything goes. If he likes you, he's your man. He'll probably start talking books, he collects books, first editions. If you could let him have one of yours, he'd do a lot for you.'

'Oh, I have first editions, nothing but; what I want is a second edition,' said Stephen.

Violet complained of a jumpy tooth. Her husband must drive fast but not shake her.

'Can I drive both fast and slow?' said Trefougar patiently.

Violet said he was trying to humiliate her and screamed bloodthirstily at a truck which kept hovering in the rear.

Emily laughed feebly and asked her family if they were hungry. They had breakfasted early. It was now nine-thirty. She hinted, 'We won't eat till Brussels perhaps.'

She reached behind, and undid a packet of beautifully made chicken sandwiches with little pots of salad and a special dressing, mayonnaise with chopped chives and hard-boiled eggs. Stephen did not want to eat. The Trefougars were too nervous to eat. Emily and Christy ate several sandwiches and drank coffee from the thermos; and then all was put away.

Emily said to Christy, 'Now darling, tell us what you know about Cicero.'

'Why Cicero?' said Violet acidly.

'Go on, go on, Christy. Cicero was – Now, who was he?'

'Cicero was, ah, was a Roman orator.'

She said energetically, 'And writer; and not a, but the greatest orator and best stylist of all time. What did he write?'

'He, eh, he wrote orations – '

'Delivered orations!'

'Eh, spoke orations and wrote letters; he wrote his orations down afterwards.'

'When did he live?'

'He lived, eh, in the same time as Julius Caesar, Brutus – '

'Ah, Brutus was a traitor against Caesar. But Cicero – ?'

Stephen said, 'He hedged!'

'Stephen!'

Stephen laughed.

They stopped by the roadside, near a café, Violet saying now that she was hungry. The Howards got out their little lunch again, and the Trefougars got out the lunch Violet had prepared. It consisted of small square-cut sandwiches with rough edges, made of ham and corned beef, with butter, no pickles, no mayonnaise, no parsley, no red peppers, no silver wrapping and no little silver forks, nothing that Fernande had prepared for the Howards. Emily, with proud, laughing face, surveyed all that they put on the tablecloth brought for the purpose (a plain white-and-red check tablecloth such as you see in Swiss restaurants). Then she put out her own delicate, elegant sandwiches prepared by Fernande and ate them, passed them to her own family, laughing every time the Trefougars took one of their sandwiches, following it with her eyes to their mouths. They ate little, being anxious to get on; and she laughed as they put up their sandwiches again in greaseproof paper, not as her own, in silver foil. Her own small tablecloth was a fine, thin, white damask.

As soon as they were back in the car, Emily once more interrogated Christy.

'Now, Christy, you know your Grandma is thinking of sending you to Cambridge or Oxford. Now, tell me what you know about the ancient Britons. That's something you'll have to know. Come on, the ancient Britons – '

'The ancient Britons, ah, were Celts – '

'And they had no culture.'

'They had no culture, they, ah.'

'Did they have any agriculture?'

'Yes, they dug the soil with antlers and they mined with antlers – '

'And what did they wear?'

'They wore – ah – funny clothes – '

'They painted themselves with woad and danced before Caesar. They ate hips and haws. Christy, now learn something. The ancient Britons were a stupid, dumb, primitive, barbarous people. They didn't know how to cook or to make clothes. They didn't know anything. They made woad, that's blue mud and they put blue mud on themselves for clothes and to keep off the lice. They didn't know how to fight, they folded

320

before everyone, the Romans, the Saxons, the Normans, they ran away to the hills and those who remained became slaves and serfs, they washed the togas and cleaned the sandals of the Romans. They were cowards. Now what was their religion?'

'Their religion? They had the Druids,' Christy said.

'Yes, the Druids! They were a sort of medicine men. They had human sacrifices. They burned sheep and goats and men for their gods. They crushed men to death between paving stones. You can see those stones on end at Stonehenge. When you go to England, Christy, you'll see that. And they made cages of willow-twigs and put men in them and burned them to death. They didn't have any navigation, they learned it from the Romans. They had little baskets they went to sea in. Of course, the Vikings took them over. Now can you remember all that, Christy?'

'I don't know,' he said simply.

'Well, now, start from the beginning and say it all just as I told you.'

'Oh, shit, it's shit, don't let me catch you saying a word of it,' said Stephen.

Stephen and Emily had a hot argument about the historical facts contained in her history of the British. The Trefougars said nothing. They quarrelled so much that Emily said she wanted Violet to sit with her because she was British and she knew Emily's story was true. Violet made no objection and Stephen sat in front with Johnny Trefougar.

Johnny suggested that they should leave the women and Christy in Brussels to go shopping or to the art museums, while he and Stephen went on to Antwerp for Trefougar's business. About this Stephen had guessed more than he said. He waited discreetly for Trefougar to make it plainer. Trefougar was quite plain. For the moment he was smuggling gold. Violet knew something about this and that partly accounted for her hysteria, Johnny said. At the frontier Violet behaved very wildly, demanding to be let through without examination because of their diplomatic status. Emily was quite calm and even laughed, while Johnny and Stephen behaved with natural dignity.

Stephen had told nothing of the true purpose of the trip to Emily. He had invested about $3,500 in a partnership with Trefougar to bring in, illegally, gold ingots of one kilogram each. They were protected by Johnny's status.

All went well. They drove to Antwerp, leaving the woman and the boy behind. They ate well, went to the theatre, had a splended time in Brussels and so back again after the weekend. Stephen came to admire Trefougar's self-control, nonchalant ambition, calm daredevilry. His control did not break down till they were nearly 200 kilometres from the frontier, when Johnny kept stopping and began drinking heavily. Stephen took no notice of this, for so far Johnny had driven like an ace, without a fault, swift and mild. But just outside Compiègne, Johnny began to behave wildly, shouted and, unexpectedly, he smashed them against a tree. He was himself in shock, but the only aid he asked of passing motorists was for them to send someone at once to pull them into Compiègne. Emily had a chipped wristbone, Christy a broken ankle, Violet had been thrown backwards and seemed to have hurt her neck but was otherwise well. They sat there, with Stephen gathering in the valises which had been thrown out and about, when suddenly, out of the back, shot some of the small ingots of gold.

Emily looked, understood partly, but she was upset with her own pain, and even more upset about Christy's injury. Stephen insisted upon the boy's being taken to Chantilly for treatment, along with Emily; but at this moment there arrived an exchange car. The ingots by this time having been safely stored in the valises, they changed to another car in which Stephen drove them to Paris, where he took them to a 'safe' doctor, designated by Trefougar.

'Why all this?' stormed Emily, who had only partly understood.

But Stephen said, 'Supposing Anna hears about this? Christy is too dumb to understand but supposing you, for instance, with your longing for full confession, say something indiscreet, that we've been taking gold around the country, crossing frontiers with contraband, with half-mad smugglers, smashing up Christy. Where will it end? You just shut up about the whole thing.'

Emily was shocked and became thoughtful. What had Stephen been doing all this time while she had been haranguing him about getting work? She now began to see the purpose of his friendship with the Trefougars.

She soon recovered from her injury, but Christy, owing to delayed treatment, was some time in bed. Emily insisted on his spending his time in their house instead of going to Suzanne and so she was able to spend her time with him, doing lessons with him and talking to him about his future, their troubles; and about Fairfield, who was soon to come.

She telephoned Vittorio, too, and he came to see her. Emily, in her anxiety, told him the whole story. Vittorio seemed in no way shocked and talked for a long time with her, when she said she could no longer trust Stephen. Imagine Stephen, the innocent and unwary doing this, getting into the toils of a British agent. For what else could Trefougar be? Now she understood his expensive car, his way of living. Poor Violet. This was the dreadful secret, secret beyond secret, which she had been unable to tell. No wonder she drank too much.

How sympathetic Vittorio was! Not like the prudes and Grundies she would have met in America. Meantime, when not working, she spent long hours with Christy; and how they laughed! She set herself to ridicule, deride, mock the silly little schoolgirl who was being sent over to be his fiancée and then his bride.

'You, Christy, think of it, a young European, with your culture and your fine instincts, you going to the Sorbonne perhaps, to the Beaux-Arts at any rate, and perhaps to Cambridge ot Oxford, they are going to tie you up even before you get to college to a dirty-minded little wax doll, for believe me, Christy, you with your sure, pure, earnest innocence, your cleanness, will never understand the mental slovenliness, the verminious' (she said) 'soul, the dunghill mind, the grasping and grabbing little smirched toilet-paper ideas of a contaminated little dunghill flower like Fairfield, brought up in corruption and moral squalor to live off others and unite her ill-gotten gains with other money, in a world of abomination. That is not for you, Christy. Your grandmother is a grandmother. A grandmother is like an old man who loves little girls and thinks them so sweet and pure and hopes he can fool them. An old woman is the same as an old man. Disgusting, revolting people. Old age is horrible. And so, Christy, she means to tie you up to this purulent little worm, this maggot of greed, so that you can both be tied to her apron-strings. Do you see, Christy love? Oh, how dreadful if you ever fell in with her schemes! But you are too good and clean, too nice a boy to like her and certainly you are far from marrying a miserable little lousy flyblown heiress like Fairfield, who has never had an honest thought in her head. And she knows nothing. I have seen her. She is not like you, honouring learning and wanting to do something for mankind. She is thinking only of herself, getting married to a rich boy, buying clothes, getting another automobile. In all, Christy, she is one of the most despicable products of our flyblown excrementitious civilization. What would your poor mother Emily feel, after all our love for you and our agony for you, if you had no more character than to fall in with your grandmother's plans like a child, like a helpless babe, like a basket-case? No, Christy, you won't do that. You won't let us down. Think of our love for you, Christy. It is rare to be loved and admired and understood as you are by us. No silly little ignorant miss, with a crippled moronic mind could understand you or love you. We do, Christy. I love you, Christy, God, Christy how I love you. Remember that. Think of me. Think of my love, my yearning, my great, great, deep love for you.'

She would go away, leaving him astounded, bewildered, sensing an enigma he had not the means to solve.

Stephen stayed alone in his room; he seemed angry and upset. He was anxious about the police and the unpredictable behaviour of his friend

Johnny. He even spoke of returning to the USA – 'nothing but hard luck has struck us here.' He thought he would go the United States to have an operation on his colon. He did not trust European medicine. But Emily would not let him go alone.

Pretty soon Emily had guessed that he still had dealings with Johnny and she was terrified when, just before Fairfield arrived, Stephen agreed to go to Switzerland with Trefougar alone.

She spent much time with him begging him to give up the trip. What was it for? Why was Trefougar constantly crossing frontiers? 'I know, he's bootlegging, black-marketing. But what? I don't want you in it, it's dangerous. These people are not our sort. We don't understand them. Stay away, I implore you, Stephen.'

He laughed at her. 'You believed in Violet and thought Johnny was a maniac, God knows what sort of a degenerate. When it turns out simply that Violet is a drug-fiend. Ask Suzanne. She knows, even if she doesn't tell you.'

'Oh, I don't believe it. Her sorrows were real. Her tears were real. I was scared myself. You can't believe she made all that up.'

'I don't know if she made it up. I know she should never have said it, and if she said it and is like that, she is a drug-taker.'

'You can't know. You know nothing about such people. Oh, you are so transported, fascinated, overpowered by this miserable Johnny. He's exactly like the people in the Resistance we met, except on the other side. They're all corrupt. There isn't anyone here that you can trust. You can't put your hand on your heart and say, Here is an honest man, or woman. Perhaps you're right. We ought to go back. What's air and life to them, is poison to us. I don't know.'

But very soon, he was packing his bag. Theirs was a short trip, just over the weekend, like the Brussels trip. 'And why not? I am doing something at last, I am making a little money, no matter how. You yourself always said not to respect money, that money was money, no matter where its roots were.'

She said, 'But you aren't the man. It's you I'm worried about. What ever would I do, or Anna or any of us, if something dreadful happened? If you went to jail? How do you know you aren't the fall-guy? Johnny won't go to jail and you, the dirty American taking over Europe dishonestly, you will go. Why this infinite trust reposed in a crafty, unreliable Briton?'

The evening before he left, she was sitting at table with Stephen and Christy who could now get about a little; and after Stephen said that he was leaving at eight-thirty in the morning, Emily said, 'Christy, my son, I have now only you to rely upon. You're my knight errant, my gallant *cavaliere servente*.'

324

'Of course, as usual, you don't know what you're saying,' said Stephen, aloof.

'I am appealing to Christy's sense of chivalry, which I know is very strong, to be my support, the oak I must cling to, when you, Stephen, go rushing about Europe on business you can't tell us about. And I am sure you wouldn't tell Anna either. Oh, Christy, Christy. To think I have you only; only you to protect me.'

Stephen said coldly, 'And I too am relying on Christy. Christy you are my son, the eldest in the house, I am placing the responsibility on you. A boy of your age and of your class is adult.'

Christy looked at them both seriously. Then he said, 'What am I to do? I will do whatever I can.'

Stephen said humorously, 'I'm putting Emily, your mother, in your charge, Christy. And don't let that fellow Vittorio come too often, nor stay too late.'

'No, Father,' said Christy.

Emily smiled coquettishly and grimaced. She had begun to have a quantity of winks, smiles, leers, cunning looks, and would ferociously flash her eyes; light and shadow of menace and grin would pass through her wild, bright, light eyes. She sat at the head of the table now, flushed, with damp eyes, hair and lips. She put out her dimpled, pudgy hand and stroked Christy. 'My darling will look after me, I won't need anyone else,' she said.

Christy was getting about but he still remained in the house. Suzanne came every day. He was getting on well in his studies now; and was preparing for an end-of-term examination for the bachot, the bacca-laureate. This examination was important to Emily for she had to show that Christy was making great progress under her care. She herself, instead of writing, spent her whole day at his studies. She made complete preparation herself for every lesson, read ten times the material, wrote ten times the essays, and forced Christy to learn everything by heart.

She had heard that Christy was going to be questioned on the French Revolution for the bachot; she had paid money to someone who was supposed to know, an old tutor.

Day and night now they studied the subject. 'By heart, every word by heart, Christy,' she insisted; and hour after hour, till the boy was exhausted, those in the house could hear, 'Danton, Georges-Jacques, member of the convention, born at Arcis-sur-Aube, 1759–1794. Attorney in the king's council until 1791, founder of the Club des Ordeliers, Minister of Justice after the 10th August, one of the greatest statesmen of the revolution. Powerful and impetuous orator. He was accused of moderation by Robespierre, jealous of his popularity. He was beheaded in

325

1794. His motto was "Audacity, more audacity and still audacity!"'

Emily became enraged on the subject of Danton, whom she soon came to think of as a martyr, destroyed by the hypocritically 'just and pure', a man of great talent, of genius, brought low by political rivals. A lion of courage, attacked because he loved luxury.

At night, at dinner, after Suzanne had gone, Emily would say,

'Now, Christy, Danton – '

'Danton, Georges-Jacques, 1759–1794 – '

He had to have it pat. She pounced on every lapse. And afterwards, until late at night, phrase by phrase, learned by heart.

'Danton said, "I don't like this fantastic St Just. He wants to make France a nation of Spartans; whereas I want to make it a land of Cockaigne." This was in the great debate where the fanatic St Just accused him of luxury and treason.'

Long, long into the night, till the boy's eyelids closed.

Stephen's absence lasted not one weekend but six weeks. Emily, to blind and deafen herself to the misery, loneliness and fear, worked all day long and did not sleep, except with pills. She took pills to work, pills to sleep, pills not to cry bitterly at her weary, empty life.

During Stephen's absence she had to entertain visitors from the USA, most of them now on their way home after their European summer. They called on her without warning, sometimes announcing themselves by a telephone call and often expected her to find room for them in her house. If she had not room, they invited themselves to the next meal, came early for drinks and stayed until all hours. Her American visitors this summer were strangely impudent, hurtful, intrusive. Was it because Stephen was absent? There were the Shokays. Shokay had been an actor, was now a successful screen writer. He had been a witness before the Committee, stood his ground, received a handsome, if silent applause from people on the left. He had been in jail for a few months but was once more in work at the studios. He had with him his third wife, a thin schoolmarmish fair girl, who said little and allowed herself to be waited on. Meanwhile, Shokay followed Emily about the house, posed in a loose, engaging manner in corners and on couches, followed her with eyes, large, moist eyes, smiled as if at a secret understanding. So insinuating was his manner that she almost confided in him her most secret fears, the first time they met. But she did not. Her fears were real; they smelled of danger and disgrace. Then she thought, 'Could I fall in love with him, have an affair with him?' She felt very lonely. 'My heart is abandoned, I am lonely.'

Shokay said he was broke, he had come over to preserve his fortune, live cheaply in Europe. He took several trips back to Hollywood leaving his wife, who was pregnant, with Emily. He came back before she had her

326

baby and, to mark that occasion, went to Switzerland to buy for himself and her two expensive gold watches. He then rented a luxurious apartment in a quiet street near the Champs-Elysées, where he lived with his wife, his child and two servants, while he worked on a script with Henri Villeneuve. He told Hongree of his poverty and Hongree worked with him for nothing. Shortly after that, he lost his own gold watch and sent the police a case of Scotch whisky to encourage them to find it. Emily was at first soft and tender towards this engaging forty-year-old. But a time came when she was without money; and she noticed that he was spending freely. He came often to her house, with his family, dined and drank well, and never brought her a gift. At the same time, people came called the Sturts, Fred and Freda. Freda, a nervous woman of forty-five, short, plump, with loose dark hair, was his second wife and they were divorced. Fred was tall, fair, smooth-fleshed, with a nice rich-boy's manner; long ago he had been fond of Emily; but now he was full of himself, his new academic dignities (he had gone back to college late), and his success with his psychoanalyst. The husband and wife, divorced, were travelling together for convenience. They made a round trip of Hollywood recounting the disasters or successes of old friends; and they drank deeply. Emily, who was out of funds, was frightened at the amount of whisky that was drunk during Stephen's absence. They sensed her helplessness; they drank more. They sneered at her, flouted her, ridiculed her in her loneliness. And Fred Sturt, who had once been so fond of Emily, before his second marriage, that he had wanted to come and live in the same house with her, now said sententiously, 'You don't know, Emily, what Stephen is writing about you, to everyone, to all your friends, all over the States. I think it fair you should know. I heard from a few of your friends that he thinks you're going to pieces, losing your grip. He says worse things than that about you. He says you have boyfriends. He says the woman you are is not the wife he wants.'

Fred Sturt talked on solemnly and piously, doing it all for the best. Then he once more discussed the decay of their friends. Alan was drinking himself to death. You couldn't leave half a bottle of whisky in the house, he would find it. He would crawl around at ten in the morning looking anxiously for whisky. If he stayed with you, you might get up at seven to find him already half-way through a bottle.

Emily looked at Sturt with horror. He himself had drunk half a bottle of whisky while talking to her. She too often drank half a bottle. Stephen objected. Did he write that about her, too?

She was so dejected by this gossip that when the Sturts asked her out to dinner, she refused, though she knew they had money and dined well. Stephen would soon return and go over the accounts with her. If only

Christy could help her out! He was a kind boy, who understood money matters well and spent very little. A little to help her out would mean nothing to him. Christy would not go back with Grandma, at all costs. She would push him in his studies here. When the Sturts had left for dinner, she ate something and then got out the lesson books, studied them and then went upstairs to bed. She could not sleep and began prowling round the house. She saw that the light was on in Christy's room and gently pushed the door. Christy, who knew he was dull and was conscience-stricken about the money spent on his board, lodging and tutors, tried to study through the night. There he was at nearly three in the morning with his head on the table. She felt remorse. She knew his feelings. To make an impression on Grandma, she was driving him too hard. She went in and woke him. She had on a charming nightgown which Stephen liked. It had a low bodice for her splendid bosom and over this she wore a rosy chiffon dressing-gown. She took the boy to the kitchen to give him coffee and sandwiches and there they sat talking over their family troubles, both weeping together. If only he was able to help her, she said, she knew her darling boy would; and she kissed him many times. Of course he understood the trouble: they had to live beyond their means to show Grandma and others that they were good parents; and nothing, nothing they could do was too much to do for such wonderful precious children as he and Olivia and Giles were; but of all the blessings she had ever had, he, Christy was the greatest, so good, loving, clever a boy.

'I know I am not clever, but you say that to cheer me up and it does help,' said Christy.

He was now a well-grown stripling, pliant, somewhat secretive, with fine, dark eyes. He was wearing Thai-silk pyjamas, a blue flannel dressing-gown and blue leather slippers.

He said to her, 'Perhaps it would help if I went back to America? Then you would have only Olivia to bother about?'

She flew to him, embraced him, tears still in her eyes from her compliments,

'My darling boy, my son, my dear one. What would life be without you? You don't know what you mean to me. Life would be empty without you. There would be a pain here always.'

She pointed to her heart, under her rosy breast. The nipple stood up at him through the thin, silky material. She looked at it and smiled at him with capricious coquetry.

'I am a woman, Christy, my precious, you know; and this is what makes a woman, this heart, this breast, this skin, this mouth, this loving mouth that I am pressing to your dear cheek; to your dear – '

328

She kissed him eagerly on cheek and mouth, holding her mouth to his and pressing his lips, drinking thirstily. He let her manage him and drew back when she released him, with moist, large eyes. He seized her hand and kissed it.

'I love you, mother, I do really love you,' said he.

She jubilated.

'And now, my darling, I am going to take you up to bed and tuck you up. Your eyes are tired, you're thinner. You are too young to be wakeful all night. Come, I won't give you an aspirin, I'll sit by you, my darling son, until you go to sleep. Tomorrow is another day. We'll study then. Do you feel you study better with me? Or with Suzanne?'

'I study better with Suzanne; she doesn't distract me. You do,' he said smiling. She hugged him and pulled him away, towards the staircase.

They came out to find Giles on the stairs. He looked at them sleepily and said, 'I'm afraid. I'm alone up there, Mamma!'

'Oh, remorse, remorse! Naughty Mamma! Run to bed Giles darling. and Mamma will be in in a moment, but she must see that poor Christy gets to sleep first. Christy does not sleep at all any more, because of thoughts and dreams and – yearnings; Christy is a man and is disturbed and upset as a man is.'

She got Giles to his bedroom, keeping Christy by her and then, herself, she saw Christy to his bedroom, took his dressing-gown from him and his slippers, held the covers for him and settled them round him. Then she bent over him, kissed him a while, with her round perfumed bosom hanging over his face and neck. Christy for one moment embraced her, holding her shoulders and hiding his face in her neck, and then blushed. She pulled her clothes round her and said, 'Oh, Christy! Not too close. Remember, darling, you are my guardian while your father is away. But, oh Christy, there is no real harm. Nothing to lose sleep over. You love me and I love you and we are a sweet united family, and all love one another. There is no harm in love. Go to sleep my darling, and think no more of it. I know you won't leave me when I need you. I know my darling boy. Remember always that Mamma loves you and most dearly, needs you more than anyone. So sleep now, my Christy, sleep as if Mother were here beside you all night.'

She left him with his eyes wide open, following her to the door. At the door she blew a kiss. She went away smiling – as if Christy would leave her now! – and went to her own room. She sat down smiling. Of course he was thinking of her, intoxicated with her, a likely adolescent with no girls. The millions were safe. Not only that, she was really lonely. There was something hideous in her mind; Stephen's betrayal. Writing all over America, writing to all their friends! It was the boy she loved truly, for this truth and innocence, his loyal heart.

'It is Christy I love, my real son!'

She heard a sound. She went inside. Giles was awake and crying, 'Where is Daddy? Why doesn't he come home?'

She calmed him, but formally, and went to bed without giving him a thought. But still she could not sleep. She rolled and tossed.

'Oh, Christy, oh, me, oh, my! This difference of the generations is cruel. And you are so young, so young as to be useless. Never mind! I won't let you go. You must stay by me, Christy, stay, stay and be mine. You must help out. I can manage you. You must help. Oh, Christy,' and she smothered the pillow with kisses.

She was putting on weight and very often wore dressing-gowns all day long. Stephen would not have cared for that; but at present she did as she pleased and so she lived with and near Christy, in exquisite house-gowns and boudoir wraps, of silk, chiffon and lace, bathed, powdered and perfumed, doing his studies with him, eating with him, sitting by his bed at night, and kissing him, kissing him, till the air of the house was to him the odours of her flesh, cosmetics, delicate underclothes and perfumes; till she would see him almost fainting from the odour, worn with sleep, desire, study, all the needs of his cloistered years.

She waited for him, dressed in a close-folding house-gown, on a short seat with a brocaded satin cover, in the hall outside his room when he came up from his work. He walked quite well now and it was time for him to go to Suzanne's. Suzanne had a three-room apartment, with corridor, kitchen and bath, the small bedroom near the kitchen for herself, then a large sittimg room for Christy's lessons and visitors and a large sunny bedroom with plateglass windows looking over a public square, and with tables, chairs and shelves, for Christy himself and his young friends. In this room was a single iron bedstead, and room for Christy's records, record-player and other possessions. At present Suzanne lived there alone waiting for him; but she had taken on one or two day-pupils.

After his work in the evening after dinner with Monsieur Jean-Claude Christy would go upstairs with his books to continue his studies in this room. At that moment, at Emily's insistence, they were working very hard on Cicero. Emily wanted Uncle Maurice and his friend William to be taken with Christy's Latinism, when they came to visit at Christmas; and she herself, caught up with her own enthusiasm, had become a frantic student of Cicero. William, Uncle Maurice's close friend, had published a defence of Cicero. This was the first intimation Emily had that Cicero had attackers, had defenders. Wishing to defend him, she began avidly to read his writings in translations; and she attempted to follow Christy in his Latin, too. Gay and eager, bursting with opinion,

330

she waited for Christy when he trudged upstairs, about ten o'clock in the evening. He knew she was waiting. With her large, brilliant eyes she saw him as he came up the stairs, her long lips smiled, her teeth shone; she laughed quietly. He glanced at the Medusa, though he expected her, as if with stupefaction, baffled and giddy, like a half-innocent college boy stealing along under the high walls of the frowning college alleys, he came along the hall, holding to the wall, his eyes fixed on her. She could see what she was to him. She smiled, 'Christy, oh my Christy, Mother's Christy.' He stared at her, standing at the door of his room. She smiled, 'Oh, Christy, don't you know Mamma? You tease, you flirt. Flirtatious lad! I'm only your Mamma, your friend. Are you creeping in there, you little toad, you little frog, – ugh! And not even blowing me a kiss?'

He smiled a little and blew her a kiss. He went in and started to close his door. She got up and went to the door.

'Don't shut the door, Christy. I'm coming to work with you. You know you do much more work with me. Let in Mamma.'

He let her in and she bent down, folding him in her arms, kissed him eagerly, wrapped her arms round his waist, kissed the top of his head, said, 'Ah, Christy! Mother adores you. Mother wants everything good for you. I dream about you, Christy.'

She took his books from him, went to the desk and put on the lamp, opening the books at once.

'Now, tell me about Cicero!'

He stood at the partly closed door looking at her. Then he closed the door, came and stood by her,

'Emily!'

'Mother,' she said, looking up at him with a fetching, bright, sarcastic smile.

'You are not my mother. You are my father's wife. But not my mother.'

She continued to glance up at him, smiling with a curled lip.

'All right, I am Emily. Sit down and work with Emily, who is crazy about you darling and wants everything good for you. Emily who adores you.'

'Emily, let me kiss you.'

She laughed, put her arms round him and kissed him, on the cheek, jawbone, ear, neck, the roots of the hair. His hair turned to fire. He drew back, quickly, put her at arms' length, and stared at her with the selfsame stare as in the corridor. Then he quickly sat down at the side of the desk, away from her.

'Let's work; I have so much to get through I ought to work.'

She smiled, but went on at once, 'What was his name? Where was he born? In what year? When did he die? Go on.'

331

He recited his lesson.

'How did he get the name Father of his Country?'

The youth answered.

'Why is he considered best of all Latin prose-writers? What are his best political speeches?'

She continued, pressed him, forced him, told him what he forgot; and continued, 'And Cicero was against tyranny. Tell me how you know that. He had a high moral standard, the highest; tell me how you know that.'

The young man, knowing her demands, blundered on.

'He fought for truth and liberty, he opposed the dictatorship of Sulla and Caesar. Tell me the dates and tell me how you know this.'

It was a week later than Monsieur Jean-Claude, for the sake of scholarship, brought Christy a book which described Marcus Tullius as a greedy depraved man, who never paid his debts, stole where he could, lived in inordinate luxury, was faithful to no one, was a frantic spendthrift, and whose letters to his family, wife and daughter, covered with fine writing a total lack of concern.

Going one evening into his room when he had gone to the movies, she began with an inquisitve sparkle looking through the drawers of his desk and found in the middle drawer a note from Frances Wilson, the American seventeen-year-old girl he had met on the boat and who like him, had been a young communist. Frances Wilson was on the way back home to college and promised to see him as she went through Paris with her brother Mike.

Rue Chomel, Paris. VIIe

'Christy darling,
Well, I made it out of bed and took a bath. Brother Mike
finally got up about nine and then we had a cup of coffee for
breakfast. After breakfast we went out for a walk and feeling
rather sleepy sat down in a café and had a small shot of
crème de menthe. My darling Christy, we did not get drunk,
you need not worry, I am not a complete alcoholic. I am OK
though not five-star favourite for the swimming finals, as you
think. I showed Mike the card you sent me and he laughed
his head off. Well, back to school soon and I haven't done a
thing. I guess there are going to be a lot of little remarks
handed out in school when I get there, the great travelled
woman who cannot get fifty per cent in French, etc., and
such things. I don't mind it. Some of them are funny as hell.
Mother started off yesterday asking how you were and how
your tutor was coming along, so I guess you're all right with

332

them. I was out only with Mike (my only boyfriend, my darling, nothing to worry about, you see). Well, see you soon; as soon as you get ensconced in Madame Suzanne's when you will have some time to think of your own life, as you say. Life hasn't been bad here. Thank God for Mike. He is one hell of a guy. Will pass by your *château* before I leave to say hell-o to your parents. But first of all to see you and have a laugh and take a walk, go to some café *terrasse*, have a cigarette (which we are not allowed) I expect I will have the energy for that. Have not had it since I saw you. Mike is now pouring a drink. Don't worry, my love: we are not getting potted. How is Madame Suzanne? Is she strict or a good friend to poor 'monstery boys' as you say? (Do you mean with monks or with monsters?) I still did not find my little red bear. Are you sure you didn't take it? If you do find him in your luggage bring him to me when you see me this week. I need that little guy, he is pretty damn lucky. So am I. So are you. Or not? Love, Frankie,'

And to this was a reply, half-written:

'My darling Frankie,
First of all, my love, I want to tell you how sorry I am about the letter I wrote you the other day. I was in one hell of a morbid mood. All I remember about it was that I was very worried about something personal and I missed you more than I ever have; and that doesn't mean I don't miss you as much now, for I sure as hell do. We said that the person who left didn't get affected as much as the other one; well, I think that I have proved to myself to my satisfaction that law to be false. I sure hope you didn't feel as bad as I did, because if you did then all I can say is God help us, because we sure have it bad.
Father has been away for a few weeks and Mother is all right, but nothing to brag about. I am afraid I am not very interesting in the house, because I am wishing you were here, but that is just tough for them, I mean Mother, Madame Suzanne and Monsieur Jean-Claude. Giles has turned into a little monster; his voice, with trying to|speak French, is changing, and what surprises me is he now sounds sometimes like a sixty-year-old man. He several times said something to me in a foreign language, he means it to be

333

French and I haven't even answered because I have been thinking subconsciously, 'Who is that? I don't know who it is.' I hope you're not getting confused because I am trying to get this finished – but I don't think I'll make it into the mail tonight. But you'll get it in time and telephone me at Madame Suzanne's. I'll make her let me see you and I can arrange everything for I have a certain influence – if you know what that means? If you don't, think it over. . .'

Emily put the papers back and went downstairs to think this over. Where had Christy received his letters from this girl? She questioned the servants. At last the porter said that the young man had given him money to receive letters for him. 'I saw no harm. He is a young man of eighteen.'

When Emily went back upstairs, the dressmaker had come to make her a new dressing-gown; Emily had become so portly that she felt uncomfortable in anything but loose gowns. 'I'm always at home; I'm a housebound wife, why should I have town suits and evening-gowns made? When I've finished my present book and can reduce I'll get out and buy something, or you, Jacqueline, can make me one. I don't know what I will weigh a month from now, so why waste money on a dress.'

Then, as she was being fitted, she told Jacqueline the story of the secret correspondence, the underhand behaviour of the lad. Jacqueline said, 'It's natural, it's a phase, Madame: don't frighten him. Ask the girl to the house. Those aren't real love letters. It is nothing but youthful loneliness. They are playing at love. This *dear darling* means nothing. But the boy is lonely. I strongly recommend you to have the girl at the house, even to stay.'

This idea at first did not appeal to Emily, but later she saw advantages in it. When the boy returned from the movies, she accosted him at once.

'Christy darling, Christy my love, let's have one of your friends here to stay. Don't you want some girl you can go out with? You could go to the movies with a girl. Don't you know some nice American girl who's fun, you could go to the café with, smoke cigarettes with – one doesn't hurt. I want you to be natural, be your age, Mother wants you to have fun, darling, not to live in a monstery.'

She burst out laughing, shouted laughter, lay down on the sofa panting, cried, 'Oh, Christy, it's such a marvellous sensation to have a good laugh. I'm tingling all over, it's like sunbathing, listen darling, I mean it, Christy. Now who would you like?'

He said, 'Emily, I see you read the letters in my drawer.'

She lay quiet for a while, but presently recovered and got up to say soberly, 'Well, Christy, I did. Where's the harm? You're just a couple of

334

kids. Let her come here to stay. Send her a letter. Father's away for a couple of weeks yet; and we can all go out together, see everything. Why you poor boy, you work so hard, you haven't even seen Paris. What will Uncle Maurice say? Yes, you and Frankie and I will tour Paris. I'll get Madame Jacqueline to make me a suit after all.'

This was all done. Frances Wilson left her brother in the hotel in the rue Chomel and came to stay with the Howards in the rue de Varenne. Emily wanted to arrange a room for her on the same floor as Christy but Madame Suzanne strongly objected, in spite of Emily's comical remarks and dancing eyes; and she was given a room next to Olivia. Then with Madame Suzanne, Emily organized sight-seeing tours of Paris for herself with the two youngsters, leaving Suzanne at home to attend to Olivia, Giles and the servants.

Stephen, who had gone away originally for a week with Johnny Trefougar, had stayed away four weeks and hinted that he might stay longer. Trefougar had leave of absence for ill-health and was visiting doctors in Switzerland. Evidently they were travelling about a good deal, and had even returned to France to border-towns several times. Emily and the boy had had postcards and letters from Annemasse, Vallorbe, Porrentruy (near Berne) La Chaux de Fonds, and St-Louis (Haut-Rhin over the border from Basle). Emily could not understand what he was doing, was discomfited and angry with him for the news about him she had received from Americans passing through on the way home. She was more than disturbed, though she said nothing about it, by the news brought that Jay Moffat Byrd and Godfrey Bowles, who had baited them in Hollywood, had both gone to jail in the loyalty investigations, convicted under the Smith Act for refusing to give names of leftists working in the studios and among their friends, and for contempt of court.

Said Emily, writing in her *Journal of Days*, 'Who would have foreseen it, for those two heavies, Pious Jay and Noble God? But then Suzanne has taught me never to bet on loyalty. We don't know. To think of them, that Jay and Godfrey are responsible at bottom for our being here, in the mess we are in and in the unhappiness we are.'

The girl Frankie came and was installed, a lively, very short, broad-faced girl, hefty who was one of the 'campus leaders' in a students' revolt and was interested in scapegoat and other unhappy, misfit children. She talked earnestly at breakfast in the latest psychological jargon and otherwise was a gay, sinless puppy, spoiled by a brilliant father and a rich mother, very serious about herself.

'She leads Christy by the nose,' said Emily the first morning to Suzanne. 'We don't know people. I never thought he was so spineless.'

Suzanne laughed, 'You are just like all mothers and mothers-in-law.'

335

Suzanne laughed, 'You are just like all mothers and mothers-in-law.'

Emily laughed, 'Emily Wilkes in "The Mother-in-Law"; that's a good idea.'

She prodded the unwilling couple to fulfil her programme. Christy had had enough of the house; Frankie was going back all too soon to the campus rituals of an American college, and had better have European culture forced on her.

'It's the only way to do it at your age, Frankie. Ah, me! I know only too well. Get Fernande to give you your lunches and come along.'

How she heckled and high-hatted and harassed Frankie! Frankie said the Louvre was 'not functional.'

'What an abysmally stupid opinion, Frankie, if it is an opinion. I don't call it an opinion. It is like a hee-haw from a hippo munching leaves, all muffled by the saliva and sap but no brain-juice in it. Don't interrupt Christy! Frankie must learn something. Why is she here? Why don't you like the cheese, Frankie? You surely don't want to live all your life on grocer's cheese? Don't you want to learn things? Heigh-ho! Les Américains. Sit up straight Frankie, you're getting round shoulders; you're overweight as it is. Well, I am. But I need it, this mountain of fat is a mountain of energy. You do nothing. Don't tell me sitting in an armchair at a desk interviewing the ragged and destitute of the mind, the poor in soul, social alley-cats, the boys kicked by their fathers and the girls half burned to death by their mothers, do you mean to say you, Frankie, who know nothing, you poor, ignorant, little sod, are going to do something for them, to heal them; when their misery and hurt comes from society and you, with your few campus slogans and your total, abysmal ignorance of Europe and of all society that went before – what can you analyse? What do you know? Don't give me that – that, social-worker talk. What do you know? Nothing, nothing! Don't interrupt, Christy. This ignorant girl that I would kick to the bottom of the class, she wouldn't get ten per cent from me, she's going into business righting the wrongs of American society with her fat-jawed, fat-eyed, fat-breasted, fat-waisted, fat-legged, fat-footed intuition and Freudian jargon. Shut up, Christy! I know America and she doesn't. She's an ignorant, selfish, vain, little maggot. Sit up, Frankie. You sit opposite me and I can see all the revolting arrogance in your fat little eyes. You're a nobody.'

The first few mornings she had insisted upon Frankie Wilson sitting in with herself, Christy, Suzanne at the French lessons. She had soon herself been ungovernable, exhibiting Frankie, whenever she spoke; and later to Christy calling her a dull little campus sex-maniac, only going into politics to sleep with boys, so stupid, so venal, 'Here you see it, where different values reign! What a success for a dumb little animal like that to

336

marry an artist, you, Christy and a rich man, a very rich man. The American dream! We'll sweep these sweepings off our doorstep, Christy! What is she but a shipboard acquaintance?'

To her astonishment, Suzanne had taken Frankie's part. 'She is an amiable child, quite innocent, with orthodox phrases from the school-room, but quite sincere, a good companion for Christy. He could do much worse. She is just a schoolgirl. You could do a lot with that girl.'

She insisted also on her taking the Latin lesson with Christy and herself, under the teaching of Monsieur Jean-Claude.

'Now, Monsieur Jean-Claude, I want Frankie and then Christy to tell you what they know about Cicero before we start. Learning has to have a foundation. Frankie, please start.'

'Well, I don't know about Cicero.'

'Go on, go on, you must know something. Haven't you even heard of Cicero?'

'Yes. He was a Roman; he wrote in Latin.'

'And he's in Shakespeare; but you never read Shakespeare, did you?'

'Where is he in Shakespeare?' enquired Jean-Claude.

In the play of *Julius Caesar*. Now Christy tell us what you know of Cicero. You see, Monsieur Jean-Claude, Christy's uncle is a scholar, a Latin scholar, and it is essential, completely essential that Christy should also be a Latin scholar. Christy, now, Cicero attacked misgovernment, he was an enemy of tyranny, of dictatorship. The republicans of the French Revolution were young people who were fired by their reading of Cicero at school and from him got their passion for freedom. Like you, Christy. That is why, Monsieur Jean-Claude, it is also necessary for Christy to be soaked in Cicero. Christy's a young communist; he must know what his spiritual ancestors said, those who attacked the enemies of freedom. Now, Frankie, what do you know about it? Nothing! But you say you led a movement for freedom on campus. But how can you, if you are just amusing yourself, looking for kudos? If you're serious you'll try to find out what a great liberator and lover of freedom like Cicero said. You won't just wave a few flags, repeat a few slogans and get married and sit back fat and cosy as a hedgehog in winter, thinking you have done your bit. For that's what you will do. I can see. You are just a talker and a poor talker at that. So I tell you to listen, Frankie and find out from Christy and Monsieur Jean-Claude and myself what a great fighter for freedom was like.'

Monsieur Jean-Claude said, 'As a matter of record and since you are interested in scholarly views of Marcus Tullius, I should like to tell our two young friends that there is a well-known book by a scholar, Monsieur Jérome Carcopino, published in 1938, called *Secrets of Cicero's Correspon-dence*. We can, if you like, go through the letters of Cicero with this commentary in mind. For instance, Monsieur Carcopino says that in these letters, "The politician is shown here so odious that his misfortunes come as the punishment of unpardonable faults into which he was plunged by the mistakes of a mind too self-centred to be farsighted and the false moves of a will too weak to overcome the crises in which his generation struggled."

'He bought a sumptuous private hotel on the Palatine, to be near the powerful whose cases he now wished to take. By this, he tells Atticus, he satisfied his private vanity and increased his prestige. Please take notes and we will refer to the letters. To Atticus: *ad aliquam dignitatem pervenire.* . . 1. 13, 5–26 Jan., 61BC. He borrows from women, from Julius Caesar. He was a money-lender. He lent to well-placed and famous men but he preferred loans to the reckless sons of rich men. His toughness in exacting his money back and the high percentage is excused by him, by his need for money, urgent bills and a pack of creditors always after him.

'After his famous consulate, he jokes (so that he may not weep) about his debts: "Know that I am now so burdened with debts that I should like to enter a conspiracy if anyone would take me in." Ad. Fam. V.6.

'In 45 BC he is reduced to getting money from women, and large sums were paid. He does not deny this.

'Brother Quintus, to simplify things, had allowed Marcus Tullius to receive in Rome indemnities from the Treasury Public fixed by the senate. He received them but never transmitted them. He writes: "I see today that I am a wretch. I understand of what criminal act I have rendered myself guilty when I dissipated in mad expenditures the sums I received from the treasury in your name." Note, Christy, *"Qua in re ipsa video miser et sentio quid sceleris ad miserium.* . . etc." He wrote this from exile, brought once more face to face with his ruin. He tried to rob his close friend Atticus to whom so many of the letters are written.

'How did he have such money troubles with his property fees and bank accounts? He could not dispense with senseless luxury. He says to Atticus, "Don't bother about my money affairs as I don't care about it; think only of what I desire."'

At this Emily clapped her hands and cried, 'Oh, how wonderful, how right he was! Why, everything was there for him to take, it was the way of the age, wasn't it? He understood his age! He was the leading man of his age! But he was right. He was respected for that. Do you want him to live in an attic with Atticus?

'But Monsieur Jean-Claude and children,' she said, thumping on the table with her fist, 'yes, he did have a weakness; it was to regret it, to apologize, instead of taking what he needed, what everyone had, what everyone thought practical, and keeping it without apology. Wasn't it a

338

time of conquest, when revenues were pouring in from all the backward, low-browed peasants, the ignorant, stupid tribes without arts or sciences or political knowledge, that the Romans conquered? And why should you conquer without getting tribute? Didn't they all have triumphs in Rome showing what they had taken from the backward peoples, the rough barbarian gold and jewels and stuffs? And wasn't it their right? They went out there and put order into the provinces, they taught them how to grow crops and build houses. There they were dressed in a rag or a loincloth or a bit of bark if they dressed at all, living on roots and painting themselves blue, and the Romans came at the height of their civilization, with their arts and sciences, their building and road-making and they taught them everything. They made the soil produce and it was natural for them to take the fruits; there was plenty because of the superior methods of agriculture. They brought civilization all over Europe, where before there had only been yelling, ignorant barbarians living in forests, building rafts and killing each other in stupid little forays. The Romans came and civilized the land and the land brought out luxury and corn. It was coming to them. Why was he ashamed? Was there anyone who did not do the same? It was because he was not an aristocrat, for aristocrats never are sorry or ashamed, they know the rules of conquest and of living better than your neighbour, but because he was at heart a mild, good-natured middle-class man. He was kind to his wife and he adored his daughter. Oh, poor Cicero; and in the end, brought to an unfortunate end, to shame, with all his kindness to his family and all the letters he wrote to his friends, showing such devotion, and his magnificent, passionate oratory defending in the courts, so that he was thought sublime, the greatest orator of Rome. Think of it! And he apologizes, he is ashamed because he lives as well as the next man. What are debts in a society where debts are an accepted thing? They are not a shame, they are a means of living. I despise those who are afraid of debts. It only shows what a mild nature he had, too mild, more milky than kind, that he was afraid; yes, it showed his lower-class origin. He would have been happier and done better and been more respected if he had told them to go hang themselves with his IOU's round their necks! Let us be realists and not schoolmasters who know nothing of the world, Monsieur Jean-Claude. I want my children to be realists in an age just as difficult and full of crises as Cicero's. I don't want you putting into Christy's head these little middle-class, scholarly ideas. Christy belongs to patrician society, he is a patrician and he must not learn the mawkish, ignoble, sheepish, humble, oh so humble and petty comments of a mean little bookworm. Christy must be trained for his class and his position; that is why he is here. Christy will never associate with anyone who thinks like that. Oh, I hate

339

and despise what is modest forelock-pulling, and demeaning. Monsieur Jean-Claude, remember that you are teaching an aristocrat, a scion, a patrician; and let us look at things from that point of view. Cicero was quite right in everything he did; why should he abase himself, get down in the dust, when no one else did? I expect it was just artist's temperament. He must have been very tired at times; and then you get the moods of subjection and self-abasement. He had to work for his money and work damn hard. That is why he felt abasement; it was fatigue. What a wonderful man he was! Christy, I want you to think about this wonderful man, the greatest, sublime genius of prose in ancient Rome who, in spite of all his worries, was so tender and good to his friends, such a good father and anxious husband, always worrying about whether he had done his duty to his loved ones. And think, Christy, that that is the duty of those in public honour, to have these doubts and these worries but never to show them. That was where he was wrong – to show them. See how now after two thousand years nearly we are picking on him like crows pecking an old rag because he was so tender, good and honest that he worried about his debts! That is something we must never do. If we contract debts it is because we have credit and if we have credit it is that we have earned it by our labour, our position, our name. When credit has been given to us we do not owe the money back. Remember that Christy. Not that you will ever owe a penny. But me, ah me – but if *you like*, Frankie, you can remember that Cicero worried about his debts and his spending for that is middle-class and that is the best they can do, as they nose their way through their miserable mean world. And that is the world you live in, Frankie, you are going to live in, you will never get out of it – you have no signs on you that you will ever rise out of the middle-class swamp and sump you were born in, so you may as well begin to worry right now about the debts no one will allow you and the luxury you will never have. That is for you, those lessons are for you, for the frumpish world of the dumb, down – dreary middle-class. Oh, what a middle class man must be this dreary little scholar, if you can call him that, who wrote this bitter and ignorant attack on Cicero; such a wretched little mental pauper should never be allowed into the forum of scholarship to spit at his betters. Oh, I despise him. You went astray, Jean-Claude. I don't like this way of teaching. Let us give honour where honour is due and let us be men of the world here, not the base, cowardly, timid gentry who are afraid to have a debt. Don't nations have debts? Could they get along without debts? Don't cities and provinces and villages and hamlets have debts? And isn't is a sign of their standing when at last they can contract a debt; and the better the standing the greater the public market in which they can contract their debts, until nations have debts on an international level.

340

And is that a shame and disgrace? Don't let us bandy these words like housewives. If you have never been in business, then debt seems a shame; but banks are there for debts, not for savings; business could not go ahead if everyone paid cash – no, they want you to contract debts. True, Cicero lived in an old-world setting where big business was unknown but still he shows his humble origins, I think. And I am very sorry he had that headache. His wife, instead of divorcing, should have said to him, It doesn't matter; it belongs to the rank you have achieved, I know. And instead of having to marry his daughter for money, his daughter whom he so dearly loved, his own child, this charming little girl whom he adored, he could have been free of this load on his conscience. Oh, dear, dear me, poor Cicero!'

Emily wiped her eyes. She sighed.

'Well, Monsieur Jean-Claude, let us have no more of this little fungus-grown pedant, this petty little jealous dominie. Let us think of the greatness of great men.'

The tour of Paris lasted two days only, when Frankie, silent, sullen, left for her little room in her cheap hotel. Emily went to the hotel with her, coaxed Mike the brother and insisted upon paying the hotel bill. When Emily herself had seen the girl to the hotel, she returned haughtily to Christy and said, 'And now Christy that you have been with this dumb Dora two days you can see the sort of necking companion you got hold of.'

Christy protested that she was not a necking companion; and during these few days, at any rate, she had not been.

'Then why does she call you "darling Christy" and write you that slush? Oh, Christy, I can't trust you out of my sight. You promised me so many things and you're just a little liar. You have disappointed Mother, Christy.'

Seven days later, when Frankie had left the capital, Emily allowed Christy to move over the Suzanne's apartment in the Park Montouris.

To him, Emily, who was now very lonely, wrote a letter and he answered:

> 'Dear Emily, not Mother,
> Yes, yes, yes, I am a wretch, I know it. I have always been that,
> I know. And now when I stop and throw a glance backwards on
> the snows of yesterday, I know more, I am a liar and with
> something of the cheat in me. I have always been that, I think.
> You should never have believed in my grand promises. There's a
> song going about here now which is very popular and which
> expresses it, "You should never have believed me when I said I

loved you for I always was a liar." Well this song is for me. But in spite of that, I'm very fond of myself; and of you too. Please love me in spite of my faults. For, in fact, he or she who has no great faults in his (her) character is nothing but a sausage. Well, so much the worse. I'm like that. Just as you say. A wretch and a liar. So much the worse for you and me and all my friends. Well, apart from that, I've been very much taken up with the work for my examinations. Everyone is at me to work; I have worked, though I always have the peculiar (senseless) feeling that people do not do it for me, but for some other reason. How can that be? That expresses my lack of belief in myself. And yet, don't weep for me. I somehow believe in myself. My preparations are finished now, but I've the habit, I still want to work. But I want to be home, I mean America, on a visit and I think it will be good to be home. There are problems here and a sort of anxiety I never did solve. To be frank, I understood you in America and I do not think I understand you here. (That was my mind going downhill I suppose?) Meanwhile, if Fairfield comes and is allowed, I think I will go with her, Grandma thinks it a good idea, to the Wiesbaden Music Festival, there will be a good many people and all kinds of madmen for music. I have a friend going through Paris – and if you could put him up in my old room? Please. He hasn't a penny. I myself will come back on my way home and see you.

'If you write to me, Emily, of course I will write to you. But no doubt I will always be disappointing to you, for I am, I know, a disappointing fellow. Not to myself, but my whole life long I must live with myself; and so must make a compromise. That is something you never did. And so, dear Emily, so that you will not catch me up and expect too much from me on any subject, I say goodbye. But only till we meet again. Your loving son, Christy.'

Emily was shocked by this letter; she cried. Stephen was absent and had denounced her to friends in America – a recent letter even said, though she could not trust the writer, that he had spoken of divorce, 'the only thing to save us both'. What was she to do now? To whom could she turn? Suzanne still came every day for her French lesson; but in the afternoon now, her mornings being given over to Christy in their own home. Emily thought with bitterness of Suzanne and Christy, in their own home, paid for chiefly by themselves and Christy; of Suzanne, just like a bride of Christy, the old hard-baked woman.

Except for the little tour with Frankie and Christy, Emily had not left the house during Stephen's absence; most of her time in her workroom, where she did three or four hours a day writing pieces for sale, and the rest of the time in the usual way, frittering her time away, as Stephen said. When exhausted with the paper world, and not with Christy, she went to the kitchen to work out fanciful menus for possible guests, Vittorio, Stephen and the Trefougars, Mamma and Fairfield; and she amused herself making special dishes for herself when the servants were out. But she was restless, very unhappy. 'I am unhappy, unfortunate, most unhappy,' she said to herself. She would say it aloud and begin to weep. What friends had she? She and Violet Trefougar had talked to each other every time a postcard or letter arrived from some new place in Switzerland or over the border. Three times Violet had come to lunch; Emily receiving her in a voluminous house-gown, or in a handsome dressing-gown.

'I shall never get into a dress again, I never shall leave the house again,' said Emily. 'Jacqueline keeps on letting out my slips and all my other clothes; I have no blouse to wear. The suit she made for me only two weeks ago is too small. She must let it out. What I want is to have people come here, stand all round me, eat around me, while I lie on my bed, some grand, brocaded bed, in a luxurious dressing-gown. Oh, what luxury! The end of care! I can't reduce. I must eat, Violet! Oh, soon, these dreadful days, I don't know whether they are days of freedom or prison; soon our men will be back and I must, I must reduce. But the only joy I get these days, the only joy, Violet, is in eating. It is a real joy and nothing else is as good. I wrote to my beloved dear Vittorio and he answers me with a scrap of paper, he says two words on the telephone. He came here once; we lunched, I in my dressing-gown. I threw my arms around him, Violet, kissed him, oh, I love him so much, what joy at last to have him here with me, to talk to him – if only – but what is the use? – he did not stay half an hour after lunch. He had a meeting and from then on, nothing doing. He can't come. Too busy. Is it the fat? He doesn't like such lardy women? Or was it the dressing-gown; not formal enough? But in high high society, women receive in a trailing, languorous house-gown, don't they? I thought he would understand. I can never be happy. Do you know I cry every day, Violet, and blame all my dearest and nearest; they are all my scapegoats. How stupid and dull I am becoming, like a backyard wife, who doesn't even go to the movies, whose husband abandoned her because of the tattletale grey in her hair! Do you know there is grey in my hair? You can't see it, because I am fair; but I am going grey. So soon! My life is finishing so soon. No one's fallen in love with me. They only think of my fame, which is imaginary, and my money, which is a debt deeper than the deepest well. They think I'm happy and

343

each time I see anyone and see those thoughts in their mind, I think, Oh, how dreadfully unhappy I am. What is the matter with me? I'm the happy one, I'm supposed to be deleerious with joy, making other people laugh. Laugh, clown, laugh! Is it true that clowns are lugubrious? Violet, I cannot go on so melancholy. I don't believe in it. It's wrong. Be my friend, Violet darling. You are such a lady, so kind, so intelligent, and you've so much trouble. Much, much more than me. Who am I to groan and squeal? Violet, darling, what do you do?'

'Don't you take anything?' asked Violet.

'Go and open the top drawer in that dressing-table,' said Emily.

Violet did so. Emily said with gay, vain eyes, 'Well, what do you see?'

'Some pills.'

'Yes, they are the ones. I take them. I'm told not to take so many. But I take them all day long if I want to. I must live, I must feel bright. I am not going to give in, get blue; and I'm not allowed to drink as much as I like, so there's just that. Do you know what they are?'

'They're not the ones I take. Mine are very good. You ought to change perhaps. Sometimes they turn their backs on you; there's a reaction.'

The two women discussed that pills and gave relief and happiness and the expense of this treatment. Emily said she had to get extra supplies of her own on the sly, for Stephen, as with all things, supervised her, kept her tethered. 'I am like a goat we once had. She was a clever goat, goatess, though. She always got away. Stephen treats me like a child. I make all this money – he never made any – and I am still in baby's harness for him. A poor, wretched woman without brains or talent, who needs his guidance.'

They talked over their troubles with their men and presently Violet offered to introduce Emily to a medical friend of hers, a society doctor who had a distinguished clientele of rich women, some titled, some famous actresses, journalists and women from the best families.

'The strain has been enormous, during the occupation and now with the people so unruly and restless, that no one knows what is going to happen. They are so unhappy, they are very grateful to Dr Kley.'

'Dr Kley?'

'We all call him that; it's a pet name, an abbreviation. The women rave about him. He will see anyone; and if he likes you, he will prescribe for you. He has helped so many people. All women. He prefers women; though I believe there are one or two men. He will see you. But you will have to get dressed, Emily, he won't come here. He has a big apartment, splendid, in the rue de Miromesnil. I'll give you the address as soon as you like. I'll take you myself. He prefers an introduction. He kept this magnificent apartment all through the occupation and I suppose he

344

helped the Germans too; but it is all medicine isn't it? Everyone can get ill and need help. He kept in with them and now he can help us; that is the way I look at it. I don't know what I'd do without Dr Kley. And you will be grateful to him too. I know he can help you. See, Emily, all we women are unhappy. It doesn't work out well for us. Our men are selfish, going their own way; they only want to make money and don't think of our happiness. Now Dr Kley knows all this and he does all he can to give women happiness. All. You don't know what I mean by that; but you will find out if he likes you. And why shouldn't you be happy too? You are a really nice, clever woman. You're an original. It's a shame you should suffer.'

Emily was excited, expectant. She could not wait to meet the zealous doctor. But it came out that since he had such a rich and well-placed clientele and since his services were so personal, his fees were high.

Now that they had become more intimate, Violet came quite often to see Emily and ate with her. Emily was delighted. She and Violet ate very good food. Afterwards they drank coffee and brandy and discussed their troubles. As for the money needed for Dr Kley's treatment, Emily's bank account being empty and an overdraft spent, Violet said she could easily get a friend of hers, who helped her, to help Emily. Emily was a very good risk. 'Of course he's a Shylock,' said Violet, 'but we don't care, do we? Let's be happy, if we can. Life is short. I couldn't face life with Johnny if I didn't have help and – I don't know how it is with you and Stephen, it's better with you I think – but you see Doctor anyway and life will be simply heaven. You won't cry, you won't be unhappy: you'll be able to smile at Stephen when he returns. Even if he did say he'd divorce you. Men say that. But he can't, can he? You haven't done a thing.'

'No. Tough luck. Very tough luck. Though I don't want him to divorce me,' said Emily laughing.

With Violet's help, she borrowed a sum of money from Violet's friend, a man named Verrai, or so Emily thought, and was promised further accommodation later on. With the money she put on her altered suit, a beautiful hound's-tooth silk, and went with Violet to see Dr Kley,.

Dr Kley, a Hungarian (some said a Romanian) was a medium-sized, fair man with a smooth manner, which sat patchily on his wary, irritable, small face. Violet had a few words with him and then Emily went in alone to explain that she slept badly and found it impossible to reduce. She wanted some pills.

'What pills have you been taking?'

He made her lie naked on a low, broad couch he had and stood for some moments looking at her fixedly, with a strange expression. Then he prescribed for her a course of treatment, six medicines to take in turn during six weeks and with them some pills which would help her to reduce. She paid him his fee in cash as she had been told to and went out to Violet, who eagerly examined the prescriptions, She said, Yes, those were her pills; she was very glad; Emily would soon feel the benefit.

At first Emily did feel better, though she laughed at her 'faith cure' and she began to plan something that would enable them to sail dry-foot over their ocean of debts. She wanted a French or European subject so that she and Stephen could work on it there without too much trouble. What subject? The French Revolution? Treated as Dickens had done it, for she felt herself sometimes another Dickens, with the humane, humorous and pathetic touch, not going too deeply into the social questions he understood very well, serving things up palatably for the kind of people who were her readers.

'No one will accept a re-evaluation of the French Revolution except in scholarly works which are expensive and hidden away in bookshops with old men with a stoop and spectacles to guard them. But any popular treatment of the French Revolution need not be – of course – filled with women shrieking and throwing petrol and working the bloody heads into their knitting – but I can't have a mob hero either.'

She discussed it with Violet who made a few suggestions but none helpful, except perhaps, 'You must have mob scenes, darling, and tumbrils and the dreadful Robespierre at the guillotine; that is what people want. And of course, Marie-Antoinette. You can have some new things in it, for your own sake, but people want to see the real things, the things that make their hair stand on end. After all, no one really trusts the French ever, do they? They remember the revolution and we must remember that they remember.'

'That's very true, Violet; that is what we in our hearts think of the French.'

'If I thought about it I'd be afraid to live here. We all think like that and we distrust them, and we hate them; for they aren't sincere. They are bloody-minded; they're cruel and relentless and they don't understand the rest of Europe, except like Talleyrands, out for themselves, France first and last, and all the rest babarians anyway. Their polite talk is the dry and cunning talk of diplomacy, and everyone of them a diplomat. I hate them, Emily; and they hate us. So give it to them. Don't be sentimental when it comes to the French or the French Revolution. Wouldn't they like to see that happen all over again?'

'I sort of agree with you, but I've got to think it over. I'd like to have a project when Stephen comes back. We need it – and I need it. And good old Dr Kley – I believe he's done me some good. I believe in myself again.'

But it was some time before Emily fixed on her subject. She knew that

346

the traditional 'French Revolution', with scenes of mob violence and hissing hate of the aristocrats, the noble demeanour of the lost on their way to the scaffold, the scenes in prison, had their appeal, but weren't they out of date? Besides she wanted to do something of her own that would make her name both in a book and in a historical movie, a blockbuster – and already she saw the great sets a-building, the troops of actors, the prison scenes, violence of the soldiers, flaring lights on the Seine. It would be done in Rome, where American movie-money now went. She became excited about it and began to sketch out scenes. But France had now affected her and she wanted too to do something that Vittorio would think well of. 'I know people of the latest revolution, that to come; I can't dishonour them, they're my best friends; and now that I'm here, I have some respect for the people and the streets, the working people, the streets where people lived their daily lives even when the guillotine was working day and night.'

18   MONEY-MAKING

Stephen returned saying that he had won a big prize in the Swiss lottery; but he was not in a prize-winner's mood. He was very angry with Christy, who had not written him a word during the six weeks; and at once telephoned him that he was to come over the next morning. Stephen complained of his internal pains and said that the worries of the past six weeks had aggravated his trouble. He would have to return to the States and go into hospital. Trefougar had assured him that neither French not British medicine was worthwhile, and he had not the money to be treated in Switzerland. When Emily asked him why he had travelled so fantastically, incessantly, it seemed, crossing the frontiers, he laughed bitterly, took a paper out of his pocket and threw it to Emily. On it was written in ink:

USA double eagle fetches around	$50
eagle	$25
sovereign	$13
Mex. fifty-peso	$25
napoleon	$10
vreneli	$10
20-mark	$13
gold bars	$35.16
gold plates	490 Swiss francs

'Well?' she said, after glancing eagerly down the columns.

'I'm in the gold business,' he said sourly.

'Oh, Stephen, wonderful! I always knew you could.'

He said something obscene.

'Stephen!'

He took back the paper, 'And shut up about it. I'm making money for us to throw out the window. I'm in international finance. That's a laugh. I'm a free-booter, smuggler. Tell Jacqueline to run us up a little flag with the skull-and-crossbones, so that everyone can see our disgusting thinking and can know how low we have sunk.'

'Stephen, you're boorish.'

'I'm ill, for one thing. I'll go to bed. This travelling about, all the anxiety over the customs, Trefougar lying and bluffing his way every-

348

where, leaving without our hotel bills paid – oh, I hate it, it makes my blood run cold, cold with bitterness, not with fear. I'm a coward, but not that kind. To look those petty, mean men in the face and know that they have a right to suspect me. But what do I really care? Can't they be bribed, isn't there one among them who can be bribed, or for all I know, has been bribed? To look at the men in the bank and think, Which one is a spotter? And have the spotter come to you and say, "I know where you can get rid of the swag" and split with him and go to the bank and have the officials there know you're what you are; a lowdown rascal, a vile black-marketeer, like the Italian boys in the streets, selling chocolate and butter and stolen bicycles. That's what Europe has brought me to, me the proud heir of the Howards!'

'Oh, Stephen. And did you make money?'

'I made enough. Though it won't last us long. I must go on and on with this if I'm to keep the house going. And now my scamp of a nephew has decamped, he's over there reading diatribes against me, against us, from his friends in the States, from Florence, keeping his pockets sewed up, learning that we're plotting to live on him, to filch the sweat from his greasy banknotes, to scrape a percentage off his laundry bills, to take a little of the food he pays for, poor relatives living off the rich young gentleman, officious beggars, *schnorrers* stabbing with dirty fingers at the full pocket.'

He went to bed, without telling Emily anything else about his travels. She was anxious to tell him about her new project, the French Revolution novel, featuring perhaps Danton, Marie-Antoinette, Robespierre, Camille Desmoulins – she was not sure yet, and she thought it would take some time to get the right angle – an angle to please serious readers, to present something new and yet old for Hollywood, to attract the romantic women who loved court dress and wept for those who died for it and yet to exhibit to their one time companions, to those who had not got off yet from 'the slow train down from the Finland station', that they had the insight of Marxism, still had that discipline. Turning the subject over and over in her hands, eagerly, Emily thought it could be done; but Stephen was the scholar, apter and stricter than herself – he was the one to trim the ship for her.

Stephen had taken to bed with him the accumulated mail. Emily, after a quarrel with her cook and a long discussion with Suzanne about Christy's freedom, immaturity in sex, sat down with a book in her hand meaning to read, but overwhelmed by her strange feelings about Christy, the anxieties and jealousies he caused her. 'I don't love him except as a son.' Jacqueline, the seamstress, was in the living-room making a quantity of French curtains for their windows, filmy net with deep borders and insets of real lace. Emily sighed and opened the great American novel, Dreiser's *The American Tragedy*, brought up again to notice, perhaps because the novelist was dead. She looked at it and sighed thinking of the enormous amount of work and the time – a year, two years? – that separated her from her French Revolution book in print. They might get an advance, probably could – but the big money would not come in till it was printed, a success, and attractive to Hollywood. Emily had never had an 'A' picture and this time she wanted to clean up, have not merely an 'A' picture but a giant phenomenon of the Cecil B. De Mille sort, a blockbuster. That would solve their problems. They could live decently, pay their debts, if necessary, move to a better house than this, though perhaps smaller, Christy being gone and Olivia no doubt going; and lead a quiet, pleasant, luxurious life, all peace and production. She sighed and fingered the novel. Certainly Dreiser had not waited for all that; but she was different, the idea of working in poverty, waiting long years, made her restless and angry. She was a money-maker, no need for her to crawl on all fours after the chariot of fortune. She would drive it. 'Pouf'! the patient waiters, the cap-in-hands at the gate of life, it won't serve me to only stand and wait. Life, life itself – what is life? Not pulsing and puking and waiting.'

She opened the book, determined to learn something from it.

Stephen later shrieked at her from above, 'Come and look at the mail with me. What am I going to do about this – about that? Do you know what laundry cost us last month? What is all this dress-making? Do you know what Christy's tutors are costing, I mean what I don't dare charge the estate? And all to play up to Uncle Maurice, who never glances our way. Why did you draw on the account like that?'

In spite of Stephen's getting up, running about upstairs and shouting and banging on the wall, she read on. This is what I should be doing, she thought. Dreiser is stupid, dull, his language is Teutonic, but Dreiser is powerful, dramatic, overwhelming; it's because he's honest. He's overcome by humble human tragedy and he doesn't care who knows he is. He's awestruck by riches, that's true – not me; but he's awestruck by human nature, too; and so am I; but he's cold, penetrating and suffering, humane, an adult. All I can do is to try to squeeze out belly-laughs and horse-laughs. Oh, my! As he says, 'I am a mental and moral coward.' Me, Clyde Griffith.

Stephen banged on the top steps, 'Where is the rest of the mail? Marie-Jo says a cable came from New York. Is it the play? Is it our book? Come here! Answer me!'

Emily called out, 'My God! What is the matter? Let me work!'

'Will they, or won't they produce the damn thing?'

'Go away! Let me work. How can I work? We live on my work.'

'Good God! Are we bankrupt or not? Do you know what cash we have in the bank? Where's the statement? I've a desk full of bills. Didn't you pay anything? Are the servants paid? Here are three blue papers from bailiffs all come this week,' Stephen said in a lamentable scream.

'Oh, heavens, who could work in this?' said Emily opening the door. There he was in his pyjamas, yellow-faced and drawn, one sock on, papers in his hand, his blue eyes sunken.

'Where's the mail? Did the agent write? What's happening?'

Emily came out and said, sobbing, hanging on to her busband, 'Dreiser is surely one of the few novelists in the world, except you, my darling – you could do a thing like this – '

'Stop boohooing, stop your damn bunk – where's the rest of the mail? Where are the bank statements?'

'Oh, Stephen, to choose such a doomed soul! Listen, Stephen! Like us, perhaps! He makes you feel it is like us. Absolutely without a single redeeming trait, betraying all and each, and himself, leading himself to doom, a worm, a victim, a sponge, a cringer, an unspeakable bit of human dust, dust before he's dust, mud before he's mud and for this wretched bit of human being, like us, like me at least – to show this severe terrible compassion – such compassion, oh, is terror, terror.' She shuddered, 'Oh, I feel so cold, such terror – suppose we were all to be shown up like that; and yet,' she said, straightening and looking at him with red face and brimming eyes, 'that is art, never would I ask for another sort of sentence from the most compassionate judge! Never for the dreamstuff. He says, Here is the remorseless, logical, inescapable doom he brought on himself and the twentieth century brought on him and America brought on all. He is not, I am not, sorry for myself, or Dreiser or Clyde or us – yes, I am. Behold his unspeakable suffering, so puny, so unworthy, his, the tragedy of the century, the century of the common man, so common, so wretched.

'Eh? Splendid! Terrible! Oh, Stephen, I have made a mistake. This is what I should have done. All this is no good! It is not good, this house, these servants, Christy and Anna and Olivia and Fairfield and Maurice – all wrong. I have made a terrible, irreparable mistake. For I, like Clyde, will end with worn, wretched, horrid little dreams! All for nothing! Our play is rejected! My book is not taken! Nothing is taken! It is all for nothing. I have sold out for nothing.'

Stephen looked at her earnestly, took her back to her chair, 'I have a poor raving lunatic for a wife! Do you mean we're ruined? What has Dreiser to do with it? If you'd written like Dreiser, who never had a baked bean to his name and not a principle either, we'd be even worse off. Pull

351

yourself together. What have you been taking? Let me see those letters.'

He read the letters and began to get excited himself, 'What! A fine agent!' He walked up and down fuming. 'I'm going to cable him. We're ruined. How are we going to eat?'

'My God, this morning, you spoke of going to Italy and said we had money enough to last.'

Stephen shouted, walking up and down and looking at her blackly, 'I was counting in the play and the book. This upsets all my calculations. We can't live another three months with all our crazy expenses and now Christy's moving to Suzanne's and paying all his own expenses, we lose even that advantage; and the miserable hypocrite, flannel-mouthed humbug is getting stiff-lipped with me; Florence wrote him such and such. My God, in a family like ours, if the poor can't live off the rich, where are we? What's the point of family loyalty?'

Emily said, 'Let's move to an apartment. I'm giving up everything for apples of Sodom.'

'Our only excuse for having Christy is that we supervise him. I didn't even want him to move to Suzanne's. Those two, Jean-Claude and Suzanne can now do whatever they like with him. And now there is this third tutor, Monsieur Laroche. You know what Christy is, a miserable little constricted mind, narrow as a sardine, self-righteous while pretending to be humble: don't I know it? Like me. We finally got the family into the habit of seeing Christy with us, one of us. Now it's ruin. Listen Emily – this journal you write. Publish it, if it's readable. You read books and waste time as if we were millionaires. You can make money – you've got to. The little bit I make on this damn currency-running, I hate it, I do it to hold my end up – it isn't what you can make with one damn movie script. You've got to make money while we're in this terrible situation. I'm away from my country, I have no contacts here but rogues and ambiguous people, I'm helpless. It wasn't I who wanted to fly from my country and live abroad, cousin to a traitor, but a thin-blooded cousin – I am a traitor, not to take my country and all that goes with that pill.'

They screamed and quarrelled. Emily said, 'I'll get dressed. Let's go to the movies. We can't go on like this. You know, Stephen, we love each other. Let's break up this terrible scene. We've got into a situation comedy or what they call comedy in the USA, husband and wife throttling each other.'

But before they were ready to go the telephone rang and their old friend Axel Oates spoke. He had come from the Far East, was on his way to Eastern Germany, and had passed through Paris only to see them. Ruth was with him. She was not going with him to Germany but to Fiesole, where a friend of hers had a rented villa. She would stay there till Axel returned to France, on his way home to America. Axel congratulated Stephen on being back in Paris and asked them if they would like to go out that evening. They had cooking arrangements in the little attic apartment a friend had lent them, but they would eat out.

'I like it and I know you hate the idea of anyone being up from dawn in the kitchen – '

'Ugh – yes,' said Emily, flushing and trying to think when she had said this to them.

'Old friends, going out on a Saturday evening, to a riverside rump-steak and french fried joint; but it won't be like that.'

'Well, sure, we're glad. I haven't been out of the house for weeks; the prisoner wife.'

They were to meet at La Régence in the rue du Théâtre Français. Emily and Stephen were cheered, Emily because La Régence had a famous restaurant and Stephen because he longed for a good talk with a man who knew the world situation, a first-rate political journalist. 'God, it's been years,' said Stephen.

'What about Vittorio and Suzanne? You have them.'

'Oh, that's like having a pipeline to the universe. I want someone who knows who's running for governor in Nebraska. To think that only two years ago I knew the name of every political punkin in every county of the USA. Now my head's useless lumber. I don't need it for what I've come to.'

'Fancy the Régence! They must have sold a book! Or a series of articles, I suppose. But to whom? They're dead ducks in the States.'

'A decent meal and plenty of good talk, that's what it means to me. They'll survive: they know how to.'

'Oh, we're so miserable, my poor darling. I am going to drink and drink; don't stop me. After all, it is not at our expense and we've given them enough dinner parties and Christmases and we had them there for a month.'

As she was dressing in the black and white hound's-tooth suit, the only thing she could now wear, though she had reduced her weight a little, she began to laugh.

'I hope it won't be like the Wauters.'

'How could it be?'

'Oh, all married people are frightful when you go in a foursome. But I feel they love us and we love them. They still believe in us. That makes them totally original.'

'All married people of any kind are frightful; only old maids, hermits and eunuchs are interesting,' said Stephen.

'Suzanne is interesting alone.'

353

'Not to me. In you there is still a lot of the night-court reporter. That's where she belongs. Suzanne would have been better as an old maid who made a mistake and is covering up. As it is she's like an old maid but a spoiled one. I hate her. I hate teachers and heroes and do-gooders. And there's something particularly dull about Suzanne. She has no sex appeal.'

'How mean you are,' said Emily laughing. They kissed. Presently they went out, leaving Olivia and Giles with Marie-Jo, Fernande and the porter. Emily said they should have had Suzanne over. Dear Anna would not approve of the child's being left *avec la valetaille*.

'With the what?'

'The menials.'

'Oh, I'll send her home if she's going to be an albatross round our necks.'

'And now the Oateses are going to see us as we now are. Not the good little reds we were in America. Perhaps they'll think us boring too?' Emily said.

'You are a public danger, a monster, a terror, but never a bore, if a bore, well, the sort that has never been seen before; and so a phenomenon. If they don't like my phenomenon, they can sit on a tack.'

In the taxi Emily kissed him. 'Oh, what a blessing to leave the worm-eaten château and all its worms. Yes, Suzanne begins to pall on me too; whatever pall means. It sounds like a funeral wrap.'

The taxi put them down in a few minutes on the pavement next to La Régence. The Oateses were not there. It was very cool and, after waiting a few minutes, they had a whisky and a sherry. Emily said, 'Oh, you pay Stephen. I want another and I can't wait.'

The restaurant was brightly lighted, cosy, expensive and already had rich young Americans eating there. Some people were playing chess at the back; others were eating the snacks for which the place was famous.

'My God – the snacks! That is why they brought us here,' said Emily in a fright.

But the Oateses came up at this moment with Daniels, a famous American journalist, whom they had known in Connecticut and an assistant who worked on his paper with him, Evelyn. Evelyn, about thirty-eight, short, plump and eager, was a hard-working journalist, the born link between parties, people and even nations. She was a fresh, country-bred woman, looking quite girlish. She was plainly dressed in suit and soft blouse, with her hair loose. She had handsome, oval blue eyes and a soft, burring voice. Daniels (called Dan), a lively, sociable man, but at first quiet in any company, had been very ill, and was now convalescing. Evelyn and some other devoted women had done all his work for him during his absence, going to Paris, Mexico City, Rome and

354

other places to make his contacts and get articles. Dan was a widower.

The Howards showed rejoicing on meeting old acquaintances; but they were embarrassed. Some letters had told them that Dan had denigrated them, denounced them, 'stabbed them in the back'. But who knew? New York and other cities where there were many radicals, liberals and men of good will, were then fermenting, hotbeds of suspicion, fear, doubt and error. The three men were having a tremendous talk; Evelyn paid polite attention to Emily but chimed in with all that Dan said; she was of course his lieutenant. Ruth and Emily exchanged friendly chat and Ruth was always calm and agreeable, but for the first time Emily felt out of it, like a suburban housewife sitting with 'the women' while the men discussed politics.

'I don't know a damn thing about upstate elections,' she said laughing.

'Oh, let them talk. They're cute,' said Ruth.

Axel was a teetotaller and Dan was off liquor on account of his ulcers, and Stephen, suffering severely, was drinking Vichy water. Evelyn preferred tomato juice. Emily and Ruth, sitting alone like two old soaks, said Emily, drank their double whiskies and waited. Axel had with some difficulty made a short trip to China and wanted to return when he could.

'I'd like to go myself, but then of course, you're kosher, friend of the left, they wouldn't let me in under the rope,' said Stephen bitterly.

'We'd like to go but we've got our plans for several years ahead,' said Evelyn, and was going on when she looked at Dan and stopped. 'You are sitting in a draught, dear,' she said, and turned to the women; 'He will wear his light overcoat although it is getting colder. Dan, you must begin to wear your winter things. Wear your coat now.'

'But then when I go out I'll catch cold,' said Dan, a little warily. He liked women's attentions but always presented himself as a healthy, outdoor man.

'It's dreadful, really dreadful to make us all worry. You should have worn your winter coat,' said the assistant sweetly and drew back in her chair, trying to control herself, anxious to show their intimacy, anxious not to irritate Dan. She said softly, 'He's afraid he'll look ridiculous. Why everyone here knows that there are plenty of sick people, and people who were deported and just returned. Who looks?' She laughed like an awkward niece, from embarrassment. 'Such vanity!' She looked at him with patient fondness, out-of-place clinging.

Emily looked at him with bright, unamiable eyes, about to burst into laughter.

Dan coughed. Evelyn shook herself nervously.

'You coughed! You see! Try not to cough! It's a habit.'

'But it tickles me,' said Dan.

355

Urged by Evelyn, he found some pills in his pocket and took one. Axel said that now they might go. He had picked out a nice little restaurant not far away.

Evelyn said, 'Oh, it's raining, what shall we do?'

'Take a taxi.'

'Oh, we'll walk,' said Ruth, 'it's only a sprinkle.'

Axel said, 'You'll like this restaurant, it's in this quarter, in a side street, a real people's restaurant where Paris itself eats, and at the same time, good cooking. The man's a born cook. I thought you'd like it.'

'Oh, I know it,' said Evelyn. 'It's unique, isn't it, Dan? Friends from *L'Humanité* and *Ce Soir* often go there and the man has not raised his prices. He gives a set meal for one hundred francs and the daily special is as low as seventy-five francs and at the same time you can get pâté de foie gras truffé, roast chicken, cooked before an open fire, right in the room where you sit – there is only one room and the kitchen – and as for snails, Dan is very fond of them – Burgundy snails – this man is a gem, a genius with snails, his sauce is one of the best in Paris, Dan says. I don't know. I'm not a gourmet, but Dan is. Well, in short, anything from the plainest to the tastiest, he has all – of course in a modest setting, so that you don't feel you're paying for the décor – well, you'll like it. It's just what you'd like, Emily. It's true Paris and you must feel very much at home here now.'

Emily was encouraged by the truffled foie gras and the roast chicken. 'Ah, well anything like that. We've never been to a place like that though we've been in Paris for so long. Well, I guess it would be interesting. *La vie*, eh?'

Evelyn said, 'But it's raining, isn't it? Wouldn't it be better to stay here this evening?'

'Oh, no the rain's stopped and it's just a few blocks.'

They set off. Stephen walked with Dan, Axel with Evelyn and Emily and Ruth together. Ruth, a husky, good-natured New Yorker who had been everywhere with Axel and before meeting Axel had travelled much on her own, said 'I don't care where or what we eat. Do you? As long as it's fun and the men are along. Food without men is no food; there's no taste.'

Emily laughed, 'Hooray! Put out the flags! Yes, I hate to eat with women. Look in a restaurant that has no men and it's a bad restaurant. I guess sex and taste go together.'

They were now all in considerable good-humour. At a street-crossing Evelyn had changed places in order to steer Dan out of drips from gutterings, awnings, cornices and lampposts. They presently turned into a long narrow lane which Stephen said he knew; 'It leads to the marché St-Honore.'

They found he didn't know. Then with Axel sure of himself and Ruth stopping every few doors and saying, 'It's here,' they at last arrived at the place in the rue de la Sourdière. It was a very small, ill-lighted place with two dirty plate-glass windows across which muslin curtains were drawn, the menu on the door in violet ink. Evelyn piloted Dan to the back of the room saying, 'He will be warmer here.'

'What's the name of the restaurant?' said Emily.

'I don't know. I think l'Escargot de Bourgogne,' said Ruth.

It was one small room painted ochre, with ten small tables arranged for the most part in pairs. The tables were dressed with new cloths of rough linen striped red and blue and yellow and had slender vases of flowers. On the walls were exhilarating posters advertising Spain, Algiers, Italy, Marseilles. There was a small counter, a switchboard with red and blue lights and a door leading to the workers' hotel upstairs. There was no one there. They were early. An Algerian worker came in soon after they were seated, saluted the middle-aged, short, dark-haired woman at the counter, drank a very small glass of muddy wine and went upstairs.

'It is a workers' restaurant,' said Evelyn cheerfully.

Perhaps because of the feeble light the Howards felt miserable. Dan cheered up however and said he would take a small apéritif. They had come early, he explained to the woman at the counter:

'Let us have a *porto* before your nice dinner.'

The woman gave him a pleasant smile, almost of recognition. Women gave this smile to Dan, though Emily considered him very unattractive, being nursed and henpecked by Evelyn and because he had attacked them as runaways and renegades – that was what they had heard. She frowned and thought of herself, 'Why are we eating with this dirty backbiter? If he thinks that of us, why does he eat with us?' She had to take a *porto*, there being no whisky there.

Presently from the kitchen came a youngish, middle-aged man in sweater and worn grey trousers who took their order for the first course: for the Howards, the truffled pâté, for Dan and Evelyn parmentier soup, the soup of that evening, for the Oateses various hors-d'oeuvres.

Stephen said pleasantly, 'I've capitulated to the local habit of eating soup every evening, but I can't eat leek and potato soup in the evening. It insults my wife. I stay up half the night worrying about my stomach.'

This embarrassed Evelyn.

Next, Emily ordered one dozen Burgundy snails with the special sauce, Stephen waited and the others shared a dozen between them. This took some time and with the snails they consumed each a glass of poor white wine. Emily declared, eating the snails with gusto, 'Well, it's grand anyway. It's a workers' dump but you tell an American truck-driver that

357

in a French workers' restaurant you get truffled cream of pâté de foie gras, burgundy snails and parmentier soup and roast chicken and pheasant, I see they have – and scalloped veal and mushroom sauce and so on, why the guy would think you were a traitor to the USA, a wiseguy, a spy, a greenhorn, a phony and all ready for the guillotine.'

'They don't have guillotines in the USA, fortunately,' said Stephen.

'I'd like to write an article, saying, listen friends, they don't eat wayside weeds boiled in water eked out with a few cans of hamburgers and pineapple juice sent over from the USA, they eat pâté de foie gras. And if I wrote down what I understood just now from this character who cooks, that these snails were fed on these herbs for three weeks beforehand, and white wine with the poor wretches – eh? They wouldn't buy it. Or else they'd say, "See what they're reduced to living on? Snails! I guess it came about that way to begin with, they were poor,"' and she looked thought- fully at the snails.

'Very funny,' said Stephen sourly. He was depressed by the quiet and modest men coming in to sit at the nine other tables, and another worker with lime on his sabots, who had just gone upstairs, perhaps without supper; by the poor light, by the smell of the garlic sauce on the snails, by the doubts about his quondam friend Dan, who seemed a little upstage with him, by the pain in his entrails and by a twinge of his rheumatism, too. The foie gras had been ordinary, not exceptional, the wine acid. He had ordered a beefsteak; he wondered if it would be cow or horse in this place. He wished he had ordered veal, along with Emily. Dan had ordered cod in black butter ('What a horror!' Emily had signalled to Stephen) and Evelyn boiled mackerel with caper sauce ('Terrible! What did you expect?' Stephen signalled to Emily). The Oateses had jugged hare and boiled potatoes; though Ruth seemed discontented.

The Howards ate their dinners painfully. The Oateses seemed very cheerful. The Howards decided not to go to a café with their friends. Stephen was suffering from the acid white wine. 'We'll go home and you'll come to us next week.' They took a taxi home and in the taxi they both groaned. Unlucky evening.

Emily said, 'Oh, I wish we had gone to the movies. It's so dull in Paris, Stephen. Everything is so dull and accepted and bourgeois; and here bourgeois I found out from Suzanne means family-style. Home-style – pot luck. We know them. They can't like it. It's fun for them like going to the fair; hamburgers and ice-cream. But when I go out to eat in Paris I want good food. Oh heck. We've moved miles away from anyone we used to know and like. Our standards were wrong! Juvenile. Like, if you're hep, you go and eat in a Jo's Diner, terrible food, hamburgers like chopped soles off the shoes of dead bums and drown it in sauce and coffee, like water the bum was found in, shoes and all. Oh, my! Stephen. They live here, they know Europe and they keep up these childhood games. The love-the-workers stance.'

'I only want to be home and sit down and begin to relax. I can't wait to get home. It pours all over me like a salve. I don't love the workers, or the friends of the workers, I just want to survive. I feel lousy.'

Upstairs was a letter from Anna saying that her visit was put off to just before Christmas and she would bring Fairfield then. The letter had been left with the porter by mistake. The courts, said the letter, after further applications, had decided that Olivia might be taken care of by her grandmother, since the Howards were living abroad. However, Grandma would leave Olivia where she was till she came over with Fairfield.

'Oh, zut, zut and double-zut! We're always on trial, always being put on our best behaviour. There's no peace in our life!' said Emily. 'Oh, how detestable the rich are, knowing their power and getting the bowstring ready and holding it over your head like a bowstring of Damocles.'

They had only been home a few minutes and were dolefully traducing their hosts and friends, when Emily had, noted down by Olivia, a telephone message from Violet Trefougar. She felt obliged to come and see the Howards that same evening. She knew they did not go to bed early and she needed them badly. Stephen said that he had had enough guilt for one evening, just looking across the table at Dan, and that Violet always made him feel guilty. Emily telephoned the Trefougars.

The maid said, 'I am afraid Madame is not very well,' but Violet sprang to the phone and cried, 'Oh, I am not well but I must come to see you.'

They heard her in fluent though foreign French speaking insolently to the maid; and then again to Emily: 'Oh, darling, if I don't come to see you this evening, I'm afraid I shall go out of my mind. I have to take a taxi because Johnny has gone off again – on one of those things, you know! – and taken the car.'

'You must stay with us tonight, Violet.'

'No, I can't because of the child.'

The Trefougars had just adopted a little boy of six, well-grown and beautiful, tall, straight, proud and amiable. Violet hoped that with him her life would change, her despair would cease.

'If I have any sanity left, Emily, it is because of this child; this little man has saved my life.'

Emily put down the phone and burst into tears. 'And we have just heard that we are losing Olivia: and we have lost Christy.'

'I told that little hound to wait here to look after you. But he turned his back on you like the others. He is very good at turning his back on people and always with a righteous reason, the dog. I hate hypocrites.'

'Oh, Stephen, we didn't like those people tonight, did we? What is happening to us? We are alone.'

Stephen's eyes were wet, too.

They waited impatiently for Violet. She came, beautifully dressed in a Worth dress, blue, simple. She was excited and nervous beyond anything they had yet seen in her.

'Oh, my dears, I'm so frightened, troubled, I live in fear! How good to have you to run to!'

They felt guilty, more touched than before, because since the Belgian trip they had been condemning her for her hysteria. During the past weeks, unknown to Stephen, Emily had become not only friendly but something of a crony. She understood Violet better and feared her.

Suzanne had said, 'She's just a selfish beast,' and Stephen, 'She's intolerable, I'm sorry for Johnny, I'd smack her.'

And during the past six weeks, Stephen had come to know Trefougar better and to fear him. They both now wondered, each privately, whether Violet's upset, her vice, had arisen from the welter of threatened violence, suicide, murder, other crimes, dirty companions and perverted sex and whether she had not for years shown, as Emily claimed, 'Dignity, astonishing perfection of manner, decency and remarkable self-control.' The story of the adopted child had altered their feelings towards her.

Violet was saying she thought of them so much. She secretly agreed with them in many things. It was Johnny who was a brutal fascist. She was for making compromises, even making amends to the East.

'We've treated them too long as if they were brutes, pigs, farm animals, without understanding, and frightful monsters. When the real brutes were the Germans, whom we admired so long for their culture.'

She brought all this in before she began on her own troubles, which were of the same sort as before. Johnny had no sooner returned than he had gone off. He had come home, quarrelled with her, given her no money, gone off. The little boy had been there, seen all, listened to everything innocently, and tried to console her when Johnny, now called his father, had gone.

'The child seemed to understand everything, though of course, that's impossible. Without him I should have killed myself yesterday.'

She had sacrificed her personal life and dignity for long years, she said, for Johnny's sake and now she had decided to do so again for the charming boy; but it was hard. She had no one to call upon.

'Either they believe Johnny's lies, or they're in with him, in whatever traffic he carries on, or they just can't be bothered taking my side; easier not to. Besides, it's a male society. Women are just part of the luggage. When I weather this, I'll be all right. Only now I need intelligent sympathy.'

360

She asked their bedtime, would only stay till then, went through the house with them, went to the kitchen where she was always happy she said, drank coffee, went with Emily to Christy's rooms, where some of his things still were, waiting for removals. Emily wept and clung to her.

'I feel for you so deeply about this little boy of yours.'

Giles hearing all the movement, got up and came down to see them in his bunnyhug pyjamas.

Violet was still talking of the mistakes Johnny had made in his diplomatic career; in a way, he was right; but she did not believe in him or in the general British policy. If they never met and were never friendly with the communists, how would they ever know their plans, come at them?

'Johnny says we know enough about them. Our job is to be lined up against them. My feelings are that they're right on some points. I'm a bit of a communist.'

Giles, who was drinking warm milk, declared suddenly, 'I'm not. Communists are Jews and I don't like Jews either. No one in our school likes Jews.'

Giles was now a brown-faced, chubby and amiable boy of seven, alert, witty.

Violet hugged him, 'Little precious infant!'

He let her hug him, ate and watched them wisely, smiling a little.

His father asked, 'What's this? You're an American. America is a democracy. We don't believe in fascism. We don't hate Jews or Negroes or Mexicans or even little boys who are too big for their pants.'

Giles grinned, 'Yes, but Daddy, the boys at school aren't Americans, they're French, one's Greek, one's Swiss, one's Italian, one's English and they all come from democracies, except the British and they don't like communists. Communists aren't democratic. Louis's father said so.'

'Who's that, Louis's father?'

'Louis is a Greek. His father's a Greek. The communists want to take away his house and his business. That's robbery. And Louis says I'm an American, an American believes in democracy; and Louis says the Americans are helping his father. So they can't be communists.'

Emily laughed and opened her mouth. Stephen said, hesitating, 'Yes, no doubt the Americans are helping his father because his father is rich.'

Giles said seriously, helping himself to a slice of apple pie, 'And because his father has a factory and we have a factory, I told him. I told him you are a communist, but he doesn't believe me. He says, no Americans are communists.'

'Well, you know Axel and Ruth and Bundy and Mike and a lot more of our friends are communists, and they're Americans.'

361

Giles said, 'Oh, they're poor. I mean rich Americans like us, who have factories and houses and automobiles.'

Stephen said testily, 'We don't have a factory, we don't have a house and at the moment we haven't even an automobile. And in America every hill-billy has an automobile and every communist, too.'

'But we have a factory. I told him we had a lot of them.'

'Well, you will have to tell him differently. Because we don't have one, not one,' said Emily energetically.

Giles stopped chewing and looked at her severely, 'Not one?'

'Have you ever seen a factory we owned?'

'No, but I know – Grandma and Grandpa and Grandma Wilkes – a lot of people and Uncle Cha in England and Aunt Dunbar Melton in England – they all have; and I know in Alexandria we have. I told Akim, we have factories in Alexandria.'

Emily said, 'Well, we don't. Other people do but we don't. And that's why we're the other side of the fence. We're communists.'

'But why? Akim and Louis and Gilbert and Giorgi, the Bulgarian boy and the others, they are all against communists, everyone in the school and they say I must be too because we have factories. They said so.'

'I can see their point of view all right, very rational,' said Stephen smiling.

'And they say I have to be on their side because if the Americans don't stand with them, there's going to be hell to pay.'

'Eh? What's that?' said Stephen.

'The whole world would go to the devil. *Ils ont raison*, they're right. Because they say if I were a communist I'd try to rob their factories and I said I wouldn't, so they said I couldn't be a communist. I said I'd fight them if they said my father would try to rob their factories.'

Stephen sighed, 'Oh, I wish I could. Never mind, their point of view is crystal clear. You boys have interesting talks for toddlers.'

'Pedro says he isn't worried because his father's factories are all in South America and at present South America is lined up with the United States; but there are communists everywhere trying to take their factories; and you never can tell, we all have to stand together.'

Stephen said, 'Well, that's a solidarity that's quite touching; and I only wish we were as solid ourselves. That's pretty good. Only Giles, we have to be solid on the other side, because we're the have-nots, have-not factories, have-not rich villas, have-not yachts, et cetera. We're on the outs and so we have to side with the workers.'

'Why?'

'Because we are workers.'

Giles studied them, baffled and anxious: 'But we aren't workers! We don't work!'

'That's cool from my own son. Come, when you grow up, Giles, you're going to work, aren't you?'

'No. I'm going to have a factory and two automobiles like Eduardo and Louis, and race-horses. We are all going to whip the workers, just like they used to do in the olden days. It is the only way to make them work.'

Stephen sprang up, 'Well, for Christ's sake. What sort of a den of thieves have we led him into? He's coming away tomorrow morning. I'm not going to support at this rate a seven-year-old fascist and peon-whipper. I'll go and see the headmaster in the morning.'

Violet asked, 'What do you expect him to think? He's only a baby. I think it's interesting to hear what they say. I think we don't pay enough attention to the other side.'

Emily murmured, 'You're right. But just the same, Vee, we pay good money for the boy to be taught, not distorted. Bad joke.'

Stephen said to Giles, 'When you grow up, my pretty child, you'll have to work; just like Giorgi and Louis, Pedro, Eduardo and whoever they are. They have a big surprise coming to them.'

'Eduardo says he will never work; he will kill every worker with his own hand first; and Gilbert is going into the Foreign Office and Louis says he is going to play along with the Americans and we all should.'

'They certainly teach a lot and fast at that school,' said Stephen.

Emily and Stephen, especially Emily, spent the next twenty minutes telling the boy what he should think and say, and explaining work and the worker to him. Giles replied, 'But it wouldn't be fair taking away Alessandro's race-horses, and automobiles and everything.'

'A new personage, who is Alessandro?' said Emily.

'A Greek boy. It's wrong. It makes him mad. It makes me mad too. Besides, I already told them about Grandma and Fairfield and everything.'

Violet said, 'Poor child. Oh, it is confusing. I shouldn't know what on earth to answer a child. Parenthood is fascinating, dangerous of course, but it makes you think. I'm glad I have a child now.'

Stephen yawned and stretched, 'Well, do what you like. I leave it to you, my boy. I don't go with those boys and I never did mix with such high-feathered birds. I don't want to preach communism in a place where they couldn't understand it. I don't want you to get into a mess for nothing. Just remember which side you're on. The side of the workers and the Soviet Union.'

'But Dr Thibault said and the teachers all say that Russia is making war against the whole world and is stirring up France and making France poor.'

'Some school. You know that's a lie, Giles,' said his mother.

'Well, I don't see how Russia is on the side of the workers and on my side. I think it looks as if everyone is against us.'

'How true! But why are your little boyfriends, Giorgi and Alessandro and Louis and so on so very scared, eh? Why are the pants scared off them, so they're worried night and day about losing their race-horses? Eh? They're scared, aren't they?'

Giles burst out laughing, 'Well, yes, they're scared, they're certainly scared. Haw-haw. Oh, boy! Are they scared!'

'They're scared our side is going to win. And it is.'

'Say, Daddy, when all the factories are taken away from them, I don't suppose we could get a factory, eh? I know how to drive an automobile already, so maybe I could get one to drive.'

They burst into a babel of talk, laughing and commenting on the opportunism of children. But Giles was thoughtful, his eyes on the wall. 'Well, I wish I knew who would win. If I knew, I'd know what to do.'

'He'll survive; even in the dark ages.'

'I wish I knew what to do,' said Stephen.

'He's a dream baby,' said Emily, leading him off to bed.

'He's very thoughtful,' said Violet.

19   THE STRUGGLE FOR CHRISTY

Emily had written to Christy's family, Grandma, Maurice and even to Florence in her exaggerated humble tone, that Christy, in spite of all her efforts, was hopeless at his studies.

'He could not even be a steam-fitter, whatever that is.' She had given Christy into the care of Suzanne and two tutors but even now he was thinking of going to Munich to music festivals, with girls; he did not care at all about studies. She had written these letters when he left her, in suffering, though she let her pain appear as disparagement and blame.

Two days after he returned, Stephen received from his mother a letter referring distantly to *letters received*, and saying, that it was evident that Stephen and Emily were not fit to bring up Christy; they had themselves retired. He was a sensitive, unusual boy who needed special understanding and that if his water-colours were at present poor and did not fit him for entry to the Beaux-Arts it was because he had been forced furiously and without intelligence. Christy was the kind that grows slowly and solidly. Anna had long been sure that a boy with the loving, delicate and thoughtful nature of Christy could not thrive in 'that domestic climate'; they were unsuitable as guardians and Anna intended to provide him with a setting of repose, calm and dignity, 'above all quiet'.

Stephen read this letter at breakfast and, beside himself, shouted out, 'What letters are these? What have you written, you goddam drivelling idiot? Losing me a boy I've worked for for years.'

Emily shut the door on Stephen, but she was overwhelmed. She wrote a note to Violet and asked the porter to take a taxi and deliver it to the Trefougars.

'Cold winds blast the miserable house, horror whines in the rooms, the servants are trembling, they listen, rejoicing, I am sure, and yet frightened, and they keep to the basement and my whole life is going to pieces. Stephen does not love me, but Christy and Christy's family. I am nothing. He would throw me into the street today for Christy's money.'

In the afternoon, Violet came to see her, and Stephen, haggard, sick, had to greet her with an almost suffocated courtesy and let her go up to

365

Emily. Violet imagined that Emily was out of the cordial sustaining drugs that kept her working and cheerful, and she had brought some of her own. 'I was on to Dr Kley; I will get some for you, and bring them to you tomorrow. I know how it is. Not a word!' She kissed her and went, talking genteelly to Stephen on the way out. The next day she came again, with drugs from Dr Kley for which she had paid, Emily having money difficulties at that moment with Stephen in the house; and soon she left again.

When she had gone Emily took as much of the drug as she thought would give her a long sleep or even carry her over the border into death. One of the servants found her, and called Suzanne, Stephen being absent; Suzanne came, brought a doctor and between them they brought her round.

'Don't tell him, don't tell,' she begged; Suzanne promised not to tell and went downstairs urging the doctor to be silent.

'Have you any more of that?' the doctor asked her.

'Oh, no, I get it from a friend and that is the last. I meant to end it all and so I took all I had,' she said; though she had more.

She struggled downstairs and only just in time, for Stephen was crossing the courtyard. On the console table where they put the letters, Emily found another letter to Stephen from his mother about Christy. She tore it open, skimmed it. The short letter consisted only of reproaches and threats:

'You took the child from us but only to torture him, make him a spy and an unintelligent person. You complain of his letters to me; but you have made him what he is. He can't go to you, he is afraid of Emily, he says so, and so he must write to me. Who else can he go to? I shall see to it that you have no more to do with him. He is too important as a person to be twisted in this way. I am quite satisfied however with his present living conditions. When I come over in December, I will see what I want to do with him; but I am extremely displeased with you, I am in fact angry. I see that you can never keep your word but let all kinds of selfish and outside interests interfere with the boy's good development and happiness. I have decided against bringing Fairfield with me in December, since it is most likely that I will take Christy back with me to the States when I go in January.'

Emily, worn out by her illness and these evil letters, took to her bed. She would lie in bed for an hour or so, but then get up and go to her typewriter, where once more she worked on a story she thought would sell, on outlines and on what she now called 'the Marie-Antoinette book'; though she was still only lining it up to present to Stephen, to get his opinion. In between hours of cruel battle and insult, shouts and yells,

366

the two would sit down and discuss their moneymaking plans, in writing.

Emily had to give Stephen the letter from his mother. She explained that she had opened it because of her anxiety and she mourned bitterly, 'How can anyone say such dreadful things, such lies? Anna doesn't mean to lie. I never knew her to lie, but those are lies. I love the boy. I never did anything for my own interest, only for his. He's as much to me as Giles. I have awful thoughts about him, about us, Stephen. I am so unhappy. You know I am not a weeper and wailer and gnasher; but I have never known such cruel unhappiness as now. Every letter we get, every visitor even, every telephone call is black, miserable, negative; each one seems to spell doom. I sometimes feel I should never have taken the child of another woman. I feel as if they are right to reproach me. Yes, I didn't tell, but I often felt that. I did it for you, too. But I was not sure it was right. My God! But out of my love for Christy and you I struggled against it. I do understand Christy; they're wrong. I've brooded over him and worked till the sweat poured down all over me, like a showerbath, worrying and helping him and teaching him – don't you believe I love him, don't they? No, they all think and you think too that it's sordid, venal; it's only greed. But I love him. I know very well he's not like others, he's different from us, perhaps like you, but sensitive, another rate of growth, another sensibility; strange, and beautiful, all the corruption and innocence that makes adolescence so fascinating and makes us long for our lost corruption. We are too dull and formalist. Just at this difficult time, they are going to take him back again. He'll never learn anything now. He'll always be a half-grown boy, never quite out of his shell. Oh, Stephen, I wonder if you understand the child-man he is, the strange unique thing, a true individual. If I could tell you what I feel about him – it's almost poetry, because I see the child in the man, and what an exquisite creature of fable that is, more than a thing half-goat and half-man. If you were to know the truth, Stephen. If you could understand my deep passionate love for Christy, you would talk to your mother and convince her that Christy never could have a more tender, devoted mother than I am. And I know how to shed the mother for the sister, and friend.'

'That's just talk. What I know is that Christy has gone and $500 monthly has marched out of the house with him.'

Blue papers began to come in, bills, debts, summonses. Stephen went over the accounts with Emily. Repairs, cleaning, laundry were not done at home; most of their personal and house linen was too fine to send to an ordinary laundry and had to go to specialists who did fine work. Emily had lent $200 to Violet, she said, and sent $1,000 to some communist friends in New York who feared investigations and were about to quit the country for Mexico. Thus she explained the calls on their bank account. In reality the money had gone to Dr Kley.

'It's little enough, and it salves a little of our consciences,' she said firmly, when Stephen stared at her angrily.

They had to put aside $1,000 for Anna's visit; and everything had to be thoroughly gone into and set right if possible, for Anna had threatened to investigate their situation. She had never pressed them about the extra quarter's allowance she had given them on their departure.

'But that is the last, the very last cent you will ever see out of her. She'd come and visit us in debtors' prison, look through the bars and push the scene away into her thinking cap, for future reference; that's all she'd do. She can't understand animals like us. To her we are not human.'

Emily went to work again, struggling against her illness, despair and vice, her loneliness and Stephen's insults. She always felt she could make money; but he was beginning to lose faith in her. At present he refused to even consider the Marie-Antoinette project.

'I have no time to do the research. It has to have something original and it would take too much consultation now. I have to get a job. If I am working when Anna comes, I can face her, point at my prospects.'

But though he tried and consulted all his friends, what could he do? He was not a toughened journalist, with hard work behind him and a name. Someone held out hopes of a job in Eastern Germany; but he thought that with this his passport would be cancelled; and he would be in his nightmare, 'the man without a country.' He refused to consider a Marshall Plan job.

'No cold war job! I won't go on record as working against the Soviet Union. They'll be indicting me as a spy next.'

All this time in their own country the political investigation, the so-called 'witch-hunting' was getting worse, they had no hope of returning there, unless willing to face investigation; and at the same time through their madcap life and wild talk they were alienating foreign communists; indeed now that they looked back at their life in Paris they groaned and saw that the communist party had taken no interest in them; that only Vittorio, and Wauters, and Suzanne, a few good-natured Resistants had taken them up.

Stephen said in a fit of despair, 'We used to be intimate with Browder and Company and here we have not once been invited to meet Jacques Duclos. We're out of it. They've humiliated us. I have no luck. I've had no luck since I came abroad. I've written to the heads of all the European Parties offering my services. I received one or two cold answers, mostly none. Perhaps some of the letters were opened or did not get there. But no man was ever in a more miserable situation. And they're right. What

368

can I do? I'm not a worker. I can't work with workers. At what? They don't want me. There are enough of them. They wouldn't know what to do with me if I went crawling on my hands and knees, salt water pouring from my eyes. I don't speak their kind of English or American or French or anything. I can't think like them. Their sufferings upset me and I can't do anything about it. I don't really believe that if I see five people starving to death on a minimum salary in one room in a slum in the suburbs that I can do anything now or ever by writing a squib about housing. That cuts me out. I'm on the sidelines. The question is what can I do on the sidelines? For us it's just spectactor sports, the whole damn social idea.'

'We are being persecuted,' said Emily.

'Yes, we are being persecuted over here too. Some of our friends must have got in their jack-knives, via the mails.'

'Oh, how can we live through this life of madness and pain? We're on a desert island, everyone sees our flag of distress and everyone says, "Drop dead"', said Emily.

Emily, with her illness and her multifarious works, had not yet finished a *Mrs Middletown* book she was working on; and editors were slow to answer about work she had sent in.

'Our reputation's muddy, no one knows where we stand,' said Emily. 'They only want a letter from us.'

Stephen grumbled, 'You know I will not write that letter. Too bad. I will not say that I've given up, denied the Party. I always hear a voice saying, Before the cock crows, you will, Peter; and so I'm damned if they'll ever get me to. I'll starve first.'

'Oh, why are you so slow and unsure – what does it matter what you tell them? You are a brave and true man; I know it and you know it. It is for them, the blind and deaf and stupid, but the ones who give us bread. Before the slaves revolt haven't they the ideas that they revolt with? But when Massa says, "Are you a good man, Sammy?" Sammy says "Yes"; though tomorrow he's going into the house to get them.'

'I'm not a brave and true man; I'm a man in doubt and misery. And I'm not a slave. This epoch is full of suffering for us all. No one wants what I can do, the people don't want my services, my mother despises me and has taken my son from me. My life is in collapse. If I had any true and brave manhood, I'd cut my throat.'

'And leave me?'

'Oh, you'd get Vittorio or someone else.'

'Oh, Stephen – you don't love me. You're throwing me to the wolves. You're selfish. Like all melancholics you're a soul-murderer. You're killing my heart, my only hope.'

369

'And you're Tyl Eulenspiegel. You die today and get up fresh as paint tomorrow.'

'That's heartless. You're shuffling off your responsibility to me as a husband and friend. I've always said to myself that you were that, a friend. You're not. I'm dismally alone. My heart is howling.'

They had a savage scene; and they went to separate beds, the first time they had done so.

The next morning a packet arrived for Stephen, from his mother. In it he found a sheaf of letters written by Emily to various members of the family and sent on to Anna when she began asking for news of them. These letters revealed Emily's irresponsible prattling, robbing Peter to pay Paul in flattery, her insolent jeering at them all, her feelings for leftists and radicals wherever she went, apparently genuine, and their relations with communists and Resistants abroad. In some, to show Stephen's determination to get a job, she had even detailed his recent letters to 'heads of Parties'.

'Why did you tell them all that?' he said, terribly angry.

'I don't know Stephen, I wanted to show our good faith. Oh, I know it's a weakness; but I like to trust people. They're your people. Why should they do things like this to us?'

'You have brought all these misfortunes on me – Christy's going, Anna's anger. Why are our affairs of interest to everyone? Why can't you leave our miserable confusion and absurdity in a decent obscurity?'

'We are not private people. We never have been private people, even before we were married. We had made our way, separately, before that and after we were married, we never left the footlights. What we do is, unfortunately, of interest to too many people. Who but us left the Party in the headlines of the metropolitan press? Rather than be misrepresented I'd say what I think in a symbolic representational truth, I'll mislead them, I'll put it any way, or at any rate, what is suited to their understandings. We're not going down the drain for the Howards. Let them burst!'

'Yes, we lie to them. All right! But you have a different lie for each one and lined up in front of the footlights as you say, they make a motley collection of grinning death's-heads. And listen to what you have pushed into Anna's head. She thinks there's going to be a revolution here and that Christy, that very precious youth, must go to Switzerland where he can prepare for the Sorbonne; otherwise dear old tattered England, where they will prepare him for Oxford or Cambridge. . . .This comes of your buttering Anna and telling her what a genius Christy is. But we know, no matter what we say in public, that Christy is too far behind and that he is too mediocre ever to get into any of the brain-shops. We must stick to the idea that the best and surest place for him is the Sorbonne. I think it's a dream; but we must stick to it. Christy's the dream-boy of the Howards. We must play this carefully. More – Anna is going to call the tutors and Suzanne together when she comes here and find out what Christy has done.'

'Oh, Jehosaphat!' said Emily, startled.

'We'll immediately call the tutors and Suzanne in secret conclave. You talk to Suzanne and get them together as soon as you can. We must tell them not to discourage the dope, too. Otherwise that will be in the next mail to Anna.'

That day lessons were cancelled for Christy and there came to the house, Suzanne, Monsieur Jean-Claude, who taught Latin and ancient history, and Monsieur Laroche who taught mathematics. Suzanne interpreted and Stephen and Emily put the questions.

Emily said, 'Monsieur Laroche, you know that your pessimistic and unfair report on Christy a few months ago upset us so much that we were obliged to report to his grandmother, who had just arrived in Paris to see to his studies. I am sure you have changed your mind by this.'

Stephen said, 'We want to know how far the boy has got. What grade is he in compared with a French boy of his age?'

Monsieur Laroche said, 'It is no use disguising the truth. The boy is too far behind to catch up and his brain is not active enough to catch up even if he had seven more years to study.'

Emily said firmly, 'I don't believe this, I refuse to. The boy is different from you and me, a special, delicate, sensitive intellect. I know how to teach him, but although I can study hard, he has already got ahead of me in Latin. He can work hard, but he is dreamy, he must be forced; and as he has an excellent, yes, superb, a remarkable memory, he must learn it all by heart, every word of grammar and the textbooks entirely by heart.'

Monsieur Jean-Claude said, 'Even if that were possible and I don't see that it is, there are the other things; ancient history, the commentaries and things that can't be learned by heart, the writing of original poetry, themes, unexpected pieces of translation, unexpected constructions. You know he must make a speech in Latin.'

Emily cried, 'How stupid, how old-fashioned! There must be some way of getting past, for boys who can't make speeches.'

'No more than you can pass a swimming examination without swimming.'

'Oh, pouah! I know someone who hired a boy to do his swimming for him; and we can hire someone here. There must be a way and we will find it. You see, Jean-Claude and Monsieur Laroche, this is enormously important to us, to his father, to me. We will explain the situation. We

371

love this boy dearly, we have studied him from the very hour we got him. We understand his genius. We know the kind of patient and loving care he needs. He was taken from an unworthy mother – '

'Emily!' said Stephen.

'It is so. A woman who raised her son in licentious scenes, sex and liquor, and the boy was given to us by a court. But the boy will be a multimillionaire and there is still obscene wrangling going on in spite of the court order. A woman who left her husband – '

'No, no, cut it out,' said Stephen.

'Now his grandmother wants to take the boy from you, Monsieur Laroche and Jean-Claude, and from us and send him to his cold, frigid, unkind relatives in England, who are backward and eat out of trenchers, sardines and rice pudding all in one trencher, or send him to Switzerland which is out of this world, no place for a modern youth to grow up. My husband agrees with me, don't you, Stephen?'

Stephen said, 'God help any foreign boy raised there. They may as well live in Mars. They live in constant terror of being at war, avoiding war and yet with the one idea of profiting by war. Now I infinitely prefer my adopted son to live in France, have French sympathies, not only because I admire the French, a great, passionate and learned people, but because later on he can easily get a job in the State Department; and God knows, I want Christy to have a job, not like me. He has radical views like mine – '

'Well, he is only a child, but we want him to be that kind of man, like his father,' said Emily.

'His views are mine exactly, only he has no theory and what worries me more than anything else is that if Christy goes to a fashionable school either in England or Switzerland they will knock all that out of him like Giles and you know the boy's a goddamn fool – '

'He is not, Stephen. He's brilliant.'

'I don't fool myself, Monsieur Jean-Claude, I know you don't. The boy has no political brains. You know better than I whether he has any other sort. Let's hope so. Otherwise, it's a dull outlook for us all. He has one argument for him I beg you to bear in mind, and that is the American system of education, their laxity, hatred of the brain and belief in rambling ignorance, their belief that genuine learning distorts the personality.'

Monsieur Laroche said, 'I do bear that in mind. I understood that at once. But now I have been with him for over a year and it is not only his mathematics which are non-existent – '

'Oh, Monsieur Laroche, he is quick and intuitive in mathematics; it is really astonishing how he sees things better than I do,' said Emily.

'No, Madame, giving him all the credit possible, he cares about

372

nothing but politics; that is the only thing that arouses interest in him and in which he shows a normally good heart, the passions of a boy. But I do not think he has any mind of his own. He can reason quite well for a sentence or two on this subject, he has some experience; and then in the fourth sentence he can reverse his position completely, once more parroting members of the other part of the family. He has an extraordinary, admirable respect and admiration for all members of his family, though particularly for Madame and Monsieur Howard and his brother and sister here, in a manner of speaking. He has not a wonderful memory, Madame, but a fragmentary, superficial, transient memory. He can remember next day, perhaps for a week, not longer, what he has learned by heart. He will eventually perhaps get through some course or other at the Sorbonne, if he has tutors always with him. I don't know why he must go to the Sorbonne. All this money is in a way wasted. There are many worthy lads of talent, even of more than talent, who need to go to the Sorbonne, boys sick and hungry, who are refused at their examinations in spite of their talent or genius because they have not even the money to buy books and there are not enough books in the library to serve all the needy students. I would gladly undertake the tutoring of any one of these boys if I could. If your idea was to help an unfortunate deserving student, I should be delighted, the work itself would be a pleasure – '

Emily looked at him furiously. She rang the bell. Marie-Jo, the maid, appeared and she called out, 'Bring in some wine, Marie-Jo, we're dry! And some sherry and port. And some sandwiches!'

Then she turned and said imperiously, 'Monsieur Laroche, I am interested in Christy. I don't give two cents for those sick students! Let them die! I care about nothing that is not mine and that I don't see and hear and touch and love! I hate those sick students. What's it to me if they don't get into the Sorbonne? To hell with them. I don't want to hear about them. They don't exist for me.'

Monsieur Laroche looked angry. 'Very well. However, I ventured to say that because last week Madame was talking about the students' misery. The bitter misery, the struggle you said. And frankly, Monsieur Christy is not worth my time and trouble.'

She exclaimed, 'How can you say that about a child? You know it will ruin his life if he doesn't go to the Sorbonne. His grandmother will say we have wasted his time, allowed him to waste his money and spoiled him for life in the USA. He must go to the Sorbonne. He must. He will have nothing to live for: he is so eager, so anxious, he dreams of being a student there.'

'To me he seems quite apathetic about it. What he talks about is politics and young company and I think he loves the communist party because there he has young company and the only friends he ever had.'

'Monsieur Laroche, you are not fit to teach children. You don't understand them.'

Stephen said, 'Emily! Monsieur Laroche, excuse my wife; she is very concerned about Christy. My wife has a very warm heart. I had better be plainer. In the first place I do understand Christy because he is like I was. I did not develop until I was about twenty-six, mentally I went through college in a fog with the aid of tutors and hard study just like Christy; nothing stuck to me. About twenty-six I woke up and I have been awake ever since, though I'm no bright star. My father naturally thought I was a goddamn idiot and washed his hands of me; and my mother always hated me, she saw I was some kind of sport. Now my mother does not see that Christy is just like me, she sees him through a granny's rose-coloured spectacles. We want Christy to stay here because we think our affection and understanding will help him to wake up sooner. We want you to help us, not to yield to your disappointment and boredom with Christy, but to help us to keep him. Tell his grandmother all the truth, but make it palatable to a doting grandmother. I want Christy by me because I want him to be a son to me later on. I'm going to need friends. We had hard luck coming here and settling in this country, but things look brighter now and I hope soon to get settled in a paying business – '

Emily looked at him in astonishment and smiled slightly.

' – which will enable me to help him. His real mother has complained about his large expenses and I am inclined to agree with her. His grandmother cannot do anything without consulting two prime parties; Christy himself, since he is in control of some of his money now, and ourselves, his legal guardians. Now, if you will help us, we will retain complete control of Christy until he has gone through the Sorbonne. You see that this will considerably lengthen his stay with us, especially if he is abnormally slow. That is what we require. For Christy is legally of age at twenty-one, but he does not come into the bulk of his estate until he is twenty-five. That is our aim: to keep him under our protection until then. You see, he has a prolonged youth: he has all the time necessary. If you will only be patient with an exceptional case, I shall be very grateful to you.'

Monsieur Laroche said, 'I understand quite well. You know it has helped me to have this pupil and I don't want to lose him either. But how can I avoid telling his grandmother the truth? It's a question of professional delicacy and self-respect.'

'And what do you think, Jean-Claude?' asked Emily suddenly of the Latin tutor.

'I think Christy will pick up and eventually make normal progress. He has promise,' said Monsieur Jean-Claude. He was a blond man with mobile lips and a sunny smile round the centre of his face. He admired Emily sincerely, for her books, her establishment, her energy. He had once said, 'I wish only that I had you to teach, instead of the boy. And if I were not a teacher, I should like to spend my life at your feet, listening and drinking in your rollicking genius.'

Emily now wore an air of triumph. 'I drink to you Jean-Claude,' she said, throwing back her head and drinking off a full glass of sherry.

Monsieur Laroche sipped his sherry. He shrugged slightly, looking at Suzanne, 'I need the money of course; and I am here to work. But it's the weariness of it, the hopeless toil.'

'Christy has a good ear, he is making progress in French,' said Suzanne.

'Ah, boys, will be boys. He means well,' said Jean-Claude.

Suzanne looked at the two tutors and said, 'I think we all understand about Christy. But Christy is really happy here. I am sure French influence is going to form him for the better. It would be a shame to see him torn from his two adoptive parents here, who love him dearly and make him feel at home in the world. Besides Monsieur Laroche, what difference does it make? We must not be prejudiced against the rich. One child is as good as another, even a rich boy has rights. Must Christy be neglected, cast off just because of his money? So many people will reproach him with it in later life. It will always be cast up at him. Let's be fair to him now. For he will suffer for it later on. His political views are a great comfort for him, a shield. A boy as tender-minded as this would otherwise feel that he was hated and despised; an unhealthy state of mind. It is not his fault, but it will always be held to be his fault. Let's help the boy.'

'That's right! Soften him up, so that some day he'll be some use to someone,' said Stephen, smiling.

Emily said, 'None of us here loves the rich, but Christy is a human being, think of what that means, a loving, suffering human being! He needs care, he needs understanding. Our whole generation is busy thinking about the poor, every damned writer in the proletarian novel period, which is now passing, thank God, spent his time jumping on the rich, muckraking, scandalmongering, showing them as monsters and spiders and vampires, forgetting that there can be rich boys hungry for love and understanding whose career can be ruined too if they don't make the grade. To be rich, and thought of as stupid, in our epoch especially! Think of it, Monsieur Laroche.'

Monsieur Laroche could not help smiling, 'Well, that is true. Christy is a charming boy, affectionate, anxious to work and I have no fault to find with his character. My English is poor. I should not like people to think me backward because of that; but in England they might.'

375

He gave Emily a melting smile. He was a dark, thin-faced man, seemed the pedant, but had very lively expressions.

Emily pressed forward, 'Surely, Monsieur Laroche, a backward boy is as interesting as a tubercular boy? Both have a failing. Why should the picturesque one, the melodramatic one, interest you more than the fate of an honest, hard-working, unloved lad who had a miserable childhood? It isn't reasonable. It's romantic rubbish. I'm impatient with the view that sees the rich as ogres, rogues, instead of realizing that most of them are good fathers, mothers, children and grandmothers, devoted to each other and leading decent lives. And if they are hated for being rich, it is their misfortune more than – my God, who among us does not like to succeed? Can you blame those who were born to success? Born with another twist, Monsieur Laroche, you could have been a rich man, a very rich man – you're top of your particular line! Why blame the others? I'm a well-known writer, some call me famous – my husband's a famous journalist – are we all criminals, rogues, to be hated and guillotined, when a guillotine stands in the place de la Concorde? Are we rascals and vampires? Or do we love each other and help each other? I don't understand your old-fashioned prejudices, it sounds like the beginning of the century and the long-dead muckraking epoch to me. The century was young, hah! We must leave a boy ignorant and lonely, jump on him with both feet and say, "Let's educate some boy in rags. This boy isn't worth my honourable and self-respecting attention because he's rich!" But you are at the top of your profession, Monsieur Laroche, and that means it is only the rich you can serve.'

Monsieur Laroche looked pained, but Jean-Claude kept laughing, 'Oh, it's so amusing; you are really wonderful!'

Emily seemed to dilate. She smiled, her eyes shone, she flushed and for at least three-quarters of an hour she continued to exhort the harassed, gloomy, restless, nauseated and, at length, depressed and exhausted Monsieur Laroche.

Stephen, with his feet crossed on the sofa, listened with varying expressions, but did not intervene.

At last, 'Emily! You've said enough! I see Monsieur Laroche's position very well. To hell with Stephen Howard and Christy Howard and all the Howards on the primrose path. I feel ashamed of course of seeing all this money spent on one boy. Monsieur Laroche, I promise that if Grandmother leaves the boy here – that is to say, she has not the actual authority but she can use pressure I would rather not see – if that happens I will help at least one of your needy students, out of compassion. I do sympathize and I feel as you do. I wish I could help a thousand. I hope the day will come when I can, or Christy can. This is another thing to think

376

of. Christy is the kind of clay that can be pressed into shape. Perhaps if Christy works side by side with a brilliant needy student, he will remember it all his life, become his friend and remain a radical forever. Do you know how I became a radical? One of my tutors at college was a boy in my own class, who was a needy student but very brilliant – he was ahead of the professors in my opinion – a Jew of course. I wish I were a Jew, sometimes. It would be useful to have a brain that worked.'

Emily burst out, 'Stephen, how can we keep students? That's nonsense. Who's going to pay for these tramps? I'm not. Is Christy going to pay for him? Grandma would never allow it and I wouldn't either. You – not unless you win the lottery again – '

'I'll find a way,' said Stephen.

'I hate it. It's a stupid idea. What have we to do with ragged, sick tramps? These things are social. We help one student and five hundred die! You know charity cannot solve the social situation. I won't have it. I want to help Christy, whom I love, and no one else. I'd hate to have that unwashed, dirty student around with lice in his hair and with a straggling beard and pale cheeks – then I'd have to feed him too, I couldn't look at him starving, then I couldn't stand his thin, dirty clothes, that means we'd have to give him Christy's old clothes – oh, pouah! I couldn't look at him. I know the sort. They saunter around the streets with a piece of bread stuffed in one cheek and you can smell them and their shoes are falling off their feet. And he's to come here or go to Suzanne's. Nothing doing.'

Monsieur Jean-Claude said demurely, 'Christy is a boy and not a social situation, I agree. However if we can help a student, let us do so; he is also one and not a social situation. But this will take some looking into.'

Monsieur Laroche said sombrely, 'I have one ready. But I don't insist on that one.'

Stephen said cheerfully, 'We have agreed upon a troublesome thing like Christy's reports; we will agree, all five of us, on the student, poor fellow – '

'I hate it, I won't have it. I want mine and only mine,' said Emily.

They had some food and drinks, and when the tutors were going, Stephen said to them,

'Well, you do think it is the best thing to tell my mother, who is just a silly old woman worried about her grandson, the usual thing: that her grandson is getting along as well as can be expected and you have hopes for him: that he works hard.'

Monsieur Laroche promised. Emily said, 'Oh, Grandma is really a lovable woman, she is gentle, timid, upright, so honourable, so anxious. You need not worry, she will believe every word you say.'

Monsieur Laroche said, 'I am really embarrassed. But I'll do this – if one student is bad, the other student is very good; and I feel happy – because you help the student. Very well, I will work harder with Monsieur Christy because you help the student. Merci Madame.' He took Emily's hand and kissed it, and when he straightened up, she saw there were tears in his eyes.

When they had gone, and they were left with Suzanne, Emily expressed her disgust at the idea of the indigent student. 'I don't want anyone else. I have enough with Christy and Giles. I hate the others. I could not see you, Suzanne, and Jean-Claude and Monsieur Laroche bustling about this homespun Yahoo. If their parents can't take care of them, too bad. Why can't they get scholarships? That's a noble thought you had, Stephen. To stick us with this clodhopper genius. If he weren't a servile, fawning toady, he wouldn't accept. He must have been crying on the shoulder of Monsieur Laroche. How do you know it isn't the boyfriend? Yeah, a fine note. When we're broke already, not a cent after the Christmas set-up and when dear Anna leaves, and you make all kinds of crazy promises. I despise scholarship people and helped people and all sorts of hangers-on. Christy's bad enough, now he's got his own money, he doesn't even get his shoes soled. You don't suppose he's going to pay for the student? My God! And this stinking, mendicant cap-in-hand with this surly domestic of ours, this vassal, Laroche, the two of them will set to it, you'll see, to snatch from Christy and to give him ideas, the ideas of the ankle-nipping and foot-licking underdog. And maybe tuberculosis too. And get him into riots in the streets! What will Grandma think of that? And maybe also show him up – show Christy for what he really is, a fizzle, a booby, an idiot who can't add two and two, just what we've been trying to keep from him – pouah! Why did you do it? I don't care what you did when you were a mollycoddle at Princeton. Christy hasn't your brains.'

Suzanne was astonished. 'But then you really think him stupid?'

'Yes, I do, Suzanne. I made my own way, wrote my own books, earned my own living, made $80,000 a year in Hollywood and never a tutor, not even a shoe-wiper or a floor-cleaner, but me serving sizzling fries and mile-long hot-dogs in the canteen when required. I despise the rich, make no mistake, all the cripples with gold crutches. The rich are only rich because they stole the feathers to feather their nest. Christy is a nitwit, a jerk, a drip, oh, what good does it do me to say so? What I really think of the farcical youngster, a runt of pedigree stock – well, it won't make me a cent to say it. If he were turned out of your apartment this evening, Suzanne, he wouldn't know how to make his breakfast, with all his knowing talk, oh, I laugh up my sleeve at him – but God, we need him. Maybe he'd become a fairy like Uncle Maurice, he's pretty enough – '

Stephen shouted, 'Emily, shut up! You're drunk; Uncle Maurice is not a fairy. He's a gentle bachelor. You're drunk.'

'I am not drunk, I hate our clan and their simmering and boiling about the offscourings of someone's left-sided – '

'Shut up!'

'But you don't want to help the student,' said Suzanne wondering and laughing somewhat.

Emily said coldly, 'That's something else. I'd rather poison him than help him. I'll do it, if he comes here with his thin cheeks and bony hands turning over Christy's textbooks. He's bothering my game. What will dear Anna think of woebegone apprentices with black nails and gutter-water running from their shoes, sitting with her Christy? My game is to hold Christy up as a paragon, the best thing in boyhood.'

'Oh, you Americans are so surprising, so hard to understand,' said Suzanne, rather affectionately.

Stephen said, 'Oh, we're savages and we're a new sort of hypocrite, the sort they had in England in the seventeenth century, and in Italy in the Renaissance. This is my game and to hell with you! I suppose we're a sort of savage Renaissance. I'd hate to think as Emily thinks, we're Rome to produce nothing new, no philosopher, no poet but an enamelled one, no economist – though plenty of economy; and to have to wait eleven hundred years for a Renaissance. It's depressing.'

Suzanne looked at them. 'It is funny the way you behave. I suppose your country is so rich it doesn't matter what you do?'

Emily said forcibly, 'That's it. And we've been struck by the god-damnedest thing in history. Just when we're getting our pinfeathers and beginning to fly around and dominate the world and becoming a demo-cratic monopolistic empire with every death-dealing weapon in the world, the world is sick of empires and monopolies and says, Down with empires and all that crap. And there we are, the young giant whose lightnings are burning a hole in his hand. Oh, I'm dying laughing at us; but it makes me sick, too. I feel so faint-hearted, when I think of it, all that power and gone wrong. It can't be? Rome didn't have a hundredth part of what we have. Surely not? Why don't we win? Why don't we burn up everyone else with the atom bomb? No one is able to understand. But something stands in our way! What is it? Destiny? A thousand years to the Mayas is an instant in our sight; the decline of the Roman Empire took so long, four or five hundred years and so many people were happy about it and money and reputations were made and no one knew anything about the decline – we can only see it now. I suppose some saw it and some of us see it. I can't bear it, to tell the truth. Why is it we have the historical eye on our own country? It's wrong. I want to love my country and believe in it and sleep happy and never think of ruin. We're the destroying force. Oh, why am I an intellectual where I must see what is wrong and be on the wrong side, for to see your country is wrong is to be on the wrong side. In other days in America there was only one side. But now there are two. In history where there are two sides and you see it, you are obliged to be on the wrong side, unless you're a cur. History is so long. Oh, God.'

She stuck her head in her hands.

Suzanne came over to her and took her hands from her face. 'What is it? I don't understand.'

Emily said, 'It's the struggle for Christy, I suppose. It's ignoble but it must be done. Why is my life tied up with these strange rich people? And they're mine. I'd be a booby to let them go. I won't. They don't feel what I feel. Stephen doesn't feel what I feel – the struggle. They're really his. If he's for the poor student, he's doing him a favour. But I belong to them and I'm famous, I'm a success, but whatever I do is wrong. I bear it all. Oh, I am lost, lost. I am fighting for the wrong things. Everyone will spit on my name, in the hereafter, if they remember it, if there is a hereafter.'

'What misery! Poor girl,' said Suzanne, looking at Stephen.

Said Stephen, 'I know. Goddamn it Emily, my darling heart, what can we do? Must we cut our throats? I'll do it. I'll give up Christy if it makes too much trouble for you. We can live simply, buy a cottage on the Côte d'Azure. I can work as a messenger boy. We'll give this up.'

'Oh, don't be annoying. You know we won't give up Christy. Would I give up Giles?'

'Well, then, you must not cry.'

After Suzanne had gone, they walked over the river to the Tuileries and walked up and down thinking about their future. If Grandmother was not convinced and Christy went to England, they would go to England, if to Switzerland, then they too, to Switzerland. They would not relinquish the boy.

The next morning, the tutors, as they had requested, sent them fair copies of the reports they intended to send to the grandmother in America. The reports were short.

Jean-Claude said that Christy was satisfactory, behind boys of his age in France but he was catching up. He had a good character, sound mind, excellent prospects, he worked hard, was not frivolous. He was impressed with his duties as a man of estate, kept proper accounts, was just, fair, courageous and warm-hearted. He seemed to be attached to all members of his family – an excellent boy preparing to be an excellent man. One drawback – he still could not compete with boys of his age abroad; but the tutor felt certain he would more than hold his own with boys of his age at home in America.

'A pity he said that,' said Emily.

Monsieur Laroche said that Christy was a very special student, a particular kind of student and he was willing to take great pains with him. With a satisfactory report from Suzanne, they sent off these two 'lightning conductors' to Anna; who, however, replied at once that these were evidently the real opinions of the tutors, and they were not like what Stephen and Emily had written in their letters. 'You are obviously unfair to Christy, you nag him, you don't try to understand the kind of child he is, not hard-boiled, coarse, outspoken, not the typical American child. You say you have struggled with him for years, but what such a sensitive, affectionate child wants is not struggle and family storms and scoldings but peace and love. You say in your letters that you made sacrifices for him; but I don't know which ones. His peace of mind has been ruined by your whims, travelling everywhere abroad, he has been left for weeks to himself and to strangers while you go sight-seeing, allowed to travel with foreign children he scarcely knows and even with communist youth groups. It shows what he's made of that he has stood up to it and is the fine boy his tutors say he is.'

Evidently Grandma had written to Christy too. When he came on his weekly visit to the rue de Varenne he was accompanied by a soft-haired, soft-formed, casual and derisive American girl of about seventeen; her name, Paula. Christy strolled in conceitedly, scarcely said good-day to Emily or Stephen, showed Paula his room and the rest of the house, evidently to impress her (his own quarters with Madame Suzanne were small) and proceeded to stroll out again.

'What are we, foreigners?' enquired Emily.

'I have a life of my own now,' said Christy.

'What are these solemn sulks?' cried Stephen.

'Christy's right. You give him no freedom. I want Christy to take me all round Paris. We have things to talk about. I found out Christy has no American friends. He has no fun at all.' So said Paula; and the two young ones left.

'That girl's an agitator; now we'll have riots and demands for weeks,' said Stephen, laughing.

'I think we should write to dear Anna, that it is time for Fairfield to come over. I'll tromp on her *cucaracha*,' said Emily.

Stephen said, 'Good idea. Christy can squire her round; but Christy won't go for any Fairfield. I know from my own youth.'

Emily then wrote to Grandma, 'We are longing to see Fairfield. Christy needs a companion of his own age, an American girl of the right background. Fairfield is a lovely child, she is so sweet and remote, far better than the usual twit of our present age and its disorders, I fear. At least she has this to say for her, she isn't a leader in campus riots, with long, dirty hair and wrinkled slacks. She's a clean, lovely, fine American girl with real values.' She read this far to Stephen and Suzanne and added, 'And more. Stephen, I'm going to write to Anna, for the struggle is too much for me, that we are not and cannot be communists or friends of such people. It's all over. If this be treason make the most of it.'

Stephen said, 'Ah, not communists – how can you say that?'

'Stephen, we are not and cannot be. Hasn't Anna shown that several times and isn't she right? Hasn't our trouble with Christy shown us that? And isn't it so? Didn't every howling parasite among our friends show us that? And it is so. Who cares for our purity? Ha!'

She laughed strongly, 'Stephen, I am going to write to Anna and when the letter is posted, I will feel spiritually free. They have not got a chain on me any more. I don't give a damn what they say. They lost me. I am free. I suffered too much. Even Vittorio, such a good man they say, made me suffer. He didn't even answer my last invitation! Who is he to crush me like that with contempt? It's the power of the Party. He is mightier than he is, because he represents the gods. Who can deal with such people? You can never be good enough for those who are messengers of the gods: who consider their presence, their words, an undeserved benediction. They lost me. I am free. I can think and write without being compelled by narrow petty mumbo-jumbo orthodox views and strait-jacket childish loyalties. Like the child who has to hit every railing with a stick, I had to hit every tenet of my faith with my pen when I wrote. Heigh-ho. Yes, Anna dear, I will say, you are as ever completely right. We cannot be communists any more and we must shun their dreary heartbreaking company. Fairfield is safe with us.'

She rang the bell. 'Will you have tea or a cocktail, Suzanne? I need something. I'll run upstairs and brush my hair. It's plastered to my forehead.'

When she was upstairs, Suzanne said, 'Do you feel the same, Stephen?'

'I realize some modification has taken place without my help in our position. We were thrown out. We can't either walk back or crawl back. We have been persecuted and neglected here in Europe and I've only been offered contemptible jobs, translator, night-clerk in a news agency. It was done no doubt after an initial bout of hesitation and after consultation with our enemies at home. We have been booted out. We have got over rubbing our bruises. We are out. It must be so. I don't put it

382

like Emily. I don't feel free. I feel sore. But I must live somehow. I don't know why exactly.'

Emily returned looking gayer and, indeed, bumptious. She said to them, 'In any case, we are, Suzanne, forever and forever outside this particular pale.'

She took a few steps about the table, in her excitement. 'I wrote that to Anna. Here is the letter. I said to Anna, "We have, Anna dearest, at last faced these facts for ourselves; we have gone through too much agony; Stephen has been too often and too bitterly humiliated and we have faced the fact that in spite of our past and our friends, for better or for worse, we aren't communists any more." Oh, thank God! Is our martyrdom over? I didn't write that.'

She threw this in their faces with almost an air of triumph, she smiled ecstatically, beat her breast, taking a deep breath and grew rosy.

'It took as much courage to do and say this, Suzanne, as anything yet done and said. But I did it. I suppose a chained prisoner has to be brave to throw off his chains. Didn't some of the Bastille prisoners want to rush back to their dungeon? All don't feel safe in the light of day. But I do. Oh, blessed day! There,' she said, handing the letter to Stephen, 'post it. Our letter of reprieve.'

Suzanne surveyed them, astonished. She said after a moment, 'Well, I suppose you have come down to earth. Your mother will be glad. When you came here she thought it was over, she told me so. But she said, she was really quite reasonable, "I suppose these things take some time to get rid of." Do you feel all this, Stephen?'

Stephen pushed back his chair and hugged his ankle gracefully. 'Well, Suzanne, I feel it as – many things, many things you can't understand. Sad, tragic, pitiful and silly. I feel I'm less the man. But I can't stand up to the avalanche of contempt and neglect. I forced myself on them; they didn't want me. Just the same, our grasp on history, on the facts of life, is better, I am sure, because we were in the movement. And as for me, though I'm not in, I can never be out. I don't feel free at all. I don't want to feel free.'

'I can't agree with that. It's just as if we'd been sick for years,' Emily said. 'We'll only slowly get back to some normal way of life. This is final! It must be.'

Suzanne said, 'I'm very interested. I have never before been present at a change of heart. I think we ought to talk about it tomorrow. In French.'

Emily cried enthusiastically, 'Yes, the facts of our life have changed. We are different, infinitely happier, free, ah, you don't know what it is like. You never had the temptation, Suzanne. You are so steady. We were like birds fluttering, fascinated before a great python. We didn't dare disagree with the Party and we trembled when a switchboard-girl gave us a nasty look. Perhaps she had heard something on the phone, that we were slipping, not in favour.'

Suzanne asked them what they intended to do. Emily, for the moment, had to write another potboiler, for their money had been spent fast and loose. Stephen said he would be willing to go back to the States at once and work for the family in one of their offices, but for the danger from the Investigation Committee. Then they did not think it right for the children, just after they had acquired some notions of French, Latin, history and other subjects in the European manner, to go back home to programmes that now seemed backward to them. Stephen considered that with his small quarterly income, and with Emily working regularly at her potboilers, and without this atrocious dilemma tearing her apart, and with Christy now self-supporting, they could make out, if the family, that is to say, Anna, would make him a loan.

'They must buy me in. I've knuckled down,' said he, with a pallid smile. It was the usual thing in rich families to make advances, gifts, or settlements for various reasons. With such an advance Stephen could set up a literary or news agency in Paris, say for about five years, till it was safe to move back to the States. All trouble connected with them would gradually die out. They would mix only with neutral, bohemian or journalist types, the literary and movie world; they would not touch politics. Stephen had charm, personality.

'Ah, yes, he is to the manner born,' said Emily.

'That means I'm used to firing cannon when they empty bumpers,' said Stephen crossly.

'What do you mean?'

Stephen did not answer but continued, 'And then I'm cynical, corrupt and rotten and sentimental enough to be able to pick out successes, I really believe. After all, in all these years, I was Emily's censor; stream-liner, corrupter. I knew what would go down. She never wrote a word she wanted to. She wrote what I said was good. I eliminated all that was tragic, heavy, thoughtful, true, even the ghost of an idea from her books; at least, I tried to, not always succeeding. But I was always right. Every time an idea has sneaked in under the canvas, that book has been a failure. Only Emily had a codlin-moth in her apple; and it's bad, for it started at the core and ate its way out. She wants also to be a great writer.'

Stephen sent off Emily's letter and one of his own, proposing to set up a literary agency in Paris. They continued meanwhile to discuss with Suzanne the project of Stephen's going into business in Paris, London and later New York; and perhaps getting a job even with Tauchnitz or another house in Leipzig.

384

'If they would have me, I could go to the east, and start a firm publishing paperback leftist best sellers there.'

'But I thought you had left the left?' said Suzanne gaily.

'The twig was bent early. I can never desert Mr Micawber; or I hope not to,' said Stephen, with more hope in him than had been for a long time.

'You are very amusing, you really are. It is extraordinary how you both always have to succeed. You are real Americans,' said Suzanne laughing.

'Is that so unusual?'

'Yes, it is rather unusual.'

20 RESCUE AND RECANTATION

Anna soon replied. Her sister in Alexandria was ill and she had decided to come to Paris, take Stephen along with her to Egypt to see their relatives there. On the way they would discuss Stephen's future. She would not bring Fairfield till the spring. During the next three days, with intervals of storm and anxiety, they discussed this new turn. Stephen said that Anna hesitated to give them money, when she saw that they were still the rakes they had become fully in their Hollywood and Connecticut days; but she still wanted to help him. In Alexandria she had a sister, Palmira, a widow and Palmira's son, Hector. Hector was very rich from his father's estate, he was a keen businessman, supported art and the theatre. There was an uncle too, a very good businessman, and a brilliant girl, Hector's sister, Jean, beautiful, about thirty-three, divorced, and another interesting fortune in the family to marry. 'Anna's getting ready to drop the Arkansas has-been,' said Emily.

Stephen and his mother had a very disagreeable time, although Stephen put himself out to be pleasant, feeling that his renunciation of communism must be rewarded by a loan or some other arrangement. Anna reproached him with everything he had ever done, his delicate, clever, spiteful essays in economics and about the monied, which he had written at Princeton; his refusal of a fine girl whose father was a member of the New York Stock Exchange, and of other girls; his behaviour about Christy and Florence; his marrying an eccentric from Arkansas, whose grandfather had been a Pennsylvania coal-miner; whose mother a house-cleaner before she married; herself now losing her grip, not making anything like the money they had made in Hollywood and on Broadway; their noisy affair with the Party; their flight to Europe, so described by the papers; and their present situation. They were attempting to keep Christy to themselves, to chisel a small part of his income, with the vague if unfounded hope of getting a loan or help later on. Emily's manners and many other things came up for discussion.

Stephen admitted he was beaten in the search for a living, and was reasonably pleasant. He walked about the room, put his shoes on and off and only retired to his bedroom when his headaches or his belly-aches became too severe.

He returned to Paris, to his wife, miserable, sick and doubtful. Anna was torturing him, she doubted his recantation; he was so shoddy, unreliable. Might he not go back to the radicals as soon as he had her money and she was in America?

'I had to give an absolute, formal, signed guarantee that I would never see any of them again. She's right too, according to her view. She's lending me money. What sort of a risk am I?'

'She's lending you money? Oh, joy!'

'Wait! She brought up all the committees of enquiry, and asked me if I am going to let the family name come up again, endangering the whole family. What with Florence and myself, you and Christy, it will look as if we are all reds. Uncle Maurice gave money to Spain, someone else went quixotically to Russia and wrote a book – what sort of a family is it? She insisted upon a definite promise and – more! A public recantation in the American press – but I put it to her, we can't do that. It's too soon. Raise the dust as holier-than-thou anti-Browder communists and four years later we've made the well-known turn. Besides, I told her, we would have to wait for the next station.'

'Next station?'

'On the renegades' train,' he said, looking down.

'Renegades!'

'She was partly convinced, but prefers us to make the turn now. Who cares what communists think? But I refused. So no money till I've talked it over with you and I give her a date and a speech.'

'Oh, damn it all, we're going to be blacklisted and hated and despised, so what difference does it make? Let's get off at any station or none – at 87th Street! If we remain communists in reality, in our hearts, what difference does it make? They'll say we're not communists but bohemians, compromisers, splitters and traitors. They'll be comparatively pleased with us, if we say so ourselves. Don't leave them in confusion: give them a bone to chew on. I want to be in the clear. You see where your compromising gets us?'

'No, I won't do it. It's my life. Otherwise, life is death.'

'But the money? If Anna doesn't give it, we're sunk.'

'I know Anna better than you. If we're patient and we're good boys, she'll come round. Don't go writing your letters to her. She hates them. The set she moves in don't write letters.'

Emily cried with conviction, 'Oh, I won't. The situation is dynamite.'

However, as soon as Stephen left to go over to Christy's rooms, Emily hurried upstairs and, after taking some fortifying pills, she sat down and wrote a plaintive, humble letter to Anna in which she said they had sown their wild oats and were willing, very willing, joyful, to agree to anything she so reasonably asked. She had perhaps led Stephen astray herself and she saw things much clearer now. She loved Anna and would do anything to please her.

Just before Anna returned to the States, Emily gave a grand dinner for her at the house, inviting the Trefougars, Mernie and Fleur Wauters, Suzanne, who had a charming smile and could sing and listened attentively to everyone; and a number of others. First she had a cocktail party to which thirty-five people were asked, including Emily's literary agents and friends of theirs from London, some new French friend, a writer, Uncle Maurice and William; and after this came the dinner of twelve. Stephen had had conversation with his mother and Maurice during the party and at the dinner.

Emily surprised them all by standing up excitedly, with her glass and crying, 'To dear Anna, to dear Mother, who has made a new life possible for us.'

They drank and in answer to their enquiring, amused glances, she then gave another toast, 'To Stephen, my dear husband, who for so many years has lived the life of the mind for which he has paid such a heavy toll without ever being allowed inside the gate – that is the gate of his needs and desires. Ah, I don't mean that, Stephen, it was no payment; it was an accident, a catastrophe that came. You take a railroad ticket, you pay and get the ride; on the way a tree falls across the line, there is a landslide. That is, our climate has abruptly, catastrophically changed. Perhaps happily in the end. Perhaps tragically. But we must face it as you face a railroad accident, glad you didn't end up dismembered. Stephen had found an avenue for his work, he was honoured for his honesty and noble endeavour; then even they came to regard it as quixotic. It was scorned and dangerous to the rest of the world. For us at that moment those people, now strangers meant warmth, human security, a future for our children. Yes, a home for our children, our ideas and our work. And we were cast out of that home. Ah, the depth of Stephen's isolation, misery. Rejected by those for whom we had given so much, estranged from our own world of ideas and feelings, we couldn't belong to any other; not in honour, and honour is Stephen's rarest, noblest trait. We remedied our immediate sufferings, if you like, by coming to Europe and were sustained by the challenge of a new life, new language, problems, friends, culture. But we have been pursued by those we sacrificed ourselves for and those who once represented our ideal. Ah, me! We lost Stephen's hope of finding a new and yet old manner of dedication and work. I say Stephen,

388

for though I was by his side always and throughout this tragedy, yet it is Stephen who has lost most, suffered the deepest wounds, been more cruelly rejected, been more painfully isolated from what he loved and those he loved; and I mean by this, dear Anna and those close to him in his family. My work, such as it is, alas, in this moment, my work which is not my work – well this toast is not to me – I could go on working in the pork-chops basement. Stephen could not. His work was always and, as we hoped, always would have been in the future for one thing only, pure, inevitable, honourable and satisfying. And all, all rejected! All, all lost! All hated. What injustice! Well, I don't want to mention that. Man goes forth to labour etc. And so our Stephen, noble and great man, has sustained in the last six months – no avenue, no hope, no job – such tortures as few men sustain, because it became every day more clear that he had no hope of work – '

'Emily! Emily!' said Stephen.

'Real work, Stephen. Seemingly not for the rest of your life. Stephen cannot work for black reaction. Dear Anna and all our friends knew that. And he is not permitted to write for his own side. Little by little in the last six months he has lost hope of working at all, ever. What despair! To have honesty, this precious jewel rejected and hated by all; and by those who talk of it most. And we needed money! Needed it desperately! And again he had no work! The effects of all this upon a man like our Stephen anyone can imagine.'

'Emily, please!' said Stephen, looking at her. Anna looked at her with hatred. Emily noticed both and seemed to enjoy their disorder.

'What can that do to a man's psyche? We have all heard very often and now I was fated to see it. How my heart sank! It often seemed to me that never had a man more suffered from the blows of fate and injustice more hopelessly! For how could he extricate himself from the trap he had somehow fallen into?'

'Become a stockbroker,' said Stephen grinning sourly.

'Ah, could you, at your age?' she said combatively.

She emptied her glass. She said laughing, 'I forgot. To Stephen!' She filled, drank and sat down, her face flushed.

Anna, she could see, was very angry and wounded. Stephen, once it was over, was cool enough. Austin Humphreys, a tall, dark, fleshy man, an English consul from a small consulate, was smiling at her with curiosity and the Trefougars were talking eagerly with Douglas Dolittle, a visitor, a tall, heavy, fair Englishman, who preferred country life, but for some reason had just started a small publishing business in the rue de Seine. Both had been brought to fill out Anna's party respectably and Stephen had hopes of going in with Dolittle.

It was a respectable company in fact. Mrs Humphreys, named Fabia, was a nervous, upper-middle-class Englishwoman, about thirty-two. They, in a yawning, offhand way, complained of their poverty, their debts, while at the same time inviting the Howards to their home in Chelsea and to the charming little rented house in the seaside town where Austin was consul. They even offered to sublet their house in Chelsea to the Howards; and in any case such houses could be got near them, for five or seven years or longer. The difficulties were maids, governesses, schools. No one had any money. Some of London's most famous women scrubbed their own floors, others took in foreign girls, who worked for pocket money. Maids if got, would hardly stay and then there was the insurance; the foreign girls gave themselves airs, many of them were graduates. It was difficult. If both members of a couple worked, there was barely enough to eat and wear utility clothing, once school fees and children's clothing were paid for. And then the summer holidays! What a nightmare! The only time they ate, however, was then, on a rare trip to Paris, Normandy, Brussels, even. Indeed the women looked as if they had a thin time. A change of government they thought would help; others believed that England had gone too far down a long decline.

'My father used to say that we would end up like the Romans and the Spaniards. It does seem to be the penalty of Empire,' said Fabia Humphreys.

After coffee they moved away from the room and conversation became general. Emily was interested in the conversation, exactly her own troubles.

'We are all bankrupt, not one of us but is head over ears in debt,' said one of the English women. It was a sympathetic company, defeated, chic and humane. Yet they wanted the Howards to go to London and settle, just as the Brussels friends wanted them to go there. It would be easier in either capital it seemed. And why not Geneva, said another? No fear of war, money safe and tight and even tax alleviations for foreigners. Switzerland was free as the air; for the right people, of course.

After dinner Emily tried to speak French and found it had nearly all gone. Stephen was speaking English to the Humphreyses, Dolittles and Trefougars. He said to Emily when she complained about her French, 'And I say, thank God, what a relief! I have not one word of French left and I wish I never had to use it again. Why must I feel guilty not to speak the French language? They don't speak mine. What freedom from a galling restraint. Always to be babbling like a child of three.'

Emily, after brandy, when they were standing about, found herself talking with great animation to Austin Humphreys. He complimented her: she was a dramatic speaker: no wonder she had had a Broadway success. Emily grimaced, 'You remind me of a film I saw. A girl wanted to go on the stage and recited Lady Macbeth's speech. The talent-scout said she would make a wonderful comic. Well, that's me. Medea in my heart and what comes out of my typewriter is the funny-mediocre.'

Humphreys was amused and kept detailing her rosy, plump but haggard clown's face, her merry smile, the curly, untidy hair, the fat-ringed neck, her excited, active, fat body. She had again become very fat and was wearing a handsome black silk suit with a skirt that folded round the waist. Emily told Humphreys, 'I am very, very happy, deleerious, simply floating! If you only knew! These last few months in Paris Stephen has been simply sick with despair.'

'Why, though?'

'Because he was treated as an outcast and his whole life, so gracious, so noble, so beautifully, effortlessly right, so dedicated, was lost. He had burnt his bridges and found himself in a howling wilderness.'

'I thought they published those articles of his you showed me?'

'Ah, yes, they did! How like them! A cent of encouragement, a dollar of contempt. It means nothing. And Stephen must keep his family; work, work, work. He wanted creation and to relearn. I worked and his adopted son was rich and he getting poorer and lonelier; he was in a torment that does not bear thinking about.'

Fabia said impatiently, 'But really why should he care? He'll come into money, he's got this quarterly allowance and you are used to making money. I think he's quite well off. I wish we were as well off.' She laughed selfishly and impatiently.

Emily, who of course had already explained all the family circumstances to her guests, said, 'Ah, he has a sensitive and deeply and often-wounded spirit. And when the last days came, our bitter hour, just before dear Anna reached us, and he went round all Paris begging for work, a final, humiliating, desperate effort to find work that he could do, honourable work, he came home desperate. I feared for him. He felt it was the end; that he had lost his dignity as a man, as a father of sons, as a husband to me. He said we would never respect him again; he was finished. He could go on no longer.'

'Well, I suppose he was in the dumps all right,' said Humphreys, looking at Emily with interest.

Fabia, though bored, liked Emily too. She said, 'But I gathered it was all right now. What happened?'

Emily smiled gloriously. She almost trumpeted, taking a swipe at her glass, half-full of brandy, 'In this darkest hour, when he was so endlessly searching, he quite suddenly touched on the idea of going into a private news service or a talent agency in literature and through a chance

391

introduction he heard of Douglas Dolittle. Dolittle is a friend of Johnny Trefougar. Stephen was broken by the many, many hopeless interviews and, more in fear than despair, he wrote to Dolittle. How unlikely it seemed!'

She called, 'Douglas, oh, come here, dear Douglas.'

Dolittle turned round slowly, looking at them with his foggily-lighted eyes; then he smiled and came towards them. Emily emptied her glass, gave it to Humphreys to fill, reached up and kissed Douglas Dolittle on the cheek, put her arms round him, hugged him, laughing excitedly and then put her arm through his and, when Humphreys came up, through his.

'It happened that Douglas also knows Dale, one of Stephen's cousins. We wrote to Dale. Dale wrote to Douglas and did a thing so beautiful for Stephen, that I feel I shall be forever touched with joy, when I hear or think of the very words *human being* and *cousin*.'

She said hastily, 'And Dale had absolutely no axe to grind, nor did Douglas, nor Johnny Trefougar. Douglas was tied up but he moved heaven and earth for Stephen, a man he hardly knew. And so Stephen is going to get this chance in Paris after all; not only because of his essential talent and passion and vision; but because of his profound knowledge of literature, his taste; and above all, his force and instinct. And what a combination it will be.'

She looked brightly into Dolittle's face.

'What a combination it will be! Douglas is interested in ideas, he is a hunter of genius pursuing genius. Dolittle and Howard, the future Gaudeamus Press. I assure you that the day before yesterday when all was settled and the conversation between Anna and Douglas and Stephen had been held and Stephen came home with an immense bouquet of roses and this silver bracelet and said, "My darling, it's to be," I burst into a howl and sobs, I fell down on the floor and it took Christy darling and Stephen and Marie-Jo to raise me. They put me on the couch and were lovely to me and I don't think I ever spent a more delicious, deleerious, strangely beautiful evening in my life. Oh, real life, a destiny! The relief! What pure, beautiful, perfect, floating grace and ease. If that could last forever, that feeling of Elysium! I felt almost as when Giles, my own child was born.'

She bore them over to Anna and put her arm in Anna's. Anna covered her first recoil but remained stiff. Emily carolled, 'Anna made all this possible for us, for she said she would lend us the money, without a word of asking, without a hint, with the simplicity of a fine heart, out of sympathy, intuition, generosity, tremendous, fine generosity. Anna made all this happiness and perfection possible. But I think, Anna, your

392

confidence in him and in us did more than all in these blissful three days to buoy Stephen up. If Anna believes in me, Stephen said, that is a new world, the world is orchestrated at last, it is new and too good almost to be true. But true it is,' she said, hugging Anna's arm, 'that is the meaning of mother and son, of mother's love, son's love. As we mothers know. So we enter upon a new chapter of our lives and may this one be a lovely, lovesome, joyful one. We have blessed our good fortune in you, Anna dear, how many times, and so often spoken of how we love you. Dear Douglas, and Dale, sweet, dear Cousin Dale, who realized at once, seeing Stephen's desperate needs, his soul needs, his genius and his exact situation in time and place, what it was necessary to do – and did it!'

Anna withdrew her arm.

Emily turned round, her bosom bursting the seams in the new tailored suit, raised her rosy cheek, rosier still in the black dress, 'And Anna really cured him of despair and complete breakdown. She changed the world. It's all over, the blackness; it's all glorious and new, the morning of our lives, the rosy dawn. Ah, I'm incoherent, absolutely, I know.'

She looked joyfully at Dolittle and Humphreys, both of whom were smiling, and at Fabia, who looked at her in curious thought, but not discontented with her.

'I'm floating, don't wake me up! But it is not a dream!'

She briskly went away from them to tell the maid to bring round more drinks. She passed them on her way back and brought out, 'Ah, well: I suppose – I know – I'm laughable. I know it's nonsense. Perhaps shameful nonsense!'

Fabia said, 'Why is it? Don't we all want to be happy? We have the right to be happy. I know what a relief it was when my aunt died and we got into the house; and then Austin got the job. I was jolly glad, I was really happy. I understand.'

Emily had come back with another glass of brandy. 'We – the world staggers about on the brink of war and war-in-peace, or even sudden doom, the end of the world, the sun blacked out for all, in peace. Paris may be a smoking ruin tomorrow morning. In God's name, it's shocking to be so happy, as if we were vegetables blooming because it's spring. I know people are starving all over this thrice-damned city, the governments are either falling or getting into the clutches of the Marshall Plan or some other steel-jointed claw of the Anglo-Saxon conspiracy to ruin the western world – '

Fabia stared at her, Douglas pulled his moustache, but Austin seemed much interested. She challenged them, 'Well, it is so. In my country, Congress runs nothing but red scares to stampede the cowards. Just see how often the word red occurs in the *New York Times* index. That is an

393

index. The lamp of Liberty is on the blink, there's terror reappearing everywhere and the Great Fascist League is springing up fresh like grass from the mouths of a million innocent, martyred, doomed stinking bodies and my heart's singing fit to burst because my husband got a job. A queer detail.'

'It's our right to rejoice, if that's the state of the world,' said Fabia.

'Your life opens before you,' said Austin sympathetically.

Later, Emily, when alone with Humphreys, confessed that she was still haunted by worry from the old days. Their old friends and even Vittorio would now abandon them, say that they had shed their faith. Said she, 'How can we bear the stinging brand? But we must live. We have not changed, we cannot change.'

He seemed surprised, 'But why worry about them? You have us.' He smiled.

'They are such a small part of the world. I know you hate to abandon the old troop, it's like leaving school or the army, but that's just a part of life. Do you respect their opinion so much? I don't.'

She said sharply, 'Ah, tomorrow Austin, I must write to my old friends, to all who were in the movement with me and who still cling to me and I must tell them what I told you at dinner but in cold chilling terms. It's an agreement between Anna and us.'

He laughed and said quietly, 'The pound of flesh!'

'Not to leave them in the dark, tell everything. Anna wants it. To show her we've turned over a new leaf. How am I to do it? It's a brutal, cruel, wrong thing to do. I lost nearly all my friends during the scandal and now – perhaps – I'll lose all the others. I've got to write a letter of provocation. I'll write it before I go to bed. Otherwise I'll pass the night in the flames of hell-fire! I will anyway.'

She burst out laughing and went to get herself another drink.

Stephen came over to her, 'Emily, don't drink so much. Anna doesn't like it.'

'Anna! Is she going to be my bugbear?'

She rolled away from him like a burly sailor, took the glass in both hands and took a big swallow. She went to Violet Trefougar with a glass for her in her hand and said, 'Ha-ha!'

'You're happy tonight, I'm glad,' said Violet Trefougar.

Emily repeated, 'Yes, I'm very happy, I'm deleerious with joy. I'm floating in an ocean of lilies. But Stephen!'

He joined them.

'Stephen, a thought just struck me! All this rudeness, callousness, cruelty, was perhaps organizational! Perhaps, Stephen, when you're a talent-scout, the well-known Gaudeamus Press, they'll remember you

394

were their friend and they'll come to you; bygones, bygones. You know the old byword: the sympathizers, the fellow-travellers get the brass bands and the big hands; the faithful get the kicks! We're no longer faithful; it's the bouquets and banquets for us now. Eh? Perhaps Vittorio will still be with us and all the others. Will we keep our cake and eat it too? After all, take the Resistance movement, why one of the biggest men in it, so Mernie Wauters says, went into it for the danger and the game, outwitting people he despised. No one would even talk to him nowadays with his automobile lined with white velvet, his house of Vita glass, his gold-plated bathroom and handmade flat silver and his mistress with cuffs of diamond and ebony! He's a great heroic monster – '

She stopped, envisaged him, opened her eyes and laughed, 'What a glorious, gorgeous monster! And helped the Resistance too. Can we too perhaps enter the annals of the red register as gorgeous monsters, human, all-too-human, a bit of Lucullus and Petronius, a bit like the Medici or even just like poor Cicero, adoring the fine life; but still faithful in our hearts, dependable, marked down to help in the next Resistance. Well, really they must think a bit like that. Look at Madame Gagneux, Suzanne. Why she is so human that she is willing to admit that her favourite writers were mostly bastards during the occupation: and that courage is an everyday virtue in need and that it passes over you, leaving you a coward. And she understands all, not exactly forgives all, but does not condemn all.'

'Every human being is a sort of monster, if you get to know them,' said Violet Trefougar.

Emily said, 'Yes, yes, that is exactly how I feel. I must write sweetness and light, but I know too well what people are like. Vittorio, who seems so kind and who makes people love him at first sight, is cruel and indifferent. He doesn't give a damn for you, you're a pawn in his game, he plays catch-as-catch-can with you. All our dear ones in the USA at the first hint of disfavour fell off as if we were lepers. Why, if I were a leper I'd expect my friends to try to get me a doctor, or offer to go with me to a leper island, and with love and sorrow. But they didn't. And now I'm going to be a damned soul, yes, to them, a damned soul. And not a letter will come, not a telephone call. And will the other side so much as take me to their bosom? She was a damn red, they'll say, what was the matter with her? To hell with her! Eh? Damned! Double damned! Emily Wilkes Booth. Oh, come upstairs with me, darling. I've got to take one of my headache powders. Don't let Stephen know. He'll rage. He might tell Mamma. I'm depressed and agitated. This brings me no happiness. I talk of happiness, joy, and I am thinking, What unhappiness, oh, what terrible unhappiness. Life isn't worth living.'

395

'Go upstairs and take one of your headache powders, you'll find some comfort in it,' said Violet.

'You are right. I owe you so much. I couldn't do all I do, without them. Man as a chemical compound, eh? But that's the me they're going to know. Come on! Bring some drinks with us.'

The two women went away and stayed away some time talking in Emily's room. When they came back they were both happier. The guests were going now. Anna left. She was to have lunch with them the next day at Jean Casenave; after that would come only one more family dinner, this time at Uncle Maurice's before she went back to the States.

The Trefougars waited some time, for Violet wanted another word with Emily. They were going to Switzerland for a weekend and wanted the Howards to go with them. Emily begged Uncle Maurice to stay a bit longer and stay he did. He did not leave till two in the morning. Emily had been very excited and even noisy; soon the fatigue and excitement wore her down again. But she found out a good deal about the Humphreys couple. The high-strung, handsome finishing-school wife had been a hellcat in her day, had run about the continent alone, got a job as a housekeeper with a middle-aged man, who tried to kill her with a hatchet; and so on. Now she lived only for the houses they lived in and for mild affairs with local men. Maurice did not know whether Austin was happy or not. He was a quiet man, smoked his pipe, walked his dog, said little, and did not mind changing consulates every year or two. Emily's eyes sparkled.

In the meantime, a fresh trickle of hope had started in her. She and Stephen would see Douglas Dolittle almost every day. Dolittle had many friends, they would be happy again. Paris was already full of interesting, liberal Americans, who lived well, had luxurious villas, apartments, went abroad, loved France, drank wine at dinner, had good cooks. Life again, thought Emily to herself, after the plague hospital. She felt she had impressed the melancholy, good-looking Dolittle; they might become fond of each other. 'Oh, God, how I long for a real affection, a love, to which a political proviso is not attached.' How long had they wasted their time treading mazes in no man's land. She sat down with Stephen after the party for a breather and talked things over. They both felt released and softer towards each other.

Emily wished they had Christy with them again: that would complete their happiness. She said to Stephen, 'Our storms are over. Poor Christy suffered from them. I hope in a few months we can enchant him back again. We will all be different. It was a tearing-apart of ourselves. Now we are convalescent. What bliss! What a paradise! Eh, a real marriage at last: the voice that breathed o'er Eden, that earliest wedding day – oh, my heaven, what bliss!'

She fell on Stephen's neck.

Stephen talked of practical things, too. He had to see his mother the next day about the actual conditions under which she would give or lend him the money. She had wanted to meet Dolittle and Stephen's present friends.

'As Anna says, you cannot get twenty-five to forty thousand dollars without a consideration. It's fair enough, as Pegler would say. Henceforward I associate only with Dulles, Walter Lippmann, Truman, etc. But she has spoken to Dolittle: she is going through with it.'

Stephen believed that Dolittle was delighted to have the support of a family like the Howards, even if the money was a comparatively small stake. Stephen was to be a partner.

'I shall have my room, my desk, my secretary.'

'And why not,' said Emily. 'Douglas is lucky to get a man like you. There are so many oddballs and deadbeats roaming around, opium-eaters of a sort, wanting to park their ragged ass in a publishing house, do anything to be the handmaids of literature. And you! He's got someone right from the top of the tree.'

'And when we really get started, we'll take your books and mine and they'll get translated, too.'

'Thank heaven; and I can write what I want now,' said Emily.

Stephen frowned, 'First, let's get on our feet. I have managed to bring my family round and get them to respect me. Let's not go wildcatting now. You have several money-books to finish. First things first.'

Emily turned red. However she said, 'Tomorrow, I must get off those letters Anna wants us to write.'

Stephen thought it of no importance. Bad news could wait; also the curses of their former friends. Emily was restless, though; wanted to know the issue. Would even Mernie Wauters visit them now?

'Why ever not? He's a man of the world. Besides he likes our food and drink.'

'Suzanne says that Mernie has had to do a lot of standing up for us, since the last visit of some character, sent especially from the USA to blacken us. Mernie has been faithful to us, she said, terribly decent and kind and warm. From him and Suzanne I learn that we never had any idea of what was really going on in this stupid inferno, fry'em and boil'em business. Surely the people over there have something better to do than fry us on a pitchfork. Oh, I hate and despise them. And if it hadn't been for Vittorio himself we would have never known what went on; and that there had been a frightful uproar among the great ones, that Cachin and Duclos and Togliatti and Palme Dutt and Harry Pollit had been warned of or knew of our taking part in a turmoil, over our miserable presences; and even our evening parties in Paris came up for discussion. Who would have guessed that such slight personages had international meaning? We're the subject of an international conspiracy! And now because of our eminence we are in outer darkness. If only we had been nobodies, we could have disappeared and never been heard of again, led the quiet life. But because we were spotlighted, top names, we are therefore the worst traitors and fomenters of sedition and in general an international nuisance – Marxian reversals, eh? We could scarcely have got so much fame or notoriety if we had been faithful sheep.'

Stephen said, 'No more of it. Thank heaven it's over. I shall never go down on hands and knees again to anyone. My novice days are over. I am now a democrat, a real one, anyone's equal. I feel as if I'd been let out of a convent.'

Emily said mechanically and sadly, 'And I as if I had been let out of prison. My heavens, every word might be guilty, every action might bring you on the carpet. How did they invent in these days such a system of crime and punishment? They do nothing to make us want them and we must give up everything for them. So what if the age is decrepit; and eventually towards the year 3000 the world will be communist? My long-mouldy bones will have reached the democracy of dust. In my life I will have been tarred and feathered and ridden the rail for nothing.'

'Well, it is over. What is there to cry about?'

But she was crying. Large tears were welling from her eyes of their own accord – she sat in her chair, the picture of misery, round, rosy and not crying of herself, but with the regret, remorse, bafflement welling out of her, a profound sorrow.

'What is it? What is it?'

She said humbly, 'It's to be free of that overhanging sensation – I guess. It's the sadness that once we were loved by people we respected.'

She sat drooping, drowned in tears.

'Don't cry, Emily. I can't stand it.'

'And Suzanne told me that Madame L' (she named a high Party name) 'said that she could never come near us, not even in the presence of fifty people. That if we were at a party with someone else, she could not come, because she would herself rather have died or committed suicide – and you know how repugnant and wrong that is to a communist! – than do what we have done! – and,' she said with a dreadful sob, 'are doing tonight. She said that even supposing for a moment that everything we say about the Party is true, to do what we do is worse than death, a filthy and contemptible thing beyond description.'

The tears were pouring down her face.

'My God, I thought we were going to be happy now. When did she tell you this?'

'Tonight. I said to Suzanne, Bring me face to face with her and I'll say to her, "You are a leader of women. Don't you understand the problems of a woman like me? What have I ever done against the human race? I am just a woman who can't live in disgrace!" '

She got up and was angrily standing in front of Stephen.

'And tomorrow or tonight I have to write those damn letters to suit your mother, in order to ease twenty or thirty thousand measly dollars out of her. When I myself made, with a turn of the hand, three times that in Hollywood in one year. She's putting her foot on my neck.'

Stephen said, 'Don't talk that way of my mother: she could be worse. Didn't you say she let you out of prison. Let's bury the episode. Tomorrow we'll get down to business. Yes, let's go to bed. Let the servants clean up for once. Don't let the ghost of your stepmother keep you out of bed.'

'No, I'll clean up and begin to mumble the text of those letters over to myself. I won't sleep unless I get that fixed. It's like Mernie said. You knew they were on your trail and at last the Gestapo knocks on your door and you're almost thankful. It's over.'

Stephen was very pale, 'Let's go to bed. Leave the ashtrays. I can't stand any more.'

They got into bed and turned off the light. Suddenly she shivered a little, but it was a giggle. It increased: she began to laugh. She laughed outright, frankly, hilariously: she roared with laughter.

'Go to sleep: the bed's shaking, Pagliaccio,' he said, touching her with his hand.

'Oh-ho-ho,' she continued.

'All right, you dumb ox, you clown, what is it?'

'We were going to clean up Europe with the Marshall Plan and already Europe has cleaned us up,' said she, strangling between laughs. She continued wilder.

He said, 'Very funny. Go to sleep.'

'Haw-haw-haw.' The house rang with her gigantic laughter, 'Ha-ha-ha, oh-hoho.' She got up and tried to walk about, 'Stephen – oh-hoho, save me!' She fell on the bed and turned on her side trying to stifle her laughter. 'Haw-haw-haw, oh, my God, oh-ho-ho, I shall die!'

She sobbed, struggled, strangled, shouted, screamed with laughter, strong, immense laughter, it seemed, not hysterical, the great roaring of big lungs and a strong heart.

Stephen turned on the light and sat up. Her face was crimson, tears poured out of her eyes. Her bosom heaved convulsively. He said, 'Stop it! You'll have convulsions. Stop! Stop it!' He slapped her.

She stopped, still heaving, and sat up to glare ferociously at him, 'Don't you dare touch me. I'll kill you.'

'Calm yourself.'

She said, 'You wretched worm. How I hate you! How I despise and hate you!'

He looked at her astonished, his mouth half-open. Her eyes fell lower, thoughtfully, and she said forcibly, 'And myself!'

She laughed a little, feebly, 'But we are happy! But we have made good. The Howards have squeezed a pittance out of Mamma. We have lost all our friends, but we have made genteel acquaintances and we'll get yet to a Walter Lippmann cocktail party.'

She laughed softly, 'I'm del*ee*rious, I'm raving, I'm so happy.'

'Have you finished?'

She turned to him, 'I'm a damned soul, I'm lost, I've betrayed everyone and everything. But it's all right, we can pay the servants.'

He dropped down on his side and moaned, 'Leave me alone. I can't cope with all this. I can't take any more. It's too much. I'd rather die. If I have your contempt like that I'd rather die. I only wanted to make you happy.'

She looked at him with contempt, 'I have given up the whole world but thank heaven, I have become a Howard. Now I must mention every one of their names with respect, four-footed, false-hearted Fairfield, four-alarm-bitch, dear Dale, who can tell you all about the Cecil Sharp collection, and the dead-head Dolittles and Mrs Humphreys with their loved Sèvres. That is to be the field of battle henceforward of Emily Wilkes, who once fought for human freedom.'

'Leave me alone. I don't know what this is all about. I only know I make no one happy.'

She was tired. She lay down, baffled. Stephen turned out the light. She began to compose her letter of renunciation to her former friends; but in a few minutes she was fast asleep.

In the morning she got up about five and began at once typing her recanting letters. The first was to Ruth and Axel Oates, now back in the USA where Axel had set up another weekly and news service. She wrote to them first, thinking they were the only ones who might still be her friends; 'and to get my bloodstained hand in.'

She began with an intense burning hatred of the Germans for what they had done – to Europe, to France, to the Jews, to children – and mingled in with this civilities towards England, which in its faded conservatism and anaemic socialism, she still loved; and to Belgium, whose great wealth and kermesse spirit and bad French she loved; and

400

towards Italy where they intended to go in spring, and to Geneva where they might one day reside. She then discussed English Labour, 'childish, on a lower level, unsuitable when we live in an epoch of absolutes.'

'What did Stephen say only last night? Ah, well, one can debate the socialist policies of parties in England and the USA. But actually it's all shadow, no substance. Neither of these countries can or will produce any significant organization of the proletariat. Let us talk about Reality, History; for example, France, Italy – and ourselves in this time and place. Stephen is taking a new step, he will be learning, writing, and the old frustration will slowly disappear. I hope he will be at once appreciated; he needs it. The whole idea of Gaudeamus Press must be revised. Stephen has so many ideas; and they admire and respect him and wait on his word, I can see that. It is true that he hankers after a thing like the *Labour English Review* which, childish as it is, would be readable if it had the editorship of a man like Stephen. This is an interim. He may go on to something like that. As it is, without a period of reassurance, he cannot go down once more into that shadow struggle with gigantic, venomous, ever-changing pygmies. For Stephen now, another kind of life, the sunlight; no wandering in the amorphous mist but battle in the sun and struggle for reason, blessed reason, independent reason, which lives apart from shibboleths and apart from the darkness and flame that surrounded the Inquisition, the mysterious sects, the devil worship, the Trotskyists and other sectaries. Yes, they say it all happened because they are small in numbers and cannot reach the people; perhaps that is so, but even in France and even in Italy where the membership is large, can it be said that the individual does not suffer? That no injustice is done? Are there no innocent martyrs whatever in the bloody dark unrevealed chronicle of Bolshevik history, no innocent people afraid to return to their loved country for fear of a rope or a shot in the dark? No people hauled out of bed and brought suddenly up on strange charges, ignorant of the denouncer, the accuser? Oh, the dread secret denunciation and private informer, meaning nothing and arising out of jealousy, envy, crime, lust or even a little cash, blackmail, pressure but ending up as only one thing– your name on the records of infamy now and forever. Your name pilloried innocently. How can the innocent person defend himself? He cannot. The innocent suddenly charged, behaves like the guilty, guiltier than the guilty. It is the criminals who get off and have false papers and friends in the police. But we, never – no, indeed, once accused how can we not take our stand with the other side? For terror and dishonour and misunderstanding await us on the side our hearts once chose. Oh, alas, dreadful dilemma which cannot remain a dilemma, for we are not obscure persons. We must live and work, bring up children nobly and why should we fail? For an error? A judicial error? And are communists, those pious stiff-necked people the pattern of the philistine, better than others? Indeed, as they used to say, Tammany is better for the poor, for you can buy them and they will listen to the broken-hearted mother who has a few dollars in her hands. And if you can buy communism, where is their virtue? So they remain unhuman. We must live on the side we belong to. I remember hearing my father talk about an engineer, Phil Brotherton, working in Mexico. He sympathized with the Mexican workers, but he said if his Mexican workers rose against the damn gringos (it was then) he would have to take refuge with the whites, and fight with them. And we too – with the whites! Ah, this waiting, this waiting; why are we always waiting? Is it a situation of our class in our age?

'But Axel and Ruth, it is not safety now. We are no longer communists, we have been through all that and we no longer feel we are with them. We are post-graduate, we understand them; but we feel we are in a sense more sophisticated than they are. Everyone knows that the frustration of sexual and perhaps the other creative emotions frequently produces the alcoholic and even the drug-taker. Therefore people who imagine they have or actually do have frustrations, tend to become alcoholics and drug-takers almost by default. Similarly, communists produce a certain type, perhaps even two or three, but to me there is one master-type and this type becomes more noticeable across the decades. It is furthered by parasitic communist conformist literature and by ignorant outsiders conforming in their way as well. Besides, most moderns, lonely in the tragic years, find comfort in behaving according to the norm. One can see this, so far as comunists are concerned, by examining personalities of the Russian Bolsheviks in exile. Say, in 1912 you have an enormous variation in personality; there were all sorts then, just men and women struggling for reason and revolution; there was no communist type in the days of struggle; but victory brought a change, conformity. Now in every country, communists strive to fit themselves into a mould. It is a good mould, perhaps honourable, perhaps even great. But people should be *free*. A form, a mould is a stereotype, it banishes the person, bleaches personal thought and dyes over it. Take our friend Vittorio, a man of great talent, if not genius, and with such gifts that he has carried over into manhood the freshness, capacity for love, sorrow and joy of a child. Surely a great trait. He has all sorts of facets and curves; an impressionist, a futurist, could depict him. He is a human being, intricate, delightful, convoluted. Or was once. Not long ago perhaps. Now he struggles to acquire a synthetic personality. He tells you about art, in which he is wonderfully learned; about literature, and they appeal to him as the high court on literature; and yet you feel too sure of his conclusions. They are

402

banal, they are languid, they are dull. How sad! All this is a grim fatal limitation of his own intricacies of perception, his delicacy and charm. He is no longer Vittorio. He is party conformist number one hundred thousand. He is a poster, a poster comrade. Most communists not so endowed fit easier into the mould and perhaps might be called victims of history.

'We don't want to be victims. We want to see, smell, hear, understand. Yes, I have been considering the communist character. Let us take, in contrast, a great individual. Take Danton. Or Cicero. Their friends were overwhelmed by their characters, their own characters, rich, various, tortured, intricate and noble because human. They fill the soul with a great nostalgia because they are right, somehow entirely right. Reason, the fullness of humanity is so little considered in our doomsday world, that it is like a shock to discover man afresh. It is the ideal of man to see life whole, and these great, though perhaps much-mistaken men, call upon one's own life-forces. And all these are the reasons, the reasons which we have suffered for, for our giving up our beliefs, Axel and Ruth, and feeling sure we are right in giving them up. Our souls were cramped, our lives miserable, there seemed no goal or hope and even our marriage was as painful as a fever. It is over. We are cured. I don't ask you to rejoice with us – but be good to us, try to understand us and know that we did not act from the base motives we are accused of.'

This letter was Emily's springboard. After it, she wrote five or six others, much shorter, signed them, typed the envelopes and brought them down to breakfast for Stephen to read. She was very sorry that Suzanne was not there to hear them.

'What is this?' said Stephen suddenly.

At the bottom of the letter to Axel and Ruth Oates, she had scribbled in her own loose handwriting, '$30,000'.

'Oh, cross it out! I must have been thinking about the money.'

21 TRIAL AND EXECUTION

Stephen was in his new job till nearly Christmas, when he found himself so ill that he went first to French doctors, then to his uncles' medical man in London and last to his family doctors in America. They put him into hospital, got him ready for an operation and kept him in hospital for a long time. Emily was uncommonly upset; but she could not go over to him, because of the children.

At Christmas, she had only Suzanne, the children and their old friend, the English journalist, Desmond Canby, whom she invited by telegram from London. Canby, once a communist, now a cautious 'retired communist' who had never denounced his former friends but, as they said of him, 'always kept the door open', was not living well and could not visit the continent as often as before. He was married to a well-to-do and titled woman, and was now living with her family, making a risky living by writing the witty articles for which he was famous and which had had a tremendous sting, long ago, when he had expressed political beliefs. The money he earned free-lancing could scarcely keep him and did not keep him, for he was fond of fine living. He telephoned from London to say he would be very pleased to spend Christmas with the Howards.

'What will I bring?' he said.

'A bottle of gin.'

'I will.'

He came on Christmas Eve and stood in the doorway, tall and bulkier than before, dark, slow to speak, with the unassembled bogey look of a very drunk man.

'Welcome to Turncoat Hall,' said Emily, who was herself drunk. 'There are only to be a couple of select apostates present, you and I. The Dolittles you'll like, just ordinary nobodies, but your class, Des, and there's Madame Suzanne, you won't like her, she's a menial, but a good friend to me. Come in, help decorate the Christmas tree. Where are your presents?'

'My presents?'

He smiled stiffly, and swayed forward, 'Oh, in my little valise, some gauds for the tree and I shall go out and get something, as soon as I've had a drink.'

404

'Did you bring the gin?'

'H'm – no. I forgot it. I'm not very flush. I had to leave a deposit for my safe return with the family you see: more gauds. Never mind. I know you have drinks.'

'Oh, yes. Come in, Des, we'll have fun. It is so dreary and I've been weeping like the widow of widows. I am so glad you came. It was very good of you, drunk or sober.'

He came in quietly, though almost toppling, not pleased by her words; but soon they were seated with drinks and then Des said he would never get to the shops. He would send her something magnificent from London.

'I promise.'

He went to bed very drunk, but got up early in the morning, apparently in good health, though he did not eat bacon and eggs.

Christy was staying in the house, and the three children still made a fuss about the Christmas tree.

They passed the morning quietly and at noon the Dolittles came with hallooings of joy and rapturous embraces from Emily; and they luckily at once took to Des.

As usual Emily had insisted upon doing the decorations herself. A large Christmas tree in a tub, arranged by the porter, had a few strings of silver and luggage labels all over it, in blue, pink and yellow, while attached to it by thin pink embroidery floss were the five-cent candy bars, which Emily had got out of a crate of confectionery sent from the States. There was one for each person. They had plenty to drink and when Christmas lunch was ready, went in to eat in a small dining-room which opened out of the hallway, a dark room in which the table was dressed. In the centre, in a fine silver-and-glass vase, were some half-dead flowers, while the cloth was decorated by the paper streamers used for humble dancehalls and public houses in that season, and a considerable number of old postcards addressed to Stephen and the children. They were postcards from holiday resorts and from the family travels.

'I did the decoration myself,' said Emily, standing at the end of the table and smiling strangely, almost with derision.

'What is this? What is the meaning of it?' asked Des uneasily, looking at the untidy confusion.

'Oh, Emily has been having fun,' said Mrs Dolittle.

'I don't understand it,' said Des, in the same tone.

Emily, still with a strange expression, saw the food coming in on the dinner-wagon and sat down. She said, 'What does it matter what you see, Des? Des Canby, celebrated lunch-detective and sandwich-snatcher, like all the English, sponges and toadies, who'll do your dirty work for a drink, why not? Isn't he here drinking my drinks, eating my food? I can't say so, you mean?'

'For shame, Emily,' said Suzanne in a clear voice. She was sitting beside Des Canby who bowed his head, plucked at the paper streamer in front of him, but said nothing.

'It's Christmas, Mother,' said Christy.

'She's drunk,' said Mrs Humphreys in a low voice to her husband. 'Take no notice.'

'Well, why not, aren't we all here to whitewash the rich, lick the spittle, kiss what should be kicked? You, Doug Dolittle, and you, Fabia Humphreys, come tell me, did you ever pay your debts? Haven't you beggared tailors, dressmakers, grocers, butchers and interior decorators? Haven't we all? And you too – oh, you'll sit here, you'll eat my food, you'll be drinking all the afternoon, what about you, Suzanne? – '

'What about me?' said Suzanne.

'Didn't Anna, dear Anna, say she would take our Olivia away from you because she thought you were a little too fond of the little rich girl; "It's not quite healthy, is she turning her wrong?" she said to Stephen. Not to me, because I'm only the poor helmet-maker's unbeautiful daughter, the poor Arkansas rice-grower! And you Christy, don't you write me foul, dishonest twisted letters? Put round the shrimp cocktails, Mario,' she said to the butler employed for the occasion, 'and eat, friends, eat. I'm the harpy who's fouled the food, but eat, it's Christmas, oh, joy. Oh, God,' she said to Suzanne, 'I wish Violet were here. Suzanne come upstairs with me a while and let me talk to you. I'm tearing in two.'

And without an excuse, she left them. They looked at each other, murmured and ate. 'What else is there to do? Something's wrong.'

'She told me she was going mad,' said Mrs Dolittle.

'Oh, she's excitable. She isn't going mad.'

'She took me down to the basement where she had a brooding-room, she calls it,' said Mrs Humphreys. 'There's a window on the courtyard, just below the courtyard and there she is working on her novel about Marie-Antoinette. She says she is too feeble sometimes to get upstairs and she has a couch there, she sleeps on it and she keeps her medicines there. Sometimes, the cook Fernande told me, she sleeps there half the day and half the night; and she has found her lying on the floor, asleep – or otherwise, something else. I went down there with her, she opened the cupboard, took out some headache powder, which she took, and she said to me, quite calmly and reasonably, that she is going mad, she knows she will never recover.'

Dolittle said, 'I don't believe it. She probably has spent all her money. Of course she tipples: she's probably been hitting the bottle. Pass the wine, Doug! Take no notice. She's upstairs taking a pickmeup. She'll be all right when she comes back.'

406

'Americans are very extreme, aren't they?' said Douglas Dolittle. Then to Christy, 'Not you, Christy, you're charming. But then you have European manners and you're from a different background.'

Canby said, 'Americans are just like Russians, that's why they're at each other's throats, brotherly hate. Just the same, I don't believe the war will be between Russia and the USA. I believe it will be between America and Britain.'

At this fascinating prospect they all began to chatter. Emily soon returned, in a good mood, with Suzanne, and the Christmas dinner from that moment went forward well enough. After coffee and brandy however, the Dolittles said they had an appointment for tea and they left.

'Oh, Suzanne, I am no better than poor Violet. I remember the first time she came to us, I didn't understand her sufferings at all and I thought she was mad. Now I know it was her misery. Well, no more of that. I was blue, very blue; but that's all over. Now children, look after yourselves. I am going to show Suzanne my workroom.'

So saying she took Suzanne down to the workroom in the basement described by Mrs Dolittle.

The next day, Suzanne found her there again.

It was a small, dark room with light from the courtyard. Glass shelves had been fixed in the windows and reduced the light: ornaments stood on the shelves. Under this structure was Emily's work-table upon which stood a new electric typewriter, which they had bought because of her increasing rheumatism. Against the back wall was a double bed taking up much of the space, over it a rumpled, dark-green cover and on the floor an old, thin, green rug, also rumpled.

Emily looked at Suzanne over her shoulder as she passed to a wardrobe fitted into the wall.

'I am going mad, Suzanne. I know it. And I think I am glad.'

'That's nonsense, my dear. You're just tired and lonely. You need Stephen.'

'Yes, I need Stephen. I need a man. I need men. I cannot live this way. What shall I do? What good are the men I meet? They're all tied up. Meet a man at my age and he has a rope round his neck, and ankles and wrists tied: he's the victim of a female hold-up. His pockets are empty and his spirit is broken. He's petty and mean. If I kiss and hug him he gives me a gleaming eye and a wet grin and a red lip and a red tongue, but he's off hotfoot to his woman's bedroom. It's safe. They're afraid of me. I always frightened them. They like tame women, Suzanne. The women are tame. What stops us, Suzanne, from living? All my life I had no joy. How I longed for it! Where is it? Why do we have this great need for joy and love of joy if there is none? I must have it – and do you know where it is to

407

be found? No, eh? Well, I know. Look! Look, here – '

She went to the closet, opened the door and showed shelves full of papers, typescripts, loosely packed together. She took a child's paintbox from a shelf, opened it and showed Suzanne some pills in the pans.

'I long for these, Suzanne, more than I ever longed for food and drink or even a man. Well, I don't know – but yes I think so. And when I have one, I feel for a moment, just a moment's length, such exquisite, unbearable, absolute joy! Do you think Stephen or success or money gave me this inexpressible, exquisite, sharp joy! Oh, Suzanne, if you knew – but only Violet knows; and then she, I don't know that she feels as I do. It isn't for long, ah me, and then the dreary ebbing away, the dullness begins to return. But where in life did I find the joy I wanted? And when I have what I want then I dream, just for a moment, of all the raptures, as if all were possible. And all was possible to me. I opened my arms to life always and received what – wooden dolls! The big empty parcels a practical joker gives you for your birthday, and inside, shavings, bits of dirty paper with the halves of words written on them.

'But down here, Suzanne, I have found myself. I am writing better. See here, this is going to be my big book – about poor Marie-Antoinette!'

Suzanne caught her glance; she had a glittering mocking smile, her eyes swam with gaiety.

A pile of yellow second-sheets stood beside the typewriter, a new ream on one hand and, on the right, a pile of typed yellow sheets. Emily stood by them, fingered them and said with a proud smile at Suzanne, 'This is it, Suzanne. While he's been away, I've done all that, down here, in my cell; this is my *magnum dopus*, *Trial and Execution*, the last days of Marie-Antoinette. He's away and this time I'm writing a real book, a prose epic, like Tolstoy; and in it, man is the pawn of immense forces; who knows how many and what kind? Man is carried along on the flood of time, whether he's in a boat or drowning; he is not even in his element like a fish is. It's not only about Marie-Antoinette, that's for the Midwestern mammas; it's about the flood of time and how they were carried along on it. I stay down here, they say I'm sleeping or eating hemp, I don't know what they say; I don't know what they tell you – '

She broke off and grinned: 'Perhaps they come in, I don't lock my doors, and you know how it is, I sleep just where I feel like it, on the floor, on a chair, on the covers, even on my typewriter – I don't get dressed any more, I'm too fat, and I'm so busy, I don't even go upstairs to wash. I think I'll have a bathroom installed here. Yes, that's better for me. I drop with fatigue, Suzanne, and I dream, strange dreams. I'm not a dreamer. Last night or the night before – when was it? – I don't know the time these days. When Stephen's away, days and nights shutter past, time

408

is just a venetian blind, light and dark – ha-ha! – I dreamed, yes, I was telling you, that I was sitting in a sort of box, like a bay window at the theatre, and hung round me were clowns, heads of clowns, all different and all me.'

She laughed, 'Isn't that just me? Well, I don't have many visual dreams. I have physical dreams because I am physical. Such strange dreams, Suzanne, dreams of fire, of pangs and agony, I dream I'm screaming. Do you think I do scream? I'm obsessed by screams, inside me, as if I'd always carried the idea with me. Do you think a baby when it's being born hears its mother screaming and remembers that? For I do remember screams. I've always heard them, but inside, as if inside all the muscles and bones and fat that make me up.'

She laughed, 'I laugh you see! And inside I hear the screaming. What is it? Do you hear screams? You must have heard plenty during the Resistance. There are places in Paris I can't go past. It frightens me, places where they tortured Resistants and anyone in fact, if they wanted some fun. I know there was a school next to one, a fine young ladies' school, think of that, and a hotel next to another. People must have heard those screams, those terrible, strangling screams. And now today they say nothing, they go about their business. It's like the time I was walking down the street with Stephen, someone called out "Murr-derr!" but no one heard it but me. When I go past those houses, I hear those terrible cries. Oh, Suzanne, my heart fails me. I want to die. And in this book *Trial and Execution*, I am putting not only the history of those days, but of ours. Many innocents went to the scaffold, denounced and misunderstood, and pure victims of misfortune, and those the police hated or even the butcher or neighbour hated. It is like that today. Terrible times! So my book is not only about then but about now. It is not *War and Peace*: it is *Trial and Execution* and we are all being tried and all go to our execution, by their hand or ours, or by time, killed, exiled, living in terror, starving, dirty, frightened of neighbours and old friends; that is the terrible time we live in. Suzanne, Suzanne! It is like brain-fever. The torture is over but we are all tortured. I dream of being burned, of pains in my body, of barbed wire round my arms and legs, I dream awful things, Suzanne! I can't live alone, that's it. How can one? How do you? Suzanne, I wish you and Christy both would come back to live with me. The staff hates me, they quarrel in the kitchen, I don't know what they are saying. People despise me, and it gets so cold.'

'Don't they have the heating on all the time?'

'It isn't that. Yes, they do. It's a terrible cold, the coldness of the bitter world. I don't belong to it now. I'm outside the warmth of the world, up there where it's cold and dark, you know the sky is black? And you are

409

crucified by fierce rays from outer space that sparkle against you and burn you. Those are my dreams. I don't dream like others, I dream of awful realities, just as torture is an awful reality. People talk about Nazi tortures; but do you know, Suzanne, they copied those, they learned them out of books? Man has always been torturing man. I don't believe we came from monkeys. Monkey's don't torture each other. We came from devils . . . It's getting so cold! Oh, how terrible it is, I'm trembling – '

She went to the wardrobe in which her pills were kept.

'Don't take another.'

'I need them. I'm in desperate need. If you knew the longing, the urgent need, the deepest, fiercest need anyone ever had – and – ' She took her pill and turned round with a grin, 'Ah, Suzanne and when I have it, the wild joy!'

'Emily, come out with me. We haven't looked after you. Come out. We'll take a walk. Get dressed.'

'Oh, it's cold. I'll throw a fur coat over this dressing-gown. We'll drop in somewhere, there's a bar near here where I go, a little place and I eat something there, bad food, heavens, how bad! But I eat and I don't have to ask Marie-Jo and Fernande to feed me and come to me with the tray and look at me with the eyes of policemen.'

'Well, get dressed and we'll also go to the bar.'

She went to another closet where she had her silk suit behind a curtain, sent Suzanne out of the room while she quickly dressed. She had shoes, handbag, cosmetics at hand and very soon came out, flushed and smiling impishly, her hair untidy, but with expensive bracelets and a string of handsome beads and smelling of a fine perfume.

She said naughtily, 'It didn't take me long, did it? I do this often. They don't know. I say I am going to put the letters in the mail-box; I'm going shopping. I just go round the corner, down to the quays.'

They trotted along, talking about Christy and family matters; but Emily seemed mischievously excited; and she presently said, 'It's here. I'm out of breath. Let's stop in for a drink. Ern petty vair.'

It was a modest-looking bar, with a restaurant at the side, which served good food.

'They know me here. I have friends.'

She saluted everyone, laughing and with a wave of the hand and sat down, sitting upright and looking brightly around. The waitress, a serious woman of about forty, came up with a knowing smile. There were greetings and introductions, they ordered and Emily detained the waitress saying, 'Did my friend come in today?'

'The big one or the little one?'

'Eh! I don't know. The little one.'

410

'Perhaps he's working.'

'He told me he would be here today.'

'Oh, well, then – '

The waitress went away and Emily put her hand on Suzanne's arm.

'You'll see my friend. One's a medical student, you'll see him come in with a satchel; the other's a jockey. Very amusing. Trays amusong. He reminds me of a stockbroker Stephen knows. But I prefer a jockey to a stockbroker.'

Suzanne was amused, 'How long have you known them?'

'Oh, a week or two. It's discipline. I said to myself, I must get dressed, go out, meet people. I want to get the book done, you see. No matter what happens to me, in the end, I'll have the book done. Oh, what joy to think I'll do it. I never would have done it with Stephen here. It's a good thing he's over there suffering, they're looking after him and I'm free here to work. What do I ask out of life, Suzanne? To work. And because of my dear beloved husband, I never did the right work. But now, you'll see. And I am writing about the people of Paris, so I must know the people of Paris. Oh, don't be afraid for me! I was a journalist for years. Nothing ever happens to a journalist. My medico tells me about the people in hospitals – I knew an ambulance-chaser before, he loved me – he loved me. And the jockey tells me hundreds of things. I love them, I love them both. They are my friends! Oh, I am so sick of the dreary circles we know. Only you, beloved Suzanne, worth talking to; only you with a heart and understanding. If Stephen had been here, I never would have met anybody but dreary, dreary literary people – I always hated literary people. But these are people. And I'm going to keep them on the side, have a life of my own, because I've been suffocated in marriage. People are always I suppose. Marriage is good and it's wrong too. Well, heigh-ho, I am letting you into my secret life, Suzanne, because I trust you.'

They sat there some time, Emily drank several whiskies, and Suzanne some port wine, but she drank sparingly.

Presently, the jockey, a small lion-coloured man with thick hair on end, dressed in tans and yellows, came in. When hailed, he came, with discretion to their table, standing a little way off, and when Emily urged him eagerly to join them, he sat down modestly and spoke with polite deference to Emily.

He talked about some races he had ridden in, some owners he knew, discussed different racecourses, and the merits of French and English racehorses. Emily was excited, making him show his paces to Suzanne, leaning forward and saying 'Et mon ami, Monsieur Damiens, promised to take me to his stables next week. I must see them. I must know about these things. God, what do I know? Nothing. I assure you, Frédéric, you must come to me, to my house in the rue de Varenne and talk to me, tell me all you know. I am a writer you know and I must learn everything I can. I am writing about Paris: you must help me.'

They had a snack, Emily paying for the three, and then she urged Monsieur Damiens to come home with them.

'You must come upstairs with me, I will write down everything you say. We'll have drinks. I'm all alone. I need friends. I need company. Do come! Suzanne is here. She can protect us both.'

Evidently Monsieur Damiens knew Emily quite well, for he accepted this invitation coolly, though with some curiosity.

'I am very anxious to see where you live,' he said to Emily.

'And once you know, you can come often, any day. Come and eat with me. We'll have talks. I'm so lonely. It will be fun.'

They set off for the rue de Varenne. On the way, Suzanne had a few words in rapid French with Monsieur Damiens and at the gate to the courtyard, he demurred; he did not think he should visit Madame now. Perhaps tomorrow, or another day. Emily argued with him, sparkling, pouting, blushing, and even pulled his sleeve.

'You are disappointing me. You are not keeping your promise. You're my real friend; but when you get here you're afraid. Well, anyway – '

The jockey said, 'Not today, Madame.'

'I see what it is. It is you, Suzanne. You have talked him out of it. No matter, listen, Frédéric, come by any time. I will go up to my room, see there, the window; you whistle, come tonight, just whistle and I will throw down to you the keys of the gate and the front door and you will just come in by yourself and no one will stop you. Suzanne will not be here because she has work to do. Suzanne has to watch over our dear son and she will be home and in bed. But we will enjoy ourselves, won't we? Will you come by then? Do just as I say.'

The little thin-faced man laughed, looked twinklingly at Suzanne, said, 'Yes, very well, Madame,' and saluting them both, went off.

'What are you doing, you silly girl? You are behaving like a fourteen-year-old, a naughty one. Really you will get into trouble. I am very fond of you, Emily. I worry about you.'

She pouted, 'I'm lonely and no one bothers about me at all. No one takes any trouble except Violet and she is a bore: she is so boring now, with her adopted son. She is worse than any grandmother. I have got to know about life. I'm a democrat. A writer is a democrat. Life is democratic. And anyway, Suzanne, Stephen left me alone. I owe him nothing.'

Suzanne came in with her, had a serious talk with her about her position. She had nothing against Monsieur Damiens, but she also knew nothing about him. He might be a good man and others bad. Emily said

412

she was an old journalist and used to knocking about with all types; no harm would come to her. Besides, she said with bright impertinence, she was going to live her own life; she paid for it, not only with money but with the servile shame of being a stupid man's wife.

'I'm bound hand and foot because of his scionage. Bah! I'm going to be myself, like any man would be.'

In the end, she promised Suzanne to be careful and not to invite strangers into the house. Suzanne promised to help her get up an evening with new friends. Suzanne then left, while Emily gaily ran upstairs to change her clothes, make other arrangements and to sit by her window. The jockey in fact was strolling up the other side of the street, at the corner of the rue de Bellechasse. He turned round to look at the building: she waved and he waved, lifting his cap. Emily was surprised to see Suzanne crossing the courtyard some moments later.

'Oh, I suppose she has been gabbling with Fernande, finding out when Monsieur is coming back. I should worry! I'm going to run my own life. I want to find out what it's like to have an affair. I want to have a real affair!'

Emily had a tray sent to her room, put on a lacy gown and sat by her window, writing and also looking with smiles towards the street, whenever she heard someone passing. About ten o'clock that evening Monsieur Damiens returned, stood opposite and whistled. Emily was delighted. She had a keyring ready and into it she had fastened a note, telling him what to do. She threw the keyring into the street, he picked it up, unlocked the gate and crossed the courtyard. Emily, looking merrily over the staircase, heard voices speaking in French, first subdued then raised. She recognized the voice of the porter and Frédéric; and hurried downstairs, calling 'Come in, Frédéric, come in *chéri*. What are you doing, François? This is my guest: I have invited him in for drinks.'

The porter hesitated. She became angry, tugged at their sleeves, separated them, and drew Frédéric towards the sitting-room.

'Take your cap and gloves off, make yourself at home. I'll get drinks,' she said. 'What are you hanging about for François? I shall look after the guest. This is an old friend of my husband. This is my good friend Monsieur Damiens.'

'Yes, Madam,' said the porter and went off shrugging, looking back dubiously, hesitating in the lobby. A little while later she heard voices in the kitchen and closed the doors. Early in the morning someone crossed the courtyard and closed the gate.

The children came down to breakfast, went to school in taxis and Emily was not to be seen. When Suzanne called, she was still asleep. Suzanne went up to her room; she was not there; then down to the basement, where she found her, lying across the bed, uncovered. She covered her and went upstairs to the porter.

In the evening she came again and brought Emily a telegram she had received from Stephen's mother, reading, *Please keep Olivia with you during Emily's illness. Stephen returning immediately.*

There was a quarrel, but Olivia said she wanted to go with Suzanne and Suzanne left with the child and some clothes in a bag, saying that she would engage a nurse for Emily. But words flew so furiously at this, that Suzanne went off with the child, after saying in a cold, reticent tone, 'You are very ill and you do not know it. I shall take measures.'

Emily, mad with anger, rushed to the kitchen to scold them and then again to the cellar room where she shut herself in and could be heard typing hour after hour with only a few moments to rest. In the middle of the afternoon, Marie-Jo knocked to ask if Emily did not want to eat, and was told merely to bring black coffee. All day she worked and went on work ng part of the evening. Suddenly, she came out, said in a tired cheerful manner, 'I did thirty thousand words! A big chunk. It was worth it! I am too tired to eat. Bring me a sandwich though and I'll see if I can take it with a drink.'

Still in her dressing-gown of the morning, she crouched in a corner of the sofa with her drink, and when the maid came in with her chicken sandwich, she said pleasantly, 'Put it there, *ma chère*. I feel wonderful now, Marie-Jo. Yesterday, I was ill: today I am better. I worked all day. Isn't that wonderful! Have a drink with me, Marie-Jo, come be my friend!'

Giles came to her saying he was lonely; and asking when his sister would return. But Emily said, 'Mamma is working, blessed work! Let Mamma work and presently we will get your sister back.'

414

22 STEPHEN RETURNS

Three people wrote to Stephen in New York: Suzanne, Violet Trefougar and the porter who, on a sheet of paper bought especially at the *tabac*, expressed it that 'there was disorder in the house'.

Stephen cabled that he would return immediately. A letter following said that he had to renew his passport and for that had first to make a trip to Washington, DC. Emily, full of joy, fluttered about the house setting things right, telephoned Suzanne to bring back Olivia and, at times, worked fast on her book also.

'Stephen will be so happy. We are going to make a fortune this time; and this book is a monster, it has everything, not only fortune but fame!' So she told Suzanne.

Violet Trefougar took her to the airport to meet Stephen. He came off, assisted by an officer and leaning on a stick. Emily threw herself on his neck and when she stood back, tears running out of her eyes, she saw the startled, the hard look on his face.

'Oh, I have been ill too, Stephen. But it is all over now. Now that we are two again, oh joy, I'm breathless with joy, now everything is right again.'

But when he got home, Stephen, after greeting the three children who stood waiting for him, and the cheerful and relieved servants, went straight to bed. He had left the convalescent home too soon, made a very fatiguing trip to Washington, though a cousin had gone with him, and had boarded the plane against doctor's orders.

'But I am glad to be home. Whatever I have had to do, it is worth it to be here.'

Emily had planned a celebration dinner; but she had to eat it with Suzanne and the children. Stephen, lying in bed and taking only soup, did not see the richly but strangely decorated table, with rosettes and scrolls of paper, all the long preserved wedding anniversary and valentine cards they had given each other since the day of their marriage, all the jewellery he had given her, and carelessly-tied ribbon bows from many Christmas days.

Emily wore her black and white suit – Stephen did not like her in dressing-gowns – and had tied a pink ribbon in her straggling hair; but she was no longer the merry oaf she had been, she looked leering and wild, her eyes swam and one half of her face, grey and fallen, seemed many years older than the other. Of this she was not conscious, but continued eating and drinking with gusto, hurrahing and talking greedily between bites, her suspicious, greedy eyes watching them all, calling to attention anyone who did not look at her.

Afterwards, Stephen called her to him and said, 'My passport ran out. Did you get yours renewed?'

'Passport! Oh, lawdy, Ah forgit dat passport!'

'We must get it renewed at once.'

'Any trouble?'

'No trouble. I was told to go to Washington. I went with my cousin. They got me into the room there and asked me about a thousand questions, you, me, Christy, Florence; but they gave it to me. I had to give assurances, which I gave with pleasure.'

'What assurances?'

'That I would not talk against my country abroad, that I would assist them if I saw traitors and things like that that it was easy for me to agree to. Though I said to them, Where would I meet traitors?'

'Then it was very easy. That's good. I thought – many times I thought, oh, Stephen – that you would never get back; and I would have to pack up and take the family back to the States. I really saw Dear Anna coming for us. I fretted and mourned; if you knew the soreness and suffering – but you, poor Stephen, have been so ill, so sick, you have been crucified. Oh, lord, I should never have let you go back to the USA. We were separated and I here, so woebegone, saw you for weeks at death's door.'

'You and I are always at death's door. I wonder why.'

'That is exactly what Douglas Dolittle said: "The Howards are always at death's door." And I wonder why? Oh, Stephen, we haven't been very happy. Yes, at times, rapturously happy, happy beyond hope.'

'Perhaps only when there were the wrong reasons.'

'You've changed, Stephen. You've been so ill, had such harrowings, you've suffered too much.'

'That was bad. They gave me the wrong drugs and I nearly died from the drugs which were supposed to ease my pain. But that's me, isn't it? Nothing goes right with me. I was the one in a thousand they didn't suit. It had nothing to do with the doctors.'

'And I was not there. Only your family.'

'Yes, I didn't enjoy that. But Emily, what brought me back before I am well, is that I had bad news of you. They said, Suzanne, that is, said, you were seriously ill.'

'Oh, I have been so well. I worked so hard on my book, The Monster, I

416

call it; The Monster is half-way finished. It will make us a million, Stephen. Our troubles at last will be over and I have planned it so that it will also be my great book; the great novel of our times. It will serialize, sell to Hollywood as a block-buster; it will pyramid forever, you'll see. It will be the success of our lives and all our troubles will vanish. I suffered from overwork, I used to stay down in my workroom day and night, days and nights together, and of course, the staff, who want orderly, bourgeois lives, for it is the working-class who are bourgeois – ' she laughed immoderately, 'the staff didn't like that. Madame should be upstairs ordering the household, seeing to the laundry and counting the coals; or if she is the grande-dame type, she should be out at *les cocktails* and *les dîners intimes.*'

He smiled, 'I don't think they want you out at *dîners intimes*: but I don't care what they want. I want to know how you've been living. You don't look yourself Emily.'

'I am not myself. I am someone else, someone better. I have begun to live my way, not yours; and I mean nothing bad by that, Stephen. I have filled in the outlines, lived as I should, working when I want to and not according to a programme. I have servants; let them look after the house. I have begun to live my life, which I never did since I was married.'

'Did you live it before?'

'Ho-hum! Does one ever, I wonder? I guess not.'

'And so that is what François meant when he said there were disorders in the house?'

'What! He wrote to you? And you dare to say you take notice of what a worm writes, a nauseating, dull, household spy? He wrote to you? I'll call him at once. Let him say here what he said to you. How dared he? All the while I thought he was my friend. I told him everything. I let him look after me, because he said he wanted to. Oh, the flunkies! An army of servants is an army of spies and enemies. I suffer so much from this terrible affliction of spying and hate and distrust. No one to look to. How bitter! And I was fighting sickness, bravely, for I know I was brave, and I worked like a madwoman. Stephen, I will go mad, if this terrible world of cruelty, pinpricks and griefs continues. Why did you leave me? Everything has got worse. I have passed the signpost. I cannot go back. I passed it while you were away. I am going downwards now. Oh, grief and despair. I am despairing. And to think you believed a porter, less than a servant, a doorkeeper! I am stung. That means that I can't think of you any more as a consolation! There never was a time in my life when I didn't think, in all my troubles, But Stephen is there, I can rest my head on his chest, on his heart, and hear it beating for me. When we were first married, every night I rested my head on your heart and knew it was

417

beating for me. It doesn't now, does it?'

'Yes, it does. I have nothing but you. More so now than before.'

'Why, now?'

'Because of what happened in Washington.'

'That was nothing. The very least.'

During the next few days, however, Stephen interviewed those who had written to him and it was Suzanne who told him the whole truth.

'Because you must look after her, Stephen; no one but you can influence her. She can't help it. She promises, in a transport of friendship, she's happy, she's going to reform, her eyes sparkle, then she goes upstairs, has her drinks, goes downstairs, has the pills that give her this unnatural energy, works, falls to the floor, sleeps unnaturally – and this is one of the strongest, most gifted natures I have ever met. It is because of the excessive energy, the gaiety, the genius, yes, the genius, that I cannot control her. You can control her because she loves you.'

Suzanne said nothing about the jockey, the café on the quays.

Emily was so insulted when she heard of this that she went down to her cellar-room, stayed there three days and nights, refusing to answer Stephen's messages. Stephen was still chiefly bedridden. She sent answer that she was working. She was very angry that he had not asked to see The Monster.

The third day, aided by Marie-Jo, Stephen crawled down the two storeys to her room in the basement. The door, as always, was on the latch. They called, pushed the door and saw the dark, small room, a servant's poor room, smelling dusty and unclean; Emily nowhere. But when they walked in, Stephen saw a bundle at the other side of the bed, and going round, he found her on the floor, deeply asleep, with sunken face. They were unable to wake her. He sent for the doctor and with the porter got her on to the bed. 'Oh, my God, she's dying!' The porter said, No, he did not think so.

'This has happened before. She has such a strong heart and physique that she can recover entirely. She will recover; but Monsieur should take her for a holiday. This house and this loneliness has been unfavourable: you might call it bad luck.'

They put her to bed upstairs and, just as François said, she soon recovered, but she seemed overtired, somewhat pale, she looked older, almost an old woman.

Stephen was unable to take her away then. As soon as he was able, he had to go to his work in the Gaudeamus Press. He took taxis there and back. He wanted the thing to be sailing along by spring, when Anna came to claim Olivia and to bring Fairfield. Anna intended an early

418

marriage for Christy and Fairfield, if they liked each other. Stephen was despondent.

'Will he have the guts to say no? It's exactly the same as when I was his age. The parade of possibilities with Mother in charge. I saw so many that I could look at them no more. That cured me. But Mother has learned. It is one at a time now.'

'Christy will never marry Fairfield: he is too refined and intelligent,' said Emily. Even Suzanne remarked that Christy had many rude things to say about rich girls.

They struggled along in this way until spring.

Anna came, bringing with her Fairfield, and at the same time there arrived in Paris from London, Stephen's cousin, Dale, a young middle-aged man, fair and gay, a bachelor. Anna hired two cars to drive Fairfield around Paris and then out to Versailles, where they were going to lunch.

Emily, in her best mood and looking well enough, sat beside Dale and kept exclaiming, hugging his arm and kissing his cheek. Christy sat beside Dale, and in front were Stephen and the driver.

Emily cried, 'Oh, superb, oh, poetic, oh, colossal, oh, joy, oh, my darling Dale. To be cousins. You don't realize how unusual, how impossible, this drive would be in the USA. We would all be biting each other's ear and kicking the neighbour's shin, yelling and insulting. But here, happy and free, innocent and really people of the world, *mondains*, innocent – Americans are not innocent. I don't know what's the matter with them. Europeans are not innocent but they know how to be calm. All Americans are hugging some ugly secret: they mope, they droop, they drink, they grouse. But here! I understood a lot of things since I came to Europe. At home you're backward and suppressed if, to get over the dreariness, you don't neck and drink at every turn of the road. In Europe people live full lives, and like each other for anything, as art, woods, motor drives, poetry, family dinners and just cousinhood! Oh, oh, joy! I'm free at last. With a great big sigh I push back to the Atlantic I hope, the last of my American bugbears. Because to feel you have to make love all the time to the opposite sex is to be afraid of it. There was one place this didn't happen: the newspaper business. They're good guys there – I wish I were back there sometimes – there guys are guys and girls are guys too. But outside any such profession, why, it's hell . . . Anyhow,' (she kissed him), 'I love and adore you, Dale; for you're not that sort. And oh, look at those heavy green sprays, those fronds, those sprays, those sprigs – in America, bah! – we don't even think of using those words, it's just plain woodlot to us. Why I wonder? We're afraid, ashamed, again.'

They drove on and on. About ten, they reached Versailles, parked the car and visited the palace. Stephen walked with his mother, Christy with

419

Fairfield, Emily with Dale, courting and cajoling.

'One cannot have *désespoir* on a day in May rolling, strolling, and with a loved cousin' (she kissed him), 'loved friends, loved husband and children. Think of the joy, oh, life is so full!'

'I'm so tired of our *hôtel*, Dale, and the grandeur. I'm glad we came here to this greatest absurdity of all. And such a quiet day! Versailles for the Howards alone! Suppose we lived here? I think I'd like it. Would you, Dale?'

'If we lived like they did. Have you read about the *fêtes* they used to have?'

'Oh, yes, oh, yes. Hunting the girls on horseback, and the parties in the woods.'

But Dale, interested in history, explained to her all about Versailles, its splendour, the money it took to build it, what the rooms meant, the way the court lived. He was very enthusiastic. He had often read about it, but not seen it before.

They walked through the halls, rooms, the salons, past long windows, through apartments as if in a crystal, past strange little corners and washrooms. The living quarters seemed small and dubious enough.

'Well, I'm glad we've done better than that in America,' Fairfield said.

Emily said, 'Oh, darling Christy, my own Christy, how do you like Versailles?'

'It has old age and crumbling charm,' he said.

'Listen to him! A European aesthete,' said Emily, delighted.

'Let's quit this boneyard,' said Fairfield.

Emily declared that Fairfield, now sixteen, was the picture of Marie-Antoinette when, as a girl-bride, she came to Versailles from Austria to marry the prince and become the *dauphine*.

'What a fairytale! And there is sweet little Fairfield, always coolly complete by herself, untouched, as if the place belonged to her. I alas, am also untouched – but with me, it is alas, old age! And look at my darling Christy, oh, Dale, explaining it all so soberly, just as you are to me; oh, wise youth, a man already! There are tears in my eyes, Dale!'

They went to lunch. Emily was delighted. There were French ladies in charming clothes, 'Just as then, but not the French of then, the French of now, of the rue de la Paix, the rue St-Honore, the avenue Matignon. We all belong here, Dale, now. Except me, the Cinderella, perhaps. But I'm a happy one, the prince married me long ago, and here I am with three or four beautiful kind sisters and brothers! Ah, me, what happiness!'

She leaned close to Dale so that her shining fair hair touched his forehead and said aloud, 'Dale, I must keep this mine forever. I am going to write *Versailles and Emily Wilkes*, their lives together! Or no, I will write it all into The Monster, my masterpiece.'

Dale laughed, 'How queer you are! But not dead, and like nothing ever before.'

'But I'm vulgar, Dale.'

'Well, you have a right to be anything you like, you're a great woman.'

She put her hands to her head, 'My goodness. The hair rose on my skull. In the USA no one would ever say that to a woman. It's the spirit of Versailles.'

'Versailles is great and vulgar, magnificent and enduring,' said he.

She said, 'We are gently and languidly involved with all sorts of pasts. Henri IV said Paris is worth a mass and I guess I would say the same. Then my past, your past, so different from mine, so enchanting and the little lakes here with their long-ago pasts and the special past of Stephen who was here when he was twelve, for he too, golden scion of this golden family, has seen it all long ago and almost forgotten it.'

Stephen said, 'Yes, I thought it was something I had dreamed.'

'Ah, Dale, what a family, to have such dreams! To be able to think that Versailles was only one of their dreams! I shall bring my little Giles here, so that he too will think it is something he dreamed. Yes, Giles shall have such dreams. Ah, my God, the beauties of this life! How strange that the rich, the bourgeoisie should have such a beautiful life! What a dilemma! What a puzzle! For surely their minds and lives are finer that those whose dreams are back streets, garbage cans, vacant lots filled with rubble, howling landlords, roaches in the kitchen! What horrible dreams they are! They make me shudder, make me suffer! Well, well – life, dear sweet, difficult, promising life.

'And now this is going to be one of Fairfield's dreams too. Fairfield had such a dream on her sixteenth birthday! I cannot say what manner of dream it was! Ha-ha. For Fairfield will not admit she ever saw the boneyard.'

She passed along with Dale to Anna and linked her arm in Anna's.

'Dear Anna, what poetic joy! Versailles is now part of the lifeblood of all of this wonderful dear family of Stephen's and mine. How strong, how intoxicating, how insistent the dead past is as it lives at Versailles. It overhangs, it is imminent, it threatens. It threatens only because it is empty. Empty – '

She broke away from Anna and said mournfully, 'Yes, it is past and grey, cold, strange, formal, inhuman. And yet, with the Trianons, the woods, the paths, the islets and the shadowy couples and the lone walkers – what are they thinking of? Not the grey and cold. Even the lovers here cannot be thinking what our lovers think of in Central Park and Far Rockaway, not quite the same nuances, eh? Oh, well – that was

421

my dream when I was young. I wish I had been Fairfield. I mean in Fairfield's lucky place.

'Think of it, the soft hush of green young May –

'Think of it – this past that is Lethe, this deep, soundless, over-whelming of individuality, this dream-past rushed on us, over us, and spoke silently to us, rushed over us without seeing us perhaps, in its tranquillity. To have lived like that, in this magnificent happy past, and to be gone now, but to have this for your life-dream. Ah, me. We are sad creatures. What are our lives compared with theirs?'

Dale, excited by her talk, was talking to her. She listened abstractedly, saying sometimes, 'What wonderful details! Oh, your memory, Dale, for all that's tender and true in the dear past!'

But she said suddenly, 'And yet, Dale, it seems to me a frozen, graven image like an old cathedral on a winter day, full of tenderness, an essentially hollow idiot, yet deeply comforting, at least for me who have lived through this rich afternoon. I taste death and total loss and I like the taste; it is sweet to the taste.

'You know, I am writing about Marie-Antoinette. It is meant to be good. I have the memory of all these Marie-Antoinettes of all degrees, all doomed; and the sadness of their stately doom, behind the unspeakably rich and voluptuous and happy life a horrid sound, coming out of the gorgeousness pushing through into the forefront, the slow-paced tumbrils, the towering guillotines, the last moment, the awful axe. And it is this most awful of scenes, itself wickedly vulgar which saves this park from vulgarity.'

Dale explained, 'Louis-Quatorze was the decadence of his own age. All the great men came to flower and withered before he came to the throne, little overdressed, big-wigged monkey. William Blake said, "A man is big if his wig is big."'

She said, 'To me, suddenly, it is terrible, dead, ossified, and what is not living is vulgar. What is this but an arid man-made, slave-made landscape, thirsty and starving and loveless?'

'That is because you do not and cannot belong to the past, Emily.'

'Dale, Dale! I am decadent, too. You don't know. Oh, Dale, you are the one to save me. Your great understanding, your wisdom – you would see what is wrong with me and bring me back to life. You would cut away all the decadence and I would be what I once was, a girl so full of life and joy and hope, you can't imagine it! No one knows what I was like. I didn't know myself. It is only now when all is lost – all is lost, Dale, I am lost!'

'You are not lost, you are tired; and if ever you were lost you would go down like they did, nobly and vigorously, to leave a legend, too.'

She threw herself into his arms. He was surprised, but he held her.

422

They were behind the others; and the others, because of their lively conversation were paying no attention to them.

'Dale, I love you. How is it that you know what words to say? What a heart you must have! What a tender, good mind. I need you. Won't you come to live with us and give me life again? Oh, I have been through such torments as no one knows; and I can't talk about them. I don't want to. I only want someone near me, just in the same house, to whom I can go sometimes and say just these words, "Help me, console me; and don't ask what I am suffering." '

Dale set her on her feet, linked his arm in hers and made her begin to walk again. He said, 'The revolutionary general, the knight of the revolution, Lazare Hoche, came from Versailles. They were not all faded and outmoded. It was this desert, as you call it, which produced revolutionary genius. The blood is there in the stones. Yes, if they had simply withered downhill into death and dusty oblivion, more and more faded, out of date, childish, figged out and silly as they seem now in the museums, they would not attract us at all, and not a woman of genius like you. Our attitude to them would be the attitude of the wild Kentuckians towards the British. What was their code? "No institution of theirs, no law, nothing to recall that wild and wicked land." But the French with their good sense and their love of all that was theirs, arranged it so that the whole monument they left behind, this most extraordinary of French gravestones, is not merely not repulsive, not merely the broken pediment of Ozymandias. We can look there and think, they lived and they had the good fortune to yield to their betters, the vulgar proles. And both sides had the splendid good taste to obliterate all of that life on the grand tragic scale.'

Emily said, 'Ah, yes, the tumbrils are absolutely necessary to Versailles.'

'How bloodthirsty you are! Memories of the Indian frontier, I suppose.'

'No, I am afraid. When I think what they could do. See that vast cobblestoned courtyard, the lifeless palace – it would be dull and vulgar if not for the terrifying memory of the furies, clawing at the cobblestones, their feet gaping with festering wounds, dirt ground in and scarred everywhere, filling the air with their rotten breath, spoiling the gilt with their fierce dirty paws; and think of the broken, yellow, torn nails, the knotted joints, overturning, tearing, breaking with hate, pocketing, shouting, jeering, lusting, and bad, bad, as conquerors are always bad, jealous, mean, and justified eventually by history. What a terrible picture! It makes me hang my head. I can't even cry. My eyes are empty. I am empty. If that can happen, why live?'

Dale laughed, 'Take Louis XIV. I have no sympathy with the talentless old monster. Louis XIV came to the throne with twenty-three million

Frenchmen and ended with fourteen million. The *soleil* ceased to shine for nine million. A record. Anyone could have done the same mischief with less damage to the people.'

'Ah, no. The image of Versailles is not Louis Exe-Eye-Vee, Louis the Fish-eye, strutting like a toad on red heels, over a crowd of half-human cowed courtiers. For me there is only one spectacle, the frightened, beautiful queen who began her days innocent and soft as Fairfield, gentle and full of a girl's senseless, impossible hopes. There she comes now to a hideous reality, the reality of monsters and ruffians. Why monsters? Nature never made monsters like human beings. She shows herself, bravely to the wild, wild, heartless, vicious mob; for jealousy, envy, murderous hate are vicious and heartless. All the green and lovely places of France are haunted, all the great places are crowded with terror; the Terror, and others. The sound of the tumbrils is heard through the land and every spring, every dread summer, every year of drought and every year of grain – we wonder, we fear! Oh, why are we here? A land of blood.'

Dale looked at her sideways. 'My eye, how you take on. I always thought you found Europe so tame. Dear old Europe, the tame, trodden pasture etc.'

'With Versailles it's all said. No phrases unturned. And it all meant nothing. The beautiful and doomed. Oh, I adore it. And I get a fierce sense of triumph from gaping at it and thinking, They're gone! Just a vulgar Arkansas maid. But alive and so triumphant. Ha-ha. Yes, thinking it over, Dale, I really do adore it and triumph over it. We have defeated you in the end, my dear friends, architects of all this noisy, silent elegance. If I could knit I would have come and spent a happy afternoon looking up at the façade and thinking a few names for future reference: De Gasperi, purl one, knit one, drop one, Paul-Henri Spaak, purl one, knit one, drop one, Governor Dewey, drop one, Sumner Welles, drop one, General Marshall and his plan in his pocket, knit one, drop one. I believe there is a strong streak of both Lady Macbeth and Madame Lafarge in my soul. I know Christy would tell me there were no knitters, no Madame Lafarges, but I would make them if they didn't exist. I'm like that myself. There must have been!'

Dale laughed, 'Ah, Emily, come on, come to England and cheer us up. Let's have some fun. Come along. You don't really like the French at all. No one really does; but they don't know what to do about it. It's a sin against culture to say you don't like the French. And your view of the French Revolution – all derived from Dickens. You yourself are a Dickens or maybe a George Sand – you haven't realized yourself yet. Come to England and I'll make you work the right way. I'll make you!'

424

Emily drew back, 'Jehosaphat! Your family is certainly one for making other people work. The true aristocratic touch, eh? Even in the woodlot in spring! Say do I look like that, I guess so; a workhorse, eh?'

They joined the others, found their cars and drove back to Paris, and that evening dined at another fine restaurant, Laserre in the Champs-Elysées. All this time they knew nothing of shortages, milk, bread, wine, meat nor sauce, nor gas nor clothing, nor money nor time. Yet secretly Emily and Stephen were gnawed by fear; their work unsold and big debts behind them and before them. With the family and in this state of mind, they visited museums, shows, shops, gardens.

Some days before the end, going back to Anna's hotel, Emily sauntered with her mother-in-law, who was to leave in two days for America, with Fairfield and Olivia. Christy was to go over to them in the summer. Anna spoke of this.

'He must always be American. I don't want to see him one of these unfortunate children who no longer feel at home in America and think of French sauces and embarrass people by speaking with a correct French accent. They are very poor company and have become exiles. They're not happy in their own country. Now Christy is not like that. He is a healthy, nice boy.'

Emily agreed enthusiastically with all of this and told Anna she could depend upon it, their views coincided.

'And dear Anna, how happy you have made us all, with your perfect sense of fitness, guiding us, your organization and genius for making a real family feeling! If you knew my feelings: the delicious guilt and terrific pleasure.'

'Why guilt?' said Anna inimically.

'I should be working.'

Anna was silent and Emily regretted her remarks. She laughed, 'Perhaps I meant g-i-l-t. I love it. Oh, if only we didn't have to worry about the future of the world and of my dear husband and babies. If only it were the nineteenth or the eighteenth century. All the time passed and the world didn't come to an end. We sit on the Champs-Elysées and lift our glasses with lovely wine and toast and love each other, dear Anna, and talk about painters and writers we all like – '

Stephen had approached, inquisitively.

' – because we came of aesthetic age with them, like Cézanne and James Joyce and Eliot and Hemingway and we love them because we're of their age. Yet perhaps they're already hurtling, rushing towards the Dark Ages which haven't been had yet. They'll be unknown along with us – '

Stephen said, 'Why that? I won't have that for you, Emily. Is Michelangelo hurtling towards the Dark Ages in any way?'

425

'Oh – no – I mean, now the party is over, we are separating, I want to boohoo and cry, Up the Family and Here's to Absent Friends who aren't even yet absent and it's even more painful to look at them now. My goodness, I think the moment of parting is much lonelier than afterwards.'

She hugged the flaccid, satin arm of Anna, who walked along without response.

Dale had come up. He said cheerfully, 'Perhaps in their day, every one was bored with and tired of Michelangelo and talked small talk about him. People like us never knew Cézanne and we wouldn't have: he was considered mad. And you can bet your boots the Cézanne of today is off starving to death somewhere at this minute. Well, everyone knows it. If you're so mad as to be an artist – you know beforehand your fate.'

It was beginning to rain. Emily held out her hand and said, 'The holiday is ended! How perfect! The sky has tears!'

Stephen laughed, 'For the Howard-Tanner clan? That would surprise me.'

'Ah, it's been noble, dreamy, poetic, all our dear ones and when will it happen again? Such a sense of warmth, love, security, of belonging together and of confidence in the future. And tomorrow – we're on our own again. Ah, me. Life! Such as we live it.'

Anna questioned her about her writing and Emily replied enthusiastically that she felt she and Stephen were working much better in Paris, because writers were more respected and appreciated there.

'Do you want to be respected and appreciated? I thought you wanted to make money,' said Anna, with some contempt.

'Oh, I like both. But you've inspired me, Anna. I've actually worked since you've been here. I can often work when I get home after a fine dinner, noble wines, pumping the joy of living into me. Well – it doesn't come out quite that way. But I've nearly finished a foul serial that I am sure will sell and that will keep us going. And as for this book I'm on, I'm sure I can sell it for $10,000 advance. We had a note about that today. It's not sure – but you may have noticed our radiant expressions.'

But Anna said their expenses were much more than that.

When they parted, she warned them again and asked them to meet some friends of the family who were coming to Paris next week. Stephen bit his lips, but said they would give them a party and a dinner or two.

'But we must work, Mother!'

'Your cousin Cherry has the very best Washington connections. I don't want you to get out of touch. You met a lot of good people while you were over this time. I know your illness prevented you from meeting all you might have met. You may need Cherry's help, with this political fever over there. I want you to get back lost ground. I'll do my best to help you, if you do your part. Cherry has always liked you, Stephen; and she'll pull strings for you, when you need them. I know you did the right thing when you went to Washington. I have been told.'

When they went to the plane, Emily wept and clung to her mother-in-law and Olivia, kissed Fairfield, weeping, blessed and embraced and flattered them all and, as they began to leave for the plane, she kept crying out, 'Love, my darlings. A *bientôt!* Oh, dear, it's so long till next time. Goodby-ye.'

She turned to Stephen, dried her eyes and said, 'Well, now – thank God that's over. To market, to market to feed a fat pig. No more chasing, nor more dreary philistine tourist fun! Oy-oy! As the Greeks used to say. Oh, fooey on all families! Let's have a celebration on our very own, Stephen, with Dale perhaps before he leaves, to take the taste out of my mouth and then I really must work. Like a dog. Our lives depend on it.'

They were very happy this evening. They left the servants and the children to take care of themselves. They were going to walk where they pleased, see what they liked. Stephen had a surprise in store for Emily; it would soon be her birthday. They were going to wash the family out of their system and not talk about anything of that sort – not about whether Christy was going to England next autumn, nor whether they themselves should take the family counsel and go to England too; and otherwise move to a small apartment; not worry about the Gaudeamus Press, not think about Emily's commitments. They walked, they felt they could not get enough, the city was once more becoming their own, getting into their legs and eyes. They walked with arms embraced, they kissed just like other French couples.

'How happy we are when t'other dear charmers are *loin*,' said Emily.

Said Stephen, 'It is for us and all; yes, my favourite city, except Vienna, Florence, New York, Rome and London, God help me. I wish I could live in Florence. It's shabby and Paris is shabby. The women aren't well dressed and the whole city spiritually is in the dumps. I know it's just the neighbourhood of May Day, the Mur des Fédérés and the approach of July 14 and the strike spirit and the realization that they are not so crazy about American bathroom culture as we dreamed. Oh, well – let's go to the Ritz or the Tour d'Argent. I am not going to cry for bedraggled Paris today. It would just stick in my throat.'

'I feel free too, liberated. It's awful the way for a family you must put on an act; and you can't get out of it. I feel like a liar, a goddamn lickspittle and a spy, for I don't agree with a word they say – except Dale of course.

427

He's the typical, educated, crafty Englishman. You pin him down and he's over the hills and far away. And when it comes to that Fairfield, by golly, she sticks in my throat, a sharp-tongued, vain little enamelled puppet. I'm obliged to be nice to her, she doesn't know any better, she's your kin, she's slated to marry Christy – oh, horrors, *horreur*! He's none too bright, he's backward, in fact, though who can say why? But to be tied for life to that bunch of paper frills – these picayune, dry, knowall babies we turn out – why, she won't even let him touch her, I guess, and you can see cheap, prim flirtations in the turn of her nose; prim and dirty.'

'Forget Christy and Fairfield and everyone. We said we would.'

They had a drink in a fashionable hotel. The cafés, now that they looked at them, were worn, dirty, spiritless, there was hardly any electricity, no cleaning, few customers, and those customers shabby. Some cafés were already shut up at the dinner hour. This Paris was not for them.

'And yet all this is irrelevant, isn't it?' said Emily.

'How?'

'There's Paris behind the scenes, marching embattled, tired, hungry, resentful and with a long, long memory. They've eaten crow and they won't forgive it. The proud French! I love them. They don't squeal, but they remember. I wouldn't like to be on the dark tablets of their memory. Paris the wonderful, the Venus, the Astarte.'

But neither of them could walk as they had used to. Stephen still had a cane and had little strength. Emily, still roly-poly, was not strong either. Perhaps she had not eaten enough, or she had worked too hard.

'I'm getting hungry, and we're near Les Halles. Dale told us about a splendid little restaurant.' They walked by the law courts, the *gendarmerie*, the flower markets, the Châtelet and the Hôtel de Ville.

'Here Blanqui stood that day, here people's heads rolled in the gutter, people smothered in their own blood. You can't live in Paris and be like we are and *not* be a red, can you?'

Stephen said, 'No, lots of people have tried to go back on their life history, their perceptions and their dedication; and you can't do it, tragedy or annihilation follows. They were scarred for life, there was a burning mark on their foreheads. You can't go back. You passed the signpost and there's no turning back.'

'You frighten me. What do you mean? How cool it's getting.'

'We were dedicated,' he said. He showed her a little plaque surrounded by humble bouquets, and some field flowers in a homemade bouquet on which was a handwritten card which said:

Ici est tombé pour la Patrie et pour le Libération de Paris –

Stephen said, 'Come on!' But Emily was crying openly, suffocated with tears. She gasped, 'I can't speak, it's so touching. It's real. Oh, Stephen, I wish we could have done that and be no more; no more harassments.'

People were passing them, going home from work, poor Frenchmen in cloth sandals, toil-stained trousers, with sunk faces, tired eyes, a desperate expression. They walked on and Emily said, 'You see, Paris stands no nonsense. It says, Here it is, the truth is evident. And passer-by, the truth of your life is evident.'

'Let's be gay, not miserable.'

He hailed a taxi and said 'La Tour d'Argent.'

'But you must have a table!'

'Oh, I think they'll take us in.'

It was all arranged. 'You like it so much and I thought we would come here together when the others had gone; to celebrate and because you're smart and we'll sell your foul serial.'

'Oh, my darling! Yes, it is my favourite, my dear beloved Tour d'Argent. We really have lots of things to celebrate and how I adore splendour. Ah, me, a weakness.'

'A weakness that I adore. I have it too.'

The headwaiter came up, kissed Emily's hands, saluted Stephen. The women, unlike those in the streets, were fashionably dressed. They had a table from which they could see Nôtre-Dame, and all the lights of Paris just coming on, and though dimmed, rich enough in the beautiful May evening. There were old furniture, a big fireplace, well-spaced tables, beautiful women, rich and canny men, ease, glitter, luxury; and the miseries of Paris, six storeys down, all forgotten.

They ate some shrimp, pressed duck, a special duck, their duck with their number on it. They rolled up the duck on a little cart (and Emily called it the 'duck tumbril') took it to the duck-press, and the duck-waiter carved it, pressed the bones, cooked the sauce, grilled parts of the duck – and with this they had *pommes soufflées*, a salad, two or three wines, and pancakes in caramel with hot cream and kirsch inside.

Said Emily, 'I am floating! After Duclos takes power, *crêpes flamandes* for the masses! Our battle-cry! Pressed ducks for the people. And this gent here with the lean, tense, haunted face, inspired and revolted at the same time by the near perfection of his sauce or the utter perfection of his duck, the triumph, the despair, he shall be head Duck Commissar; oh, certainly that is a thing that will happen in Red France.'

They looked at each other and laughed. Emily said, 'If the people here knew what we thought! Supposing we told this respectable little man with his white collar and muttonchop whiskers that we are looking at him as a handpicked candidate for the guillotine! – and we look just like swinish, American Middle-West, luxury-bound two-cent rakehells. Oh, poor man!'

429

They looked with sympathy at the poor man who was with his well-dressed, plump wife, strangely cobwebbed with wrinkles, and two long-legged, long-haired modern daughters, all bent over their duck.

The waiter came and took away some crumbs, a cigarette butt.

'What service!' sighed Emily.

Stephen said, 'The cigarette smell upsets the other diners. We ought to have some courtesy.'

'Oh, I can't when we're so happy. The tumbrils will be here soon enough.'

They started to laugh, a little, much, wildly. Emily cried, choking, 'Oh, if they only – in this setting, in this restaurant, knew what we thought!'

After a while, with the coffee and brandy, they began to talk about moving. They had better look around for a smaller, better place, with a garden or near to a park for Giles. Stephen said, 'There is the parc Monceau, which I hate; there is the avenue Foch, too dear. I'll go to an agency tomorrow. And no cellars in this one; no cellar workrooms for you.'

But Emily began to talk morbidly of their futures, if they had any; and whether they could keep on living in Paris, and what they would do, poor hunted creatures that no one wanted; and she began to complain of the cold. She was afraid to be out, like this, in a pressed, too-suffering city. Why were they here with these dreadful, heartless people? Let them go home!

'I must go home, Stephen, I'm afraid: something will happen. I must get home and look at my work and sleep and sleep. I sleep so little. Let us go home.'

They went home. Emily went at once to her basement and after a while he heard her typing. He went down, told her to stop; but she said, Oh, no, now she was here she felt happy, she had a function, here she was herself, here she had freedom from all the fears.

430

23   FINAL ARRANGEMENTS

Time passed. But there came the old round of arguments, fierce disputes, savage accusations, regrets for folly which had seemed happiness once, casting up of accounts for things which had been only innocent joy at the time. She asked wildly, 'I make $8,000 a year even in my worst years, Christy provided for – you have $12,000 a year – why are we broke? Why am I driven like this to slave so that I can't sleep and need stimulants and doctors? Does Vittorio need a wife earning $8,000 a year? And yet Vittorio is not a hero: there are hundreds, thousands of men like him in Europe. He gave up all this to do what he's doing.'

Vittorio had come and gone, had spent an evening with them, from seven until three in the morning and it had been one of the best evenings of their lives. Would have been if only Vittorio had let anyone speak but himself! said Stephen. But Emily had been triumphant, catching ball with Vittorio, laughing at his gold. Stephen cried irritably, 'Oh, go and marry Vittorio. I can see you living in Belleville, huddled over one gas flame with Vittorio, listening to his eternal chatter, getting shoved out of one country after another – losing touch with everyone. You like to rough it – at the Ritz. You have illusions about yourself. You love luxury. What's wrong with that? The poor get a damned bad deal. Everything sold to them is rotten, poor, bad workmanship, worst materials. I can see you trying to eat with Vittorio or any other hero on twenty francs a month. With Vittorio you'd never eat in the Tour d'Argent or Véfour in your life.'

She defended him. Vittorio had eaten in all those places and given it up.

Stephen enquired, beginning to laugh, 'But why must you give it up? I don't see why he had to give it up. He could have gone on working at his profession and been a communist.'

'He knew that was playing at it. The company he kept was rotten.'

'And so he still is wild about a thoroughly bad society woman, an adulteress, a lesbian, a thief, a prostitute, a hanger-on of rich men, and from what I hear, she's famous in two capitals for her dirtiness!'

Emily blushed. She said more humbly, 'I don't know what his motives are, but I am sure they're noble ones!'

431

Stephen said, 'What rot! It's sympathy for those noble Roman wounds on his face.'

'She, too, I suppose. Everyone would say, she married the communist martyr with the crucified face! How many of us try to quit our past via some other person. It can't be done.' She looked sad.

Stephen said, tenderly, 'You're a passionate, hot-hearted, great-natured little girl and you're really only a girl. Every woman suddenly shows what a girl she is.'

Emily implored, 'Stephen, take me seriously. I am not a girl. Can't I admire Vittorio without wanting to marry him?'

Stephen said laughing, 'No, you want to marry him. And I won't let you.'

She turned away, 'I'm bitterly insulted, humiliated. Vittorio represents to me what we ought to be and are not.'

Next time they went out he took her up the rue de Belleville, almost to the Buttes-Chaumont where, in a side street, above a painter and decorator, he showed her the black-faced, eighteenth-century apartment house where Vittorio lived. He had one room on the fourth floor. He had to walk up dusty stairs from a cobbled street of poor children and little food-shops.

'You couldn't write even one of your stories in a setting like that.'

'I could. I started out with nothing.'

'You were using up your adolescent strength. You couldn't now. You've other habits, some of them bad habits, you've been ill, you're worn with feasting, with working on drugs, with me – worrying about me.'

He took her back to the centre, to 'their dear Véfour', asking her if she did not feel happier then. She ate a great deal, but resentfully.

'You're buying me off. I ought not to give up my feelings. They're real; they're honest.'

'But they're not practical.'

'But you haven't told me why we have to live in such grandeur?'

He smiled in the elegant, trifling way that she had admired first of all in him, 'I'm a gentleman. I can't live any other way. I have to have clean and good clothing, my two baths a day. Think that you've never lived with a man who doesn't wash enough and who changes his shirt – maybe once a week.'

She was restless. Teasing, trifling, annoying, Stephen detailed his advantages.

'You're pinning me down with a hundred pinpricks,' she exclaimed.

The next day, instead of her taking her lesson with Madame Suzanne, Stephen took her out and bought her a beautiful blouse, a new hat and a pair of gloves. Then he sent her back to work.

432

But she became morally ill again and questioned everything.

Their happiness was injured by the system they had, of each reading his manuscript to the other. She and Stephen tore the work to pieces, especially Emily's, for hers was to sell. The next day she had to do it again, worn and frustrated, 'bleeding' as she said; and she vented her weariness and disappointment in recriminations.

'You've ruined my talent, with your expensive tastes and selfish idleness. You've sponged on me, you're a parasite. I'll never forgive you.'

Emily took to her bed.

Suzanne came to her bedroom and gave her lessons, reported on Christy and Giles. Emily furiously confided in her, begged her to bring Vittorio to see her.

'Tell him I'm very sick; I want him to tell me about Danton!'

'Read about Danton!'

Emily explained that she had become passionately interested in the monstrous figure of the corrupt revolutionist. She cried laughing, 'No, I must have someone to tell me, from Vittorio's viewpoint. Tell him I want to know all about the *gula-immense, gula-immensa!* Vittorio says there is hope for everyone. So let him tell me what hope for the *gula-immensa!*'

'This is no way to learn.'

'It is the only way to learn for a backward, blank-minded, selfish American like me,' she cried viciously.

Stephen said quietly, 'Please bring Vittorio along Suzanne, and let us have a ray of sunshine for a change. All that she says about Americans anyway is not for her but for me.'

Emily smiled radiantly. She wrote a note to the revolutionist and when it had gone off, she lay back and thought about Vittorio's poverty, which irked her and stood in her way. It must be remedied somehow. She said to herself, 'If I had the decency, I would go to work, sweep the field as I can if I try and keep them all – all my poor friends.'

If she made a lot of money, she could send some to Vittorio, anonymously, have a false legacy sent to him! But then he'd give it to the Party? That would never do. Or to the serpent in Rome? Worse still! Yes, of course, he'd buy some Paris trifle for the Roman woman, a rope of emeralds, say. How could she, Emily, improve his lot, make him happier, fitter company, yet not give him that slippery thing, money? *'Twas mine, 'tis his and has been slave to thousands.* No, no. Last time she had seen him he mentioned some trouble he had been in. He had said with a twisted smile, doleful and comical, 'You see, it is easy for them to recognize me,' and he had touched the scars; 'and then I cannot see them coming anything like as well.'

Emily looked at Stephen with a smile next time he entered her

433

bedroom, 'Oh, for a million dollars!'

'All I can offer you now is the equivalent, a letter from Vittorio, saying he's coming. Did you mind my opening it?'

'Oh, it's a bit late now to ask, isn't it? One of these days though – but no one is trying to get me away from you. Worse luck!'

'Worse luck!'

Vittorio came to dinner. He came early for aperitifs as requested, with his usual large bouquet and some fine chocolates. As usual he charmed them all. He sat by Emily's bedside before dinner and in between her fits of violent coughing, brought on by a bad cold she had caught lying on the floor in an unheated cellar, he told her about Danton, H. T. Buckle (with Stephen), Kafka (with Christy), Jules Verne (with Giles).

Vittorio went away at three in the morning, all of them, with Christy, having laughed, argued, coughed, drunk, eaten, expostulated, expounded, denounced, vituperated and rejoiced their way through the evening. Vittorio had done a fair part of his translation of Emily's *The Wilkes-Barre Chronicle*. He took away with him Stephen's latest manuscript, said he would write a letter to friends, Italian and French publishers.

Vittorio said, 'The book looks good. It must be published. All our lost literature, ours on the left, all the good writing of this world today must not be lost. We must work to have it published. We must not let them crush or uproot all our flowers, for the west is not going down but coming up; and books like yours and Emily's are some of those flowers. Your works are fine politically, and aesthetically fascinating, an honour to your country and should be known here, all over Europe, in the Soviet Union, in the eastern democracies, in all those places where they fancy American culture is represented by your mucker and immodest writers; they despise you wrongly, but accordingly. This is valuable writing; for the America of the future, for the Party and for me, my dear friends, for me your dear friend.'

Stephen said, 'Ah, Vittorio, thank you. I longed to hear that just once. I feel happy, warm, good again. I was beginning to regret my whole life, to wish I'd been trained to be a fine, second-rate clerk or a tea-taster; something at least useful everywhere.'

'Why should you feel like that at any time? Whatever happens there is always hope for everyone.'

When Vittorio went Stephen smiled at his wife, 'There's a fine, warm, civilized, literate, decent person, my God. I wish there were a few like him in America, who understand that life is what it seems and also complex, not what it seems. He's enthusiastic, good, generous; he believes in people. He even seems to think it's part of a friend's duty to believe in people's work and not to squash hopes and ruin fervour.'

434

Emily sighed and laughed, 'Oh, leave Vittorio alone. If only this thing goes well darling and we can make it into a play and a musical comedy, we'll buy a car and go all over Europe. We'll put Giles in an expensive, good school and roam Europe. Damn the Party and all its works. We're not made for the garret and the backroom and we're never happy but when we're alone together spending money in a nice genteel way, but never counting. That is the only way to live. We're not made to be these serious, philistine, dumb, bureaucratic things, commissars and gauleiters and party hacks, how dull; too bad for them and us. Take Vittorio. He's boring after all, compared with what he must have been as a wit of Roman society. Do you suppose he talked to his wily serpent dame about Danton, Marat and Blanqui? No.'

Stephen said, 'Who knows? They may have thought it very cute. Oh, I hate that guy too. He's always stealing thunder, he's a show-stealer.'

'Oh, he cheered me up when I was so low and dull but he can talk you into the ground and five fathoms under. Still he is better than those who know nothing but the machine and the line, nor know there is any other culture than Five Year Plans. My God, what people! How did we ever put up with them? It was after 1929. Everyone lost his shirt. The other world looked like the only hope and all through the hungry thirties, the USA did not look like the hope of mankind. Well, we were Marxists and we ought to have seen so far ahead as to know the USA would pull out of it, with such resources, such unexpendable bottomless resources. A young giant. It doesn't matter what it does, really. We were crazy to get into that mess.'

'But that mess was the only organization you ever knew,' he said laughing, and kissed her. 'Your head is made of wool, inside I mean.'

'Yes, but it cramped my style forever. And I saw you too as a hero riding on a green horse into the tombs; and my, it seemed such a big thing to me.'

She howled with laughter.

She received some unpleasant mail from the United States, however; not only a request from the *Literary Monthly* asking her to state her views plainly, to say she was against the Soviet Union; but a strange query from the editor of a popular manual of biographies to whom she had written very fully. He said, 'Do you intend to return to the United States? If so, when? If not, I don't see how I can publish your biography in a dictionary which will be of intense interest only to United States teachers, chemists, executives, treasurers, national organization heads, newspapermen, manufacturers and librarians. These will be interested in knowing if you are living in the United States, what your plans are with regard to the United States. If you are unable to answer in the affirmative, that you are

435

contemplating an early return to the United States, the biographer does not think he can include you in a normal United States contemporary biographical dictionary. Kindly answer by airmail.'

This strange letter at first made them indignant, later it upset them. To be excluded would lose them sales. They answered him. Why not? They expected to return to the United States very soon. They were merely getting some facts, figures, helpful data to write a book between them about Europe 1950 and would return home in the near future.

'That will hold him off, the goddamn blackmailer, I'm not obliged to return to my own home country for him. I'm free,' said Emily.

'By the way, what about your passport, Emily? Did you get it? It's out of date.'

'Oh, Jehosaphat, I'll get it tomorrow.'

She went while he was at work and when he returned, that was the first thing he asked her about. He was very anxious. She, though, was merry, sparkling and naughty, with a demoniac twinkle. She laughed, 'You thought there would be so much trouble! Why, I got it right away. There was no hesitation, as you said there might be. You scared me for nothing. It's my country isn't it? They were very nice and helpful and co-operative.'

He was very glad to hear it. She said she felt free, now; she had never felt better. It was true, with the way all these people wrote to her, she had been under a cloud. Now the sky was clear.

'We are free. And never let us get into such a mess again. The record is wiped clean, Stephen. We're OK.'

'It must be Anna's doing,' said Stephen. But he was very glad.

But their year was full of ups and downs; their festivals prepared by Emily were scrappy, strange and made them unhappy. Emily spent much time in her cellar workroom and was beginning to look like an old woman, though she was not yet forty, and still had her great strength.

At the beginning of April, 1950, Stephen received a message from the Embassy. They wanted to see him at his convenience. He went without misgivings, because of the good treatment Emily had received. He spent all day there and for the next two days went to them and was very well treated, very politely and with good taste, just as Emily had said.

He returned home on the third day calm, gay and boyish, reposed.

'How did you get on?'

'Very well. They were very pleased with me. I did my duty to my country. I am a patriot, a good citizen; I am not a man without a country. They have written into my record: good citizen.'

'That's swell, absolutely marvellous. I knew there was nothing for you to fear.'

436

'You knew? You thought! And I know why you thought so!'

'Why?' she said truculently.

'They wanted my co-operation and I gave it – just as you did. In the same way but better.'

He was smiling, debonair.

'Better?'

'Yes, I talked. I sang. I talked and sang for three whole days. I gave them names, all the names I ever heard of, boys I knew at school and at college, librarians, doctors, nurses; it was astounding what names came to my memory, as I began my new and original system of total recall. Of course, I gave names of Party people that they know very well and my friends; they know they are my friends – and Vittorio, a great contribution – and Jacques Duclos and Earl Browder; and Godfrey and Jay, who are already in jail, in fact, mostly I gave names of those in jail. I did a good job. There is nobody I ever knew I did not name; and I don't think they can make anything out of that biographical dictionary!'

'Why are you so pleased?'

'I am pleased because there is no more ambiguity. I know what my future is; I know what has to be done. What is to be done? I know. What a relief. Yes. I suppose it is.'

'I am astonished, Stephen! I never thought you would do that.'

'You see, they told me that you had already done it, so I thought I'd make the record perfect. The renegade husband and wife: the perfect American couple, loyal to each other and to the country.'

'Why are you so cynical? Now we are free. No more questions. They can ask no more of us.'

'Oh, no, I'm not cynical. I am satisfied.'

Stephen was very busy during the month, not only working at the Gaudeamus Press, but spending some of his evenings with Christy. Emily was annoyed with him for neglecting her and in rebellion spent much of her time in her basement workroom, working fitfully and passing long silent hours there. Because of her lonely restlessness and partly to defy Stephen, she bought whisky and vodka and took them down there, where she would sit drinking with herself and her phantasms, sometimes talking aloud to them, or uttering defiant or miserable exclamations. But Stephen remained calm and tender, helping to bring her to herself when he was at home. Stephen saw the Trefougars at their home and visited others; but he would have no one at the house. In the middle of the month Axel and Ruth Oates were in Paris and invited them to dinner. Stephen made an excuse, Emily burst out in ribald laughter at their ideas of entertainment, but was anxious to have them as guests. She was very tired of being alone.

But Stephen said he had no time then for entertainment: after May 1 she could have guests. He was tied up until then. He went also to see Uncle Maurice, ate with him and spent a whole evening with him.

Uncle Maurice had a large apartment on the avenue Président-Wilson, near the museum of orientalia, the Musée Guimet. He himself had a small, costly collection, which he intended one day to donate to the museum, to be the Howard Gift. Uncle Maurice's apartment had two large rooms on the square, kitchen quarters, bathroom, bedroom and large but cosy sitting-room where he entertained his intimate friends. He was very fond of Stephen. They did not understand each other, but were friends. The staff of two, man and wife, took a small round table into one of the front rooms, and the two men ate there. The meal was not meagre nor scanty but prudent. Maurice always dieted and Stephen, since his operation, was infirm and dyspeptic. They had anchovies in flaky pastry, an omelette, chicory *au gratin* and apple *compote* with meringue on top, wine, coffee, brandy, a little of each. Uncle Maurice was about fifty, with a Rhineland face, short nose, receding forehead, bright blue eyes and a slash across his cheek and jaw on the left side, which, fortunately, made his face interesting. He had the mild manner of an alert, kind boy who knows the world is cruel but is prepared to laugh at it; he was charming, gentle, humane. As soon as the coffee and brandy were in and the door shut, he began to complain to Stephen about his servant Hortense who had been with him, as everyone knew, ever since he returned to Paris from New York. At first she had been very good to him. She still looked after him and cooked well; but her picking and stealing had at last become exorbitant. He laughed helplessly. She now had her husband in the kitchen all the time. True, he helped. But instead of going home for meals – they had a little room, with conveniences, in a workers' hotel – he came early and stayed late, eating all his meals there. Maurice produced some figures he had noted in his diary. The diary was the sort that had at the side of each day's notes, a place for noting the expenses; Received, Disbursed. Maurice had not noted anything of the kind, but he had noted in the back, *220fr. a day on the average.*

He said, 'Tonight we had a sort of gala meal. I eat more frugally; because that is my way. Even when William dines with me, we eat frugally. He likes that. When we want a little more, we usually go out to Chez Francis, not to burden Hortense. But she charges me 220 francs a day for food. Don't you think that excessive? Of course, she is good to me. She brings me flowers from their little cottage in the suburbs. They have recently bought a little cottage which has plenty of ground and he is a good gardener. She brings me flowers every Monday. Of course, they don't work for me Saturday or Sunday, so I have to cook eggs for myself; and William and I go out.'

With some pleasure he showed Stephen a few flowers in two small vases, some drooping: it was Thursday.

'I don't like to speak to her; but I do think she is charging me excessively. Dale was here and he liked her cooking, but he said he felt sure they were robbing me. But how can I say, "You're robbing me?" And what other way is there to deal with it? I ask you, Stephen, because you live in Paris and you have several servants; you know what to do.'

Stephen was not very helpful. They talked about Maurice's problem a few minutes and were interrupted by Hortense, who sailed in with nervous belligerence and took away the things.

'Anything more, sir?'

'Oh, no, thank you, Hortense: we can manage for ourselves.'

'Then we will go in a few minutes, sir.'

'Very well, Hortense.'

'Have you any orders for tomorrow, sir?'

'Well, Monsieur William is coming and we might have *coquilles St-Jacques*, he likes them and it is Friday.'

'Yes, sir. Anything else?'

'What do you say? *Fromage à la crème*? You know, Hortense.'

'Yes, sir. Well, goodnight.'

After they heard the serving couple depart, close the front door, Stephen said, 'I wanted to ask you a favour, Maurice.'

'Anything I can do.'

'Maurice, it's about Emily. I'm not happy any more and I've decided to leave her. But I can't tell her directly. I have bought a small car today and I am going to tell her I have to make a business trip to Switzerland. I've done it before; she won't think it strange. I'm dropping everything, because everything binds me to her, the business, the house, the children. I am sorry about Christy and Giles, but I can't do more than I have done. I haven't the strength. I have spent a lot of time with Christy this month. I've always felt he was like a son to me because he is like me. I am sorry he is. I had a long talk with him, Maurice, about Fairfield and Mother, not disrespectful, I assure you. I find that he is quite decided on his own account, not to marry Fairfield. He told me the astounding news that he has a girl in mind to marry, a young French girl, an artist who sings folk songs in a cabaret manner. I've been with Christy to hear her. She is really good, Angèle – she's at the Lune Rousse now, I think. I forget. I've met her. She's genuine, a nice girl, not a gold-digger. He certainly won't marry Fairfield if he's in love with this girl. You'll like her, Maurice: so will William. I know you appreciate genuine artists. I don't say he'll

439

marry her. They've fixed it for him to go to England in the fall and study for one of the English universities. They've decided his French will never be good enough. Though it was good enough for Angèle. Never mind. I've asked Christy to be good to Emily. He loves her, I'm sure, though he's afraid of her – a volcano like that is not for a small boy. And Christy will be a small boy for some time to come. Then he may marry a volcano. There is Fate standing ahead of him, like a giant woman. Fate seems friendly, even maternal. And like all mothers, you never know what turn she is going to give to the play . . . So I have spent most of my time with Christy. He has promised to be good to his mother, Emily that is, and to his brother; by that he means Giles. Olivia is in safe hands.'

Maurice was silent for a while. He sipped his brandy. He said, 'Did you meet a woman you like better?'

'You may take it that there never was and never will be another woman for me. Anyone who has known Emily as a husband has had everything a woman, any woman, any woman past or present, can give. And suffered all that a woman can make you suffer. You cannot be a husband to Emily and think of other women. There are no other women, when she is there. Are there other winds about when a tornado is in progress? And afterwards when someone says, of a wild wind, "Quite a breeze!" you think, what ignorance of natural forces!'

Maurice nodded. 'And what will you do then?'

'I am leaving her. But I don't want her to suffer in any way. She can't help what she is or what has happened. She has caused me disappointment and misery, I can't say how much; too much to talk about. I've been always horribly unhappy. Yet I know if I were young again and she came along again, I would take her. This must be fate, Maurice. Otherwise what is it? And I suppose, with me, not the perfect husband for her, she has been horribly unhappy; and what she has become is partly my fault. But I can't have the wife she is now. She is so outrageous – Maurice, lying there in the basement, drunk and dirty, living on drugs, rushing out shouting, insulting me – I won't go on with it. I know I have a duty to her. Unluckily, I have deserted higher duties; I am getting quite used to being a bastard. I don't want to get too used to it. It's better for me to go. I just want to ask you if you'll go over there and help her when she finds out I have left her. I'll leave you a couple of letters, one for her, one for Christy, and I want you to give them to him when they find out. I'll see they find out very soon. I hope you'll do it for me, Maurice. I won't ask anything more than that. I know you like and appreciate Emily. Many people do. But the trouble is they're afraid of her too. They don't understand her. I do. I have. I would have made a good captain. I rode out the typhoon. But too many typhoons wear a man down. That is all.'

440

'May I ask what decided you, Stephen?'

'No.'

'I didn't ask.'

'Then you will?'

'Of course. I will be good to Emily.'

Stephen got up, went across and kissed Uncle Maurice on both cheeks.

'A French salute. Thank you, Maurice.'

After a few words, Stephen said to Maurice, 'There will be no money troubles involved. I've settled on Emily the $3,000 I get every quarter from Anna. That is my money and I can give it to her. I've arranged for her to get any profits that arise from my participation in the Gaudeamus Press. She won't starve, even if her writings don't sell. She has great hopes for The Monster, as she calls it. I'm not sure. Marie-Antoinette – she's identified herself now with that heroine – seems to me a bit out of date for Hollywood. Now we have our own wars and social problems. She may be bitterly disappointed; but she will never starve. Nor will my son.'

'But where will you be, then?'

'Yes, well, Maurice, I decided to make a clean break. I had better take off for South America or the South Sea Islands or anywhere, where she can't find me; for she is very determined, very tenacious and I can't resist her. Even in the state she is now, in the hands of doctors, of a doctor, one of the few bad ones, of bad friends, of – what has happened to her, she would find me – I could never get away. So I am taking a run-out powder. I am not proud of myself: it is not brave. But then my whole history shows that I am not brave.'

'But you'll let me hear from you?'

Stephen smiled very gaily, 'Oh, I'll try to.'

Stephen, towards the end of April, told Emily that he had made sure that Christy would walk in the huge Paris May Day procession – some Americans were doing it; and he too, Stephen, intended to do it.

'Stephen! My God! And the Embassy!'

'They didn't make me give my hand and seal on May Day processions. They never thought of it. I just want to make sure Christy feels we are with him.'

'But we aren't!'

'We'll see. You never know with children. It is better to believe in them to the end.'

As to Ruth and Axel Oates, he refused to let Emily see them or to have them at the house or to eat with them; but early one morning, just after breakfast, he went to see them. He had learned that they wanted to go

441

again to China; a first-hand report on China as it was at that time, would help Axel's magazine. He had learned too that they could not do it because of the expense. He went to see them and took with him his own cheque for $1,000, which he gave them for their trip to China. He said, 'You don't know: you may not come back. You may forget us. I am sure you will. This is not to make you remember. It is just a cheque. There are millions of cheques. This is one. You owe me nothing. On the contrary I owe you something.'

As he was going, he bent to kiss Ruth's cheek, then with a tender look, he refrained, stood up straight and looked sweetly at her.

When he went home he told Emily all about it. Emily was shocked.

'You gave them a thousand dollars! We need it, Stephen. Well, heigh-ho. OK. They're decent people: they're friends. To hell with expenses. I don't see why I couldn't see them and say hello. I haven't had friends here for a month. We could have given them a good dinner, something they don't often get.'

'Do you remember the dinner at the Escargot de Bourgogne, if that's the name?'

'I couldn't forget it.' She laughed insolently.

'Do you remember how we wondered how Daniels could eat with us, after he'd stabbed us in the back or so we'd heard, denouncing us as Trotskyists, renegades?'

'Yes,' she said sulkily.

'I don't feel like eating at the same table as Ruth and Axel, when we've both given their names to their enemy.'

She smiled, coaxed, 'We had to do it, Stephen. They'll be all right; they know how to get by. It doesn't mean anything. You know they knew their names, they knew them long ago.'

'Just the same, I can't eat with such people. You know the story Vittorio told us, the time he was in concentration camp. The children were waiting to go to the gas chamber; but something was held up, so the young Nazi soldiers got the order, Play with them, amuse them. And they did, with a good heart, with the best spirit, glad I suppose to be kind for once. They played with them, tossed the ball to them for forty minutes, though everyone was shivering with cold; and then the fault was fixed. They stopped playing and the children went to the gas chamber. And Vittorio, who told so much – for once his voice faltered.'

'Well, what about it?'

'I prefer not to be out there playing ball.'

24 THE MONSTER

On May Day, though Emily was dubious, Stephen marched with Christy from the place de la Nation to the Bastille. The two Howards waited on a café *terrasse* till the great flood of Algerians, wearing the green of Islam, poured into the square, not in fours or eights or twelves, but as a flood; and right behind them, the Howards fell in, though the workers coming after were French metallurgists. Stephen said to Christy, 'Christy, this is the happiest moment of my life: the best; also the most foolish.'

At the end of the march, the Howards separated. Christy had friends to meet. Stephen went home, kissed Emily and Giles, shook hands with the servants and said he had an appointment out in the country, not far away.

Passers-by notified local people and also the local police that there was a car in a distant field, burning fiercely, so bright that although it was clear daylight, no details could be seen. The police found that the car had burned totally and that there had been a man inside; and the man must have been drenched in gasoline to burn like that. But at last they identified the car and so the man. It was Marie-Jo who answered the telephone. She telephoned Suzanne, who spoke to the porter; and in a short time Suzanne, and Christy with her, were over at the house in the rue de Varenne.

Evening came. Emily now knew all that was known. She sat in an armchair in the sitting-room on the first floor, flushed, crying and gay and excited by all the attention being paid to her. To everyone who entered, she hospitably offered a drink. On a console table near the door stood two bottles of gin, one of vodka, two of scotch whisky and bottles of other drinks, with an ice-bucket and other fixings. She obviously was uneasy when anyone stood or sat without a glass in his hand. Suzanne was there, Maurice, the Trefougars, all sitting down and drinking, when Douglas Dolittle and his wife and Desmond Canby, summoned by Emily by telegram, came through the door. Emily greeted them all with smiles and tears, waved them to the bottles; Christy, on his feet, stood by the telephone. It rang – a Paris acquaintance was summarizing politely her shock and her sympathy.

'Who is it?' cried Emily.

'Madame George.'

'Oh, get her off the phone. The phone must be kept open for the AP, UP and for calls from the USA. We don't want these local calls.'

Christy got her off the phone and waited by the telephone. In a moment it rang; Emily exclaimed joyously, 'At last. It must be the UP. They haven't called yet. Reuter's called half an hour ago. How slow they are! Imagine letting Reuter's get in ahead of them!'

She sat there, her crazed and fallen face gay, while she sucked at her drink. She was very genial, kept insisting on one or the other filling up the glasses; and when at last Christy said, 'Chicago calling,' she jumped up, ready to speak to Anna, who was then in Chicago with one of her daughters.

'Oh, dear Anna – '

But Anna, speaking to Christy, said she did not want to speak to the widow; she just wanted to know what the latest news was and whether Maurice and Dale were there. Christy said that Emily wanted to speak, but Anna refused, 'No, I can't speak to her.'

Christy had a short conversation with his grandmother, then called Maurice to the phone. Emily was hurt. She could not understand why Anna would not speak to her, above all.

'I am the widow. I am her daughter-in-law. I am the closest.'

She ran to the phone and tore Maurice away, and spoke with tears, 'Oh, dear Anna, it's Emily. Oh, dear Anna, what a tragedy, poor Stephen. This to happen to us, when we were all so happy. Oh, everyone is here, dear Anna, Maurice, dear Maurice, Christy, Des Canby is here, Dale is coming and everyone is looking after us. We are expecting a call from California. We had a call from London earlier this evening. Oh, everyone is so shocked and upset. Everyone so loved Stephen. Oh, Anna – Anna – he left me! Oh, Anna – he left me!'

She began to cry in earnest and Maurice took the phone from her and spoke quietly to Stephen's mother.

'No one knows what happened. It's better for me to write to you, Anna. There'll be an inquest and then the funeral. Yes, of course, we'll send Stephen back to the States. I know you want him buried with our own. We're all doing all we can and Dale has already arrived at the airport. He telephoned. Don't worry. There is no need for you to come over. You can't do anything here.'

Emily meanwhile had thrown herself into the arms of Douglas Dolittle, crying and saying, 'He left me, Doug! I can't believe it: I was sure he never would. Oh, Doug! Look after me.' And when later Dale entered the room, she did the same with him. Maurice sat at the back of all the chairs which had been assembled for the company, his hands to his face. Christy, obeying Emily's orders, stood near the telephone.

Emily was annoyed, astonished, 'UP haven't called yet. What's the matter with them? Here in Europe they certainly haven't the zip they have in the USA. I see now why we get such stale news. No reporter worth his salt in the USA would let a news item like this slip through his fingers. My God, if only I were on their news service, I'd have telephoned two hours ago – when did the news come through, Maurice? You don't know. Where's François? Well, Suzanne, you know. My God – anyway keep the line open. We must keep them open for the news services.'

Axel and Ruth Oates turned up. She got up to greet them and eagerly offered them drinks, while they were weeping.

'This is the first big party we've had in months. And for such an occasion. Well, life, life! My God! Everything in reverse. Oh, poor Stephen. He loved me so. He wrote such beautiful letters to me and to Giles and Christy. He was just going away on a business trip for a couple of months, and he wanted us to know how much he loved us. The police have taken the letters, but I can tell you what he said. To me he said, "My darling wife; you were always the perfect wife, I have never had anything to reproach you with. You were perfect. Your loving husband Stephen." He wrote to Christy that he had been the perfect son; and to Giles that he loved him and always would; and he even wrote a letter to you, Axel and Ruth, that you had always been the perfect friends. I would show them to you, but the police took them all, because of the accident and because there must be an inquest. Of course, the idea that he planned it is stupid. No one would write such beautiful letters and plan a thing like that. It was a terrible accident. The only thing I know is that he loved me and us all and he knew it and he lived for us.'

After a while and when they had all drunk a little more, and she was still waiting for the news services, disappointed and put out, she said sulkily to Axel and Ruth, 'And do you know what is going to happen now? Uncle Maurice and Dale are closing the house and they are sending me off to Switzerland, second-class in the plane. I am not used to that. I am used to luxury travel. They don't understand that Stephen would never allow it. He always had the best for me. They never understood Stephen. Stephen would be furious if he knew the arrangements. I might as well have no seat in the plane, like on the floor, have people walking over my hair, tramping on me. That is what they plan for me. Christy is looking after his brother; Suzanne is taking them both till it is all worked out. The servants are going. And I am to go to a cheap hotel, bed and three meals a day, not even a sitting-room and they will write to me, pay my board and send me to a doctor. I can't choose the doctor. If Stephen

445

were here he'd be crazy-furious to see me treated this way.'

Christy, standing by the telephone, said, 'Mother, I will always look after you and Giles. Don't feel like that. You won't have to live that way. It is just till we get everything settled. I promised Father that I would always look after you and Giles and I will.'

'When did you promise that?'

'A little while ago, last month. He said he had to go away on a business trip and I promised, in case anything happened then or any time, to do as he would always have done for you.'

She, with her tormented face, half-merry and half-morose, drunk but very keen, looked at him with a cunning smile. She smiled fully, got up, put her arms around him, and thanked him with many kisses.

'Oh, my dear good boy. Thank you! Bless you!'

In the end everyone but Maurice and Christy left and she seemed not sorry to get rid of the consoling company, standing between the festive console table and the telephone which was still being kept open for AP and other newspaper services.

When all was settled, Christy and Maurice saw that Emily packed and got ready for the plane trip to Lausanne, where she was to visit doctors and possibly go into hospital. The estate had enough money: she could have a long course of treatment. But when they came for her, she had gone. No one knew where she had gone. The truth is she had taken another plane, to Rome; and with her she had only a valise, filled with papers, The Monster.

Someone who had known her long ago in Hollywood days, going through Rome, which at that time was full of Americans, passed her in the Forum Romanum, without recognizing her and then stopped, came back and looked again. This old woman, with the straggling half-grey hair, the droll, hanging-fat face, the untidy silk suit, was still unmistakably only one person in the world, Emily Howard. He came up to her.

'Emily! What are you doing here?'

Emily was sitting on the stones near the Trajan Column. She had a handbag on her lap and beside her a worn valise, of snakeskin with gold fittings, which lay open. Some loose papers lay on the steps and in her lap were letters it seemed.

'Emily! What are you doing here?'

Emily looked up into the face.

'Don't you know me? I'm Jim Holinshed. Here's Vera!'

Emily looked strangely at them.

'Oh, I'm waiting for someone. Hello! He comes by here.'

446

'Emily, what are you doing here?'

'This is my office.'

She looked up at the sky, shook her head and held up some letters.

'This is my office. I have no other office. Stephen would never have wanted to see me like this. But there is someone will help me. He believes in me, in all of us. He will help us. Vittorio! You know him? I am waiting for him. I get my mail here. I send letters. This is the only good place.'

She put her hand in the valise and brought out papers, which she strewed about the steps.

'Emily, where are you staying?'

'Staying? I am staying here.'

'No, where is your hotel? Can we take you there?'

'Oh, I live here.'

'Where do you sleep, we mean?'

'Oh, I sleep here. You know the saying, The son of man has nowhere to lay his head? That is absurd. You can lay it anywhere. I lay my head on the steps. And I stay here.'

'Emily, come and have a meal with us.'

'Oh, no, I don't want to play ball with the little children; that's too funny.'

'What do you mean?'

She began to laugh and could not stop. She lay on and rolled about the steps, endless laughter.

'Oh, Jim – Jim Holinshed! What a funny thing. It is all so funny! Everything is so funny!' She kept on laughing, until she cried 'If Stephen could see me now! But he's in jail. He's in jail for contempt. They took him from us in the end.'

They left her, in the end, and went to the American Embassy. They did not know what else to do.